The Legacy Series
Volume 3

The Convicts

The Soldier

The Outlaw

The Deviants

Sheritta Bitikofer

MOONSTRUCK WRITING

Cover art by Angela Quincoces Rivera at http://www.dream-designz.com

ISBN: 978-1-946821-43-0

CONTENTS

The Convicts

    Contents   #

    Dedication   #

    Content Warning   #

    Terms to Know   #

    1. Chapter 1   #

    2. Chapter 2   #

    3. Chapter 3   #

    4. Chapter 4   #

    5. Chapter 5   #

    6. Chapter 6   #

    7. Chapter 7   #

    8. Chapter 8   #

    9. Chapter 9   #

    10. Chapter 10   #

The Soldier

    Contents   #

    Dedication   #

    Foreword   #

1. Chapter 1 #
2. Chapter 2 #
3. Chapter 3 #
4. Chapter 4 #
5. Chapter 5 #
6. Chapter 6 #
7. Chapter 7 #
8. Chapter 8 #
9. Chapter 9 #
10. Chapter 10 #
11. Chapter 11 #
12. Chapter 12 #
13. Chapter 13 #
14. Chapter 14 #
15. Chapter 15 #
16. Chapter 16 #
17. Chapter 17 #
Terms to Know #

The Outlaw

Contents #
Dedication #
Terms to Know #
1. Chapter 1 #
2. Chapter 2 #
3. Chapter 3 #

4. Chapter 4   #

5. Chapter 5   #

6. Chapter 6   #

7. Chapter 7   #

8. Chapter 8   #

9. Chapter 9   #

10. Chapter 10   #

11. Chapter 11   #

12. Chapter 12   #

The Deviants

Contents   #

Dedication   #

Prologue   #

1. Chapter 1   #

2. Chapter 2   #

3. Chapter 3   #

4. Chapter 4   #

5. Chapter 5   #

6. Chapter 6   #

7. Chapter 7   #

8. Chapter 8   #

9. Chapter 9   #

10. Chapter 10   #

11. Chapter 11   #

12. Chapter 12   #

13. Chapter 13   #

14. Chapter 14   #

Epilogue   #

Afterword   627

About the author   #

Also by Sheritta Bitikofer   631

The Convicts

Legacy Series Book 9

Sheritta Bitikofer

MOONSTRUCK WRITING

CONTENTS

Dedication #

Content Warning #

Terms to Know #

1. Chapter 1 #

2. Chapter 2 #

3. Chapter 3 #

4. Chapter 4 #

5. Chapter 5 #

6. Chapter 6 #

7. Chapter 7 #

8. Chapter 8 #

9. Chapter 9 #

10. Chapter 10 #

Dedicated to my father and all my family in Louisiana. I will always remember, with immense fondness, the days spent sitting on the back porch with mason jars full of sweet tea, the baying of basset hounds in the yard, and smell of a delicious Cajun dinner cooking in the kitchen. I love you all more than you will ever know.

CONTENT WARNING

Some language and situations within the following pages may be of a sensitive or offensive nature, due to trying to stay accurate to the historical era in which the story takes place. The book includes racial slurs and incorrect historical interpretations of the institute of slavery during the antebellum era. These are not the views of the author, nor is this story meant to propagate these harmful interpretations of American history.

TERMS TO KNOW

New Orleans – Founded in 1718 Jean-Baptiste Le Moyne de Bienville as a French colony. Struggling for years, slaves and immigrants were brought in from France to settle the area. What is now considered the French Quarter is the original layout of the land, which was designed after the famous cities in Europe with their straight streets and a central plaza. It became an ideal trading port since it was settled right at the south of the Mississippi river which leads up to St. Louis. Irish, Acadian, Haitian, German, French, and Spanish settlers came to New Orleans for varying reasons. Some established farms and plantations along the river or started their own trades within the city. The Louisiana Territory changed hands to the Spanish in 1762. During this occupation, the city suffered two fires, allowing the Spanish to rebuild nearly a quarter of the city according to their cultural architecture, which can be seen today. The territory became French again in 1800, but only for three years until America purchased the Louisiana Territory. The territory claimed statehood in April of 1812. One remaining peculiarity about Louisiana is that instead of counties, the region is divided into "parishes" and still retains much of its French and Spanish roots in the Creole and Cajun culture.

Battle of New Orleans – The final battle in the War of 1812 between England and America. Although the setup took place between January 8th and January 26th, the final engagement lasted approximately half an hour just east of New Orleans along the Mississippi. Andrew Jackson led the American forces consisting of Choctaws, Creoles, Free People of Color from New Orleans, Kentucky sharp shooters, and Baratarian Pirates. General Pakenham led the British in the battle, but was killed during the engagement, along with many other officers. It was an American victory, though they were outnumbered. There exists a historical debate as to whether the battle took place after the war ended. Though the peace treaty had been signed prior to the battle, it had not been officially ratified in Congress or Parliament, wherein lies the controversy.

Natchitoches – (Nack-ah-tish) Established in 1714 Louis Juchereau de St. Denis, it is the oldest permanent settlement in the Louisiana region. Named after the Natchitoches Indians who resided there.

Andrew Jackson – Major General at the battle of New Orleans on the American side.

Free People of Color – Freed African slaves. They either bought their freedom or inherited it from their free parents. These people enjoyed the same rights and privileges as free white citizens, including the right to own property and have their own businesses in town. These people varied in skin color from black to mulatto (half-black and half-white) to quadrille (one-part black, three-parts white). They were often encouraged to carry documentation that proved their freedom.

La Place d'Armes – What is commonly known as Jackson Square today. The literal French translation is "Place of Weapons" or "Place of Arms". This was because the armory was traditionally located on the square/plaza. The most notable landmark is the St. Louis Cathedral, which was rebuilt in 1793 after fire, as well as the Cabildo used as the courthouse until the 1850s.

Rougarou – A Louisiana myth, similar to the werewolf in Europe. They were said to inhabit the swamps and turn into a half-man, half-wolf creature by night. Depending on the story, they either ate misbehaving children or Catholics who didn't honor Lent. The curse usually lasted for 101 days and then whoever the rougarou bit next would become a rougarou too.

Jean Lafitte – (Jahn La-feet) A notorious French privateer who operated under contract with what's now Columbia. Born in Bordeaux about 1776, he arrived to the Caribbean in the 1800s with his family. He harbored a deep hatred of the English and Spanish due to an influential grandmother. He was said to have gone to a military academy on St. Kitts. After this, he partnered with his brother and set up privateering operations on Barataria Island just outside the mouth of the Mississippi in the Gulf of Mexico. He was said to have a fleet of ships that attacked the Spanish and English. It's rumored that he and his brother had a blacksmithing shop in New Orleans on the corner of St. Phillips and Bourbon, but this is inconclusive. He often smuggles slaves and alcohol out of the port city. He made an enemy for himself with Governor Clairborne, but redeemed himself after offering his men and services during the Battle of New Orleans. Afterward, he earned the status of a war hero, but this didn't last long and he was forced out of Louisiana. He set up operations out of Galveston Texas.

Baratarian Pirates – (Bear-ah-tare-ee-ehns) Pirates and privateers that served under Jean Lafitte and whose base of operations were on Barataria Island.

Algiers Point – Right across from New Orleans, it was the ideal crossing point. Ferries ran from Algiers Point to New Orleans. "Black Ivory" – Another term for slaves.

Rebellion in Haiti – Between 1791 and 1804, slaves rose up against their French masters and plantation owners in Haiti. Led by François Dominique Toussaint-Louverture and Jean-Jacques Dessalines, it has been one of the most successful slave revolts in history. Many slave owners escaped with their slaves to New Orleans in the early years, but others stayed. This rebellion incited fear in the slave holders in America, thinking that their own slaves might be inspired to do the same.

Le Code Noir – A list of rules and articles set down by the French government for its citizens and colonies, dictating the proper treatment, punishment, and few rights of slaves in their settlements. Some rules laid out the guidelines for the proper care of slaves in the way of how they should be dressed and educated in religion. Others about how to handle runaways, marriages between slaves, and children. Some rules forbade the separation of families if they should be sold, and the various ways that negligent slave owners would have their property confiscated due to ill treatment of the slave. When Louisiana came under Spanish rule, many of these rules were no longer enforced.

Voodoo – An African based religion that focuses on the utilizing of spiritual energies through herbs, rituals, and supplications to a wide pantheon of deities. It gained popularity through media as being an evil or Satanic cult, but nothing could be further from the truth since voodoo practitioners don't believe in heaven, hell, one Satan or one God. The foundation of their belief is to do no harm to others and this shows in many of their practices. Voodoo dolls, for instance, are not to cause harm to others but as a form of self-healing. Most commonly seen in media would be what is called a "Bokor", which is someone who practices voodoo in order to make money. A Hougan is a fully initiated priest, while a Mambo is a female initiated priestess. A Houngenikon is something of a ritual assistant to the Hougan or Mambo. A houngenikon is normally a "hounsi canzo"; that is, a woman chosen from among those whose initiatory status is just below that of the Hougan or Mambo. In a complex ceremony, more than one houngenikon may be responsible for its smooth running. Typical attire during ceremonies is white robes and women often wear matching white turbans. Spread of voodoo into Louisiana can be linked to slaves coming over directly from Africa or from Haiti, where the religion as thrived.

"Lobo" – Spanish for "wolf".

Mulatto – A light-skinned individual who has mixed parentage. One black parent and one white parent.

Quadroon – An even lighter skinned person who has one part black and three parts white heritage.

Creole – A person whose heritage can be traced back to the original settlers of Louisiana during the French or Spanish rule. Sometimes white, mulatto, or black, or any combination of the two, Creole is as much a culture as it is an ethnic group. Traditional Louisiana food such as gumbo, music like the Zydeco genre, and a unique dialect of French, can all be attributed to the Creole culture.

Acadian – French people who immigrated to an island in modern day Nova Scotia to escape Catholic persecution. Many originated from Poiton, France and fostered good relations with the native tribes of Acadia when they settled. In the 1760s after the French and Indian War, they were forced out of their land by the British and many scattered in the ethnic cleansing. A large majority of these people fled to Louisiana because the primary Christian denomination was Catholic and they could practice their faith openly. They also liked the seclusion of the swamps and bayou areas. Many of them were given subsistence farming grants all the way up to Opelousas. Described as passive and hardworking, they didn't mix with the rest of New Orleans or Louisiana society after the Civil War. Maintaining their history, culture, and way of life has been a struggle ever since. We would know them today as "Cajuns".

Gris-gris bag – (gree-gree bag) A sack of herbs that had been "blessed" by a voodoo practitioner for a special purpose.

Loa – (Loh-ah) A voodoo term for "spirit" or "diety". The exact number of Loa in the religion isn't exact and varies amongst believers and different geographical sects. It's safe to say there's an indeterminate amount, but many have similar qualities or names across the religion as a whole. Communion with the Loa through prayer, ritual, and contact through possession is highly sought after. They are divided into groups or "Nanchon".

Petro Loa – A particular grouping or category of Loa who are considered dangerous, malicious, and tricksters. One notable Petro Loa is Met Kafu, which could be the closest thing to the devil in the voodoo religion and is feared by its believers.

Rada Loa – Considered to be the oldest and most benevolent Loa in the voodoo religion. Papa Legba is the most notable and is said to be a commuter with an even higher Loa that goes between the believers.

"Connards" – "Bastards" in French Grand Chemin du Bayou St. John – Literally means "the great road/street to Bayou St. John"

Congo Square – Once a sacred piece of ground by the natives just north of New Orleans, it became a popular meeting spot for slaves. Congo Square could very well be considered the birthplace of jazz music in the New Orleans area.

Chapter 1

March 30th, New Orleans 1815

The odors and sounds of the city met Bart even before they rounded the final bend in the river. The creaking of merchant ships, and the shouting of men on the docks as they loaded and unloaded fresh cargo were distinctly heard from his place at the bow. Now that the British blockade had been lifted, the peace treaty ratified in Congress, commerce and trade could continue.

Bart was fortunate enough to miss the battle just down river a couple of months prior, along with nearly all of the martial law limitations that Andrew Jackson had enforced over the citizens. Though the trip to Natchitoches was far from convenient, he was able to bypass a rather messy altercation. Now, he returned with one less reformed loup-garou and with more questions as to how his own enterprises had faired during his absence.

Bleached sails came into view, their masts swaying with the wind as they navigated down the muddy Mississippi. Ships from all nations were anchored at the docks or easing their way out of the harbor. Bart held fast to the line as he leaned over the railing to catch a glimpse of the port. Not part of the Americas for even a decade, New Orleans was steadily becoming a booming hub, just as the politicians had predicted. Situated upon the mighty river that snaked north along the borders of her neighboring states, it was the ideal place for all incoming and outgoing trade to help fuel westward expansion.

But Bart had never been interested in the efforts of the French, Spanish, or the Americans that owned this land over the last century. This place wasn't only ideal for trade, but for a certain mission of his that few knew about, but nearly all had speculated. The unique terrain became his ally when hiding his activities along the edges of the cypress swamps to the south of the river.

For now, he had a few men to see and some affairs to settle with the customs house. Then he could return to the place that had been his home for almost a hundred years.

He felt an uncanny wash of relief at the sight of the port city. It was emitted by his inner wolf, but not necessarily shared by him. Bart was one of the few loups-garous he knew that enjoyed sailing, whether it be across the ocean or down a river that concealed deadly sandbars. His wolf, however, did not agree and as soon as his boots made contact with the dock after walking down the gangplank, he was overcome by a silly urge to kiss the stable ground.

Of course, he refrained and carried himself like the gentlemen his reputation demanded of him. Anyone might have seen him as a man just past his prime with touches of silver that streaked through his hair and beard. No one would have ever suspected that he was older than this very city and the country they now called home.

His dark eyes trailed up to the impressive stone buildings with their arcade facades - indicative of the Spanish influence from their relatively short period of reign over the territory – and mansard roofs that reminded him of the great homes and government buildings in France. Down the straight, dusty avenues and roads that were laid out like a sprawling grid, carriages, carts, and pedestrians made their way from shop to shop.

The voices that drifted out of every window and rose to a dull roar all over the city were as varied as the faces they belonged to. French, American, German, Irish, Spanish, and the Free People of Color all mingled together in an inspiring display that brought a smile to Bart's lips. Despite his status as a well-off merchant and plantation owner, he was often lumped in with the later aforementioned people group due to his lighter, mulatto complexion. And ever since the Americans had come, he'd suffered for it.

His status, wealth, and fabled generosity made him infamous within New Orleans amongst every class. It either made him enemies or blessed him with connections. As he passed St. Louis Cathedral on La Place d'Armes and continued down St. Peters Street, several men looked his way and either smiled or sneered. Women who also met his gaze covered their blushing cheeks with their fans as they turned to giggle with their companions. He smirked to them, and touched the brim of his hat in greeting, but it was rare that he ever stopped to speak with any of them. It was a habit of his not to spend too much time within the city, unless absolutely necessary.

And if he were to speak, he'd have to check himself before uttering a single word. It was a chore to mask his British accent from the public and slow down his enunciations to emulate the speech of those around him. If he were to reveal his true drawl, especially after the most recent war, he'd certainly raise suspicion. It was only with a select few that he could relax, only because they knew the truth.

He turned left down Royal Street. Years ago, two fires had eaten away at the establishments here, allowing for stronger brick homes to be erected with their elaborate wrought iron balusters and overhanging balconies that shaded the walkways along the roads. Another architectural gift from the Spanish after nearly a quarter of the city was destroyed in 1788. Bart remembered it as a terrible year for New Orleans and he stayed close to his home during the reconstruction.

Craftsmen of all trades could be found here, and Bart followed the scent of barley, yeast, and beer a few blocks away. Inside the brewery, the back of his skull tingled, alerting him to the presence of more of his kind. More loups-garous.

He had heard them in the back room, arguing in intermittent German and Gaelic. Bart shook his head ruefully and passed through the public tavern where working men came to refresh themselves with a glass of beer. This brew had earned a notable reputation for itself over the last few years. One benefit of being a loup-garou and incapable of becoming intoxicated was that when it came to matters of alcoholic beverages, they focused on the taste and not its ability to put men in their boots. Lorenz Hiedenhem and Carney O'Malley may have been the best damn brewers in the whole southern region, and Bart had the good fortune of claiming to be the one who brought them together. If only they could stop bickering over every batch.

He stepped through the archway into the back room and found them screaming at one another, voices raised. Even without his sensitive hearing, he would have known they disagreed on the amount of molasses that was added to the last brew all the way from Burgundy Street. The air was saturated with the aroma of hops, yeast, and other herbs used to help give their brand its unique flavor. Word of their success had reached all the way to Boston on the east coast and merchants from all across the states would make a point of stopping by their tavern when they came to port in New Orleans.

The brewery consisted of three stories. Three steps down from the entryway was the bottommost level. Barrels brimming with beer were lined against the stone walls, awaiting transport or consumption. Several barrels were reserved for beer that was in the final stages of fermentation, a leather hose trailing from their spouts to the second-floor landing.

Bart didn't attempt to silence his ascension up the flight of stairs, looking for the two younger loups-garous. A strong fire burned in the second-floor furnace, its heat making the water in the brew kettle above him simmer and steam.

One more flight of stairs brought him to the place where Lorenz and Carney stood near the railing that skirted around the opening to the mash tun below. The German waved wildly with one arm while his other mindlessly stirred the half-processed brew with a giant dipper. Carney put some distance between himself and the loup-garou who was older and far more dominant and stood on the other side of the chillers where recently heated beer was cooling after being boiled for a couple of hours in the brew kettle.

Bart had never been interested in the brewing process, but he had heard it explained so many times by either Carney or Lorenz during conversation that he could most likely brew his own beer from beginning to end in his sleep.

As soon as Bart crossed his arms, they finally took notice of him near the top of the stairs.

"You're back!" Lorenz exclaimed, coming forward to give him a hearty slap on the shoulder. "It feels like you've been gone for months."

"It's only been one month," Carney corrected, his pale red brows furrowing.

"I said it only *feels* like months," the German loup-garou snapped back at his apprentice. "Not that it literally was months since he left."

"Is it just me, or do you two seem to look for an excuse to argue about everything?" Bart asked, his deep English accent contrasting so frankly with the other Europeans.

Lorenz replied in the negative, while Carney gave a decided affirmative. It never ceased to amaze Bart how these two managed to maintain an operation as delicate as beer brewing with only themselves to man the facilities.

Sometimes he wondered if it had been a mistake to let them both stay in New Orleans together. Lorenz had established the brewery even before Carney was born in Belfast, but the Catholic loup-garou had few other options than to flee to one of the rare places in the New World who took kindly to those of his faith. He and Lorenz cracked each other's skulls on more than a few occasions. But once they were on any other subject than work, one could look past the fiery red hair of the Irishman and the dark blonde of the German to see that they were as close as brothers.

"How was your trip?" Lorenz asked.

Bart gravitated toward a small table near the dirty window and took one of the chairs. Carney took the other while his business partner was trapped in the task of stirring the mash as the barley and wheat blend steeped in the hot water.

"It went well," Bart replied, smirking to the two loups-garous. "Nashoba seemed to get along well with the Chickasaw around Natchitoches. I think he'll be a fine fit there."

Carney's blue eyes looked heavenward. "Lord knows I didn't think that one could be turned around, but you've surprised me again."

Bart smiled, though he would never admit he concurred with Carney's first impressions. The rogue Choctaw native was a savage loup-garou before he came onto the plantation. It took several months to break him, but after a while, Nashoba stopped craving the flesh of humans and could conduct himself like any other civilized man. It was difficult to let him leave, especially since his home had been in the Louisiana wilderness for as long as he could remember. But sometimes complete relocation was required for these extreme cases.

"How many more convicts are on the plantation?" Lorenz questioned as he leaned against the railing.

Bart didn't often appreciate the slang that others applied to those loups-garous he rehabilitated at his home near the swamps. They were criminals, but to dub them as convicts, or rougarous as some of the locals would have unkindly labeled them, seemed like a sort of condemnation. He hadn't met a loup-garou yet that he couldn't break.

"Just three," he answered.

They continued to talk, mostly about business both with his plantation and at the brewery.

"That reminds me," Lorenz said as he scratched beneath his neckerchief, which hid a nasty scar he had earned when he became loup-garou, "a man came here looking for you a few days ago. I told him you were out of town, but he didn't seem to mind."

At this, Bart's wolf stiffened. If someone was looking for him, it could have meant a number of things. Either it was another loup-garou in search of help, a potential business connection who thought they could make him a proposition, or someone who did not mean him well.

"Who was he?"

At this, Carney chimed in. "He was werewolf," he replied in a lower voice in case anyone might have heard him over the simmering brew kettle. "I think he was a soldier, but they all left after Andrew Jackson sailed back up the river to Kentucky."

Bart leaned back and laced his fingers over his stomach, feeling the cool metal of his vest buttons under his palms. "What did he want?"

Lorenz shook his head. "He didn't say. Only to tell you that he'd be waiting at the inn on the corner of Bourbon and Du Maine. Said he wanted to take you up on an offer you made a long time ago."

Bart squinted, peering through the many years' worth of memories for any unkept promises or abandoned offers. At first, he could think of none. And then it came to him in vivid relief.

"It couldn't be," he muttered, more to himself than the other two. He looked up, refusing to hope but daring to venture a guess in his heart. "What did he look like?"

"Looked like he'd been in the sun for a long time," Carney said as he folded his arms over the edge of the table. "Black hair, brown eyes."

"No, they were green," Lorenz contented. "Maybe a really dark green, but they weren't brown."

"I got a closer look at the man than you did. They were brown."

"Hazel?" Bart asked quickly.

Lorenz snapped his fingers. "I believe they were."

"Oh, and he was from England too," Carney added.

He didn't need to hear anymore. Bart stood from his chair, nearly knocking it over. He paid them a hasty goodbye and hurried out onto Royal street. If he was right, which he dearly hoped that he was, he had been waiting for this reunion for nearly a hundred years.

Those smiles and nods he so generously gave to any passersby before were reserved, his mouth set in a grim and determined line as he weaved through the crowd down Royal Street. One left turn onto Du Maine and the tavern came into sight. His nose picked up the old scent, the one he remembered from so long ago, faint traces of a memory he had been afraid to hold onto for all this time.

His wolf spurred him on to walk faster, but he slowed as he reached the tavern. His senses spiked as they had outside the brewery and he took a breath to steady himself before rushing through the doors.

Bart's eyes skimmed through the faces looking for him. Tavern goers, including merchants, traders, sailors, and some citizens of New Orleans, all congregated around tables. Laughter and conversation roared through the long room, but it all dimmed to Bart when he spotted his son toward the very back. With a mug in his hand, his dark hair was combed back and tied with a black ribbon; much like in the same fashion as he had worn when they first met. The lines of his swarthy, handsome face were more distinguished, matured from the youthful looks of a man in his twenties.

Hazel eyes met his and a smile curved over his mouth, one that Bart never expected to receive in his lifetime. They had parted on bad terms. That was never denied. Bart had told himself a thousand times that he would look for James again when the time was right, but all his inquiries in the Caribbean brought up nothing, just like they had before. His son had a marvelous talent for disappearing without a trace.

But now, James came to Bart. The prodigal son who had once hated his father had come to New Orleans and sought after him. If he hadn't known beyond a shadow of a doubt that he was awake, he would have thought he was dreaming.

James stood from his chair and Bart realized his legs were carrying him across the bustling tavern hall. They met in the middle and clasped arms as if they were old friends.

Still in a daze, Bart wasn't sure what to say. James must have seen that, so he spoke first.

"It's been a long time," he said. His voice had barely changed over the century. Deepened, perhaps, and matured along with his outer appearance, but mostly the same except for the loss of his accent, which he attributed to their public setting, reminding Bart as well that he needed to be careful in case anyone heard him.

"It has," Bart replied, keeping the overpowering emotions at bay for now. "You've grown a bit."

A sparkle of mischief shone in his son's eyes and he reached up to pluck at a bit of gray hair at Bart's temples. "So have you."

He laughed and his gaze was drawn back to the table where James had been sitting. There was someone else with him, younger than the both of them and watching the crowd with a pair of bright blue eyes that contrasted so sharply with his dark hair. He dressed the same as James, in clothes that held a distinct fragrance of seawater, gunpowder, and wilderness. His thumb grazed over the handle of his mug in a thoughtful manner, as if his mind were miles away.

"The German at the brewery said you were out of town," James said, interrupting Bart's assessment. "Did you just return?"

"I did. Who's your companion?" he questioned, jerking his chin to the other loup-garou.

James glanced over his shoulder as if he had forgotten the young man was there. Then, his smile widened. "His name's Robert." Then, he turned back to lean in closer as if what he was about to say were a secret just between them. "He's your grandson."

Bart shouldn't have been as shocked as he felt. Looking now, Robert bore a stunning resemblance to his father both in features and in build. Some things about him gave a nod to his mother's lineage, but he was certainly a Croxen.

The last time he'd seen James, his son had a mind to court the daughter of Kingston's governor. From what he heard through gossip and headlines later, Grace Norrie was kidnapped by a rogue pirate. Her father searched across the Caribbean for the Devil Dog who had reportedly kidnapped her previously to this crime and returned her. But neither pirate nor lady were ever seen again. It wasn't Bart's place to get in the way of James' happiness, so he never volunteered what little he knew or suspected.

Knowing that James fathered a son made him both proud and terrified. What kind of hell had the boy been put through by his adventurous and sometimes wild guardian? Had James trained Robert well enough to know what it meant to be a loup-garou, as Bart had failed to do?

Despite all these unanswered questions, Bart felt his cheeks hurt with the force of his grin. "I'll be damned," he chuckled.

This drew Robert's attention and he looked up to the two men of his family, curiosity in those eyes he had inherited from Grace.

James led Bart to their table, which was pushed well out of the way of any moving traffic across the tavern and the noise seemed to echo less in this corner. Introductions where made and as soon as Robert was informed of his relation to Bart, he seemed relieved.

"All this time, I thought he was taking me to meet an old pirate friend," he said.

"It wouldn't surprise me if James never spoke a word about me to anyone," Bart returned, unashamed to be little more than a footnote in his son's more colorful history.

Robert shook his head. "Actually, he mentioned you quite often."

At this, Bart was surprised, and James looked to him with a shrug.

"He asked, so I told him," his son explained, as if to crush any ideas Bart might have of James' mawkish sentiment toward the father he never knew.

"You're such a liar," Robert laughed. "I remember you talked about the famous privateer plenty of times without being prompted."

James gave his son's shoulder a tight squeeze and shook him a bit playfully. "Either way, Robert is aware of your existence," he said to Bart.

With formalities out of the way, they could move onto topics that were far more important. "How did you know where to find me?"

They all took their seats as James elected to answer first. "We've been around New Orleans for a few years now. We've heard all about your rather... unconventional sugarcane plantation. Not many planters actually pay their workers."

Bart shrugged his brows and lowered his gaze, only mildly offended that he should be so known for his liberal work practices, rather than other things. "Well, not many planters share the same values as I do."

"Even some Free People of Color have slaves to run their fields," Robert remarked. "How many do you employ on your plantation?"

"Only thirty," he replied and then pointed a cautionary finger to his grandson. "I don't employ them. I allow them to live on my land and they share in the profits of the sugarcane they harvest. And just because other darkies have slaves doesn't mean it's right to have them at all."

James held up a hand as if to intercede. "Don't mistake us. We don't agree with it any more than you do. You forget I had several freed slaves aboard my ship."

Robert rolled his eyes, but more at the mention of James' pirating days rather than his sentiments toward the institution of slavery. And Bart could understand why. James began to carry on about his former crew and how the men came from all walks of life, faces of every color were welcome aboard his ship as long as they served him faithfully and didn't ask questions about his seemingly unusual behavior. Making port at an isolated island once a month and boasting a pair of golden eyes while in battle would have made any sailor suspicious. But the Devil Dog made sure that each man knew their place.

Bart saw Robert's annoyance with the subject, so he cleverly diverted it back to where they had begun. "You've been near New Orleans, but you're just now coming to see me?" he asked.

At this, James looked a little embarrassed. "We were working, so we never quite had the chance. But with Lafitte allowing the men to –"

"Lafitte?" Bart interrupted. "Jean Lafitte?"

Now it was Robert's turn to jab a warning at his grandfather. "Governor Clairborne pardoned all the Baratarians after the battle."

James gave a nod in agreement. "We served on the artillery lines under Andrew Jackson himself. We're heroes to New Orleans just as much as Lafitte is."

Heroes indeed. Bart sat back in his chair and let out a long sigh. "I had hoped settling down with Grace had tamed you a bit, but I see now I was wrong."

James narrowed his eyes upon his father. "Grace has been dead for almost sixty years, all of which you weren't around for. So, don't make assumptions about whether my character has changed or not. You only knew me for two days. The rest was filled in with lies and tall tales about what you thought was true."

"And if it weren't for those lies," Bart bit back in a hushed tone, forgetting all vocal disguise in his frustration, "then I would have never had those two days to begin with, and you wouldn't be here, would you?"

His words held a double meaning and James was smart enough to understand. If it hadn't been for those mythic tales about the Devil Dog, he would have never come out of his retirement as a privateer to hunt his son down in the Caribbean. And if it hadn't been him, the unlikelihood of James escaping the gallows or a worse fate at the hands of the law would have been greater. And if that was true, then Bart could be thanked for Robert's very existence.

James, much to his astonishment, lifted up his hands in surrender and eased back from the table. "I didn't come here to fight or argue about what did or didn't happen between us. Like I said, you don't know me nearly as well as you should, and Robert deserves to know his grandfather. I'm here so we can help fill in the gaps for each other, if you think you can tolerate being in the company of a former pirate."

It didn't take Bart long to make up his mind about that. Pirate or no pirate, James was his son and Robert was his grandson. He'd visit with them for as long as they were willing to put up with him as well.

He smirked. "A twice former pirate," he corrected jokingly. James returned with a half-smile of his own before Bart continued. "I don't mind at all, but perhaps we should continue this conversation in a more private setting." He gave a pointed look toward a small group of Americans who were cutting their eyes toward the only mulatto-skinned man in the room, who dressed far too well for their tastes. "The company here is far more disagreeable."

CHAPTER 2

"Of course," James continued, "Robert wasn't too pleased with the idea of joining, but he didn't have much of a choice in the end."

They continued to walk along the road that ran deep into the wilderness to the east of the Mississippi. Ever since they had left the tavern on Bourbon Street and taken one of the ferries that crossed the river to Algiers Point, the three men talked – as discretely as they could in the company of humans – of their lives over the last one hundred years. Some details were carefully omitted or hinted at, knowing that their conversation may not have been as private as they wished.

But the only creatures to hear them now were the cicada bugs who droned on in the dense forests that enclosed both sides of the dirt road. Spanish moss like the graying beards of old men drooped from the contorted branches shading their path. With Robert walking along one rut in the road, his thumbs slung in his vest pockets, James and his father let themselves wander further into the middle. Bart assured them that few people passed down this lane and the well-worn ruts were made by his own wagons and not a neighbor's. The last plantation they passed was at least five miles behind them. They were completely safe to speak as freely as they wished.

"I would have been just fine as a clerk for Mr. Levins in Charleston," Robert contested. "The only reason I agreed to follow you into the Continental Navy was to keep an eye on you. I had a choice to stay behind."

James knew damn well that his son knew better. He was perfectly capable of taking care of himself. "I didn't need you to keep an eye on me. And Mr. Levins wasn't going to take you on as one of his clerks while his daughter was putting a good word in for that boy she fancied. That's the only reason you didn't fight me when I said we're joining the navy."

As always when mentioning the young Miss Levins, Robert's face scrunched as if something in his clothes made him uncomfortable. Bart chuckled lightly at his grandson's expense.

"Oh, I fought you," Robert rejoined. "For days, I tried to make you see how foolish joining the navy would be."

James slipped him a devilish smile. "But it was worth it."

Robert scoffed. "Yes, being shot at by the British, nearly blown to pieces by cannonball, and on the edge of starvation was far better than staying safe in Charleston on our farm."

If being raised by a retired pirate and a strong-willed, sassy mother had given him anything beneficial, it was his quick wit and sarcasm. It didn't emerge often, but when Robert stopped pretending to be the kind of man who preferred to be behind a desk rather than manning a cannon, that sardonic banter shined through. He was his father's son.

"But, you didn't die," James ribbed.

Robert's brows furrowed angrily. "Do you realize how much we lost in assets alone by leaving the farm? Not to mention all the livestock."

The amused smile never left Bart's face as his gaze flitted from one Croxen boy to the other.

"You never let me forget," James replied, knowing he would hear the figures despite his answer.

His son then proceeded to list off every piece of farming equipment and acreage of real estate, along with its going rate and what they could have been sold for. They could have gone off to serve in the war for American independence as richer men than they had been before or invest the money in something worthwhile. Robert certainly would have been an excellent clerk if Miss Levins preferred him over the son of the livery owner.

The sound of other human voices disrupted Robert's long dictation of their former estate's inventory, drawing their attention toward the path once more. The aroma of simmering stew and cooking meats floated to them, breaking through the swamp odors that had become so prevalent as they traveled even further from civilization.

The spices in the dishes alone made James' mouth water already. Remembering the days they spent aboard the *Alliance* brought back the gnawing sensations of hunger and frustration with the strict military protocol. Luckily for them, one of the officers was also a werewolf and aided them in concealing their secret from the rest of the crew. However, that didn't keep them from suffering more cruelly at sea than any other. It certainly was challenging to keep their unique and enhanced abilities to themselves.

Bart turned to them, unbothered by their approach to the plantation. "What did you do after the war?" he asked them.

James looked to his father, still in some disbelief that he had made the decision to seek him out after all this time. He had toyed with the idea for some years since they learned that Bart owned a plantation near New Orleans, but the timing was never quite right. Lafitte's infamy barred them from even stepping foot in the city on most occasions. How brothers Jean and Pierre snuck in to make their deals with the merchants of the town, James never quite understood.

But as he had told Bart earlier, the general pardon issued by the governor for services rendered during the final battle of the most recent war between England and America had allowed them to not only enter New Orleans, but partake in its society.

"Since our farm in Charleston had become irrevocably removed from our possession, I decided to take Robert to St. Kitts and show him where I was raised."

James had thought such a confession might wound Bart in some way. He had learned to forgive since he became a father himself.

He had been responsible for grown men who didn't need help in procuring the basic needs for life. Neither did he have to constantly protect or shelter Grace all the time. But becoming a father, responsible for the life of a small, helpless being had changed him forever. Things that used to enrage him were more bearable. Patience not only became a virtue, but a mantra when it came to raising Robert. All the hell he gave his mother had reincarnated in his little boy, and James paid dearly for it.

Being a father also allowed him to understand Bart more fully, and therefore the once despised man became worthy of pardon for his past sins. He could only hope that James could earn the same.

"And how did you like St. Kitts?" Bart asked his grandson, leaning a bit to watch the youngest of the three werewolves on the far side of the road.

"Not at all," he replied. "It was insufferably hot, just like Louisiana. Only the mosquitoes were worse. Its one redeeming quality might have been the beaches."

Bart nodded in approval. "I liked their beaches as well."

"We were there for a few years before we met Jean Lafitte for the first time," James carried on. "He was acting too big for his breeches and after he nearly failed a duel, I taught him a thing or two about how to properly aim a pistol."

"You conveniently failed to mention that it was you he lost the duel to," Robert murmured.

Much expected, Bart gave James a reproving look.

"Lafitte was drunk and insisted on it," he said defensively. "But I earned his respect when I didn't kill him that night, even though I could have easily."

Robert edged closer to the men. "It wasn't until five years later that we heard from him again, asking if we wanted to join his crew. He offered father a ship of his own in the fleet."

James lifted his chin proudly. "All I had to agree to was raiding English and Spanish ships. A portion of the cargo went to Lafitte and I could keep the rest."

"And those raids against the English didn't help our situation in this last war," Bart said. "Governor Clairborne's been after Lafitte for quite some time."

James grinned. "And now, the privateer under contract with Columbia is a pardoned war hero."

Bart gave him a sideways look. "Call him a war hero or privateer all you want, but Jean Lafitte is still a pirate that has made too many enemies. The governor doesn't like his illegal trade of black ivory either. After what happened in Haiti, I don't blame him."

Perhaps one of the only aspects of Lafitte's enterprise that James disagreed with, was his sneaking fresh slaves from the Caribbean to New Orleans to be sold at the slave auctions near the docks. He firmly believed the enslavement of another human being for the sake of earning money was one of the few unspoken sins. There was a special place in hell for those who thought they were doing right by forcing a once free and innocent person into a life of hard labor and cruelty.

That's why, when James heard about what Bart practiced on his own plantation, he couldn't have been more honored to claim him as his father. If his business system flourished, then maybe it would catch on and this abhorrent blemish on their society could be phased out permanently. It might have been too much to hope for, but the impossible happened every day.

"Joining Lafitte was as much a decision of the heart as it was of the mind," James said after a pause. "I won't lie and say that I don't miss those days when I was a captain of my own ship. But we couldn't stay in St. Kitts forever and this offer allowed us to travel and possibly gain a fortune we could use to retire somewhere in America."

"Somewhere cooler," Robert said as he hooked his finger on his cravat and tugged in an attempt to loosen it. It was only spring, but Robert had always preferred the colder climates of the northeast as opposed to the stifling humidity of the south.

"When Lafitte told me he went to Andrew Jackson and extended his help in defending New Orleans, I thought he had lost his mind." James shrugged. "Now I see it was a rather strategic move to win ourselves back into the good graces of the governor."

Bart didn't seem so convinced as they drew closer to the plantation, though it hadn't come quite into view yet. "You do realize it won't last." He said it in such a way that it was both an assumption and a question.

James, as much as he esteemed Lafitte and his shrewd mind for business, understood that all good things must come to an end and this season of good will in New Orleans was no exception. "Yes, but it will give us time to plan and choose where we will go next."

The elder of the werewolves, who boasted far more gray than James was comfortable seeing, looked to them with enquiring eyes. "So, you won't stay in New Orleans?"

Robert shook his head. "We haven't had much chance to discuss it."

James watched his son's face, searching for any hint as to what might have been percolating behind those sapphire eyes. The last forty years of their lives had been completely shaped by what James wanted to do. It was his decision to join the navy, his decision to travel to St. Kitts, and then ultimately his choice to take up on Lafitte's offer. Now, he would let his son make the next move. They would go wherever Robert wanted and do whatever he pleased, even if it meant going back to a simple life of farming. His wolf might have preferred that to the open sea. And though he was still a pirate at heart, James was one beast who could be domesticated, as much as his father didn't want to believe it.

The sound of negro voices became more distinguishable and they rounded the bend until they spotted a house some distance off. A great two-story mansion, one like James had seen a thousand times in the Caribbean and in the areas around New Orleans. Smooth white columns supported the roof and second floor landing. Tall, latticed windows with open shutters looked out on the drive. A few chimneys poked out from the roof, smoke curling upward into the evening sky.

The land around the house was cleared and well-trimmed, free of tall grasses and weeds. James could hear movement within the house and beyond where he could just barely catch sight of a kitchen house and the corners of shacks. Every building was bustling with activity, as if they knew the master of this plantation was approaching even before he was announced. If his nose was correct, he could smell fresh fish being seared in a cast iron skillet within the kitchen house, along with a simmering pot of okra soup. The spice of the peppers made his nose tingle. Somewhere on the property, he could also detect a pen for livestock and a rich, plentiful garden used by the cooks of the plantation.

And there was something else James noticed. Amongst the very human presence on the plantation, he was bombarded with a more intense sensation, warning him that other werewolves were nearby. At least five, maybe six. This was also accompanied by a single, trace scent of something from years back. There was someone within the mansion house that he knew, but it couldn't be possible. The last time he saw that werewolf, his face had disappeared into the watery depths of the Caribbean. He looked to his father with the unspoken question.

Bart saw his confusion and smiled. "Well, this will make one conversation a little easier. You probably wouldn't believe me if I told you without material proof."

Beside him, Robert was more enamored by the scene and the so far unseen people who lived here than the slight tremor of panic James felt deep within his bones.

Just as James began to second guess his decision to come to his father's plantation, the massive mahogany door opened to admit a man onto the front porch. He wasn't a negro, but his skin was darkened by years in the sun, just as James' was. This man had also been a sailor, but now he was dressed as another laborer, a tradesman. The splattering of dark dust on his white sleeves marked him as a blacksmith, and he was built for the job.

Dark eyes were trained upon them and James' wolf urged him to edge himself a little closer toward Robert to protect his son. Bart, of all people, wasn't troubled by the appearance of Will Ainsworth on his porch. After all these years, James still remembered that face and the name that brought his crew so much trouble in the final days of his command on the *Burning Rose*.

But there was something altered in his countenance. The man who fought like a wild animal on his deck now seemed tame and civil. The glint of maliciousness in his eyes was gone. There wasn't the look of deception and conniving intent about him as there had been before. No one would have supposed him to be a devious man. Perhaps he wasn't. Not anymore. Just as time had changed Bart and James, maybe it had changed Will.

The lingering mystery of why he was in Louisiana remained, but James kept moving one foot in front of the other until they climbed the creaking steps to meet him. Will and Bart exchanged a few words about his arrival to New Orleans before they turned to their guests. He noticed a subtle change of accent in his old adversary, as if his lowborn childhood had been worked out of him in some way.

"I suppose you two know one another, but let me introduce Robert Croxen. Robert, this is Will Croxen."

James did a doubletake. "Croxen? I thought your name was Ainsworth."

Both Bart and Will laughed at his puzzlement. Robert, poor boy, was in the dark about the connection.

"There's much to tell you, but come inside," Will insisted. "Emilie just brought in a fresh batch of lemonade."

Dazed, James followed them into the cool foyer and then into the parlor to the right. Lavishly furnished with heavy patterned drapes, it was every inch what he had expected of a plantation mansion. Their footsteps were softened by the intricately designed rug that covered the polished floorboards of the room. The thinly padded upholstery of the sofas and armchairs didn't make for comfortable seating, but it was far better than the wooden benches and chairs James was used to.

The fireplace was bare and cleaned of ashes, bare just like the mantle and many of the other surfaces around the room. A tray, arranged with a decanter of lemonade and a few tall glasses, sat on the center table between the sofas.

Robert and James took a seat while Bart poured them each a glass of the tart, but sweet refreshing lemonade. Will sat across from them in his own armchair and for a moment, James wondered if he cared that he might sully the woven fabric.

Another thought, as disturbing as the others that had flown through his mind in the last sixty seconds, was that he had never been in the company of this many werewolves before. Not only were there three in this room, but three more somewhere else on the property. Then there were the two others in New Orleans he had met. In Charleston and even St. Kitts, he and Robert had been the only werewolves in the area. To know there were so many so close unnerved him, but he wasn't quite sure why.

"This man has come a long way from the sandbar I found him stranded on," Bart began, referring to Will, as he handed them the filled glasses. "It took three months for him to speak a single kind word to me after we arrived in New Orleans."

"I think it helped that you were nearly starving me," Will quipped with a teasing smile toward the older werewolf. All the while, James scrutinized the man's face and mannerism, looking for a hint of the rogue he had met on the seas so long ago. That blackguard simply wasn't there anymore. Could this be the same Will?

Bart took his own glass and sat on the vacant sofa. "Once he did talk, though, we discovered that he is also my son. By a different woman, of course."

James' eyes went wide and if he looked to Robert, he suspected he would see the same alarm. All thought ground to a stuttering halt at this seemingly casual confession from Bart, as if this kind of news wouldn't have been so startling.

"Your son? So he is..."

"Half-brother," Will finished for him. "I wasn't aware of it at the time when we met, I assure you. And even if I was, I'm sure I wouldn't have behaved any differently."

That, too, sounded like a bold and rather controversial admission. "You would have still stolen from my cook and deceived me into going after Bart?"

Will nodded without a hint of shame. "I would have. I'm sure there wouldn't have been a soul alive who could have convinced me to abandon my mission to kill Bart."

He finally blinked, only slightly recovered. "But you two... You're here now, so..."

James hated to see his father so thoroughly amused. "Do you remember what we talked about in the brig aboard your ship?" Bart asked.

Searching his memory, he nodded. "You had asked me if I ever ate human flesh and I told you I didn't."

"You didn't, but Will did. After I helped myself off your ship, I continued looking for him. I never went into detail about the crimes I once mentioned to you, nor did I tell you about what I had become known for across Europe." Bart shifted as if trying to get comfortable on the sofa, which wouldn't have been an easy task as it was. "I'm not sure you ever fully understood what happens to a loup-garou when he eats human flesh. You might have instinctively shied away from the idea, but some like Will, didn't. When a loup-garou gets a taste for it, they become feral and unstable. They lose all sense of sympathy for others and make decisions that gratify their own needs, no matter what they may be. Theft, murder, rape, all of it could be attributed to this derangement of the mind that happens when a loup-garou makes a habit of eating humans."

James glanced to his son and saw the total look of disgust. Bart was correct in what he said. James never had to instruct Robert in the realm of common sense. They naturally detested the notion of eating another person, no matter how hungry they became. A loup-garou had to be desperate to resort to such methods. Then, he looked to Will. What could have driven him to such extremes? Was it his before professed hatred for Bart? Or did something else happen before James picked him up in that lone rowboat out in the middle of the Caribbean?

"I've made a reputation for myself as being someone who can break a loup-garou of their addiction. In fact, that's what I've been doing for the last one hundred years in New Orleans. I have connections across the states and territories. If one of them comes to me and reports some strange murders or if another loup-garou knows someone who needs rehabilitation, I go to investigate and bring them here."

The laughter and voices of the sharecroppers behind the mansion grew a little louder in the silence after Bart finished his speech. James' gaze dropped to the table where the one remaining glass was left turned over on the tray.

All this time, he believed his father had gone after him because of all the untruthful stories that might have been spread about his days as a pirate. Sure, he was cruel and ruthless at times, but he never ate the hearts of his captives as some believed. Bart chased James because he thought that he had turned feral as Will had.

Robert leaned forward and rested his elbows upon his knees. "How do you do it?" he asked, intrigued. "How do you break someone of the addiction?"

Bart went on to explain how he separated the loup-garou from society, kept him in a specially made shack toward the back of his property, and simply deprived him of the flesh he craved for a few months. Instead, they provided more wholesome meats such as chicken, pork, rabbit, and the occasional alligator. Other wild poultry was given when it became available.

"When they've become accustomed to their new diet, I release them and have them serve on my plantation or in town for a few more months. Once I'm convinced that they can return to their packs, I escort them home. If they have no pack, I find a place for them. I just returned from depositing one reformed loup-garou native to Natchitoches in the north. There are three more who are still here. Two are past the first stage of their rehabilitation, but I still have one in the shacks."

Still engrossed by this topic while James tried to make sense of it, Robert asked, "How do you keep them contained? A simple wooden shack can't hold a werewolf."

A wicked grin split Will's face. "It wasn't easy at first."

"It took constant supervision and I couldn't keep humans on the property as I do now," Bart added. "But New Orleans proved to be our ally and silversmiths crossed our paths over the years. I'll show you the shacks later, but you'll find the bars of the cages are coated in silver to keep any loup-garou from escaping."

James finally grasped the reality of what this place was. As happy as the voices sounded outside, as lavishly decorated as the mansion appeared, as successful as his methods were, James understood the truth. "This is a prison," he said flatly.

All turned to him. Will was the only one who didn't seem upset by the assertion, validating it without ever having to say a word.

"I don't like to think of it that way," Bart replied with a shake of his head. "Some call the recovering loups-garous convicts, but I would think of them more as... patients, really. They are sick and I'm helping them along the road to wellness."

"By starving them," James pointed out, remembering what Will had said earlier.

"We aren't starving them. Not really. They believe they're starving, because they crave something they can't have. The food we provide is more than enough to satisfy them, but that's part of the sickness. Their stomachs and pallets tell them what they are eating isn't enough, even when it is."

"But they're suffering. And you're holding them here against their will before putting them to work in your fields." James' expression hardened. "Do you pay them the same as you pay your sharecroppers?"

Bart nodded. "Just the same. They never leave here without some of their own money in their pockets to help them along the way. Most of the time, these rogue loups-garous come here without any etiquette, no social skills to speak of, no manners or sense of law and order. We teach them that as well, so they can blend in with the rest of society."

James glanced to Will, who remained strangely silent during this debate. "And do you agree with his methods?"

The former rogue werewolf didn't move, didn't blink. A few heartbeats passed before he finally nodded. "As inhumane as you may think they are, his methods work. The results justify the means."

None of it settled right with James. Not because he believed that what Bart set out to do was wrong in some way. The thought and sentiment behind rehabilitating werewolves who were a danger to humans was noble enough. It was the way in which he did it. Forcing the men into the withdrawal from what made them turn violent and trapping them in cages. It might have been the old pirate in him that grimaced at the procedure, but James couldn't come up with a better way. Just like Will said, nothing could convince him that he was in the wrong, so why should any other feral werewolf listen to advise that what he did was sinful? If words alone couldn't cure them, and if this type of imprisonment was too sadistic, then what other option was there?

From the other side of the house, James heard a door open and lumbering steps hurrying from room to room. That was the only reason he curtailed his questions and comments, which were in no short supply. Less than a moment later, a man stopped just outside the doorway behind Bart. He didn't turn to see who it was, but waved him forward anyway.

"Come in, Simon," he said softly. "They're friends."

A negro stepped forward, dressed as any other free man in a cravat, waistcoat, and matching vest. Not a speck of dirt sullied his trousers either. His black eyes looked between the new visitors and an unabashed smile split his ebony face to reveal two rows of perfectly white teeth. Black hair was neatly trimmed no more than a quarter of an inch, but by the way the ends curled a bit, James could guess how unruly and wild it could become if left unmanaged. His face, though clean of scars, seemed to profess his hard life in the roughness of his complexion and the deep lines from frowning – or perhaps screaming – so often. His attire said he was free, and the joyful light in his expression declared it, but his body told another story.

Will gave a short nod of greeting as Simon came forward.

"Robert, James, this is Simon. He's not a sharecropper here or a patient, but he is a fellow loup-garou."

James could sense that from the moment he stepped foot into the mansion, though he was slightly embarrassed to admit he hadn't thought he'd be black. The number of werewolves he had met in person could be counted on one hand and none of them had been of African descent, though he was sure it was possible.

"Pleasure to meet ya, sir," Simon said, offering out his massive hand to James.

He took it and shook it firmly, impressed by his strength and brawny stature that surpassed every other werewolf in the room. His shoulders were wider, arm muscles straining against his coat sleeves as if they were far too small for him, and at least a few inches taller than any of them. James imagined the man would certainly be a fearsome opponent in his wolfish form.

He then went to shake Robert's hand, who couldn't stop staring.

"Simon's been with me for about seventy-two years," Bart explained. "He's been a loup-garou for sixty-nine."

James shot a look to his father, but he didn't have a chance to ask.

"Mass'r Bart turned me," Simon said, his chest expanding with pride.

A ripple of astonishment was shared between James and Robert, but the burly black man wasn't fazed by it at all.

Simon then looked to Bart and started asking how his trip went. Bart, of course, found their amazed looks humorous again and carried on the conversation with his friend as if nothing were wrong. Will, on the other hand, rose from his chair and motioned them to follow him out of the room.

James and Robert set down their half-finished glasses of lemonade and trailed behind Will down the corridor toward the back of the house. He led them onto the back veranda that looked out over the rows of wooden shacks, which were in slightly better condition than he expected. Men, women, and children of all varying shades of blackness walked about and talked with one another while their supper was prepared in the kitchen house off to the left side of the property, away from the mansion.

"Yes, Bart turned Simon a few years after they first met," Will said, obliging himself to settle their confusion. "I had advised him against it, but once I learned Simon's reason for wanting to become a werewolf, I washed my hands of the business."

Robert leaned against a rounded column, watching the sharecroppers as if he were studying them, while James and Will stood beside one another. This day had proved to be an interesting one. He had expected the reunion with his father, but to find out he was running his own werewolf asylum, then meeting the man who had been his half-brother all along was almost too much to process.

"Simon was a slave once. Born in Georgia and then sold when his owner passed away. He came to New Orleans and was purchased by a French planter who was known for mistreating his... property." The venom in that last spoken word told James that he was not alone in his opinion of slavery. "In New Orleans, Bart caught Simon's owner beating him for supposedly stealing money after he was instructed to conduct some business in town. In reality, his owner simply gave Simon too little money for the necessary purchase. If Bart hadn't stepped in, Simon wouldn't have a hand right now. His owner was trying to maim him, which went against Le Code Noir at the time."

"Code Noir?" Robert questioned, apparently still half listening in their conversation during his inspection of the plantation.

James, having been acquainted with the term since he was a boy, replied, "It's a set of rules laid down for slaves and their masters in French colonies. It's not so widely implemented now, but seventy years ago when Louisiana was still French, I'd imagine it was taken seriously."

"It was," Will confirmed. "And according to Le Code Noir, Bart was able to turn Simon's owner into the authorities and his property was confiscated from him. Bart purchased Simon before he could be sold at the next auction and then made arrangements for him to be freed. Simon, however, wouldn't leave Bart's side. Said he owed Bart his life for taking him from his previous owner, so he wanted to repay him for it."

James smirked. "I take it that Bart didn't like the idea."

"He didn't, but Simon simply wouldn't go away, so he allowed him to stay and help him with the plantation. When he learned about werewolves, he immediately wanted to become one. I remember when I asked him why he wanted to be a werewolf, he said 'So no white man can evah hurt me again'. I couldn't argue with that logic."

"So Bart bit him," Robert said.

Will nodded to his nephew and then turned his stare toward the sharecroppers' cabins. "He did. And he's been here ever since. He takes care of the plantation when Bart's away and helps me keep the other werewolves in line."

James spotted a couple of white faces amongst the other negroes, the other werewolves who were here to recover from their wicked lifestyles. They had glanced in their direction while helping carry planks of wood to a new shack being built at the end of the lane, but nothing more. No wave, no nod or look of inquisitiveness, as if new werewolves showed up on the plantation all the time and their arrival meant nothing.

"How do you really feel about all this?" James asked, keeping his voice low so few could hear them – human or werewolf – beyond the back porch.

Will's head turned to him, his dark eyes serious as he carefully gave his response. "As I said before, the results justify the means... I have a wife and blacksmith shop in New Orleans. I've been – for lack of a better term – sober for almost a century. I can't imagine what my life would have been like if Bart hadn't taken me in. I'm not so sure I would be alive right now." He stepped closer. "And you were a damned fool for not going with him when you had the chance. You may not have eaten human flesh, but our father knows far more than either of us can imagine. You could have learned from him."

James, used to being reminded of his folly plenty of times, gave just as hard of a look as he received. "If I had gone with Bart, I wouldn't have married Grace, and you wouldn't have a nephew."

Will's gaze briefly flickered toward Robert. "At least you're here now. I presume you're staying?"

James couldn't give an adequate answer. Instead of lying and assuring that they would be here for years, he only looked away. "We'll be here for some time. I can say that much."

"If you're smart, you'll get what you can out of Bart before you go." A moment of silence stretched between the three of them as they watched the families of the sharecroppers, oblivious to what might have been truly taking place on this plantation just beyond the sugarcane fields. "I know you must have hated Bart for leaving you and your mother. I hated him for the same reasons. We can't change the past. I'm sorry for what I did a century ago. I suppose I've made amends with everyone I could except for you."

The two brothers regarded one another. James had made a point of forgiving Bart all those years ago, but never had he considered forgiving Will for what he did. He didn't think he'd have to. But, as he said, they couldn't change the past.

"Knowing what I know now, I suppose your actions were beyond your control," James said. "You couldn't help being what you were. There's nothing to forgive. If things had played out differently, we might not be standing here today."

A corner of Will's mouth tilted up in a crooked smile. "I guess you're right. All we can do is move forward."

Every bit of it was strange and James still couldn't wrap his mind around it. This place, these people, and the extraordinary undertaking they were so committed to. James wanted to think it was a good thing, but something in his gut - in his wolf - told him that there was something wrong. He couldn't put his finger on it, but it was there beneath the smiling faces and good intent. Going against what society dictated for people of color was going to make Bart plenty of enemies, and if anything should go wrong with one of his "patients", James couldn't fathom the kind of chaos that would ensue.

For all their sakes, James hoped that his father was prepared for the inevitable.

CHAPTER 3

Robert would have rather stayed in the cool indoors once supper was served, but Bart said they rarely used the dining room. Instead, they were escorted outside and given seats on the front porch of one of the shacks behind the mansion house. Every sharecropper living on Bart's plantation assembled around this porch, bowls and utensils in hand. Seated in the grass or upon stools they brought from their own cabins, they waited for the meal.

James and Robert silently watched and listened to the unique collection of dialects and languages amongst the negro and mulatto faces. French and an interesting accented English dominated the conversations as they asked Bart about his travels. The two new guests were warmly received, but Robert lamented the fact that Will had to leave them for his home in New Orleans, saying that his wife would hang him by his toenails if he was late for supper again.

Simon, the freed black man whom Bart had turned, sat close to James and soon, they were deep in conversation about how they came to New Orleans and their own connections with the man who saved his life. Robert, once again, felt out of place.

His eyes skimmed over the faces, watching how they interacted, studying the smiles and gestures of a people he had rarely seen up close. Negroes were common within New Orleans, the Caribbean, and Louisiana, but it wasn't every day that he could observe them in such an informal setting. Here, they were free to talk with their families. Dark faces that he so often saw downcast and creased with fear, were lifted up and cheerful here. Deep negro voices he had heard rising in supplication to God for mercy and deliverance, now spoke of the many blessings they enjoyed because of Bart's kindness and generosity.

When he thought on it, these people were truly free and given a kind of autonomy that was rare in other parts of America. Even in Charleston, the streets were not crowded in by black men and women who had either purchased their freedom or were granted it by their masters. Bart's sharecroppers could easily leave, without the need for anyone's permission. They could find other places of employment. They could travel if they wished. They could be anywhere but here, and they chose to stay. Given what else was happening on this plantation, Robert was astounded again.

He looked to the two other werewolves in the group. They, too, seemed happy and free. Not free from the unjust system of slavery, but from something far more oppressive. It was nearly impossible for him to imagine what it would have been like to be trapped within his own mind, imprisoned by a dependency on human flesh. His wolf, usually docile and passive, writhed at the very thought of it. Robert couldn't fathom what would have driven men like his uncle to such an addiction.

But neither could he understand why man enslaved fellow man as they did, why it was accepted and even paraded about like a sign of wealth and status. The world needed more men like Bart, who fought against the unjust and liberated the afflicted. Why his father, James, seemed to doubt the endeavor was beyond him.

The squeal of door hinges toward the kitchen house drew the attention of every werewolf in the group. All heads turned in unison to watch a young girl struggle down the walkway, her long skirt tangling in her legs as she walked. The heavy pot she carried between her mulatto hands sloshed with the okra soup they had been smelling for the last hour.

Bart pushed himself up from the porch and immediately went to help her. No others moved and a deep line wrinkled between Robert's brows. Out of all the strong men who were perfectly capable of helping her, the owner of this plantation was the only one to come to her aid.

"Let me take that, Emilie," he heard his grandfather insist.

Much against the lady's wishes, the handle was transferred from servant to master and Bart brought the soup to the hungry people around the cabin. The woman, Emilie, appeared only a little younger than what everyone might have supposed Robert to be; perhaps just at the start of her second decade of life. Silky black hair was pulled back and tucked beneath a cloth rag tied around her head. Her thin limbs and waist explained why she wasn't able to bear the load of soup, but the strong set of her jaw and clear, dark eyes made up for what she lacked in physical abilities. He was sure she could win any argument and scold even the toughest of men on the plantation and they would instantly concede to her silent strength.

Robert watched her with purely platonic interest as she ran her forearm across her brow and then straightened out her skirt. More than anything, he felt a stirring fascination for these people and how they could have endured being enslaved, oppressed in the harshest way possible. What was Emilie's story? How did she come to be here and who had put that fire in her eyes?

Bart had already taken the ladle and began to spoon out the chunky soup for each of the sharecroppers and their families.

A portly woman, with the blackest skin Robert had ever seen, hurried after Emilie and handed off another tray loaded down with golden fillets of fish that had been fried earlier. The soup, containing little meat at all, wouldn't satisfy the werewolves in the company. But this would.

The negress wrung her empty hands in her apron and turned back to the kitchen to retrieve something else while Emilie carried over the platter of fish. Robert hadn't realized how hungry he was until he caught sight of the long, thin fillets. She knew exactly who to deliver the fish to and went first to Simon, who plucked up the top five fillets for himself. Then, she went to the two nearly rehabilitated werewolves who took their share.

Her dark gaze met Robert's and Emilie hesitated. With a bit of uncertainty, she looked to Bart for direction. He nodded in approval and with timid steps, she approached the guests that she must not have noticed before.

James gave her a kind smile to assure her, but Robert went one step further when he took his portions.

"Thank you."

Emilie's skin was just light enough that he could see a bit of blush creep into her cheeks as she nodded and walked away, her shoes clapping against the rough boards of the porch. James passed his son a look, but Robert wouldn't return it. He was too hungry and his father too presumptuous to bother arguing.

After the kind of crushing rejection Miss Levins subjected him to in Charleston, Robert had abandoned thoughts of romance. Even in St. Kitts when the local women batted their eyes and giggled behind their fans, he didn't feel the least bit of compulsion to court or indulge himself in their company, much against James' encouragement.

Emilie would not change that for him, but he could show compassion and respect for a girl who tried to carry a pot brimming with soup that was far too heavy for her.

Bart was the last to take his fish and sat down beside Simon. The heavyset woman, whom Robert assumed was the head cook in the kitchen, rushed out with cornmeal cakes for each of the sharecroppers. He looked at the disks that were no bigger than his palm, browned on both sides and rimmed in a deep golden color with specks of seasoning that he guessed could be red pepper.

The humans took the bread and dipped it into their thick soup, scooping up bits of the tomato, onion, and sliced okra that made up the broth. If he weren't a werewolf, he would have asked to taste it. However, his fillets were just as delicious as the okra soup smelled.

"What is this?" he asked Simon, leaning past his father to address the man.

Simon grinned, those white teeth gleaming in the waning light. "That there's catfish, sir. Freshly caught dis mornin'."

Robert wasn't sure he had ever eaten catfish before. "It's certainly different," he said, rather impressed how the cooks could season the fillets in such a way that didn't turn his stomach. It was rare to find a meal cooked by someone other than himself or his father that agreed with them so perfectly.

Bart also leaned over so he could see his grandson. "Emilie and Ruth are aware of our special needs," he said, just loud enough over the clamor of spoons tapping against wooden bowls and murmuring voices around the porch.

His stare traveled to the young woman as she joined the head cook toward the back of the assembly to sit with a few other ladies. They were the single, hard-working women of the plantation who had neither husband nor child.

"How many more know of our... special needs?" James asked his father, carefully choosing his words.

"Very few," Bart replied before taking a bite of the fish.

"Folks 'round here don' like talkin' 'bout rougarous," Simon stated with a chunk of fried fish stuffed into one of his cheeks.

"Rougarous?" Robert repeated.

A few who were close to the porch heard him and stopped with their spoons halfway to their mouths to stare. The smell of their fear at the very mention of the word mingled in with the savory aromas of the dinner, spoiling even his appetite.

The two recovering werewolves stiffened, and Robert could see flecks of gold spiral in their irises at the triggering scent. Bart only had to give them one look to set them back in line and they ate their fish more greedily to stave off their old cravings.

Bart then turned to his sharecroppers who put off this fear and said something quickly in French to explain himself. They visibly relaxed and went back to their meals. The older werewolf then stood up and walked around to sit by Robert so they could converse in secret. James, too, kept a listening ear open.

"It's a twist on the typical loup-garou legend from France," he said. "And I suppose I've made it worse in some ways. They say it's a beast that lives in the swamps. He's a man with the head of a wolf and depending on who you ask, he goes after misbehaving children or Catholics who don't honor Lent. Some say he's only a rougarou for one-hundred-and-one days then transfers the curse to the next human he bites."

Robert, understanding that Louisiana and New Orleans were founded by the French, wasn't too surprised that the people of this region would develop their own flavor of the myth to explain disappearances or strange sounds they heard coming from the bayous. That would make the secrecy of Bart's endeavor that much more vital. If anyone were to learn that Bart or any of his associates like Simon were something similar to the rougarous, it would be much more readily believed than in other places like Boston or Charleston. There were few superstitions there, if any at all.

"But how did you make the propagation of this myth worse?" James asked, probably eager to find a fault with his father's side-business of reforming werewolves.

Bart set his fish down and leaned forward on his knees, once more keeping his words soft and low so others wouldn't hear unless they had ears like a werewolf. "Gossip spreads fast in New Orleans. I suppose some people who have visited the plantation or worked here for a time might have suspected something and came to their own conclusions. I've only ever had one loup-garou escape and he caused a slight panic, but that was decades ago before we had the silver cages."

"But not since, right?" Robert asked Bart as he slid a pointed look to his father.

"Correct," he replied. "But the damage was done and if you ask any of the superstitious people in New Orleans, they may say something about the rougarous they believe to be here."

James, however, was not pacified and clung to Bart's confession that something bad did come from this venture to help addicted werewolves. More willing to forgive, Robert continued to eat and watched the dark faces around him. When he exhausted this study, he turned his eyes to the impressively well-maintained shacks down the lane.

Bart changed the subject and went into detail about how the sugarcane was harvested and how this season would yield the best this plantation had sold in two years. This was due to the nature of how one planting of sugarcane could last three harvests, each batch maturing and deepening in its sweetness. Though sugarcane was easy to grow in this part of the country, there wasn't a lack for other work around the plantation. While the bright green stalks of sugarcane continued to grow, the sharecroppers could make repairs to their shacks, clear more land for planting, take care of the livestock and gardens, or offer out their services in town as long as they produced papers that stated they were free. Bart made a point to encourage his sharecroppers not to work on any other plantation, lest one of the slave owners decide to deal nefariously with him and force one of them back into bondage. It had happened before many times with other Free People of Color and Bart couldn't bear if such a fate befell anyone he knew.

Emilie rose from her place near the back, catching Robert's eye as she made her way toward the porch. He could see the way she reined in a bit of her spirit before approaching Bart, hands clasped neatly against her flour-dusted apron.

Bart finished his sentence, then turned to give her his attention.

"May I go to the Duplantiers this evenin'?" she asked in a voice that puzzled Robert. It was neither as strongly accented as some present who were French, but neither was it touched by the southern influences as Simon's was. It was a strange blend of both.

He might have focused a little too fixedly upon her, because he could see how she glanced his way and then squeezed her fingers nervously to hide the way they trembled.

Bart nodded. "Of course. Remember to take a lantern with you and please be back by morning. Take a pass from the hook by the sitting room door on your way out."

Emilie gave her thanks and rushed away.

"A pass?" James inquired. "I thought you said all these people were free."

Bart nodded. "They are, but there are plenty of people between here and the Duplantier plantation that would cause trouble for Emilie if she didn't carry something to prove she was both free and under my protection. The pass allows her to go wherever she wants and if there's any question to the contrary, they can come to me."

"You're going to let her go without an escort?" Robert asked his grandfather.

James, once more, relished the apparent turn in his son's attitude toward women, but Robert wouldn't play along.

"The Duplantier plantation is less than a mile from here and she goes frequently. I'm not too concerned."

Simon shook his head and made a dissenting noise in his throat, wordlessly expressing his opinion on the matter.

Robert smiled at the differing sides and inquired further.

"She meets with a woman at Duplantier's every other day," Bart explained. "It's the only thing she ever asks for, so I allow it."

"What for?" James asked, brushing out the crumbs from his plate into the grass near the steps.

"That Miss Marceline been teachin' her magic," Simon replied, unable to keep his peace any longer.

A low growl rumbled in Bart's throat in warning to his friend. "It's not magic and she's not hurting anyone, so there's no harm in it."

Now, Robert was thoroughly intrigued. "Magic?"

"Not magic," Bart corrected again. "Her mother was from Haiti and she came here with her master during the slave rebellion. They settled on a plantation down the river and ever since her mother died, she's been interested in voodoo, so I let her learn it from one of Mr. Duplantier's slaves."

He had heard of voodoo from some of the other sailors and pirates amongst Lafitte's crew. It was mostly spoken as a thing to be cautious toward and feared by the white folk, but Robert didn't want to believe any of it. Just like the rougarou, voodoo seemed like just a myth to convince white men to take care of their black slaves or else a bad curse would fall upon them and their plantation. To think that there were actual people who practiced the craft was intriguing.

Robert was ready to ask more questions when Bart's eyes snapped toward the house. Simon saw the distress in his master and was the first to his feet. Once he pulled his focus in the same direction, he could hear the soft wailing of a baby coming toward the mansion. The wind carried with it the scents of three people, fear and misery strong in their signatures as they came closer.

Bart handed his plate to Robert and hurried after Simon, but his curiosity wouldn't let him be still. Robert, in turn, handed the two plates to James and ran off before his father could stop him.

When they entered the house, Bart turned on his grandson. "Stay in here," he ordered, the words laced with a string of dominance that Robert couldn't argue against.

He stopped near the stairwell that led to the second floor landing, safely concealed in the shadows as Simon and Bart opened the front door. He could see their distressed faces as they half-tripped and half-ran to the mansion house.

Both the man and woman were dressed in tattered clothes, torn and stained by mud as dark as their faces. The woman, presumably the mother, held a child who was somewhere between an infant and a toddler against her hip. The baby suckled its own fist to stifle the cry, but it rang in Robert's ears as loudly as if he were the one holding him.

Simon went to the negress' side and helped to stabilize her as Bart faced the man. All three looked exhausted and even if his nose were completely dysfunctional, he could tell they were terrified for their lives.

Before Bart could speak, they were already begging him for protection.

"Mass'r McCarthy is threatenin' to sell us to get back what he lost durin' the war," the man said.

The woman stepped forward, her child's screaming deaf to her own ears by now. "We come all the way across the swamp. Please, Mass'r Bart. We is tired and hungry."

Bart rubbed the back of his neck, looking to Simon for some advice. If Robert had been asked, he would have quickly agreed to harboring the fugitive slaves, but only his grandfather would understand the consequences of such a decision. Now that the territory sat squarely in the American's hands, the citizens of New Orleans and Louisiana who were accustomed to the old ways would have to admit to new laws, new practices, and new punishments.

In Charleston, if a slave ran away from their master, it was the duty of every free man to capture that runaway and return him to his legal home. But Bart was no ordinary free man.

Risking his plantation, the safety of his own slaves, his wealth, and status within the community, Bart nodded and led them into the foyer. They tracked in dirt across the wood floor, but as soon as they were brought into the darkened hall, Robert could see the dread seep from them.

"Take a seat in the dining room and I'll have Ruth bring you something to eat," he told them.

Simon relieved the child from his mother and Robert stood just outside the invisible bubble of comforting dominance that the black werewolf emanated. While dominance could be used as a tool to make others obey, it could also be used to sooth and provide a feeling of ease for those who needed protection.

The couple continued to mutter thanks long after Bart walked away, leaving them in the care of his manservant. He stopped in front of Robert and gave a heavy sigh.

"You're doing the right thing," he said to the older werewolf.

Bart, not so convinced, wouldn't meet his stare. "Mr. McCarthy and other plantation owners like him to the east of New Orleans must have lost a lot to the English when they came to Louisiana. If he's willing to sell off his property to re-coup the losses, he's desperate. Many may choose to rebuild, but not consolidate everything."

Robert recalled seeing the devastation Major General Edward Pakenham left along the Mississippi. Plantations were sacked, slaves were freed to join the British army, and fields were raided for what little supplies they yielded. Mr. McCarthy could very well lose everything if he didn't sell out now and reestablish himself on a smaller scale. Then again, so could these poor souls who ran from the fate their master had in store for them.

"I've seen the slave auctions," Robert said. "It's likely they wouldn't keep the family together. With how young the child is, they would have to purchase the mother too and unless their buyer was wealthy enough, the father would be overlooked."

Bart nodded quickly and passed a hand over his eyes. "I'm aware," he grumbled. "I'll have a talk with Mr. McCarthy tomorrow. Perhaps we can work out some arrangement."

Robert tilted his head. "Will you buy all three like you did Simon and free them?"

By the sour look on Bart's face, he dared not to hope for it. "I don't have enough. All three will easily go for over a thousand, maybe two."

He swallowed hard at the sum. To think that the price of a human soul could even be calculated was appalling.

"But I will figure something out," Bart continued. "My conscience won't give me another option."

Night closed in on the plantation. Lanterns and candles, one by one, were blown out in the shacks down the lane and inside the mansion house. Though Bart professed that he rarely entertained guests, several spare bedrooms were available in the upper story. Two beds were gathered from storage for both of his guests so they could share the same dorm that overlooked the back of the house.

Robert slept soundly, his usual light snores breaking the silence. The family of three were peacefully resting in an adjacent room while Bart was just now settling into his own bed down the hall. Under the circumstances, Simon stationed himself downstairs on a cot so he could be close by the doors in the event that the slaves' master or patrollers came looking for them.

As the grandfather clock tolled midnight, James was the only one still awake. He stood in front of the glass-paned doors that opened out from the bedroom onto the upper balcony. His view of the shacks and sugarcane fields beyond were tinted in a bluish haze by the moonlight as all other lights were snuffed out. In the distance, he could hear the occasional barking of a hound and thundering of horse hooves upon the soft earth. He had heard this same collection of noises and upon asking Bart and Simon, they told him about the patrollers.

Each plantation owner hired his own team, employed expressly for the purpose of searching the swamps and river sides for runaway slaves. This occurred almost every other night and it was rare that a slave escaped them. It was a wonder Eliza and Solomon had arrived to Bart, eluding the patrollers completely.

But he wasn't thinking about the sharecroppers, the patrollers, or any runaway slaves at the moment. His eyes were fixed upon three shacks near the far back of the property, past the sugar processing buildings. He could just barely see its gabled peak against the tree line. He knew their purpose and why they were so far sequestered from the rest of the plantation. Earlier that evening, after the rest of the tenants ate their fill, Simon took a platter of leftover catfish into the fields. He returned nearly an hour later, not a single fillet missing from the plate. Whoever he was delivering to had refused the meal, and James wanted to know why.

Glancing to his son, he reached out and unfastened the latch on the doors. Without making a sound, he stepped out onto the balcony and vaulted over the iron railing between the columns. His landing was little more than a soft rustle against the green lawn.

Simon stirred from inside the house and James' keen ears waited until his breathing became regular again. James had snuck aboard enemy ships in the dead of night, gliding across old creaking boards without alerting a single sentry. He could surely slip away from the plantation under these conditions.

He paused only once before using his inhuman speed to dart down the lane between the shacks and around the growing sugarcane fields. The screaming of the cicada bugs drown out all other sounds as he neared the reserved shacks.

James slowed and when he came within just five or so yards of the only occupied building, he stopped dead in his tracks. It was as if he had just breached through an unseen wall dividing the safe and peaceful from a pure evil that made his wolf urge him to run.

One word came to mind, one that he had just learned earlier that day. Rougarou. The evil counterpart to the true creature that was far more than a myth in Louisiana, France, or anywhere else for that matter. Whatever was trapped within that cage inside the shack, James had never felt its equal before. Not even Will emanated this penetrating malevolence.

It took a moment for him to breathe again before he forced his way through the thick mire. The raspy breaths of the beast served as one last warning before he past the point of no return.

James pushed open the door, the hinges noiseless in the command, much to his surprise. He had expected the state of the shack to be further dilapidated than the ones back on the plantation that housed occupants more worthy. Moonlight angled across the floor and gleamed against the silver bars, but didn't touch the prisoner that crouched toward the very back wall.

The stench of sweat, dirt, and months of confinement within this shack made James want to gag, which never happened even when he cleaned out the bilge water on his former ships. He stood in the doorway, watching the rougarou from this safe distance. The silver bars were at least six feet from him, out of reach from the beast if he should choose to try and reach through.

Matted and tangled black hair draped past the rougarou's shoulders, golden eyes that seemed to be lit from within glared through the darkness. His tanned skin, shape of his face, and slope of his nose couldn't label him as a native of these parts, but neither was he a negro like the sharecroppers. His clothes were torn and discolored, just as a prisoner's might be. Barefoot and filthy, he bared his teeth like a cornered animal.

James didn't move, refused to blink. This is what starvation and incarceration did to a werewolf, feral or not. But however much he pitied the beast, he wouldn't touch the lock or make any promises to free him. If this creature were to be set free, he would surely hurt someone. But how long before he could be released? How much longer would Bart keep him here?

The man's lips clamped tight suddenly and the snarl was subdued. The gold left his eyes, leaving dark voids in the shadows, but James could still easily make out his silhouette.

"You're Bart's son," he said, his words heavy with a Spanish cadence that James recognized all too well. "You look just like him."

He would neither deny it nor confirm it, but stared and waited, forcing himself to refrain from any cues that could break the balance of control. James had to remember that he was the free one. He was free to leave whenever he wanted, but he was determined to see this through and learn what was on the other side of this scheme Bart implemented.

"You didn't take the food Simon offered you," James said, keeping his tone even and unoffensive. "Why?"

The man crawled into the moonlight, just inches from the bars that could burn him if he so much as grazed his skin against the metal. Now, James could see the full depravity to which he was subjected. The dirt smeared on his cheeks, the dark circles around his eyes, the haggard and crazed quality in his movements all professed that he had been suffering for a long time.

"Do you think we were made to eat fish?" he returned. "Or pigs or cows? Why eat what the humans do? We are above them. Stronger, faster, more powerful. Why make ourselves equal to them by eating as they eat?"

"Because it's wrong to eat humans."

The wild man cackled like a true villain. "You sound just like Bart too. 'It's wrong to eat humans', 'humans are our friends', 'humans are our allies'," he mocked and then spat on the space of floor between them. "Humans are weak and senseless. They destroy the world they were given. They cut down the forests and kill one another out of hatred."

"How is that any different than if we killed them? Wouldn't that make us just as wicked?"

The rougarou gave him a toothy, yellow smile. "There is no such thing as wicked. It's all a matter of perspective."

"As is weakness or strength," James observed. "What you see as a weakness isn't weak at all. Compassion, for instance, I'd assume you'd think is a flaw."

"Compassion is a lie," the man replied scathingly. "A man who cares fools himself into thinking others are greater than himself. Why waste one's time and efforts tending after those who don't want to take care of themselves? Why waste such precious energy caring for someone who is inherently selfish too?"

"So, you believe in the principle of every man for himself."

"I do," he said. "And you should too. That's what Bart does. He doesn't care about those negroes and half-breeds he takes in. He doesn't care about me or the other lobos. He only wants glory for himself. He's prideful and wants to boast about the people he helps. He feels no compassion. He just wants recognition."

As much as he didn't want to admit it, James could see the man's point. From the outside, it might have appeared that way. Bart was willing to kill him a century ago over a rumor that he was a rougarou like the monster he faced now. James wished he could say that he knew his father better than that, but he didn't. Nearly a lifetime spent apart told him nothing about his father's true character. He could have been altruistic, or completely self-righteous as the rougarou suggested.

"Do you believe that his motivation somehow disavows the good he accomplishes?"

"Good is also a matter of perspective." The rougarou drew dangerously close to the bars, but James was not about to warn him against that nearness. "Do you believe teaching these people to be dependent on a rich man's hospitality, even in part, is good for them? What will they do if they didn't have Bart to clothe them and care for them? They will forever look for handouts and welfare from people who are better off than them. All they would know how to do is work as laborers in the fields. No opportunity for advancement. No freedom. They're still slaves, just as I am... Just as you are."

"I am no slave," James barked, his composure shattering from this accusation.

"Aren't you? How long will you stay here? Until Bart tells you to leave?... Until your own son tells you to leave?"

At the mention of Robert, he growled. "You know nothing."

"I know plenty." The rougarou lifted his hand and wrapped his dirty fingers around the bars. Flesh burned and sizzled as it came into contact with the silver and he didn't even flinch. Wisps of smoke curled up from his palms, the odor of charred flesh assaulting his nose as blood dribbled down the bar. "And because you're the only one who has ever honestly talked with me, I'll tell you a secret. If you and your son don't leave this place soon, you never will."

James didn't want to know what he meant, didn't want to speculate how he knew about Robert or anything else. He gave one last look to the rougarou, gathered up his calm again, and left. It wasn't until he was well down the lane between the sharecropper houses that he was able to shake off the last of the unease that pervaded his bones.

Even when he crawled into the bed on the other side of the room from his son, the convict's words echoed in his mind, replaying on loop, refusing to let him sleep.

CHAPTER 4

The house slave led Bart through the main foyer and into the sitting room. From across the house, he could hear the McCarthys eating breakfast. The two girls, as well-mannered as they were, talked incessantly while the two parents nodded in agreement to their stories.

Bart regarded the slave, knowing the man had been recently whipped. The stale scent of blood lingered over his skin and clothes, though he was well dressed, as was the custom for slaves who were the first ones to greet any guest onto the plantation. The weapon of choice still hung in a rawhide coil by the front door, unashamed and displayed so openly that even Bart felt sickened at the sight of it.

His dark eyes never left the floor, his black face roughened by years of hard labor. This must not have been his usual post, symptomatic of Mr. McCarthy's dismal situation. If he was already bringing field slaves into the house, there was either a lack of work outside the home, or an abundance of it inside. By the crates that lay open in the far corner of the sitting room, straw packing material dangling over the rim, Bart could establish it was the later assumption.

Even since before he arrived on the property, he could hear the voices of those miserable slaves in their shacks, quietly sobbing over whatever future they believed they had with another master, or singing those lovely negro hymns as they commenced the first chores of the day. The songs of these oppressed people might have been the only beautiful thing to be born out of such sadness and brutality.

"Mass'r be in to see you soon, sir," the slave muttered nervously before shuffling out of the sitting room and down the hall.

Bart was ready to tell him not to bother Mr. McCarthy, that he could wait, but the slave was too quick to do his job. Soon, the tiny voices of the Misses McCarthy's were abruptly cut off and the grumbling complaints of their father supplanted them.

"I told you I'm not receiving guests," the plantation owner said, followed by the ruffle of material that Bart guessed was the tossing down of a linen napkin to the dinner table.

"It's Mass'r Croxen, sir," the anxious, displaced slave quickly said. Bart hated how some slaves took to calling every free man his master, whether they were white or not. "He say he knowed somethin' about – "

"Hush," Mr. McCarthy interrupted. "I'll see him."

Heavy boots thrummed across the house and Bart straightened to his full height, preparing for a meeting that he had been dreading since the evening before. Mr. McCarthy was an easy enough man to get along with, but only if one's skin and ancestry were as white as the petals on a flowering magnolia. Being a direct descendant from some of the first families to colonize Louisiana, he had the privileges of class to help him build a small empire on this side of the Mississippi.

But war was no respecter of wealth, of class, or family. War only destroyed, and Bart learned long ago that the lives it stole were not worth what was gained after peace treaties were signed. The war that had started just three years ago was no exception. No new boundary lines were established, no new lands were conquered or lost. It was pointless, all of it. The war for America's independence, however, might have been one of the most noble causes worth dying for.

Mr. McCarthy appeared in the doorway, looking less than presentable as he hadn't been expecting guests and from what he said to his slave, hadn't a mind to receive any either, especially at this hour. He wore no vest over the loose shirt that was tucked into his trousers, nor did he wear a coat to contain the billowy sleeves of said shirt. His hair was combed, and that might have been his only saving feature in the present moment to prove that he wasn't a naturally unkempt person.

Knowing full well what kind of opinion the slave owner held for him, Bart gave a cordial nod of greeting, but didn't pay him a smile that wouldn't be returned. Mr. McCarthy strode forward and knotted his fingers behind his back, nose proudly lifted as if to prove that he was the better man of the two, even though his guest was better dressed. Bart didn't give a damn about status at a time like this.

"You have some business to conduct with me?" Mr. McCarthy began, his pure New Orleans dialect rivaling the one that Bart would have to fake for the sake of his image.

After living in the same place for one hundred years, he learned how to make subtle changes to his character to throw off the next generation. For the time being, he was a Creole, a man born free in Louisiana and raised by Free People of Color to explain his complexion and inherent wealth.

"Last night, two of your slaves along with their child came onto my property, begging me for asylum." Bart ground his teeth to feign annoyance.

Mr. McCarthy scoffed and let his eyes settle on something behind his guest to show that he wasn't even worthy of his full attention. "You've made a reputation for being soft toward the darkies. I should have known they'd run to you."

"I'm not so much upset that they arrived on my doorstep as I am about what they had to tell me about you and your plantation."

Mr. McCarthy's lips puckered into a scowl. "You can't trust whatever these people say. They'll lie for self-preservation, you know this."

"Yes, I do know this," Bart replied, stepping ever so slightly to the side so the slave owner was forced to look at him. "I also know how you treat your slaves, so what they said is not difficult for me to believe."

Unused to being spoken to in such a way, Mr. McCarthy bristled like a badger ready to protect his den. "They're my property and I may do with them as I please. This includes selling them, beating them, or killing them. And it's your responsibility as a citizen of this state to return my property to me." His countenance twisted in resentment. "Or do I need to report to the authorities that I've been robbed? That three of my slaves were coerced into running away. I know your tricks, Mr. Croxen, so don't even begin to think that you can buy your way out of this."

Despite himself, Bart smiled in the face of the man who hated him without due cause. "I don't know what tricks you're talking about, but I will say that I'm willing to buy Eliza, Solomon, and little Henry from you."

He grumbled under his breath, "Darkies owning darkies. I can't wait to leave this backwards territory."

For a man who came from a family that might have once been tolerable of freed slaves and colored people owning estates, Mr. McCarthy was growing too high from his roots to retain any sense of morality or nobility at all. Families who had been settled in Louisiana for half as many generations had become familiar to seeing people like Bart and Simon walk through town without the burden of a master to tell them where to go and what to do.

"By the looks of it," Bart observed, "you're preparing to do just that. Where will you go? Georgia? Kansas? Virginia? Someplace you can walk down the street without having to see these black faces uplifted because they know they're free and no man can take that from them? Someplace where you may never hear their laughter and only their screams for mercy? Someplace where men like me are shunned and detested because we give a damn about human suffering."

"They are property!" Mr. McCarthy barked. "Not humans. They are less than humans. I've seen wild beasts with more sense than some of these darkies."

Bart, knowing he had broken more than a few codes of etiquette, wanted to break even more and show him what kind of wild beast lurked behind his own dark eyes. His wolf had more sense than this self-righteous bastard who couldn't

see the plain truth through the lens of entitlement and racism. But there was more
to consider than Bart's own gratification in seeing the man dead on the floor of
his own sitting room. There was a wife and two daughters who, even though Mr.
McCarthy was not a good man in any sense of the word, needed to be cared for.
He hated to think that someday, those two little girls would grow up to be just as
callous and unfeeling toward people of color as their father was.

"How much for the three of them?" Bart asked, realizing they had digressed
from the point of this meeting. As much as he would have enjoyed pounding this
man into the ground with moral logic, he didn't have the time or the patience.

For a moment, Mr. McCarthy didn't speak and a veil of seriousness dropped
over him. To Bart, the silence which might have been ringing in the human's
ears, was filled with the voices of those who depended on this poor excuse of a
businessman for safety and provision.

"Two thousand," he finally said.

"We both know they aren't worth that much," Bart argued. "The child only
isn't worth anything but an encumberment to the mother for another year or so."

"Solomon's a capable field hand and always picked double what the others
could."

He had seen those fields of cotton on his way to the big house. Instead of the
expected tufts of white, like a blanket of clouds that had been brought down from
the heavens to settle over the green stalks, stretching as far as the eye could see,
Bart was greeted by barren fields that had been burned by the English. Stems and
leaves were left charred and blackened, the worst nightmare of any farmer.

"I'm not interested in a cotton-picker. I need a man who can cut down sugarcane."

One of Mr. McCarthy's hands finally came up to jab a finger at his guest. "I
know exactly what you're going to do with him after you buy him. You're just
going to free him and that bitch of a wife. I don't even understand how you can
keep a plantation going with how much money you waste on these – "

By the raised tone, Bart knew that Mr. McCarthy was prepared to throw
around more derogatory names referring to the slaves and he would not abide by
it. He talked louder, nearly shouting to be heard. "What I intend to do with them
is none of your concern. What you should be worrying about is how much it will
cost to move you, your family, and what slaves you do choose to keep, to that
blissful country where you can beat and mutilate your property how you choose.
I offer five hundred for all three."

The man's blue eyes nearly bugged out of his head. "Five hundred? I knew you
were a pretentious Creole, but I didn't think you were insane. You can't possibly
expect me to – "

"I expect you to do what's right for you and your family," Bart said. "If I just returned them to you, they will run away again until they find the freedom they need. Do you really want to contend with such a hassle when you have more important things to do?"

"I paid five hundred for Eliza alone."

"And now she's lost value because she has a child. We can haggle over the price all day, but once again, you have better things to do with your time." Bart glared at him, wishing he was free to assert some of his loup-garou dominance to win this negotiation. "Five hundred for all three or I turn them into the swamps and you'll never see them again. You'll get nothing."

It was a common fact that the cypress swamps that nearly surrounded New Orleans on both sides of the river were fraught with dangers and perils – such as the rougarou. Poisonous snakes, alligators, bottomless mudholes, and many other natural things that could turn on a straggling adventurer in a split second. There were too many things that could kill a man in the swamps, and Mr. McCarthy knew it. Many plantation owners had bewailed the loss of property to the land that wouldn't dare be cultivated or tamed by man. Not even Bart had navigated the winding, confusing paths of the rivers and marshes beyond the edge of his plantation.

This threat, though Bart would never carry it out, seemed to be taken seriously and Mr. McCarthy turned pensive again. He walked to the window, whose gauzy curtain was pulled back to let the morning light stream through. Several silent moments passed before he declared his final judgement over the fate of his property.

"I'd rather count those negroes as a loss than sell them to you," Mr. McCarthy said softly, voice just loud enough that any normal man wouldn't have heard him from where Bart stood.

His arrogance ran even further than his greed, which Bart hadn't been expecting. He waited another moment for Mr. McCarthy to recant, but when he didn't say a word to the contrary, Bart only nodded.

"Very well. I'll run them off my estate and their blood will be on your hands because you were too stubborn."

The slave owner would not suffer another word out of the free mulatto and turned, his face pale with rage. Bart was too quick and wouldn't hear another conceited word out of his mouth. He quitted the room, the house, and the plantation in as much time as it would have taken Mr. McCarthy to come back with more hateful speeches.

"When the wort is pumped back into the brew kettle," Lorenz explained as he pointed to the boiling vat of unfermented beer, "we then add our hops, molasses, and sugar."

James might have been interested in the operation, but Robert was not. He leaned against the edge of the window, looking out onto the view of Royal Street as his father endured this lesson in brewing from the two other werewolves they had met earlier in their stay in New Orleans. He watched the shoppers and merchants hurry past one another, listening to bits of conversation as they passed by.

Earlier that morning, Bart had returned to the plantation after his visit with Mr. McCarthy regarding the slaves. The meeting hadn't gone as planned and now, they were in New Orleans giving closure to that same bit of business, though his grandfather was less than forthcoming about the means in which he was to do that. He said he would go to meet with Will and his wife, Lottie, but James requested that they separate for the afternoon. And his father gave just as much explanation for his actions as Bart did.

Robert glanced back to James who asked questions about the portions of hops to sugar that should be added to the brew kettle. From the moment he awoke, his father seemed to be in a haze of deep thought, his forehead and brow wrinkling several times within the span of an hour as he seemed to be pondering something that troubled him. His few attempts to coax the truth out of James was fruitless, and he was left to wonder.

As far as he was aware, nothing had occurred which could explain this silent brooding, but he was given subtle clues as the day progressed. James' aversion to spending more time with Bart than absolutely necessary was a clear sign that it involved the old werewolf somehow. It seemed to contrast with his previous attitude toward personally becoming more acquainted with his estranged father. His occasional question posed to Simon and other members of the permanent staff at the plantation in regards to their happiness and intentions to someday leave the estate also hinted to his unexplained reflectiveness.

But Robert, who was normally quick-witted and easy to solve such puzzles, could still not account for his father's behavior. It wasn't like James to be thoughtful or reserved at all. If they'd had a moment alone without other supernatural ears attuned to their conversation, he might have interrogated further.

He partly wondered if this trip to the brewery was merely something to distract James from whatever haunted him. As long as James was occupied and enjoying himself, Robert wouldn't complain even when the acrid stench of beer stung his nostrils.

He turned back to the window, once more scanning the crowds and wishing he were out in the open air instead of in this stuffy and slightly dank atmosphere. His gaze was diverted from a stray dog prowling by the outer wall of the brewery – no doubt suspecting there was another animal encroaching on his territory from within – to a lady walking slowly on the other side of the street.

Her hair, as bright as a gold five-dollar coin and equal in color as in luster, was tucked beneath a blue bonnet that matched her eyes. Loose curls trailed out around her flushed cheeks, bouncing with each step and tossed in the light breeze she walked against. Her smile was directed to her black maidservant who accompanied her, but Robert wished she would chance to look up to his window just so he could be the recipient of that same smile.

Her dress, light and a shade of blue darker than her bonnet, flattered a portion of her figure as the fashion of the times mandated. The white, lacy ribbon tied across her upper torso drew his eyes to the almost milky paleness of her smooth skin around the neckline of her dress. Gloves covered her hands, but he supposed if he were to unsheathe her fingers, they would be every bit ladylike and feminine as the rest of her.

Robert stared, all senses closing in on the woman and her companion. They were talking about some gossip regarding another young woman in town and a scandalous affair with an overseer on a plantation, but he wasn't interested in the subject. Her voice was as lovely as her face and he could listen to her soft drawl for days on end.

She was, by far, the most beautiful creature he had ever seen, more stunning than Miss Levins a thousand times over. Instantly enchanting. Even his wolf drooled and his leg muscles twitched as if they were ready to bolt down the stairs and give chase. Robert moved from window to window, following them along the street until he came to the end of the building and they turned to continued down Conti Street.

Without a thought, he rushed to the stairs. He vaguely heard his father shout for an explanation, but Robert heard nothing. He was more focused on the lady's laugh, knowing that as long as he could still hear her or her servant, he could track her throughout New Orleans.

He came to the street, now in the fresh air, but still unsatisfied. If his heart mandated his speed, he would have startled many by blurring through the crowd.

Instead, he reined himself in and took off at a more discrete pace. Her blue bonnet and slender neck emerged through the mass of heads and Robert forced his wolf to be silent and let him think for the first time since he had seen the lady.

What would he say? How could they be introduced? What would be his excuse to approach her? If a good gust of wind would just rip her bonnet from her head, he would run to fetch it. Or if she were to trip and stumble into the path of a merchant cart, that could be a good excuse for an introduction. He'd gladly risk exposing himself as a werewolf if it meant he could rescue an angel.

The lady and her servant stopped outside a dressmaker's shop and Robert slowed, keeping his ears open while his eyes skipped ahead in the event that she were to turn and see him. When he heard the shop door open and her sweet voice became muffled through the wall that separated them, he cursed under his breath.

There was no reasonable excuse for a man to go into a dressmaker's shop. Instead of taking a moment to reassess this plan or discourage himself from the pursuit any further – as he should have done – Robert gradually steered himself to the shop door and entered.

Bolts of material lined up against one wall in racks, while stuffed mannequins displayed articles like dresses, bonnets, shawls, gloves, and other accessories that the womenfolk obsessed over. The lady and her servants stood by a counter toward the back of the shop where an older woman attended them.

"I just finished hemming it this morning," the dressmaker said. "The cloth was very fine, but I believe you will be satisfied with the work."

"I always am, Gemma," his lady – for he already foolishly considered her to be his – spoke, a smile in her words.

The dressmaker, Gemma, seemed bashful under the compliment and then turned to Robert. "I'll be with you in a moment, sir."

This accomplished what Robert secretly hoped for. The lady turned upon hearing that a man had entered the shop, brows arched in surprise. Her lips closed over her teeth, but her smile did not falter. She and her servant curtsied and Robert somehow had enough sense to bow, though his eyes never left hers for a second.

Gemma left them alone to fetch the lady's order from the back workroom and he wished he could somehow get the slave to leave as well so he could be alone with the ethereal vision he had been hounding for several blocks.

After a customary greeting was exchanged, the vision spoke. "It's not every day a man enters a dressmaker's shop." Her gaze swept over him teasingly.

Robert would not be embarrassed, even when the servant giggled at his expense. His keen mind that had been drawing a blank on how to explain his presence there, did not fail him in the moment of his need.

"I came to commission a dress for a close friend of my grandfather's," he said, glad that all anxiety that he felt in his chest was not present in his voice.

The lady, though given a perfectly reasonable explanation, still retained a glimmer of humor in her dazzling blue eyes. "I believe I know everyone in New Orleans and I've never seen your face before."

He was merely glad that she had taken these few seconds to study his face enough to know she didn't recognize him. "My father and I are visiting my grandfather."

She nodded and he relished in the way her lips turned up to give her grin a more coquettish property. "And where are you from…"

Robert perceived that she dragged out her inquiry so he could make the proper introductions. "Robert," he finished. "Robert Croxen. I like to say that I'm from Charleston, but I've been many places."

As soon as he uttered his surname, he knew he had done wrong. Both her and her maidservant let their smiles wilt, leaving them in a state of apparent confusion.

"Croxen?" she questioned. "Surely you're not the grandson to Mr. Bart Croxen. The man barely looks old enough for the title."

His senses didn't fail him again and Robert simply shrugged and gave her a helpless gesture. "He holds his age well, Miss…"

She caught onto his implication and the ghost of that former smile reappeared. "Isabelle Burnett. My father owns the largest cotton plantation upriver from New Orleans."

If she thought that would impress Robert, she was sadly mistaken, but he allowed her to brag as long as she was bragging to him.

"It's a pleasure to meet you, Miss Isabelle."

Gemma reemerged from the backroom with a dress draped across her arms. It was a fancy garment, lined with lace and dotted with beaded appliques across the golden satin. It might as well have been pointless to try and enhance the beauties of one as fair as Isabelle Burnett, but this gown just might do the impossible.

Isabelle turned to inspect the dress and nodded gleefully, her excitement restored. "I can't wait to wear this tonight at the party," she exclaimed, inciting Robert's interest once again.

While Gemma labored to gently fold the finished work in a parcel box for her customer, she turned to Robert.

"And what can I do for you, sir?" she asked.

Now trapped within his own lie, he had to see it through. "I need to commission a simple dress."

"Do you have the measurements?" Gemma asked, as amused as Isabelle had been upon learning of his purpose in the shop.

Robert shook his head. "No, I'm sorry. I don't. This is meant to be a surprise for a friend of the family and that prevents me from acquiring any measurements."

Isabelle now spoke up to aid him. "Gemma is a genius seamstress. If you give her some estimates, I'm sure the finished product will be close enough."

The dressmaker, once again, bowed her head. "I can do my best, sir."

Robert looked to the mannequins, but none of them seemed the appropriate size for the woman he had in mind. Then, he looked to Isabelle and saw his opportunity.

"The woman is about Miss Isabelle's height," he began. "Well, perhaps about two inches shorter." He took a step forward, now able to examine her up close with a proper reason. "She has wider shoulders, as well. She's much skinnier than Miss Isabelle in a lean sort of way, and not nearly as... endowed. The woman is slimmer in the hips, as well, and doesn't have Miss Isabelle's shapely neck to compliment any lavish collar. As for the color, I'd think something close to the shade of Miss Isabelle's eyes would be stunning. Though, I'm sure no other lady could wear a color as well as she does."

The negress maidservant suppressed a giggle as a blush rose to Isabelle's cheeks, her smile widening with each sly compliment.

"Will these measurements do?" Robert asked, never lifting his eyes to Gemma, just as Isabelle wouldn't disengage from him.

Gemma agreed and after tying up the parcel, took down the specifications on a scrap piece of paper on the counter. "When do you need this by?"

"As soon as possible," he replied, speaking more of his need for Isabelle Burnett than the dress.

The heiress to a cotton empire bit her lip and finally turned to take her package. "Gemma's genius cannot be rushed, Mr. Croxen," she implied, sneaking in her own hidden meaning under the cloak of well-bred conversation.

"I am a patient man, Miss Isabelle." He dared another step closer until he could hear her heartbeat skipping rapidly within her chest. "Especially when it comes to something I desire this ardently."

He trod upon dangerous ground, but Robert had never felt this pull toward anyone or anything. It was like gravity and he couldn't fight it. He was a leaf circling a whirlpool, powerless to stop himself before drowning in those eyes that beckoned him to claim all that he saw.

Isabelle handed the parcel to her servant and curtsied to Robert. "I hope this dress is everything you expect it to be."

Robert bowed again as they made their way to leave, but he would not sever his stare until she had walked past the front window and out of sight completely. That was only after she had glanced back and smiled flirtatiously, daring him to hope and plot their next encounter. It would have to be executed carefully.

The plan took form even before he was finished making his deposit on the dress commission.

CHAPTER 5

"Where the hell did you run off to?" James thundered when he spotted his son coming around the corner from Conti Street. Out of respect for Lorenz and Carney, who were so openly enthusiastic about their craft, he stayed until the tour of the brewery was complete before excusing himself to pursue Robert.

His eyes alight with some kind of happiness that James couldn't begin to guess, Robert met him halfway to St. Louis Street. "I apologize for leaving you like I did, but..." he simply shrugged his shoulders and smiled as if he were in the midst of a dream.

It was then James smelled the faint traces of perfume. "Where did you go?" he asked.

Robert gave no answer. "Are you finished at the brewery?" he asked, glancing down the road to the establishment.

Though he wasn't too keen on his son keeping secrets from him, if this had to do with a woman as he guessed, then he'd allow the evasion. They turned and proceeded down Royal Street in the direction Robert had come, intending to turn on Bienville Street until it connected with Bourbon, where they were told Will's blacksmith shop was situated.

"I am," he said with a sigh, disappointed in how effective he was in his design for meeting with the two werewolf brewers.

Robert knew him too well and chuckled. "Not that impressed, are you?"

This was their first moment alone since meeting with Bart the previous day. Much had taken place and now might have been their only chance to discuss the things that pressed on his mind. James turned to his son, who had also served as his best friend for the better part of almost a hundred years. Quartermasters and crewmates came and went, but Robert had been the only constant James had ever known in his life. They told one another everything and it pained him to keep this corked for just the last few hours.

"What do you think of Bart's plantation?" he asked. "Be completely honest."

Robert's smile weakened under such a somber question. "I think he's doing a good thing. He's helping people, negroes and werewolves alike."

That's not what he wanted to hear, but James had to accept that his son spoke his candid opinion. Still, he could see the rougarou's dirt-smudged face, sneering at him from the shadows as he spoke of perspectives and entitlement. Its spectral image haunted his sleep and the words continued to pound between his temples the more he let himself linger over the idea.

Bart's apparent altruism lost its glamor with every passing hour and neither Lorenz nor Carney could provide him some relief. Before he took his leave of them, he asked what they thought of Bart and his business with the rougarous and sharecroppers. They replied in the same way that Robert did now, with confidence that Bart was doing a good and righteous thing.

James continued to straddle the fence between wishing his father to be a good and wholesome man, and wanting to tear back the curtain to reveal the nasty truth behind the operation. Was torture implemented? Did the sharecroppers not receive equal royalties? Did the rougarous revert back to their old ways as soon as they were away from Bart, leaving them more demented than they had been before?

If the answers to these questions were all affirmative, everyone was keeping it hidden behind carefree smiles.

"This doesn't satisfy you, does it?" Robert asked, but before James could reply, he continued with, "I don't understand why you can't accept that Bart's not the man you thought he was so long ago."

A ripple of dominance escaped him and he turned angrily upon his son. "Why do you think I wanted us to come here?" he questioned, minding to keep his voice down for the sake of the crowd around them. "I wanted to get to know him better."

"And what you found doesn't settle with what you truly wanted," Robert observed. "You wanted to think him an evil man without moral or sense, so you could congratulate yourself on being right all along."

"Not true," James barked.

Robert, who had inherited a dominant streak from the Croxen line, returned as potent a force as he received. "Isn't it? Why interrogate everyone who knows Bart? Why can't you simply open your eyes and see the good for yourself?"

"What if what we see isn't the truth? What if they are hiding something?"

His son rolled his eyes. "Why do you believe that everyone is hiding something?"

"You're hiding something," James charged lightly. "You won't tell me where you ran off to, but I know it has to do with a woman. Average men may not practice deceit on a daily basis, but the common man will hide his faults from the world if it will save him disgrace or punishment."

Perhaps seeing the wisdom in what his father said, Robert confessed about the young woman he had seen from the upstairs window, how he followed her all the way to the shop and now was bound to pay for a new dress for Emilie on the plantation.

"And I thought you had lost all vigor in that cock of yours," James teased, jabbing an elbow into his son's ribs.

Never quite as appreciative of his ragging, Robert gave him a playful shove in return. "My cock is working just fine, which is more than I could say for you."

James let out a boisterous laugh that turned some heads on the corner of Bourbon Street. The thought came to him that he should have opened himself to Robert much earlier. He needed this release, but his son was not one to abandon their touchy conversation so easily.

"I challenge you," Robert began, "to put aside whatever it is that made you doubt him. Bar it from your mind completely and, for once, don't assume that every man you meet is a scoundrel."

Too encouraged by his son's early comment, James could not argue. "I will do my utmost."

They had often challenged one another in this way, daring the other to be bolder or more reserved, to be more outspoken or to keep silent for the sake of self-preservation. The result of such challenges were always to their benefit, and James enjoyed this rare bond he shared with his son. Robert would always be his first mate in life, and he couldn't foresee that ever changing.

They spotted the plaque above the blacksmith shop and couldn't help but hear part of the conversation within before they gripped the door handle.

"How long should Teddy keep them?" a feminine voice asked, presumably Will's wife whom they had yet to meet. James was surprised to hear the familiar French cadence.

"Just for a few months," Bart replied, "or until Mr. McCarthy leaves New Orleans."

"Did he say he would send authorities to search the plantation?" Will questioned.

At this point, James and Robert entered, met by a wall of thick, diminishing smoke. The modest establishment was unlike most blacksmith shops that James had visited over the decades. Normally an open and airy place, the smoke and heat had opportunity to escape so the lungs and throat wouldn't become congested. In a city like New Orleans, where space was becoming more and more scarce, professions like blacksmithing were restricted when it came to easy ventilation.

Though the two-story home was built of brick, the center of the room was reserved for the forge, whose embers glowed hot amongst the ash and dying flames that needed stoking. Tables and workbenches were littered with tools and prefabricated wares that Will sold to customers who were in need of a quick fix. Other custom orders were either hanging across the walls with tags tied to indicate who they belonged to, or currently being fashioned against the anvil near the forge.

Bart, Will, and Lottie stood toward the very back near an open door that led into something of a grassy courtyard where more tools of the trade were strewn about, warming in the afternoon sun.

James evaluated his half-brother's prize, and highly approved. The woman seemed strong, her shirt sleeves rolled up to display a pair of forearms that had known labor. Her skin was not fair - which was considered a mark of beauty - but tanned and smudged by soot from the forge, almost as much as her husband's. Hair the color of raven feathers was smoothed back against her head and knotted into a tight bun at the nape of her neck. A few long tendrils that escaped from said bun dangled down around her ears. Her eyes, a pretty shade of honey brown had a determined, brash look about them that, in some ways, reminded James of Grace when she was cross with him.

She turned to look at the two werewolves as soon as they walked into the shop. Robert froze under her stare, but James was used to defying brazen women and came forward to join them.

"Who's getting arrested?" he asked nonchalantly, knowing that he had intruded, but not caring in the least.

Bart looked sideways at his youngest son before saying to his eldest, "He didn't say that he would, but he implied that keeping them on my plantation was a form of theft."

Emboldened, Robert broke free of Lottie's spell and came forward. "Are you talking about Eliza and Solomon?"

Lottie folded her arms. "We are," she replied, looking from James to Robert and back. "You must be the rest of Bart's family."

Quick, impatient introductions were made by Bart and then he returned to the more pressing matter of the slaves he had acquired the night before. This must have been the reason for their visit to New Orleans.

"Do you think Teddy will take them or not?"

The blacksmith's wife glanced toward the back courtyard and made a face that would give any man cause to doubt. "It is hard to say. Because you ask him, I believe he will say yes, but you know his concerns."

Bart rubbed at the back of his neck. "I can't simply let them live in the swamps until it's all over. They'll be in far more danger out there than on my plantation."

"What if we kept them here?" Will offered.

His father quickly shook his head. "Someone will see them in town. If they're recognized, they'll alert Mr. McCarthy or the authorities and we'll be no better off."

"Who's Teddy?" Robert finally inquired, speaking the question that had been bothering James.

Will was more forthcoming than Bart. "He's another loup-garou. He and his pack live in the swamps with their... extended family."

The accentuation in his words riled his wife and she turned to him with a glare and began spouting off a light reprimand in rapid French. To James' amazement, Will fired back with just as much passion, but not in a harsh manner. When Grace would scold him, it took a mountain's worth of self-control to hold in those biting words that would put her back in her place. He refrained out of respect for her and said nothing, enduring the verbal whipping. Will, however, didn't do that and it might have been another testament to Bart's sufficient training.

While the husband and wife bickered, Bart finally turned his attention to James. "Teddy Desmoillon and his clan, for lack of a better term, are from Acadia, a country to the far north that was settled by the French. They were driven out some years ago and a large detachment of them came here to Louisiana. Half of those displaced people were also loup-garou and took up residence along the bayous to avoid detection. Lottie's great-grandmother was part of that first group of Acadians who came here, so she has close ties with Teddy and his pack."

James looked to Lottie and could see where she inherited her fire from. If her ancestors married in with werewolves, she'd certainly receive the stubborn quality of dominance even though she would never shift into a wolf.

"So Teddy would be concerned about Eliza or Solomon finding out about the pack," Robert assumed, but James could hear the slight note of wonder in her words, as if he wanted to ask more about the Acadians and their special community.

Bart nodded. "Exactly. But, I can't think of any other solution. They can't stay with me."

"What if someone were to go with them into the swamps and keep them safe?"

"I can't spare Simon for that long," he asserted.

James lifted his hand as if offering out the perfect solution in his palm. "Just take them up the river like you did with that one reformed werewolf you took to Natchitoches."

Once more, Bart shook his head. "If I disappear, it will raise alarms and my guilt will be even more certain."

Robert's words came back to him, reminding him that men who were wholly selfless wouldn't worry about guilt or a tarnishing of their name if the cause was right. Why should Bart be afraid of retribution if it meant saving the lives of these three slaves?

The challenge to be objective came to mind and James shut down his doubt long enough to understand that if Bart was arrested or put on trial, it would endanger his sharecroppers and his efforts with the rougarou. His hesitance was then justified, because it's source was from his worry for the lives of those who depended on him.

Lottie and Will fell silent and James looked back to see them staring down one another. Words lacked the power to convince, so their wills clashed in a storm of human versus werewolf dominance that amused James more than it should have.

Finally, the woman turned to Bart, the conflict with her husband unresolved for the time being. "I will speak to Teddy on your behalf, but I still feel it would be a waste of time."

Bart grinned. "There's no harm in asking. The worst he can do is refuse and we will find another way."

James sensed a different emotion than his hopeful and passive words might have suggested. He was truly anxious, but for whom was uncertain. Was it for himself, for the slaves, or for his plantation - which might as well have been something like a pack in itself?

"Perhaps you could speak with Jean Lafitte," Robert said, shocking them all, even James.

"Lafitte?" Lottie gasped before prattling on her grievances toward the plan in her excited French tongue, which fell on ears that couldn't comprehend their words. One thing James had never taught Robert was French, though it might have been useful in hindsight.

Will, too, joined in with his own complaints, but in English. "Lafitte sells slaves. How can you possibly suggest that he could be trusted with the runaways?"

Bart might have been the only one seriously considering the plan, but said, "Lafitte's base of operations on Barataria is remote enough that it might work, but it is likely they could be sold right out from under our noses."

Robert raised his hands in supplication. "Hear me out. Lafitte may have the reputation of a pirate, but he does have a sense of loyalty toward his men. If James asks for help, he'll give it and if any man tries to double-cross him, he'll shoot them."

"We've seen him do it," James admitted.

This quieted Lottie's discourse, though the heat in her eyes could not be banked for all the assurances in the world. Will only looked to Bart for a final decision.

"When could we meet him?" he asked, and then held up a hand to check any reproof from his eldest son. "I only entertain this option as a backup plan. If

Teddy is unwilling or things become too dangerous, I want to know that Eliza and Solomon will be safe no matter what may happen."

A spark of mischief and hope brightened in Robert's face, too imperceptible to anyone who didn't know him well enough. But James saw it and smirked.

"There's a party tonight and I'm sure Lafitte will be there," he said. "We could go and speak to him then in private. After a few drinks, he'll be open to discussing business."

After a careful moment of deliberation, Bart nodded. "I hate parties, but I suppose it's necessary."

James wanted to make a crack about just how necessary it truly might have been, but he bit his tongue and let his son have his way. And *he* was the one who said not all men were naturally deceptive.

Emilie kneaded the dough, her bony black fingers coated in flour as she pushed and rolled it into the right consistency. Sweat dotted across her forehead and occasionally she had to shoo at the chickens that pecked at the bits of grain around her feet.

Outside, she could faintly hear the other workers on the plantation, talking and tending their own gardens in the waning afternoon. Across the kitchen, Ruth stuffed the seasoned ground pork into their thin casings, twisting the sausage links every five or so inches. Abraham had slaughtered one of the fat hogs earlier that morning, providing them with meat for Bart and his new guests who were loup-garou, just like him.

For the thousandth time that day, she thought of the younger of the guests, the one they called Robert, and she hated herself for it. Hated the way his blue eyes followed her in spirit the entire day through every chore, how his smile and kind words made her stomach clench. His face appeared behind her closed eyelids each time she blinked and while she slept. His strong jaw, the set of his dark brows, the way his arms filled out his coat sleeves, and a bit of tanned skin that peeked out from just below his cravat where his shirt collar could not reach as it stretched across his broad chest. It was enough to make her scream, but she wouldn't dare open her mouth. Not even to confide in Ruth, who knew that something was off with her young kitchen assistant.

Over and over, she told herself that Robert was not interested in a half-blood negress like herself. He looked just as white as any other high-born male of his free class, though his father still carried some resemblance to Bart in the way of skin tone. Though, he gave off no airs of superiority with her or any of the other people of color on the estate. He was kind and gentle, even when he caught her slipping her way past the big house at dawn. She had broken her word and stayed out much longer than she had vowed to Bart, but Robert wasn't angry. He simply gave his greeting and made a hasty promise that he wouldn't tell his grandfather about her transgression.

The relief of his discretion washed over her as powerfully as it would have if she were a slave and had been spared a whipping that she rightfully deserved for her disobedience.

She wasn't too old to forget the first fourteen years of her life where she woke up each morning and faced the day with consuming dread. Would she be beaten? Would she displease her master – who was also her father? Would she be harassed by the overseer as she had been so many times before? Would she be unable to escape the shadows of her despair when she was cornered in the dark by men who only saw her as an object of lust?

Emilie froze in her kneading and squeezed her eyes shut against the memories, against the way she felt when she pled to her father for safety and he turned the other cheek. She swallowed hard and pushed her palms into the dough more furiously.

"Chil', if you beat at dat dough any harder, it won't rise," Ruth scolded from where she stood, the sausage stuffer propped against her stomach as she squeezed more meat into the casings.

Emilie looked down and immediately released the battered mass before she could do any further damage. It had been five years since she last saw her father or any of the other slaves on his plantation. Five years since she was assaulted for the last time and left a bruised and bloodied mess at the hands of the overseer. Five years since her father did the most merciful thing in his life and turned her out of the plantation with a promise not to follow or pursue her. How many more years would it take for her to be fully and completely free, not just in body but in soul and spirit?

"Sorry," she muttered before she tore off a small portion of the dough. After setting the loaf to rise, she'd take that disconnected piece and store it in a container of salt so she could make a batch of sourdough later in the week.

"Dem ghosts still botherin' you?" Ruth asked as she twisted off more links.

Emilie only nodded. Her past was not a mystery to those on the plantation, and it was better to let them all know the truth so nothing would be assumed in the end. That included what she did when she slipped away in the evenings to go to the Duplaintier Plantation.

One crucial benefit to her turn through the crucible is that it left her with an attitude of perseverance and absolute disregard for what others thought of her. She didn't care if they thought she was a witch, or that she was foolish for taking up the practice of voodoo. Everyone had their way of coping with trauma and she had hers. If they didn't agree with it, it wasn't Emilie's problem.

After carefully molding the loaf, she set it in a floured bowl and covered it with a piece of linen cloth before moving on to the next task of preserving the ball of dough.

"Din't Miss Marceline give you a gris-gris bag for all dat?"

As Emilie walked across the kitchen to take a jar of salt from a shelf near the fireplace, she could feel the gris-gris bag Ruth mentioned rubbing against her leg beneath her skirt. The tiny cloth sachet was filled with herbs and blessed with a spell to ward off evil spirits. The formula was slightly different than her previous gris-gris bag and it appeared as if Marceline would need to make another for her. It wasn't an exact science. Nothing about voodoo was. They could supplicate to the spirits, the loa, but if one aspect of the ceremony was not to their taste, it was all voided. She assumed that was the fault in her last gris-gris bag, so Marceline was happy to make her another. Anything to help Emilie sleep at night.

"She did, but..."

Her voice trailed off, not for lack of anything to say, but in order that she could listen to the new commotion outside. With the jar of salt between her floured hands, Emilie turned and peered out the dirty window.

Simon had bounded off the back porch of the big house, hollering for the other two white men on the plantation to come to him. She knew both of them were also loups-garous, brought onto the plantation under an act of charity by Bart, but Emilie wasn't told all the specifics of their purpose there. She knew they came for a few months and then left, a constant revolution of strangers permitted to live and work with the rest of the negroes.

Before she came onto Bart's estate, she couldn't even fathom the existence of such creatures as loups-garous or rougarous. She had never heard of the legends and stories that surrounded the uninhabitable swamps. After a few months of watching her new master, or rather employer, she began to suspect something wasn't quite right with the men. Their behavior, though cordial, was strange and reserved. Their monthly disappearances, the way they seemed to know everything that was spoken and done on the plantation without being present, the flash of gold she sometimes saw in their eyes, all of it lent to the thought that they were not normal.

It wasn't until Bart finally confided in her about their curse that she understood the truth. This truth, however, was easier to swallow than it would have been six months prior to that long talk in the sitting room at the big house. By then, she had met with Marceline and learned about the loa and ways of the spirits.

Emilie reasoned that Bart, Simon, and the other loups-garous who came to the plantation, were merely being ridden by some spirit that the believers of voodoo hadn't known before. Whether of the Petro class, who were tricksters and aggressive, or of the Rada class, who were older and more benevolent, she wasn't sure. Marceline always said there were a thousand and one loa, but sometimes one-hundred-thousand and one loa. The number changed constantly, but Emilie came to accept that it was an indefinite number, incalculable by mere human minds. The loups-garous were just the vessels for one of those many loa, and unlike the ritual possessions that sometimes lasted between two hours or two days, this possession was permanent.

Emilie didn't fear them because of this, but sometimes envied them. Bart and the others were gifted with a strength of mind and body that she could never obtain. If it were possible for a frail woman like her to receive the loa they share, she would have petitioned for the change just as Simon did before she was born.

Beyond the black man's shouts, she could hear something else. It was fainter, like the distant wailing of a dying animal. Ruth, her hands employed with the task of filling the links and unable to set the project down, jerked her head toward the door.

"Go see what dem boys be yellin' 'bout," she said with a sigh, probably thinking that some of the hogs had escaped from the pen again.

By the way Simon seemed so concerned, Emilie doubted it. She set down the jar and rushed out, wiping her hands over her apron to dust off the flour. Out of the hot air of the kitchen, she could hear that far-off cry more distinctly. It certainly did sound like an animal, but it wasn't dying.

The roar held a strong note of fear and palatable rage that made her shiver and shrink against the wall of the kitchen house. But whether it was her curiosity or the gris-gris bag pressing against her thigh, Emilie felt a burst of courage and charged forth to get her answers.

She managed to catch up to the three men, now armed with the special guns Bart kept in the house with his silver ammunition. Each one of them wore gloves and loaded the short-barrel weapons with the utmost care so they would not be burned by the bullets.

"What's happenin'?" Emilie demanded, coming up alongside Simon who was more likely to respond to her than the other two.

"This ain't none of yo' business," he said. "Get back to the kitchen."

The bitter yowls of the creature grew louder and Emilie grabbed Simon's arm to hold him back from rushing ahead. "Is it another loup-garou?"

Simon glared at her and for a moment, she thought she could see those tiny flecks of silver sparkle like stars in his eyes. His belligerence, more than his words, confirmed it. The loups-garous that hid in the swamp were always a sensitive subject for Bart and the others, though she didn't know exactly why. Was this wailing a sign of trouble or potential danger?

Now, she wished she had thought to have Marceline make a gris-gris back that could fight the power of a loup-garou. Bart and Simon had always been kind to her, ever since the day they found her half-starved and sickly in the swamps after she left her father's plantation. If it wasn't for them... well, she didn't want to think about where she would be. But it would have never occurred to her that she would need protection from any of the loups-garous that stayed at the plantation. Not until now.

"Mind yo' own, Emilie," he growled, low and serious. "There are some things you don' need to know 'bout. This be one of them. Best you not know about everything that goes on 'round here. And you can tell Miss Ruth that too."

With that, he tore away from her and hurried to catch up with the two white loups-garous who waited on him. They disappeared around the budding sugar-cane fields and Emilie stood listening. Birds were scared away from their nests near the edge of the bayou and took to flight, black figures against the blue afternoon sky. She watched them soar, chirping and cawing their warnings to the other critters that might have been close by. How she wished she could fly with them or at least understand what they instinctively knew. Something was living in those bayous and Simon knew exactly what it was.

A sense of unease coursed through her limbs, but she refused to crumble beneath the terror. If it was a loup-garou and they were taking silver bullets, then it must have been evil and needed to be killed. She muttered a quick prayer of protection over the men and tried not to let her restless mind meditate on all the possibilities. She had to trust that whatever was out there, it wouldn't come close. Not while Simon and the others protected them.

CHAPTER 6

"Are you watching for Lafitte?" Bart asked Robert, whose expectant gaze wandered about the room.

All around, men in their finest suits and women clad in dresses made of the richest materials the port city offered, reeled and danced to the band who played in the mezzanine at the other end of the ballroom. The choking fragrances of expensive cigars and flowery perfumes was enough to make Bart lightheaded. Laughter, whispers, the whine of the string instruments, and clatter of heels upon the polished tile floor made it nearly impossible for him to enjoy himself.

His son's voice was just barely intelligible on the opposite side of the hall where he continued to tell his account of the battle, a favorite topic amongst the locals who saw nothing from the safety of their homes. They had only heard the boom of the cannons and report of the rifles from the city, and James was more than happy to fill in the gaps with every exaggerated detail.

Robert, on the other hand, volunteered to be Bart's liaison to Lafitte as soon as he entered the ball. They had arrived half an hour ago and there was still no sign of the war hero.

Bart would have much rather been at the plantation, where it was quiet and he wasn't the object of hushed censure by half of the partygoers. He couldn't make out their words, but by the furtive looks and tense way mouths were drawn tight at the sight of him, he knew that he wasn't welcome here. He wasn't the darkest man in the room, but he was the darkest *free* man.

Before the Americans arrived, the air used to not be so rife with antipathy. Free men and women of color were welcome into all circles because the French respected the fact that they were either born with the right to socialize with them, or they had earned it fairly through hard work. Now, the papers showing that a colored man was free and not the property of anyone but himself meant almost nothing. They still talked and gossiped as if his ankles were clad in chains where he stood.

"I don't see him yet," Robert mumbled, craning his neck a little higher to check one entrance into the ballroom.

Bart heard a whoop of laughter and turned to see the pirate in question approaching James's group. No doubt Lafitte's ears were burning as James continually told of the way the man selflessly loaned out hundreds of men to the aid of Andrew Jackson.

"There he is," Bart said, then looked back to his grandson.

Robert wasn't listening, but those eyes which had been scouring for someone besides Lafitte all evening, had finally found their intended target. He followed his line of sight until he caught a glimpse of shimmering golden satin and curly blonde tresses pinned up with white feathers shaking with each turn of her head.

Letting out a deep sigh, Bart smacked Robert's shoulder to get his attention.

"Do you know who that is?" he said, speaking to the young man as if he were a child who knew no better. He coveted a priceless trinket that was not for sale.

"Isabelle Burnett."

"Exactly," Bart replied with a nod and then pointed to the woman who began to make her way along the wall, smiling and curtsying to everyone she greeted. "That is trouble. Leave her be."

Perplexed and taken aback, Robert asked, "Why should I leave her be?"

With a gentle hand, Bart pushed Robert's chin to follow Isabelle's progress around the room. "Do you see what every virile man is doing?... The exact same as you. Drooling and fawning over a young lady who doesn't give a rat's ass for anyone but herself."

Robert jerked his chin away and glared. "We met earlier today," he said in defense. "She was completely charming."

Bart might have let the matter go if he were talking to anyone else, but this was his flesh and blood, and he couldn't allow Robert to be so deceived. "It's all a ploy, I assure you. Miss Isabelle is kind to everyone she meets, no matter their class, but she is no better than her father who is extremely prejudice against anyone below their station."

"She complimented the dressmaker on Conti Street," Robert replied. "She's almost generous to a fault when it comes to doting on the lower class. And she was especially kind to her maidservant."

He scoffed. "That's because her personal slave grew up with her on the plantation. They are as close as sisters, and in consequence is spoiled by her good luck of being Isabelle's companion. As for the dressmaker, Isabelle has been taught how to be polite and courteous, but her heart isn't in the flatteries she gives out so freely. It's all a show, Robert. Don't let her pretty eyes fool you."

A long pause followed this speech, and heedless of his warnings, Robert left Bart's side and strode across the room to where Isabelle congregated with a few other belles of New Orleans. He watched as his grandson presented himself in the manner that was expected of any gentleman, and then offered out his arm to the lady.

Bart shook his head, but was at least thankful that they had procured suitable attire for the ball. There was no time to go back to the plantation to change, and what they wore while journeying into town might have been adequate, but just barely. Fortunately, one of the many tailors in the town owed him a favor and three fresh jackets and vests were procured before the ball that evening.

It must have been this new change of clothes that helped in recommending Robert to the young lady, because she smiled and a blush colored her powdered cheeks before accepting him. They walked hand-in-hand to the floor and joined in the circuit of dancers that orbited continuously around the room. With grace and poise, they seamlessly became part of the ranks, and Bart had to wonder who he had inherited such natural skill from. It couldn't have been James.

Missing his liaison, Bart was at the mercy of his son and slowly made his way to where Lafitte told of the final climax of the battle.

"Andrew lifted up the note to read it and I heard him mutter, 'Who the hell is Lambert?'."

At this, many let out chuckles or bursts of laughter. Bart listened further and pieced together the story of how the last surviving major-general of the English had sent a letter to Andrew Jackson across the lines, petitioning for the time and opportunity to collect his men so he could make a full retreat with the wounded.

Bart was content to be seen and not heard as each man in the circle, French and American, asked their questions and gave their passing strategic opinions as to why the battle lasted only half an hour. He was more amazed at the lopsided lethality of the battle to care about the factors that played into its short duration.

James finally caught sight of his father in the group and edged closer to Lafitte during a lull in the conversation. The pirate's hazel eyes spotted Bart amongst them, the first time he had so obviously been noticed by anyone and nodded with a grin.

"If you gentleman will excuse me," he said to the small crowd that had gathered, "I have some business to attend to."

The three moved away and weaved through the throngs of dancers and tipsy guests to make their way toward the nearest exit that led to a private wing of the hotel. Along the way, greetings and brief, lofty toasts were given in the pirate's honor, and somehow Bart's accompaniment neither waned Lafitte's reputation in this assembly, nor aided his own.

Once they were safely shut away from prying eyes inside one of the empty smoking lounges of the grand hotel, Bart's ears were given some relief from the constant noise. He could still hear the activity down the corridor, but it was far more manageable than if he were in the thick of it.

"So, you are the father of James Croxen," Lafitte said with a toothy grin as he took a seat in a plush wingback chair near the center of the room.

"I am," Bart answered. "I have been away from New Orleans for a while, so you'll have to forgive me for not having met you sooner."

Lafitte, casual and amiable in his own way, waved off the apology. "Oh, don't try to flatter me. I know most of those connards in the ballroom don't like me at all. They only tolerate me now because of the battle. It was my plan from the start. I told myself that if I showed a bit of patriotism, they will love me, and New Orleans will throw themselves at my feet." He held out his arms as if to display his immense success. "And I was right."

James shot a smile to his father, who wasn't too amused with this confession, but took a seat across from the pirate to begin. "Then I congratulate you on your victory," he said. "Did my son mention why – "

"Why you wanted to meet with me?" Lafitte interrupted, spurring a bit of Bart's irritation that had to be doused quickly. "No, he did not. What is it you wish to discuss?"

Bart was then given the floor to submit his petition for Eliza and Solomon to be taken into Lafitte's care until Mr. McCarthy left the area. Knowing the pirate dealt in the slave trade, he attempted to appease whatever morals or conscience the man might have had. He talked about their son, Henry, and how there were few other options available to them. If they returned to McCarthy, they would be whipped or killed for their run for freedom. If they were turned loose into the swamp, they would surely die there too. Keeping them on the plantation was even more risky for both him and the slaves if the authorities were to come and look for them there, which would culminate in a similar fate as the previously mentioned options.

Lafitte listened, his fingertips touching to form a steeple just below his bearded chin. The thoughtful way he pursed his lips gave him cause to hope, but Bart would not allow himself to rejoice for the slaves' safety until the pirate gave his word that they would be looked after.

"Mon Dieu," he mumbled when Bart was finished. "You are in quite a predicament, aren't you?"

"My son has spoken of your generosity and loyalty to those who have helped you in the past. So, it's not only I who asks you, but James as well. You would be doing both of us a service by granting this request, as well as saving the lives of three innocent people who deserve compassion."

Lafitte was silent for another moment longer and then let out a tight breath. "I would naturally be inclined to accept. However," he continued with a bit of pain feathering his words, "because of recent events, I would not be able to guarantee their safety on Barataria. I could give you my word that I would not venture to make a profit off of them, but James knows the type of men I employ to run my many enterprises. They are not honest men, such as I am. I fear that your little pets wouldn't last a week on Barataria, much less a few months."

Bart struggled not to show his disappointment.

"Is there any other place you can think of where they would be safe?" James asked of his commodore. "Another island perhaps? Or another hideout?"

Lafitte shook his head, just as saddened by this hard truth as they were. "None that I know of. I would suggest they stay on your plantation. At least there, you can watch over them. I'd be tempted to bribe off the authorities myself, but things are different now and I wouldn't want to upset this happy turn in my reputation for anything, not even a few runaway slaves."

Rubbing at the light stubble on his cheek, Bart considered the idea of bribing. The five hundred he had planned to use in order to buy the little family could still be used to make blindmen out of their potential enemies.

But as Bart was debating on the shrewdness of such a plan, he could hear his name being called from down the hall. James, upon hearing it too, bid a quick goodbye to Lafitte, promising they would meet again before leaving New Orleans, and fell in beside his father. They left the room and followed the frantic, but familiar voice.

They came upon Andre, a young boy just barely growing into his teen years with lanky limbs. He was the son of Ruth, born free on the plantation, and also an excellent messenger. Bart often joked how the boy could run across the country and back without breaking a sweat. But now, the boy panted for breath, but not because he was tired after running all the way from the estate. Fear broke through the dense clouds of tobacco and verbena sachets and Bart rushed to him.

"What is it?" he demanded, pushing through the other men who were more concerned with getting the boy and his dirty bare feet off the clean floors. Andre looked like a beggar amongst all the finery, but he was more determined to find Bart than listen to the other white folk.

"Somethin's happenin' at the plantation," he gasped out. "Simon and them otha' white folk went out inna' the swamps. Heard lots of screamin' and howlin'. Mama told me to fetch ya from town to come help."

The unspoken truth hit Bart in the gut, making him almost sick to think of what might have happened in the time it took Andre to reach them. He didn't say a word, not to the boy, to James, or to Robert who must have heard the commotion and left his dance partner to investigate. He simply turned and charged past the crowd, pushing his way through the elite of New Orleans, forsaking their company and hoping he wasn't too late to help protect his pack.

Robert stood, his feet cemented in place on the back porch of the mansion house. Unable to move, unable to speak, he stared out over the devastation. Some cabins were completely wrecked. Others were partially torn down, the plank siding of the walls just barely hanging onto the frame posts by loose nails as part of their roofs collapsed in. Across the grassy lawn, victims of the rampage lay on blankets and cots as the women and children tended to the gaping wounds.

Some didn't make it so far and Robert saw out of the corner of his eye, two men carrying shovels toward the edge of the property beyond the gardens and animal pens.

Blood and fear were so potent in the air that he couldn't even smell the ripening sugarcane or the fire smoke of the kitchen chimney. The soft whimpering of children, terrified that their parents wouldn't survive their injuries, and the inconsolable crying of one mother whose husband had been torn apart filled his ears. The pairing of such noises he would never forget, as it broke his heart into pieces. He had seen war and carnage before, thanks to his father, but never had he witnessed this kind of indiscriminate violence toward human lives.

James and Bart, who seemed unaffected by the scene, were in counsel with Simon and the other two werewolves at the end of the lane of shacks. From his place, fixed on the veranda, he could hear their conversation break through the haze.

"Diego was fine yesterday," said Claude, one of the reformed werewolves. "He didn't eat what Simon brought to him, but he didn't seem unstable."

The other werewolf's skin was just a shade darker than Claude's with a noticeable tilt in his eyes to denote his native ancestry perhaps two generations back. Miko added his confirmation of what Claude said. "When we heard him shift, we ran to the holding shacks as soon as we could."

"The silver on them bars was all broken to bits and the shacks was tore up," Simon finished. "He tricked us into thinkin' he went north, but then we heard the women screamin' and came runnin' back. He woulda tore the whole place down if we didn't fill him full of shot." He lifted his empty rifle as if to prove his point.

"And he still kept running?" Bart questioned, eyes widening. "You all unloaded on Diego and he kept running?"

"Never seened anythin' like it," Simon remarked with a shake of his head. "I knowed he bled some, though."

"Some?" Claude laughed. "The man was covered in blood. How could you even tell?"

Simon slid a contemptuous look to the werewolf he helped to rehabilitate. "I know what rougarou blood smells like," he said. "It's different than any other blood I know and I been doin' this for years. You best know I mean what I say."

Bart let out a pulse of dominance to bring the men back to the issue at hand. "Which way did Diego run?"

Miko pointed in the general direction of the Mississippi.

"I already sent out a howl to the swamp wolves," Simon said. "Teddy's expectin' us."

Robert saw Bart close his eyes and struggle to keep his cool. "You sent out a howl to Teddy?" he ground out.

Simon stepped forward to stand in front of his alpha, their vast differences in size and fortitude plain. If Simon had any inclination to strike at Bart, he could send the older werewolf rolling into the sugarcane fields.

"Diego's gone crazy. We can't take him alone. We need help."

Those few short statements might not have been enough to convince Bart of the gravity of the situation, but he let go of whatever kind of reproach he was ready to give for making a decision without prior approval. He nodded and looked to Claude and Miko.

"You two stay here and protect the others in case Diego tries to double back again." Then he turned to his son, who was shifting his weight from one foot to the other. "You and Robert come with us. We'll need all the help we can get."

As if instinctively, James looked to the porch and met his son's eyes. Through a series of slight, almost imperceptible movements, they argued about the prudence of going or staying. Robert, of course, would have rather done anything else than go after a rampaging rougarou, but James had been taken hold of by some unaccountable bravery and insisted that they help Bart.

In the span of just a few seconds, James made the decision for him. Robert would not be a coward. "We'll go."

Bart nodded and told Robert where to find three more rifles inside the mansion house. As heavy as his limbs felt, he found the strength to move and carried himself back inside. To get to the makeshift armory on the ground floor, Robert would have to cross the sitting room where Ruth and Emilie were tending to three of the sharecroppers who were only lightly beaten during the attack. Bart had allowed them to be nursed inside the house, because none of them were likely to bleed on the upholstery.

One nursed a sprained ankle, another was determined to have a broken rib, and another was completely unconscious after hitting his head on the corner of a cabin step. Ruth sat on one end of a sofa, wrapping up the ankle while Emilie applied a cold washcloth to the forehead of the man who hadn't woken up for at least an hour.

Robert would not make eye contact, knowing that either of the women were likely to ask questions about what happened that night. He couldn't explain, nor did he want to. His mind and body were numbed by the desolation of the plantation. He had prided himself on having the ability to disconnect from tragedy, to approach terrible situations with a kind of aloofness that would help him to process solutions. But right now, he felt on the edge of an emotion that neither he, nor his wolf, wanted to experience. One look at another aching soul, one more tremor sparked by a grieving mother, and everything would come unraveled.

He fetched three more rifles, three pairs of thin calfskin gloves, and pocketed as many silver bullets as he could carry. Before he could even leave the armory, Emilie stood in the doorway, her apron splattered with darkened blood that mixed with flour. Her face, pinched with worry, implored him to stop.

"You're goin' with Mass'r Bart and Simon?"

Mutely praying she would ask nothing further, he nodded and stood still, waiting for her to move aside. But she didn't.

"You're goin' after that monster."

It wasn't a question, and he wasn't quite sure if he agreed with her word for the rogue rougarou, but he nodded again.

The worry in her face morphed into a calm, but grave expression before she said, "Good. Take this with ya."

In a move that made him take a quick step back, Emilie turned and lifted up the edge of her skirt. He could see nothing from his angle, but heard the muffled pop of a string broken after she slipped her hand underneath. She came out with a tiny bag, that once out from the cover of her few layers of clothing, let out a pungent aroma of mixed herbs and something that prickled at his chest and rose up his throat. Unaccustomed to the feeling, he let out a gruff cough to rid himself of it.

"This will help ya," she said as she took liberties by tucking it between his vest and shirt over his heart. "That rougarou don't stand no chance against y'all. Anger and hunger gonna blind him, but ya gotta keep a level head yourself, too."

Its effects were almost instant and the tingling he had felt before dissipated into something relieving, as if a spike had been driven into a rising loaf of dough. The anxiety was released and he could almost sense himself deflating until he could think clearly again.

He looked with alarm to the young woman and didn't regret that he had to buy her that dress anymore. Emilie deserved it. Whatever she had just done, no doubt with some voodoo magic, Robert no longer felt on the border of madness. How did she know what he was feeling?

"Thank you," he said.

She gave him a smile and then turned to flee into the sitting room again. Letting this unearthly serenity finally settle over his spirit, Robert waited a moment longer, and then made his way out of the mansion house.

CHAPTER 7

Two boats were taken, each one captained by a man who knew – at least in part - the complicated twists and turns of the swamps. James kept one hand gripping his wooden seat and the other clamped over the side of the rocking pirogue canoes. Simon navigated the narrow, winding canals, but due to his hulking frame, the boat continually tilted from one side to the other until James thought they would capsize. The water wasn't as much of a concern as the pairs of eyes that would occasionally emerge from the dark depths to watch them paddle by.

If the situation were at all different from the current, urgent state of things, James wouldn't have volunteered them so readily to make this trip to the Acadians. But after seeing the ruin of the plantation, after knowing that one of his own kind was the cause of so much suffering, James couldn't distance himself from this any longer.

He couldn't help but feel responsible somehow. He had heard Diego's irrational speech and could have foreseen this disaster after they spoke the night before. He should have warned someone, but he was silent against the lurking threat. If he had told Bart what the rougarou said, then perhaps they could have saved lives that night. He still cringed to think that anyone could exact such blind, senseless vengeance upon people who didn't deserve his hatred. It wasn't the loup-garou way, that much James understood.

Robert and Bart were situated in the lead as they came closer to their destination. The constant trilling of the nocturnal bugs and frogs of the swamps couldn't drown out the music and laughter that floated to them across the bayou.

Flickering candlelight dotted both sides of the banks, interspersed with greater fires that lit up the dark night, casting golden reflections along the rippling surface of the river. If he weren't so distressed by the importance of their mission, or by the constant anxiety at the idea of their canoe turning over, James might have smiled at the festivities taking place along the banks.

Men, most of whom were werewolves, and women of all ages danced and clapped in time with the fiddle players and wheezing of the accordions. Their campfires illuminated the modest huts made out of cypress wood harvested directly from the swamps. The shingles of the roofs were either covered in thick palmetto branches or of that same cypress, obviously adequate to keep out the heavy rains that were so common in this region.

Their dress and manners were informal. Their clothing was clean enough, though the evidence of hard labor and dirty work were plain on the men's shirts and on the women's white aprons. But despite a long day of living so far disconnected from society, they rejoiced in their independence. They were self-sufficient with their own gardens and abundance of livestock that wandered about freely without corrals or pens to keep them close by. Porches with forward sloping roofs were the ideal place to congregate, if one wasn't out in the yard dancing and twirling around the fire with their partner.

Dogs that weren't bothered by the presence of so many other predators, lounged with bones between their paws, gnawing at the marrow or sleeping. Children were having their own celebrations, like the adults, giggling and darting in and out of the shadows in the midst of some game.

Not one dark face was among them, but the predominate language appeared to be French or a heavily accented variant of English. He recalled from earlier that day when Bart explained that Lottie's ancestors were French refugees from the north who settled in Louisiana. These were her people, and also the swamp wolves.

James had never seen so many of his own kind in one place. The sensations and smells barraged him until he became transfixed by this completely new and strange world. He didn't care so much about the alligators waiting by for a chance at an easy meal anymore. In fact, he didn't spot a single one anywhere along the banks of this community. When he saw what was roasting on the spits above the fire, he grasped why. He had never tasted alligator before, but by the smell alone, he imagined it would certainly be a delicacy worth trying.

Robert, probably finding this display exceedingly strange, looked over his shoulder with a disbelieving grin. James only shrugged to his son, unable to explain any of it.

Bart slowed when they neared a particular home near the middle of this long procession of cabins and huts along the river. A man, dressed a little neater than the rest of the Acadians, leapt off his porch and ran to meet them.

A smile reached up to his slightly wideset, dark chestnut eyes dancing beneath a heavy brow. His wavy hair, a reddish brown in hue, was let free to fall around his neck and shoulders. As werewolves go, he was muscular, but in a lean way that wouldn't have turned heads, which might have been to his benefit. The alpha of a werewolf pack this size needed to stay inconspicuous, while still maintaining his authoritative presence amongst his peers.

The man greeted them warmly in a somewhat less marked version of French that James was so used to hearing, and Bart replied in the formal way he always did.

The alpha, Teddy, hurried onto the slightly crooked dock that jutted out from the cattail-covered banks as Bart and the others pulled alongside it. He then grabbed Bart by the arm and helped him to his feet, the planks groaning under so much weight. James wouldn't leave his boat until Simon and the rest were safely ashore, fearful that the boards would snap under the load of five werewolves at once.

"This is incredible," Robert commented as they walked up the cleared path to the shack. Tall weeds and grasses lined the walkway and James spotted a hound sleeping by the edge of the steps, floppy ears touching the ground as bags of skin rested on thin outstretched limbs.

Detecting not a single trace of sarcasm in the statement, James decided to reply with his own. "Which part? Their cleanliness, the fact that not a single alligator comes within a mile of here, or that these dogs don't so much as bark at our arrival?"

"All of it," Robert explained, stopping to stare out over the countless families who walked from one hut to another, bowls of food in hand, simply to go and sit with their neighbors and visit. "Everyone seems so happy here, but they're all werewolves. How can they coexist in one place so... harmoniously?"

James also stopped to admire the view. There was a certain kind of assumed comradery about this place. They relied on one another for company, entertainment, and there was probably a fair amount of sharing amongst the Acadians. "Living in the wilderness can do that," he remarked. "It can make families out of complete strangers."

Robert's head tilted, a look of total beguilement falling over him that James hadn't seen in years. "These people must all be descendant from the same settlers that came here decades ago. Remember what Bart said?"

Of course, he remembered, and James snorted. "I wonder how many of these people are inbred."

With that, he turned and trudged up the steps, finally rousing the hound from his sleep. Bloodshot eyes watched the two werewolves mount the porch and go inside where two oil lamps were lit in each of the glassless windows.

"Have you seen him?" Bart asked after explaining their situation with the runaway rougarou.

Teddy's once joyful face soured into a look of effusive worry and pain. "No, I have not," he replied. "If any of your convicts came through here, the dogs would have smelled him and told me so right away."

James should have guessed that the dogs that seemed to come accessory to every cabin would be trained to detect true danger, not just a werewolf.

The creaking of a chair in the far corner alerted him to another tenant of the cabin. A man, werewolf, lounged back casually with his arms folded across his barrel chest. Boasting the same chestnut eyes and dark auburn hair as Teddy, James wondered if this man was somehow related to the alpha. The key difference in their physiques might have been enough to refute such an idea. This man was just as burly as Simon and could probably rip an alligator apart without much trouble at all.

He silently watched the group, the toe of his booted foot swaying from side to side as he listened. Nothing about him could suggest that he was concerned or amused, but simply waiting for his turn to speak or be acknowledged.

"Can you gather some men to help us find him?" Bart continued hastily, bypassing all customary forms of introduction to James or Robert for the sake of time. They didn't have much left, especially if Diego was still in his wolf form.

James still shuddered at what that crazy Spaniard might have been capable of. Just from their brief, but terrifying conversation at the detention shack, Diego was liable to kill everything and everyone in his path. Add to the fact that he must be starving and out for revenge against Bart, they needed every available hand to help. And in his opinion, more guns than the ones they left in the canoes.

Teddy nodded eagerly. "Absolument," he replied, and then gestured toward the man in the corner of the main room of the cabin. "My brother and I will go with you."

Bart's gaze darted to the man and then back, as if in total disregard. "We need more than just you two."

At this, Teddy propped his hands on his hips and cocked an eyebrow at his superior – perhaps not in rank, but in age. "Mon amie, we have known one another for quite some time and you know that Uriah and I are excellent trackers. We will help you find this rougarou. The more we involve in the hunt, the harder it will be to corner him. Too many hands in the pot and the soup will spoil."

James didn't quite understand the metaphor, but with how eccentric these people proved themselves to be, he decided not to bother. "Two men are better than none," he told his father.

Teddy gave a nod of appreciation for his agreement and then took charge of the search party, listing off the many paths and routes Diego might have taken from the plantation.

"It is unlikely he would go across the waterways, so he would naturally stay on dry land for as long as possible. The swamps have many avenues. We will have to split into two teams."

Each man looked to the other, already choosing their partners, which made everything imbalanced.

James stepped closer to Robert, who had been looking to Simon, who in turn had picked Bart. Naturally the older werewolf wanted both of his sons, but all four couldn't be in the same party.

"I'm not going anywhere without Robert," James announced.

Bart met Simon's gaze and then nodded, but not with a little regret. He might have wanted all three of the Croxens together, but his bodyguard wouldn't settle for being by anyone else's side. Teddy offered out his hand to James to shake.

"It would be my honor to take you and Robert downriver," he said. "Uriah can take your father in the other direction."

At this, Uriah stood to his full height and strode across the floor, his heavy boots thudding against the floorboards. "If Diego has been on this side of New Orleans, I will certainly find him."

His booming voice matched his towering stature, much different than Teddy's. How the smaller and less intimidating of the brothers became the alpha of such a pack was beyond comprehension, but once again James wouldn't bother with these quirks. They were now divided into teams of three and with luck, they would find Diego before anyone could be hurt or killed by the insane rougarou.

Will leaned against the iron railing of his balcony, watching the streets below while keeping his senses open. Bart might have been the alpha of the plantations, and Teddy the alpha of the swamps, but Will liked to think that he was the alpha of New Orleans. Nothing happened here that he wasn't aware of. Every crime, every celebration, every ball, and every hanging, he was privy to the details, because he listened and waited.

The shutter doors that led into the upstairs hall of their home on the corner of Bienville and Bourbon were wide open and he could hear his wife washing off the soot and dust from the day's labor before dressing for bed. He, on the other hand, still fashioned the dirt and stain of ashes and cinders upon his open vest and linen sleeves. The wind, laden with the scents of the town, brushed across his brow and through his hair, cooling his forehead while imparting secret messages through what traces it conveyed to him.

The city was expanding. Crews worked all day long, extending the roads in all directions and building new homes for businesses and families who were coming to New Orleans in droves. The reputation of the port city, though well known throughout the nation, reached a new level after the war. Now, everyone wanted to visit and see the delights of what many considered to be a small taste of Paris on American soil. Will didn't like it one bit. More people meant a higher risk of exposure, not just for him, but for his father and the plantation.

He was aware of what was taking place on the bayou on the other side of the river. He'd heard Andre's pounding little feet as soon as he jumped off the ferry at the docks. The ball carried on without even a pause for the loss of a few guests. But it didn't go unnoticed by Will. He had stayed vigilant ever since they left, knowing some danger might have been close by.

All the while perceiving each scent and voice that came to him on their corner lot, Will thought of James and Robert. He wouldn't confess to anyone, not even his wife, but he was glad they finally made themselves known in New Orleans. He would have gone to them the moment he realized they were staying at the inn, waiting for Bart, but he knew that such an introduction would be made easier by his father's presence.

Seeing James brought back too many painful memories that he never guessed would have resurfaced after so long. There was the regret, the shame, and need for absolution from his half-brother after nearly a century of festering in the knowledge that his actions had irrevocably altered the lives of so many people during his time in the Caribbean.

For now, he would be content just to know that James considered him a new man, and he had earned forgiveness for all the hurt he had caused. His half-brother might have his doubts about Bart's methods, but Will hadn't lied when he said that the ends justify the means. The results should have spoken for themselves, but he knew that as soon as the holding shacks with their silver cages were mentioned, James would shut out any positive impression that might have been made.

Will understood the mentality of a former pirate. Freedom, above everything else, was vital. Knowing that the rougarous, no matter how unhinged they might have been, were kept in cages appalled him. Will had spent a lifetime learning to distinguish emotions, and if he was correct, James was utterly disgusted with Bart and this whole affair. Maybe a prison break like this one would make him think differently. It may have seemed like the rougarous were captives, but the silver cages were nothing compared to the kind of prison that existed within their own minds and souls. What Bart did for the rougarous was humane and appreciated, but James couldn't possibly understand that, unless he could become a rougarou himself and experienced the rehabilitation first-hand.

"Will?" Lottie said from the bedroom. "Are you coming to bed or will you stay on the balcony all night?"

He didn't move or turn to call out his reply. He only let out a tired sigh and continued to listen, knowing he would stoke the wrath of his wife if he didn't come to bed, but also knowing that one moment away from his post could be disastrous.

Soon enough, he heard the whisper of thin fabric and soft, slow steps of his wife coming to get him. He didn't have to turn to know that she had let her ebony hair down, the dark curls swaying in the breeze. The temptation to turn was strong, but Will continued to stare at the drunkard stumbling across the intersection to see if he would pass out or make it down Bourbon street.

Two strong hands slipped around his waist and trailed up to the front of his chest, fingers lingering as if she were commissioned to hold him there for the rest of eternity. Her scent eddied around his head, clouding his mind until the drunk teetering on his feet below was no longer significant.

"Bart and the others will find the convict," she mumbled, pressing her lips against the fabric that stretched across his shoulders. "You don't need to police the whole city."

Will closed his eyes, giving in for just a moment to enjoy the feel of her body leaning into him.

She was in her nightgown and out in the open air. Though there were few awake at this hour, one glance out an upper story window might ruin her. But Lottie never cared for her reputation. Not when she left the swamp wolves to live with him in town, and not when she served as his assistant in the shop below. But the shame of her more masculine and bold tendencies couldn't overshadow the pity she received from the other ladies of New Orleans. Still in her prime, and unable to bear a child. Two stillborn babies and three miscarriages might have broken any woman, but not Lottie.

"Just a little longer, mon cherie," he begged.

Lottie didn't listen and playfully nipped at his arm in the way he liked so much. Her bravery and her dominance might have been attributed to her Acadian bloodline, but there was so much more she inherited from the werewolves that resided in the swamps.

Will let out a low growl of approval when the tips of her fingers curled and raked down his shirt. Her nails dragged across the ridges of his abs to settle over the front of his trousers and stayed there, toying with him.

"Now," she demanded like a lusty vixen, pulling him away from the railing without further protest on his part.

Just as he seized her mouth with his own in a kiss that would certainly lead to more, he felt it. The sign he had been waiting for. His growl of pleasure turned into a snarl of irritation and he let go of his wife to turn back to the city.

"What is it?" she whimpered, stamping her bare foot in the shadows between the balcony and the hall.

Will felt it long before he could find the scent or hear the scraping of claws. This wasn't a stray dog that slunk down the alleyways and through gardens near the harbor. The hatred, the hunger, the sheer aura of evil that emanated from the rougarou told him enough.

Predicting both its path and its motive, the beast was headed for the hotel ballroom, where most of New Orleans' society would be found. Soldiers would be there and veterans of the war, but none of them would know how to put down a monster like a rougarou.

"I have to get Carney and Lorenz," he told Lottie, kissing her one last time before buttoning up his vest and making his way down the stairs to the shop.

"Is it Diego?" she asked, trying to follow him, but far too slow in comparison to his wolfish speed.

"I believe it is. Stay inside and keep that dagger under your pillow."

Will knew he wouldn't regret having an old knife handle refashioned with a silver blade. The risk of relapse, not only in himself but in other reformed rougarous, scared him too much to leave Lottie unprotected, even against her own husband.

Careful not to be seen, he hurried through the alleys and backways to the brewery where Carney and Lorenz were unaware that anything was amiss in the city. He pounded his fist on the back door and called for them by name. Carney was awake, tending to their current batch to make sure every step was meticulously regulated, while Lorenz was fast asleep. It took a moment for the German to answer.

"What the devil are you about?" Lorenz questioned, rubbing at one of his eyes while the other remained half-shut by drowsiness. Carney came down the hall and grabbed their coats before Will ever had to answer. They were both oblivious to the escaped convict, but they should know that if Will came banging on their doors, it was a serious matter.

"I'll explain on the way," Will directed, keeping one ear attuned to the beast that was steadily stalking his way across town.

Lorenz grumbled and took the coat that was shoved into his hands while Carney stayed two steps ahead of him all the way toward the hotel. Will's explanation of the situation might have been a little rushed and he might not have had all the answers they needed.

"What's important right now is that we get Diego and take him back to the plantation," Will said hurriedly.

One sound, a cry cut down by the lashing of fangs, and the subsequent soul-splitting odor of blood made him lurch to a stop. Carney and Lorenz smelled it too, and now the German was wide-awake. Heedless of who saw them, they bolted into a run and kept away from the golden glow of the lanterns that hadn't been extinguished along the streets.

They were too late. The mutilated body of a Creole woman lay slumped against a bakery on Du Maine, just a block from Dauphine Street. Carney gagged at the sight, but Lorenz and Will were desensitized to the savagery. They had both experienced the unadulterated ferocity of the rougarous, in one way or another.

This, however, seemed different. The short stretch of time between the scream reaching his ears to the time they arrived on the scene might have been around fifteen to twenty seconds. Diego would have still been feasting on the carcass by the time they arrived, but he had vanished again. But this woman was only ripped open. Her insides hung from the open cavity of her chest and torso, dress torn, and he could see a bit of the white bone of her spine through the gash in her throat.

Diego, as starving as he might have been, didn't eat her. He simply killed her and kept going, leaving a speckling of blood for them to follow.

Will stared into the corpse's open eyes, vaguely aware that Carney was vomiting in the gutter on the other side of the street. "She must have just been in his way," he mumbled, skeptical about Diego's motivations. If this was a hunt for food, he passed up a perfectly good prize in exchange for a bloodbath. This kind of murder was senseless, psychotic, almost human. Only humans killed one another for sport or vengeance and not for food.

Whatever was running through Diego's mind, it wouldn't bode well for New Orleans.

Lorenz went to his apprentice and urged him to hearten himself as Will left the body to track down the beast. The authorities would find her, and Will didn't want any of the werewolves to be around when it happened. Bart stressed the importance of keeping one's nose clean when it came to hiding their identities.

They continued on and soon spotted the gleam of dark fur in the moonlight just before he ducked into the shadows of an adjacent building to the hotel. Muscular shoulders shifted beneath his pelt as a tail swept the ground. Will slowed and dodged behind the corner of a butcher shop, hoping the smell of the meats would roughly mask his approach.

The beast prowled closer toward the hotel, so hidden in the dark that no human would be able to see him coming forward, despite his size. Will and the other two could just make out the ruffled edges of his form and the pointed tips of ears that pricked forward. Then he stopped and crouched low, his belly almost resting on the ground as golden eyes watched the silhouettes interrupting the steady glow of candlelight from inside.

Laughter and music floated through the open windows, the scents of a couple hundred people blended together in a mass of humanity that must have been making Diego's mouth water. Then again, what was he looking for here? He could have made a meal out of the woman he left in the street. Was he after a meal or a panic? He understood, more than Lorenz or Carney could ever know, what the smell of fear could do for a loup-garou who had gone feral. It was an obsession, a vice as consuming as the taste of human flesh once they became insatiable monsters.

If this was about causing terror in New Orleans, Diego would certainly have what he wanted if he ran into the hotel and began tearing the guests apart. Not only that, but the secrecy of their existence – of the existence of werewolves – would be jeopardized. Will couldn't allow it.

He took a noiseless step forward, preparing himself for the ambush when two ladies and a man exited the hotel. One was a slave attendant, perhaps a chaperone or personal maidservant. The man he recognized as a decorated veteran from the war, escorted the other lady, whose milky white skin and golden hair matching her gown.

Diego let out a slow, rumbling growl that Will could feel in his bones, even from this distance. The humans turned and were walking in their direction, right into a trap that would escalate into chaos. Calling on his wolf for the strength and speed he would need, Will felt his eyes burnish a deep gold.

Muscles tensed in both him and the rougarou just before they sprang forward, simultaneously rushing for the same target.

A scream shattered the night air. Will's arms enveloped the dense mane of the beast as he tackled him back into the shadows. Claws lacerated his chest and torso, but he continued to wrestle him into an alleyway. Not a moment too soon, Lorenz and Carney joined him.

It wasn't enough.

He heard the fleeing footsteps of Miss Isabelle Burnett and her escorts, but Diego thrashed at his detainers to chase after them. One burst of strength and all three werewolves were carelessly tossed off as if they were nothing. They crashed into empty crates, barrels, and the brick walls of the buildings that formed the alleyway.

By the time Will could see straight again, Diego was gone. Half of the guests at the hotel had come out to investigate the screaming, but none had thought to look down their alley yet.

"Come on," Will ordered. "We need to drive him out of town."

Lorenz and Carney looked to him as if he had grown a second head.

"Are you daft?" Carney exclaimed. "He just threw us off as if we were wee gnats!"

Will radiated dominance and growled, sobering both of them out of any other argument they would have given.

"Then again," Carney corrected with a shrug as he brushed off the seat of his trousers. "I do like a good challenge."

Lorenz, too, stood and waited for Will to lead them on. In all reality, Will might have been just as apprehensive as they were. He had helped his father with these kinds of rougarous before, and even helped in catching a runaway years ago, but none were like Diego. None had been this bloodthirsty, this absolutely determined to be the monsters that humans feared werewolves to be.

CHAPTER 8

The moment Bart heard the solid, echoing tune of Will's distinct howl, he directed Teddy and Simon toward the Mississippi. Abandoning the plantations, they rushed around the boundary lines of the properties and farms to Algiers Point. The ferry port had been retired for the night and the operator was sound asleep in his home near the docks. This would have left them stranded if it hadn't been for the early arrival of James, Robert, and Uriah.

On this clear night, with a spread of bright stars accompanied by the silvery moon above, the loups-garous, who could see just fine in the pitch blackness, were afforded some extra light that helped them to see even farther through the clusters of trees and bushes. On the docks on the southern side of the river, they could easily make out the figures of their friends huddled around the moored boats.

"We were following Diego's trail to the east of here," James told his father. "We guessed that he might have swam across because his scent ends right at the banks. We didn't think he'd risk getting in the water, but it looks like we were wrong."

Robert frowned at the dark, murky waters, probably assuming they would have to cross the Mississippi in the same fashion. Uriah and Simon, however, were equally deterred by the notion and were working to free one of the ferryboats from its mooring on the docks so they could steal the vessel for their own use.

"Careful, lads," Bart advised as he moved forward to assist. "Don't cut the lines."

"We don't have time for that," Teddy argued as he unsheathed a set of claws to displace his normally rounded, human fingernails. With one quick motion, he cut through the ropes that kept the flat-bottomed boat from going adrift. Uriah did the same as his brother, while Simon stood on the other side of the boat and hastily ripped open the knots instead.

"How are we to moor the boat back when we return?" Bart asked, giving the swamp alpha a condemnatory look as they boarded the platform. Robert and James took up the long oars and began passing them out to the other men as they finished the job of cutting the boat loose.

"We'll find some other rope," Teddy answered with a careless shrug.

This was exactly why he preferred to send any correspondence through Lottie, rather than go directly to Teddy for anything he might have needed. The alpha was reckless, sometimes to a fault. Not much older than James, Teddy was far less experienced and showed little respect for his elders, whether they were within his pack or outside of it. While Bart's thoughts were three steps ahead of their current situation, Teddy stayed in the moment and did whatever seemed best at the time, heedless of the consequences. They couldn't afford such negligence here.

One thing they could agree on was that they didn't have time. Will's howl broke out a quarter of an hour ago, and even with every loup-garou on the ferry rowing toward the New Orleans harbor, it'd take another ten or fifteen minutes for them to set foot in the streets.

Once they were on dry land again, they skirted around the city's northeast side and met Will, Lorenz, and Carney some distance outside the city on the Grand Chemin du Bayou St. John that led further north. The German and Irishman stood some distance down the path, listening to the general sounds of the swamps and smaller plantations beyond New Orleans. They must have been attempting to find the general direction Diego had run, but Bart had a fairly good idea where the rougarou was going. The soft beating of drums and chanting voices of slaves could be heard through the maze of oaks, elms, and palmetto bushes.

"He's gone toward Congo Square," Will reported. "He almost ran into the hotel, but we caught up with him in time."

Robert tore himself away from his father long enough to come by Bart's side. "Did he hurt anyone?" The streak of panic in the young loup-garou's voice told Bart exactly what was on his mind. Or rather, who.

Will went into unnecessarily gory detail about the Creole women found dead in the streets and how Diego almost attacked Miss Isabelle Burnette and her company as they exited the hotel. As soon as the vixen's name was spoken, Robert turned to run back into New Orleans. James caught him about the collar and yanked him back to stay with the group, nearly choking him in the process.

"She's fine," James said, chiding his son for the rash impulse.

Bart agreed. Probably accompanied by a man she met at the ball, Isabelle was safe and out of harm's way since Diego was diverted away from the city. The same couldn't be said for the gathering at Congo Square. Slaves and natives from the surrounding area met on that patch of sacred ground to dance well into the night. Thinking that the free people of New Orleans were enjoying themselves at their own ball, the slaves decided to have a revel of their own. If only they knew what was being drawn to them in that very moment.

The mind of a rougarou, though sometimes enigmatic and volatile, could be predicted. When in a state, such as the one that Will described, rougarous were after one thing. Chaos. They would feast in their own time, but they first wanted to cause as much havoc and bedlam as possible. Running through crowded places, slaughtering everything and everyone in their paths, and drawing attention to his beastly form were typical signs that it would take real effort to detain him.

Will had never reached such a stage, and Bart had only witnessed such senseless aggression a small handful of times. It didn't surprise him that Diego would be given to this level of madness, but it never failed to scare him a little.

Looking to the other loups-garous, he wasn't so sure they could take on the rougarou. But they had to try.

"Let's stay in our groups as before," Bart instructed. "I'll take Teddy and Simon up the north path. James' group will come around from the east, while Will's can come from the west. I want to pen him in and keep forcing him north and away from people."

"What if he reaches St. John's Bayou or Lake Pontchartrain?" Will asked. "There are still some humans living on the fringes out there."

"Try to make sure that Diego doesn't find them before we do," he answered. "We have to get him alone, away from humans, and then we can take care of him."

His eldest son glanced to the rifles in their hands and understood. "You're going to kill him."

Bart grimaced. "If he gives us no choice, then we will."

Out of the corner of his eye, he saw James prop his gun against a tree and quickly unfasten the buttons on his vest. "And I'm not taking any chances." He shrugged out of the garment and let it drop to the ground before tugging his shirt tails from his breeches. Robert saw this, abandoned his gun, and followed suit, discarding his own coat and slipping off his shoes.

Teddy and Uriah excitedly agreed and shed their own clothing as well. Simon and Will, who still retained a bit of respect for Bart, looked to him for approval. As humans, they could track Diego to a point, but if the fight turned too violent, they didn't stand a chance against the rougarou, even with silver bullets.

Either way, the four guns between them couldn't go unused. If they had five fully shifted loups-garous, that allowed the others to be armed. "Go ahead, Simon."

The black man nodded and handed his gun to Will. "I think you're a better shot anyway."

Diego crashed at the thickening wall of consciousness between himself and the beast that had taken control of everything. Twenty years of disgraceful existence had driven him to this madness, slowly building until the monster had finally created a life of his own. It happened so gradually, stealing upon him with such subtlety that he hardly realized what took place within his soul until it was too late.

He could see it all. He saw the bushes and palmetto branches slashing at his face and shoulders. He heard the hammering of the drums that kept time with his heartbeat. He could smell everything from the traces of wildlife that fled from his presence and the sweat from the dancing humans who were totally unaware of the peril they were in. He even felt the burning of the silver that was still imbedded in his flesh. He could still taste the blood on his tongue from when he cut open the stomach and throat of the woman that had spotted him in the streets.

Every sickening moment, awake or in sleep, as a man or as a wolf, Diego was a witness to it all. But he could do nothing. No matter how hard he tried to pull himself from the darkness and break the hold of madness which he was under, it did nothing. The choices he'd made so long ago had set him on a course that could not be directed, could not be changed.

The more he fed on human flesh – whether living or decayed by death - the worse he became. Words that were not his own came out in angry outbursts. Thoughts, sinister and disturbing, paraded through his mind. Diego attempted to take those thoughts and words captive as soon as he understood the destructive path he was on, but it did him no good. The cravings came so strong that it was nearly impossible to resist. Blackouts would end with him waking beside a mutilated woman or half-eaten child. The hunger knew no limits, would not give into his muttering pleas to abate or cease all together.

And then, he became as he was now. Completely shut out from every decision, possessed completely by the wolf within him and reduced to a prisoner in his own mind and body.

Diego wanted nothing more than to retreat back to the swamp, to lock himself back in that silver cage – as mangled as it was after he escaped. He wanted to subjugate himself to Bart's form of rehabilitation. Anything to keep him away from the innocent people the beast wanted to devour.

As he drew closer to the gathering, the spasmodic light of their torches came into view. Their dancing and laughter became louder, and Diego fought himself harder to steer him away from the people, as he had tried to do in New Orleans outside the hotel.

Just as all the times before when he told his wolf not to do something, or not to say those mean and upsetting things, Diego was powerless. His paws barely made a sound as they drummed against the ground, the soft earth deadening any sign that he was coming upon the slaves so quickly. Only the heavy pants expelled from the wolfish nose at the tip of his muzzle would give him away, but their music was far too loud.

That same nose alerted him to something new. Diego saw them as his saviors, but the beast hated them. The other lobos, the ones who had imprisoned him and the ones who'd saved him from attacking the people in New Orleans, were closing in around him.

He screamed inside, pleading with them to end his life for good before he could hurt anyone else. But the beast, as mindlessly vicious and bloodthirsty as it was, still clung to life and the chance for the thrill of murder.

The wolf ran faster, pushing on through the thicket that grabbed at his pelt and dared to slow him down. Then, a force collided into him, sending him rolling into the sturdy trunk of an oak. The lobo that intercepted him was Diego's hero, while he had earned the hateful title of enemy to the beast.

The lobo, far larger than any he had encountered before with fur as black as a moonless sky, charged forward and tackled him along with another from the same direction. Diego, if he had any control, would have let himself be submissive and give into the dominance that only proved to rile the beast further.

In this state of lunacy, Diego's monster could throw them both off with relative ease, and he did so before darting to the east, hoping to skirt around to come at the gathering of humans from a different angle.

But everything was ruined for the beast when a gun was fired from somewhere behind him. Expecting to receive the bullet, he ducked lower, but he soon learned this wasn't the purpose of the shot. The dancing and music stumbled to a stop and the dancers began talking about the risk of discovery. They ran to the north and west, away from where the gunshot originated.

Diego slid to a halt and snarled at the unfairness of such a trick. Now, his prey was scattered and all the enjoyment would be taken out of seeing them flee from his gnashing fangs and wild, golden gaze. He couldn't leave dead bodies strung out upon the forest floor and taste their lifeblood as it ran out in rivers between the blades of grass.

More lobos descended upon him - five in their full wolfen forms - seemingly storming in from every side. He roared, waiting for their challenge with a kind of fierce eagerness. If he couldn't kill the humans, then he would kill them.

Diego fought harder to restrain himself, to force his legs to stay still as they came sprinting forward, set in determination to take down the creature they deemed insane and rogue, too feral to ever exist in respectable society. They were right, but Diego's cries for help and hope would never be heard. Not until they ridded him of the beast.

The battle commenced. Claws and fangs ripped through flesh on both sides as he was overcome by his oppressors. Blood splattered against the smooth bark of the nearby trees as yelps and growls broke out in a din of beastly rage. Bushes and smaller trees had been flattened as all six wolves engaged one another. Diego could feel every talon dig into his skin, every set of jowls that tried to sink through his bristled mane. And he couldn't stop the beast from fighting back, defending his right to kill and rampage through Louisiana. All the while, he kept screaming for the sweet release of death or exhaustion to end this infuriating duplicity that had torn his psyche in two.

Somewhere on the edge of the fight, he could hear the very human voices yelling and arguing at one another about when or where to shoot so that none of their allies would be hurt. Interspersed in his own repetitive, muted pleas, Diego implored them to take any shot they liked, as long as it was between his eyes.

Finally, the crack of a gunshot rang out. But it wasn't him that suffered. One of the smaller lobos whimpered and recoiled from the fight. Diego's beast saw his chance and leapt upon the weakened one, snapping at the lobo's neck and back.

Another bounded upon Diego with a kind of ferocity that he hadn't seen out of any of them thus far. His assault upon the injured lobo instigated a selfless, merciless fury in the other. Through the haze, Diego could just barely recognize the raving lobo. It was Bart's son, the one they called James.

The lobo fought him with such intensity that even the feral beast's tail began to tuck between his hind legs as they rolled and tumbled through the clearing they had created. Even with one wolf out of the fray, the others were stimulated into a similar frenzy as James to seek revenge for Diego's ill conduct toward the weakened lobo, whom he began to assume was the grandson of Bart.

This move, done under a savage impulse to kill, would prove to be his undoing. The lobos fought harder, and the gunmen aimed more precisely.

One silver bullet found purchase in his shoulder. Then another in his haunches. One arm was completely shot through, but the wound crippled him momentarily so he couldn't stand on all fours. One of his ears were mangled and ripped apart while his nose became so gnarled by their continual slashes he couldn't smell anything but his own blood.

Diego was losing too much blood and his healing abilities couldn't compensate for it. Weakness overcame him and the fight in the beast leaked out as quickly as his depleting stamina. He crumbled to the ground and growled in ragged huffs of breath. The four lobos stood over him, ready to deal the deathblow. If Diego could have spoken in that moment, he would have thanked them.

Just as he thought the victory was within reach, Bart ordered them away. Diego wept within his soul, but the beast only growled, sprawled across the bloody lawn as the man came forward. The other lobos stayed close, incase Diego decided to strike out one last time. But thankfully, he was too weakened, too tired, and too drained to move.

Bart crouched down and pulled a tiny sack from his waistcoat pocket that reeked of herbs and something that made his marred flesh tingle from the tip of his muzzle to the last bit of his tail. He took out a pinch and blew it into Diego's face.

He flinched back only for a moment, but blackness soon closed in, making both Diego and the monster he was trapped within fall into a deep, dreamless sleep. For the first time in years, he felt and sensed nothing. All that remained was a peace, a complete void that brought him no turmoil or pain. For an indeterminant amount of time, he ceased to exist while his heart continued to beat.

"He ain't gonna be none too happy when he wakes up."

Simon said what they all were thinking as they stared at the unconscious body of the rougarou behind the silver bars. The knock-out powder Bart had been given by Marceline – with Emilie serving as the deliverer – did its job well. Diego had shifted from his beastly form and wasn't roused from his sleep, no matter how roughly they handled him on the ferry across the Mississippi. That was at least an hour ago, and Robert might have assumed he was dead if it wasn't for his shallow breaths.

Through the open doorway of the cabin, a film of emerging dawn blanketed the sky in a matte grey. Just bright enough for them to see by without too much difficulty, but still dark enough to cast deep shadows within the cabin itself. The constant drone of the bugs in the swamp was gently interrupted by cheerful birdsongs. It was as if the world knew nothing of the drama that had rocked New Orleans just hours ago.

Bart, who sat in a chair on the opposite end of the shack with his chin resting on top of his laced fingertips, wouldn't take his eyes off the convict. So intense was his gaze that Robert doubted he had blinked for several minutes. And so captive in his own thoughts, he probably hadn't heard a word any of them had said.

Robert flexed his shoulder, more out of a strange impulse to make sure it had fully healed than out of pain or discomfort. His father devotedly watched him each time he made the slightest movement in said shoulder or let out a grunt or sigh that could be perceived as a bad sign that he wasn't fully recovered from the silver. They had removed the bullet as soon as Diego had been apprehended, but that didn't make the experience any less traumatic.

It was the first time Robert had ever been shot with silver. The only thing he could equate it to was the sensation of a live flame burning him from the inside out. How Diego could sustain so many shots and not even slow down was perplexing. They had taken out those bullets as well, but due to Diego's weakened state, he was slower to heal. Blood-soaked bandages encircled his arms and patched over the holes in his sides, but Diego had the convenience of being unconscious during the process.

If he could help it, Robert never wanted to touch any silver ever again.

"I know you are not too comfortable with our methods," Teddy began, "but I have a suggestion for curing the rougarou."

They all – save for Bart – looked in the swamp alpha's direction. He, along with Uriah, elected to stay with them until a solution could be found for Diego. Will also chose to accompany them to the plantation while Lorenz and Carney went back to their brewery, which still needed constant supervision, even after all the excitement.

"Cure?" Will questioned incredulously. "You say that like it's something that can be fixed overnight."

Teddy, the more vocal of the two brothers, replied, "Not so much overnight, but it could be faster than simply waiting out the cravings. There's a method we use with oleander flowers."

"What the devil are you talking about?" James asked, his tone rife with conde-scension.

Encouraged by the question rather than deterred by the manner in which it was spoken, Teddy became more animated in his explanation. "It's an old trick I learned from my grandfather when he traveled to Portugal. The plant grew wild there centuries ago and now it grows here in Louisiana. All parts of the flower are poisonous and loups-garous can get sick when it's eaten in large quantities."

"You're suggestin' we make Diego eat some oleanders?" Simon asked, deep lines of confusion furrowing on his forehead.

"Not directly," Teddy said. "What we do is take the oleander and boil it into a tea, and then marinate some human flesh in it. We feed that to Diego, he gets sick, and after a while he won't want to eat human flesh anymore."

Robert, who had remained quiet since they returned to the plantation, saw some sense in the plan. "You're tricking his mind and palette."

Teddy snapped his fingers excitedly. "Exactly."

"It will never work!" Will exclaimed with a laugh. "If Diego, or any rougarou for that matter, is willing to eat rotting corpses, then poisoning him will do no good."

Siding with his half-brother, James added, "Besides, how do you plan to get human flesh? Cut it from the arm of some volunteer?"

"The graves around New Orleans are all in mausoleums," Teddy pointed out. "The ground is too wet for the humans to bury their dead. It's easy to steal a body these days."

The four who were not in the habit of having to steal bodies or even think of disturbing the restful dead, looked to the two swamp wolves in revulsion. Arguments of a moral and ethical nature erupted between all but Robert and Bart, the latter of whom had yet to speak or even acknowledge the outbursts of those around him.

"We just need to put a few bullets in his skull," Will finally declared, throwing his hands up as if to rid himself of the discussion now that he'd added his own opinion on the matter. "Silver cages won't keep him in and if he's progressed this far in his psychosis, it's too late. Nothing can be done but to kill him."

Finally, the elder spoke, pulled from his meditation by Will's remark. "We're not killing him."

The words were so softly spoken that if there was no firmness in the conviction, they might have gone unnoticed. But every man, even Uriah who defended his brother ardently in his offer to use the oleander plant, fell silent when Bart made his assertion.

"As soon as he's strong enough, he'll escape again." Once more, James partnered with Will. "Next time, we may not be so lucky to corner him as we did tonight."

The others added their input, petitioning to Bart to agree to their suggestions. Bullets or oleanders. Those were the choices he was given.

"Let the man think!" Simon roared, effectively startling them all into silence. The only sound within the cabin was their steady breaths, which was then interrupted by light footsteps upon crisp grass. The approach of this new intruder surprised them all.

Robert was the first to move, knowing that he might have been a more welcome interceptor. Emilie didn't need to see Diego in this state, or at all, even if she knew what he was.

She came unburdened, her hands empty, but face flush with the exertion of crossing the plantation to reach the secluded collection of cabins. For the moment, she stood and stared at the wreckage of Diego's former holding cell. A tangled, demolished mass of wood and silver bars that caught the fading light in just the right way that their previous purpose couldn't be disregarded. The only other feature that might have been distinguishable was a portion of the roof that lay tilted to one side, sheltering a division of the rubble.

Her eyes flitted over the pile of debris and went still. Whatever she had convinced herself the night before, Robert doubted that this is what she had expected. He wasn't sure if she had ever seen the cabins before, or only knew of the rumors that surrounded this part of the plantation. It must have taken a great deal of courage to come all the way here, unescorted, and unprepared for what she'd see.

Reminded of the idea of courage, Robert reached into his vest pocket where he had kept the sachet of herbs safe while they hunted down Diego. None of the others had asked him about it, and he wondered if they could even smell it on his person. The barrier of a layer or two of clothing seemed to smother whatever vestiges it could emit. But its effects, whether completely psychological or spiritual, were felt and it came in handy for him while they searched and then shortly after he had shifted back into his human form.

Unlike his approach, which could have been heard by all the men in the second cabin half an acre away, Emilie was completely unaware of Robert until he was nearly upon her. She turned and started. Upon seeing that it was a friend and not a ravenous monster, she pressed her hand to her chest as if to keep her heart from pounding clean out of it.

"It's only me," he said to ease her, then offered out the sachet. "I assume you came for this?"

Her dark eyes glided from his face to his hand, and then shook her head. "No, I came 'cause... Well, I just knew you were out here." Taking a breath as if to fortify herself, she announced, "I want to help."

Robert admired her bravery, not only for coming all this way on a hunch that there would be someone to meet her, but also for her willingness to give what little assistance she could. If it took five shifted werewolves and four marksmen to take down a beast like Diego, it was laughable to think that a woman like Emilie could solve their problem.

Then again, the little bag of magic in his hand and the knock-out powder Bart had used on Diego, proved that even someone as small and seemingly weak as Emilie could do something incredible. He pocketed the sachet again and looked her up and down, wondering if she'd produce another herbal miracle from under her skirts.

"How?" he asked.

Emilie glanced to the cabin where the rest might have been listening and waiting just as he was. From where they stood, she wouldn't have known who was inside, even with the door open. "That rougarou spirit is evil. It's ridin' the fella and got some mighty powerful hold over him. I think we can break it."

Robert wouldn't pretend to know half of what she was talking about. "Break it. Like taming him?"

Emilie smiled bashfully. "In a way," she said. "It's hard to explain. Kinda like when Jesus cast out the demons in the Gospel."

He shook his head. "But this isn't exactly a demon." That was his first lesson as a werewolf. The wolf was bound to him until the day he died and there was no force on earth or in heaven that could sever the connection. "Your voodoo can't make him human."

That coy smile took on a playful, almost mischievous quality like Emilie knew far more than she was letting on. "We ain't gonna make him human. But we can take the starch outta him."

CHAPTER 9

No one was quick to offer their back to the unconscious rougarou. Though the knock-out powder was still in effect, they were unsure for how much longer. Diego had already been suppressed for over an hour and though the Duplantier plantation was only a short run away, they feared the jostling might wake him.

Bart made up a parcel of silver chains and a pair of gloves in the event Diego showed the smallest sign of wakefulness, but no one, not even Simon, wanted to have a wild rougarou laid across their shoulders if such a thing should occur.

Robert elected to carry Emilie, who would be a much lighter and more docile burden, though a slightly fearful one at that. In the course of a day or two, she had been privileged to observe the nature of the werewolves far more than most on Bart's estate. Now, she would come to realize how fast they truly were.

James, who had as much to fear from the rougarou – if not more – as any of the rest, stepped forward and said he would take Diego. Simon, Teddy, Uriah, and Will, ran with him, each of them with one eye focused upon the path through the dense forests between the two plantations and the other trained upon the limp convict.

A few times as they vaulted over patches of tightly packed bushes or dodged around trees that stood defiantly in their way, James heard Diego's breaths hitch as if he were gasping or having the air beat from his lungs. He didn't give a bilge rat's ass for the rougarou's comfort, but he did care if the ride was too rough. So he did his best to maintain a smooth gait as he swerved around the obstacles or jumped over what he couldn't avoid.

They neared the edge of the Duplantier plantation in good time and the sun hadn't yet risen over Louisiana. Still, he could hear many slaves and workers already out of their shacks and preparing for the long day of work ahead of them.

James crouched low, his sleeping cargo still upon his back with one leg and one arm firmly hooked in front of him. It made for an easier conveyance. Something he had learned early in his career as a pirate when carrying an injured sailor across the untidy deck of a ship.

Ahead of him, Robert lowered Emilie to her shaking feet and saw that the rag she usually had tied about her head had fallen off somewhere in the journey, revealing a mass of black silky hair riddled with tangles from the ride. Bart took her hand and helped her to gain her balance before striding straight onto the plantation to find Marceline.

Will came up and inspected Diego, checking his heartrate and other vitals to ensure he was still mostly comatose.

"I can feel him twitching," James whispered as his own muscles stiffened, ready to fling the madman off at any second.

Emilie, who might have been in the most danger, stayed close to Robert's side during the inspection. Robert, who had taken on the part of her protector, had also been her advocate while trying to convince Bart that they had little to lose in allowing Marceline to try her voodoo magic on Diego.

It was a preferable alternative to killing the rougarou or taking a risk at feeding his addiction by actually providing him with human flesh. It was of James' opinion that even if the meat was poisoned, there was no guarantee that it would hinder the cravings, and there was still the challenge of grave robbery. Whether it would be helpful was debatable.

Simon slid off the satchel containing the shackles in preparation for the inevitable, but James didn't drop his load just yet. He kept his ears and eyes open for his father and the voodoo priestess. A long quarter of an hour passed before footfalls were heard coming down the path between the cottonfields just beyond the tree line.

With Bart was an older woman, whose black face was wrinkled and dimpled. It wasn't often that a slave could live so long, but Duplantier, unlike many other slave owners in Louisiana, took good care of his workers from what Bart had told them before. Many luxuries and allowances were given to the slaves, including the right to practice whatever religion they wished, heathen or not. It might have been the only reason Marceline was permitted to wear a white turban to contain the wiry gray hairs that managed to poke out around the nape of her neck, despite the capable wrapping.

Dark, slanted eyes surveyed the group and she cradled between her boney hands, a woven basket of supplies she'd need for whatever it was she intended to do to Diego. She didn't seem a bit surprised or frightened and James wondered how much Marceline knew of what exactly she was being called upon for. Did she know they were werewolves? Did Emilie tell her at some point in her apprenticeship?

Emilie hurried forward to take the basket from her mentor and looked to the contents, nodding in understanding at a few of the articles she found there.

"Let the man down," Marceline scolded James in her crackled but wispy voice, waving her hand at him as she stepped over the vines and dead branches in her way. Bart offered out his hand, but she refused to take it, though her slightly hunched frame and slow bend of the knees might suggest his help could have been useful. The hem of her white skirt continually snagged on the dull tips of limbs and she impatiently tugged to free them.

James did as he was told and they laid Diego on his back, straightening his legs and positioning his arms so they were against his sides. With his hands protected by the gloves, Simon withdrew the chains from the bag. Once more, the voodoo priestess waved him off.

"We don't got no need for them, Simon," she said.

"He could wake up any – "

Marceline cut Will off with one stern look. The closer she came, the stronger her presence was felt by all the werewolves. Her countenance was proud, but not unpleasantly so. She carried herself with an air of dignity like a woman who had seen much and suffered equally. A wealth of knowledge and wisdom could be seen, not just in her eyes, but in her movements and mannerisms as she knelt down by Diego's sleeping form to assess his condition. She behaved as if she had done this a thousand times before and had become a master at taming wild werewolves. It might have boosted his confidence in her abilities if he hadn't known what Diego was truly capable of.

Making them all nervous, she lowered her ear to Diego's broad, bare chest, presumably to listen. When she straightened, she flicked the back of her hand at certain joints, making a dull slapping sound upon impact that made each of them flinch and stiffen. The rougarou was liable to wake at any minute and this woman was far too close and reckless. Simon tensed with the silver chains still gripped between his mighty hands, ready to apprehend the beast if he should strike out against her.

James, still squatted where he had twisted his body to let Diego down onto the ground, watched the blank face of the rougarou, searching and waiting for any bit of consciousness. It seemed strange to him how such a vile, vicious monster could look this calm and tranquil at all. The scowls he had first seen the other night when they met might have been assumed to be permanent. But now, the harsh lines were smoothed out, lulling James into feeling something of pity for the way Diego's life had been destroyed by this hunger.

Marceline turned to ask Emilie for a tied-up bundle of herbs and the flint needed to light up the incense. Within the span of less than a second, James saw the corner of Diego's mouth pull. His hand, still coated in blood from the fight near Congo Square, shot out to grab James by his shirt sleeve.

All werewolves rushed forward to seize some part of Diego. A leg, an arm, his torso, anything to keep him lying flat on his back. Marceline was pushed aside and Emilie let out a shriek, stumbling backward until she tripped over her dress and fell to the ground. James and a few others let out a low growl, but the rougarou made no move to rise.

Diego's grip was firm, his fingernails ripping into the fabric he clutched so tightly. Slowly, his face contorted in a look of pain rather than rage. His dark-rimmed lids cracked open to reveal bloodshot eyes that immediately searched for James. Once the Spaniard found him, lips that had been made parched and chapped by the drying blood caked upon them, parted and he wheezed out a plea that sounded strangely self-possessed.

"Kill me," he whispered, his voice too weak to speak any louder. "Please, kill me."

James, who had been unwilling to take his eyes off the rougarou before, looked straight to his father. The convict was his charge, his responsibility. Diego's fate rested completely upon Bart's good graces. He had the power to let him live, or wrap the silver chains around Diego's neck until his head hung on by a single piece of skin.

Faced with a similar situation before, James knew what would have been best. The only way he knew to deal with Will a hundred years ago was to let him drown in the Caribbean. At one point, Bart thought he had no choice but to capture and kill his own son for his presumed crime against humanity. Would he be so convicted now in Diego's case?

With his own convictions aside, he would have been inclined to give Diego exactly what he wanted. It was his wish to die, to be free of this life and the torture he must have endured under these mad appetites.

But after a moment of thought, Bart shook his head. He still wouldn't see the logic in killing the beast.

Disappointed, James grabbed Diego's wrist and pried his sleeve free without a word of comfort to the convict. Simon, heedless of Marceline's earlier insistence, unlatched the silver cuffs and used them to restrain Diego.

Brown eyes plumed into a wolfish gold as flesh burned under the metal. A tear slid from the crease of the rougarou's eyes and James wasn't sure if it was from the pain or the utter misery that had been so audible in his earlier request.

Behind the wall of werewolves, Marceline calmly struck the flint at the bundle of herbs. The tips burned red as wisps of incense curled upward. A fragrance permeated that part of the forest and its effects were instantly felt by all.

While it calmed his mind, James felt a deeper, visceral sensation in his chest and core. The wolf within him stirred and his body quivered in response. The closest he could compare it to was that strange moment between sleep and awake when his body felt as if it was falling without end, but he tensed to prepare for the crash that never came. Soon, he gave into the feeling and let out a long, slow breath that eased every muscle.

All around, golden eyes receded to let the human irises come forth again. Even Diego, whose wolf had every reason to be pressing through the wall of consciousness that separated them, dissipated and withdrew. The same evil aura they all associated with the rougarou also began to fade, and for the first time James wondered if this would truly work.

Marceline nudged her way through the slightly inebriated werewolves and began her voodoo ritual, wafting the incense over Diego's body and mumbling a chant. Emilie soon came to her side and joined in, their beautiful black voices lifted up and echoing one another in a language that none of them understood.

James watched through a slight haze as ointments and salves were rubbed over the rougarou's chest, arms, and face with the utmost care. No other werewolf moved, or even made much of an effort to apprehend him anymore. Whatever the bundle of herbs and sticks was comprised of was debilitating all of them, allowing each to experience just half of what Diego did.

A slight dizzy spell overtook him, but James forced himself to stay alert. Diego's eyes were the first to close and his lips parted as if he were falling asleep again. Robert swayed and leaned, nearly falling over had Will not grabbed for his shoulder to keep him upright. But his half-brother didn't look to be faring well through the experience either.

The only werewolf who seemed totally unaffected, whether mandated by his pride or a genuine insensibility to this magic, was Bart. He had knelt down by Diego's head, his stoic face watching each of them, along with his convict.

Through the drowsiness and the euphoric lightheadedness that descended upon him, James carefully studied his father's expression and the concentrated look in his eyes. Maybe it was the incense or the inexplicable peace that cleared his head, but James realized something so revolutionary, so tangible that not even the disturbing words of the rougarou could make him doubt it now.

Bart did care. Taking on feral werewolves wasn't a show of pride or arrogance. He cared for every werewolf present, whether they were Acadian, black, or a former rougarou. He stayed alert, though the effects of the ritual were hard to ignore, because he wanted each of them to be safe if Diego should react badly to what Marceline was doing.

Saving the rougarous wasn't a matter of prestige, and neither was freeing runaway slaves. James had always believed humanity to be full of deception. They can shake your hand one moment and then stab you in the back the next. Loyalty was possible, but every man had his price and his reasons. He didn't want to think that werewolves could be the same way, but his first experiences with Will and Bart had made him cynical.

Now, after meeting more of his kind and seeing his father's true character, James recanted every hateful thought toward the man. There were good men in the world, and he was glad that his father was one of them.

Bart leaned against the smooth column and turned his eyes upward to the clear afternoon sky. Diego and Simon were still with Marceline, along with Emilie – much to Ruth's dismay. He could still hear her in the kitchen house, muttering under her breath about losing her assistant for the day. Diego's recovery would take more than just one ritual as Marceline warned him. But this was the first battle in a spiritual war that only the voodoo practitioners could see, so Bart left the rougarou in her capable hands. Even if Diego would be unconscious for most of the treatment, it was a better alternative to keeping him on the plantation where Marceline couldn't help him.

Men on the estate were rebuilding the cabins and shacks that had been dismantled in the previous night's raid. Teddy and Uriah called upon the other loups-garous of their hidden pack in the swamps to assist the sharecroppers, who were completely unaware of who they worked beside. Acadian women also came with their holistic medicines to help those who were still healing from their wounds.

Explanations were not demanded of Bart, though dissenting whispers fluttered around the plantation like bothersome mosquitos. They were all free to stay or leave. It would neither hurt his feelings nor his pride if they couldn't cope with what they had seen.

Diego might have been in good hands, but there was so much more now that Bart was forced to address as a result of his escape and subsequent rampage through New Orleans. The silver cages had never been broken before. Bent, perhaps, but never broken and twisted as he saw upon their return to the plantation.

What the others might have perceived as resolute strength in the face of this crisis was, in actuality, a desperate need for a new plan which resulted in this quiet preoccupation with his own thoughts. How should he reinforce the silver?

Should he make the cabins closer so he can monitor them more carefully or move them even farther away from the sharecroppers, so senseless injury could be avoided in the future? Or should he abandon the whole notion of trying to reform these loups-garous in favor of a more tranquil living as a farmer? Or should he try harder and push forward through the hardships and trials until he accomplished what he had always set out to do? Total peace might have been too much to hope for, but Bart knew that if he totally forsook this mission, he'd regret it for centuries. Then again, was his mission worth risking the lives of these people who had put their trust in him so completely?

His eyes roamed over the black and white faces, remembering their stories and how they came to be here. He saw Claude and Miko, only two of the former convicts who had benefitted from his help. Then there was Eliza and her son, who stayed close to Solomon as he helped pass along freshly planed boards to Teddy on the roof of one cabin. Plans for the runaway slaves' safeguarding were already in place with the swamp wolves, who didn't give a moment's hesitation to taking them in until their disappearance was forgotten.

Bart was torn. He could not keep both the sharecroppers and the rougarous, but his heart felt split in two directions. One wished to help the humans, while the other still wanted to help his own race. Due to the fragile nature of humans, giving up one would still jeopardize the other. Rougarous could not be allowed to run free, but neither could they be allowed so close to humans during the first stages of their recovery.

He passed a hand over his damp brow, feeling the building heat of spring in the air. Soon, it would be summer and the heavy work of harvesting the sugarcane would commence. While he had Diego on the mend and the other holding shacks empty, he had to make his decision soon.

Behind Bart, his family sat back in chairs upon the veranda, quietly talking amongst themselves about various things as they took a break from helping with repairs. The nature of their conversation momentarily drew him out of his pensiveness.

"This truly is remarkable, though," Robert said, his voice piqued with a kind of fevered excitement that he hadn't seen since their arrival. Granted, they hadn't had much time to get to know one another apart from their first evening on the plantation.

Bart turned to watch them over his shoulder.

"This is normal," Will chuckled. "Werewolves were never meant to be alone, but in packs so they can help one another."

"I'm not talking about packs," Robert insisted, gesturing to the rows of working men. "This kind of human and werewolf integration. It's fantastic."

James leaned forward on his knees, a glass of fresh lemonade in one hand. "It can be dangerous too."

"Not if they're all aware of one another."

Will shook his head at his nephew. "But most of these people aren't aware they're working with werewolves."

Robert shifted in his chair and set down his own glass on the table between them. "But what if they were? What if there was a community of werewolves and humans working side by side and there were no secrets between them? Imagine how much could be accomplished if Teddy's pack could use their full strength in front of the others as if it were nothing."

"You're talking nonsense," James laughed, taking a draft of his bitter but sweet drink.

"Not necessarily," Bart said, wedging himself into the conversation. "It's been done before, but on a smaller scale."

His thoughts went back to the network of packs his own father, John Croxen, had created in France. Loup-garou packs abroad were sometimes, by necessity, assimilated as Robert suggested. Though, the proportions were often unbalanced, and the only humans permitted into the packs were the females who were willing to mate with the loups-garous. Even amongst the swamp wolves, who were a glorified exception to this widely accepted rule of no-integration, were primarily made up of loups-garous. Humans were the minority.

Glad that someone could agree with him, Robert hurried along in painting this picture of cohabitation. "Such a community could break the stigma that surrounds our kind. People of different races would work together, maybe even live together. There would be schools of both human and werewolf children learning about one another. They'd be introduced to the concept of a werewolf from an early age and they wouldn't grow up to fear them as most adults do."

Will couldn't suppress his laughter, but James continued to listen and Bart saw a glimmer of thoughtfulness about him, as if he might have been changing sides in this argument.

Bart crossed his arms and found this a slightly easier topic to handle than the one he had been previously engrossed in. "You'd have to start with a decent-sized group. Preferably an even number of humans to loups-garous and plenty of females. The risk of inbreeding would be an ongoing concern, but if you have a steady influx of new members in the community, it could be done."

His eldest son looked to him, slightly aghast. "You can't be serious. It's far too dangerous to allow humans and werewolves to live so close together. Look what happened here." He jerked his chin toward the back part of the plantation, but Bart didn't need to be reminded.

"Ignorance could be just as dangerous," James said. "It'd be nice not to have to hide for a change."

Robert, whose keen mind was now fully set upon the task, continued with added eagerness. "We would have to find a good piece of land away from most other cities and towns. Some place close to a water source, as well as a trading post – at least in the beginning. But not too close so the risk of discovery won't be a problem."

"You could make inquiries in New Orleans about surrounding parcels of land for sale," Bart offered, secretly hoping they would settle close by.

James looked to his son, probably searching for any sign of agreement or refusal, but the young loup-garou was too enthralled by his scheme and merely acknowledged his offer as a wise step in this long process.

"We'd have to find members who can benefit the town as well. We'd need bakers, farmers, blacksmiths..." At this, Robert looked to Will, eyes bright with hope that was soon to be dashed to the floorboards.

"I want no part of this," he swore emphatically. "Maybe it will work, and maybe it won't, but I don't want to be there if it does fall to pieces."

"What could possibly happen?" Robert asked them.

No one gave an answer. If seclusion was achieved and, as James put it, ignorance wasn't a problem for either race, then harmony might be conceivable.

"I can reach out to my father in France," Bart said, breaking the silence between them. "I stay in touch with him on occasion. He has connections with alphas who might be willing to relocate their packs."

James straightened and looked from Bart to Robert, more than a little alarmed. "Are you two going to truly conspire to do this? Maybe you should give it some more thought."

Robert shook his head. "I had actually been thinking about it since we visited Teddy's pack in the swamps. The idea started then, but I've been thinking about it even more since we left Duplantier's."

He held up a hand to stop him. "You've been thinking about this for one day and you're making arrangements for Bart to send a correspondence to France for volunteers?"

To his chagrin, Robert only shrugged. "It just feels right. What have we to lose?"

"Our heads," Will grumbled.

"Not if we're careful," Robert argued.

The discussion continued, each man giving their respective opinions on each benefit and disadvantage that this kind of undertaking would involve. But no matter Will's pessimism, James' apprehension, or Bart's complete confidence that he could be successful, Robert had made up his mind. The only question now was what they could do to ensure the realization of this project.

Bart, though his profit margins were low in comparison to some other plantation owners in this part of the country, would contribute what he could in the way of monetary resources. John, likewise, upon hearing the plan, would feel the same and want to do what he could to help his great-grandson's efforts. In time, Will might come to see that the endeavor wasn't a complete folly and he might join the community with Lottie and maybe a few of the swamp wolves if they would be willing to depart from their clan.

What he did here on the plantation might not have been so significant, but Bart could recognize a calling when he saw it. Robert had a sharp mind and a level head for analysis. He'd think of every pitfall before breaking ground in this new community. He'd sketch out their defenses, organize everything down to the finest detail of how these classrooms were to be arranged or the layout of the town to optimize efficiency. He might not have been so adventurous as his father or as dominant as his great-grandfather, but he had inherited Bart's tenacity. Once his heart locked onto an idea, it wouldn't be released.

Seeing that slow kindling of fervidness in Robert's expression reminded him of a younger version of himself that he had lost in recent years. Bart went day to day, doing what he thought to be best and caring for those who depended upon him with a tepid passion that needed rekindling. He had forgotten that feeling of naïve confidence, when he thought he could take on all the injustices of the world and win.

He looked back to the plantation, to those people who relied on him, and knew that he would have to find a balance somehow. He couldn't neither abandon his mission, nor his morals.

CHAPTER 10

Robert's eyes skimmed across the fine print of the advertisement column of the Louisiana State Gazette. James, likewise, sat beside him at the tavern table with his own stack of newspapers and currently held the latest issue of Le Courrier de la Louisiana, since he was the only one between them who could read French. They needed to find a good, inexpensive track of land, far from any major city, and with potential growing space. Their search had taken two hours already.

The opposition he received upon voicing his plan was expected, but the genuine support that was given by his father, Bart, and even Teddy, was a surprise. He expected someone to highlight a flaw that he had overlooked in the excited formation of this scheme. But every point made by Will was quickly rebutted, leaving no room for doubt that this community would be a success.

All they needed now was the land and the people to settle it. Bart was already at the postmaster's office, scrawling out his transatlantic correspondence to every alpha he knew in Europe. It was a short, but polite invitation to come to America with a brief mention of the town in which they would live, asking them to send word or come straight to Louisiana to meet him first. The only part he omitted was the fact that there was no town yet to speak of. Once the land was found and the plan financed, however, the werewolves in France, Germany, and England would be packing their trunks for the voyage. If they elected to come, that was.

The rowdy noise of the tavern didn't distract him nearly as much as the scent that snuck through the open doorway as two men entered. Somewhere between reading about a runaway slave in Mississippi and a piece of land somewhere north on the river, Robert stopped and took a second whiff to confirm it.

Without a word to his father, he hastily folded the newspaper backwards and rushed out the door, heedless of who saw him. James hollered, but Robert was already halfway down Chartres Street, following that familiar perfume.

He hadn't forgotten about Isabelle. Through the chaos of trying to find Diego, fighting him, and then rebuilding the plantation, Robert hadn't stopped thinking about her. This trip to New Orleans to make inquiries and search for properties had a dual purpose that he wouldn't tell Bart about.

If he confessed this ulterior motive, they might have ordered him to stay on the estate and well away from the coquettish lady who was believed to be playing Robert for a fool. But they didn't dance with her the other night. They didn't hear her whispered flirts as they twirled about the dancefloor, the envy of everyone at the ball. They didn't understand the deep connection they shared. He felt as if he had known her for a thousand years instead of a few days and he couldn't expect his father or any other werewolf to empathize with him.

He saw her in the street, and one heartbeat later, she looked up to meet his gaze. But there was none of the usual warmth in her stare. No smile graced her lips, no bashful coloring of her cheeks. Instead, her eyes widened in shock. Within a few seconds, she quickly recovered to maintain an unruffled outward composure to fool the crowd that moved around them.

This first reaction kept Robert from taking another step further. He watched her just as intently as she watched him. Neither moved toward one another, neither made any serious effort to come together as they should have. Dozens of people saw them at the ball and would naturally assume they were courting. Fear of exposure or a supposed scandal couldn't have made her so timid. Something else must have been the matter, but for the life of him, he couldn't figure what it could be.

In those long moments spent fixed upon one another, her slave stood patiently and waited until her mistress ordered her into one of the shops. This fleeting break of eye contact jolted Robert into action and he hurried on to meet her.

She smoothly guided the point of their interception closer to the mouth of a bystreet that provided a shortcut to Toulouse Street.

Once in the shadows, Isabelle finally betrayed her feelings and let her troubled heart mar her pretty face.

"What's the matter?" he asked gently, reaching for her arm so he might provide some comfort.

But she didn't want him. Isabelle withdrew her arm in the most minute way to avoid his reach, but she might as well have struck him.

Robert froze, feeling his body stiffen and ache with this subtle rejection.

"I had hoped I wouldn't see you again," she replied, so softly that if he weren't a werewolf, he might not have heard her at all. The slight tremble in her words added to the injury their meaning inflicted upon him.

Struck dumb by this admittance, Robert could say nothing as he went on.

"I can't ignore what you are any longer, though I might have been inclined to overlook everything before the night of the ball."

What he was? His first thought made him question if he had done anything to make her suspect he was a werewolf. But though he was convinced of the beautiful mind between her lovely eyes, no one would naturally conjecture such a thing without full and undeniable proof, which he hadn't given.

Terror, panic, and agony knotted within his chest and the sheer power of his raw emotions finally gave him a voice. "What are you talking about?" he asked, ready to laugh off whatever explanation she gave.

Isabelle's eyes took on a dewiness as she continued, throat working out the syllables as much as her feminine disposition would allow. "You told me who your grandfather was when we first met and I shouldn't have led you on as I did, but you looked so... so white that I thought if I simply didn't tell my father anything about you, then it could be possible for you to court me. But then, at the ball, I saw your father and heard how he talked about serving under Jean Lafitte. My father is a patriot, but he has never liked pirates." She sniffled and opened up her purse to retrieve a handkerchief. "After you left, I heard so many things about you and your father, but I didn't want to believe any of it. I wanted to believe it was just men boasting as they often do, but then Lafitte himself made some comments and..."

At this pause, she dabbed her handkerchief at the corner of her eyelids to mop up unbidden tears. "And then your uncle showed up outside the hotel with that beast."

Robert felt a cold, tingle skitter down his spine at the mention of Diego. "A beast?"

She huffed a laugh. "Surely you heard of what happened."

"I heard it was a rabid dog, not a beast." That was the story that had been circulating around New Orleans and he would stay true to it.

"I was there," she insisted. "I saw it with my own eyes. It wasn't a dog. It was something bigger with glowing eyes and... I'm not so silly and superstitious, but I've heard of the rougarous that live in the swamps. If there ever was a creature that looked like a rougarou, that was it. And your uncle tackled it as if it were an escaped hog or something."

Robert could no longer look at her frightened, weepy face and cast his eyes to the ground, waiting for her to say what he had feared.

"And I saw your uncle had the same eyes as the beast... I don't know what he was or what that makes you, or any of your family, but I can't have any part of it."

"I'm only a man, Isabelle," he insisted, closing his eyes against her refusal. He knew someday he would have to tell her the truth, especially if they were to court and marry. But he never thought he'd try to defend himself like this. "A man who... who loves you and wants – "

"Don't say it," she retorted, struggling to control the cry that wanted to echo down the brick walls of the alley. "Don't say you want things that will never come true. You have dark blood in you, even if you have no ties with whatever your uncle may be. I've thought it through and there's no way I could ever disconnect you from your grandfather. Even if that could be concealed, all of New Orleans knows you served under Lafitte and my father would never allow us to court."

Robert looked up and hastened toward her, forgetting all rules of propriety and conduct in the tidal wave that overwhelmed him. Desperation made him into a man that couldn't accept this was the way things had to be between them. He wanted to love her, to marry her, to take her to the new settlement they were to build, and live the next several decades wrapped in her arms. He knew it wouldn't last forever since she was human, but he wanted just a bit of her sunshine in his life before being subjected to a lonely darkness without her.

His hands groped for her, but Isabelle must have seen hints of his gentlemanly degradation and slipped from him once more.

"Please, just leave me be," she whimpered before running from the alley, the handkerchief pressed to her mouth to muffle the sobs.

Now he wished he had never run out of the tavern. Wished he had never stepped foot in New Orleans at all. Robert staggered back and leaned against the side of the building, the rough and gritty edges of the bricks snagging on the fibers of his coat. He stared at the ground, trying to make sense of it all, needing to feel something other than this anxious nausea in the pit of his stomach. Each breath he exhaled, he felt as if he were losing a piece of his soul, leaving him and his wolf numb and grieving for the loss of hope.

Some length of time passed and he barely noticed his father coming into the alley. James only had to look at him and smell the faint remnants of Isabelle's perfume to make whatever assumption he wished.

He offered no words of consolation, no "I told you so" speech that Robert had received the first time he felt any predisposition to love or care for a woman. James only leaned against the wall beside him, quiet and as neutral as a carved statue.

Robert wasn't sure how long they were there until he couldn't take the silence any longer. "Aren't you going to say it?"

James slowly shook his head. "I'm not going to say a damn thing."

"And you suppose that would be enough?"

"I don't need to say things you're already telling yourself."

For once, his father didn't come back with some biting or sardonic remark. If he actually understood how Robert felt, how he mourned this sudden loss, the end of times must have been upon them. James had very rarely ever refrained from glorying in these kind of humiliations. When Robert failed to be the kind of cutthroat pirate his father expected him to be, jokes and laughs were given out like a form of sadistic remedy for his shortcomings. As if ridicule would challenge him to be better. James was capable of compassion, but never expressed it when Robert needed that kind of gentility the most.

Robert looked to his father and could feel a tiny wisp of the spirit he lost return to him.

James reached up and took a firm hold of his son's shoulder. "Let's go. I found a piece of land you may like."

"Please say it's far from Louisiana," he pleaded as they ambled out of the alleyway.

"Is the southeast part of the Mississippi Territory far enough?"

His face pinched in displeasure. "I suppose India wouldn't be far enough if you had offered it... Close to Georgia?"

"Remember Fort Mims?" James asked, but then continued without his answer. "It's a little further east of there."

"On the border of West Florida? Isn't that land crawling with natives?"

James proudly nodded. "It is. You won't ever have to worry about seeing Miss Isabelle in a place like that."

As much as he adored Isabelle, the thought of her following him now made his stomach turn. The image of her beauty was now both a pleasure and a torture to even think of. How long would it be before she would fade from his memory? Would she ever?

One other thing besides time could erase her from his heart forever. Sense. Her reasons for forsaking any chance of courting were vain and prejudice. She had some cursory knowledge that he wasn't a normal man, but she showed no desire to learn or understand. She defamed his heritage, admitted that his family would be a detriment to her reputation and good standing with her father, and any romantic association with him would taint her in the eyes of society, even if the Romani blood wasn't apparent.

Isabelle rejected him because of who he was, and there was nothing he could do to change her mind. A mind that had been molded by twisted views on race and the color of one's skin. A mind that thought of nothing but rank, class, and what was acceptable. Robert saw past skin, past bloodlines, but he couldn't see past ignorance.

Reentering the streets of New Orleans, Robert took a deep breath and turned to his father. "Will this ever stop hurting?" he asked honestly, hoping that James would continue to be serious.

No such luck.

"Sure, it will," he said haughtily with a big smile. "You just have to bed enough whores until you forget her name."

Robert sneered and shoved James' shoulder as they made their way back to the hotel to discuss their plans for the new settlement. He already had a name chosen for the place. Devia. From the Latin word for straying, trackless, wandering. Because, as werewolves, that's what they did. They wandered. But in this town that would hopefully flourish, those who wandered could finally have a permanent home.

The Soldier

Legacy Series Book 10

Sheritta Bitikofer

MOONSTRUCK WRITING

CONTENTS

Dedication   #

Foreword   #

1. Chapter 1   #

2. Chapter 2   #

3. Chapter 3   #

4. Chapter 4   #

5. Chapter 5   #

6. Chapter 6   #

7. Chapter 7   #

8. Chapter 8   #

9. Chapter 9   #

10. Chapter 10   #

11. Chapter 11   #

12. Chapter 12   #

13. Chapter 13   #

14. Chapter 14   #

15. Chapter 15   #

16. Chapter 16   #

17. Chapter 17   #

To the memory of the fallen and their families. North and South, Confederate and American. To those who are fighting and dying for the country they love, even today. To them and all who follow, I thank you.

FOREWORD

The views expressed by the characters in this story do not necessarily reflect the views of the author – whether political or moral. However, it is the author's intention to describe the horrors of the Civil War, as seen through the eyes of those who lived through it. War cannot always be accurately depicted in the literary sense. Flowery prose and words fail in comparison to the deep, visceral feelings and ideas that only battle can bring into being. No tongue or mind can possibly conjure an image to do the thing justice. All war is hell, as General William Tecumseh Sherman once said, but hell is different for everyone, just as the Civil War was experienced differently by all. Soldier and civilian, North and South, Union and Confederate, man and woman, white and black, the elderly and the young, infantryman and cavalryman, spy and sailor. However, in this story, the prospective of a soldier in the Confederate army is told to the best of the author's abilities. Memoirs, battle reports, and historical records have been read and reread in order to truthfully explain the movements of the army and the feelings of someone who would have served in the Army of Northern Virginia; and then for the loved ones left at home behind the battle lines. History is often written by the victors, and the glory of battles are given to the generals, and it is the intention of the author to peel back the layers in order to show the untold story that isn't often studied in the classroom.

Although this is a work of historical fiction and incorporates the existence of paranormal beings, many characters and figures mentioned were actual soldiers that lived and fought in the Civil War. Please refer to the end "Terms to Know" section for the list of names.

It is the hope of the author that every representation of the soldiers, commanders, and civilians are faithfully portrayed and if any offense is given to the decedents of these honorable dead, it is unintentional. It's for those men who fought and died for the cause they believed in, that the author dedicates this story.

If the reader is intrigued and wishes to learn more about the Civil War, they are encouraged to visit their local library for further reading, or to the nearest Civil War battlefield that has been preserved for the education of future generations.

Walking in the footsteps of the fallen can be a more powerful experience than imagining the events in one's mind.

"We were inured to privations and hardships; had been upon every march, in every battle, in every skirmish, in every advance, in every retreat, in every victory, in every defeat. We had laid under the burning heat of a tropical sun; had made the cold, frozen earth our bed, with no covering save the blue canopy of heaven; had braved dangers, had breasted floods; had seen our comrades slain upon our right and our left hand; had heard guns that carried death in their missiles; had heard the shouts of the charge; had seen the enemy in full retreat and flying in every direction; had heard the shrieks and groans of the wounded and dying; had seen the blood of our countrymen dyeing the earth and enriching the soil; had been hungry when there was nothing to eat; had been in rags and tatters. We had marked the frozen earth with bloody and unshod feet; had been elated with victory and crushed by defeat; had seen and felt the pleasure of the life of a soldier, and had drank the cup to its dregs. Yes, we had seen it all, and had shared in its hopes and its fears; its love and its hate; its good and its bad; its virtue and its vice; its glories and its shame. We had followed the successes and reverses of the flag of the Lost Cause through all these years of blood and strife." – Sam Watkins, 1st Tennessee Infantry, Company H

Chapter 1

The smoke from the dozens of fires sprinkled across the countryside did little to mask the stench of army life. Dustin could still smell the odors of the men who hadn't bathed in weeks – perhaps months – and the spicy signature of fear that hovered over the camp. Like a constant cloud of dread, it followed the Army of Northern Virginia from Manassas to Leesburg, to Frederick, to South Mountain, and finally here.

They all knew what would come the following day; more fighting, more blood and whizzing bullets, more death and suffering. If Lee hadn't heard of Jackson's good news from Harper's Ferry, they might have retreated back into Virginia, instead of making this run to Maryland for support, which they had yet to receive.

But the Confederate army and the generals who commanded it were in good. They were finally in Yankee territory and under Lee, who had been instrumental in the defense of Richmond months earlier, the Confederacy was considered to be well on its way to winning this war in its entirety. What they didn't know was that they were still outnumbered, and though they had continued to whip their enemy time and time again in this most recent campaign, their winning streak wouldn't last forever. Not while McClellan had been afforded this particular advantage that Dustin helped to provide.

Dustin leaned against a tree, just on the edge of the firelight, his hands tearing at a long weed he had pulled from the ground a moment before. Only occasionally did he reach up to scratch behind his ear like an irritated, flea-ridden dog. The lice accompanied the hunger and filth that every soldier was issued once they joined the army. But that was a drop in the bucket compared to the multitude of complaints and grievances amongst the regiments.

Like the other men, he couldn't sleep. Not only because of the ominous foreknowledge of what would come at dawn, but because every little sound within a radius of three miles rang so loudly in his ears that sleep was unattainable on nights like this. If the army weren't so troubled and they could hunker down for the night, then it might have been possible for him to settle onto his army-issued blanket in peace as well. But for a loup-garou - a werewolf - enlisted in the Confederate army, peace and quiet might have been a futile hope.

Amongst the countless white steeples of tents, he could hear every muttered curse over a lost card game, the soft clattering of the dice as men gambled away at Chuck-A-Luck, every whispered conversation, and the crackling of burning wood. It all kept his mind active and pinging to one sound or another without reason or aim.

Darren had taught him well over the past ninety years, but fatigue and hunger had worn him thin. He hadn't forgotten his training. He could still hear his alpha's words echoing their warnings at every turn. But when his body and wolf were so strained, so ragged like the other men of the fifth Alabama infantry, it was hard to ignore his surroundings. If his stomach wasn't growling and he had any rabbit left in his haversack, perhaps his senses wouldn't have been so overwhelmed.

From where his regiment was bivouacked by the Piper farmhouse, he wandered south to Boonsboro Pike where it seemed slightly quieter. Some fifteen or so yards away, at the nearest campfire, he could hear a group of men under Anderson and Jenkin's Brigade talking amongst themselves or obsessively cleaning their weapons.

South Carolinians and Georgians exchanged stories about their time marching through Virginia and Tennessee. Not a single one of them spoke of the battles, or the bloody fights against the Federals. No one wanted to talk about those things, because no one wanted to hear them. As long as their rifles were propped up against one another in that typical tent-like fashion with their bayonets fixed, they didn't want to think about the fighting and moments of pure terror they experienced as they were fired upon.

Dustin didn't want to hear them either. The average soldier was only aware of what was happening directly in front of them during any given battle or skirmish. Unfortunately for him and his acute sense of hearing, he was aware of much more than the enemy he engaged. He heard the death wails of men across the field, well out of sight and human earshot. He smelled the blood of hundreds of soldiers cut down in their advance or retreat from the field. The gunpowder, the trodden grass, the loosed bowels of the boys who would become men by the time the fight was over.

He hated it. All of it. The only reason he was even here, enlisted as an infantry volunteer, was because he wanted out. Out of America, out of the south, out of the Confederacy and the Union alike. When he had told Darren that he was ready to leave and see the world, his alpha released him with more than a little grumbling. He said it was foolish to try and cross enemy lines, but it would have been equally foolish to try and smuggle his way past the Yankee blockade that encased the south.

If only they hadn't left France fifty years ago when they'd answered the call for volunteers to help a new settlement in what was now lower Alabama. He would have rather stayed in France and butcher the language every time he tried to speak it than suffocate his Irish accent to appear just as southern as the men in his company.

This would be his last battle. The commander of the sixty-ninth New York infantry was expecting him as soon as McClellan was done destroying Lee's army. The arrangements had been made, his betrayal of the Confederacy complete. All he had to do was fake his death tomorrow and he could gain safe passage to Washington. From there, he'd make his plans and buy his ticket for the next Atlantic voyage to Europe. He'd come back after the war, but as he told Darren, now that he had a firm hold of his abilities, he wanted to explore and travel. He couldn't do that in Devia, Alabama.

"If only I had taken that job with my cousin with the railroad," one private griped, "I could've stayed home."

"What would that have done any?" another asked chidingly. "Ol' Jeff still woulda conscripted ya."

The first private, one he recognized as a Palmetto Sharpshooter, reclined against his knapsack. "Nope," he said. "Any man doin' some job for the Confederacy was exempt from the Conscription Act. My paw read it in the papers to me."

"Well, hell!" another from across the campfire exclaimed. "If that was true, I don't deserve to be here. I gots a big ol' farm to run down south. I'd be doin' heaps for the Confederacy."

"Bull shit!" another called out. "You can't have a farm. You ain't got no brains for farmin'."

The soldier pinched up a bit of dirt and flung it at the other man from the sixth South Carolina Infantry. A few of the men chuckled and began tossing around good-natured insults. Some of these men had been with their companies from the start of the war, enlisting as soon as their states called for volunteers. Others were fresh recruits, hoping to revel in what false glory a soldier received during his enlistment term.

Parading through towns and basking in the cheers of its citizens was the only glorious part that Dustin could see. Everything else, the marching, the deplorable rations, the drilling, the harsh generals and commanders that would sooner shoot a man for a small infraction than build up his morale, all of it was far from the preconceived image most citizens held of their proud boys in gray or blue.

"Didn't you have a farm, Ben?" one soldier from a Georgia company asked. "You coulda gotten out of gettin' conscripted, right? Bet you've got a ton of darkies waitin' on ya back home."

Dustin glanced up and let his tired eyes focus on the one soldier who had yet to speak. He sat quietly, his gray kepi wrinkled between his hands, wringing it until the wool was worn in places. It was the kind of fretful, nervous habit that he had seen amongst many soldiers, especially young ones who didn't want to fight again.

The young man's face, however, was smooth and free of the worried lines that was usually paired with this kind of mindless behavior. The orange glow of the fire brought out the golden hue of his thin, slightly curly hair. The light twinkled in a set of light brown eyes that still retained a distant, faraway look after the other soldier had addressed him.

He was much like the other soldiers. It was clear that his boyhood years had been spent in labor. His uniform jacket was laid across his lap, allowing Dustin to fully see the strong curve of his back and shoulders. Ben wasn't a stranger to work, and that's why his answer didn't surprise him.

"We didn't work with darkies," he said, his gaze fixed on the fire with a lazy kind of concentration.

At this, several of the other soldiers looked to Ben in bafflement that such a statement shouldn't have inspired. It was as if none of the others could even fathom a farm that didn't have at least a few slaves working its fields. To his own chagrin, Dustin might have understood their confusion. Even in the deep south, it was rare to come across a wealthy landowner or merchant who didn't have at least one African bound to him through the unjust practice.

In the stunned silence, Ben finally blinked and looked up, which broke the spell of bewilderment over his comrades.

"Who picked your cotton?" the other Georgian asked. "Y'all did grow cotton, right?"

Ben nodded. "We grew it, but it wasn't ours."

It was then that Dustin understood, along with the rest.

"And you get paid to do that?"

The farm boy nodded again, but showed no shame or pride in the admission. "Our employer didn't own any slaves. He had two-hundred acres of cotton and paid plenty of other folks to help him pick it."

Some gasped at the sheer amount of acreage, others were still too puzzled to believe Ben was telling the truth. Dustin, however, knew he wasn't lying. What reason did he have to lie about his job when it was a more prestigious thing to own another human being and force them to toil away without pay?

"Ya some kinda darkie-lover?" asked one of the more ignorant of the South Carolinians. "Like one of them abolitionists?"

Rather than offended or riled by the question, Ben just shrugged. "I'll admit they make it hard for a farmhand to earn a livin', but I don't hate 'em or love 'em."

"Then why are ya even fightin'?" his neighbor asked, just as incredulous as the others. "Don't ya know the Yankees wanna come and free all the slaves?"

"Ain't nonna my concern," Ben said. "But I don't reckon they can do that from what I been hearin'."

"They ain't gonna free the slaves," another soldier drawled. "They just wanna take away our constitutional right to have 'em."

At this, a fervent argument erupted around the fire. All the while, Ben remained mute on the subject and resumed his study of the smoldering and popping logs in front of him. Dustin, though thoroughly amused by the turn this gathering had taken, watched the Georgia farmer. In one moment of honest confession, he set himself apart amongst his fellow Confederates. He wasn't a slave owner, nor did he seem to endorse the system. He didn't join in the debate over what they were fighting for, and he didn't respond to any of the somewhat biting comments that could have been linked to his apathetic attitude toward slavery and the southern cause.

Before he could realize it, Dustin had pushed himself off the tree and slowly started toward the congregation around the fire. The soldier who had been sitting next to Ben had risen from his seat and was now in a hot verbal sparring match with another man. This left Dustin a spot to slip in and sit beside the farmer.

"So, if you're not fighting for slavery," Dustin began after leaning back on his hands and stretching his feet out toward the edge of the fire, "then what are you fighting for?"

Ben, probably startled by his arrival into the circle, looked to Dustin with blonde brows arched. "Same as what everyone else is really fightin' for, I guess. States' rights and all that. I don't have a head for politics, but I don't get why the people in Washington are makin' a big fuss about the slaves. It maybe ain't right, but it sure as hell ain't why we fired on Fort Sumter."

"So you're fighting for Georgia?"

Again, he nodded, making the tips of his curls bounce with the movement. "It's my home. Who wouldn't fight for their home?"

A feeling of envy rose up in Dustin. His boyhood country, Ireland, was nothing more than a distant memory. It was his Eden and he had been cast out from its gardens forever. If he could return home, he would. Though Dustin could lift a house off its foundation, he didn't have the strength to go back to Glengarriff.

Ben, however, could point to a specific spot on the map and claim it as his. His hometown, wherever that may be, was filled with memories and a family that waited for his safe return.

Dustin offered out his hand. "Dustin Keith. Fifth Alabama, Company D."

For the first time that evening, Ben cracked a smile and received the handshake, briefly pausing in the crinkling of his kepi. "Benjamin Myers. Seventh Georgia, Company G." Upon release, he asked, "What are you fightin' for then? Alabama?"

Dustin had to resist the urge to roll his eyes. France was more of a home to him than the budding town of Devia where he came from. "Nah," he said, remembering that he had to hide his true nationality. "I'm only here because I got conscripted."

Many soldiers had grown to resent their new country, especially in the spring of that year. Jefferson Davis had called every able-bodied man into service, though many were eager to go back to their homes since their first term had ended. It seemed as if no one ever expected the war to last this long. Some didn't expect it to even begin, saying that neither side would take up arms against the other. He had heard so many times that it would be a quick and relatively bloodless war. Manassas and Shiloh proved them wrong.

Now in its second year, both Johnny Reb and Billy Yank began to realize just how long this war would be. And no one wanted to fight it anymore, except for those who let themselves be blinded by pretty ladies tossing flowers and kisses to the handsome soldiers as they passed by their windows.

"I could've gotten out of this monkey show this past summer, but I chose to stay."

Dustin looked to Ben's twisted kepi with its bent leather brim. In that same glance, he saw the private didn't have any shoes. The tops of his feet were almost blackened by mud. Where tan skin peeked out from beneath the layer of muck, he saw the thin pink lines of healing cuts and blisters. He wasn't all too amazed to see this. If anything, he was surprised that Ben hadn't picked up a pair of new shoes off a dead Yankee like so many others did. "You don't look like a man who'd want to stay."

Following his stare, Ben finally looked to his mangled hat and smoothed it out again. That did little good. Unless the hat got shot to pieces, those creases would be there until the end of the war.

"It's really not all bad," he said with a slightly nervous laugh. "We get paid, plenty of fresh air, and I haven't had to pick cotton for a year and a half."

Over the raised voices of the other Confederates around them, the squealing growl of an empty stomach reached his ears. Every word that came in precedence from the soldier might as well have been a lie.

Dustin smirked, admiring his bravery in the face of starvation that made no cause truly worthy. He then reached around into his haversack and pulled out a handful of hardtack that had been issued to him in the last payout of rations. Being a loup-garou, there was little he could eat outside of meat and fruit. The pan-fried flour cakes were not on his list of allowable snacks.

Ben's eyes went wide. "Ain't you gonna eat 'em?"

Dustin let his face pull in a look of repulsion that didn't have to be faked. "No. They're just going to go to waste if I don't eat them. Got some coffee to soften them up?"

Reaching for the gift, he looked over his shoulder toward another fire where he could smell the pot of roasting "coffee". "I think they've got some over there," he remarked before excusing himself to investigate.

Dustin watched him swing his haversack around to pull out a tin cup before approaching one of the other soldiers. Ben petitioned for some of the brownish muck the soldiers called coffee, though it didn't adhere to the conventional ingredients of what he knew to be coffee. Instead of a traditional bean brew, Dustin had seen soldiers boiling everything from peanuts to beets to rice, corn, and even wood chips. The end result was a warm, flavored drink that gave no vitality to the drinker. Dustin found the concoction to be disgusting to say the least, but many soldiers loved it.

On the other side of the fire, a soldier had pulled out a banjo and began carefully plucking at the strings to tune it. Dustin had heard this man's playing across the campground on previous nights as they traveled from Boonsboro to Sharpsburg.

Some of those who were deep in their naïve and single-minded discussions on the matter of war and economics, cut off their rants to listen and wonder what the musician would play to lift their spirits. No soldier would ever deny the calming, morale-boosting effect that music and song had upon the weary soul of men who had seen too much.

But within the first few chords, Dustin knew the man had no such intentions. A song that pulled at the heartstrings of every veteran present could have the total opposite consequence.

He began to sing, drawing the attention of others around the fire. "*We shall meet, but we shall miss him, there will be one vacant chair...*"

"Don't sing that!" shouted an officer standing nearby at the mouth of his tent. Accompanied by others of the same rank, Dustin saw they weren't pleased with the choice of ballads.

The musician immediately ceased his melody and started in on another. "*Let us pause in life's pleasures and count its many tears, while we all sup sorrow with the poor...*"

"God dammit, Watson!" the same officer hollered. "Not that one either!"

Dustin tightened his lips to keep himself from bursting into a laugh.

The musician, Private Watson, let out a sigh and paused before starting in on his next attempt. *"Just before the battle, Mother, I am thinking most of you."*

Instead of receiving opposition from his commanding officer, Watson was shot down by his fellow privates. "That's a damn Yankee song!" they screamed.

Frustrated by the utter lack of appreciation for his efforts, Watson nearly slammed his banjo down beside him. "Well how the hell was I supposed to know that?"

About this time, Ben came back with a steaming cup of the imitation coffee and after checking that the hard crackers had no weevils, dropped a few of the bits into the brew. He, too, seemed to be entertained by the scene of the downcast musician.

Giving it one more try, Watson settled the banjo in his lap again and plucked at the strings in a slow and lilting rhythm that was nearly shot down before he could sing the first line. *"The despot's heel is on thy shore. Maryland, My Maryland!"*

"No!" Was the resounding answer from almost every soldier in the camp who could hear the tune of the song. Some songs, like that one, had been worn as thin as the soles of their shoes during the long marches.

It might have been considered safe enough to the officers, but no private wanted to hear that song again for as long as they were in the state. They had been marching for days to that ballad under orders by General Lee. It was presumed that it would hearten the people of the state to their cause and any Secessionist sympathizers would give their aid. Nothing of the sort happened, song or no song, because all the rebels who felt oppressed under Lincoln's rule had fled south already.

Dustin heard Watson grumble a few curses as he racked his brain for another song. Solemn and slow, he started in on what became his last try. If he recognized it correctly, Watson wouldn't get far. *"There's a low, green valley, on the old Kentucky shore. Where I've whiled many happy hours away..."*

"Are ya blind?" one irate soldier from Tennessee shouted toward their group from another fire. "This is a long way from Kentucky!"

In a slightly comical turn, Watson sighed, propped his chin in his hand and simply stopped trying. Sympathetic to his plight, some soldiers shouted out their requests. Eventually, one was settled upon that most men were eager to join in the chorus. *"Wait for the wagon! The dissolution wagon! The South is the wagon, and we'll all take a ride."*

Dustin listened, as did Ben, and the two sat beside one another. Two men who were on the same side of a confrontation, but for entirely different reasons. They were of two different races, different backgrounds, but they did share one thing in common. They were both farmers. However, the connection Dustin felt toward this stranger went deeper than that.

It wasn't until he tried to search for the explanation that he realized it. His wolf approved of Ben, even perhaps liked him. That sentiment was rare for Dustin. Besides his alpha, he didn't typically take to someone so quickly. It took years, sometimes a couple of decades, for both he and his wolf to be content in another person's company – loup-garou or not.

For a moment, he almost regretted the course of fate. Ben and the other soldiers around him were wholly unaware that they shared a fire with the man who might have expedited the coming battle. If he hadn't told the Union soldiers were to find the abandoned copy of the marching orders directed to D.H Hill from General Lee himself, McClellan might not have known where to send his army to confront the rebels. It was a great deal of trouble to intercept that message – Special Order 191 - along with stealing the cigars to reward the finders of such confidential plans.

In a move that Dustin tried so ardently not to feel guilty for, he might have signed the death certificates for many of these boys who would go marching into battle the following morning. Espionage might have been the only way to secure his escape to the north, but at what cost?

As if to mirror his own dark thoughts, the clouds began to loose a drizzling shower over Sharpsburg. It was just enough to dampen their shoulders and hats, but not enough to douse the fires. The musician immediately stood to find good cover to keep his instrument safe while the other men began to complain about the rain, the rations, and the lice.

But beneath it all, Dustin heard their confident boasting.

"We'll whip them Yankees and march right onto Washington!"

Such a statement always proved to encourage the men to the southern cause once more and every heart around that fire beat strong with the determination to do just as they said. That is, all but two.

CHAPTER 2

March. March. March. Just keep marchin'.

Ben focused all his energy into taking one step after another, following the man in front of him with his rifle propped against his shoulder. All around, the thunder of canons, the faraway shouts of troops, and the general stomach-turning fact that he was about to join the fight, made him want to turn tail and run.

But he couldn't allow himself to think. He took Brigadier General George Anderson's advice and stayed all hands and all feet. Alert and yet numb to the battle and the dizzying thoughts of what they were getting themselves into. He couldn't think about the shredded bodies of his old pals. He couldn't think of Thomas Brittain who was shot at Manassas just a few weeks ago. Nor could he recall Henry Hester's death mask when he lay dying from his wounds after the battle at Malvern Hill in July. And he couldn't replay the last conversation he had with Jack Wilson back in June at Garnett's Farm where he died at the hospital.

He briskly shook his head and began muttering to himself, "March. March. March."

He, along with the rest of Anderson's Brigade had been guarding Boonsboro Pike with the other regiments that made up D.R Jones' Division. But that's not where the fighting was. Farther north toward the cornfield he had seen when they arrived, the battle having commenced early that morning. The ground, wet from last night's rain and the sky still overcast to give the day a gray and somber feel, it was proving to be a miserable dawn that would no doubt turn into a bloody day.

Lee – whom they teasingly called Granny Lee for his snow-white beard and grandfatherly deportment toward his troops – made a habit of riding up and down the field of battle, assessing every situation carefully and coolly. Rarely raising his voice in anger toward the privates and giving clear instruction to his subordinate officers, Ben knew he would never serve under a better general. He was the picture of military strength and leadership. Under Lee, they couldn't possibly lose.

And that's why when he ordered Anderson's Brigade north to fight back an encroaching band of Union soldiers who were ready to take a good piece of strategic ground, Ben didn't quake in his boots as some of the other men did.

Already the victor of several battles, Ben had the good fortune of never sustaining a wound. He had been shot, but never in a place that mattered. Twice through his cartridge box, and once through the sleeve of his jacket. Each one narrowly missed its intended mark and each time, Ben thanked the good Lord above that the angels were looking out for him, even in the midst of so much death and carnage.

Anderson's Brigade had been ordered to join ranks with McClaw and Walker's divisions, so Ben and the seventh Georgia infantry made their way toward a patch of woods. To their right, he could hear the roar of canons and feel the earth tremble beneath his bare feet with each deafening volley. Farther ahead and to the left, came the hurried orders from officers and a procession line of wounded men being carried to safe ground.

The few glimpses of their beaten and battered bodies emboldened Ben. If Lee thought them capable of plugging this hole in his line, then he would do so and stop any advancing Yankee. Pride for his state, his country, and the cause for southern independence galvanized his courage.

Ben trudged through the thicket – rather loudly due to the constant crackle of parched leaves and fallen branches beneath their feet - and could see the white brick of the church building they had passed the previous day. Empty of all its congregation and riddled with holes from artillery fire and rifle shot, it remained standing on the edge of the battlefield. He heard some other soldier say it belonged to some pacifist Germans. How ironic.

Ahead, coming in at a slow and casual march, he could see the line of Federals through the trees. As soon as they spotted one another, the orders were given. Halt. Load. Aim. Fire.

The air became alive with bullets as the enemy fired upon them.

Ben, now a seasoned veteran of war, loaded his rifle with mechanic accuracy, speeding through the nine-step process. All those summer days spent hunting turkeys and bucks back home in Georgia with his older brother served as practice for shooting down his fellow men as he did now. He wasn't quite as good as any of the sharpshooters in the army, but he rarely missed his target.

Giving leave to take cover behind trees and bushes in the patch of woods to the left of the church, Ben shoved the soldier beside him – a man by the name of John Beck, who was also part of the Franklin Volunteers – into a cluster of tall pines.

"Don't forget your cap!" Ben told him, mostly out of a need to be helpful. He had wished some fellow soldier had reminded him of that during his first battle at Manassas. So often in the chaos of firing round after round, a man forgot one step or two in loading his own rifle, no matter how many times he had done it before.

He grabbed another cartridge from the hard leather box on his belt, tore off the paper tie, poured the powder in and chased down the bullet with his ramrod. And taking his own advice, he made a point to grab a percussion cap from his other pouch and positioned it before taking his hastily aimed shot. All the while, he felt the vibration of the occasional bullet hitting the trunk of the tree he leaned his shoulder against. Splinters of wood and bark stung at his cheeks when the adjacent pine was struck in the same way. Beside him, John fumbled constantly with his ramrod. Once, he cursed himself for forgetting the bullet and accidentally firing nothing but powder.

One by one, the Yankees in blue were mowed down as the cougar-like, explosive roar of the rifle fire split through the woods. Some Confederates fell and let out shrieks of pain or moans of agony, but Ben tuned them out. He had to or he'd lose his concentration for sure. The dead began to litter the ground, blood soaking into the earth and staining the grass around the fallen.

The order was given to advance. Ben and John darted out from their safe cover and ran toward the enemy, firing off one more shot each while others fixed bayonets to the end of their rifles. The color bearer of the seventh Georgia Infantry preceded them, the red and white thick bands lazily waving above their heads, rallying them forward.

"We got 'em on the run, boys!" shouted Lieutenant Colonel George Carmical.

The rebel yell swelled and rattled the very leaves in the treetops as the units realized they had taken the ground for the Confederacy. The Yankees turned tail and retreated from the woods, falling back to Hagerstown Pike and the open field beyond where the rest of the battle seemed to be drawing to a close.

Hurriedly trying to load while sprinting through the brush, his pulse hammering in his ears like the booming sound of the artillery units to the south, Ben hardly noticed when he was no longer running with John Beck. He slowed and turned to look behind him as the rest of his company and regiment filed ahead, shouting in their small but glorious victory over the Federals.

There, trying to scramble out of the way of the stampede, was John with a gaping hole in his chest. Blood seeped from his wound and decanted over his torso to darken the butternut brown fabric of his jacket. Risking a severe reprimand or punishment from his colonel, Ben ran in the opposite direction of their charge.

John gasped for breath, a trickle of crimson oozing from the corner of his mouth as arms flailed to grab at the air. Ben was by his side, his gun dropped for the moment beside his comrade. He caught the desperate arm and held it tight, staring at the wound that he knew was fatal. There was no use in screaming for an ambulance or a stretcher to carry him to a hospital tent behind the lines. John Beck wouldn't survive this day.

"They still runnin'?" John choked out, wide eyes staring up into the face of the man who had enlisted with him on the same day in Atlanta.

They stuck by one another in almost every battle, at every skirmish and engagement. They even tried to request furlough together and agreed to help one another with the train fare for the ride home to Georgia. Those requests were never approved, due to the sheer impossibility for the paperwork to please each and every officer in the chain of command whom it passed through. But they had tried together, and if they had gotten that furlough in the springtime, they would have gone home together too.

Now, there would be no more chances for furlough.

"Yeah," Ben answered, forcing every ounce of strength he had left to be there for his friend in these final moments. "They're still runnin'."

A mocking smile spread over John's lips, which were colored a deep red by the blood he coughed up. "Bunch of cowards," he wheezed.

Ben tried to return the smile, but knew he had failed miserably and only nodded. "They sure are."

With shaking effort, John reached up and unfastened two of the brass buttons on his coat. It took him a couple of clumsy tries since the metal was slickened by his blood, but once they were undone and he was admitted access, he pulled out a piece of folded up parchment.

"Give this to my folks," he ordered to Ben, handing him the letter. "You're gonna make it through this hell. I know it."

Ben swallowed hard, and though he didn't want to take it, knowing it would be as if he accepted John's inevitable death, he couldn't deny his friend this last request. He took the letter and tucked it into his own jacket, a bit of blood transferring from John's fingertips onto his own in the exchange.

"I'll give it to them," Ben assured, squeezing his arm tighter as his friend became racked with coughs and gasps that told him the end was near.

He remembered where John stowed away the tintype of his mother and younger sister and immediately fished it out of his haversack. He remembered they had talked about wanting to see their families one last time if the end should ever come on the battlefield. Obviously, John wasn't in the position to remind Ben, and he was even surprised that he could recall the moment himself as bullets continued to whiz past him. One struck his kepi and knocked it clean from his head. Another lucky miss.

But by the time Ben found the tintype, John had gone still and his arm no longer tremored. The spark of life in his dark eyes faded. Ben stared, taking the moment to recollect his last words. *You're gonna make it through this hell. I know it.*

How he wished they had a few more seconds, just one more minute so Ben could lift the tintype to Johns' eyes. He knew that once this battle was over and his body was laid to rest with the other fallen soldiers, Ben would write a letter to John's mother and tell him all about how bravely he had fought that day. He'd talk about how they'd driven back the Yankees and reclaimed the church for the Confederacy.

Just as these thoughts entered his mind, as soon as the voices and tramping feet of the army moved on through the maze of trees, Ben heard the report of a gun from not too far away. At almost the same time, he felt the bullet pierce his side. He let out a cry and fell back with the impact, reflexively reaching for his gun as he searched for the one who had shot him.

Twenty yards away, he saw the wounded Union soldier propped up against a pine just as his arms became too weak to hold his rifle.

Ben, feeling a burst of panic, kicked at the ground to help him crawl toward some sort of cover. His back hit a bush, the tips of its branches jabbing into his shoulders as he lifted his rifle. Despite whatever wound kept him from retreating with the rest of his regiment, the Yankee gathered up what was left of his strength to slowly load his rifle one more time.

Already two steps ahead in loading, Ben took aim. Just before he did, through the pain that blurred his vision, he remembered the percussion cap. It wasn't seated.

His fingers wrestled with the flap of his cap box and fished out his last one from the very bottom. He let out a tight breath as he took his final aim and shot the Yankee. The man jerked and then went limp against the tree, leaning to one side as blood ran out from the hole in his forehead.

Now, with the last threat eliminated, Ben reached for his side. So much for his lucky streak. His whole body went cold at the sight of the wound. Part of his jacket was ripped open, showing the gory mess of blood and a gaping hole where the bullet had plowed through him.

It was the worst pain he had ever felt in his life. Worse than when his brother broke his arm with the blunt edge of an axe blade when they got into a scuffle about something – as boys so often did. He felt the shakes spread through him, just as John had before he died and Ben refused to let himself think it. He couldn't let his friend's last words be a lie. He'd make it through this hell. He just had to hold on long enough for another regiment to pass by and find him. Then he'd go back to the field hospital.

However, the longer he sat there, the jabbing bed of broken bush limbs digging into his back, he couldn't hear his company returning. And each new marching regiment that happened to pass between the patch of woods and the church couldn't hear his pleas for help. Pain and weakness had stolen his voice and every shout came out as a hoarse whisper that he could hardly hear himself.

Each time he tried to lift his arm to wave for their attention, he realized it took far more effort and exacted more pain in his side with each movement and he gave up. With his rifle laid across his lap, Ben decided to be patient and wait a little longer.

Every passing second felt like an hour, and every moment like a day as he suffered in this pain, feeling his hot blood chill the skin around his stomach. Trails of blood curved around his hips to soak the seat of his pants. Each labored breath left him hurting even more than the one before. But he had to keep breathing, had to stay awake and listen for aid that would surely come soon.

He had to make it through this war. He had to make his family proud of him.

Sunken Road

The air fizzed with the constant crackling of rifle fire as both sides reigned down bullets upon the other. Lying on his stomach on the embankment behind the rail fence, Dustin thought he was relatively safe from the enemy. The Napoleon canons belched hot smoke and lead across the battlefield, creating great chasms in the Union lines as they advanced and retreated in response. Dustin hadn't been in the army for long, but if there was ever a more proper looking military ensemble, Dustin would have doubted its true existence. Complete with a band that failed to play their tunes over the thunder of the canons and the neatly formed rows of soldiers in blue, these Federals knew how to come into a battle.

It was only too bad that they didn't know how to stay in one.

Despite the elbows and ramrods that jostled him from both sides on the tightly packed entrenchment, he still managed to fire a rifle and kill a Yankee every five or so seconds. As soon as the men from the Alabama regiments and North Carolinians took cover on the Sunken Road, it was agreed by all that the better shots should take places by the rail fence while the greenhorns loaded rifles and passed them forward.

Dustin had never missed his mark and was the first to be pushed forward with a rifle in his hands. Behind him, Colonel John B. Gordon continued to shout his encouragement to the troops, even though Dustin knew the man had already been wounded more than a couple of times in the course of this battle. In the midst of one tirade against a soldier who wasn't firing fast enough, he was struck again in the shoulder, but continued to scream his orders.

Bits of dirt that had been flung up by bullets and shelling on the ground ahead of him got caught in his hair and rolled down the front of his shirt underneath his jacket. Bullets whistled past his ears, striking the poor soul behind him that had been handing up rifles for the last ten or fifteen minutes. The stench of blood, soil, gunpowder, sweat, and unabashed fear hovered like a smog over the battle. There was hardly any perception of time as one minute passed to the next with the same volleys, the same peppering of shot across the field as shrapnel exploded and snapped the rail fence in places.

The dead became too many to number, but no retreat was issued. Dustin eagerly waited for it. He wanted to run from this damn trench as fast as his loup-garou legs would carry him and he didn't give one picayune who saw him do it. But he kept shooting, aiming for officers, color bearers, and privates alike. If the rifles were better equipped for the range, he would have shot at the men who controlled the canons on the far hill.

His wolf rose up at every battle, pressuring him to fight harder, longer, and fiercer than any other Confederate dared. The shackles of discipline didn't bind so tightly on his wolf as it did for his more human side, who wanted to be far from the battlefield and all this violence. It was a wonder he hadn't been court marshalled for insubordination after the countless times he had charged ahead of his regiment to pursue the fleeing troops under the provoking of his wolf. Or that his secret hadn't been exposed when his eyes flashed a hellish gold every time he had been shot or given over completely to the primal instinct to survive.

Ahead, another regiment appeared over the crest of the hill. He first saw the tip of their flag, an emerald green with gold and crimson embroidery. Then, he saw the emblem of the cláirseach harp and he cursed aloud.

He knew, simply by the old folksongs he had heard from the Union side of the battlefield the night before, that some of the Irish Brigade had turned out for this battle. He just hadn't planned on fighting them.

Below the harp, sewn in upon a red ribbon across the bottom read, "Riamh Nar Dhruid O Spairn Lann."

"They shall never retreat from the charge of lances," Dustin translated under his breath with a shake of his head. "Just my luck."

The rifle was useless in his hands. He would not fire upon another Irishman. These men were the ones he was supposed to meet with after the battle was over. They were the ones who would get him out of the Confederacy.

"Fág an bealach!" one of the Irish commanders cried from across the field. If only Dustin could clear the way, then he would have.

"Fire that rifle, private!" Colonel Gordon shouted at Dustin, who incurred the wrath of the vehement commander.

Thankfully, providence made a way for Dustin and a bullet slammed into his left shoulder just above his heart. It shattered his shoulder blade. Dustin let out a partially staged cry of pain and tumbled back and out of the way, so another shooter could take his place. Rather dramatically, he tossed aside his rifle and crawled across the piles of dead and wounded men to reach the other side of the road.

It was the first time he took the opportunity to see the kind of destruction the Federals had wrought. Bodies, at least two or three deep, were piled haphazardly in the center of the lane. The lifeblood caked in the dirt after inching along the ground like a creek escaping through a leaking dam. The tattered clothes of the men who were torn apart by shrapnel lay everywhere.

The pain in his shoulder wasn't so terrible and the flesh already began to knit itself back together, closing over the wound after the foreign metal had been pushed out. The fractured and split edges of bones reformed as good as new, leaving only the hole in his uniform and the trail of blood down his shirt to show that he had been wounded.

In any other battle, he would have continued fighting. Laying sprawled out across the ground with the other injured soldiers would guarantee that a doctor would at least inspect his body. When he looked, he'd find nothing. Not a trace of a bullet hole. Not even a scar. It was that kind of exposure that he couldn't risk. But now, he wanted to be left alone by the officers and generals who barked out their orders. If they presumed him to be dead or at least incapacitated, they would leave this part of the battlefield – whether in retreat or advancement – without so much as paying him a single glance.

In his charade, Dustin continued to watch the bullets and canon fire soar overhead and listen to the orders that came less and less frequently from the Confederate captains and colonels. It was then he realized that the officers were being slowly picked off by the enemy. First Colonel Gordon, and then Brigadier General Robert Rodes. More wounded commanders followed from the twelfth infantry, rolling through commanders as time dragged on.

Regiments and companies were left without commanders, and without direction.

Forgetting their training and the blind discipline that had been pounded into their skulls for months, soldiers began to retreat under no one's orders but their own. Soon, confusion broke out amongst the troops and Dustin was nearly compelled to stand up and correct them.

Questions and baffled looks were exchanged, and many of the companies began to think that they had missed the order to fall back. So, rather than stay one moment longer in the battle, they retreated.

Boots and bare feet clambered up the opposite slope as the Union took advantage of their disorder and flanked the Sunken Road. Now, Dustin laid flat and closed his eyes to wait for the chaos to pass over him. The Confederate line had officially broken.

Two impressions, and two impressions alone were felt on his part. Pride for his fellow Irishmen who took the centermost piece of Lee's line, and then utter shame for his own Confederate regiment, the fifth Alabama, who couldn't think straight enough to realize that they were not ordered to retreat. However, upon seeing the dead at Sunken Road, a retreat might have been the best order given all day.

He had heard it said that some generals were better fit to be privates, commander of no regiment or brigade, while some privates had more sense to be generals and colonels. Maybe those men, who would later be labeled cowards and deserters, were right to run when they did. If they hadn't, all of the Alabama and North Carolina regiments might have been totally and systematically murdered that morning.

Dustin lay still, waiting for the pounding feet to fade away, leaving only the moans and pleas of the dying that should have been drowned out by the sound of war. Instead, it became the supporting notes in a harsh song of desolation. The clash of bayonets, the heavy drumming of canon, the boisterous shouts of brave men who were not afraid to die, and the shrill cries of boys who were too young to endure so much, all mixed together in a symphony that had been playing since the beginning of time.

The gears of war were lubricated by the blood of its combatants and the tears of its civilians. And as long as they were willing patrons, Dustin knew he'd live to see more fighting, more destruction, and more sorrow than any one man should be allowed to witness in a lifetime. If ever there was a time he didn't want to be a nearly immortal loup-garou, it was right then upon the battlefield near Antietam Creek.

CHAPTER 3

LATER THAT AFTERNOON - NEAR DUNKER CHURCH

The constant shelling slackened as the sun rose higher over Sharpsburg. When he knew that every living soul had left the entrenchment at Sunken Road, he pushed himself to his feet and cautiously picked his way over the innumerable dead and wounded.

More than once, he had to stop and felt compelled to look upon the slain, all lying in bent, unnatural positions in the road. Lifeless faces gaped open, eyes rolled or fixed upon the blue sky that had cleared since earlier that morning. Jaws were slackened in their final moments when the last breath escaped over their lolling tongues. The only thing in or out of their mouths now were the flies that wasted no time in gleaning what they could from the corpses.

Other men looked to have died in peace with their faces relaxed, eyes closed, and lips sealed; a strangely sad and less disturbing image than their fellow soldiers offered. The only suggestion to their time spent in the battle lay in the wounds that killed them. Some looked to be still alive, faces blank as if they were only struck into a stupor from which they would never recover. Others, those wounded men who had been hanging onto life when the Union charged the road, had been sent into the ether by bayonets. Those death masks were the most hideous and heart-wrenching of all, pinched and contorted by the final blow they received by some vindictive Federal.

Limbs that had been blown off at the knees or hips hung on by tattered strips of their uniform or patches of skin alone. Belly wounds allowed guts to drop out onto the ground or into the faces of the dead soldier beneath him. Sucking chest wounds drew in the edges of the torn shirts. Men lay with their faces shredded, eyes hanging from their sockets, skulls busted open to the point that Dustin could see the mashed, bloodied mess of brains beneath white bone. Blood that was still slick and fresh, glistened in the noonday sun that heated the bodies and made them reek all the more.

The rabbit that he had eaten the night before wouldn't stay down and Dustin gripped a stretch of fence as he relieved his stomach of its contents, all the while avoiding the vacant stare of a young, but very dead boy who couldn't have been more than fifteen years old and lying with his torso shot to pieces.

This was worse than Seven Pines, Malvern Hill, and Boonsboro. The carnage hadn't been so concentrated as it was here. Those soldiers who had been wounded died before ever receiving attention due to the regiment's hasty retreat. This oversight only added to the death toll. And if his nose and senses were correct, and not made completely useless by the overwhelming input, this same story wasn't restricted to this piece of ground. To the north, it was the same.

A mist of death covered the fields and roads around Sharpsburg. The wails of men who were being treated at the hospital behind the lines echoed to him. The steady marching of those soldiers who were still living after this first onslaught shook the earth with the resounding mantra. One more push.

Dustin, made weak by the overwhelming view of so much death, couldn't bring himself to run as he'd wanted before. No one was around to see him except the few stragglers who were rushing to catch up with their companies. But he couldn't will his legs to carry him faster than a slow, ambling pace. A few times, he slipped in the pools of blood that had yet to congeal, and he made a respectful effort to not step on an outstretched, insensible limb. All he could do was force himself to keep walking and hope he came upon a Union soldier who might take him prisoner so he could ask for an audience with Lieutenant Colonel James Kelly in command of the sixty-ninth New York Infantry and who he was instructed to meet after the battle.

Blood and mud had dried over the tops of his shoes and no matter how far he distanced himself from the battlefields, the smell of death lingered around him like a leech that refused to be peeled away.

The white church along Hagerstown Pike came into view, all but battered and gleaming in the sunlight as more dead and wounded soldiers littered its hallowed yard. The Confederates who had put up an admirable fight along the fence that skirted the road were lined up as if they had been assembled for the firing squad. Each one was shot down where he had lay, rifles still in hand or tossed a few feet aside in the dirt. Union men who had fallen in the charge over the road were mixed indiscriminately amongst their enemy. Death was no respecter of rank on this battlefield. The bayonets that topped their rifles were darkened by the blood of those rebels who fought to defend this tiny patch of seemingly useless ground until the last possible moment.

Uniforms of blue and gray lay across or beside one another, death and the color of their spilled blood as the only equalizer in this whole conflict between the north and south.

In the distance, he could hear the aftermath of the slaughter. Men called for their comrades, horses nickered for their riders who had been shot from the saddle, and the superiors decided what next to do. A detachment of officers and soldiers were in conference at the edge of the woods beyond the church, some of the only calm voices he could detect in the vicinity.

Some conversations were purely military, speaking of where they would move next and where regiments would be positioned. But Dustin, once more stunned, nearly fell to his knees when he heard this simple question.

"General, are you going to put us back in again?" a young man asked of the valiant General Robert Lee, whose soft yet commanding drawl was unmistakable amongst the others.

Lee replied, "Yes, my son. We all must do what we can to drive these people back."

More fighting? Dustin let his gaze drift over the cornfields, the expanse of open ground where the dead were abandoned, the rolling hills were artillery was being moved, the tree lines where he could just see the enemy army moving further south toward the creek. Lee was going to send his men back after what had already taken place here?

He closed his eyes to it all, wishing that he wasn't standing in the disturbed dust of the road were the speckling of blood had darkened the dirt. He would have rather been in Alabama where the blockade slowly strangled their supplies. He would have rather been in France or England, or even Ireland despite this self-imposed exile from his homeland. Anywhere but in Sharpsburg.

Driven by the need to escape, he hurried forward, but saw a group of men on horseback directing the movement of artillery down Hagerstown Pike. They, like the Union army, were headed to the creek to hold the line there. Dustin diverted into the patch of woods by the white church.

The carnage continued into the woods, dead men shot down in the cool shade. Here, the stench of death had no way to escape and the breeze that snaked its way around the trunks wasn't enough to carry it away from his sensitive nostrils.

The limbs and brushes provided some concealment from the passing regiment, but he knew that he wasn't the only living man amongst the pines and elms. Somewhere, further into this perpetuating blanketing of corpses, he could hear the rasping call for help.

Dustin went rigid. He didn't want anyone to see him, especially not a Confederate. But if this man was a Federal, maybe he could save his life and that would give him some clout with the Union army, just as his small but monumental act of espionage had. What if he was a Confederate? Should he try to help and risk being turned in as a straggler or potential deserter?

When the withered voice rose up a little higher in its appeal, Dustin thought he almost recognized the voice.

And that familiarity drove him to turn and find the soldier. Stepping carefully over the many boys in blue who had fallen on this side of the wood, he found him. Ben was leaning against a sturdy bush, the rifle between his pale, limp hands and face blackened by the discharged gunpowder left over from the battle that took place here.

How long had he been there? The fighting moved on from this place hours ago, if he remembered correctly, before the engagement at Sunken Road. Whatever had happened here, he put up a hell of a fight.

His brown eyes had lost all luster, his hair flattened and darkened by sweat. His wrinkled hat sat a few yards off, a bullet hole torn through the wool. The soft, spastic rapping of the farm boy's heartbeat told Dustin that he was close to death. There wasn't much he could do. Even if he managed to dig out the bullet in Ben's side, he had already lost too much blood. The evidence of this was all over his lap and pooled around his britches, nearly covering the lower half of his body.

"I don't think I can help you," Dustin admitted sadly with a shake of his head.

"I don't need help," Ben whispered, his lips barely twitching as his tongue formed the words he needed to say.

In a move that astounded him, Ben reached up and dug around in the open flap of his jacket. He pulled out a letter and handed it to Dustin, the bit of parchment dabbed in one corner with dried blood.

"Give this... to John Beck's family in... Heard County, Georgia." The request came out gratingly, halting as Ben tried to take a breath between each few words, but managing to intake little in the effort. "Tell 'em he died... pushin' the Yankees back... He died a good death... As will I."

Dustin felt hot tears prick at the corner of his eyes as he took the letter. Ben let his hand drop and it tightened over the barrel of his rifle.

"Find my wife near Franklin," he continued. "Tell Abigail that I love her and... I'm sorry for not comin' home... I shot the man that killed me."

His gaze dropped to something behind Dustin and he looked to see the Union soldier against the tree. Shot through the head. Ben had somehow managed, after being wounded so fatally, to shoot his own killer. Dustin had heard plenty of stories about heroes, but they always lived to embellish their own stories. Here, he was privileged to see it first-hand.

"Tell my folks," Ben murmured, "that I'll see 'em again."

Dustin couldn't stand it. None of it. His wolf whined and begged him to do something, anything to save this boy's life. But there was nothing. He wasn't a doctor and he wasn't a priest who could administer his last rites. He was just a man who didn't belong in this war.

That thought made him nearly stop breathing. He wasn't just any man. He was a loup-garou. He *could* do something for Ben.

He looked back and saw the haggard, tired face of his new friend begin to sag as if he had been holding back the angel of death himself, just to speak these last words, but now had no more strength to resist his spirit being purged from his body.

"You will see them again, much sooner than you think."

Dustin grabbed up the rifle and tossed it aside, spurred into action by this sudden realization that he was about to commit the most heroic deed in his life. He was going to save Ben from certain death. He was going to snatch the man out of God's greedy hands and make sure he lived.

Only once before had he watched a human be turned into a loup-garou. Darren hadn't been the one to do it, but he understood the concept. It only took a cognitive decision from both him and his wolf to administer the venom that would initiate the change. One, long bite was all it took, and Ben would live.

His frantic eyes searched for a good place and decided upon his arm. Beyond sensing pain, Ben hardly protested when Dustin tugged him away from the bush and proceeded to yank one of his arms out from his uniform. Pushing up the off-white sleeve of his shirt, Dustin let his wolfish fangs extend and then latched on.

He hated the taste of blood as much as he hated the smell, but he continued to tell himself it was necessary. It took a moment, but soon the residual leakage of venom mingled with the blood and flowed over his tongue. He dug in deeper, willing nothing to be wasted. A coolness washed over his eyes and he knew they had turned golden; gold like the eyes of the wolf who eagerly agreed to this course of action.

From the corner of his fixed stare on the ground, he could see Ben's fair brows pinch in confusion. Then, his face wrinkled with the searing pain that coursed through his veins. The venom was taking hold, instigating the change and instilling him with a piece of Dustin's own wolf. He didn't understand the scientific or medical implications of the change. All he knew was that after the bite, Ben would be loup-garou, just like him, and live. That's all that mattered and that's all he cared about.

Soon, Ben fell unconscious under the immense pain that might have rivaled the wound in his side, but Dustin kept time with his pulse throbbing against his fangs. It was slow and weak at first, but then strengthened and quickened as the venom spread.

1850

Franklin, Georgia

"Get the lead outta your britches!" Ben's father called over his shoulder.

Phillip was ahead of him, five years older and with stronger arms to carry his pitchfork. Ben continually adjusted his own on his scrawny shoulders, a boy of only ten years who was gradually being introduced to the world of farming. Up until now, he had helped mother in the kitchen and around the house with some small chore or anything to keep him busy. But now, his father wanted him to start helping on the Rider Plantation.

Ben hastened his steps as they approached the big red barn where they kept the horses and mules used for plowing the fields. They were almost ready to plant another batch of cotton for the season, but their first job was to feed the animals. His arms weren't as thick as his older brother's, or his father's, but Ben promised he would do his best if they just let him try. If hauling the hay from the loft was too much, he would go back down to the house to stay with his mother for the day.

That was the last thing Ben wanted to do. He wanted to be with his father and Phillip. His mother's company wasn't terrible, but he wanted to be like the other men in his family and work. Ever since he was old enough to know how to talk, he'd heard of nothing else but farming. It was what was discussed at the supper table every night and was the first conversation of every morning. He knew the name of his family's employer, Mr. Calvin Rider, just as well as he knew his own.

Of course, that name took on two different meanings for his parents. His father was disposed to admire the man and respect him, while his mother complained incessantly about the working conditions of her family or the slight variance in pay that wasn't a variance at all. She'd say her husband's wages didn't come on time or that he was paid a little less than he was previously. Every time she accused their benefactor of something malicious, his father stepped in to defend Mr. Rider with one excuse or another.

Phillip and Ben, of course, were not asked their opinion on anything. Not until Phillip started working with their father. Then, he was allowed to make comments at the table about business. Ben could not. And that's why he hopped out of bed before the sun rose and was dressed before anyone else had rubbed the sleep from their eyes.

His father unchained the latch to the barn doors and Phillip turned back to watch Ben struggle with his pitchfork. "Come on, slow poke," he upbraided.

"I'm comin' as fast as I can," Ben whined, leaning to one side as the heavy prongs of the pitchfork threatened to throw him off balance.

Phillip grimaced and, once Ben was closer, took the tool from his hand and repositioned it on his shoulder. "Hold it like this." Now, the prongs were just behind his head, the long handle stretching out in front of him. "Just don't hit me in the back of the legs."

Ben eagerly nodded, having resolved earlier to do everything they said and commit it to memory so he'd never forget their advice.

Their father took to leading the massive animals from their stalls and into the pasture while the boys made their way into the loft to shovel down hay to the floor of the barn. Phillip gave a few quick pointers before letting Ben try his hand at the task.

Of course, he tackled it with vigorous enthusiasm and tried to lift up too much at one time. He heaved and grunted against the surprisingly heavy weight of the load and eventually had to withdraw the prongs to try again. This time, he settled for a smaller load and managed to throw it down to the barn floor without falling over.

Ben looked to Phillip and envied the way he made this chore seem so easy and fluid. He had the advantage of age and a stockier frame to handle the work, but that didn't stop Ben from trying to compete with his brother. He might have had to take smaller forkfuls of hay, but he made up for it by hauling and tossing it more quickly to make Phillip's one trip equal to two of Ben's.

Several minutes into this one-sided competition, he approached a new stack of hay and was ready to ram in the prongs. Before he could, he thought he saw something move beneath the straw. He paused and waited, but whatever it was didn't move again. He cautiously poked the tips of the fork into the stack, thinking it was a hiding rat or tomcat.

When no skittish animal slipped away and he heard nothing but the rustle of hay from across the loft where his brother worked, Ben thought he was clear to keep going. Phillip was getting ahead of him anyway.

The prongs then touched something hard and the haystack let out a frightened screech.

Ben fell back when the culprit finally burst from the pile, straw tumbling to the floor in a golden cascade. What emerged was a girl he had seen only once before, but from a far distance.

Up the hill from the barn, the fields, their home, and the rest of the plantation, sat the mansion where Mr. Rider and his family lived. He had never been there, never stepped foot on its wide porch or even on the rich green lawn that sloped into the valley. When he glanced up to the big house, he sometimes saw the family pile into their open carriage to ride into town. Other times, he saw Mrs. Rider standing by one of the tall columns on the porch, watching the goings on down below.

Only once did he ever see this girl with her raven curls and bright blue eyes that reminded him of a clear summer sky. It was one evening when he looked up to the Big House and saw her standing in front of the second story window. Ben had then watched with fascination as she proceeded to shimmy down a makeshift rope of white fabric that was tied together at the ends. As soon as her feet hit the ground, she ran off into the woods behind the house.

And now, it seemed she had tried to escape again.

Ben and the girl, presumably Mr. Rider's young daughter, locked stares while Phillip called down for his father to come back to the barn. All the while, Ben had only two thoughts. The first was that he was thankful to the good Lord above that he hadn't skewered her. The second was that she might have been the prettiest girl he had ever seen. The one happenstance that long ago evening didn't do her justice at all. Her lilac dress with white ruffles around her wide collar and cuff sleeves made her eyes and fair skin that much more radiant in the morning light.

Their father hurried up the ladder and let out a breath of relief when he saw the girl. "Boy, you made me think Ben had hurt himself," he scolded to Phillip, who only shrugged and gestured toward their stowaway.

"She popped right outta the haystack. I don't know how she got in here iffen the door was locked up."

Mr. Myers stepped onto the loft and folded his arms over his chest, taking an authoritative stance as if this girl were his own daughter. "How'd you get in here, Miss Abigail?" he asked reproachfully.

Abigail, with sticks of pale straw sticking out from her collar, cuffs, and hair, looked up to Ben's father, bottom lip quivering. "There's a hole in the wall toward the back of the barn. I've seen cats sneak in and out of it all the time and it was just big enough for me to slip through."

Ben looked between the girl and his father, hoping he wouldn't rebuke her for running away or turn her over to someone else who would.

"Just because you can slip through a hole, don't mean you should. Does your ma or pa know you're here?"

By her hesitance and timid look, they all knew the answer.

Mr. Myers finally sighed and offered out his hand to Abigail. "Come on. I'll take you back home."

She didn't move toward him right away. Only after staring at Ben for what seemed like a long and blissful eternity, did she then lift up her skirts and step out from the haystack. More bits of straw fell from her as she walked, each swaying and bobbing step making her dress swish with the movement. Ben watched her go, willing for her to look back just one more time so he could see her blue eyes again.

She did, just before her head disappeared below the edge of the loft and though she must have been thinking about how much trouble she would be in when she came home, Abigail blessed him with a soft smile.

Once she was out of sight, he responded with his own crooked, goofy grin a little too late. He knew in that moment that he liked Abigail Rider, and his eyes would forever look up to the mansion house to watch for her next daring escape.

CHAPTER 4

Dustin bit at his dirty thumbnail, his stare fastened upon Ben's face in the waning evening light. A newly promoted fourth sergeant by the name of Noah Culpepper allowed them to use his tent while the sick soldier recovered from his fever. That was the story Dustin propagated to the troops who clamored to know what had happened to poor Ben when the battle was over. He told them all it was just a sickness brought on by the intensity of the fighting and he would recover soon.

The truth was far more disturbing. Dustin didn't know what was wrong. The one bitten loup-garou he had seen didn't take this long to recuperate. It had been almost an entire day and he was no better. Ben lay unconscious upon the cot the sergeant had provided, seemingly trapped in some fitful sleep brought on by the fever. His forehead and cheeks were damp with perspiration, but there was no mistaking that he was a loup-garou now. That slight tingling in the back of Dustin's skull told him enough that the bite had worked.

Something else that he noticed, which he hadn't expected, was the alteration in Ben's features. His hair, once blonde, was now a few shades darker, much closer to Dustin's color. Likewise, even in his face, Dustin could see a bit of his youthfulness give way to more mature, bolder lines. Dustin remembered seeing the change in born loups-garous when they shifted for the first time. Some grew taller, others bulked in their arms and chest. Ben already had these muscles, so the shift wasn't so obvious, but he wondered if that would change upon his first transformation, which would come in just a month's time.

When it came time for Ben to shift into his full loup-garou form, he'd be wild and untamed. He would need the dominance of an alpha to control him. Dustin could maintain himself during the shift from man to beast, but he only understood the general concept of what a breaking entailed. He had never executed one himself.

He spat out a bit of grit from his mouth and tore away from his careful watch over Ben to listen to what went on outside the tent. The battle was over, the casualty figures were coming in from the fields, and it wasn't good. He could still hear the moans and wailing pleas of the dying men who hadn't been collected. They begged for water, for a helping hand to ease their suffering, a fortunate turn of events that would end it all quickly, or for the company of loved ones far away from Maryland who would never hear them.

Over ten thousand had been killed, injured, or were missing completely from the roll calls. Those figures were solely on the Confederate side. He was too far from the Union headquarters to hear what totals they had come up with, but it had to be fairly close in comparison.

Ben was numbered with the injured, though Dustin had been careful to assure the other commanding officers that he had been taken care of by a field surgeon prior to being brought back to camp. That was the only way he could guarantee that no man would try to peel back the bloodied fabric of his coat to see that there was no bullet wound anymore. The loup-garou venom, after turning him, would have flowed straight to his injury and began the slow process of healing him from the inside out. Dustin made sure to keep the bullet that was pushed out of his side, just in case Ben was the sentimental type to keep such things.

Another thought, one almost as distressing as the fact that there was no alpha to help tame Ben, was that Dustin hardly knew anything about him. Darren, as well as many other alphas, had said that turning a human into a loup-garou was not a thing to be taken lightly. New initiates were thoroughly interviewed and often lived with other loups-garous for at least two or three years to ensure that this life was what they wanted.

It was impossible to properly gauge what sort of punishment Darren would exact if he had found out that Dustin turned a man after only talking with him for one evening. What had he been thinking?

There were far too many variables and uncertainties. What if Ben had an explosive temper? What if he wasn't mentally capable of dealing with the shift? What if he became what he had come to know as a rougarou, a werewolf who hungered after human flesh? He had learned about those feral counterparts when he arrived in Devia and spoke with the alpha of the town, Robert Croxen.

Through all of it, Dustin couldn't regret what he had done. He had saved the life of a man who didn't deserve to die. None of the soldiers who perished on the battlefield today had deserved to die either, but once more, Dustin's wolf showed that Ben was special somehow. That bond only became stronger when he turned him. He couldn't give a name to whatever invisible trait that endeared him so much to the young man, but it was there and couldn't be ignored. It was as if their paths had crossed for a reason. As if fate had consecrated this place and time just for this chance meeting.

Outside and across the campground, he heard General Lee's tired voice give the order. They were to cross back over the Potomac, back into Virginia.

Dustin muttered a Gaelic curse under his breath, finding the English language not to be potent enough to intimate his exact sentiments. It wasn't that he was afraid to move Ben with whatever mysterious sickness he was mired in. But somehow, he had been holding out for a Confederate victory that would take them further into Maryland. Deeper into the Union territory, he could more easily escape – with Ben – to the north and continue his plans. All hope of joining with the sixty-ninth New York was as dead as those poor wretches on the battlefield. He had missed his chance to rendezvous with their commander.

They either had to escape now, while the armies were still close together and desert the Confederate camp, or travel with them across the Potomac. Dustin was inclined to go with the former option, except for one problem. He was responsible for more than just himself now. He had to take Ben's well-being into consideration. And what was best for Ben was to go back south. Back to Alabama where Darren could supervise his training in Devia.

Dustin covered his face with his hands and leaned back in the rickety folding chair, murmuring more curses into his palms, as if that would make things any better. He couldn't get away from this war or this country now. He had wanted to do the honorable thing by saving Ben, but he had sabotaged himself in the process.

One thing was certain, however. Their days in the Army of Northern Virginia were at an end. No more drilling, no more battles, no more hardtack.

1851

Franklin, Georgia

Ben cut into his fried egg with the edge of his fork as he listened to the sizzling of bacon in the pan on the stove. Phillip sat beside him at the table, wolfing down the last bits of his breakfast, so he would be ready to go to the fields with their father when he returned from Mr. Rider's.

Their mother busied herself with mixing the batch of dough that would be baked for their lunch later that day. Everyone was occupied and ready to start their

day, except for Ben. He had been working with his father and brother for over a
year now and he wondered when a day's worth of labor would become nothing
to him as it was to the rest of his family.

His endurance and longsuffering in the Georgia heat had improved since he
first started with them, but his muscles seemed to be in a constant state of fatigue.
He wished that the Lord had set aside more than one day of rest for his children,
so Ben could have a chance to recover. But never a complaint was heard from
him. He knew that if he spoke out against his father for whatever task he had
been given, not only would his hide be tanned for the complaint, but he'd be a
disappointment to them all. Phillip never complained about the work and was
constantly praised for it by the Riders and every other family in town who knew
him to be a good young man. He was always willing to go the extra mile for his
family and employer. Ben looked up to him, wanted to emulate him in every way
he could, but knew that he failed often. Phillip made it all look so easy.

From outside their house came the frantic flapping of chicken wings as the hens
and roosters cleared the way for Mr. Myers' return. All three pairs of eyes looked
to the front door of their small farmhouse as he entered. His father took off his
wide-brimmed hat and wiped his brow upon his sleeve that had been christened
by the first drops of sweat of the workday.

Ben looked back to his food and continued to cut up his sausage and egg into
tiny pieces, rather than stuffing them in his mouth as Phillip did. His father started
in on the report Mr. Rider had given him for the day, about what they would need
to do in the fields and which workhands were to join them.

Like the Myers family, there were three other field hands who were permanently employed on the Rider Plantation. Others were men looking for temporary
work, who sometimes showed up and sometimes didn't, leaving the others to pick
up the slack until further help could be found.

On extremely rare occasions, a slave from a neighboring farm would come to
work alongside them. But that was only when Mr. Rider needed all the help he
could get and there were no other white folks who could come.

Ben learned years ago that this infrequent practice had nothing to do with Mr.
Rider's preference toward a black man or a white man. Their employer wasn't
quite an abolitionist, as some of the townspeople thought. He didn't actively
speak from pulpits or hand out flyers that detailed the horrors of slavery as they
did in the north. Instead, he quietly protested against the system by hiring slaves
for a day or two and paid them more than what their master mandated. This extra
allowance was given because Mr. Rider believed that if a man worked, he should
be paid, whether he be white, black, yellow, or red. And he paid the slaves just the
same as he paid Ben's father.

Ben ignored much of what they said, too tired and too sore to care, even though he should have.

"Oh," his father said, "and Mr. Rider said that he wants one of you boys to go up and sit with his daughter for a spell."

At this, Ben felt a cool, excited rush plunge through his core and he looked up to his father to see if there was a mocking smile on his lips.

His mother stilled her dough mixing and set down the spoon. "Why does he want one of our boys?"

Mr. Myers fixed himself a plate of bacon, trying to pick up the strips from the hot grease with his calloused fingers. "Said he wanted her to practice some etiquette and needed a boy to do it. They don't have any male house servants, so he asked if one of our sons could help."

Phillip's eyes cut toward Ben. "Send Ben, pa. I'm sure he wouldn't mind. Besides, I've gotta - "

Before his big brother could even finish his sentence, Ben was out of his chair and running toward the front door, forgetting his weary legs and aching back.

"Hold your horses!" his father called out to him, a free hand grabbing for Ben's shirt collar. "They won't be needin' anyone 'til this afternoon."

"Get back in here and eat your breakfast!" his mother added impatiently.

Though he escaped his father's grasp, he skidded to a stop halfway to the gate after he leapt from the porch. Ben bemoaned the unfairness of life as he trudged back up the steps. He had been looking for an opportunity just like this for months. Staring and watching for any glimpse of Abigail's black tresses and blue eyes wasn't enough anymore. He wanted to face her, to speak to her. Ben continually berated himself for not even saying hello when they first "met" in the hay loft before the last planting season.

He was determined to make up for his cowardice, but his father and Mr. Rider kept him busy in the valley while he continually turned his eyes to the house on the hill. Now, he'd get to speak to her, maybe even touch her hand. His heart hammered in his chest as he sat at the dinner table once more. This time, he scarfed down his breakfast and seemed just as eager to start his chores as Phillip. Because once those chores were done, he'd get to see Abigail. And that made every sore muscle worth the trouble.

September 22ⁿᵈ, 1863
  Virginia
  Dustin nervously paced outside Ben's tent. The army had bivouacked far south of the Maryland state line, still in full retreat since Lee had decided to take advantage of McClellan's delay in reengaging the army at Sharpsburg. Once more, Lee put his brilliant, strategic mind to good use and admitted that he was not in the position to fight back again. The campaign into Maryland was effectively cut off, but he could already hear the generals planning their next moves from the other side of camp.

During the retreat, Dustin carried Ben across the miles of wilderness. He refused help from any other man, even from his own company, because if Ben had been unconscious for this long he wasn't sure how he'd react upon waking up. If he lashed out in a rage, Dustin wanted to be the target and not a Confederate who didn't fully understand his condition.

To his relief, Ben did seem to be improving. His fever had broken, and he no longer tossed his head from side to side. His limbs didn't twitch in his sleep and now he only muttered the irregular word or phrase that made no sense. Names sometimes surfaced, but they meant nothing to Dustin.

Still, Ben didn't wake up. For the last hour, he hadn't mumbled a word; hadn't stirred from the blanket he had laid out on the only dry patch of earth he could find on the edge of the campground. The nearest campfire was at least twenty yards away, the nearest tent another twenty yards beyond that. They were almost completely isolated, and that's the way Dustin wanted it. When Ben woke up, he didn't need a host of soldiers crowding in to ask questions that he couldn't answer.

With every step he took, its counter measure was repeated in Ben's chest. That might have been the only clue that Ben was still alive. Dustin wondered if he had administered too much venom during the bite. He certainly gave enough to turn him, but would it slowly kill him if it couldn't process through his body fast enough? Darren would have known all those things, but he was over a thousand miles away.

His answer came when he heard Ben move for the first time almost all night. It was a slow, gradual slide of a limb on top of the blanket that disturbed the stiff grass underneath. Dustin ducked through the tent flap just as Ben's eyes were cracking open. But instead of seeing the brown eyes he had expected, they had shifted into their wolfish gold already. Bright, almost luminous in the pitch blackness of the tent. He would be able to see well enough that no candle or lantern was needed.

Dustin went to Ben's side and knelt down, still unsure how he would explain all these things. Ben had one crucial advantage over so many other loups-garous. Like Darren, Dustin had awoken in a strange place with no memory of his first shift and no one to guide him through the initial days of his new life. Ben was lucky and he hoped the soldier would realize that much.

The iridescent eyes of the wolf peered around the tent, confused and disoriented. But when they landed upon Dustin, a myriad of emotions paraded through them. Confusion gave way to fear, then to anger that quickly escalated into a boiling rage.

Before Dustin could even get a word out, Ben lunged for him. The wool blanket was tossed aside as fangs and claws came at him with such blinding ferocity. The growl that erupted from Ben's throat was anything but human, and Dustin was far more baffled than he was frightened.

Two gashes were made in his throat and face, but he managed to apprehend the newly turned loup-garou with minimal effort. As Darren had taught him long ago, fighting with passion was useless. A level head was the only way a loup-garou could come out as the victor in most scuffles. That contradicted his typical Irish temperament of striking first and asking questions later, but he had acquired some level of patience over the years to train him out of the habit.

The growl, however, could not be contained and he soon heard the rush of boots headed for their tent. Dustin pinned Ben to the ground, craning his neck away from the wildly gnashing fangs of the once meek and demure farm boy.

He had no time to try and talk Ben down as the other soldiers were coming closer. He briefly let go of one of Ben's arms, grabbed for the metal canteen that Dustin had stolen from a dead Union soldier weeks ago, and bashed it against the side of the raging loup-garou's head. The metal split under the force of the impact, but it did its job.

Ben was unconscious again with only a small cut at his temple from the makeshift weapon. Dustin scrambled off of him just as the fourth sergeant, Noah Culpepper, threw back the tent flap to enter.

"What was that?" he demanded. More privates pushed their way through to get a good look at Ben. Thankfully, his eyes were closed and every sign of his beastly nature retracted before they had a chance to see it.

"What was what?" Dustin answered, his hands slung casually in his pockets as he worked to keep his heavy breaths under control. It was a blessing that humans couldn't hear as well as a loup-garou, otherwise they would have heard how his heart threatened to pound straight out of his throat.

"It sounded like a cougar or somethin'," one soldier remarked.

Dustin feigned understanding and thumbed toward the back of the tent. "I think that was just something prowling around in the woods."

"It sounded like it came from this tent," Noah asserted, looking between him and Ben. "Is he all right?"

Dustin didn't have time to replace the blanket or reposition his arms to make it look like Ben was still peacefully sleeping off his sickness. "I think he was having a nightmare earlier. Kept rolling around and asked for some girl named Abigail."

A look of recognition sparked in Noah's eyes and he nodded. "That's his wife. Ben hasn't seen her since last Christmas, I reckon."

More bodies crowded at the tent opening, asking the same questions that Noah had and, together with Dustin, they endeavored to force the men back. Their excuse was that Ben needed more time to rest and they were only going to wake him. But Dustin had other motives. As soon as the tent was cleared of visitors and the rest of the camp was sound asleep, they would leave.

He still had no idea what was happening to Ben's body or mind. Loups-garous were not this instinctively violent from the beginning. This kind of fury was reserved for their first shift when the wolf was more prevalent in their behavior and appearance. Outbursts may happen here or there, but never a full, unwarranted attack. This went far beyond his realm of knowledge and the safest thing now was to make sure that Ben was far away from any other humans. If this kind of unchecked savagery happened again, Dustin might have another situation on his hands, as with what happened to Cassandra. And he had vowed long ago that nothing like that should ever happen again. Not to him, and not to someone he cared for.

1851
Franklin, Georgia

This was the first time Ben had ever stepped onto the front porch of the Big House. Already, he could hear the halting notes of the parlor piano. From what his father had said, Mr. and Mrs. Rider would not be home that afternoon and only their elderly house servant would chaperone Ben and Abigail.

When Miss Peters opened one of the massive doors, he took a shy step back. At first, the old woman's wrinkles deepened with severity upon Ben. He stood for a moment, unsure of what to say with his cap gripped between his hands and wishing to appear even smaller than he already was.

"My pa sent me up here to – "

The house servant waved her hand and smiled in comprehension. "Oh, you're one of the Myers boys. Come in."

He did as he was told, but not before kicking off the dirt from the bottoms of his shoes. His mother made him clean up a bit before making the long trek up the hill to the Big House, but the sweat he had washed off not ten minutes before had returned, giving his face a glistening effect.

He gazed at the magnificent interior of the house with its flowered wallpaper, smooth hardwood floors, and paintings of people whom he assumed to be other members of the Rider family. Miss Peters led him through the foyer and into the brightly lit parlor. The window curtains, made of a heavy and soft velvet, were pulled back by golden tasseled ropes, but the view outside was still veiled by lace that filtered the afternoon sun. Sofas of elaborate upholstery designs were situated in the middle of the room upon a heavy-looking rug that complimented its pattern. Mahogany tables were scattered around and topped with vases of oriental design or lanterns that would be used later in the evening.

Then, in the far corner of the parlor, sat the biggest – and only - piano he had ever seen. Seated upon the bench with her back turned to him, was the object of his visit.

Miss Peters motioned for Ben to step back beyond the threshold and into the hall. He did so, slightly more entranced with the way Abigail's head turned to watch her own fingers glide across the keys. He was shooed away until completely out of sight from the piano.

"Miss Abigail," the house servant began, "there's a Mr. Ben Myers to see you."

Ben heard the subtle creaking of the piano bench as Abigail must have slid off. "You may show him in," she responded cordially.

At this, Miss Peters ushered Ben forward and he stepped cautiously into view. Abigail's cheeks reddened at the sight of him, but she managed to curtsy with graceful poise. The hem of her blue dress brushed the ground, the stiff taffeta whispering as it bunched.

Miss Peters had to clear her throat to remind him of the proper way to answer her curtsy. Just like his mother showed him, Ben placed his hands behind his back and bowed a little more deeply than he probably should have. A bit of dirt fell from his blonde locks and pattered to the floor.

Abigail's lips tightened as if she was tempted to laugh. "It's a pleasure to meet you," she said, once more keeping to safe and formal pleasantries that Ben could have done without.

To him, they weren't strangers. Not completely. He wasn't sure how much she knew of him, but Ben had found out all he could about her from other work hands who frequented the Big House and while eavesdropping on conversations between his parents. She was as wild as a mustang and as sly as a vixen, bound to burst from the mold her parents tried to force her into. Ben longed for the day when he saw her do just that.

"Do sit down," Abigail solicited, gesturing toward one of the sofas.

Ben obeyed, still entranced by her, and waited for further instruction from either the house servant or his host. Seeing that the two children were off to a fine start, Miss Peters quitted the room and told them she would be in the back garden if they should need anything.

A pregnant silence filled the parlor. Ben hadn't uttered a single word since he entered the house and never felt more shy in his life. He knew that he was only there because Abigail needed someone to practice her manners with, but what was he supposed to do? How could she properly learn if he didn't know anything to begin with?

"Would you like to hear me play?" she offered, her eyes roaming to the parlor door, which remained wide open into the foyer. The way her gaze deviated told him that she was waiting for something, or perhaps watching for someone.

"Yes, ma'am... Oh, miss. Sorry. Yes, miss." Ben could have kicked himself for the misspoken address, but Abigail didn't seem to mind. Her focus was torn two ways as she sat at the piano once more, smoothing out her skirts and positioning her hands to start her song again.

It wasn't until both Ben and Abigail heard a door open and latch shut from somewhere toward the back of the house that she stopped playing and slumped, forsaking the perfect posture she had been maintaining since he arrived.

"What's wrong?" he asked, standing without consent, thinking he had done something to upset her. "I did want to hear ya play, I really did."

Abigail turned in her seat and rolled her blue eyes at him. "I've been practicin' for two hours and I'm sick of the piano. Pa bought this last month so I could learn, but I hate it."

With wary steps, Ben approached the bench, glancing between her and the ivory keys. "Why don't ya tell them ya don't wanna play it?"

She barked a laugh. "Tell them I don't want to do somethin'? I might as well be waggin' my tongue at a brick wall."

There was just enough room on the bench for him to slide in and Ben wordlessly asked for her permission. She nodded and he settled down next to her. This was the closest they had ever been to one another, even closer than the time he almost stabbed her with a pitchfork in the hay loft. They were a year younger then, but Abigail was just as spirited and lively.

"I think ya were playin' real nice," he complimented as he began an inspection of the piano.

There were some golden words painted on the panel above the keys, standing out against the dark, polished rosewood. A tall booklet was set against the delicately carved stand, lined with strange symbols that must have translated into the music she had been trying to play.

"What's all that mean?" he asked, pointing an eager finger at the golden letters first.

Abigail turned to him in astonishment. "Can't you read?"

He shook his head, hoping no dirt bits would fall on her pretty dress.

"Oh, I forgot you're just a farm boy."

Just a farm boy. Those words cut deep and he tried not to let hopelessness creep up on him. She was a fine, well-bred lady, and far above his class in every way. She'd never have to work a day in her life, while he toiled away with his hands in the soil. But that didn't mean they couldn't be friends.

"But what does it mean?"

Abigail reached out and underscored the words with her fingertip as she read. "Robert Wornum and Sons. That's who made the piano. Pa had it shipped all the way from England."

"Them boys sure make a pretty piano," Ben remarked, then turning his attention to the sheet music. "And that?"

"Those are the notes."

Then, one by one, she explained each of them and demonstrated what they sounded like when played. She drummed out one line and then another, teaching him a skill that he would never use.

When she scooted over, giving him room to play the same notes, Ben fumbled for a place to toss his hat. He tried to imitate the way her fingers so elegantly flowed over the keys, but the going was slow, and he missed the right note several times with his clumsiness before she had to intervene.

For as long as she would tolerate him, Ben sat and willed himself to be a competent pupil, listening closely to everything she said as if her lessons were the gospel and she was the evangelist that would save his soul. And as long as he was sitting beside her, the subject of her undivided attention and recipient of her smiles, Ben might as well have been in heaven and in the company of God's most precious angel.

CHAPTER 5

The soft piano notes faded. The ghostly laughter of the two children in his memory died away. In their place, destroying the peaceful sleep, came too many smells and noises to distinguish one from the other. Nothing but a rabble of sounds as if he were standing in the heat of a massive battle. But there was no canon, no rifle, no shouting, or sharp rap of the drums. What supplanted them was the familiar cadence of wilderness, broadcast as if Ben were an omnipresent being.

The swaying of the leaves, the chirping of a million birds, a creek somewhere in the offing babbled against its pebbly shore, and a thousand smells assaulted him as if their sources were pressed up into his nostrils. Earth, wood, his own bodily odors, the fur and droppings of forest animals, and a faint trace of something that belonged neither to him nor to the wilds.

This one smell, out of all the others, sent a shiver of unmitigated fury through Ben like nothing he had ever experienced before. Something deep and fiery within his gut threatened to spread and consume him. He could feel himself tremble and his skin grow warm with this seething hatred for something he couldn't even recognize.

He opened his eyes and found himself propped up in a corner of a one-room shack. One cutout window, doorway, and busted aperture in the roof permitted bright light into the space. Verdure grew through the cracks of the floorboards, vines curling through knotholes. Ben could see everything in such vivid relief that he had to blink and squint to dull the details. He could see particles of dust floating in the slanting rays of sunlight, the flight of gnats and other bugs as they wove and spun their way through the weeds.

There was no clear way to tell where he was, other than in the thick of some rough country that had reclaimed this cabin. Through the confusion, Ben gathered that he was tied up with ropes that bit harshly into his arms and chest. His legs, too, were bound. Behind him, the same rope cinched his wrists together.

This realization, that he was trapped, only proved to enrage that thing within him that so contrasted with what Ben truly wanted to feel. He wasn't angry, but confused and slightly scared. Where was he? Where was his regiment? Who had brought him here and tied him up?

Every logical thought proclaimed that he must have been taken prisoner by a Yankee. The last thing he remembered was lying against the bush in the patch of woods by the white church. He had been on the edge of death's abyss... Ben looked to his stomach and saw the dark blood upon his uniform jacket and the frayed hole in the fabric where the bullet had entered, but he wasn't injured. He felt no pain, and none of the faintness that had preceded death. Nothing to suggest that he had been wounded at all.

If it was a Yankee that took him prisoner, he was certainly treated better than he had anticipated. He had heard so many stories that once a Confederate soldier was captured, they were tortured and barely looked after before being sent to a prisoner of war camp. There, the Confederate soldier could expect sickness, starvation, and ultimately death if they weren't exchanged quickly enough.

Listening closely, Ben began to doubt his assumption that he had been captured. There was no one near the cabin. He couldn't hear the jangling of horse bridles, the deep voices of the officers, or any sign that the shack was guarded. He was completely alone, but it didn't feel like it.

Reflexively, he tugged against the ropes and to his surprise, they easily unraveled and snapped. The heavy cord dropped around him, thudding against the floorboards. Ben paused and inspected the ends of the ropes. The strands appeared new and not worn or corroded by time and abuse. With a simple tug, he managed to break free. But how was that possible?

Footsteps in the tall grass around the cabin alerted Ben to the approach of someone. Whether friend or foe, Confederate or Yankee, he couldn't be sure. In the room was a table and chair that looked to be half-eaten by an army of termites and wouldn't provide him cover. Tucked in the opposite corner was his haversack and bedroll, accompanied by the supplies of another soldier. Judging by the canteen kept with the stranger's bundle, he was a Confederate. That, in itself, was encouraging enough.

The footsteps quickened and Ben went rigid as a new smell met him.

Meat. Fresh, raw, bloody meat.

What happened next, within the space of a minute or so, terrified Ben beyond comprehension. That burning, loathing part of himself was fanned into a howling, uncontrollable inferno. All at once, his movements were not his own and the sounds that came from his throat were anything but human. He watched the door, his shoulders slowly rising like a hunting dog stalking his prey.

The scent that had riled him became stronger, more potent, as powerful as the aroma of what Ben began to identify as food. Muscles tightened and bunched as he leaned forward, his fingertips pressed into the rough boards.

His nailbeds tingled, and he heard something sharp grazing across the grainy surface of the wood. Ben couldn't glance down to confirm it, but he knew he was the one gripping the planks with his nails, as if readying himself to dive forward.

A shadow passed across the threshold and the figure entered, almost completely in silhouette. Ben didn't take the time to find out who the man was, why he had come to the cabin, or why he was holding three dead rabbits by their ears. Quicker than the time it took for the eye to blink, Ben was on the stranger, much against his own bidding.

It was as if he became possessed, seized by a force of savagery too great for him to command. The only reverberating thought he could extricate from the discord of growls and shouts was the single-minded need to kill and feed.

By the end of that long, horrifying minute when Ben denied his own humanity, he was pinned down on his stomach. The trickling bristles of a shooting weed chaffed against his neck as he thrashed, trying to right himself.

"I'll batter ya if ya keep acting the maggot," the man grumbled in what Ben didn't recognize as a familiar southern drawl or the bland tongue of a Yankee.

Even if he could articulate words, there was no time to ask him anything or demand explanations. Because shortly after this unusual threat, two of the rabbits were tossed up just inches from Ben's face. Their pelts were previously torn, probably by the same claws that greedily reached out and snatched them out of the stranger's hands.

Ben, a mere inner spectator to this horrendous display of animalistic barbarity, stopped short before plunging his teeth into the flesh. A spark of sanity emerged and he hesitated.

"Go on," said the man who straddled over is back, keeping him down and secure against the floor that threatened to give way beneath their combined weight. "It isn't going to bite you back."

That wasn't what concerned Ben. It was the whole affair. His senses exploding, the uncontrolled viciousness, and this ravenous hunger for meat that hadn't been cooked – though he had eaten raw meat before on long marches where there was no time to prepare food. It was all too much, too extraordinary to believe.

He squeezed his eyes shut and released the rabbits to let them drop in front of him. He wanted to go back to dreaming, back to the image of Abigail when she was a little girl and he was just beginning to feel the stirrings of love in his breast. Not this, whatever this was.

His fists slammed against the planks and they splintered. The man on top of him heaved an aggravated sigh and began muttering something in a foreign language that Ben couldn't begin to guess. Soon, a tiny piece of meat was thrust beneath his nose, the smell inescapable, even when he turned his head to refuse the handout.

"Quit being stubborn and take the damn food."

That creature within him, that second self that needed the meat, was in agreement and Ben was conquered again by its ferocity.

He not only took it, but also the two other rabbits that he had been offered first. As the man rose off of him and took a few paces away, Ben pushed himself up and crossed his legs, the open carcass of the rodent in his hands. Ben shut his eyes against what he was doing. He didn't want to see it. Didn't want to believe it. What had he become? What had happened to him at Sharpsburg? Was this man to blame? Or was this a kind of hell that wasn't spoken about from the pulpit? Had he died? And if so, what had barred him from heaven? Or was this all a continuous nightmare, just like the war that tore the nation apart?

Warm tears gathered at the corners of his eyes and escaped to roll down his cheeks. Tears of anger, of fear, and of pure sorrow that could only be experienced by a man who had everything stolen from him.

1862

Franklin, Georgia

Abigail hated the way her hands gently shook each time she pushed the tip of the needle through the folds of fabric. All around, eight other women were able to sew their uniform projects with ease, hardly looking at the work as they gossiped. How could any of them make their stitches so evenly spaced and precise without putting half as much effort into the task as she did?

These ladies, some old friends of her mother's, and some close acquaintances of her own, met two or three times a week to sew and share any news they may have gathered in the days they spent apart. Today, it was her family's turn to host the gathering.

The mass of homespun butternut fabric in her lap was meant to be a new jacket for Ben. It was similar to the one he had been given when he was mustered into his company. The fabric was an appealing shade of tan, uniquely fashioned with thick black sleeve bands featuring three spare buttons and two more shoulder bands to match. In one of his previous letters, he mentioned that the inner lining of the coat he now wore into battle was wearing thin. And with winter on the horizon, she knew it would be cold in the north, not like it was in Georgia. She wanted her brave soldier to be warm, even if he couldn't return home for Christmas as he had last year.

Her lips curled into a melancholy smile as she remembered those few days he had been allotted in December. Four days and three nights with her Ben. That's all she had of him. Nine months had passed and she only had a single photograph of him to keep her company. She kept it by her bedside and kissed it every night, but the image of Ben in his new uniform, taken just a week after he enlisted, wasn't enough. Not anymore. Not when she dreamed of him almost every night. Dreamed of how they were children in this very room, young and oblivious to the future that awaited them.

She realized she loved him in this parlor when they danced together during a Christmas celebration her father hosted. He proposed on the very sofa where three other ladies crammed their hoops together now. They were married by the window where the piano used to sit for so many years – now sold off in order to donate the profits to the war effort. So many wonderful things took place in this parlor, in this house, and on this plantation.

"What's that smile for, Abby?" one of the older women asked teasingly.

"She's thinkin' of Ben," said Elsie, one of her oldest childhood friends.

The other ladies, all ranging between the ages of fifteen and fifty, either began to talk about their own beaus and sweethearts far away, or smiled quietly to themselves, because they understood how Abigail's heart ached for her husband. The older matrons of the group didn't stop them from glorifying their men in battle, but they would eagerly silence any despondent comment. Abigail once heard her mother remark that a healthy morale must be maintained, even for the women who stayed at home. No talk of death, sickness, or the errant thought that one of their own from Franklin could ever be listed amongst the wounded after a battle.

Abigail thought them ignorant. War wasn't all glory and victory. She knew that despite their brave dispositions in the face of a possible Confederate defeat, they all hungrily skimmed through the newspapers after every major or minor battle, looking for a name they even remotely recognized. She, too, was guilty of it, and was thankful never to read the name of Benjamin Myers amongst any casualty roster thus far.

Many of the strong, able-bodied men from Heard County were enlisted or conscripted, fighting for Georgia's independence. In the first few weeks, the loneliness had been easier to bear. Abigail could keep herself busy with cleaning the house her father had given them as a wedding present, or making sure that the fields stayed free of unwanted weeds or pests that would ruin the harvest they intended to plant when Ben returned.

When the weeks stretched on, and then months, and news from the two battlefronts were far from favorable, Abigail knew that there was little point in tending the fields. She stayed in the company of friends and family after that, until her mother insisted that she return home to the Rider plantation. Such a move, though she balked at first, proved to be a godsend, especially this year when she needed the support the most.

"When was the last you heard from Ben?" Elsie asked beside her, her needle darting in and out as she sewed together the tan sleeve for her intended uniform. Without a beau for herself, she relied on what news other women gleaned from the letters and newspapers.

The sad smile returned to Abigail's face as she recalled the last correspondence she had received from her love. "It was dated August thirty-first, the day after they fought the Yankees at Manassas Junction."

It had been one long month since she last heard from Ben. Secesh Mail was not the most reliable when it came to timeliness. Anything could have happened. Certainly a lot had happened on the Rider Plantation in the last month.

"I thought they had already fought there," replied a young girl about sixteen years of age by the name of Missy. She had just formed an attachment to a soldier from the nineteenth Georgia infantry that served in the Army of Tennessee. Before he caught her eye, Missy had never cared for the war or Confederate cause. Now that she was emotionally invested, she attended every sewing circle with her mother and elder sister.

"They did, dear," said her mother beside her. "But that was last year. They fought a second time."

"Why would they fight in the same place twice?" Missy asked, setting down the bright yellow sash she was knitting for her beau, who was recently promoted to a rank that required such regalia.

This sparked a new conversation and Abigail's Ben was soon forgotten as the delicate feminine brains tried to make sense of the army movements. Some imparted what their men mentioned about Lee, Jackson, and other generals that had become household names like Robert Anderson, J.E.B Stuart, James Longstreet, Jubal Early, Braxton Bragg, A.P Hill, Beauregard, and Joseph Johnston, whom the men affectionately called Old Joe.

Abigail absently listened as she tried to steady herself, so she could make the next stitch perfectly aligned with the others. She had always been inept at sewing and all the things that women were expected to master by their teenage years. Her spirit and skills were far more analogous with that of her husband's. She could more easily plant an even row of cotton or corn than she could manage a simple stitching pattern as this. Much to her mother's dismay, she had grown up stubborn, headstrong, and determined to challenge the role society wanted to box her in. Heaven forbid she walk around the house without her stays or plunge her hands into the soil as her old nanny, Miss Peters, so often did.

Mrs. Rider thought marriage and raising a family would finally temper her wildness. But Ben only fed that fire within her, encouraging it to burn all of society to the ground, because it dared to define her life. Even now, under her parents' care and protection, she rebelled against them in the small ways; just enough so that she knew she was getting away with something, but not enough to cause a scandal.

Over the soft feminine voices of the ladies in the parlor, Abigail heard the wagon pull up to the front of the house. Glancing toward the window that looked over the porch, she could see the hazy image of her father alighting from the seat. In the back of the wagon was a mound of supplies and she let out a long breath of relief. The blockade that choked the Confederacy was not only making it difficult to procure certain luxuries, but was beginning to deprive them of necessities as well.

But instead of helping one of their workers with the parcels, her father bounded up the porch steps, a newspaper rolled in his fist.

Either by a natural lull of conversation, or by the sudden arrival of their host into the parlor, the sewing circle fell deathly silent. Abigail looked to her father as he entered and a coldness passed over her when she saw his expression. A mixed look of horror, sympathy, and personal loss was written there and she wondered what name he found today.

Her father had scoured the casualty lists as dedicatedly as any of the other women who regarded him with suppressed wonder. They, too, wanted to know the name. With so many families connected by marriage or close friendships that stretched back almost a hundred years, everyone knew everyone in this part of the state.

But her father didn't look to Missy, to Elsie, or any of the other women who had men invested in this war. He looked to Abigail, and her hands began to shake all the more.

Her legs had no strength, her body unresponsive to any command she might have given it. She simply sat as she tried to remember to breathe.

Let him only be wounded, she thought to herself. *Just wounded and then he'll come home.*

But by the grave, sullen countenance of her father, it was much more serious than a wound.

It had to be a mistake. She would have felt Ben die. Her own soul would have been split in two if he were taken unto the Lord by this cruel war. But she felt nothing lately. There was no way he could have died without her being awoken in the middle of the night by a terrible premonition. Their love was too strong, too true to allow her to be informed of his death by a telegram or newspaper.

Her next thought came in response to the new sound that rose through the Rider household from the nursery. The cry of an infant not two weeks old, calling for his mother who now sat like a stone statue, fixed with grief and disbelief.

He never knew.

Blue Ridge Mountains

Three days. Three, long, fecking days of hunting as quickly as Dustin could so he could return to the derelict shack, only to find Ben still rooting around like a wild animal. It was like when his family, back in Ireland, had adopted a shepherd puppy from another farmer in Glengarriff. They would find something destroyed every time they turned around. Back then, Dustin could forgive the pup for its behavior, because it didn't know better. He didn't know how to forgive Ben, because he didn't know what was wrong.

It had been almost a week since he'd turned Ben into a loup-garou, but there was something terribly amiss about this process. The human side of the man, the side that could reason, might as well have been erased. He was the same in body and looks, but Ben had to be restrained by a set of chains that Dustin had found behind the shack.

Ever since he'd awoken from his second spell of unconsciousness, Dustin was forced to board up the one window and doorway to keep the freshly turned loup-garou inside. When he figured out how to pry up the floor, Dustin resorted to the chains. But that was only after everything else had been scarred by his claws and gnawed to splinters. The gap in the roof also needed to be patched, or he'd jump clear out of it when Dustin wasn't paying attention.

Along with this need for thoughtless destruction, Ben's stomach had become a bottomless pit. It was all Dustin could do to keep him from trying to rip off his arm when he came back from foraging with a meager, but adequate meal that should have satisfied him. It didn't, and the animals along this side of the mountains became aware of the beasts that had invaded their territory. Food was becoming harder to find, but the skills Darren had taught him – especially tree climbing – had finally become something useful.

Perhaps attributed to all these things that Dustin was forced to address hourly, Ben's eyes never returned to their human brown. They were never anything else but a deep golden hue. The eyes of the wolf shouldn't have been so permanent, but since Ben perpetually conducted himself as a wolf, it might have been a natural side-effect. The beast was too close to the surface, but why? There was absolutely no reason for this. He should have been cognitive within the first twelve hours at the most.

Dustin arrived to the shack, bearing the last of the mountain's deer across his shoulders. His approach was noticed, and the rattling of chains rammed against the floor and walls of the shack, echoed by grunts and growls. Ben was not improving.

With one hand steadying the deer, the other unlatched the makeshift locks upon the door. Once all three had been undone, he tossed the deer inside and barricaded it shut again. Links that had been straining against the loup-garou strength for the last two days finally snapped – as he predicted – and Ben was loose within the shack once more.

Dustin, almost numb to the whole affair by this point, listened to the ripping of hide and cracking of bone under powerful jaws. He also found it odd that, though the wolf was so near to breaking free of its human host, he never transformed beyond the extension of claws and fangs. It was as if the human mind and soul had vacated him, leaving only the wolf in its place.

It was in the midst of these thoughts, as he racked his brain for the thousandth time on how to quickly solve this problem, when a still quiet fell over the shack. No snarls, no chewing, no shuffling movement across the creaking floorboards.

Dustin wondered if the moment had finally come, if Ben's human mind had somehow reemerged from the inescapable depths of his new nature. When he turned and cracked open the door to look for himself, he was sadly mistaken.

Ben leapt and knocked him to the ground, breaking the door off its rusty hinges. The man was on him for only a moment before running off into the forest. Once Dustin was able to comprehend what had happened, he jumped to his feet and ran after Ben. He was completely inexperienced, bashing against trees and crashing through bushes, leaving behind a trail that could easily be followed.

This part of the mountains was uninhabited. Dustin made sure of that before ever commandeering the shack for their own use. There were no paths, no roads, nothing to guide Ben as he loped on all fours through the dense wilderness. Dustin found it difficult to keep up with him, even at full speed. Ben's use of both hands and feet to propel himself forward might have had something to do with that.

Dustin suspected that the new loup-garou didn't even know where he was going. A few times, he had arched about in a wide circle before plunging in a completely different direction. But he didn't slow down. Not until he reached the decline of a particular ridge just to the west of the shack.

One yelp and a string of rustling sounds told Dustin that Ben had lost his footing somewhere along the rocky slope and began tumbling over the side of the mountain. He came to the crown of one ridge and watched the young loup-garou groping for a hold on the grade as he rolled through the maze of trees. If he had been in his wolf form, maneuverability in this terrain might have been easier. His human hands had no traction and his claws could only do so much.

A few times, he had managed to put his feet underneath him and redirect his fall or right himself so he'd narrowly miss a sinister cutoff. Other times, he collided with a tree that only momentarily paused his uncoordinated descent.

Below in the valley was a narrow portion of the Shenandoah River. Rocks peeked out from the steadily moving current, creating white foaming crests against the clear waters that flowed to the south. The river had cut a route through the mountains, the rise on the opposite side correspondingly steep and difficult to traverse.

Dustin hurried after him, set to either catch his ward or intercept him just before the river. He used the forest to his benefit, launching himself from the trees as he slid upon the dried leaves and leaping over the moss-covered boulders. Soon, this became less about catching Ben and more about saving him. If Ben rolled into the water first, it was likely he would be swept away in the rapids.

Within a moment, however, Ben had caught himself on a sturdy pine. His arms wrapped around its trunk, golden eyes fixed in horror upon some distant point on the side of the mountain. Dustin could see, even from a distance, that he was trembling fiercely. His bare feet shook as if he had just clawed his way out of a frozen lake. But his open, panting, terror-stricken countenance told him enough.

This was Ben, not the wolf. The wolf wouldn't have been this scared. Even if it was, it wouldn't have displayed it in such a human way.

Dustin closed the distance, but for fear of startling him, he stayed back a few yards, allowing Ben time to adjust and cope. He remembered what it was like to awaken from the beast's hold in a new environment, with questions and confusion fogging his mind. Once more, he considered Ben to be a privileged man. He had a mentor. He didn't need to search for one as Darren had to, nor did he have to stumble upon one by sheer dumb luck as Dustin did.

"I know you're scared," Dustin began, hoping his attempt at true consolation wouldn't be taken as a meaningless platitude. "But I can assure you that everything is going to be okay."

Ben's head slowly turned to look at him. It took a few seconds before the dawning of recognition came. "I... I know you... Don't I?"

Dustin nodded. "We met at Sharpsburg. I gave you some hardtack... Do you remember?"

Once more, it took a while for Ben to register. "Dustin."

He took another step closer, but that was enough to bring on the flood of memories. Ben jerked and flew into hysterics. He let go of the tree, inspected his body and his arm, looked around him, and then to Dustin.

"Where am I?" he demanded in a panic.

"You're in the mountains," Dustin answered. "You're safe."

"My company... My regiment... Where...?"

He thought it odd that Ben's first thoughts wouldn't even naturally go to the fact that he could now hear and smell for miles or feel that wild stirring. His first questions were about his fellow soldiers.

"It's a long story, but I need you to – "

When Dustin took another step forward, Ben's lips peeled back in an impulsive growl that even shocked him. It wasn't long before Ben began to understand his situation a little more plainly.

"What happened to me?" he brokenly questioned, one hand gripping at the front of his uniform, as if it were too snug over his chest.

"Again, it's a long story. But you have to trust me that it's all going to be all right."

Ben shook his head in disbelief. "You did this, didn't you?" He offered up his arm. "You did somethin' to me."

Now, he remembered more. Dustin held up his hands in a placating manner, ready to pat down the steadily mounting flames of distress. "I did, but – "

"What did you do?" Ben screamed, anxiety displaced by that rage Dustin had witnessed over the last few days.

Another step closer would further provoke him, so Dustin stayed rooted in his place. "It's a – "

"Don't give me that horseshit! It's not a long story. Tell me what you did!"

Dustin, whether out of admiration for this new spunk in his friend or out of a wish for him to stop bellowing, answered coolly. "I turned you into a werewolf to save your life."

Ben's jaw went slack. "A werewolf?"

"To save your life," Dustin repeated just as flatly. "You're welcome."

Golden eyes slowly lowered to look once more to his hands and body that seemed unchanged, at least in his outward appearance. The claws had retracted, leaving dull and dirty nails in their place. The only thing left to return to normal were his eyes, but the longer they talked, they refused to dim.

"A werewolf?" Ben echoed, still skeptic.

"Do you remember the last few days at all? The shack, the meat, the – "

"Chains," Ben interrupted. "Yes... I remember now... A werewolf."

The word became more confident now, as if Ben were already accepting this new life. But Dustin wouldn't hope for it.

"Yes, a werewolf."

His fist tightened over the fabric of his coat, pressing the knuckles into his chest. "So, this thing I feel in me is..."

"That's the wolf," Dustin said. "It's far more complex than I can explain in one sitting. Even I don't understand it completely, but you'll get used to it."

It took him months to fully grasp the many facets of what it meant to be a loup-garou, to be both man and beast. It was too much to think that Ben could even be grateful at first, which is why what he had to say next came as no surprise.

"You should've let me die," Ben growled. "Who the hell gave you the right to do this to someone?"

Dustin dropped his hands, at least glad that he wouldn't have to continue his efforts to convince him of the truth. "No one. You were close to dying."

"You thought you saved me?" Ben asked, rising to his feet. "You thought doing this to me was a good alternative? You thought givin' me this... this thing was better than dyin'?"

"Anything's better than dying," Dustin retorted angrily, ready to defend his decisions. "Would you rather be food for the worms on that battlefield? Because that's where I would have left you."

A kind of quiet rage came over Ben as he glared at the man who claimed to be his preserver. "Do you have any idea what you've just done to me?" Every word dripped with a kind of loathing that Dustin had only ever felt toward himself. It was strange to be on the receiving end of it from another person. "I hate you. I barely know you and I hate you."

There was not a hint of pity or remorse left in Dustin. He only shrugged wryly. "It wouldn't be the first time someone said that, and I'm sure it won't be the last. You may hate me, but right now I'm the only man on this mountain who can teach you how to live with the wolf. You can run away and try to figure it out for yourself, or you can be the open-minded man I met around the campfire and let me explain everything."

Ben's chest heaved as he tried to sort through the war of emotions that swirled behind his eyes. He was smart, probably smarter than half the Confederate army. If he knew what was good for him, he'd choose the right path, the one that could eventually take him home.

CHAPTER 6

OCTOBER, 1862 - ARMY OF NORTHERN VIRGINIA

The groans of the injured as they were pulled to their feet reverberated in Noah's ears as he looked through the mass of bodies and suffering men in the field hospital. The stench of sweat and gangrenous flesh could be smelled yards away from the collection of tents. The wounded from the battle were receiving the care they needed, but for some it wasn't enough. Limbs that were supposed to be healed by now from minor cuts or shallow bullet holes were now piled in a morbid heap at the end of the surgeon's tent. Noah refused to look at them as he passed through to look for his friend.

He hadn't seen Ben in days. Not since they all rushed to the tent on the edge of the encampment that night. The Alabamian from Hill's division didn't seem nefarious in any way. Noah had no reason to doubt the man's intentions to make sure Ben became well again. The thought that he would run away with the private had never entered his mind.

It was far more likely that since the army went its separate ways after reentering Virginia, the man would have had to return to his unit and leave Ben in the care of the doctors within his own brigade. But the longer he searched, the more his heart sank into his new boots. Along with his new commission came certain privileges, though he wished he could have passed them down through his fellow soldiers. So many went without new clothes or extra rations, which is why he loaned the use of his tent to Ben while he recovered from whatever wound or illness had befallen him. The Alabamian wouldn't even allow another doctor to examine his friend, so Noah was still in the dark about what had happened at Sharpsburg.

The regiment was moving out again, still routed from their defeat and making damn well sure that McClellan wasn't following their retreat. There was talk of turning to the East, toward Richmond and Fredericksburg, but orders and reasons were only carried down so far in the chain of command.

He spotted the thick, dark mustache and goatee of Dr. James Cotten as he finished tying off the new dressing on a soldier's arm. Noah hurried toward him, being careful not to trip over the discarded tin cups and bowls full of bloody water on the ground where they had been left.

"Dr. Cotten," Noah said, grabbing the man's blood-stained sleeve. "Was a soldier from Company G admitted a few days ago. Blonde hair, complainin' of a fever. He's about our age, from Heard County."

It hadn't occurred to him that so many men their age were being put into positions that might have been too much for them. Cotten couldn't have been a day over twenty-three, same as him, and yet he was expected to tend and care for hundreds, maybe thousands of wounded men alongside the other doctors and assistant surgeons appointed to their division. Likewise, Noah was fairly new in his appointment, but scarcely knew how to act. He couldn't imagine moving up to third sergeant or even lieutenant during the course of this war. God willing, the war wouldn't last long enough for him to have to bear such insignia on his collar and sleeve coat.

The doctor's close-set eyes looked to him, slightly frazzled by the strange question. "I see a lot of boys your age come through here. You expect me to remember one with a fever?" he asked, raking his hands through tousled locks.

Impatient for an answer, he did his best to describe the quiet, sometimes timid farm boy from Franklin, whom he had talked with plenty of times in the course of the war thus far. His wife's family were more acquainted with his in-laws, but they hadn't been thrown together until Jefferson Davis called for his first batch of troops.

Dr. Cotten's mustache and beard moved in such a way to tell Noah that he was grimacing behind all that wiry hair. "Sorry. I don't recall seein' him."

One of the assistant surgeons called out to the doctor and he dashed away without another word. Noah, despite his rank, was gently pushed aside by a pair of men carrying an amputee soldier upon a stretcher, and he knew then that he wasn't going to find Ben in all this mess.

He left the hospital sector of the camp and decided to check one more time amongst the rest of Company G. If they were to move out one more time, he didn't want the boy to be left behind or be accused of deserting. Everyone knew the price of desertion.

But instead of seeing the golden hair of his friend, he saw someone else who could help him just as well. Through the rushing of gray and butternut uniforms breaking down tents and packing up what little they had into their haversacks, he spotted the Alabamian. He walked briskly, with purpose and confidence, making his way straight for Lieutenant Colonel George Carmical's tent, which was in the process of being released from its stakes.

Noah urged his tired legs forward to intercept him, but the man was abnormally quick to weave through the soldiers and officers in his path. There was an otherworldly look in his green eyes that Noah had noticed the moment they first met. A vastness and wisdom that seemed uncommon for someone his age. Everyone else, from private to commissioned officer, no matter how seasoned they were in battle, still retained a quality of rawness about them, as if they were still unsure of what their role in this war truly was.

This Alabamian, though, reminded him a lot of Ben in some ways. He seemed to understand the full-scope of what exactly was happening to this country, and like some cowards, wanted no part of it. That understanding made Noah skeptic and he wanted to call him a spy for all his cunning looks, but he had no evidence.

The man reached Lieutenant Colonel Carmical before Noah could and stopped dead in his tracks. For several minutes, the two talked and Noah edged closer to the encampment, hoping to catch a word or two.

Seeing the Alabamian and the colonel side by side, Noah was once more dumbstruck by how this war was making boys into men. George was scarcely into his second decade of life as he was being given command of an entire infantry regiment. The sleeves, though usually baggy and loose around the elbows due to the style of the day, seemed even bigger on the lieutenant colonel's frame as he faced the private who was at least half a dozen years older than him.

Noah was drawn from his mission for just a moment to reflect on this trend. All around, he saw boys who bore a variety of ranks, all of them trying to make light of this upending of the army. But he saw the truth behind their eyes, just as clearly as he saw the truth in the Alabamian's. They were scared as rabbits and half starved. The battle at Sharpsburg toughened some, while it broke others.

When he turned back, refusing to look deeper into what this war was doing to the men of his country, the Alabamian was gone and George was standing alone with his hat off. His stare had drifted to the darkening sky with a silent supplication. Noah feared the worst and came forward to pose his questions.

"No, I don't know where we're goin'," the young lieutenant colonel said before Noah could even open his mouth.

"I wasn't gonna ask about that, sir. I was gonna ask what you and that man were talkin' about."

George looked to him and, upon recognizing him as the sergeant from Company G, Ben's company, he sighed. "He was just givin' me a report about one of your boys. Ben Myers died a couple of days ago. The fever got the better of him. Private Keith buried him up near the mountains... I trust you can inform the family, since he was part of your company."

Noah closed his eyes and bowed his head, his fears finally validated.

George gave his apologies, along with another letter that was put into Ben's care before he died, now entrusted to Noah to deliver safely. It was addressed to John Beck's family, another of his fellow soldiers who had fallen at Sharpsburg.

His superior officer then turned to direct some of his staff, leaving Noah with his grief.

Death, especially after what they had seen at Sharpsburg, was a constant in war. It shouldn't have struck him so hard. They'd lost plenty since this campaign had begun. They honored each of their fallen brothers as well as they could, but with so much tragedy and so many lives lost in this conflict, it was impossible to give each of them a just veneration for their service and devotion.

Noah passed a hand over his eyes, remembering the long fireside chats he and Ben had shared, talking about lofty things that he'd never expected a farm boy to know about. Things about life, love, and what it meant to give themselves to a cause like the one they fought for.

A few men ran past him, canteens and haversacks banging against their hips as they went to join up with their company, bringing Noah out of his daze. The war and the army would stop for no one, not even a brave and gentle soul like the one they had just lost.

Blue Ridge Mountains

It might have been an impertinent thing to do, but Dustin reasoned it was better to let them all know that Ben Myers was dead, rather than let them believe he was a coward and had run from his post. His family might have preferred the story that he died as a result of his wounds than the report that he had gone missing without leave. Soldiers left the army all the time for a few days. French Leave, he heard them call it. But this would last far more than a few days. If Ben's incompetency was any indication of how long it would take him to become accustomed to his new life as a loup-garou, it might take nearly a year or two.

It also might have been cruel to make Ben sit on the uppermost peak of the mountain range, naked as a jaybird and shivering from the cold autumn wind that made the orange and auburn leaves drop in heaps. He at least provided the young man a blanket to keep warm, but Dustin couldn't help but feel a little guilty that he was clothed while Ben was not.

"How much longer?" Ben growled, that sneer seemingly a permanent fixture upon his face these days.

Dustin turned to look at the sunset sky. "Not much longer," he said. "You should be feeling the pains pretty soon."

"And this is gonna happen every month?" he asked, his voice quivering as a cold wind seeped through his blanket.

Dustin nodded. "Every month."

That might not have been a consolation to the young loup-garou at all. After all he had tried to tell Ben since he first regained human consciousness, the boy was not enthusiastic about his new life in the least. Dustin didn't quite expect him to be, so the string of colorful southern expletives wasn't a surprise. Apart from educating him in the ways of the loup-garou and training him as often as they could, the two never spoke. There was never a kind of casual, personal conversation between them and it unnerved Dustin. He hadn't envisioned them to be the best of pals instantly, but there was a level of assumed respect from his pupil that had yet to show itself. Ben still hated him with a kind of passion that he hadn't expected. It made him wonder how difficult it would be to break him once he completed his first transformation.

The last two or so weeks were spent in basic training. Dustin had never personally trained another loup-garou, but he put Ben through what drills he remembered from his first months with Darren. Running, jumping, climbing, and of course the finer points of hunting, since they were limited on supplies and the ability to go into town for food. But the fresh meat they found in the forest was far better than the stinking, fetid excuse for provisions that the army offered them.

The mountains and valley were copious in the way of ample game for two loups-garous, but Ben's hunger would prove to completely wipe out the squirrel population of the entire north-west district of Virginia if he continued at this rate. From the moment Dustin allowed him to hunt at his leisure, confident that he wouldn't try to run again, Ben was on the side of the mountains and running after the rodents for hours. He was sure that was why the forest seemed so quiet nowadays.

Something Dustin had become aware of over the last few weeks was a deep, visceral tie between himself and Ben. They hadn't even formed the pack bond yet, but already he could tell they shared something between their wolves. He couldn't compare it to anything else he had ever known or experienced. It was a lesser, less potent pull than the one created when Darren broke him and became his alpha, but far stronger than a simple feeling of affinity with a close friend or relative. He cared for Ben as much as he cared for himself, and perhaps that was why he pushed the young soldier all the harder to become a better loup-garou.

One thing troubled him even more than this inexplicable tie with the soldier. Even when Ben was calm, as he was now, the golden eyes of the wolf remained.

They had never gone away. It unsettled Dustin to see the wolf in the man, always there, just waiting to burst loose. But it never did.

It became another facet of his appearance that he didn't even seem to be aware of. Dustin was the only one who could see and worry over them as he did. And as long as he could help it, he wouldn't tell Ben. With luck, they would go away with time and more training. When the anger in him died, so would this looming threat of the wolf.

He looked to the sunset and marveled at the glaring splash of orange and crimson that draped across the sky, skirted by the steely gray and blue mountain peaks in the distance. Patches of mist blanketed the hills and treetops, giving the landscape a blurred silhouette. How could such beauty and serenity exist on the earth while men were blowing one another to pieces just a hundred miles away?

Twilight would come swiftly over the region, and so would Ben's first shift. That was why he couldn't bring himself to appreciate the beauty of nature as much as he would like, knowing what would come at any moment now.

When it did come, when Ben first gasped and convulsed under the immense pain that Dustin remembered all too well from his first time, he had to force himself to watch. Ben bent over his lap, pressing his face into the ground as the searing heat would swell from his stomach and through his limbs.

He cursed under his breath and attempted to stretch out his arms and legs, thrashing upon the ground as he tried to find some comfort. There would be none. Not until blessed darkness overcame him and blocked out all memory of the transformation. At what point that would happen was different for every new loup-garou. Sometimes he would remember the dark hair sprouting from his skin or see the muzzle extend from his face. Some wouldn't recall how their hands grew rough pads on their palms or how their spine would extend into a tail down their backside.

Darren was lucky to only remember the pain at first before blacking out. Dustin remembered so much more during his first shift in Ireland, that first night he was to spend with his wife, Cassandra. But how he wished he could have forgotten her screams and the way it felt to have her flesh beneath his claws.

Dustin shrugged out of his suspenders and pulled his shirt over his head to ready himself for his own inundation of anguish. It would take him less time to change into his loup-garou form than Ben, but he struggled to keep himself attentive to his friend's condition. Anything could go wrong, as he'd learned while under Darren's tutelage in France. Especially for one loup-garou who was so unwilling as Ben. The thought occurred to him that they should have changed in the valley where he didn't have to worry about high cliffs.

After several agonizing moments, both were shifted into their half-man, half-wolf forms. Ben's pelt gleamed a raven black, while Dustin's featured a marbling of brown with darker, distinct markings across his muzzle and chest. With the coming decades, he knew he'd see more tan and white variations appear in his coat to resemble his alpha's fur. The older and more experienced a loup-garou became, the more it showed in their wolven forms.

Dustin, also, could be in complete control of himself during the shift, unlike Ben, which was all the more reason to keep him contained upon the mountain. With his size and unmatched strength, Dustin could easily dominate Ben in the initial breaking. All loups-garous needed this initial taming. Any who went without it were wild, rogue, and dangerous, just as Dustin had been during his first shift.

Ben rose, the wool blanket falling from his massive shoulders. Dustin braced himself, ears forward and tail erect to ready himself for the fight that would come. Darren had told him once how difficult it could be to conduct a breaking without help or support from another pack member. He didn't have such luxuries here in the wilderness.

The younger loup-garou looked and locked stares with Dustin, two sets of golden eyes meeting. At first, Ben didn't seem bothered by this show of mild aggression and alertness. There was none of the usual hostility that came from an untamed loup-garou. He only snorted and turned to walk away, uncaring of Dustin's presence at all.

He wouldn't get away so easily.

Dustin sprinted forward and blocked his path. Only now did Ben bristle with rage and growl. Instead of opening the fight, however, he simply turned again and walked in another direction to avoid a clash. Too alarmed and confused by this turn of events, Dustin wasn't sure how to react. This wasn't how he had behaved when Darren broke him. He had been unruly, brutal, and nearly killed his future alpha. Ben wasn't interested in a fight whatsoever, but that didn't mean he could go without being broken.

He lunged for Ben, digging his claws and fangs into his back. The loup-garou let out a cry of pain and spun to buck Dustin off. The struggle began and as darkness fell, the night was filled with the sound of two warring beasts upon the mountaintop.

Ben continually tried to run, slipping out of his grasp at every given chance, while Dustin forced him to stay. He wouldn't let him go until the loup-garou was whimpering for release and submitted to his dominance. And unlike when Darren tamed Dustin, Ben didn't so much as retaliate with his own innate power that came with being a loup-garou.

They all possessed differing degrees of dominance, ranging from alpha - who possessed the most - to omegas - who possessed none at all. From what Dustin observed, Ben might have been the latter, an omega. Or he wasn't experienced enough yet to know how to wield this gift.

Whether out of a desire to appease Dustin, or a true effort to submit, Ben exposed his stomach with his tail tucked between his wolf-like legs while two human-like arms held Dustin at bay. Ears folded back and the shrill whine silenced Dustin's vicious snarls.

He latched his jaws around Ben's throat until he could feel the vibrations of that whine in his teeth. Once he was satisfied and convinced that this wasn't a ploy to get Dustin to ease off his attack, Ben was free.

The younger loup-garou curled onto his side and followed Dustin's pacing with a pair of frightened eyes, stricken immobile by the fear of upsetting his superior again. But he couldn't allow Ben to stay so fearful. He licked at his muzzle, as sign of amnesty and forgiveness between their wolves. At this, he responded back in kind and a bit of vitality returned to him.

It was a far easier breaking than Dustin predicted after being the sole focus of Ben's undimming hatred and loathing. He had half-expected to fail and work all night just to keep Ben from running off to terrorize the towns and farms in the valley. Instead of pondering on this turn of attitudes, Dustin counted his blessings and was glad that the worst part of their training was complete. All that was left were the months of drills and schooling Ben on the finer points of how to be a wolf in human skin, a beast amongst the civilized mob. As long as those golden eyes could be forced back, Ben shouldn't have had any problem with reintegrating into society or returning to his family in Georgia after leaving Alabama. At least, that's what Dustin hoped.

CHAPTER 7

Abigail stared unfeelingly out the front parlor window, sitting upright in her chair as the rest of the family visited behind her. Her eyes were riveted upon the drive that led up to the veranda and burning as she had neglected to blink for much longer than she was used to.

Phillip, Ben's older brother, had come home for a short Christmas furlough, glad to be a little further south and away from the fighting in Tennessee. Like Missy's beau, he served with the nineteenth Georgia infantry, proudly sporting the title of a member of the "Heard Guard", a name that had been given to the regiment upon its formation.

His return home made her hope again. Hope that Ben would come walking up the drive, kicking up a bit of Georgia clay with his usual shambling walk. She envisioned him climbing the steps as he did in the days when they secretly courted under her father's disapproving gaze.

These hopes were founded upon a single word. "Supposed".

The newspaper that her father brought that day at the end of September only listed Ben as "Supposed to be killed at Sharpsburg". She had seen this kind of listing before beside the names of other men they knew in the county. They would be listed as "Supposed to be killed" and would show up weeks or months later. The only way a man was declared dead or missing was by the word of a fellow soldier who knew them, or the manifestation of a body for the family to bury. Ben could have simply been wounded and looked to be dead. Then, he could have been picked up by a Yankee soldier or perhaps rescued by a civilian who helped tend to the dead on the battlefields.

There was too much room to speculate and nothing for certain. For all they knew, Ben was alive and well somewhere and the papers had lied. No one came to know what she had harbored in her heart, until the day when her mother brought home three black outfits. One for her, one for Mrs. Myers, and one for Abigail.

But she refused the garments, exclaiming, "Don't you dare bring any of that black crepe near me! I will not mourn! He's not dead! He's not dead, until I see a body!"

They all, even her father-in-law, tried to convince her that people would talk if they saw that she was the only one of the Rider or Myers family who didn't show her mourning. But they didn't understand. None of them did. They didn't know how she and Ben were bound together, not just in love, but in a deep and soulful friendship. If she didn't believe him to be dead, if she didn't feel it in her spirit, then he was alive and she wouldn't mourn no matter what her family or society said.

The conversation behind her went silent and the tiny gurgle of her infant son brought her back into the present.

How she wished she had told Ben about their son, Turner. But not because she lamented that Ben had died without knowing he had a son – because he wasn't dead. She regretted not penning the letter that she was pregnant, because it might have taken him away from the fighting. If he had known that Turner would be born around September, then he might not have been at Sharpsburg where he was "supposed to be killed". He might have tried harder to request that furlough he had talked about once in their correspondence. He might have been safe at home and been there for the birth of his son.

Instead, she wanted to keep it a secret. In a hushed condemnation that she didn't dare utter around her mother, she damned herself for her silly womanly sentiment. She wanted to surprise him when he came home for Christmas, while the camp wintered somewhere in Virginia. The thought that she didn't want to worry him about her condition had also come to mind, so she wrote to him about other things, like the plantation and the gossip around Franklin.

"Darlin'," her mother said softly, "come away from the window."

Abigail didn't want to. Ben could come up the drive at any moment and she would miss it. She had to be ready, but her common sense broke through the hysteria and she rose from the ill-padded chair to join them.

It was Phillip's turn to hold his nephew and the momentary responsibility did him some good. After being in the war for only a year and a half, the man who had become as much of a brother to her as he was to Ben had hardened somehow.

When she was a girl, Abigail had often lamented the fact that she would grow up to be a lady. The life of a soldier was far more preferable. However, after seeing the transformation in Phillip, and hearing the bits of stories that were often too gruesome to tell in the company of a woman, she gave up those ideas and thanked the Lord that she was not conscripted with the rest of the Confederacy.

There was a saying that the army was for soldiers, not warriors. Before secession, Abigail thought they had always been one and the same. But she quickly learned that this was not the case. Those who could take orders, those who were malleable to authority, were soldiers who would dive into whizzing bullets and defy their survival instincts for a noble cause. These men - men like Phillip - rose quickly through the ranks and served as the backbone of the Confederacy. They were the ones who paid the highest price for southern independence.

With Turner in his arms, his uniform coat laid across the back of the sofa, a ghost of Phillip's former self returned. His eyes no longer seemed hollow and vacant, his face lifted with a soft smile as he stared down into – what he believed – to be the last shred of his little brother on God's green earth. Even if Abigail didn't agree with such a belief, she wouldn't take this subtle joy away from Phillip for anything.

He might have been the most cheered one out of the bunch. Ben's parents, still solemn and passive after hearing the news about their youngest son, sat across from their employer, willing to make conversation because of their long-standing friendship. But Abigail could sense that they would have rather not been there.

Mrs. Myers had wanted to flee to the north to find Ben's body and bring it back. After much convincing, she gave up on the notion. Even with the two armies camped for the winter, it was a long journey to Virginia and there was no guarantee that he would be found. Ever since that day, the woman had lost a bit of her starch. She was no longer the upright, strong, dependable planter's wife she had once been. The death and reality of this war for southern independence had broken her into a soft-spoken, and inert creature. Abigail favored her old mother-in-law over this replacement. At least then, she would have known where she stood in Mrs. Olivia Myers' great opinion of the world and those within it.

Mr. Jedediah Myers, on the other hand, bore the loss a little more bravely than his wife. They had all known what would happen when their boys went to war. They knew they would be shot at and forced to live under less than ideal situations. But they were the Myers boys, raised to work hard and endure adversities. They had also believed, like so many southerners, that the war would end within a few weeks. Now it had been over a year and a half with still no sign of a treaty or surrender agreement.

Abigail sat beside her mother and folded her hands neatly in her lap as the talk resumed. Her father stood a short distance from the pair of sofas, smoking what little was left of his tobacco in his pipe. Such indulgences were becoming more and more scarce, but on this particular day, he felt the need to treat himself. Upon Mr. Myers' arrival, he had offered some to the farmer, but he refused a little begrudgingly, as if he thought the relief tobacco would bring was necessary as well, but refrained anyway for whatever personal reason.

It wasn't until a few moments later when her father finally broke the news.

"When spring comes," Mr. Rider began, "I'll be joining up with the thirty-fifth infantry."

A stunned silence fell over the parlor as all eyes turned to him.

"As will I," said the farmer as he kept his gaze upon the rug between the sofas.

A heaviness settled in Abigail's stomach. The master of the plantation and his best workhand were joining the army. Her mother erupted in shrill protests and exclamations against her husband. She demanded reasons or some explanation as to the train of thought that had led them to such a foolish decision.

"This is a war for young men," Mrs. Rider insisted. "Let them fight it!"

Her husband replied calmly with, "They have generals serving who are older than I am. Jeff Davis has opened the enlistment age to forty-five and if I wait another year, I'll have to lie in order to serve. And besides, if they call for another conscription, I'll have to leave anyway. Nowadays, only men with twenty slaves can get out of conscription and I'm not going to stoop to such a low just to get out of defending my country. The war could end soon and I want to do my part."

Abigail's mouth hung open as she stared incredulously at her father. He had never sounded more irrational, more patriotic, or more childish.

Mrs. Myers was no less distressed, but chose to quietly beseech her husband with imploring looks and hushed words instead of boisterous shouts. It was as if both women had forgotten themselves in the moment and behaved as the young girls who begged their beaus not to enlist. Only Abigail and Phillip remained silent out of pure shock. In the uproar, Turner wailed in his uncle's arms and beat at the air with tiny fists, wishing for the noise to cease.

Her little boy echoed her sentiments exactly, but it wasn't her place to requisite anything from her father like a promise to stay home. Abigail would let her mother do that as she went to take the baby from Phillip.

The tortured look returned to Phillip's eyes and she pitied him, because he was the only one on the plantation who knew what kind of hell for which these two old men were bound. And just like the boys at the front who had signed up the moment war was declared, there would be no swaying their decisions. They were like children who eagerly lined up at the enlistment offices, hoping they would have the chance to kill a Yankee before the war was over. Like them, they would fall in with the ranks and taste the bitterness of combat first-hand.

As she left the room, she turned to give one more glance to her family. Her parents were now face-to-face, still arguing with the bull-headed dispositions that she had inherited from them. Her father continually spoke of some delusional duty to his family and country, while her mother suggested safer alternatives, such as serving in the hospitals or becoming part of the home guard that could defend Georgia from within its state boundaries. At least then, he would be closer to home and away from the heavy fighting.

Ben's mother and father, the complete opposites, were now in one another's arms with Mrs. Myers muffling her sobs against her husband's coat. She had accepted that nothing in the world could dissuade her man from leaving her behind, while Mrs. Rider hung on until her knuckles were white.

Before her was the portrait of a family torn apart, of a conflict that had come sweeping into the hallowed sanctum of her beloved parlor. This war had poisoned everything she held dear, and it seemed determined to steal away those she loved.

Her gaze fell to her baby boy's scrunched face as he wailed and cried for some peace. She couldn't bear to see those eyes, Ben's eyes, glistening with unshed tears. Turner was so much like his father already, in both temperament and appearance. This sweet, usually quiet, infant would grow up to be just as handsome and meek as Ben. God willing, he would never have to play a part in a war like this one.

Abigail bounced him in her arms, shushing him as she made her way down the hall and away from the angry adults. When shushing didn't work, she began to hum and gently sing the only song that soothed him when he was in this state.

"*The years creep slowly by, Lorena. Snow is on the grass again; the sun's low down the sky, Lorena. The frost gleams where the flowers have been; but the heart throbs on as warmly now, as when the summer days were nigh'...*"

She didn't have the heart to finish the verse. Turner hiccupped and fell silent as it became his mother's turn to swallow back sorrowful tears.

Blue Ridge Mountains

Ben stared out of the glaringly white valley, the slate gray sky stretching from one horizon to the other and thick with the clouds that dumped the snow flurries over the mountains. He sat upon the rock ledge, the snow mounding upon his shoulders in the same way the evergreen branches were weighted down. Other trees, who had lost their leaves in the fall, stood like barren skeletons, their trunks sprouting out of the thick white layer of powder that covered the landscape.

The view was certainly pretty, he thought to himself. But it couldn't come close to home.

The cold seeped through his clothes and numbed his feet to the point that he couldn't feel below his knees anymore. He hardly cared. He knew, from the talk about werewolves he and Dustin had over the last few months, he would never lose a toe or limb to frostbite. Nor would he contract pneumonia. He'd never be sick again a day in his life. The wolf, that thing that now dwelled inside of him, wouldn't allow it.

If anything, Ben's rage kept him warm. He lived every day of this new existence hating Dustin for what he had done. He hated what he had become as keenly as he missed his home and wife. Not a moment went by when he didn't think of Abigail. The only consolation, the only hope he clung to was the promise the he could return to her when he had a little more training. When exactly that would be was all Dustin's decision.

Unfortunately, his homesickness couldn't match the apprehension he felt toward the idea of returning to Georgia. Months ago, he had wanted nothing more than to board the next train bound for Atlanta and walk all the way to Franklin if he had to. Shoes or no shoes. Now, knowing what he was, knowing the kind of devastation he could inflict upon his family, Ben wasn't sure if he wanted to go home just yet. Dustin had contaminated those longings with stories of werewolves who killed and hurt the ones they loved without ever knowing it until the dust had cleared and the man had shifted back into his most natural form. Ben didn't want that for Abigail, for his family, or anyone else in Franklin. That's the only reason he hadn't run away. There was still much to learn, but leaving Dustin would only prolong this education, and he couldn't afford making a mistake.

So every day for the last few terrible months, he had been drilled as he had in the army. He woke up to the same tasks, the same rigid schedule of running and climbing, until Ben was sick of it. If he had to choose which was worse – werewolf training or infantry training – he would have gladly gone back into the army, even if it meant he would be shot a thousand times. At least in the army, he could shoot at a man and feel a sense of accomplishment when that man fell down dead. But training to be a proper werewolf who was worthy of reentering society was much harder and much less rewarding.

According to Dustin - who failed to effectively encourage - Ben was improving. But he knew better. The only thing he was getting better at was hiding his disappointment when he failed time and time again. If he didn't get better at controlling his extraordinary speed and strength, he might never return to Abigail.

Then there were those days, those dark and miserable days, when he reflected on what had happened a few times already. Ben had shifted into the beast that possessed him and gave him these abilities. It wasn't the pain that bothered him, because he had experienced the worst a man could suffer. It wasn't the hunger that made him crave meat or want to kill everything that so much as moved out of the corner of his eye. It's the knowledge that he became something that would horrify his family.

In those long hours between training sessions, hunting trips, and the less than restorative sleep, Ben often slipped into these moods where he barely blinked or moved a muscle.

On the frigid winds, he could hear the noises from faraway towns and villages in the Shenandoah Valley. Regiments were wintered in those towns, enjoying this break in the fighting with the loyal civilian Confederates who lived there. Some would be with their families for holiday furlough. Others, who had families too far away, would enjoy the company of pretty girls and families who wanted to honor the cause by inviting soldiers to their dinner tables. There would be balls held, despite the cold. Satin and silk dresses would spin in a flurry of dazzling colors as bands played songs to enliven the hearts of belles and gentlemen throughout what was proudly called "The Breadbasket of the Confederacy".

Ben would have rather been there, in those warm barns or by the fireside visiting with some stranger than sitting on this ridge by himself and only listening to these festivities from miles and miles away. It would be a lonely Christmas, because Ben didn't count Dustin as company. Not the way his family or his old regiment would have been for him. And he certainly didn't count the wolf. If he could help it, he'd never give a second thought to it unless the circumstances warranted his consideration for the wild spirit that had ruined his life.

Interrupting the steady stream of music, laughter, and the reduced din of wildlife noises that surrounded Ben, came the crunch of footfalls in the pristine snow behind him. The slight tingling in the back of his skull broke through the gripping numbness, one of the first signs that another werewolf was approaching. He despised the feeling and all it meant for him and his situation.

Dustin sat down heavily beside him, his legs and lap disappearing beneath the snow. He grumbled some snarky comment about the cold, but Ben scarcely grasped the words. The man, whom he thought he could call a friend after their first meeting, the night before the battle, tried so hard to lighten everything. Sarcasm and remarks like the one he had just made came frequently enough to make Ben scream.

Before Sharpsburg, before the war, he actively looked for excuses to smile and laugh. When he got his first taste of war, of bloodshed and violence, it was enough to make him sick. The only bit of sunshine was left in Georgia, and the thought of home was the only sustaining thought through every battle and engagement. Now, it was what drove him through training and helped him to endure the company of this man that might as well have been as bad as a Yankee. The war had ruined his life, and so had Dustin.

Several moments passed, but Dustin didn't fill the silence between them. He said nothing about the voices drifting up from the towns, nor the way the sun began to steadily sink below the westward mountains. The gray sky darkened and the brilliantly colored sunset didn't burst across the horizon as it usually did.

"I think," Dustin began, "once the snow melts, we can make our way south."

Ben turned, loosening the packed snow on his head and shoulders. Some patches slid down the back of his shirt and dropped to his thighs. "I'm not improvin'," he stated unfeelingly.

Dustin shrugged, as if that didn't matter in the least anymore. "There's plenty of time to improve while we're making our way to Alabama."

A snapping fire came to Ben's eyes and Dustin must have seen it. "Alabama? Don't ya mean Georgia?"

Ben imagined that once his training was complete in the mountains, he was free to go on to be with his family again. Then, Dustin would do whatever it was he wanted to do before he inconvenienced his own self with a conscience.

Dustin seemed to struggle with the words at first, but then he seemed to give up on saying it in the most pacifying way possible. Instead, he was blunt. "I'm not an alpha. I may have been able to break you the first time you shifted, but I know I'm not doing right by you in this training. My alpha is in Alabama and he can help you."

That fire burned hot and Ben worked to bank it before he tried to throw Dustin off the mountain. "Maybe ya shoulda thought about that before ya did any of this."

The man looked hard into Ben's eyes and nodded. "I should have."

The words were a damp to his anger and he was more easily able to rein in the wolf. It was the closest thing to an apology Dustin had ever given him.

Ben looked back to the valley and steadily waning light. Soon, night would close in around the mountains and with this cloud cover, it'd be as dark as the inside of a hog's stomach. The snow wouldn't reflect back the moonlight in that mystical, silvery way it always did. Ben had never experienced snow before joining the army, but he had to admit that despite the bitter cold, it made the countryside sparkle at night.

He thought back to the maps Abigail had shared with him when they were younger. Heard County shared a border with Alabama. It wouldn't be wrong to assume that they would pass through his hometown, or at least close to it. If he was any better by then, he could sneak away from Dustin for just a few hours to see Abigail...

"I heard President Lincoln's got some big plans for the Confederacy in January," Dustin said suddenly, giving one more try at bridging the distance between them. "He called it the Emancipation Proclamation. It's going to free all the slaves in the territories that are at war with the United States."

Ben scoffed. "Leave it to a Republican to think he could pull off a cock and bull move like that."

He didn't have to look to Dustin to know he had elicited a rather strong emotional response from him. "If the president wants to free the slaves, he very well can."

"Not in a state that don't belong to him. He ain't my president, and he ain't the president of the Confederacy. He ain't got no right to take away property from people that ain't citizens of his country."

"So you do think that blacks are property." The softened, disappointed tone was enough to make Ben feel a little sheepish for his words.

"I ain't sayin' they deserve to be property. All I'm sayin' is that I don't know a single man who's fightin' to keep his slaves. They're fightin' to keep their rights. I heard my pa's employer talkin' about how the south's lookin' to free the slaves gradually over time anyway. Slavery is dead, but freedom ain't. It never will be. Lincoln's just tryin' to make this war about slavery, so he can get all them pacifist abolitionists to join the army. He's makin' it into some righteous war, instead of what it's really about. The states have a right to govern themselves and decide what's best for them."

"But look at what happened with Kansas," Dustin said, "Their neighbors were tearing each other to pieces over the decision to make their soil free or slave. Congressmen were beating each other senseless in the capital after this whole issue. The government gave them their right to decide and look where it got them. It's like handing the lives of thousands of negroes into the hands of two spoiled children, expecting them to make a compromise. Some things should be left for the government to take care of."

"But the government has no right to govern morality either. That belongs to the state. And you expect a president like Abraham Lincoln, who practically has all the bordered states – includin' Maryland – held hostage to keep them from seceding with the rest of the slave states, to make a better decision? Just look at this proclamation you're talkin' about. Some big time planters don't have any other means to support themselves, except on the backs of slaves. Now, I ain't sayin' it's moral to make a man labor without pay, but it ain't right to take away his livelihood either. Lincoln's tryin' to cripple the south and play dirty instead of winnin' this war the honorable way. He's still tryin' to control a country that doesn't belong to him."

A pause settled before Dustin replied with, "I don't disagree with what you're saying, but I will offer this: not all Yankees are fighting for the slaves. Some are genuinely interested in preserving the Union."

Another snort from Ben riled Dustin enough to hurry his words to explain himself.

"No, really. Listen. Do you know what America means? We're the only democracy that has survived so far. I can't expect you to know what's going on in the rest of the world, but here in America, we have so many rights and privileges that no others have. We have the freedom to speak our opinions, no matter how bold or controversial they are. I've heard about how men from the south would threaten death on anyonr who talked about abolition and that's violating their constitutional rights. We can have a voice in our government, we can remake ourselves into whatever we want. And no offense against Georgia or your mock country, but the Confederacy is trying to destroy that. They seceded just because they didn't like who was elected, because they let the fear of a president who didn't line up with their motives and ideas get the better of them. Now, the world is laughing at America, because we can't keep the Union together. I hear so many Yankees talk about how the south is full of uppity aristocratic planters who enforce their views of race and class just like the English do. The north's fighting for freedom and what freedom means for all people, not just blacks, but the immigrants who come here thinking that we'll offer them opportunities they would have never had in their home country. If we can't keep this Union together, we've got no chance of upholding the constitution or maintaining that freedom for all men."

Ben narrowed his eyes. "What about our freedom? What about the south's freedom to make a new life for themselves apart from the Union? Don't we get that chance too? What about them Copperheads in the north that are havin' their homes burned just because they think this war is a bunch of bull? Didn't they have rights to freedom of speech too? I won't say nothin' about the gentlemen planters who think they're better than any other folks. But when we see that our rights might be endangered by some Republican from Illinois with a hidden agenda, you best believe every mother's son is gonna take up their rifle and fight for what they think is theirs and not the government's. We're fightin' the same war our ancestors did against the English. We aren't tryin' to go against the constitution. We're usin' it's very words to state our cause for secession. Now, Lincoln wants to come and tell us that we don't got that choice to leave? Whose freedom is really bein' stolen here? The south's, the darkies', or the democracy's?"

Dustin had no words, and as if the celebrating soldiers and southerners in the valley were rallying behind Ben's speech, a refrain of "The Bonnie Blue Flag" came lilting from some unseen party. They were quiet for some time, listening to the words about southern patriotism and the cause for which so many were fighting.

"Then here's to our Confederacy, strong we are and brave, like patriots of old, we'll fight, our heritage to save; and rather than submit to shame, to die we would prefer.

So cheer, cheer for the Bonnie Blue Flag that bears a single star. Hurrah! Hurrah! For Southern rights, hurrah! Hurrah for the Bonnie Blue Flag that bears a single star."

The discussion was closed, the first they had engaged in that didn't involve werewolves since that night around the fire. It felt like a lifetime ago. A cry of glee rose from the valley at the close of the song, and Ben wasn't sure if his case had been won or lost in the end. But now, they both were enlightened to one another's beliefs. It might have been enough to recommend Ben to be civil.

When he glanced back to Dustin, the werewolf was still staring so intently that a faint line formed between his brows. It was as if he were studying Ben or searching for something. He had donned this look many times over the last few months.

"Why are ya lookin' at me like that?" Ben finally asked, frustration seasoning his words.

Dustin averted his gaze and shook his head. "Just trying to make sure you're tame. That's all." With that, he rose to his feet and shook off the frost from his trousers. "Are you going to stay out here all night?"

Ben didn't answer him, though he should have fired back with more questions about this alpha in Alabama or probed deeper into Dustin's queer interest in making sure all was right with his new wolfish soul. He sat mute and brushed off the mounds of snow from his shoulders. Expecting Dustin to turn and walk away toward the shack, he was surprised that he stayed.

They should have been closer, and Ben knew it. They should have found some kind of comradery in one another when he realized that Dustin was the only one who could help him. But the blame and innate hatred of the choice that was stolen from him had erected a brick wall between them. And Dustin was the only one willing to dissolve the cement that bound the bricks of that barrier, to break it down and dismantle it so they could be something like the packs he always talked about.

Each time his mentor managed to pull down a bit of his defenses, Ben was quick to putty it all back up. But now, knowing that he would be getting that much closer to home in the springtime, he had no more energy to put one more brick on top of another. He found the strength to stand and walk back with Dustin to the shack, kicking his way through the banks of snow.

CHAPTER 8

MARCH, 1863 - FRANKLIN, GEORGIA

Abigail propped the broomstick against the rough oak column for just a moment so she could refasten the neckerchief across her nose and mouth. The dust had gathered inside her home over the winter months, and though she had made sure the furniture was covered before she went to stay with her mother, that didn't prevent the floors from becoming coated in a fine layer. As she and Miss Peters swept from room to room and down the halls, that veneer of dust upon the floor and baseboards transferred to her dress and every exposed bit of skin. It was a thankful thing that she had remembered to bring the strips of heavy cloth to cover their faces. Otherwise, she'd be sneezing and coughing for days and unable to enjoy the balmy spring weather.

She was also glad that Miss Peters – much to her mother's disapproval – let Abigail borrow one of her rope petticoats so her movements wouldn't be so hindered by her regular hoops. Though, with the added exertion of moving briskly from room to room, she once again regretted that she couldn't simply don a pair of pants like her father.

It wasn't entirely necessary for her to be there. Her mother would have preferred her to stay at home where she could sew or go visiting with the other women in Franklin. Abigail refused her, knowing she couldn't sit and let her mind wander. She couldn't stay in her parents' house or even at her in-laws, not while knowing that all the men of the plantation had gone off to war just a couple of weeks before. Nor could she bear to listen to any of the other women talk about the war. That's all anyone talked about and each time someone mentioned the movements of the army or the state of their new country, she thought of Ben. She thought of him too much as it was, and that familiar prickling of anxiety would torment her stomach and nerves until she was tempted to fall down on her face and weep. He hadn't returned to her yet and it was all she could do to not constantly watch the roads.

Everyone, even Miss Peters, wore mourning gowns for Ben. All except for Abigail. She continued to fight off the black crepe, lace, bonnet, and dress, though more and more women were donning the costumes as the fighting resumed. It seemed that there wasn't a girl in town who wasn't mourning the loss of a brother, father, lover, or family friend. Missy, who had only been in love for a little more than six months, was eager to tie the shackles of mourning about her ankles when word came that her beau from the nineteenth infantry had died of pneumonia in camp the previous month. It wasn't the valiant death that any soldier would have wanted, and it couldn't be glorified like Ben's.

Abigail stamped her foot at the thought, the sharp thud of her worn heel banging against the planks. Then, she took up the broom again and began brushing away the heavy piles off the edge of the porch. A cloud was stirred up and she squinted as her eyes misted from both the thought that Ben could very well be dead, and the particles that flew up into her face.

There hadn't been a word from him for months. He hadn't even come to see her for the holidays, if he had been wishing to surprise her. She waited up at night all through December and January, watching the road from her childhood room, which had been made into a nursery for Turner. No one asked why she looked so haggard and fatigued the next morning at breakfast. They all assumed she had been up thinking of what had become of Ben's body on that lonely battleground in Maryland. But Abigail was still waiting for him to return to her - to return home.

Ben isn't dead, she repeated to herself. *He isn't dead.*

When she had exhausted her short burst of aggression against the dust on the porch, she tramped back into the coolness of the farmhouse. It would be a while before she would live there again, not until Ben came home from the war, but she wanted to at least keep it maintained while she was away.

Her mother and Miss Peters both thought her mad for not boarding up the place and permanently moving in at the Rider Plantation until the time of mourning was over and she could explore her options for remarriage. They said a young and pretty girl such as Abigail shouldn't be in want of suitors when the time came. Suitors, of course, were the last thing upon her mind. Abigail was far more concerned with cleaning each of the rooms from top to bottom and then evicting the family of raccoons that had taken up residency under the house.

She passed by one of the front rooms that, as of yet, held no purpose in the home, and found Miss Peters standing with her back to the entryway. Abigail pinched at the neckerchief and tugged it down to free her mouth.

"Are you all right?" she asked, seeing the way her family's longtime servant stood so motionless in the middle of the room with her own broom caught in the crook of her elbow.

The old woman slowly turned. In her hand was a letter with crooked cursive scrawled upon both sides. A plain, thick envelope was held between two fingers and Abigail could clearly see her name written upon the face of it. She took two bounding steps forward, and then looked to Miss Peters' ghostly white face.

"What is it?" Abigail demanded more urgently, her heart caught in her throat.

The paper trembled in her old nanny's grip before she slowly offered it out to her. Her eyes had gone glossy and wide with shock at what she had just read, inciting both fear and curiosity within Abigail.

"I found it earlier in the hall," Miss Peters murmured. "It was underneath a table. Someone must have slipped it under the door while ya were gone."

She snatched it and devoured the lines of poor grammar and spelling. In the top left-hand corner of the paper, she saw it had been dated for some time in mid-October of the previous year, a full five months earlier.

Mrs. Abigail Myers,

I don't know when my letter will reach you, but it's my hope that I may shed some light on what has become of your husband, Ben. He was part of my company in the seventh Georgia infantry and we were well acquainted with one another by this past September when he disappeared. It's true that we experienced heavy casualties at Sharpsburg, but Ben was not among the dead when we retreated.

At this, Abigail didn't know whether to feel relieved that Ben wasn't dead, or terrified that he was still unaccounted for by the army. She read on.

I believe Ben was wounded, but he was put in the care of a soldier from an Alabama regiment. I didn't know him, but I lent him the use of my tent until Ben was well again. He became stricken with a fever and this man took extraordinarily good care of him, for being a stranger and not even part of his own regiment. I thought it strange that this man should take such an interest in Ben, so I watched them closely. But not close enough. One night when we came back into Virginia, both Ben and the man from the Alabama regiment disappeared. A few days later, I saw the Alabamian talking with Lieutenant Colonel Carmical. He left before I could talk to him and when I asked Carmical what was the matter, he told me with a heavy heart that Ben had died. The Alabamian took the liberty of giving him a proper grave near the mountains. He didn't give any other specific directions that I could relay to you. I am sorry for your loss and I hope you will pass on this news to his family, as they must be worried for him as well. Ben was a brave soldier and a credit to this company, this regiment, and the entire Army of Northern Virginia. He served his country with pride and dignity.

In your services, Sergeant Noah Culpepper

P.S – Enclosed is another letter that I wish you to give to the family of John Beck of Heard County. He was amongst the fallen at Sharpsburg and this letter was given to Carmical by the Alabamian when they spoke.

The room tilted from beneath her feet and Miss Peters wasn't quick enough to catch Abigail before she fell to the floor. Her shaking hands wrinkled the paper, creasing the edges and faded pencil scribblings that tolled this new tragedy.

All the impulsive thoughts and feelings that had been thrust upon her in the first moments when her father came to the house with the newspaper came back to her like a gust of hot wind that knocked her to the ground. Her breaths came short and shallow. Darkness rimmed her vision until she almost couldn't see Miss Peters kneeling beside her.

Abigail fought through the urge to faint, willing herself to stay conscious and face this truth. Ben was dead. Here was the testimony to prove it. Sergeant Culpepper hadn't seen his body, but if the report of this Alabamian could be trusted, then it must be true. She recognized the family name of the letter writer as kin to another family in Franklin, so this could be reliable witness enough.

But what if the stranger was lying? Why was this man so interested in Ben when he fell ill with the fever? Did he do something to Ben? Maybe he took him to a hospital instead of tending to him in the field and he was still alive? Then, why would he have lied to the lieutenant colonel?

Along with forcing herself to stay conscious, her addled brain tried to come up with an excuse to disbelieve the letter and everything it contained. She didn't want to think that Ben was truly gone, moldering beneath a layer of sod on some mountain in Virginia. Her heart didn't feel buried until this moment when the very home they were to spend the rest of their lives in wanted to crumble down around her ears.

Her sweet, gentle Ben was dead, never to come home, never to embrace her in his strong arms one more time. Abigail shook with rage at the war, at the unfairness of life, at the reaper himself, all for taking her Ben away. The preacher reassured young widows and bereaved loved ones with the lesson that they would be reunited with their brave boys in the hereafter. But death and heaven were too far away, too distant a consolation for her to be comforted by. What would she do in the years and decades to come without her Ben? Was Turner to grow up without a father?

Everyone else had grieved for their soldier, but Abigail hadn't. This was all fresh, so raw a truth to be thrust upon her that she couldn't cope. The words swelled and pounded against her ears until she could think of nothing else. They cut so deep that she wondered if she would ever heal, or if time would stitch her broken heart back together again.

Ben is dead.

Waynesboro, Virginia

"Keep your head down," Dustin hissed to Ben roughly as the first sight of civilization came into view.

"Ain't gotta tell me twice with all this rain," he replied as he tugged down the wide, dripping brim of his hat.

Several supplies had survived the young werewolf's earlier episodes at the shack, one of which was Dustin's hat that he had used to keep the sun out of his face on long marches. Now, he loaned it to his friend out of pure necessity. With Ben's kepi lost somewhere on the battlefield at Sharpsburg, he had nothing to conceal the pair of golden eyes that hadn't diminished in their brilliance. Each morning, he checked to see if they had finally vanished to be replaced by a pair of more human eyes, but he was saddened each time.

He might have been slowly improving over the last few months of winter, but as the days, weeks, and months drug on, Ben hadn't been able to shake this one peculiarity.

Some part of him held tight to the hope that with enough training, the golden eyes would finally go away. Only then could Dustin breathe a little easier, and have some surety that he had not completely muddled up this turning affair. And if Ben's brown eyes could return before they arrived in Alabama, all the better. He could already hear Darren asking probing, almost condescending questions as to what Dustin had done to the poor boy to ruin him like this.

But if they ever hoped to reach Alabama, they needed a map, and they could only follow the Shenandoah River for so many more miles to the south. Once they were at the North Carolina border, Dustin's sense of navigation would be of no use to them.

A larger town like Staunton, to the west, would have certainly had a general store with an accurate map. However, Dustin was mindful of Ben's still sensitive hearing. A larger town that would be most likely occupied by Confederate soldiers would be far more overwhelming. Waynesboro seemed a better option.

Dustin glanced to Ben's bare feet, caked with the mud they sloshed through as they made their way down the road toward the town. Perhaps if he could find a cobbler or some kind of clothing store, they could swipe a pair of shoes as well.

Dustin's weren't in any better condition; the leather worn thin with tears around the soles. Cold rainwater and muck chilled his feet and he resisted the urge to shake them out once they reached slightly dryer ground, knowing they would only become dirtier the longer he and Ben walked.

Beside him, Ben took a deep breath. "I can smell some bread bakin'."

Dustin caught the unspoken question and he shook his head. "You can't eat bread. Not a lot of it anyway."

For the last six months, they had lived off the land, doing just as any wild wolf would. They hunted for their meat and foraged for berries or fruits before the winter frost destroyed them. Never had the words "bread" or "hardtack" crossed their lips. As former soldiers, they were eager to expel the food article from their vocabulary anyway. But fresh, warm bread was still something Dustin missed periodically. It had been almost a hundred years since he tasted his sister's sourdough that was so prized amongst their community in Glengarriff.

Ben looked to him, droplets of rain upon his cheeks and nose despite the sheltering rim of the hat. "No bread?" he questioned, almost horrified by the notion. "Then what're we gonna eat?"

Dustin watched the road, thankful that no wagons or riders would come out willingly in this weather. "What we've been eating. Meat and fruits. That's all you can have. Otherwise, you'll get sick."

He was silent for a second and then asked, "Like dysentery sick or..."

Dustin already knew where the young loup-garou's mind had gone. He was debating his chances, wondering if he could risk being sick if it meant being able to taste his favorite foods again. Dustin had done the same in the first few months after he turned.

"Like your entire body is rebelling against you. It's much worse than dysentery, trust me." A memory replayed of the time Dustin stole a shepherd's pie from the windowsill of a farmer in France. Darren had been so furious with him and provided little to no comfort as his bowels seized and twisted for days to rid themselves of the food.

If Ben was dejected, he didn't show it. Perhaps he would doubt Dustin's admonishing, just as he had with his own mentor so long ago, and try it anyway. If he did, Dustin would do the same as Darren had and not feel an ounce of sympathy. Ben had been warned.

Dustin gave one last cautioning word about keeping his head down as they entered Waynesboro. He pushed back the sopping hair from his brow as they hurried toward the nearest general store. Some men passed in the streets with their collars turned up and heads ducked as they hustled by. Even if Ben glanced in their direction, they wouldn't have cared to look up. The rain afforded them that much.

But once they neared the store, he realized that the weather was truly against them after all. He could already see the inside of the shop packed with civilians and some soldiers in their gray uniforms. The sudden downpour had driven them to seek cover in the shops and stores along the main road. Ben could be jostled and the temptation to look at those he passed would be too hard to resist.

"Stay out here," Dustin commanded, grabbing Ben by the arm and guiding him to the side of the shop door before he could open it.

Ben's brow furrowed with the effort to understand the order. "You're gonna make me stand out in the rain?"

"Yes," Dustin replied pointblank. "And remember to keep your – "

"Eyes down," Ben interrupted heatedly. "I know."

All the same, Dustin pushed him into the space between the door and wide window before shoving the hat even further down over his forehead. Now, it nearly covered his face entirely. He'd take no chances. One look into those golden eyes and any sensible person would react adversely to them. They might not have suspected Ben of being a witch as Darren's generation had, but they certainly wouldn't take kindly to it.

He drew himself to his full height and entered the shop, hoping that his stench would allow a bit of a buffer between him and the other customers who loitered inside. He made no eye contact and headed straight for the clerk's counter where an older man stood chatting with a couple of young soldiers.

They were saying something about a battle happening out west in Tennessee, but Dustin was too sick of war and battles to pay attention. He approached the counter and waited to be noticed, which didn't take long at all.

The clerk's nose wrinkled for a brief second before he took in Dustin's ratty appearance. He must have looked a sight, indeed. He hadn't bathed for at least three weeks and without a shave or proper comb to groom himself, he would look every bit the backwoodsman that he wished to portray, even if he wore a relatively new frock coat that he had stolen off a clothesline outside of town. They had long discarded their soldier uniforms on the mountain, knowing that any sign of their involvement in this conflict would raise suspicion.

"Can I help you?" the clerk asked with a note of impatience, most likely eager to return to his conversation with the soldiers; who were in turn giving Dustin a rather patronizing look. Right now, even the most ragamuffin rifleman looked better than he did.

"I need a good, reliable map," he replied firmly in his most convincing uneducated southern accent.

The clerk scratched at his white beard and thought for a moment. "I might have given my last map to one of the captains of the last brigade that came through some time ago, but let me go look in the back."

With a bit of a limping walk, the clerk made his way toward the back storeroom, leaving Dustin waiting beside the soldiers. Behind him, he could hear a threesome of ladies whispering about the odor that reached them from across the room. By the door, a middle-aged gentleman who looked to be a well-off merchant was eyeing him shiftily. Despite what he must have thought, Dustin would cause no problems for any of them. He learned well enough during his training in France that a loup-garou was meant to blend in, to not draw attention, and not to be provoked under any circumstances.

Dustin now regretted leaving Ben alone outside. He could certainly hear him and smell him by the shop door, but he couldn't see him well enough to know if he was doing as he was asked before. He could make out little beyond the heavy curtain of rain that dumped from the sloping roof and filled the gutters in the street.

The clerk emerged from the storeroom with a rolled-up piece of parchment about two feet long in width. Dustin's heart sank. He needed something he could easily stow away in his haversack and this was something more suited for a wealthy man's wall – and pocketbook. He only had a few greenbacks and confederate bills that might not get him what he needed. He didn't want to have to use the last bit of his money, especially not when the necessity of shoes was still in the forefront of his thoughts.

Ignoring his customer's dismay – or perhaps glorying in it – the clerk unfurled the map to reveal the states of Virginia, Maryland, and North Carolina in wonderful detail. Towns were clearly noted, along with roads, railway lines, rivers, and even the subtle geography of the mountain range. Pastel shadings outlined the dividing edges of counties as well. It was dated for the previous year, but Dustin knew that little had changed except the movement of the armies and the potential size of certain towns. War could be a booming industry for some places like Atlanta or Richmond.

"This is my last one," the clerk said.

Dustin feared that and gave up on the notion of asking the man if he had one smaller.

"How much?"

The clerk gave the price and the sum settled heavy in his gut. It must have shown in his face and the older man said, "Now you know why it's my last one."

Dustin would have been content with a small, colorless map with not so many intimate details. He only needed to know where the major towns and cities were so they could avoid them, and perhaps know the general direction of certain rivers.

He let out a sigh and stared at the map, studying it and committing it all to memory. Darren had taught him how to make the most of his sharp loup-garou mind, which could retain vast amounts of knowledge without ever having to rehearse facts or revisit resources like maps or reference volumes for information. If he could just examine the map a little longer, he might not have a need to buy it.

Outside, the wild knicker of a horse and stomping of hooves into the soft earth drew Dustin's attention away from the map long enough for the clerk to think that he was finished.

"Can I look at that for one more minute?" he asked before the clerk had a chance to roll the map again.

"Are you going buy that, son?"

"No, but – "

"Then, I'm sorry, but I'm going to put it back."

Dustin opened his mouth to protest when a few gasps rippled through the shop. Tiny feet and swishing skirts fled to the shop window. On the other side of the street, the agitated horse that he had spotted earlier had thrown his rider completely. The man lay on his back, his coat and trousers now generously speckled in mud as the horse madly threw its head about. There was nothing obviously spooking the horse from what he could see.

Then he moved a few paces closer to the door and saw exactly what had startled the animal. Ben was standing in the middle of the street, his arms upraised as if he were trying to sooth the horse from a distance. Ben had mentioned something about being handy when it came to working with horses and mules like the ones they used on his plantation in Georgia. The fool must have thought it was a good idea for him to try and calm this horse, but he neglected to remember one thing. He was a werewolf now and few prey animals could tolerate their company.

He cursed under his breath and shoved his way through the crowd and heard the heavy footfalls of the soldiers following him. He had to be quick before they saw anything or decided to try and use those rifles they carried.

Dustin rushed back into the torrent of rain to see the exact moment when the thrown rider lifted his eyes to look at Ben, whose head was not down at all, but raised to regard the frightened horse. There was no sedating the beast when faced with an unknown predator. Some pack animals could be trained to be comfortable in the presence of a loup-garou, but he knew of no cases where they could become adjusted to one so quickly. With the rain and added terror of its master, the horse was liable to hurt itself or Ben.

He didn't care that Ben was ready to take the discarded reins to take control of the situation. Dustin grabbed him by the back of his coat and yanked him away.

"What the hell did I tell you to do?" Dustin growled as they escaped from the scene. One look over his shoulder told him enough. The rider shook his head and felt at the back of his skull. With luck, he'll think he simply imagined the glinting gold. With this much rain, it was hard to see anything to begin with.

"That horse was about to – "

"I don't care!" he snapped. "When I tell you to stay put and keep your head down, I mean it. Even if someone comes up and talks to you, don't look at them."

Once they were a safe distance from town, Ben turned and jerked out of Dustin's hold. "Why not? You said yourself that we could be just like everyone else, right? What's wrong with what I just tried to do?"

Dustin gave him a hard look and lifted his hands as if he were trying to grasp the right words out of the air, but couldn't find them. So he did what his old mentor had done almost a century ago. He made sure the road was clear and then reached into his haversack. His fingers found the wooden edge of the folding mirror he had taken off a Yankee soldier last year after a battle. He thought he would use it for shaving, but after losing his only razor just before arriving to Sharpsburg, it had been useless until now.

He swiveled it open and held it up so Ben would finally see his own face since the transformation. At first, he stared unblinking, motionless when faced with the eyes of the wolf. Then, he reached out and took the mirror for himself to get a closer look. Dustin almost thought Ben would take the news rather passively. But then he slowly closed the mirror and held it tightly in his fist.

"How long have they been that way?" he asked, so low that any normal man wouldn't have been able to hear him in the downpour.

"Ever since you woke up," Dustin replied, wishing with every fiber of his being that he didn't have to reveal these truths at all. If Ben's turning had gone as it was supposed to, this might not have happened. But Dustin still didn't fully understand what had gone wrong.

"Are they supposed to…"

He shook his head. "No. That's why I need to take you to Alabama to meet with my alpha. He might know what to do, how to make your eyes return to normal. They're only supposed to be like that when you're angry, hungry, or scared."

Ben glanced up and Dustin wondered if he knew something more. "I'm always angry," he said so calmly. "I'm always… I'm always scared."

If that were the truth, then that would certainly explain everything. "You don't have to be either of those things," Dustin insisted. "You can't live that way."

Ben thrust the mirror back into his hand and his gaze turned flinty with the hateful words he wanted to spit out. "And what if I can't help it? What if your alpha can't fix them? Will they be like this forever?"

He didn't know the source of the brokenness that he detected in Ben's questions, but it filtered through the unwilling bond they shared. Dustin hadn't felt such sadness and hopelessness in decades. "You won't be like this forever. Just give me time."

Chapter 9

This damn trip seemed to never end, and Ben was on the fence toward how to feel about it. After seeing the golden eyes of the wolf that lived inside of him, and learning that this outward show of his condition might be completely out of his control, Ben knew he didn't want to see Abigail anymore. Not like this. But his heart still longed for home and the warm embrace of his family.

He thought of nothing but his mother, father, and elder brother as Dustin continued to run him through the training that was supposed to make him a better werewolf. He excelled, but fractionally, and the golden eyes were still there. He knew because he asked Dustin every day as they lingered in the mountains, long after he had promised they would go further south. He was sure the man was growing tired of the question, but Ben had to know if he looked any more like a man. And when he was given the same, disheartening answer, he fell quiet and melancholy in his own thoughts. Would he ever be normal again? Would he be able to look into his wife's blue eyes and not have her recoil in horror?

"So, that plantation you work on," Dustin began, "what do they grow again?"

Ben smirked at his lame attempt to dislodge him from the black thoughts that plagued him. "Cotton, mostly. They had enough horse sense to get the best piece of land in Heard County from what we'd been told. Most of the land around there is too rocky for big-farmin'. When my pa went to work for Mr. Rider as a young man – that is, our current employer's father – they grew corn and peanuts."

"They would have made a killing in this war if they still grew peanuts," Dustin said with an amused grin. "Think of all the imitation coffee that's been made with the stuff."

Ben hadn't thought of that before, but nodded. "He might have, but that was back when they had slaves to work the fields. When the current Mr. Rider took over the business after his pa died, he freed the slaves and hired on more laborers. My pa was the only man willin' to stay on with the slaves in the beginning."

"Not an ounce of prejudice in him, huh?" Dustin asked as they continued down into the short valley between the mountain peaks.

"Not a bit," he said with a shake of his head. "My pa wasn't exactly an abolitionist, but he believed a man should be paid for his work. Slavery didn't sit right with him. And he taught us right."

Ben heard the distant rumble of a locomotive coming from the east. It was still a good ways off, but he had learned how to gauge an object's distance based purely on the sound he heard. No other man could say he could hear for five miles in any given direction.

"A lot of young men in the south say the same thing, but it's rarely seen to be the truth."

He peered at the loup-garou. "What're you sayin'?"

Dustin neither seemed concerned by his confusion, nor troubled by what he was about to say next. "The south has a twisted way of looking at things. We already talked about that. They think just because their skin is a certain color or that they came from some fictitious cavalier bloodline that makes them gentlemen, they can subjugate another human being. It's not right. But you and your family – "

"Are just as southern as anyone else in the Confederacy," Ben bit back the more hateful words he wanted to say. "I'll admit there are some men I wish could be strung up by their toenails for the way they treat darkies, but no one can ever take the title of gentleman from them."

Seeing that he had hit one of those many veins of anger, Dustin immediately dropped the subject and nodded his concession. "All I was saying is that you at least have your morals in the right place. Maybe that's why I couldn't bear to see you die last year in Maryland."

Ben was silent, thinking over those words. He couldn't recall what would have made Dustin believe he was better than anyone else on the battlefield that day. They all deserved to live, morals or not. But no one, not even a Yankee deserved this existence. This constant, day-to-day fretting over what he would do if provoked, what the wolf would make him do next. He couldn't stand this feeling inside that he would never escape this beastly duality. There was always a furlough from the war, an end in sight when the white flag of surrender was flying. There was no end to this; no reprieve, no rest from the hunger or undying fire in his belly. This wolf would be with him until the day he died.

Instead of allowing Dustin to draw him out of this mire, he pulled himself out and did something he hadn't done before. "What about you?" he asked. "If you think we southerners are just pompous bigots, you must be from some place better than Alabama. You been actin' a lot like a Southern Yankee or Union Loyalist."

He had never asked something so personal of the man who had destroyed his life. He never cared to know, but sometimes he could feel a nosiness rise in him. Especially when Dustin became too angry or too excited, and a certain accent came out that sounded more natural than the flat cadence he daily maintained.

Dustin caught this abnormality as well and gave Ben a slightly astonished look before replying. "I'm from Ireland."

Ben would have never guessed it. "The Irish are pretty decent, I guess. Georgia's got its own Irish Brigade. The twenty-fourth, I think. Mr. Rider hired an Irishman once when I was little. Ma didn't invite him to dinner 'cause he had a foul mouth, but he worked hard."

Astonishment turned into a cool vexation. "So that's the only way you view Irishmen? That we're hard workers?"

Ben shrugged. "I don't know no different."

"And I didn't know anything different of southern men and their cause before I met you. Now, we're even."

Suddenly, this turned into a lesson in judgement, rather than an effort to finally get to know one another. Just when Ben thought he could be free of a lecture for a little while, Dustin proved him wrong.

"How did an Irishman – hardworking or not – come to be in Alabama?" Ben asked, turning to the east to watch for the train that would come rolling by soon.

A corner of Dustin's mouth tilted up in self-mockery. "More like how does an Irishman come to France and then end up in Alabama." When he saw Ben's brows arch, he continued. "I was born in Ireland and lived there until I first turned. I went to France where I met with my alpha and he trained me. Then, there was a call for loups-garous to come to America. Darren thought it a brilliant idea to leave France, so we booked passage on the next ship sailing for New Orleans. We stayed there for a while, making arrangements with the founders of this new settlement in Alabama. I would have been content to stay there, but my alpha thought I was causing too much trouble. We've been in Alabama for close to forty years. Darren thought I was ready to be on my own and I wanted to tour Europe, since I didn't have a chance to under his guardianship."

"And that's why ya joined the Confederacy?" Ben laughed. "To find some way out of the south?"

"And now I'm going back. Bully for me," he said, sarcasm feathering his words. He rolled his eyes. "You must be thrilled."

A seriousness dropped over his countenance when he returned, "I'm glad I'll be getting you the help you need. And then you can go back to your family and farm."

Ben saw the rising stack of smoke floating over the treetops as they neared the bottom of Buford's Gap. "We could get there faster with a little help."

The two werewolves looked to one another, a silent communication exchanged through the most minute twitches of brows and curling of lips as the train whistle sounded.

"Ever jump a train before?" Ben asked, feeling a bit of his old self return.

The Irishman's eyes twinkled with a bit of mischievousness that was so unlike him. "No. But I have derailed one once."

Ben chuckled for the first time in almost a year and spotted the tracks just about half a mile from their place on a ridge. If they timed it right, they could be at the bottom of the gap and find a good railcar to board without alerting anyone to their presence.

"That train's headed west, though," Dustin suddenly opposed as they bounded down the slope.

"That's the Tennessee-Virginia line," Ben called back over his shoulder. "It'll take us to Knoxville and from there, we can go to Alabama."

Yes, to Alabama and to Georgia. It'd be better than taking the previously planned route through the Carolinas. He'd be that much closer to his family and maybe, by then, his golden eyes wouldn't be so obvious. If all went well, he could enact this secret plan he had been ruminating around in his head for the last couple of months. If his eyes were returned to normal, he had no intention of going to Alabama. He'd go straight home to Georgia with the renewed confidence in his werewolf abilities. It had been almost a year since he'd turned. He wasn't as green and scared as he had been. Maybe he did have a chance for a normal life, but he had to get away from Dustin first.

Concealing themselves behind a dense cluster of trees near the tracks, they watched the train come barreling westward and through Buford's Gap.

"Passengers are in the front five... maybe six cars," Dustin said. "And on top of some of the cars toward the rear, so keep a lookout."

Ben passed him a disconcerted look. "Funny, how ya can tell that much."

He shrugged nonchalantly at the passing compliment. "Trust me. Knowing how many humans are around and exactly where they are comes in handy."

Though Ben could see the prudence in such a skill, he hoped he would never feel the need for it. If he was with his family and tending to his own farm, he wouldn't need to be so hyper-aware of his surroundings. Once the war was over and they could all go back to living in peace, he wouldn't have to look over his shoulder.

The train passed, and Ben winced at the thunderous racket caused by the constant pumping of the pistons and rods as they moved the wheels upon the tracks. The strong odor of coal burning in the furnace and the rolling column of smoke from the chimney of the engine made him gag and cough.

Images of war and battle flooded back to him in volleys of canon fire. He cringed at the harsh, unforgiving ghosts of battles past and willed himself to stay present, just to keep his mind focused on the task instead of freezing, as he had done once or twice before. A sudden noise, the faraway reminder of the Yankees' presence to the north of the mountains would sometimes startle him out of his sleep. Though, Dustin never seemed bothered by it at all. Ben knew in those moments that his mind was slipping.

"You're sure you want to jump a train now?" Dustin asked, being mindful to be just loud enough for Ben to hear, but not too loud as that it would add to the dissonance of noise he was already dealing with.

If he were being honest with himself, he would have told Dustin to forget the idea and wait for the train to pass, so they could cross the line. Quiet would have been preferred over this discourse of mechanized racket for endless miles as they chugged along westward. He only needed to wait until he could bear the noise, until the haunting reminders of his time in this war had passed.

But then he thought of Abigail, his mother, and everyone else in Georgia whom he wanted to see again. He thought of the hills of cotton and the smell of apple pies cooling in the Big House on the hill. He needed to be home, needed the comforts of his family and loved ones. He had to be strong for them.

He saw the first few railcars pass and saw the faces of Confederate soldiers in their homespun uniforms. They, along with their fellow passengers perched upon the top of the other railcars, were focused on the path ahead or talking amongst themselves and paid no mind to the two werewolves hiding in the trees.

He waited for them to pass and then ran forward without answering Dustin. The months of training to stop upon command came in handy. He jumped at just the right time and felt his feet connect with the floor of an open railcar that carried military supplies. He stumbled at first and caught himself on a stack of shipping crates.

Dustin followed suit and landed beside him with minimal effort, as if he had just stepped onto the platform with no trouble at all. Ben envied him as he staggered to keep his balance. When he did right himself, he looked to the crate that saved him from flying out the other end of the railcar. When he saw the label, he let out a laugh that startled Dustin.

"What is it?"

Ben pointed to the black painted label on the crate. "I think this is the first time I've ever been thankful for hard crackers in my life."

When Dustin read the label, indicating that the contents of the crate were army issue rations, he joined in Ben's laughter before poking his head out from the boxcar opening to look down the tracks.

"This train will take us through Christiansbury, Newbern, Wytheville, Marion, Abingdon, and Bristol before we can set foot in Tennessee. We might need to get off at any of those stops to avoid being seen, but you're right. This will expedite the trip."

Dustin didn't seem too pleased with the idea, but Ben felt a warmth spread through him, revitalizing that deadened part of himself he thought he had lost. It was like when he found out he had been approved for furlough two Christmases ago. Now, like then, he was going home to see his family. Going home to Abigail.

Franklin, Georgia

Abigail picked up the silver spoon and began polishing it as she had with the rest of the cutlery. An hour had been spent in the task, readying the utensils to be sold in town. Her mother had already made arrangements with a local merchant who planned to send them on with a blockade runner, who would then smuggle them to Europe. Through the chain of commerce, Abigail's family would be given just enough money to hold them until the fall. After that, she wasn't sure what would happen to them.

They didn't even have enough to give the government, who had requested at least ten-percent of all the yield from farms and plantations to help feed the boys at the front. They managed to wiggle their way out of such provisional taxes, because they barely grew enough to feed themselves. The crop they had been hoping for was non-existent without hands to work the fields. With what little the women of the house could manage, they were better off not trying to plant cotton at all this year.

All the men had either joined the army or had come home too injured to work in the fields for her family anymore. Though her father was the head of the plantation, her mother had been the one to juggle the books and make sure everyone – including themselves – were paid appropriately. That's why, when she said they needed to sell the silverware, Abigail didn't argue. Her stomach didn't either.

They were all suffering in Heard County and across rural Georgia. The ladies often joked that they took their money with them to market in their baskets and came home with their purchases in their pockets. Yankee gold was far more valuable now than the printed Confederate money that circulated through the country. The price of a barrel of flour was rising every day. And if one couldn't afford the basic needs, they starved or had to rely upon the charity of their more affluent neighbors.

There was far more objecting when it came to the decision to sell the house she and Ben were given. They could handle the taxes on the plantation, but the second, smaller farm was too much for their family to afford. Abigail wanted to pitch a fit when the idea was brought up at the supper table one evening, but the complaint wouldn't rise in her throat any more than the sobs would. Every tear had been spent, leaving only the dull ache in her bones that made her feel exhausted by grief every hour.

So now, she was without a home, without a husband, and this war didn't look to be coming to an end anytime soon. Her only hope and shining ray of joy left in her life was the infant that tugged on the hem of her dress now.

Abigail glanced over her shoulder to Turner, his honey-brown eyes looking up at her imploringly and his tiny fist lightly knotting into the black cotton of her mourning dress. She gave a weak smile that never seemed to reach her eyes and put down the rag and spoon. Her hand felt raw and slick from the cleaning agent, but she stooped down to take her little boy's hands in her own.

He was still young for walking, as babies went, but despite the hunger and hard times that had fallen upon the plantation, Turner was growing like a weed and seemed almost eager to learn how to walk and talk as the other women did. It was as if he saw the need for a man in the house and wanted to mature ever faster to meet that need.

"Don't grow up too fast," she muttered. "Or they might give you a gun too and send you to Virginia."

She meant it jokingly, but the words were like needles jabbing into her heart. Letters were coming more and more infrequently, though both Mr. Rider and Mr. Myers made sure to write as often as they could, no matter the condition of their company, the slowness of the mail, or the shortage of paper.

Sometimes, her old letters would be sent back with the replies written between her own lines, along with a marginal request to send them more paper so they wouldn't have to be so thrifty. If they had any paper to spare, Abigail would have sent a bundle readily. But no one was more frugal in their household than her mother. They treated their supplies as if they would never be replenished. Instead of sending more paper, she simply restricted her letters to one page and told her husband to write on the back side. Her father – Abigail's grandfather – had served in the Mexican War and came home to tell his family of the kind of hardships and depravity he had experienced. She knew, better than most, of what to expect if this conflict continued.

As long as the letters continued to come, as long as they heard from their men, life was a little more bearable.

Abigail gently pulled Turner to his pudgy feet and guided him away from the table. At first, he couldn't balance and leaned to one side or the other, tripping over his little legs as he turned. But as she helped him straighten, he gained a little momentum. Soon, he was walking, one foot haltingly put in front of the other until they were well into the foyer.

She grinned and he opened his gummy mouth to smile back at her. Seeing her child happy and gurgle with pride for what he accomplished made her almost forget about the war, the hunger, and the utter lack of provisions. Abigail was glad her mother had set herself to tending the garden behind the house, so she could enjoy this moment without her nagging voice harping about something new and seemingly catastrophic. She never passed up a chance to gripe about the humiliating turn in their roles as women, forced to labor just to make it from day to day. Abigail didn't mind it so much, because she was never afforded a moment to think about Ben, even at night when she was on the edge of sleep. She was too tired, too worn out, and too busy to linger in her grief as she had in March and April. Abigail hadn't moved on from her husband's death, but she endeavored to keep moving, keep active both physically and mentally so her emotions wouldn't devour her. Only then could she be given some reprieve.

But soon, she'd learn that her mother and the postman weren't the only ones who could bring bad news to the Rider Plantation.

The hurried hissing of skirts up the drive made her stop near the stairs. Then came the heavy rap of heels upon the planks and the front door burst open. Mrs. Myers stood there, her face flushed and streaming with tears. Abigail's heart felt sick when she saw the letter in her hand and the splotches of dark, dried blood upon its center where it had been folded.

She dropped to the second tread on the stairs and let her son fall onto her skirts. Who was it now? Mr. Myers? Phillip? Or someone else they were close to? Mrs. Myers was given to this type of crying lately, even if a distant cousin had been reported dead or wounded. But she wouldn't have come running to her benefactress if this were a relative living across the county. This could only be news pertaining to the two men who had proudly served this plantation.

Turner, somehow understanding the coming tumult, hung tight to his mother's pliable hoops until she could recover from her own alarm enough to hold him.

Mrs. Myers left the door wide open as she stumbled into the foyer and looked into both the dining hall and the parlor.

"Where's your ma?" she asked, sniffling back the urge to sob while in the presence of her daughter-in-law. There was no use hiding her trauma, but Abigail wouldn't interrogate her. Not yet.

"She's in the garden," Abigail replied softly, hoping that her calmness would transmit into Mrs. Myers somehow so she could explain herself rationally.

She nodded and looked down to her dress and shoes that had tracked in soil from outside. "Oh, I'm so sorry," she mumbled distractedly. "I just came from the valley and..."

Her voice trailed off and then she closed her eyes, visibly fighting the words so they wouldn't come pouring from her lips too soon. Abigail, though usually unsure in how to comfort someone who had lost another loved one, set Turner on his stomach and rushed to gather her mother-in-law in her arms.

Mrs. Myers let out the cries she had been trying to choke back, dampening the fabric on Abigail's shoulder. It was a while before either of the women spoke.

"It's Phillip," she finally confirmed. "He's gone. My husband wrote to me and sent... sent..."

More tears flowed, and Abigail twisted her hand to take the letter from her so she could read it herself, one arm still wrapped around her waist to hold her close as she wailed.

One piece of paper with writing on both sides had been sent to her. One contained the penmanship of Mr. Myers, the other of Phillip. Seeing that it was her eldest son's last farewell letter, she refrained from reading it out of respect and gave her attention completely to the account of his final hours.

They were in a small town in Pennsylvania called Gettysburg. Under the command of Brigadier General Edward Thomas, they were told to support the artillery units at Long Lane. Phillip had been shot through the leg, but continued to fight. It was only until shrapnel from an exploding shell tore into his chest that the soldier laid his gun down for the last time.

"But..." Abigail stammered, "I thought the nineteenth infantry was with Col... Col-something in Charleston."

She didn't have a mind for these general names and only recalled the most popular ones of the time.

Mrs. Myers swallowed and answered brokenly, "Alfred Colquitt's brigade. He was, but then he transferred to his father's unit... Oh, if he had just stayed in Charleston!"

More cries came, and Abigail continued to read the letter. Mr. Myers went on to explain how the three-day battle at Gettysburg was some of the best and worst fighting he had ever seen thus far. The Confederacy had been beaten back into Virginia, but he left a detailed description of where they buried Phillip. It was more than they could have done for Ben.

The next words sent a chill through Abigail.

I could tell you of the battle, but no minds are equipped to read the string of words that could do no justice to the slaughter I have witnessed. Indeed, no eyes should have to behold it either.

"I have to go to him," Mrs. Myers said, taking the letter from Abigail's loosening grip. "I have to go to Pennsylvania."

She was almost unaware that her mother-in-law was making her way to the back door, still tracking dirt across the floor, until the gravity of her words finally dropped.

"You can't go to Pennsylvania!" Abigail beseeched, scooping up Turner before rushing to catch up with Mrs. Myers. "It's in Yankee territory."

But the older woman, who had now lost both of her sons, wasn't listening. She continued to say, "I have to go to Pennsylvania. I have to go to Pennsylvania."

Most likely due to the pandemonium inside the house, Abigail's mother entered from the back porch and nearly collided with her. "Mrs. Myers, what – "

Abigail stepped up and hoped to be a mediator between the two older women who were likely to clash on this subject. Her mother had mentioned more than a few times that Mrs. Myers' presence on the plantation was a consoling one when all the men were away. Out of all three of them, she was more trained to handle a rifle and was as brutal as a mother bear when it came to protecting those she cared for. But looking at the woman now, no one could have guessed that. This war was stealing more than sons and fathers, but spirits too.

"Phillip is... Phillip is gone," Abigail said, propping her child on her hip and letting him play with the lacing around her collar.

Mrs. Rider pressed a hand to her bosom and took Mrs. Myers into her arms to comfort her. When the details were relayed, once more the farmer's wife repeated her mantra. "I have to go to him. I have to bring his body home. I can't let him lie there in Pennsylvania all alone."

Abigail felt ashamed for how dry her eyes were through the whole affair, but though she loved Phillip as a brother, her tears had been so spent upon Ben that her entire family could fall in one evening and she might not have been any more broken than she was now. The worst had happened, and the war could do no more to break her.

The two women joined hands and Mrs. Rider shook her head. "It isn't sensible to go all the way to Pennsylvania. You won't be able to make it past the Yankees all by yourself. Maybe wait for Mr. Myers to come home and you can both go together to get him. Or wait until the war is over."

In a kind of accepted hysteria, Mrs. Myers shook her head. "This war will never end. Even when the last canon is fired, it won't end. The war has done too much for it to ever be finished lickin' us."

Despite such a radical statement, Abigail could see some truth in it. The war wasn't over, and all wars did come to an end, but this one would be different from all the rest. So many men had given their lives on both sides. No matter who won in the end, they would forever be a defeated nation and they would know it. And if this last battle was any indication of who would be the victor of this conflict, it was the Yankees.

As loyal of Confederates as her family was, Abigail knew they couldn't last much longer. And once the smoke cleared and the destruction was finally addressed, it would take generations before life could return to what it used to be – if it ever could.

She looked to Turner and wondered what kind of future lay for her son in a beaten country. Would he be hungry forever? Would he honor the fallen or think his father and uncle fools for fighting a lost cause?

Chapter 10

"I knew when all that ink spilled out on the rug, we'd be in a heap of trouble," Ben said with a shake of his head and a nostalgic smile. "It got all over her dress too, and I think that's why her pa didn't believe me when I said I knocked over the table."

Dustin listened, silently exalting in this moment of pure openness between them. For the last few hours, they weren't loups-garous. They weren't on opposite sides of the war in their hearts, and the world outside the boxcar didn't exist. They were just men, talking. No conversation was forced on his part, and there was no resistance on Ben's. They were coming upon another town soon, but he was in no position to disrupt his story.

"I got my hide tanned when I was sent back home, but it was worth it. For half an hour, we forgot that I was just a farm boy and she was expected to marry up in the world." His golden eyes swam with an emotion that Dustin knew all too well. "I think from that day, she forgot about those differences for good. I can't think of any other reason why she'd agree to marry me otherwise."

But Dustin could. "You're a good man," he said, hoping to frighten away those demons for a little longer. "Better than most, I'd say. And she must have seen that too."

Ben looked up and smirked. "What about you? Got any sweetheart back in Alabama?"

It had been almost a hundred years and Dustin still felt the bitter pangs of loss for his Cassandra, but he wouldn't tell Ben about that, no matter how candid he became in return. To tell him about Cassandra meant he would need to tell him about the night they were married, the night he turned for the first time, the last night they were together. And though he had told the story a couple of times since that fatal hour when he last looked into her heavenly blue eyes, he couldn't tell it to Ben.

"No, I don't," he said calmly, hiding every bit of emotion that threatened to bubble up from his wounded heart. "Never met the right girl who could handle a man like me."

"You ain't kiddin'!" Ben exclaimed. "After all that shit ya did in New Orleans, I'm surprised you ain't behind bars or hung by now."

He let a wicked grin split his face. "They can't hang you if they can't catch you."

They felt the first grinding lurches as the train began to slow upon its approach to the station at Abingdon.

"And speaking of catching..."

Dustin didn't have to say any more. Ben bolted from the spot where he had been leaning against a box of hard crackers and slunk back into the shadows of the boxcar.

He slid between two barrels and crouched behind another stack of crates, ignoring the way the already rotting meat made his stomach turn. The train screeched to a halt and the engine hissed to relieve the pressure in the boiler. Voices and shuffling footsteps from the passenger cars became clearer now that the din of machinery had diminished. Then came the shouts of the officers who were tasked with inspecting the boxcars.

Since Wytheville, they had learned that Confederate officers were on the look-out for deserters stowing away on the trains that ran across the states, especially from the east. Though they couldn't be mistaken for soldiers because of the way they were dressed now, they would still be kicked off the train and prosecuted for not paying their way like the other passengers.

Dustin listened, tracking their progress as they rifled through each car, making their way toward the back of the train where they were hiding. He glanced in Ben's direction and saw him poised, leaning upon his fingertips as if he were ready to run for the forest on the other side of the tracks. He was concealed so well that even his wolfish eyes didn't glint as brightly as they used to when peering through the darkness. But Dustin knew that if one soldier got too close, Ben would disappear in a blur before anyone had the chance to ask questions.

He hoped it wouldn't come to that.

A tussle ensued in a neighboring car and Ben met his gaze. The deep voice of a negro resisting arrest told them enough. Dustin eased back and moved to a place where he could see out the car. Two Confederate privates were dragging the black man down the dusty path running beside the railroad tracks. Another was interrogating him, asking where his master was or if he had any Free Papers to show. By the man's tattered clothes, Dustin knew he wasn't a liberated slave. Not by his master's consent anyway. If he could reach a Union occupied territory, the man could be free. Though, how free could a former slave be in a contraband camp where he was put into bondage all over again for the Union army?

The Confederates, however, wouldn't be so merciful to give him a false hope as the Federals did. They would find his master and send him back to wherever it was he came from, or resell him to another white man who could keep his property from running away. The Emancipation Proclamation might have been enacted several months ago, but there was no way for Lincoln to enforce it in places where the Union hadn't reached. The Shenandoah was still safe for slave owners who couldn't afford to lose their property.

Dustin looked to Ben and wondered what he must have thought of the business as the train unloaded its passengers and some cargo from other cars. Did he think the slave deserved to be caught? He believed a man should be paid for his works and that the president had no right to confiscate another man's property in that way, but Dustin was unsure of the full moral depth of his opinions on slavery. It was a sensitive subject, even after knowing him for almost a year. Could he broach upon the topic again?

After the soldiers concluded their check of the boxcars and any new passengers embarked, Ben emerged and searched the station ahead on the tracks.

"Get back," Dustin warned.

But Ben paid him no mind and didn't turn away until the train was well past the station platform.

Only then did he utter the words, "Poor fella."

Dustin had his answer, but felt enticed to probe further. "Who?"

"That darkie they caught."

Dustin saw they had pulled out of sight from both the city and the platform, and only then did he step out from his hiding place. He could hide his moldering grief for Cassandra, but he did a poor job of concealing his reaction.

"Don't look so surprised," Ben grumbled with a sneer. "I can understand how he feels. Kept against his will by a force he can't contend with... Trapped by a fate that he can't escape from."

It took a moment for him to apprehend his subtle meaning. "You're not trapped, Ben."

"Aren't I?" he asked, the aggravation soothed from his tone. "You told me that there's no cure for this. I'm going to be a werewolf forever, aren't I? You don't think that's a trap? You don't think that's a form of slavery?"

Dustin was stunned and couldn't find an answer for him. He might have been right. It was the exact sentiment he felt in the beginning when he had first turned. They were bound to the wolf spirit for the rest of their lives. It was their personal shackles, the fetters that clanked within their souls with every breath.

He wanted to say that it didn't have to be that way, that they could learn to co-exist, to accept this life and all the benefits it came with. But could he say the same to that slave? Could he speak the same words to a man who was free in spirit, but not in body, while they suffered in the reverse way? Dustin couldn't be so hypocritical.

Therefore, he grimaced and gave into the silence.

September, 1863
Franklin, Georgia

Abigail slid down the door casing until her rump made a dull thud upon the floor. From this strategic position on the second floor, she could hear the women talking in the parlor below. Something about the way the planks were spaced made this spot a perfect place to eavesdrop while also making sure that Turner stayed down for his nap. She remembered all the times she had sat there, listening to her parents' conversations about Abigail's future, about whether to send her away to boarding school or let her continue courting Ben. It was there in that doorway when she heard Ben ask for her father's blessing to marry.

She stared at her toes that poked out from the hem of her dress. They couldn't afford a cobbler to fix the torn leather on her shoes, so she went without slippers on most days. That suited her fine, but her mother worried for the condition of her feet walking around through the dust and hard dirt. For a lady of her status, callouses were frowned upon, whether they be on her hands or her feet. But Abigail reminded her mother of the times and the situation that they were in, successfully hushing her criticisms. Who could think of the condition of one's feet when they were in the middle of a crisis such that had befallen their state.

"I'm thinkin' of openin' my home as a hospital," came the timid voice of Mrs. Featherstone, a spinster woman who had no men to speak of in the war. "It's the least I could do for our boys."

A huff of sardonic laughter came from Mrs. Glover, a woman who was still chubby and round even in the midst of these hardships. "My dear, you aren't a nurse and the only doctor in town is thinkin' of goin' to the front himself. You're better off tryin' to make do with your farm."

Ruffled by this show of opposition, Mrs. Featherstone retorted with, "I can't do much else for the cause. Besides, I can't get any more work out of my darkies. They're all waitin' for the Yankees to come in and free them."

At this, Mrs. Glover had more to add. "That Emancipation Proclamation is the most dastardly, cowardly act ever performed by a man. Yankee or not, someone needs to shoot that darky-loving Yankee."

Another voice, just as firm but not so condemning, chimed into the conversation with her own bit of news from the northern territories. "I've heard that there are more and more Confederate sympathizers risin' up every day," said Mrs. Hopson. Unaccompanied by her daughter, Missy, she still frequented the Rider household to show her support for the family. "There are anti-war movements every day from what I hear. They're run by those Copperheads."

And Mrs. Hopson heard quite a lot, given that her son is a known spy on behalf of the Confederacy. He, along with so many others, had reported their discoveries to Richmond in order to bolster morale among the southern states. But, sometimes, good news wasn't enough.

"Lincoln has even called for more drafts," Mrs. Hopson continued, "and do you know what those blue-bellies are doin'? Hirin' replacement soldiers to fight in their stead!"

The other matrons gasped and clucked their tongues in disgust.

"What cowards!" they cried. "How shameful!"

"Is it true they've started to allow darkies into the army?" Mrs. Featherstone asked eagerly.

"It is!" Mrs. Hopson replied. "Though, I don't have any idea where they're gettin' them. If the cowardly Yankees won't fight, those freed darkies won't want to either."

"They will after Lincoln made this entire war over slavery," Mrs. Glover grumbled. "I'll bet my last good stocking and garter that they're draggin' those darkies out of the contraband camps. They're shovin' guns into their hands and tellin' them to go kill their old masters."

Mrs. Duffy, whose opinion seldom mattered because it was so pacifying and unpopular, whined, "How barbaric!"

And upon realizing that Mrs. Duffy was ready to plan an active role in this gossip, Mrs. Glover pounced upon the chance to patronize her. "That bloodless, cold-hearted president of ours is no better! Did you hear about the riots in Richmond? Women, just like us, were degraded to the level of common thieves and scoundrels because they couldn't afford to feed their families. You all know how the prices have risen because of the blockade."

When she received a satisfactory total of nods and agreements, she added, "That man, Jefferson Davis, he had the gall to go out into the streets and throw money at those starvin' women and beg them to blame the Yankees, not the government. If he were runnin' the government any better, we wouldn't have to worry about these outrageous prices. We would barely feel this war."

"He's doin' the best that any man in his position would," Mrs. Duffy said stiffly.

"Our own governor, Joseph Brown, doesn't like him any better than the people do," Mrs. Hopson retorted, supporting the treasonous banner which Mrs. Glover proudly flew. Abigail couldn't blame any of them for being angry with the government, but like Davis insisted, she hated the Yankees more than the sickly-looking officials in Richmond.

Mrs. Duffy wasn't done in her own tirade. "None of us knows the kind of pressure he must be under. He's having to make decisions all the time that affect the future of our beloved country."

Mrs. Hopson shifted on her stool, readying herself for a rant. "Where was the government when Grant took Vicksburg? Now we don't have the Mississippi."

"We haven't had the Mississippi since they took New Orleans," Abigail's mother finally stated, joining in the rest of the war talk that she so often despised.

"Indeed!" Mrs. Glover agreed. "But Davis wouldn't send help anyway. If we could have beaten Grant back, then we could have fought our way to the Gulf of Mexico."

"Instead of that horrible defeat at Gettysburg," Mrs. Hopson finished with the thought that was still fresh in their minds.

Once more, Mrs. Glover nettled in her hatred of both the disorganization of her own country and the dreadful successes of the Yankees. "Who knew that damned old goggle-eyed, snappin' turtle Meade would have beaten us out of Pennsylvania."

It was the last major battle of the summer besides the fall of Vicksburg. Unconditional Surrender Grant, as he was so often called, sieged the city past the breaking point of its proud and sturdy citizens. It was a great blow to the Confederacy, but no more than the slaughter at Gettysburg.

"We would have beaten the Yankees back in both places if we still had Jackson."

If Abigail were in the parlor, she would see each of the women bow their heads in reverence for Stonewall Jackson, the man who had been as much of a hero and gallant soldier as Robert E. Lee.

"Everything has gotten so much worse since Fredericksburg and Chancellorsville," said Mrs. Featherstone. "We need another victory."

"We need another general."

This last statement by Mrs. Glover crossed the line and every lady, even Mrs. Duffy and the usually meek Mrs. Featherstone, turned upon her with shouts and reprimands. Anyone in the Confederacy could speak ill of their president, Joe Johnston in Tennessee, Beauregard, Hood, or even Nathan Bedford Forrest. But no one dared speak a word against Bobby Lee. He had won the hearts of everyone, and even the respect of Union officers and generals who thought his strategies to be wonderfully crafted masterpieces. But they all knew it was this pride that cost them Gettysburg and the one route they might have had into the north again. Lee may never step foot in Union territories again, unless God granted a miracle to their struggling cause.

Turner stirred in his cradle and Abigail jumped to her feet, sure that the squalling of the ladies below had awoken him. But he didn't open his eyes and only stretched out his little arms and legs before settling comfortably back into a deep sleep.

Miss Peters appeared in the doorway, somehow always knowing when the little man of the house might have needed extra care.

Abigail passed her a tight-lipped smile, the only one she could muster nowadays with all this talk of war. Gone were the days when the ladies could talk about anything else. And the men weren't much company at all. They, too, were either thinking of the war or talking about it, rehashing the battles as if any alterations they could have made could be of any use to them now.

The old housemaid came to the crib, her silver hair pulled back into a tight bun and wrinkled face crinkling further at the sight of the sleeping babe. "I know ya too well, Miss Abigail," she said softly. "You don't want to be in this house any more than I do. I've got a basket for Mrs. Myers in the kitchen. Why don't ya go take it to her?"

Thankful for this short remission from the incessant and depressing conversation in the parlor, she kissed the cheek of her former nanny, thanked her, and went speedily to take up the task.

Abigail's bare feet sank into the damp soil as she carefully made her way down the hill into the valley. If the war was so prevalent in the parlor of her home, it was even more evident in the rest of the plantation. The cotton fields and orchards beyond were bare, overgrown with weeds and thorny vines. As she looked out over the once proud and prosperous plantation, she couldn't help but compare it to the state of the whole south.

This ground, overrun by a plague of neglect that only a few women were unable to tame back, personified the war in every way. Their livelihood and their hope were being strangled by the Yankees, just as the withering stalks of old cotton plants were encircled by the deep red coils and pests of all kinds fed upon the leaves. Rotten fruit had fallen from the trees, but not even the crows and scavengers that passed through their land would take of the refuse.

Something deep within Abigail told her that nothing would be right after this war. Not even if they proved to be the victors. Life would never be the same after this cruel war was over. Some of Mrs. Glover's pessimism was bleeding onto her.

One thing was a relief. That the lack and want they felt on a daily basis was not suffered by Turner. They all made sure that he had enough to eat before anyone else. He was the next generation to help rebuild their country. The only one to carry on the Myers family name. With Phillip and Ben gone... Abigail shook her head once more and tightened her grip over the basket of provisions. She couldn't think of them now.

They had all assured her that weeping for one's dead husband was acceptable. Encouraged, even. But Abigail couldn't. Even on the anniversary of his demise at Sharpsburg, she couldn't let one tear drop. It was a waste of energy that could be used for better, more useful efforts. Crying over him would not bring him back. And no matter how long she stared out her bedroom window in to the black night, she would never see a lantern come bobbing up the road to bring good news or a body they could lay to rest in the proper way. Both the Myers boys were buried far from home, possibly never to return again.

The Riders, thus far, had escaped tragedy. Her father was still well and due to his age, given menial tasks around the camp instead of being sent to the front lines with the rest of his regiment. But they rarely heard from him anymore. Still, they searched for his name in the occasional newspapers that came to Franklin giving reports of the battles that he may or may not have been in. The army arrangements changed so often, and transfers were not uncommon – as they discovered in Phillip's case. If the old man was even in the same regiment anymore was anyone's guess.

But as long as Mr. Myers was gone, Abigail took it upon herself to care for his wife in what way she could. Her mother-in-law didn't come up to the hill anymore but stayed confined within their tiny farmhouse at the bottom of the valley. The Riders were all she had since her own family was far away in Kentucky – if they were still there at all. If the Yankees weren't closing in through Tennessee, she would have urged her mother to convince the grieving woman to return to her people.

Mrs. Myers wasn't herself. The woman she had once thought to be strong and defiant in the face of adversity, had been broken completely. Some days, she was lucid and could remember that there was a war going on. Other times, like today, she couldn't see the desolate fields. Her mind deceived her, filling the void of silence with the sound of grunting pigs, clucking chickens, and the anticipation of receiving her hardworking boys after the workday was finished.

Abigail stepped over the tall weeds that had come to cover the front lawn of the farmhouse, her skirts getting caught around her pantalets since she wore no petticoats. Along with shoes, she had dispensed with such modest garments so they could conserve what little soap they had left when doing the laundry. No man was going to see her out here, and no woman – especially Mrs. Myers – would scold her for being unladylike. If anything, she might have thought Abigail the most sensible and practical of the lot for doing it.

The stench of something burning reached her as she stepped up the walkway. Abigail hastened onto the porch and didn't bother knocking on the door before entering. Inside, the potbellied stove put off such stifling heat that Abigail had to catch her breath before looking around further. Four place settings decorated the table, complete with utensils and the fine porcelain cups her mother had gifted to Mrs. Myers several Christmases ago. Platters, garnished with sprigs of herbs, were barren otherwise, as if the feast was invisible and existed only in the mind of the cook herself.

Mrs. Myers was at the counter, kneading her hands into a bowl of what appeared to be water and cornmeal. And by the knotted state of the dough, she had been kneading for a while. The cast iron pot on the stove smoked, the source of the burning smell.

Abigail quickly dropped her basket to the prepared table and used the front of her calico dress to take the scorching cookware off the stove. There was nothing inside.

"What're ya doin' child?" Mrs. Myers cried, her hands still matted with bits of dough. "That was almost done. The boys will be back any minute from the fields and they're gonna be mighty hungry."

Abigail tightened her lips together. Mrs. Myers couldn't help it. She still believed that her men were coming home to her. Unlike the rest, she couldn't move on. Now she understood what the other people of Franklin must have thought of her when she couldn't accept the news of Ben's death. Crazy, ignorant, and stubborn to a fault.

She looked to Mrs. Myers, who stared at her with a dumbfounded look that slowly morphed into that coming realization. Soon, tears would be shed and questions asked that Abigail didn't want to answer. Not again. Not to her.

Instead, she set down the pot onto the table, risking a scorch mark upon the raw wood surface, and ran to her mother-in-law. They embraced, dough clinging to the flyaway hairs on her head as Mrs. Myers received her. And together, they did cry. Cried for Ben, for Phillip, and this whole cruel war that couldn't end too soon.

CHAPTER 11

It all happened as if he were reliving it. The smell of the gunpowder was so strong, as if the rifle were being discharged right in front of him. He could see the eyes of the Yankee who had shot him, see the dark abyss of his pupils dilated from the agony of his own death. Ben heard the screaming of shells in the distance as the battle continued to rage on without him. He fell endlessly as the pain seared in his side. The metallic scent of his blood choked him, the prickle of the bush branches bit into his back again, his world spinning in a kaleidoscope of leaves and blue sky.

The rebel yell rang in his ears and he could feel his mouth open to return it when his whole body jerked awake.

His eyes shot open, but the chaos of battle continued. Over him was Dustin's worried expression, backed by a clear night sky. It was then Ben felt the perspiration upon his face. Reflexively, his hands searched for his rifle that should have been by his side. But he grabbed only dead leaves and grass beyond his bedroll.

Despite the residual dizziness from his sudden awakening, he sat upright and hunted for his missing rifle, feeling his pulse hammering through his veins, urging him to fight the Yankees that must have been closing in. Where was his regiment? Who were they fighting? Where was his knapsack?

Dustin grabbed for his shirtsleeve and kept him seated. "You were having a nightmare."

As Ben's eyes scanned through the darkness, he found it to be true. There were no soldiers and none of the usual signs that battle was raging just beyond the veil of trees. He let air fill his lungs as he realized where exactly he was.

He wasn't with a bivouacked regiment. He wasn't on a battlefield. They had traveled for a few days on the train before deeming it too risky. The station inspectors and stops outside of towns became too frequent and they would have been found out eventually. Now, they were in east Tennessee, where the fighting had spilled over from Kentucky.

From what they had heard from the snippets of news they caught at the train stations in Virginia, Bragg had beaten Rosecrans back to Chattanooga and had the city under siege. Meanwhile, the rest of the countryside was pocketed by isolated battles and skirmishes. The Union had poured in through the Cumberland Gap since the beginning of the month, taking the rugged land of Eastern Tennessee by storm, almost unopposed. And Ben could hear them fighting from miles away, hear the dying cries of Confederate and Union soldiers and the crackle of rifle fire.

It was as if he was there with them. His proud southern heart ached to fight too, despite the fact that the war wasn't going as they had planned, the constrictor hold the Union had over his country, and the threat of men invading his home state. No one thought the war would last this long or that they would get so far through Tennessee. They had come close at Chickamauga from what he had heard, and perhaps that's what inspired this new surge of patriotism. His family, his wife, and everything he held dear, was endangered like never before.

He looked to Dustin and hated the way he regarded Ben with such pity. What could this Irishman know about losing his home to invaders or see the country he loved slip through his fingers? What did he know about losing it all to a force he couldn't fight back?

Ben yanked free of his hold and tried to reason through it all again and compose himself.

"Are you all right?" he asked.

What a dumbass question that was. "Yeah, I'm fine."

"Try to get some rest."

Dustin moved away and laid down, but he knew he wasn't falling asleep right away. Like Ben, he was still listening to the war in the distance. He wondered where it was, who was engaged there, and the outcome. Small battles sometimes didn't make a lick of difference in the grand scheme of the general's plans, but they would mean a world of change for countless lives. The families of the fallen and the citizens whose town was under fire would forever remember this night when the war came to their doorsteps.

An hour passed and Ben couldn't bring himself to lay back down upon his bedroll, though the slightly groaning snores of Dustin added to the repeating chorus of gunfire and artillery shells. When that hour was over, the sound of battle died away. In its place were the rushed orders of officers and hastening footsteps of their subordinates as they moved out. Then came the moans of the dead and dying.

It was the typical symphony, what he - as a seasoned veteran - would know by heart. It was what fabricated those nightmares and haunted his steps during the day. It was the reason he was backsliding in his training as a werewolf, too.

Over the last few weeks, he had gotten worse. Unfocused and disinterested, Ben found it harder and harder to stick his landing when climbing through the trees or stopping upon the designated mark when Dustin told him to. His temper, however, did change. Instead of fulminating against his travel companion out of a burning hatred, it was out of unchecked fear for the future that awaited him back home. If he wasn't careful, he'd never be able to leave Dustin when the time was right. He'd never be able to sneak away to Georgia and see his family. And even if he could, would he be ready to face them? His eyes were still golden and if he couldn't manage his strength or speed, they would surely know something was wrong. Heaven forbid if he should hurt anyone because he hugged them too tightly upon arriving home.

With each passing day, he flipped back and forth between wanting to see them and deciding to follow Dustin to Alabama where he could receive some help for his new condition. The time was coming close, that if he were to escape at all, he had to make the decision soon. Fear and pure despondency mixed in him until his nerves could bear it no more. And now, spurred toward the plight of his fellow soldiers, Ben felt moved to do something. Anything.

Hardly understanding his own motives, Ben rose and soundlessly made his way out of the clearing. He didn't feel the sharp thorns and twigs jab into the bottom of his feet. Neither did he feel the branches scrape against his cheeks or snag in his hair. He barely bothered to even push them aside as he continued to walk toward the battleground.

He could still hear the pop of rifle fire as one army was retreating from the other, but there would be no silence in these woods until the dead were finally collected.

Dark, ghostly shapes crashed through the bushes, frightened heads swiveling as haversacks banged against their hips, and rifles were used to clear the way in their escape. As Ben drew closer, the color and insignia on their uniforms became visible in the moonlight. The Confederacy lost that night.

Instead of ducking out of sight, Ben stood erect and watched his comrades flee from the encroaching Yankee skirmishers. He saw them stumble and catch themselves upon the trees before hurrying on. Some turned to shoot at those that followed, only to be shot down by the bullets that whizzed through the air. They fell, one by one. And instead of a victorious rebel yell, the wails and cries for mercy echoed through the forest.

His limbs weakened at the sight, not because the Yankees were now firing in his direction, but because this humbling defeat shook him to the core more penetratingly than he ever thought possible. The Confederacy had started out so strong, so self-assured. And now they were being mowed down like a band of renegades, nothing but rebels to the Federal's cause for unification. How many of them could remember what they were fighting for? How many still cared?

A bullet whistled just next to his ear and it compelled him to find cover.

He dove for the nearest cluster of bushes and was met with the gaping, gasping face of a soldier that had been struck down just moments before in the retreat. Ben rolled to avoid him, but stared and watched the light fade from the soldier's eyes. It was the first time he had been confronted with death so closely since he'd knelt beside John Beck in Sharpsburg.

A violent hand reached out and grabbed for Ben, rasping out a plea for water, but he only shook his head. He had none to give. Less than a few seconds later, the soldier was gone, his spirit passing into the ether to leave behind the shell of a man who died trying to protect what he held so dear.

Ben slipped out of the corpse's grip and scrambled away, suddenly unused to this play of tragedy, as if he were freshly enlisted.

He stared at the frozen expression of the soldier, recalling the faces of his dead friends whom he had tried not to think of for months. They soon melted into hundreds, and then thousands in his mind. How many had they lost in the name of southern independence? How many more would die? Why couldn't he have died with them? Died for something he believed in?

All of the sudden, Ben felt something he hadn't since the war began. Guilt. Guilt for being a coward. Guilt for not having a rifle in his hands at that very moment so he could repel the Yankee advance. Guilt for being this powerful creature with little control over his own body so that he couldn't rejoin the army, instead of going to Alabama to wait out the struggle.

His friends and fellow soldiers were fighting and dying without him, and he was staying on the sidelines, stalked by his nightmares and kept in chains by a fate he didn't ask for. He was a deserter, betraying his country, his friends, and his family. He remembered, before Sharpsburg, when men were court marshalled for such a crime. The price for his crime would have been execution. Death by a firing squad from his own company. He deserved the same sentence, just as much as those poor souls did.

Now, more than ever, he wished that Dustin would have left him in those woods beside the church at Sharpsburg. It would have been better than living all the years to come with the knowledge that he didn't give his full measure of devotion as so many others had.

As he was backing away from the dead soldier, his heel struck something hot. He winced and recoiled his foot to reveal a coin pressed into the soil, glinting in the moonlight. Not too far away was the dead boy's haversack, its contents spilled onto the ground. A tintype, some hardtack, a housewife kit for sewing, and a makeshift coin purse lay open next to a bundle of letters from home.

All the Confederate money was in paper form now, but he had heard of this almost mythical, precious metal currency floating around amongst the southern states.

Ben stooped down and brushed the tip of his finger on the face of the coin, only to receive a minor burn. It must have been silver. Dustin had warned him about the effects of the metal to werewolves. He touched it again, testing his own resilience to the pain before taking it up in his palm completely.

He hissed as he squinted at the one side that featured Lady Liberty with the date of 1861 cast below. Then, he turned it to see the American eagle emblem and the currency value of a half dollar. There were enough half dollar coins there to buy a proper train ticket home, along with as much meat as he could carry, with plenty to spare. These coins were invaluable to a soldier or anyone in the south, since they bore the seal of the "United States of America" and could be used in the north or the south.

His flesh became charred as the coin remained in contact with his skin, but after a while, he barely felt it. He could feel nothing in the wake of so much shame and homesickness.

His strength and resolve to see Georgia, his hope for ever having a normal life again in a conquered country as a dysfunctional werewolf was like gunpowder smoke in the wind. The coin, as deadly as it was to him now, seemed the only friend he had in the world.

In one swift motion, he brought the coin to his mouth and swallowed.

The burning sensation roused Dustin from his rather fitful sleep. Years spent sleeping near battlefields could never acclimate him to the sounds and smells enough to allow him to get enough rest. But the searing pain in his throat was new and as soon as he saw Ben's bedroll was empty, he knew what must have happened. The light pack bond they shared could alert him to any number of dangers and threats. With Ben unaccounted for, Dustin knew this wasn't some effect of the acrid smoke he breathed.

From what he could determine, the battle had broken up now, sending the Confederate forces in retreat and deeper into Tennessee. But Dustin didn't give a damn about either army. He needed to find Ben.

Following his senses, he found the loup-garou curled upon the ground, his fists gripping at the autumn leaves as he coughed up mouthfuls of blood. Not too far away, he saw the dead body of a soldier with his open haversack. When he spotted the silver coins and took a moment to understand the inner turmoil that Ben emanated through their bond, Dustin filled in the rest.

He cursed angrily under his breath and dropped down to pull Ben onto his side. His golden eyes rolled wildly in his head and Dustin knew that asking questions would get him nowhere. All he knew was that Ben was a fool if he thought he could end it all quickly this way.

The silver would make its way slowly down his esophagus and then tear him apart from the inside out as it ate away at his stomach and intestines. Eventually, the metal would enter his blood and it would be a matter of hours before his insides would be charred and eroded away.

Dustin made one of his claws extend to displace the dull and dirty fingernail and with the calmness of an experienced surgeon, he cut into Ben's throat, careful to avoid anything important so he could dig around for the coin he must have ingested. The boy grabbed for the hand that tried to save his life, but Dustin fought him off.

"A chonách san ort!" he chided. "Shouldna done it in the first place, ye cúl tóna."

He knew it did little good to curse the boy now that he had done it, but it felt better somehow to let out a few of his native words, because English certainly wouldn't do his feelings justice. Dustin didn't want to think about the guilt that would follow him if Ben didn't see the dawn.

Despite the silver, Ben's loup-garou nature was operating efficiently. Within seconds of Dustin making the jagged incision, the skin and flesh stitched itself back together, making him lose track of the coin. He couldn't even find a way into his gullet before the cut would seal again. He continued to cut, sending Ben into a new torrent of agony with each frustrated swipe of his claw.

Heedless of the harm to himself, Dustin grabbed for a few of the other coins that Ben had left alone and tried to use them to help pry open the wounds he made. Silver was the only material on earth that could keep a loup-garou from healing.

Even this method proved difficult. The coins wouldn't stay in place to hold the flaps of his skin apart and Dustin couldn't handle the coins for long before the pain became too much for him. If Ben had any notion whatsoever of the torture suicide would cause him, he was the bravest loup-garou on the planet.

His efforts proved clumsy and futile, causing more damage than desired. He couldn't even slow the progress of the silver down his throat.

When the coin slipped into his chest, Dustin knew that there was little he could do on his own. A single claw alone, or even a set, couldn't keep his body open. Now that the coin was proceeding slowly into his chest cavity, he'd have to possibly break ribs and rupture other organs to keep them aside while he worked. The excess blood would make it too difficult to see.

He chucked the coins into the woods with a growl, irritated by this state of helplessness in which he found himself. The easy thing to do would be to try and kill Ben now, knowing the outcome would be the same in the end. It was what the boy wanted after all. Why not give it to him and be done with the whole affair so he could go back north and escape this war and this country?

But his wolf and his conscience couldn't allow it. He had to keep trying somehow.

Assessing his options, he knew that the only way to get the silver out would be to force it out. However, the only thing that could help him was the very thing that was killing him. If he had a better tool, something similar to what a surgeon would use and at least plated in silver, Dustin had a chance to save his life.

But who in this God forsaken war had that much silver?

Middletown Tennessee

The rolling thunder of canons echoed across the night sky. From her upstairs bedroom window, Nancy could see the spark of the gunpowder as they exploded with powerful force. With each report, the glass panes of her window gently rattled. If she were asleep like she was supposed to be, she would have awoken anyway.

She could hear the creaking of the old floorboards as her nervous mother lumbered heavily back and forth across the width of her bedroom, which shared a wall with her own. The war had come to their part of the state at last and it was all Nancy could do to keep herself from donning her late father's coat and slipping amongst the ranks of whatever Confederate regiment happened to be closest.

Her heart was more than ready to feel the thrill of battle, to fire her own rifle and do more for their glorious cause. Her mother, on the other hand, had been packing for weeks since they first heard the news that the Yankees were pressing their way through this portion of Tennessee.

Crates, half-filled with their family heirlooms and personal possessions, were strewn about the house in various rooms. Cloth had already been draped over the furniture and padlocks fastened to what they couldn't carry with them. There was no logic in the plan to flee to South Carolina like this. If the Yankees were to force them out of their home, they would only be able to carry what they could on their backs. The army would confiscate the last of their wagons that were not already donated to their great southern cause.

But Nancy indulged her mother and packed as she was directed, all with a roll of her eyes and a biting comment when she left the room.

She, unlike most southerners, had no fear of the Yankees. Only an insatiable desire to meet them on the battlefield like the other boys in gray and butternut. She saw the casualty lists, the endless roster of honorable names, and they did not dissuade her in any way. If she had to cut her hair, bind her chest, and smear her porcelain pale face to mask her femininity, she would do it. Her homemade haversack was tucked under her mattress, ready to leave with her. She only needed the chance.

Their home was situated on the very edge of town, far from the prying eyes of nosy neighbors. She could slip out the back door as soon as the cannonade was silenced, and her mother was allowed to rest. Of course, if she got the notion to try and uproot her family that very hour, Nancy's plan would be ruined.

Just as the bursts became sporadic and less frequent, Nancy tensed. Now if her mother could crawl back into bed...

She hated the way she jumped at the sudden banging upon the front door. Her mother let out a short cry of surprise. All of their servants had been released days ago and neither Nancy nor her mother were accustomed to receiving guests on their own. Certainly not at this time of the night.

"Is anyone home?" an impatient voice demanded from the porch.

Nancy was the first to move. This couldn't be a Yankee. They would have barged through and broken the hinges off the door. A true southern gentleman knocked.

She quickly wrapped a shawl about her shoulders and snatched up the only lit candle of the house from her night table before rushing down the stairs. The man rapped more urgently and called again. Upon opening the door, she was met by two men.

Neither were dressed in uniforms, much to her dismay. The taller of the two – and the one uninjured – was the first she noticed, his green eyes blazing in the candlelight. The other was nearly drenched in blood from his chin to his chest. He looked to be on the brink of unconsciousness, his eyes closed and head lolled against the shoulder of his healthier partner who supported him.

Her lips parted to ask what they wanted, but the tall – and decidedly more handsome – man answered for her. "I need to use your dining table."

The sternness in his voice rendered her compliant as she simply stepped aside to let them in. Half carrying and half dragging, the man brought his friend through the house as if he had known its layout by heart, even in the dark.

Her mother appeared at the top of the stairs and made her typical stammering, blubbering sounds as she looked upon the scene. No doubt she thought of what the town would think about them allowing two men into a widow's house without a chaperone or protector of any sort.

Nancy followed after them, feeling the cool slickness of blood on the bottoms of her feet from the trail they left from the front door to the dining room.

"Do you have any silver?" the man asked her as he threw aside the chairs that were pushed under the table.

Nancy blinked and paused in her speedy clearing of the table's surface. "Silver?"

His green eyes flashed in her direction. "Yes, silver. Silver utensils. Cutlery. Even a fork. Anything silver."

Thrown by this odd request, she could only nod and then left the dining room as he hoisted his friend onto the table with no effort at all, or any consideration to his friend's comfort while doing so. The only sign that the man was even still alive came from the gurgling, choking, and groaning sounds he made.

Nancy's mother intercepted her just outside the door.

"Who are these men?" she asked. "What do they want? What was he saying about silver?"

She could answer nothing and in the moment, she didn't care. All she knew was that she needed to do as she was asked, which was a desire completely out of character for her. Commands were usually disregarded, rules ignored, social standards forgotten, all for the sake of her own stubbornness and pride. Her mother had often said that if she had in her mind to do something, and then someone told her to do that exact thing, she would abandon the very thought of it just for spite.

But something had inundated the house the moment she opened the door. The air seemed different somehow. More tense, and yet calming at the same time. She couldn't put it into words, nor could she explain it to her mother in between the time it took to retrieve the small box of silverware.

One feeling, however, continued to hum through her heart. She liked being ordered about by him. She liked, after being under one roof with her mother for far too long without servants or other family, to know that someone was in charge and took the lead so seamlessly. By the way her mother was hurrying with an armful of spare linen cloth and old clothes from the rag-box, she must have felt this imposing, yet settling energy as well.

The sight she was met with when she reentered the dining room made her nearly drop the tray of cutlery. The invalid's shirt was torn open, exposing his bloodied, convulsing chest, with his soon-to-be surgeon hunched over him.

"What in the world are you doin'?" her mother cried, horrified.

The man only stretched out his hand, silently requesting the silver Nancy held. She gave it and remained near the table to watch what would happen. From where her mother stood, she couldn't see the way the man rifled through the utensils, his lips tightened and pulled as if he were immensely frustrated with the task of having to pick through the silver.

"Can one of you get me a pair of gloves?" he asked franticly, finally withdrawing his hands from the tray.

Nancy didn't move. Her eyes were riveted upon his fingertips and how they appeared blackened. Was that from dirt or gunpowder? Had they been that way when he arrived? They appeared to be bleeding a little as well. Was he injured too?

Her mother dropped the cloth to the table and rushed out again, prodded on by the firmness of his request. That didn't keep her from mumbling her worried concerns under her breath as she went.

The injured man's legs pulled and jerked as some unseen torment racked his body. Nancy could see no wounds, though there was more than enough blood to suggest that he had been badly hurt somewhere. His face contorted with that pain and she could see the glistening of tears streaming from the corners of his eyes in the candlelight.

"Do you have any rope?"

It hardly seemed possible that Nancy's eyes could open any wider, but they did. "Rope? I..."

"Or cord," he suggested. "Anything I can use to keep him from moving."

Nancy set down the candlestick and fled to the curtains. She whipped off the ties that kept them pulled back, making the thick drapes drop to cut off the moonbeams from slanting into the room. Now, the only light came from the single, flickering candle on the table.

She offered the sets of silky fabric to her guest. He took them and tested their strength.

"I don't know if this will hold him, but we can try."

He handed two back to her and instructed her to tie his limbs together at the ankles just as her mother returned with a pair of white gloves. Nancy recognized them, but said nothing in protest. If her mother wanted to sacrifice her favorite pair of gloves, then so be it.

After securing his friend's arms by tying them to the carved table legs, he took the gloves from her mother. Within a few seconds, he was back in the silverware and picked out his utensils carefully. The patient continued to groan and writhe.

"Hold his feet."

Nancy obeyed, using what little strength she had to grip the man's ankles. He continued to buck and attempted to jerk them out of her hold, but unlike her mother who had quitted the room with a whining complaint regarding her nerves, Nancy wouldn't abandon the men. If she were to join the army in secret, then she needed to be exposed to this kind of gore and tragedy.

What she witnessed, however, defied explanation and something told her that this would not happen in the army every day.

Gloved hands, wielding a dull, silver butter knife, cut from the middle of the man's breast down to his navel. The flesh burned, and she could see the wisps of smoke rise in the dark. A scream shook the walls and Nancy shuddered under its incomprehensible anguish. She struggled harder to keep him still. It took a moment for her to realize it was the silver that produced this effect.

The man was unphased and grabbed for forks and spoons, bending them in such a way to make them hook around the opened flaps of his patient's skin. The thick handle of the knife was used to break open the center of his chest. The man applied such incredible force that it only took one hard strike to break the bone.

None of it made sense until more steam and the stench of burned flesh made her nearly gag. The wound was internal, as if he had swallowed acid or something corrosive to make his insides this seared and glowing like the dying embers of a fire. By the symptoms of this foreign object within his body, she guessed it must have been some level of silver as well.

This wasn't normal. She could already see some of the bones trying to force themselves back together again to close over the expanding lungs and throbbing heart. She had only ever glimpsed such grotesque things in anatomy drawings from a book she once tried to read. But his physiognomy was remarkable. Downright preternatural. No man could heal so quickly from broken bones or lacerated skin.

"He shouldn't be awake for this," she whispered, disturbed by the display.

"He brought this on himself," the man replied as he continued to work to keep the repairing flesh from closing back in on itself.

Nancy tried to make sense of it all. The silver, the way the man healed, the scorched fingertips of the surgeon when he touched the silver himself, and the way he didn't need her to hold the candlestick closer to the body so he could see what he was doing.

For several minutes, Nancy was wholly occupied with wrestling the legs and watching the man use the clean cloth to blot away the excess blood that drooled from every cut he made. She didn't mind his curses as he continued to probe and search for whatever it was that needed to come out.

All the while, she tried to think of what they were. They couldn't be normal men. Silver was supposed to be harmless. It wasn't until she saw the eyes of the patient pop open and she saw the golden irises that she understood.

Werewolves.

Her grandmother's family were from Germany and often spoke of these frightening creatures who could be a man by day and beast by night. Silver bullets were the only thing that could kill them, but she never explained why. They were the monsters that killed unprotected women and ate babies. They were cursed by the devil and doomed to live on the fringes of society as hermits and outcasts.

Could this handsome man personify the terrible myths and legends? Did that explain his strength and dominance? And if silver injured them, why did the man on the table intentionally ingest some?

Nearly half an hour passed and soon the patient stopped thrashing as violently as he had before, too weak from the loss of blood and interminable suffering of feeling silver cutting into his guts and chest. She thought he would fall unconscious, but his eyes continued to roam around the ceiling and squeeze shut in intervals.

When the silver half dollar was pulled from the body, the man lifted it up into the light and then slammed it down angrily onto the tabletop.

"Damned eejit," he grumbled as he withdrew every improvised surgical tool from his friend.

Nancy remained, watching as he tossed a blood-saturated towel over the opening, so she couldn't see him healing. But she knew it was happening. The way the patient let out a long sigh told her enough. The worst was over, and he finally passed out from the relief. His legs went still and head rolled to the side, and if it wasn't for the motion beneath the cloth, she would have suspected him to be dead.

When she moved her bare foot, she realized that a puddle had formed beneath the table.

"I'll clean up the mess," he said in answer to her unspoken concern. "Do you have a spare room where he can rest?"

She nodded, unable to speak or even lift her eyes from the body.

"I need a needle and some thread. Can you get that for me?"

Again, she nodded and let go of the man's ankles, feeling her fingers ache with the sudden release of tension. Her body felt numb with stupor as she moved past him. His eyes followed her as she left the room and a cold chill swept down her spine, knowing that she was being watched by the wolf. She liked it almost as much as when he first came into the house, giving her direction like no other man on earth could ever do.

CHAPTER 12

Dawn peeked through the lacy gossamer curtains, washing the room in a soft amber glow. Dustin barely blinked as he watched Ben sleeping from the station he took beside the four-poster bed. The young woman prepared the room closest to the top of the stairwell for them, so they wouldn't drip blood throughout the home.

The stupid loup-garou hadn't moved since he was laid on the mattress that was now stained with his blood. He'd have to make a point of apologizing to their hosts for the mess he had cleaned up the night before after they had both gone to bed. His full appreciation for their hospitality would also need to be made known. It couldn't have been easy or natural for them to so willingly lodge two strangers in this way. God only knew what they must have thought of him, what they may have suspected.

He could already hear the two women rising from their beds and making their way down the hall. The younger one paused at his doorway and a tense silence made him wonder if she would try to enter. But soon, she continued on and Dustin could breathe easier. He still didn't have an answer for everything she witnessed, nor did he have the constitution to face her.

He made a good show of stitching up the jagged edges of the incision down Ben's torso, but something in the young lady's lack of curiosity made him second guess his methods.

Maybe he shouldn't have asked her to hold Ben's ankles still. He should have ordered her out of the room and done it himself. But there was something in the way she responded to him so readily that made him want her to stay. She was so pliable to his dominance. She acted quickly, decisively, and didn't even shy away from the grisly operation. There was hardly a whimper or gagging sound from her, though plenty of women would have fainted soon after Dustin made the first incision. He didn't have to be in the same room with her for very long to know that she had a spark of something fierce, something he liked a little too much.

Over Ben's screaming and moaning, the sizzle of singed flesh couldn't be heard easily. And he hoped that in the dim light, she wouldn't see anything beneath the gushing blood. He had tried to angle his body as much as possible, but he knew she had occasionally leaned to get a better view.

He pinched and pulled back the edge of the loose bandages he had wound around Ben's torso. Some blood had transferred when he first applied the linen, but apart from the stitches, it looked as if he had never been cut open. This inspection caused the first bit of reactive movement out of the loup-garou since he had fallen unconscious.

Dustin watched his face for any sign of wakefulness and was rewarded with the first glimpse of golden eyes that squinted in the morning light. Relief and unchecked resentment coagulated within his chest and it took all of Dustin's self-control not to throttle his pupil for his idiocy.

Instead, he waited, hoping that this brief moment would help to sooth out Dustin's ire. But by the time Ben's gaze fell upon his mentor, it was plainly evident that he was far from pleased.

"Choose your next words very carefully," Dustin drawled, the sneer audible in his voice. "Because what comes out of your mouth next will determine if I shove that silver coin down your gullet again."

A muscle in Ben's jaw flexed as he did precisely what Dustin asked. "I... I lost my head for a minute."

"Damn right, ye did." A bit of Dustin's Irish brogue slipped through his guise. "Do you really want to die? And if you do, why would you choose a method like that? Didn't you know it'd be painful?"

Ben had no answer for him this time and let his eyes wander about the room. He would have seen the patterned wallpaper, the hand-carved accents upon the crown moulding, and the copious amounts of crates and boxes that were ready for shipping to some place in South Carolina. This left the rest of the room bare of trinkets and valuables that would have decorated it rather well. It gave a kind of echoing emptiness to the chamber that was only populated by furniture and two loups-garous.

"Where..."

"Middletown," Dustin snapped. "Closest city I could find that wasn't burning. Apparently the battling was in Blountville a little west of here. That's what I gather from the conversations further in town."

The quiet morning allowed voices and news to carry far, even to this corner of the city limits.

"There were women," Ben muttered, closing his eyes as if still fatigued from the surgery.

"It's safe, for now. I want to leave as soon as you're able to walk. The prolonged exposure to silver will slow your healing, but you'll be fine in about a day at the most."

He didn't want to wait a day and Ben must have picked up on it, whether through his edgy tone or the pack bond they shared.

"It's been so long since I've slept in a bed," he said gratefully.

"Don't get used to it. We still have a long way to go until we reach Alabama."

The finest of wrinkles formed along Ben's brow at that statement. "Did they see..." Ben's mouth clamped shut as a minor tremor passed through his throat and chest. The flesh might have been mending together, but Dustin didn't expect him to be as good as new after all the poking around he had done the first time.

"I'm not sure," he replied, assuming that he was referring to the golden eyes or the way his flesh burned upon contact with the silver. "It was dark, and the girl might not have seen anything in the candlelight."

Ben gave him a look of skepticism that needed no verbal support for Dustin to understand its meaning.

"You're not the only one allowed to make stupid decisions." He looked away, trying to find the right way to say what he had to ask next. "What did you think would happen? Did you think I wouldn't come after you?"

A stretch of silence made him look back to see Ben's forehead furrowed with guilt. He was all too familiar with that look and this feeling he emitted. Something weighed upon his heart, something far greater than Dustin could imagine or give a name to. He had seen it in other loups-garous and in his alpha. Everyone who dared to look deeper into Dustin's own character would see it within him as well.

Ben had either done something or failed to do something, and now he paid the heavy price of shame. And he was the only one who could ever speak it into the open and break the chains that bound his soul. Once it was said, it could be defeated solely because Dustin was there to help. No matter if Ben tried to swallow a whole purse of silver coins, Dustin would be there for his pack mate, just as Darren had been there for him almost a century ago.

Unlike those moments of openness, Ben didn't speak. He swallowed hard, which seemed to cause him some pain, but he didn't say a word about it. Dustin, however, wouldn't push. He would confide to him in his own time.

Downstairs, the two women began softly talking to one another in the kitchen while breakfast was prepared. From what he could tell, their selection of loup-garou appropriate foods was nearly nonexistent. No bacon or ham. He grimaced when he heard the mixing of cornmeal dough. Ben might not have been in any condition to eat, but Dustin could already feel his stomach roll in hunger. That same stomach roiled further when he realized they were talking about their two strange guests.

Ben was listening too and, for a moment, he let himself forget about his past troubles.

"You get some rest and I'll go downstairs."

Just what he would tell them, he still wasn't sure. Dustin had been in worse situations and talked his way out of every one of them. This should be no different.

"You can't force them to leave," Nancy hissed to her mother as she followed her around the kitchen.

"I can, and I will!" Mrs. Raymond exclaimed far too loudly.

If what Nancy suspected was true, both of the men upstairs could probably hear their heartbeats. This conversation would have been better left unspoken because of the sensitive nature of the situation, but little could be done now that it was brought up.

"What about that poor man who's injured? He needs a place to rest."

Her mother fumbled into her apron pocket, looking for her tinted spectacles. "I don't care," she whined. "You should have never let them in to begin with."

"I couldn't turn them away and you can't either."

She donned the spectacles and gave a huff of irritation. "Dear child, one day you will be as old as I am and understand that not every handsome face belongs to a kind man."

Nancy started to give her rebuttal to that statement, but had nothing truthful to say. Part of her reasons did lay in the captivating green eyes of the werewolf that she met last night.

"What if they're some of our own boys who were separated during the fighting at Blountville?" she offered.

"I didn't see any uniform or rifle with them. You don't know if they're soldiers. You don't even know their names!"

Under the circumstances, no names could be exchanged, so they were all still complete strangers to one another. As soon as he came down to the kitchen, she would remedy that. She would have done so earlier when she passed his door, but lost her nerve and hurried on to join her mother in the kitchen.

"We'll find all of that out soon enough," Nancy replied. "What would father think if we turned these men away when they needed our help?"

It was unfair to bring up her father. The memory of the former preacher was still fresh in the minds of those in the community, despite his being buried for nearly five years in the church cemetery. His sermons in Middletown were well loved and stirred the hearts of all who listened to him on Sunday mornings. Their home was a sanctuary for the lost, the weary, and those looking for a word of wisdom from the Lord.

To ask this famous question of what her father would have done in any given situation immediately set her mother into a charitable mood with that glassy look in her eyes like she was on the verge of tears, despite her sudden understanding smile.

The boards above them shifted and they both listened to their more lively guest descend the stairs. He appeared in the doorway to the kitchen, standing to his full and imposing height to make her heart flutter in a nervous, but exhilarating way. Those eyes that she had dreamed of all night darted from her to her mother. There was a new, softer element in them that hadn't been there before.

Now that the crisis was over, he was even more striking, more dashing with his dirt-smeared cheeks and ruffled hair. The fact that his clothes needed mending didn't bother her. Neither did the idea that he was in want of a good cleaning himself – which she would have gladly assisted in. This supposed werewolf captured her imagination and incited almost no fear whatsoever. If all werewolves looked this roguish, it was a surprise they could be painted as murderous beasts that roamed about under the full moon.

Her mother curtsied first and she followed suit, almost forgetting herself. He gave a short, slightly awkward bow as if he wasn't expecting so civil a greeting.

"Is your companion well?" her mother asked, the picture of cordiality, despite her previous quick judgements about her new houseguests.

"He's resting," the man replied, his voice bringing a rise of color into her cheeks. "I expect him to make a speedy recovery."

At this, Nancy couldn't be silent. "Speedy recovery?"

A slight flicker of worry passed over him, but it was gone before she could blink. "Yes. I know it must have looked bad last night, but it wasn't too serious. He had swallowed something that was stuck, and it was too far down for me to remove via his mouth."

How much did he believe she saw? How much should she pretend not to know? She saw enough last night to make any woman faint. The way he broke that breastbone and pried apart the ribs, so he could easily access the organs was incredible and indeed, very serious.

But Nancy kept her mouth shut. By his reply, she could infer that he wanted to keep his identity – and the identity of his friend – a secret from both of the ladies.

"How dreadful!" her mother gasped, a hand pressed to her chest. "And were you able to extract the culprit of the blockage?"

He nodded and seemed to take a special interest in Mrs. Raymond, though he only showed it in a subtle concentration that Nancy wouldn't have been able to pick up if she hadn't been attentive to every minute change in his expression.

"We did," he said. "Thank you for the use of your table and silver."

Her mother grinned and dipped her chin. "Anything for a few of God's children in need."

Again, there was a twitch of some emotion, but Nancy couldn't decipher it before it vanished again.

"My name's Dustin Keith and my friend upstairs is Ben Myers. Might I have the pleasure of knowing whose home we're in?"

Her mother stammered with the words, but only briefly. "I'm Marjorie Raymond and this is my daughter Nancy."

Dustin regarded her once more and her heart trembled again, making her unsure of what to do with her hands while he was looking at her.

"Thank you for your assistance last night, Miss Nancy. Not many women could witness a surgical procedure like that."

How she wished he would have dropped every formality. Why couldn't they be alone? She had so many questions, so many things to say and confess. Knowing his name was just the beginning. She wanted to know more about who and what he was. She wanted to know everything.

"It was my pleasure, Mr. Keith," she replied warmly. "I do hope your friend makes that speedy recovery you mentioned... for his sake, of course."

Straddling a fine line between politeness and coquettish insinuations had been the thing of novels and gossip amongst the older women of the town. Nancy had never felt the impulse to say anything so flirtatious in her life. Then again, she had never met a man as alluring as Dustin Keith.

If he understood her meaning, he didn't show it, and only gave a slightly strained smile before repairing his attention to her mother. "Is there a general store in town?"

"There is."

"I need to go purchase some things. If you'd be so kind as to look after Ben while I'm away – "

"I will," Nancy jumped eagerly.

Her enthusiasm was barely noticed. "Thank you again."

A few more pleasantries were exchanged, including an invitation to some breakfast before he left, which he declined. All the while, she wondered what it was he could be getting from the store. Her curiosity would be left unquenched when he left the room and soon departed from the house.

Nancy, seeing an opportunity as her mother turned her back to continue cooking, rushed to the window and watched him hurry down the path and in the opposite direction of town. He must have thought he was at a safe distance, because just a few yards from the tree line, he hastened into a run. His figure blurred and disappeared into the woods just on the edge of their property.

This incredible speed could only be accounted for by his supernatural condition. She caught herself smiling, wondering what other abilities he kept secret and anticipating the moment when he would reveal all of it to her.

Ben gave himself permission to rest, now free of the obligation of training and traveling, at least for a day or so. Though he could admit freely that his behavior the night before had been irrational, the sentiments that conceived his act of suicide had all but disappeared. Even in his sleep, he was haunted by the faces of those who were far beyond his reach. Those who couldn't be brought back from beyond the grave and those whom he missed so completely that it was almost a worse pain than what the silver had wrought.

However, if given a second chance with those coins, he wouldn't take it. Not because his grief had lessened in any way, but because he now didn't feel so alone as that dead and abandoned soldier in the forest.

When Dustin had asked his questions, especially "Did you think I wouldn't come after you?", it made Ben realize that this man, who might have ruined his chance for a laudable end to his rather short but fulfilling life, was truly a friend. He could have let Ben die last night. He had surpassed all hope of redemption the moment the coin slipped down his chest, but Dustin didn't give up. He came here, not knowing if this family would have what he needed to perform the surgery and risked both of their secrets just for the chance to save his life.

One of Ben's last thoughts as he fell asleep again that morning was that he had been ungrateful. Dustin had saved his life twice when he didn't have to. He had been a hero when no one was looking. If the Confederacy offered such a thing as a medal of honor, Dustin deserved one if not two.

A period of beleaguered dreaming ensued, only adding to his guilt. A slight tickling in his ribs awoke him and, thankfully, his senses told him the hand that was peeling back a bit of his bandages did not belong to Dustin. The scent was feminine and reminded him of Abigail, though he had enough clarity of thought to realize this wasn't his wife who sat by his bedside.

Knowing this, he kept his eyes closed and took a deep breath as if he were just awakening. Her hands jerked away from him. He let his head list toward the other side of the room where he knew the window to be and took the slightest of peeks to try and ascertain what time of the day it was. He must have been asleep for a few hours, because it was well into the afternoon already.

"I was just checking if they needed to be redressed," the soft voice explained.

Ben felt his throat to be well enough to speak. "They're fine."

"My name's Nancy. I helped Dustin last night when he... I must say I'm surprised you're even conscious after all you've been through. You're probably the bravest man in boot leather that I know, apart from your friend."

When he and Dustin had talked earlier, there was a clear note of uncertainty in his voice, just like there was a note of pretense in hers. The two observations helped him to make the connection and Ben knew she must have seen too much last night. He could tell when someone was lying. Officers lied about casualty lists to maintain morale. He had seen enough lying in the last three years to make him see all the signs as if they were glaring beacons in the dark. Being a werewolf only intensified his awareness of those tells.

"Thank you for your help," Ben grumbled, feigning weakness so that she might be compelled to go away.

She didn't, and that only added to his suspicions that she knew too much. He couldn't fool her.

"If I may ask without seeming too forward... I saw what you had swallowed. It was a coin, wasn't it?"

Beneath the blanket, Ben's hand flexed into a tight fist. Damn Dustin for not being more discrete. He should have snuffed out that candle. Then again, that might have looked rather odd to be operating on a man in complete darkness.

"I don't know... Maybe."

Nancy let out a short, nervous laugh. "Maybe? You don't remember what you swallowed?"

He might have been proficient at detecting lies, but not fabricating them. Neither did he have the time to collaborate with Dustin on a story that they would tell the ladies of the house. It didn't help in the matter that neither of them was sure how much Nancy had seen. Her silvery voice might have been terrible at concealing the truth of how much she knew, but not so revealing on the specifics.

"It was in my food or somethin'," Ben replied.

Either resigned to accept that Ben wouldn't disclose the truth she must have thought she knew, or in a desire not to rile him unnecessarily, Nancy changed the subject to something far more distressing to his raw and wounded spirit.

"You were saying a woman's name in your sleep... Is Abigail a sweetheart of yours?"

Her name brought with it all the feelings and memories that were forever connected with her wild beauty and tender love. "My wife."

If he weren't trying to screen his golden eyes, he would have looked to Nancy to find out why she had fallen so quiet. He couldn't bear this waking stillness and would have preferred to be asleep than in the presence of a girl whom he couldn't read.

"Are... Are ya alone here?" he asked, returning with his own level of pretense, since she would not be the bold and outspoken female.

"I live here with my mother. She's downstairs."

"I'm sorry I'm such an inconvenience to you both."

There came the rustling of fabric, as if she were scooting to the edge of the chair. "It's no inconvenience. It's been dreadfully boring around here lately, to be honest. You and Dustin are the first bit of excitement we've had in a long time."

Ben lowered his brows as if he were confused. "What about the fightin' in Blountville? That ain't far from here."

Once more, a bit of whispering movement and a weight pressed against the edge of the mattress. "We weren't affected, if that's what you mean... Are you a soldier?"

Whatever answer he gave would need to be carefully worded. Admitting that he was a soldier would mean that he had also abandoned his regiment, which he did. But it would lead to a score of new questions. Where was his regiment? Which side was winning? Would the Yankees come further into Tennessee? And then if she was the curious type – as he had assumed already – then she would ask about previous battles and his life in a soldier's camp.

Ben couldn't tell her any of these things. His ignorance and guilt prevented him.

"No," he said pointblank.

Some of that weight eased off the coverlet and he sensed something like disappointment coming from Nancy. "Oh... And I suppose because of this injury, you won't be joining the fight anytime soon?"

"I don't reckon so."

It was a shameful thing to admit. He remembered the way some in Franklin had jeered and taunted those who refused to enlist. They were called cowards, and that was usually enough to persuade them into signing up, more than the flyers that were posted around town. To tell this girl that he had no intentions of fighting might as well have been like hammering in the final nail of the coffin for his pride.

"Do you and your wife live close by?" she asked.

Ben didn't want to talk about Abigail any more than he wanted to talk about the war, but it was a far easier subject to handle at the moment. "I'm from Georgia."

"You're a long way from home," Nancy said. "What brings you into Tennessee?"

"We're on our way to..." Ben paused for only a second and hoped that it didn't give away his hesitancy. "We're goin' back south."

"Is Dustin from Georgia too?"

His lips tilted into a wry smile. "Ya sure are nosy," he said with a laugh that made his stitches pull.

The desired effect – a soft laugh – dammed up the flood for a time. "I'm sorry. Like I said, it's been a while since we had this much excitement... And I have a bad habit of being curious."

"I can tell."

"Can I ask just one more question?... Is... Does Dustin say any names in his sleep?"

In the darkness behind his eyelids, Ben learned all he needed to know. At first, he assumed these questions were borne from a pure feminine inquisitiveness. Now, the truth was out. It was Dustin she was interested in. The aroma that seeped from her direction declared it so strongly that he almost grinned at the irony of the situation.

"No, he doesn't."

Whatever disappointment she had felt earlier deteriorated in the blinding ray of joy that was so potent, it tingled across his skin. Nancy was ready to burst.

Ben, however, felt that thrumming vitality course straight to his skull and he knew that Dustin was close. There were no footsteps to sound his approach and his scent was still relatively stale. Instead, a commotion originating from downstairs called to their attention.

Though he doubted that Nancy could hear as much, there was a metallic pop somewhere coming from outside the house and then the frantic, panicked clucking of chickens. That much alerted her mother.

"Nancy! Come help me!" she cried. "The chickens have gotten out!"

A sharp gasp and permission to depart was given before the girl left the room. Once he was convinced she was gone and in no position to return immediately, Ben opened his eyes and worked to sit up in the bed.

Once more, the stitches smarted and tugged at his flesh. Dustin had done a fair job of sewing him back together, but they were no longer needed. Feeling well enough to do so, Ben unraveled the bandages and extended a claw to cut the thread.

His lips curled as he pulled the stitches from his skin, just as the bedroom window slid open to admit Dustin. In one hand was a brace of recently killed, but rather thin-looking rabbits.

"Looks like you've got an admirer," Ben commented.

Dustin tossed one of the rabbits onto the bed and gave a mocking laugh. "Bully for me."

When Ben looked up, he saw a white fluff of chicken feather sticking out from his dark locks.

"And that wasn't too nice," he added.

"How else was the girl going to leave the room?" Dustin took the soiled bandages and used them to sop up the blood as he tore into his own rabbit carcass.

"I've had to wrangle chicken's before. It ain't fun." Ben, being careful not to make a bigger mess in the bed than what he had already made, mimicked Dustin's precision methods in de-furring the meal and cutting away the meat from the bones. "How'd ya plan to sneak back out without them seein' you?"

Dustin only shrugged and ripped out a strip of sinew with his eyeteeth. "I'll find a way to get around and help them round up the chickens once we're done."

Flinging the last bit of dark string from his chest, Ben bit into the meat. In the woods, feasting upon the raw meat of a dead animal didn't seem so out of place. Here, in a bedroom that reminded him so much of the Rider mansion in Franklin, there was a queer feeling of blasphemy and disrespect to the cultured surroundings. His stare roamed about the wallpaper and fine furnishings, then to the crates and boxes that littered the room.

"You suspect they're ready to refuge somewhere?" he asked Dustin.

He only gave a shrug. "I think I heard them talking about South Carolina. All the better reason to leave soon, so they can leave as well."

A dull numbness swept over Ben. "Do ya think the Yankees will be comin' this way too?"

He felt Dustin's eyes upon him, but wouldn't meet them for anything. He sounded like a scared woman, the way he asked about the movements of the Union army. Though he knew there was little hope for one final push from the Confederacy, he wanted to hear the lies just as much as the civilians did. He wanted to hear that the boys in grey would do all they could to defend their country through sickness and starvation.

"We'll be long gone by the time they're close."

It wasn't exactly encouraging, because Ben knew they were still bound for Alabama and not Georgia. And now, with the Yankees pressing in from the north, their path might likewise be altered to drop down into the Carolinas to completely avoid both armies.

"I almost forgot," Dustin said suddenly, startling Ben out of the unpleasant thoughts that were slowly creeping into his mind. He turned to see his friend pulling out something from his trouser pockets. "I saw the mother wearing these this morning and snuck into her room a short while ago to steal them."

He held out a pair of spectacles, the oval glass pieces tinted a deep amber hue. Through them, little variation of color could be distinguished. A bit of hope rose up in him, the first he had felt in so long that he hardly knew how to react.

"I saw Mrs. Rider wear somethin' like these once. Said they helped her eyes adjust in the bright sunlight."

Dustin offered them to Ben. "I saw how dark the glass was and thought you could use them to hide your eyes. At least until you can find a way to make them normal again."

With his fingers greased by the blood from the rabbit, he took the spectacles and timidly slipped them onto his face. He had never worn spectacles before and only knew a small handful of people who needed such aid. The world was washed in the amber color of the lenses, and he knew that his golden eyes were perfectly masked behind them.

Once they left Middletown, they wouldn't have to skirt their way around cities or farms. They could freely ask for help without Ben's condition blowing their cover. It was far from the ideal solution to the problem, but it was a small step in a more comforting direction.

CHAPTER 13

Nancy plucked at the brown loose curls that hung over her chest, as equally dark eyes stared at her reflection in the mirror. Her mother had retired to bed an hour ago, and she had been waiting for the gentle masculine voices to fall silent for some time since. She couldn't make out their words, but could feel the vibration of their conversation through the floorboards. Patience was never a virtue of hers, and as the clock continued to tick by with frustrating slowness, she wondered if they would ever go to sleep.

For what seemed like the thousandth time since she began this tedious waiting game, she checked herself over, making sure that she looked her best for when she would confront Dustin. She was tempted to dab her cheeks with a bit of the rouge she had swiped from her mother's vanity, but thought it would be too much. In the dim light, the werewolf would be able to see the difference. Though she might have been considered plain, Nancy didn't want to appear as if she were trying too hard to impress him.

All day, she had planned this meeting. Another room had been freshened and prepared for Dustin. The night before, he had been too attentive to Ben to bother with having his own room, but her mother mercifully insisted upon the private accommodations. The one blessing in this arrangement was that once Dustin left the convalescing Ben to his sleep, he would have to walk right past her bedroom.

And when he did, she would be there.

She leaned her elbows against the top of her vanity and stared unblinkingly at her image. The candle that was nearly all burned down cast a dancing light upon the face that she wished could have been prettier. Her nose was too wide, her eyes not as bright, and her sharp chin gave her an intimidating look. Since her coming-out party just three years ago, before the war began, she had waited in vain for suitors to line up outside her door. Her father had always said she was a handsome girl, but when no callers came, when no soldiers asked to fight for her after Fort Sumter had been fired upon, she wondered if her righteous father had lied.

Nancy took a deep breath and let it out slowly to settle her nerves. While Dustin did do all the things to make her believe he wasn't interested, she knew that she had won his respect earlier that day. And it was that instance that made her hope for more. She'd make the effort to ignore the bad and nurture the good between them.

The voices died away and Nancy could feel her heart hammer in her ears as she listened. The door opened and dragging footsteps ambled in her direction down the hall. Being careful not to seem too eager, she snatched up her candle, took one last look in the mirror, and calmly walked out her bedroom door.

Just out of reach from the light, she saw Dustin stop and stare at her with no hint of surprise. If there was one thing she had learned about him, it was that he was incapable of being caught off guard. She almost wondered if he could sense her intentions. Dogs were blessed with a kind of innate sense about strangers and whether they were good people. Perhaps, since he was a werewolf and they were so close in relation to the canine beasts, Dustin could assume the same.

"You're not in bed yet?" she asked, putting on the smile she had been practicing in all the time she waited for him to appear.

"Ben and I were discussing something," he replied in a low tone, his eyes shifting. They wanted to fix on anything but her.

Nancy wouldn't let him avoid her. Not again.

"I was just going down to the kitchen for a drink of water."

He nodded and stepped forward to move past her. "I'll leave you to it, then. Goodnight."

When they were about to pass, Nancy feigned to collide with him. They stopped and began that kind of awkward dance two people did when they were trying to move around in a tight space. Nancy tried not to giggle, but let this game go on for a few seconds longer before Dustin took her by the shoulders and swiveled her out of his way.

To have his hands on her, warm and firm, sent a shivering thrill down her back. She was so close to the epitome of danger and relished in it.

Instead of lingering there, Dustin turned his back to her. But Nancy wasn't finished.

"Thank you again for helping us with the chickens this afternoon."

More or less in an effort to be respectful, he paused. "You're welcome," he replied distantly.

Every line of his body screamed to her that he wanted to be left alone, but Nancy wouldn't accept it. She had to find a way through his armor and, if what she suspected was true, she was running out of time.

She took a few cautious steps, feeling the cold wood flooring beneath her feet. He didn't flee from her this time. "I'm sure we would have been out in the yard for hours chasing after the hens. But you scooped them up rather expertly."

"I've had to do it before."

The closer she drew to him, the more rigid his frame became until he was as a stone statue in her hall. A monument as gorgeous as Michelangelo's carving of King David. Perhaps more.

"Have you worked on a farm? I should have guessed as much, given how... endowed you are."

If he was affected by the compliment, he didn't show it. But she wouldn't be discouraged.

"I did, but... that was a long time ago."

"Before the war?"

It was harder and harder for the people of the south to remember what life was like before the war, before their independence, before death came to each and every household in one way or another.

Dustin gave his affirmative and now they were just a couple of feet from one another, standing between her mother's bedroom and his own on the far side of the hall.

"Where? Ben said he was from Georgia. Are you from Georgia too?"

She wanted to know so badly. She wanted to know everything. His childhood, his family, his habits, his likes and dislikes, how he became a werewolf, and everything in between. He dominated her every waking thought ever since she first saw him standing on her doorstep. Every task, every step, every word she spoke to Ben or her mother, all centered around this one objective. She would know him, even if she had to let honey drip from her tongue with every word.

"No, I'm not."

"Where are you from then, if I may ask?"

Dustin glanced behind her as if he were anticipating something coming down the hall to whisk her away. "Alabama."

It wasn't what she expected, especially after all those uniquely flavored phrases he uttered under his breath while wrangling the chickens in the yard. "Really? I didn't know the men from Alabama could be as charming as you are. A regiment of them came through some time back and they soured my opinion of the state."

She wondered if she had spoken wrongly, but Dustin didn't seem to take offense.

"It's not all bad," he replied with a shrug of his brows.

"You don't talk like any of them either," she said, letting the compliments flow freely from her lips. "You seem to have a better concept of grammar than Ben does. But you say you've worked on a farm."

The light of the candle must have been deceiving her, because she thought she spotted a bit of color rise under his shirt collar. "I... Alabama wasn't my first home, but it is my most recent one."

"And where were you before Alabama?"

Silence made her panic as he opened his mouth to answer, but only jerked his chin toward the stairs. "Didn't you say that you wanted a drink of water?"

Nancy grinned and bowed her head, as if ashamed for getting sidetracked. "I did, but I just thought... thought I'd talk to you since we haven't had much of a chance to get to know one another."

"There's not much to tell," he said, his voice lowering one more octave, making her shudder with delight. His voice was so musical, so pleasing that she could have listened to him talk for days on end.

"Oh, you're being too modest. I knew the moment you came here that there was something special about you. I just can't put my finger on it."

And for the first time, she looked to him as she had wanted to look at him from the beginning. Interested, engaged, fascinated, awed, and completely love struck. It was a gamble, a risk that she believed all women needed to take at least once in their lives. The war could be on their doorstep. The Yankees could burn the Confederacy to the ground to leave them starving and homeless. But right now, in this moment while their circumstances were not as dire as they could be, she could find love and passion in this man who had unwittingly captured her heart.

Something did soften in Dustin's expression, melting that frigid ice in his stare until she knew she had him right where she needed him.

"I don't know what it is you're seeing, but it's better that you leave well enough alone... I can't be responsible for... for what would happen."

Nancy smiled. "Don't you know that's the wrong thing to tell a woman? It only adds to the mystique." She took another daring step, the candlelight flickering in his eyes like two twinkling stars. "But I think I do see something in you that I'm drawn to... So don't push me away. It'll only make me want to seek it out that much more."

They were both on the edge. She could feel it radiating from him, a building aura of self-control that was ready to collapse. His gaze, for the first time, was fixed upon her so intently that a warmth stole through her whole body, making her tingle and her heart race with expectation for what he would do or say next.

Dustin's lips parted, words just on the tip of his tongue, but he could find none. All hardness left him and with one more step, she was inside his defenses. The candle in her hand began to dim as it reached the end of its wick, but she wouldn't be afraid of the dark. Not while he was with her.

"Do you see how hard I've tried to fight you all day?" Dustin whispered, barely perceptible over her own pulse and the popping of the candle flame.

Nancy wouldn't celebrate yet. Not until she knew she had him. "I've seen a man afraid of showing weakness. A man with a secret that he thinks would ruin everything."

"Wouldn't it?"

She slowly shook her head. "I promise. It wouldn't."

Now Dustin seemed the hopeful one, but it only showed in those eyes that gradually darkened. Soon, the blackness of the night closed in. No moonlight reached them on the second floor, but Nancy could still envision the outlines of his face as they had been before the candle had snuffed itself out.

Her hand reached out to grab his shirt, but instead it met a set of fingers that enclosed around hers. They were quivering too.

"I'll take you downstairs," he said, his hot breath suddenly pluming across her forehead.

"I'm not thirsty anymore," she whispered, letting herself savor this closeness. "Not for water."

Dustin was so near now. Near enough that his heat added to her own and a dampness pooled in a place that ached and craved for his touch. An electrifying energy pulsated between them until she could barely stand. He must have sensed this weakness, because an arm encircled her waist just before she fell.

She caught herself against him, feeling his solid body against her own and sighed. The release of what seemed like a lifetime of longing rushed through her. Naturally, her head tilted back and her silent appeal was satisfied. Lips met in a tender, almost timid fashion at first, and then deepened with the repressed yearning that they had confessed just a moment before.

He had been toying with her all this time. While she had been pining after him, openly making her feelings known, he had been battling against his own emotions. All this time, he had wanted her just as badly, just as ardently. At least, that's how it seemed. And even if it wasn't, even if he was playing her now, Nancy wouldn't deny him for the world. He would be her wolf by the end of the night.

Just before dawn, Dustin slipped out from under the covers. Nancy was still asleep, exhausted and dreaming as he tugged on his pants and silently berated himself with the cruelest words in both English and Irish. How could he have let himself fall so far? How could he have let her beguile him with her words and sincerity? He hated himself for what he had done, but if he had the opportunity to rewind and stop himself from making this grave mistake, he wouldn't have changed a thing.

He hadn't lied when he said he had been fighting her all day. Ben said that Nancy fancied him, but he didn't want to believe it, didn't want to see it. He wanted to let himself be blind and dumb to her subtle advances as long as they were there. Last night was the crescendo of her performance, the climax of an entire day spent in getting him to notice her. If only she knew that she didn't need to try so hard.

He paid her one more glance and committed her face to memory. She was fair, pretty, and strong in spirit. Everything that attracted him and made him stiff with need to have his way with her. But the longer he stared, the more he breathed in her arousal and feminine scent, one thought continued to beat within his mind.

She wasn't Cassandra.

She wasn't his wife and never would be. The last one hundred years, he had slated himself for the carnal passions he was occasionally given to when in the company of a woman who was nothing but a mere shadow of his true soulmate. They all had the same boldness, the same ferocity, and brazenness. He had sought after alpha females like Nancy and countless other women, because they reminded him of the wife he lost too soon.

Shame weighed upon him as he snuck out of his bedroom and down the hall to Ben's. No one was awake at this hour, but the grey-blue sky would become brighter over the next half hour as the sun made its appearance to start another day. With luck, they could be halfway to Knoxville by the time anyone in the Raymond household knew they were gone.

He shook Ben until his golden eyes popped open and looked to him in reviling confusion.

"We need to go," he whispered, grabbing their haversacks from the floor and shoving one into Ben's arms. "The women are asleep, but they won't be for much longer."

Ben sniffed the air, probably smelling the sex on him. "Did you – "

"Get your arse out of that bed and let's go."

A look of deviousness shone in his face. "Ya know, I think I need another day or two."

"Oh shut your feckin' gob!" Dustin hissed, tossing him another shirt. "Pick up your feet and let's go."

Ben, thoroughly amused by the whole affair, obeyed, but moved slowly out the door and down the stairs. Hurrying him on, Dustin let some of his true beta dominance bleed out. Once they were far away from the house, he could let himself relax.

"Leavin' them ladies ain't right," Ben remarked as they breached the tree line. "You shoulda at least left a note."

Dustin shook his head. "It's better this way."

"For who?"

He turned and growled to his subordinate. "Listen, I said we were only going to stay until you were well enough. No more."

"What's the big hurry to leave?" Ben asked. "It ain't like your alpha's gonna leave Alabama anytime soon, right? Why not stay a few days? Ya didn't seem this eager to get goin' before."

"It's too risky to stay."

"Again, I ask for who?"

Dustin lurched to a stop and turned on Ben, his wolf sidling dangerously close to the surface. "This isn't any of your business."

Ben folded his arms, completely unafraid of whatever wrath the older loup-garou could rain down upon him. "From where I'm standin', it is. If this is gonna make ya a mess, I deserve to know why."

"And I deserve to know why you tried to kill yourself, but I don't press you for an explanation. Therefore, I don't owe you one."

They glared to one another and the warbling songs of the morning birds was cut off by the rush of dominance that collected around them. Ben was still unfazed, his nostrils flaring and muscles bunching beneath his tanned skin.

Finally, the pressure released.

"I swallowed that coin because... I felt like I shoulda died for my country and I didn't. I should be with my regiment, but instead I'm with you and goin' some place I don't care to go. I wanna go home. I wanna see my wife and my family. I don't wanna be a werewolf and I'd rather... I'd rather be dead."

Dustin understood the sentiment. He remembered the day his whole world fell apart and how he thought he deserved death over living with such a burden as murder. Although he wasn't happy with Ben's methods, he could empathize.

"I had a wife a long time ago in Ireland," he began. "I lost her and... I've never been able to love someone since. I don't love Nancy. I don't think I ever could, but I lose my head when I find a girl who reminds me of Cassandra. Sometimes, I think I'll fall in love again, but it's not the same. It's never the same. If we stayed any longer, it'd only get worse and I don't want Nancy to think that there could be anything between us."

Now, it might have been Ben's turn to commiserate with his mentor. Their expressions softened with understanding, but neither moved for some time. The dominance fragmented, leaving peace in the void where turmoil used to be.

A voice broke the stillness. A woman crying out for the lover who left her. Instead of pushing again, Ben proceeded down the path, away from Middletown. Dustin's legs, however, wouldn't respond to his need to run. For a while, he stood there and listened to Nancy's calls that rose in pitch and urgency. Then, they were reduced to quiet sobs.

His heart ached for a moment, but he knew there was nothing he could do. They had to leave. Not only was she on the verge of falling for him, but also on the brink of discovering what they were. She knew there was a secret about Dustin, and if they stayed she would find out the truth. And even if she said his secret didn't matter, it did.

She wouldn't love a loup-garou. Not for long. Let her see his full, beastly form and stare into the eyes of a monster. Then she wouldn't want him anymore. She wouldn't understand, no matter how hard he would try to ease her fears. In this one thing, he would take after his alpha. One day, Dustin might find the daughter of a loup-garou like he did. They understood the hardships of a life spent with one foot in the human world and one foot in the supernatural.

CHAPTER 14

Her father's last letter was clear enough. They needed to leave Franklin and soon. The plantation was of no consequence, as he believed the south was already on its knees. Anywhere away from Atlanta, a vitally important supply depot for the Confederacy, would have been the safest place for them. But as Abigail looked to the few pieces of luggage that contained all that was left of her worldly possessions, she didn't feel safe at all. Bainbridge might have allies, but it wasn't home.

Turner, only aware that something had happened to make his family distressed, was restless and on the verge of crying every half hour as the women of the house bustled from room to room. Her mother took what valuable belongings they had left and stowed them beneath the floorboards in the event that the Yankees invaded Georgia.

The devils had already come close at Chickamauga. Just over a hundred miles from their home and even closer to Atlanta. Their boys were holding back the Federals at Chattanooga, but God only knew how long they would stay there. The fact that they had come this far into her home state was disturbing enough. Which was why when her mother received the letter from Virginia, demanding that they escape deeper into the south, she didn't hesitate.

In the parlor, she sat down heavily in one of the armchairs, watching Turner waddle across the floor, his tiny arms outstretch to catch himself on any and all surfaces. Every day brought with it new terrors, new worries, and new challenges. The only constant was the love of her family and her son, who found new ways to make her smile through the trials, just as his father had once done.

On the front porch, she could hear the matrons talking, plotting their travels from Franklin to Bainbridge to the south. There, it was believed they could start a new life with a new plantation. The Union hadn't seized the Flint or Chattahoochee rivers yet, which fed into the growing inland port city. A friend of her father's had offered his farm to them for refuge until the war was over and the fate of the Confederacy was decided.

The only voice missing from this important conversation was that of Mrs. Myers.

Keeping a close watch on Turner, Abigail rose and went to the window that looked down upon their suffering fields and the modest house at the bottom of the hill. The chimney didn't smoke, though the weather was chilly enough for at least a small fire. Daily, someone went to check on the woman, half expecting her to be found dead due to some fatal accident that she brought upon herself as a result of her slipping mind.

Gradually, her madness was altered, but not for the better. Instead of expecting her boys to return home, she simply sat and stared at the wall or bit of floor beyond the tips of her shoes. She wouldn't eat, wouldn't drink, and Abigail wondered if she slept at all. As her condition worsened, the need for a helper was seen as a necessary expense and Missy Hopson was employed to do the job. She came to see Mrs. Myers when she wasn't otherwise working as a nurse for Mrs. Featherstone's hospital on the edge of town.

But Mrs. Myers' bags were not on the porch with the others, and the old woman had not come out of her house in days. A few snippets of muffled conversation reached her.

"If she doesn't want to come, then I won't make her come," her mother said crossly.

"We can't leave her here," Miss Peters weakly insisted. "That Missy hasn't been comin' around as often as she should and if the woman doesn't recover from this... whatever it is, then she'll surely starve."

"I share in your concerns, but we don't have enough money saved to afford to bring along another person."

Abigail gripped the curtain she had been holding back and watched the house more intently, hoping that at any moment, Mrs. Myers would come out and give some proof of a clear and lucid mind.

"Then I'll stay, Mrs. Rider. I can't bear to see this family break apart over a lack of money. It just ain't right after all you and your husband have done."

"I could never let you stay behind. You're part of the family, too. If Mrs. Myers won't listen to reason or at least admit that her husband won't return – "

"What do you mean?" Miss Peters curtly interrupted. "I thought Mr. Rider said – "

Her employer hushed her quickly and their voices dropped even lower so Abigail could no longer hear them. But she already knew what they were saying. She had stolen the letter in the middle of the night and read it herself.

Mr. Myers had gone missing at Bristoe Junction. Though the casualty reports for this minor campaign in Virginia was reported by the newspapers, his name wasn't listed as Ben's had been over a year ago. There was still hope that he would reappear during roll call, but Mr. Rider said that his health had been failing either way.

Two sons and a husband lost in the same conflict, for the same futile cause that infuriated her more and more every day. Such a waste of good men. If only this siege upon Chattanooga would fix it and push the army back again into Tennessee.

"She's all alone, Mrs. Rider," Miss Peters continued. "That's all the more reason to take her along."

"I don't have the patience for any woman who can't accept her losses."

Abigail huffed a laugh and wondered what her mother must have thought of her a year ago. In those days, she waited for Ben to come home, just as Mrs. Myers was waiting for her family now.

"That's easier for you to say. You haven't lost anyone. You still have Miss Abigail and your husband."

"Almost every woman in town has lost a son, father, brother, or husband. You don't see them losing their senses."

"Not every woman lost everything they had."

Abigail bit her lips together and closed her eyes, surprised that even she could muster a tear for her mother-in-law. Miss Peters was right. But if Mrs. Myers couldn't be moved, couldn't be reasoned with, then what was left for them to do?

Feeling her son tug at her worn skirt, she looked down to meet his troubled gaze. How could she ever raise him, knowing that she hadn't done all she could for his grandmother? Abigail picked Turner up and propped him against her hip before hurrying out onto the porch.

They were still in the midst of this moral argument when she declared, "I'm stayin'. I won't go to Bainbridge."

Both elder women looked to her in wonder.

"Absolutely not," her mother said resolutely. "I won't leave behind my only daughter."

"And I won't let you leave behind my mother-in-law. We're all she has left. Pa made sure that the Myers were looked after all these years and I'll continue his work if you won't."

She had bowed up to her mother before, but all those fights had seemed so petty. Rebelling against curfews, etiquette lessons, and all the things that society had mandated for her were nothing compared to this one cause for justice. She'd look after the lonely widow herself if she had to, but she wouldn't let her mother do such a heinous thing as abandoning Mrs. Myers to an unknown fate.

"We can't bring her along and I won't let you stay," Mrs. Rider shouted, her face reddening. "Missy will look after her."

"Missy doesn't come often enough and if we can't pay for her passage to Bainbridge, then we can't afford to pay Missy to stay here all the time."

Turner let out a soft cry and swiveled away from the angry words, putting his back to the women who were deciding the fate of his paternal grandmother.

"We don't have enough time to hire another helper," Miss Peters added. "The girl is talkin' sense. Let's just take her with us."

"You both are forgetting that she doesn't want to go!" Mrs. Rider pleaded. "I've already tried to talk to her and she won't come with us."

"She doesn't know what she's sayin'," Abigail replied vehemently. "We have to do what's best for her and she doesn't understand what she needs. If the Yankees come into Georgia... I don't even want to think of what might happen to her."

"G'amma!" Turner wailed.

All three women looked to where the fussy toddler was reaching and realized that somewhere in their disagreement, Mrs. Myers had come onto the porch. Her dark eyes stared at them. Abigail slowly lowered Turner from her arms and let him go. He immediately rushed to Mrs. Myers and fell into her skirts as he had done so many times before.

Dazed and probably still reeling from whatever mental strongholds had kept her prisoner, she scooped him up and hugged him tightly. More out of protection for Turner than in an attempt to be cruel to Mrs. Myers, they hadn't brought him to visit the house in the valley for weeks. They had missed one another dearly, and rarely a day went by when Turner didn't make some run for the back door, as if he would go to pay a call all on his own.

Abigail passed a look over her shoulder to her mother, knowing that the child had proven her point. Mrs. Myers deserved to be with her family. Bainbridge was all the way on the other side of the state and it was unlikely that they would ever see each other again if Mrs. Myers stayed in Franklin.

What she heard next deflated her gratification.

"I won't be the reason y'all are fightin'." They all looked to Mrs. Myers, who had one of Turner's hands in her fist and bounced him affectionately on her hip. "I ain't goin' anywhere."

Abigail's shoulders sank. "They're... They're not coming back," she said, risking an episode.

Mrs. Myers only smiled to her grandson and nodded. "I know."

Shocking everyone on the porch - except for Turner who was just thankful for a kind voice - Mrs. Myers had driven the final nail in her coffin.

"You can't mean that," Miss Peters said. "You've been feelin' poorly for a while."

The widow still wouldn't look to them while her grandson played with a strand of her graying hair. "And I'm sorry to have caused y'all so much trouble because of it... But I assure you, my thinkin's fine now."

Abigail came to her side and straightened the collar on her son's shirt while also trying to get a good look into Mrs. Myers' eyes. There was none of that clouded impression, as if she were looking, but not truly seeing. Perhaps she truly was sound of mind now. Something must have happened to snap her out of the fantasy she lived in from day to day.

"I don't think we'll be comin' back," she muttered sadly, feeling a heavy weight upon her chest as she watched them grin to one another.

"And that's all right. Ya just gotta get this boy away from them awful Yankees."

Turner may not have understood where they were going or what was happening to their broken family, but he did understand the word "Yankee". His smile disappeared quickly.

Abigail wanted to fight her on this, wanted to insist that she came along even if they had to sneak her aboard the train without any ticket. But there was one thing she had learned quickly about Ben's family. They were just as stubborn and feisty as she was. Telling Mrs. Myers that she couldn't do something was pointless.

So instead of arguing or making up every conceivable reason why she shouldn't split her family apart like this, Abigail embraced her mother-in-law for what might have been the last time.

"I'll make sure someone comes by to look after you," she whispered into the older woman's ear.

With one hand supporting Turner, the other wrapped around Abigail's waist and pulled her closer. "I can take care of myself now, darlin'. Thank you for bein' here for me."

Emotions that she couldn't put a voice to clamped around her throat and Abigail struggled to push back the tears again. Leaving Franklin meant leaving behind her home, her family, and a piece of her life that this war was trying to destroy.

November 21st, 1863

Outside Knoxville, TN

"Slow down!" Dustin cried from almost a quarter of a mile behind him. "You're gonna hit something!"

Ben knew he had riled the Irishman enough to make his burr emerge, but he didn't care. They had been moving too slow through Tennessee and it seemed that the added motivation for them to distance themselves as far from Middletown as possible did nothing to accelerate their progress toward the Georgia border.

Union detachments were everywhere, spilling in from the north in waves to reinforce their occupied towns and cities across the eastern portion of the state. The tide of war wasn't flowing in their favor anymore and Ben could feel the earnestness to return home so keenly that it ached in his bones every day, sang through his blood with each mile they conquered. He knew his eyes weren't as they should be, but with the spectacles, hope had been revived.

It all came to a head just a few days prior when Ben and Dustin came upon a lonely homestead being raided by a few strangling Union soldiers. The farm was ransacked, livestock and supplies carried away under the arms of vile Yankees who didn't care for the family they stole from. Normally, Dustin urged them not to be involved in these minor conflicts. It wasn't their place. But a change had taken place in him. It was barely perceivable, but Ben could sense it somehow. Dustin was struck with a compassion that was unlike him and insisted that they help.

Using their werewolf abilities, they chased down the soldiers, stole back the provisions, and returned them to their rightful owners. Ben then learned the value of his golden eyes when he terrified the Yankees into submission, but his takeaway from the incident struck him even deeper than this hounding notion that he truly was a monster.

He thought of his family, thought of Georgia. They might be suffering from the same scourge of Union deserters. What if it was his own family's home that was being pillaged? What if his in-laws were being robbed? What if Abigail was assaulted by a soldier? He had to leave and make sure they were safe. He had to leave Dustin, however imprudent a decision it might have been.

Today, he'd endeavor to do it. He couldn't wait for Dustin any longer and, as much as he owed to the Irish werewolf, he owed more to the family that waited for him. This portion of his training allowed him to gain some ground and make his escape.

The dense forests on the southern side of the Tennessee River was the perfect place to lose him. He'd run and dodge through the trees until he couldn't hear Dustin anymore, and then plunge into the river to mask his scent. The width of the river stretched five hundred feet or so across, but on the other side was the two warring armies. Dustin wouldn't follow him through the bivouacked camps and breastworks around Knoxville. And with the spectacles safely stowed in his pocket, he was prepared to blend in with whatever regiment he could find. Then, he'd double-back after he knew Dustin had moved on and make his way to Georgia.

Ben didn't allow himself to think of the consequences or how he would be reprimanded if Dustin did find him. This had to work. After he saw his family and assured that they were out of the Yankees' way, he would go back to find Dustin. Maybe he'd even go to Alabama with him, though after his second brush with death, Ben had been able to focus on his training more successfully. He was still a long way from fully grasping certain aspects of his abilities, but he could maneuver through these trees and propel himself down steep slopes without tripping over his own feet. His shoulders only occasionally collided with the trunk of a passing tree, but those were insignificant.

When the moment came, when Ben could no longer here Dustin's Gaelic oaths or crashing feet through the brush, he turned north. He slammed into the water, still running at his full speed. The icy winter current threatened to sweep him downstream, but he swam on, trying to splash as little as possible and hoping that the cover of night would mask his bobbing head above the surface.

Once he reached the other side, dripping wet and shivering from the cold, Ben only glanced back momentarily to make sure he wasn't followed. Nothing. The tingling sensation in the back of his skull had lessened, making it clear that he was the only werewolf for at least a few miles. That was all the clearance he needed before sprinting toward the Confederate army.

He kept to the shadows, moving just outside the firelight of the numerous encampments. A warm feeling of comfort came with the sight of so many tents and gray uniforms that weren't bloodied and torn apart by shrapnel. Though the faces were downcast and pinched by the winter chill, Ben missed this. He missed the comradery, the talking, the music, the laughter that echoed through the tents as men tried to make light of their circumstances with jokes and stories. As much as it used to turn his stomach, he missed the smell of their peanut coffee and the multitude of bodies huddled together to keep warm on these long, suspenseful nights before a battle.

He continued on, his damp clothes stiffening with frost as he searched for a smaller encampment, one where he could sneak in and not stir too much notice. His belly was full from a meal earlier that night. Dustin had warned him about the dangers of eating old army foods, so he wouldn't impose upon any of them except to maybe ask for a blanket or cloak to warm himself.

Most of the men, as he neared the far western portion of the camp, were asleep upon the frozen ground. But one man was awake, playing a harmonica with a distinct warble that Ben thought he recognized. The more he listened, the more sure he was of the musician's identity.

He hastened his pace and came to the tent of an old friend, a fellow Georgian and superior officer. Noah Culpepper sat just outside the open flap, the harmonica pressed to his lips and eyes closed as he blew out each bouncing note of "Goober Peas". Ben grinned, remembering how he and the others of Company G would belt out the rather ridiculous lyrics as they marched from one battle to another.

It might have been the same harmonica and the same man, but the gray wool uniform coat had one major alteration that made Ben's grin widen. The golden, double-strand sleeve braid and three bars upon his collar told him that Noah was no longer a sergeant. Had it been so long since Sharpsburg that he could have risen up through the ranks to captain?

Ben donned the tinted spectacles, then emerged from the trees to wait for Noah to notice that he wasn't alone anymore. His old friend opened his eyes and his dirt-smeared face went pale. The harmonica lowered into his lap and they stared, one dumbstruck and the other shaking with the need to reunite with one of the men with whom he had enlisted.

"Is... Is that you, Ben?" he asked in a hushed voice. There were three other men sleeping close by on their bedrolls, chins tucked under the covers to shield themselves from the biting wind.

He nodded. "It's really me."

Noah stood and looked him up and down, the questions just waiting to bubble out in a babbling confusion. But all he said was, "I thought you were dead."

It didn't surprise him. Many who disappeared from their regiments after a battle were thought to be amongst the dead or fled with the gutless deserters. Though Ben felt he belonged to the later classification, he now had a chance to explain himself – if an excuse would even be accepted by now. One solace was that he knew Noah, and though he was a loyal soldier, he was an even more loyal friend and wouldn't turn Ben in for the crime for which he so justly deserved to be sentenced.

"Nope," he replied. "Not dead."

Noah stumbled forward, his limbs rigid by the cold and disbelief of seeing his missing friend again. When he was close enough, they embraced, and Ben was disappointed to feel that he had lost weight since September of 1862. Maybe the added bulk to his own arms and chest only made the captain seem thinner.

"What happened to ya?" Noah asked as he pulled away to inspect his friend one more time.

In a moment of panic, he wondered how well the spectacles were working and how much of a change had taken place in him.

"It's a long story," Ben replied, hoping that he wouldn't have to give any details. "But what happened to you? Captain?"

Noah didn't seem impressed by this promotion and shrugged. "It happened in February. Took another month or two to get the uniform."

They wandered, step by step, closer to his tent as they talked.

"How is everyone?"

Noah mentioned only a few names that he recognized, a few men who he knew were with him at Sharpsburg. But there were more that weren't mentioned. Men like John Duke, whom he last heard was convalescing in a hospital in Winder. William Favor, James Taylor, Will Pitman, and so many others he had wondered about for over a year.

All dead, wounded, or captured.

He didn't know what he had been expecting. This was war and when they fought at places like Fredericksburg and Gettysburg, casualties were inevitable. Perhaps some part of him had wanted to think that the seventh Georgia infantry would be held in reserves, away from the fighting, so there would be no tears in the eyes of their women and families back home. But then again, some privates, like Alman, Spearman, Lane, Stewart, Rooks, and second lieutenant Thomas Brown, wouldn't have wanted to die any other way, but in the defense of their country.

"They were all brave," Noah said mournfully, "Even to the end."

Ben nodded, knowing they would have punched him in the arm if he shed a tear for any one of them in that moment. So he kept his eyes dry and asked the questions that were just as important.

"How are we doin'? I mean, really? Is it as bad as the newspapers are sayin'?"

Noah made a face. "I don't reckon I know what the newspapers are sayin', but it's bad. We ain't even supposed to be here. Lee transferred us from the Army of Northern Virginia back in September so we could help Longstreet at Chickamauga. We mighta won that battle, but Chattanooga's a waste of time. Bragg's drivin' the men crazy – as always. He works us like we're some damn darkies on his plantation. We were starvin' and scared for our lives the whole time on that mountain. We had most of their railroads and supply lines, but it didn't do us a licka good. And you know General Grant himself is there now. Says he's gonna relieve the whole city. I suspect there'll be a battle there any day now. In the meantime, we're just busy catchin' lice and pneumonia."

"Then why are y'all here and not in Chattanooga?" Ben asked incredulously. The movements and orders of the army never made sense to him, but he wasn't the one with the West Point education. If Lee, Longstreet, and Bragg thought laying siege to these towns would truly help the cause, he had to believe it.

"General Burnside took Knoxville back before we fought at Chickamauga. Barely encountered a bit of resistance from our boys either. Damn shame. And the people inside the city actually welcomed him! Apparently there's a bunch of yella-bellied loyalists up here. Anyway, Bragg and Longstreet weren't gettin' along anyway. I guess they thought if they could take Knoxville, it would help Chattanooga fall. I can't rightly see how, but I'm just a captain. When I'm a lieutenant, maybe I can question my orders. We marched almost all the way from Chattanooga to Sweetwater, sometimes ridin' on a train that couldn't do the job of ten mules. We were supposed to get supplies at the depot, but there was nothin' there. We're runnin' on what rations we've had since Chattanooga – which ain't many. I heard Longstreet wanted to attack Knoxville yesterday, but he's draggin' his ass, thinkin' someone's gonna send him reinforcements or somethin'. The longer he waits, the worse it's gettin'. Burnside's sittin' comfy in the town right now probably laughin' at the whole army."

Ben shook his head, angry at the entire mess. "Y'all shoulda stayed in Chattanooga."

Noah leaned forward, brows arched. "Have ya met General Braxton Bragg? Because iffin ya had, ya wouldn't be sayin' shit like that. We might be starvin' and freezin' here, but at least we don't have to deal with Bragg."

The condemning reputation of the general from North Carolina had been circulated throughout both armies. Harsh and unsympathetic to the plight of the common soldier, he was the nightmare of his division. But no one would second guess his ability to gain the victory at the end of the day.

"The last time I saw ya..." Noah's voice had dropped and was no longer the frustrated captain, but the concerned friend of a man who had quite literally disappeared off the map for over a year. "Ya weren't lookin' too good. That fella that was with ya said ya had some kinda fever after Sharpsburg."

Ben was well aware of what he had looked like. Blood-splattered, unconscious, carted around by a stranger from an Alabama regiment, and totally out of his mind with the first stages of the transformation from mortal to werewolf. He was inclined to feel embarrassed, until Noah continued.

"And then when ya disappeared for a few days, I didn't know what to think. When the Alabamian came back into camp, sayin' you'd died of that fever and were buried somewhere near the mountains, all of us were just torn to pieces about it. They're all gonna wanna see ya in the morning."

Ben's stomach clenched. "He said I was dead?"

Noah went on to tell him how Dustin had come into camp and went straight for Carmical to account for Ben's absence. "I wrote home and told your folks that ya was dead too. I figured I shoulda done it since my wife's family knew yours."

Ben bowed his head into his hands. Dustin had ruined him, and saved him in one single lie. Carmical wouldn't have pressed for an investigation into his disappearance or issued a court martial, since it was said that Ben was dead and therefore – obviously – relieved of his duty from the Confederate Army. But in that same confession, his family was put through hell. One letter from Noah and his name listed on a casualty report would have sent his entire family into mourning. Black dresses, sobbing eyes, and broken hearts. They wouldn't have even had the chance to bury his body, which would have added to their grief.

Dustin not only betrayed his trust, but disrupted the lives of those he loved the most. Ben could always return to his family. He had heard stories of supposedly dead soldiers going home on a furlough to relieved wives and sweethearts. Ben could be numbered with these cases, but that didn't bother him as much.

What flamed that wolfish, beastly rage within him was that Dustin went behind his back and signed his death certificate without consulting him. They were supposed to be allies, friends, packmates. Yet, he went and did something like this. Ben could feel his cheeks burn with fury.

"Are ya gonna stay and help us take Knoxville?" Noah asked. His question woke him from the hateful thoughts, making him look up and think about an answer.

As a werewolf, he could help the army. He could hear the battle plans of the enemy from well out of artillery range. If needed, he could sneak into the city and sabotage their weaponry or cause a confusion that could buy his regiment precious time. And if that wasn't acceptable, he could offer his services as a soldier once more. He might not have been any more effective in firing a rifle, but if it came to hand-to-hand combat, he'd be unstoppable.

But something else had burst through the indignation and the hurt that Ben was tempted to drown in, through the spiraling train of thought that he could be a soldier again. The back of his head tingled, meaning another werewolf was near. And he was fairly sure who it was. How Dustin had found him wasn't a concern, but getting away from Noah was.

"I... I don't think I can," he replied, willing to talk a little longer until Dustin was right upon the encampment. "I've got plans. I've gotta go see my family and show my wife I'm alive."

Noah seemed puzzled. "Ya haven't been with them this whole time? I thought if ya wasn't dead, you'd be with them for sure."

Ben shook his head. "No, I've been... I've been busy. It's a little hard to explain."

His friend threw up his hands. "Ain't none of my business, but... now that you're alive, they're gonna see ya as a deserter. Or maybe just captured at Sharpsburg. Either way, it's gonna take a lot of explaining to get out of a death sentence. You've been gone for way too long."

"Ya can't tell anyone I was here," Ben implored quickly. "Don't even write to Abigail. I'm gonna see her soon. I've gotta... I've just gotta do something first and then I'm goin' to Georgia. Not even the devil can stop me now."

CHAPTER 15

FRANKLIN, GEORGIA

Olivia Myers noticed the tremor in her hands as she scraped the ladle against the bottom of the stew pot. This was the last of it. After this bowl, there would be no more of the thin soup she'd been living off of for the last week. The garden was bare now, and she couldn't remember when Missy said she would call next. Was it today or next week?

With one hand cradling the cold stew bowl and the other holding together the flaps of her last good shawl about her shoulders, she sat down to the empty table in the middle of the kitchen. Three chairs, vacant. She wouldn't look at them in the light of the single candle flame. Not when her stomach smarted with the need for some food. And not as long as every glance about the echoing house brought her one nudge closer to insanity again.

She found that as long as she didn't think of them, didn't remember their faces or their laughter, she was all right. Her mind would stay clear and she wouldn't imagine that it was summertime. Because the mind was a terrible trickster, and though her hands were nearly numb with the cold, she could pretend it was a blistering hot afternoon. Though she heard nothing but the tap of her spoon against the sides of her bowl, if she let her imagination wander, she could hear the grunt of mules and shouts of her husband as they tilled the fields.

No, she couldn't give in to such absurdity. They were dead. All of them. Taken by this useless war. She couldn't even remember what they had been fighting for. Only that the men of Franklin and all of Georgia had gone to be butchered and slaughtered by the thousands. Some returned. Most didn't.

But she was still here. Still dressed in her only black mourning gown, with her hair undone and cascading down her back in tangles. When was the last time she brushed it? The last time she washed her face? Or her clothes?

Soon, the bowl was empty and Olivia absentmindedly stood up and went to the pot for seconds. She was puzzled when she found it empty. She could have sworn there was more left. Setting the bowl down onto the counter, she resolved to go to the garden to pull up more of the carrots and cabbage she knew to be there.

Suddenly, it felt very cold and Olivia looked to her dirty bare feet. The floor was filthy too. When had she cleaned last? She'd get one of the boys to sweep it up while she made another batch of stew. She couldn't understand why she was so ravenous. They all had a big breakfast of toast, eggs, and ham. Looking to the wash bin where she kept the used dishes, she found it just as empty as her stomach.

Her brows wrinkled in confusion. Maybe Ben cleaned their plates. He was always so helpful around the house. Then, she noticed how dark it was. Those boys should have been in from the fields hours ago.

Stepping out her front door, she peered into the darkness, toward the barn and fields beyond. No lantern light could be seen, no sound of rattling harnesses or baying of the labor animals.

"Jed! Phillip! Ben! It's time for dinner!" she called out. "I've got soup waitin' for y'all!"

No answer. Not even a cricket chorus replied to her yells and she waited a little longer.

Soon, she could hear something. Deep, negro voices from over the rise just to the south of the fields. When had Mr. Rider hired on negroes to work the fields this late? With them came a sprinkling of torchlights upon the horizon. A dozen at least, if not more. The voices grew louder, meaner, and it took that change in pitch for her to awaken out of her daze. It was no longer spring in her mind, but a cold and bitter winter season. And she was alone. Utterly alone.

Olivia dashed back into the house and rushed up the stairs to look for her husband's rifle under their bed. He had showed her how to fire it before he left, but couldn't be sure of the last time it was cleaned. It had to be several months.

She dropped to her knees and reached blindly under the bed, her fingers scraping across the dusty floorboards until she found the equally neglected rifle. With fumbling earnest, she went to her dressing table and rummaged through to find one of the cartridge packets he had left for her.

Nine steps to load the rifle and she was ready to defend her home – or what was left of it.

A bright glow, like the coming sunrise, streamed through their bedroom window. When she went to peer out the dingy glass, what she saw made her limbs feel weak.

They were burning the fields. The dead and withering cotton stalks would be reduced to ash, the plantation purged of its former crops.

The figures of the negros were now discernible as half of them carried on, spreading the fire from their torches, while the other half went to the barn. They wouldn't find much. Mrs. Rider sold the equipment to an old farmer up the road for travel money so they could escape Georgia. Who would have thought that the plantation would fall to these runaways before the Yankees could step foot in the state again? Or, maybe the Yankees were already there, and these darkies weren't runaways at all, but freed men. What did that mean for Olivia?

From her bedroom window, she watched the inferno rise and spread like a gangrenous plague across the home she had known for years. The barn and stables were soon lit up from the inside, the dry and rotted wood structure catching quickly.

Then, they were headed for her home.

Olivia tightened her grip over her rifle and rushed down the stairs, no longer cold or caring about her rather frightening state with bare feet, a black dress, and unkempt hair. These darkies would know the wrath of a woman who had nothing more to lose.

She stood on her front porch, stance firm and eyes flinty as she watched the burly black men stomp up the path. They busted down her fence and looked through the barren garden, dropping their torches so close to the soil.

A few men hurried up toward the front steps, but before they could alight one foot onto the creaking treads, she raised her rifle.

"I'll shoot any man who comes in this house!" she warned.

One or two of the darkies laughed, but a few others took her seriously and backed away.

"Ya ain't gonna shoot us, ma'am," one of the laughing negros said. "Ya only gots one gun n' one shot. How ya suspects ya gonna fights us all?"

Olivia glowered at him, refusing to show any fear, even though he was right. She didn't grab any extra cartridges from upstairs and she was far too weak to fight any of them. From their looks, they had to be former field hands. They could easily overpower her.

Another darkie stepped up, coming dangerously close to the steps again. "Hows about ya jist move on outta da way n' nobody gonna git hurt tonigh'."

She quickly placed the percussion cap and cocked the hammer back on the rifle. "Or you men can just move on. There ain't nothin' in this house for you."

From behind the lot, a man pushed his way to stand between the porch steps and the mob. In the light, she recognized his kind features. Mr. Rider didn't keep any slaves on the plantation, but he did hire them out when he needed the extra help. One slave from a farm on the other side of Franklin was frequently called for.

Muscled, but a gentle giant among men, Hiram had come often enough for them to know him intimately. She remembered baking a loaf of bread for him to take back to his family, and more than a few times he stayed for dinner in this very house.

"Don't ya be threatin' Miss Olivia!" he contended. "She's nice folk and don't need no trouble. Move on, now!"

Olivia refused to lower the barrel of the rifle until all the hostile negros were on the other side of her slightly dismantled picket fence. Only Hiram remained, a looming sentinel in the dark who had saved her and her home. When he turned, she took the cap from the seat on the rifle and eased the hammer back down.

"Thank you, Hiram," she said, keeping one eye on the group of men as they marched their way up to the Big House.

"T'was nothin', Miss Olivia."

"Why are they here? Are they..."

Hiram, knowing he was welcome into their home at any time, stepped up onto the porch without fear of being forced back. "They's runaways, ma'am. Some from Mass'r's plantation, some from other farms in the next counties over. They been doin' this all night."

"But why?" she pleaded. "We ain't never done nothin' to deserve this. Ya know the Riders ain't never owned slaves."

Hiram nodded. "You know that, and I be knowin' that, but they don't. They think all white folks in Georgia all the same. I been followin' them since they came around our plantation just a few hours ago. Wanted to make sure they wasn't gettin' into some big trouble. Mass'r probly thinks I done ran off with them."

Olivia reached out and touched his sleeve. "I'll tell Mr. Cartwright that ya didn't have anything to do with all this." Her eyes wandered back to the burning fields of old cotton and wondered if the flames would try and spread to her homestead.

Hiram shook his head. "No need for that, Miss Olivia. I'm runnin' away too. Just not with them."

She looked to him in astonishment. "Runnin' away? Don't ya know how dangerous that is now? Why not just wait for the Yankees?"

The words didn't seem like her own. Just wait for the Yankees? She spoke as if they really were the deliverers that the darkies had been praying for during all their years of bondage. In some ways, they were, but Olivia knew better. Not every Yankee and northerner was an abolitionist, and not all of them would simply let free labor go unused. Contraband camps were no better than any plantation. The work changed a little, but the darkies were still slaves with a new master who might not have appreciated their value as much as the people of the south had.

"I ain't gonna wait for no Yankee to come tell me that I's free when I knowed in my heart that I always been free. Maybe not free in body, but my soul sho' is. No, ma'am. I gotta take my life in my own hands now. As much as Mass'r Cartwright treats me good, it's about time I moved on."

"What about your family? Are they comin' with ya?"

Hiram nodded proudly. "They gonna run as soon as this rabble moves on. I told them it ain't safe as long as they's goin' around and burning up folks' homes."

The shattering of a window drew her attention to the Rider household on the hill.

"Someone has to stop them," she breathed, watching them mount the rise and start their raid. It was a thankful thing that the other women had moved on south.

"I don't think I can do that, Miss Olivia," Hiram said regretfully. "I can tell them you's good people, but one of them older negros remembers being a slave of the late Mr. Rider and I don't think he was a kindly man. Why else would he be lookin' for revenge?"

Olivia had never known the man personally. Only through stories told by the Riders when she had first come to the plantation. "But that was a long time ago," she said.

"Some men hold grudges for a whole lifetime, Miss Olivia. A negro never forgets a beatin', and he never forgets a kindness either. That's why I come to save ya."

Olivia somehow found the will to smile and patted Hiram's arm. "And ya were so good to do that for me. Thank you."

Hiram touched the brim of his hat and jumped off the porch to run down the pathway. "Like I said, t'was nothin', ma'am. You take care of yo'self now!"

Olivia called a feeble, "You too." And then turned back to the Big House on the hill as the first fire was lit from within. By morning, the only thing left standing would be her and her home, the only survivors of the war that was tearing the south to pieces.

"Good God," she prayed, "End this war before it ends us."

Knoxville, Tennessee

Dustin didn't need to scream or even whisper the command to Ben. All that was needed was one pulse of dominance through their pack bond. One silent, wordless command for the pup to heel. It took a while for him and the other soldier, Noah, to say their goodbyes. Then, Ben made his long, solemn walk away from the Confederate camp and to the place where Dustin waited in the sheltering forests near the Tennessee River.

To say he was furious would have been an understatement. The ice that formed across his clothes had no chance to solidify as his body grew hot with that alpha-rage that he had once heard Darren describe so ineloquently. There were no words, no proper analogies that could explain what he felt toward the younger loup-garou who had tried to run away from him.

It had slowly been building since Ben swallowed the coin. An intolerance like nothing Dustin had felt in his nearly one hundred years as a loup-garou. He thought that he had reached the end of his fuse when he found Ben dying. But that was nothing compared to this.

And somehow, Ben knew it. He thrust his way past the low-lying limbs that blocked his path, eyes cast down as he came into Dustin's daunting presence.

"What the hell were you thinking?" he growled, well aware that his golden eyes, fangs, and claws had made an appearance as a result of this storm brewing in his chest.

Ben calmly took off his spectacles and tucked them away in his trouser pocket before answering. "I can't stay with ya."

Dustin might as well have been blasted through the gut with canister shot. He had said something to Noah about going to Georgia, but he didn't want to think it true. Or better yet, he wanted to think it was a lie, so his friend wouldn't worry.

"Excuse me?"

"I'm not goin' to Alabama," Ben repeated, leveling his stare upon Dustin as if he were taking aim to fire another round.

"You think you're going to Georgia?" Dustin scoffed.

"I know I'm goin' to Georgia."

He laughed and pinched the bridge of his nose, in total wonder that they were having this conversation at all. After all he had done for Ben, all the training and late nights spent shifting with him. All of it just so Ben could repay him with this. "You're not going to Georgia," he said, the mirthless laughter finally dying away. "You're not ready. We've talked about this before."

If Ben's resolve wavered at all, he didn't show it. "How long did it take you before you were ready? How long before you got to see your family again?"

"That's not a fair comparison," Dustin said. "I had no one."

Ben's lips curled. "And that's what ya don't understand. I do have someone. I have a whole family who thinks I'm dead because of you!"

He wondered when that truth would rear its ugly head in this discussion. He heard the end of Noah's story, how he had written to Ben's family. "I had to do it," Dustin furiously asserted. "If they just went on thinking that you were alive and missing or had deserted the army, inquiries would have been made. People would come looking for you. It was better that they think you were dead and you'd show up later alive and well. Don't you understand?"

Ben ground his teeth. "I do understand that, but you hurt my family. Don't ya feel any sympathy for them? They've been mournin', cryin' over me like I'm dead and gone. They didn't have to if ya just kept your damn mouth shut."

Dustin felt a vein throb in his neck as his dominance intensified. "I did it for your own good. Everything I've done for you was for your own good! And when I tell you that you can't go back to Georgia, I'm not just pullin' a laugh on you. You aren't ready. You may think you can go back to your family and act like nothing ever happened, but you can't. You're a loup-garou now. Things are different. You can't just walk into their lives and think it'll all be fine and safe. Precautions have to be taken that you don't even know about yet. You can't control yourself during the shifts. Your eyes are – "

"I know about my eyes!" Ben thundered, the final threads of his composure fraying. "My eyes wouldn't be this way if it wasn't for you!"

Dustin shook with the need to strike out at him, but refrained. "I'm so sick of hearing you complain! 'I wanna go home. I wanna see my Abigail. I wanna be with my family.' You get the morbs quicker than any man I ever knew. When the time is right, you can go to them, but it's not now!"

Ben didn't take kindly to his mocking and charged a few paces forward, his wolf just as ready to fight as Dustin's.

"Maybe I'm not ready because you've been a piss-poor excuse for a trainer. You've been drillin' and drillin' and drillin', but I'm no better than I was the day we started."

"All the more reason I need to take you to Alabama to my alpha," Dustin retorted. "He trained me and if I'm getting something wrong, he'll correct it."

"And then he'll keep me for another year. Maybe two. I'm sick of waitin'! I'm gonna see Abigail and there's not a damn thing ya can do about it!"

Dustin hardly knew why he said what he did next. "I'll betcha a hundred greenbacks that Abigail's already moved on and found another beau to replace you. She's better off for it too."

Ben lunged for him, partially shifted as the fury of the two loups-garous finally clashed. They latched onto one another, claws digging and ripping through flesh. They fought like dogs, rolling across the cold ground and sending a showering of blood and dirt in every direction. Dustin held back the shift for as long as he could, but felt his wolf pressing to the surface with each second.

Minute after minute dragged on seemingly with no end. Wounds healed quickly, stamina restored itself, and no amount of dominance could make Ben submit long enough for them to talk civil to one another again. In some ways, Dustin didn't want to. This had been building for much longer than a month since this homesickness took a turn for the worse. The last year had been one ceaseless nightmare of angst, stubbornness, and interminable frustration on both of their parts.

Ben wanted to go home, and Dustin wanted to go to Europe.

Ben didn't want to be a loup-garou, and Dustin didn't want to be his alpha.

Ben wanted to die, and some part of Dustin wished he had left him alone in Sharpsburg.

Ben wasn't improving, and Dustin knew it was his fault.

The southern patriot collided with the bull-headed Irishman.

Those few moments when he thought they were bonding, when they could put their differences aside and be the packmates they were supposed to be, were few and far between. And Dustin had finally had enough.

He threw Ben off and threw everything he had into one last burst of dominance. He finally gave up the fight under the immense spiritual force imposed upon him. Ben rose onto his knees and elbows to stare at Dustin, breaths coming out in great, panting huffs as claws and fangs sheathed themselves.

"If you go to your family now," Dustin warned, "you could kill them. You could kill Abigail, your brother, all of them. Their blood will be on your hands. Believe me when I say that you don't want that on your conscience. We're going to live a long... long time. And you don't want to hate yourself every day of it."

The obstinate loup-garou was quiet for a moment, and then shook his head. "That's a chance I'm willin' to take."

He was a fool. A damned fool. If only he wouldn't have let his loneliness blind him, then maybe Dustin's words would have fallen upon receptive ears. But in this moment, all reason took a vacation. Neither were thinking clearly.

With a shake of his head, he held up his hands in surrender. "Go then. You'll figure it out for yourself, and I won't be there to clean up the mess."

Dustin turned to the north and took a few steps before he saw the reflective gleam of something on the ground. There, half covered in a thick layer of blood, was a sizable shard of tinted glass. The spectacles must have broken during their fight and torn loose from Ben's pocket.

He passed a hand over his face and let out a heavy sigh. "Good luck to you," he mumbled. "God knows I didn't intend for any of this to happen."

Ben didn't say a word, didn't move. If he noticed what Dustin had spotted, there was no need to wonder what he meant. Without the spectacles, there was no way for Ben to hide his eyes from the rest of humanity.

But that wasn't Dustin's problem now. None of it was. Ben was released from his care and now a new weight settled on his shoulders, one that he hoped would pass with time. Leaving him meant letting him fend for himself in a world that wouldn't accept loups-garous. He'd be making the hard choices, facing a life without the protection of a pack or alpha. Dustin might have condemned him to this fate, but he was the only one who could save him from it too.

"If you change your mind, find Darren Dubose. He's in Devia, Alabama."

Those were the last words he spoke to Ben. The last friendly advice he would give. The last they would ever see of one another, because Dustin was going to make sure he wouldn't step foot on American soil again for a long, long time.

CHAPTER 16

Life in Bainbridge was nothing like Franklin. Nothing like home. The citizens bragged about its size and importance in the southwestern portion of Georgia. Here, so close to both the Alabama and Florida border, they were far from much of the fighting and commerce hadn't slowed as it had in Franklin or even Atlanta. The supplies that were brought in by steamboat along the Flint River provided some stability for Abigail, her mother, and Miss Peters.

Though, as she sat beside Georgiana Fleming in the pew, the hymnal open in her palms, Abigail still didn't feel at ease. She hadn't since the moment they left Franklin behind in the cloud of dust kicked up by their wagon wheels. The people were friendly, and Mrs. Fleming was the perfect hostess for her family. It was a fortunate thing that her father and Lieutenant Colonel William Fleming had struck up a friendship at Gettysburg, otherwise they would be without a place to rest their heads at night.

Everything should have been fine now that they were farther away from the two warring armies, farther away from the threat of Yankee invasion. But as she looked around to the singing faces of the congregation, smiles and eyes bright with the joy that surpassed all understanding, Abigail still felt dead inside. Her heart was in the grave with Ben and it took this spell of peace for her to realize it. With nothing to do and nothing to occupy her thoughts, the sorrow drained Abigail until she was given to spells of irritability and despondency.

"Miss Abby," came a hushed voice next to her.

She turned and saw Alexander Carter with his one hand holding the hymnal and the other sleeve draping in a knot. The rest of the church had turned the page – except for them.

"Sorry, Alex," she whispered in return as she lent the extra hand that he didn't have.

He gave her a smile and appreciative nod, and then continued to sing off-key. Alexander was another boarder beneath the Fleming roof, and quite possibly the silliest man who ever fired a rifle on this side of the Mason-Dixon line. He, too, was well acquainted with the lieutenant colonel and was fortunate enough to be offered a job upon their farm after he lost his arm at Chancellorsville. So few employers in Bainbridge were willing to give an amputee any opportunities, and there wasn't a day that went by without Alex's profuse imparting of thanks for everything Mrs. Fleming and her family had done for him.

Abigail looked back to the pulpit and sang the last few verses by heart before the service was concluded and the congregation dismissed. Her family, along with Alex and Georgiana, occupied a pew all to themselves toward the very back of the sanctuary. Turner was just as uncomfortable as his mother and fussed constantly during the sermon, so they all agreed that moving to the back would be best for the assembly. Though, if Abigail had her way, they wouldn't have attended church at all. It was only a reminder that she was obligated to continue in society like the war and disaster had never ravaged her family. She couldn't pretend. Not anymore.

One advantage to sitting toward the back of the hall was that once the pastor released his flock, they were some of the first to exit. Down the steps they went and were halfway to their wagon when she heard the hurried footsteps of someone coming up the path behind them.

Alex, the ever-observant, was the first to turn. Then Miss Peters, who carried Turner in her arms, subtly moved herself between her employers and whoever was coming toward them. Abigail didn't bother to look until the disabled soldier let out a loud, energetic cry like he so often did when he was excited.

"Warren Taggart!" he greeted, hustling toward the man with his one arm outstretched.

Now, she stopped and looked. Alex hugged a man that was at least half a head taller than him, dark blonde, curly hair tossed in the breeze like he had been riding horseback. The mud splattered on the pantleg of his cavalry army uniform was a testament to that assumption.

A deep, husky voice that stole the breath from her very lungs answered the soldier. She didn't even register what had been said, but only knew that her world spun out of focus for a brief moment as bright green eyes landed on her. They were the shade of a leaf that was backed by the noonday sun. His face was tanned, probably from all his days spent riding in the army. By the three-strand weave on his sleeve and three matching stars upon his collar, he was a full colonel, one step below general. The highest-ranking officer she had personally met thus far had been a major.

Abigail stared, hardly knowing why. She had never met him before. Never heard the name Warren Taggart in her life. Yet, there was something familiar in the way he looked at her, as if he recognized her or had known her for years.

She took a step back, feeling her heart beat faster like the wings of a humming-bird. Whether out of fear or elation, she wasn't sure.

Colonel Taggart thankfully diverted his attention to Mrs. Fleming and came to kiss the back of her hand before being introduced to the rest of her semi-permanent guests. One by one, names were given, saving Abigail for last. Standing like a frightened doe, she forgot to offer her hand, not that she would have wanted to anyway. Now, she knew what she was feeling. She was scared of Warren Taggart.

"I do believe you're the prettiest face beneath a bonnet I've seen in a good many years, Miss Abigail," he drawled. His accent marked him as the son of a southern aristocrat, which must have explained his rank.

Something within her balked at the informality of the flattery. "I'd beg you to call me Mrs. Myers, sir."

The colonel's smile widened, making the outside corners of his eyes crinkle with amusement. "Very well, but my statement still stands true. A rose by any other name would still smell as sweet as thee."

Abigail felt her timidity burst into annoyance. "I also ask you not to flatter or quote Shakespeare, Colonel Taggart."

"And I'll ask you to call me Warren."

"I'll call you anything I wish," she spat viciously, unsure where this fire had come from all of the sudden. "And if you continue to be so informal, it won't be anything nice."

His impertinence, and her spitfire replies only evoked smiles and titters amongst the group that watched on. Even her mother, who would have harshly scolded her for such an outburst, patiently supervised the meeting.

Alex was the first to intervene. "Better watch it, Warren. She's a regular wildcat."

This didn't deter him either and Abigail began to wonder what would throw the man off her trail.

"I like a girl with a sharp tongue," Colonel Taggart said. "Too many ladies nowadays are as meek as newborn kittens. I welcome gumption any day, even if it is directed toward me."

"You'll be singin' a different tune when she's got you on the business end of a rifle," Miss Peters chided. "Better be careful what ya say. She's gettin' mighty good with her aim."

He chuckled as Abigail's face reddened, this time with embarrassment. It was common knowledge that she had been practicing her shooting in the afternoons toward the back of the field, but she never thought her improvement would be used in her favor this way.

Thinking of one thing that would finally deter him, Abigail spun and held out her hands to receive Turner, who was looking on with mild awareness at the scene. He willingly leaned into her arms and dug his fingers into the black braids of her hair that gathered on the back of her neck.

"Mrs. Fleming neglected to mention my son, Turner Myers."

There was no flicker of apprehension in the brave colonel whatsoever. In fact, he came closer and tugged on Turner's sleeve to get his attention. The toddler turned to look at him with the brown eyes he had inherited from his father, but he seemed about as enthusiastic to be in Colonel Taggert's presence as Abigail was.

"He's normally shy of strangers," her mother chimed in, being maddeningly unhelpful. A part of her wondered if this introduction had been staged in some way. Her mother was far too allowing.

"I'll just have to pay a call then, won't I?" Colonel Taggart said eagerly, looking to Mrs. Fleming for approval.

"Come by any time you like, Warren. You know where we are."

"I heard your husband is resigning at the end of this month."

Mrs. Fleming nodded. "Thank the good Lord above, he is. He'll be on his way from Tennessee and I hope he'll be home for Christmas."

"I look forward to seeing him again," the colonel said, still pushing his luck with Turner by tickling the boy's leg. Abigail finally moved away to deny him any further access, even though her son wasn't showing much discomfort.

"Are you also in the fiftieth Georgia?" Mrs. Rider asked.

He shook his head. "No, I belonged to the first Georgia Infantry under Colonel James Ramsey during the first couple of years of the war. Then, I transferred to the second Georgia Cavalry. I met William when we mustered in together in Macon."

For some time, they spoke of where Colonel Taggart had served and how many horses had been shot out from underneath him. All the while, Abigail was barely aware of the stories. Instead, her mind was caught up in the comforting and steady cadence of the man who had managed to set her teeth on edge.

What was it that unsettled her so? Was it the way he stood so tall and confidently? Or in the way the brass buttons on his coat gleamed and sparkled as if they had been freshly polished? Abigail wasn't one to be starstruck by rank and pomp. Nor was she one to be impressed by a man who could smooth talk his way into getting what he wanted. And by all accounts, it appeared that he wanted her.

Maybe it was just her youth that attracted him, or perhaps the challenge she had unwittingly presented to his pride. Now, since he knew that he couldn't have her, he wanted her all the more. Could he not see that she was still wearing a wedding band? Or had her mourning gown negated its golden glimmer?

The congregation funneled out the doors and the pastor gave them each a final blessing before they hurried along their way. This was the cue to the rest of their party that it was time to leave as well.

"Do come by this evening for supper, Warren," Mrs. Fleming insisted, affectionately touching his sleeve as if he needed any extra encouragement.

"Thank you for your kind invitation, but I feel I must decline." Green eyes found Abigail once more. "I know my coming would be inconvenient to someone and I wouldn't wish to stoke the rage of the wildcat."

Now, all stares were on her and Abigail's cheeks flushed a deeper hue. A tense moment passed as they all waited for her to concede. If she were to refuse him, the other ladies would have called her rude and impolite. Snide banter was one thing, but flatly negating her hostess's invitation to supper was another. It wasn't her place to say whether the colonel could join them or not, and she didn't understand why they had handed her the gavel to make the final decision one way or the other. If he did come to dinner, she would be forced to sit across the table from him and endure his stare for the better part of the evening until she could feign a headache and retire from company.

Damned if she did, damned if she didn't.

"It appears I'm overruled," she grumbled, turning away so the others wouldn't see the way her lips tugged into the faintest of smiles.

He might have incensed her with his compliments, but there was something endearing in the way his eyes sparkled with genuine intrigue. It had been so long since she was noticed by a man. It was unseemly for him to give her any notice, considering that she had a child and she was still in mourning. The others, however, might have thought this was Abigail's chance at happiness again.

It had only been a little over a year since Ben died. It wasn't right for Colonel Taggart to hound after her. And it certainly wasn't right for her stomach to tighten and tingle as it did now. She hadn't felt that since Ben left, since they last kissed and said their goodbyes in Franklin.

For once, she wanted to think of her late husband. She wanted to linger on his memory, replay every heartfelt moment until she was on the precipice of despair once more. Anything to make this uncanny attraction to Colonel Taggart go away.

Franklin, Georgia

Ben stood before the charred rubble. The Georgia wind had carried the scent of the ash over two miles, but he didn't want to believe that it came from his old home. Not even the framework of the house had withstood the fire that consumed everything. No furniture, no paintings, none of the priceless ceramic or valuables that he remembered had survived. Nothing but blackened beams that lay in a mangled heap. He could only step over the brittle planks and imagine what room he would have been in as he moved through the debris.

His bare feet, hardened by miles upon miles of running across the countryside, were now begrimed by the remaining dust. As green as he was in this new life as a werewolf, his nose did tell him one thing. There were no human bones. No charred flesh in the wreckage. That was a relief, but it gave rise to more questions.

What happened here? Where was Abigail? What about his family? The ache in his chest would not ease unless he knew what had become of them.

Ben forced himself to keep breathing, to keep searching, to keep hoping. They might have escaped this disaster. They could be somewhere far away and safe. He couldn't allow himself to think the worst, or he'd go mad with grief.

The fight with Dustin was still fresh in his mind, another bit of proof that what the older werewolf said was true. Even if Abigail could escape this inferno, could she survive him? Would she accept him? Coming here in the broad daylight was a risk in itself now that the tinted spectacles were broken beyond repair. His thoughtlessness proved to be his undoing.

His eyes roamed for any clues in what remained, but when he found none, he looked to the valley. The story there was the same. The barn and fields were burned, but the house he had grown up in was still standing. Dilapidated perhaps, but still standing.

Within the home, he knew someone had stayed behind. The womanly signature in the scent told him it was his mother, but there was something off about it. He heard mutterings, unintelligible grumbles. There was once an old man in Franklin who lived off the charity of neighbors who made similar noises, usually paired with a lazy eye and skittishness that painted the caricature of a feral cat rather than a man.

Ben made his way down the hill and toward the half broken, half dismantled picket fence. He remembered how he would take a stick and drum it against the planks, running up and down the length of the yard until his mother yelled at him to do something more useful and less infuriating. The garden was barren, the soil rife with the traces of strangers. Their footprints had trampled through the rows and scattered dirt across the path that led up to the porch.

The incoherent murmuring frightened him more than any threat of enemy fire or loaded artillery. Inside the house was his mother, driven insane by something he could no longer protect her from. Ben didn't want to see it. The last time he saw his mother, she was smiling and told him how proud she was to have her son go off to defend their home. He had failed them in so many ways, but if she needed him now more than ever, he couldn't stay on the rickety porch.

A gentle push on the door sent it squealing open. Inside, the devastation had carried over. His mother had always kept the house immaculately clean – or as clean as a country farmhouse could be – but it was as if she had never risen from the chair she sat in now. The stove was cold, though there was a hefty mound of firewood sitting beside it. A pot that contained the remnants of some stew was just as cold and he wondered when she had eaten last. The floors were covered in a thin layer of dirt and dust that he felt scraping against the bottoms of his feet.

His mother, dark brown hair now graying with the fatigue of braving this war, stared vacantly at some point across the room. Skin was stretched thin across the bones of her hands, which were folded neatly in her lap. Her whole body rocked forward and back to the minutest degree, lips twitching and pulling as she mumbled about things he couldn't understand. Partial words, disjointed phrases, monotone ramblings of a woman who had reached her breaking point.

Ben no longer cared about his eyes, about the shock it would give to be seen in this way. He fell to his knees in front of her and grabbed for her hands.

"Ma... Ma, I'm home."

It took a few times for him to say it before she finally slowed in her rocking and looked to him. Eyes that seemed unfocused at first, came alive as they had been before he left. Ben smiled, and she mirrored it, but there was still no sign of recognition. He had expected her to wrap her arms about his neck, cry, and say how glad she was to have her baby boy home.

She said nothing like that.

"No one told me we'd be expectin' company," she said. "I would have cleaned up."

She rose to her feet and shuffled to the corner were a leaning broom collected cobwebs. Ben watched as his mother took it and began to diligently sweep, massing a thin rolling cloud of dust as she went.

"Just give me a minute or two and I'll have this all fixed right."

He went to her and took her hands again, halting the madness for only a moment. "Ma, it's me, Ben. I'm home. I'm home from the war. Ya don't have to clean nothin'."

Once more, she looked up, but this time in confusion. "Ben... That's a nice name. My son's name is Ben... He's dead though. Died in the war."

Ben felt his throat constrict. "No, ma. I'm Ben. I'm not dead. I'm home."

It was as if she hadn't even heard him. "My eldest, Phillip, he was in the war, too. Died at Gettysburg. Do you know where that is?"

He could say nothing, but dropped his hands and staggered back. "Not... Not Phillip," he breathed, wishing this was all some vivid nightmare like the ones he had before. All his senses told him that this was no dream. This was real. Phillip was truly dead, and his mother had lost her mind.

She went right back to sweeping, talking about those who had left her as if it were nothing. "My husband's gone too. He went with our employer a while ago. I forget how long. Haven't heard from him in a long time now. I suspects he's dead too, though no one's tellin' me anythin'. The folks up at the Big House all left. Went south, I reckon. Someplace called Bainbridge, wherever that is. Doesn't concern me. I'm waitin' for my boys to come home. They're in the war, ya know. Brave boys, fightin' for a good cause. Fightin' for the rights of all us southerners. Last I heard, we got them good at Manassas Junction. The newspapers were callin' it 'The Great Skedaddle'. Sent them Yankees runnin'. My boys were in that fight... Brave boys."

Ben eased himself down into the chair she had been sitting in. Now he was the perplexed one, reeling from this news that everyone he had loved was gone. Some dead, some missing, others removed to some place called Bainbridge. He thought he had heard of it once or twice before, but didn't know how far away it was.

His mother began humming a bouncy tune. *Bonny Blue Flag*. It was enough to make him sick. Damn the war and damn independence. He wanted his family back. He wanted his old life back before the world fell all to pieces.

"Ben?"

He looked up, hoping against the odds that his mother had come back to him. She did, but it wasn't how he intended.

Her eyes went wide when they met his and he suddenly remembered that he didn't appear like any normal man. He was a beast now, a werewolf. Though the inside of the house wasn't lit all that well, she would have still been able to see the golden eyes staring back at her.

Her face, lightly wrinkled by the age and stress of all she had been through, distorted until she no longer looked like his darling mother. She screamed and began shouting insults and threats upon him. The word "demon" was thrown about far too much for his comfort and then she brandished the broom as her weapon.

The straw bristles smacked fiercely into his shoulder and back, driving him out the front door and off the porch. He didn't have the heart to fight her, to try and calm her down from this panic. They were far too gone for that and with her sensitive mental state, there was no point. She'd likely forget what he was saying and fly into this invective again.

He ran from his home, away from quite possibly his last surviving family member. Would she remember him? Would she go telling everyone in Franklin that her son had returned from the dead possessed by a demon? Who would believe her?

Ben let the silent tears fall down his face and curve around his chin until they dropped into the ashes of the plantation fields. Everything he had loved was gone... but one thing remained. He just had to find it.

CHAPTER 17

DECEMBER 11TH, 1863 - BAINBRIDGE, GEORGIA

In the near silence of the parlor, Abigail sat in her chair with a pair of knitting needles in her hands. The new pair of socks she had been making for Turner were nearly done, and she was thankful to Mrs. Fleming for not only showing her the pattern, but for providing the yarn. It had seemed like an eternity since they'd had so much at their disposal, so much to use and waste if they chose. Extravagances such as a new dress and shoes were nothing to the Fleming family, when Abigail and her mother had gone without new things since all the men went off to war.

The crackling of the fireplace and the soft tapping of the needle tips were occasionally interrupted by the rolling of wooden wheels across the rug where her son played with a new toy, the first he'd had in months. The painted train engine was just big enough for him to grip and push across the course weave, and though he had never seen a train in person, Colonel Warren Taggart taught him the sounds they were supposed to make.

Abigail didn't mind when Turner banged the toy against the floor, nor did she mind the screeching imitation of the whistle. What she did mind was looking up to see her son so happy with something that shouldn't have been given to him in the first place.

This was the first night in almost two weeks that the colonel hadn't called on the Fleming household. She assumed he was with the rest of the town at the early Christmas bizarre. Mrs. Fleming had volunteered her services and it was expected of her to attend. And since Mrs. Rider and Miss Peters couldn't remember the last time either of them had been to a party or social gathering on such a scale, they went with her. Alex served as their escort and though he promised to dance with Abigail if she decided to come, she starkly refused.

All because the colonel would likely be there.

Since their first meeting, they had grown close – quite without her conscious effort. There were times when he complimented her, and she became vexed with the impropriety of the gesture. She had become even more indignant when no one stopped his tireless efforts to court her.

They all couldn't understand what was in her heart and the guilty conscience that weighed upon it. They didn't know how his presence, though it thrilled her, also made her revile the handsome colonel. They couldn't see the restraint she employed whenever he opened his mouth to speak, or whenever he looked at her in that caring and considerate way. They couldn't hear the way her teeth ground together whenever she wanted to laugh at his jokes.

Abigail wanted to hate him, but her heart wouldn't let her. It had returned to her for the first time since she learned that Ben was truly dead and gone. And it sang another name, another refrain of love for someone whom she barely knew.

Feeling her nose sting with frustrated tears, she took a deep breath, her ribs pushing against her stays as she prepared to do the only thing she knew to do. She'd give herself to sorrow one more time to keep Ben's memory alive. She had almost forgotten what his voice sounded like, what his kisses tasted like. His stoic face in the tintype she kept by her bed didn't do him justice anymore and with each visit from the colonel, she forgot more and more of the little things that her longtime sweetheart did to make her giggle and adore him. She was forgetting the love of a man that she never thought she could leave behind.

"Dearest love, do you remember when we last did meet, how you told me that you loved me, kneeling at my feet? Oh! How proud you stood before me, in your suit of gray, when you vow'd to me and country, to be true always."

She let her singing voice fill the empty house, confident that no one would hear the way her sadness was poured into every line.

With these words, she remembered Ben, Phillip, and the still-missing Mr. Myers. The men her father had trusted and employed for years were dead on a faraway battlefield, casualties of a war that no one seemed to want anymore.

"Weeping, sad and lonely, hopes and fears, how vain. When this cruel war is over, praying! That we'll meet again..."

"Such somber words were never sung more beautifully."

Abigail jumped at the voice that she hoped never to hear that evening. She needed a respite from him, but the colonel had come to her anyway.

Turner pushed himself to his feet with a gleeful smile and hobbled to the door where the colonel stood in his uniform. She rarely saw him in anything else than his nearly flawless cavalry jacket with a golden sash tied about his waist. The officers were always dressed so much more elegantly than the privates. Not like her husband had been before he left.

She allowed that knife to be twisted in her gut as she laid her knitting project in her lap. There was no point in hiding the way she brushed off the tear on her cheek, and she wouldn't stand to receive him.

Warren squatted and opened up his arms to Turner as he fell into him at a run. "Soon, everyone in the house will have to keep an eye on this boy. He's a regular runner."

Abigail nodded in agreement. "He'll get into plenty of mischief, if he's anything like his parents."

At every given opportunity, she exploited Ben. Every conversation would be shadowed by him if she could help it, even when her mother was quick to change the subject and encourage this blossoming relationship between her daughter and the colonel.

Warren propped Turner against his waist and strode across the floor to her, and she tracked his heavy steps while avoiding his stare. She didn't want to see the way those green eyes looked in the firelight. Not again. A few days ago, she made the mistake of sitting across from him in this very spot and she swore she couldn't breathe for a full ten seconds when he turned and asked her a simple question. She couldn't even remember what that question was, but she'd never forget the way he made her feel in that moment.

"When I asked your mother where you were, I was pretty surprised to hear you were staying at home."

"I'm in mournin'," Abigail bit back as she took up her knitting again. "It isn't right for me to be at a big party."

"Darlin', I don't know if you've noticed, but everyone's in mourning. There isn't a house that hasn't been visited by the reaper. The old rules of decorum don't count anymore."

Abigail's brows snapped together, and her knitting became a little more aggressive. "Is that why you've called on me so late in the evening without a chaperone? Do those rules mean nothing to you?"

"I asked your mother if it was all right to have a private audience with you and – "

"But did you ever ask me?" she spat cruelly, finally deeming it safe to glare at him to make her point known that he was not welcome here.

He didn't appear wounded or offended. He just calmly stood there, gazing at her as Turner's tiny hands tried to tear off the gold stars sewn on his collar. Never breaking eye contact, he lowered himself into the chair beside her. "Why do you pretend to hate me?"

"I don't pretend. I never pretend."

"Sure you do. You're pretending right now. I know you don't hate me as much as you let on. I see the way you smile when you think no one is looking, and how you watch me. Yeah, I notice that too. I didn't become a colonel by chance, you know. I earned it because I was observant in the field. I saved men's lives in the heat of battle because I notice things... And I'm trying to save you, because I see so much in those pretty blue eyes. You want to be happy again and I want to see you happy too."

Abigail shook her head and she could feel the fire doused by his honesty. "It's not your job to save me. I don't need savin'. I don't need some arrogant cuss comin' into my life, tryin' to take the place of my husband."

Warren held Turner firm as the toddler tried to wiggle and fall off his knee. "I'm not trying to take Ben's place. I could never do that. There'll always be a special place in your heart for him and I know that as long as you live, you'll never forget him. This country, this Confederacy, will never forget his sacrifice either... All I ask is that you make room in your heart for one more soldier who... who cares for you without knowing how or why. We barely know each other, but I feel like I've dreamed of a girl like you for years. I've prayed to the Almighty every day for a woman who's just like you. And I believe He's made good on his promise. Ask and ye shall receive... But the Lord also works in mysterious ways. This war for example," he said with a slight laugh. "The Yankees think God's sided with them, while we're so sure that it's His will that the south be independent. Now that Bragg's lost Chattanooga and Longstreet failed to take Knoxville, and it looks like the New Year's going to bring us a whole other year of death and loss, I'm thinking God's got other plans for this nation... I just hope I know what kind of plans He's got in store for me... And that they'll involve you."

It was underhanded to bring God into his proposal. Now, whatever way she answered, she'd either be going for God or against Him. It'd been a long time since she gave one picayune for God's plans and what kind of design was laid out for her in heaven. Whatever she did on this earth was going to be what she wanted, not what the Lord wanted. That's why she married Ben when everyone said it was beneath her to marry a poor farmer.

But would it be right for her to court or marry a colonel who was clearly above her in station before the war broke out? Was that the will of God? Was that why Ben died?

She shook the thought out and sternly rebuked herself for such thinking. God didn't kill people. Men did. All this war and hate had nothing to do with God and everything to do with His children running amuck with what they had been given.

Warren set Turner down on the ground and managed to slip his hands into hers, taking the place of her knitting needles. "I'm leaving for Atlanta in the next day or two. Everything is pointing to a Union invasion of Georgia," he said. "But I can't leave without knowing if you'll wait for me."

Abigail gazed into the eyes that begged her for the love that she was completely capable of giving, but unwilling. Hesitance captured the refusal on her lips and she paused, thinking.

If what he said was true, if the war was sure to go on for another year as the south was demoralized into surrender, then there was a chance that he could be killed. Officers were so often targeted and with Warren sitting atop his horse, he could be shot down in any battle between now and the day of capitulation. If she were to promise this simple thing, then he would die a happier and hopeful man and she'd be free of her oath. Then again, if she denied him this simple hope, what would happen? Say she changed her mind over the course of a few months and realized that she missed his company – as much as It frustrated her. If she refused him, he was free to search for any other woman after the war was over and she'd be left heartbroken all over again.

Time was not their ally. Fate couldn't be toyed with. Her answer might not have fully determined their future, because so much could still happen. But she had to take a chance and let her heart confess what it wanted.

"I'll wait," she whispered.

The guttural growl shook the leaves around him. Ben could feel the branch splintering in his grip as he watched Abigail from afar. The wolf within him foamed at the mouth, urging him to charge across the field and kill them both.

Thoughts, destructive and maddening, shot through his mind, leaving trails of heinous emotions in their wake. How dare Abigail accept this man when she was still in mourning. How dare the colonel even propose such a thing. If she was so adamant about rejecting him, about hating him, then why didn't she turn him out of the house and be done with it? What could make her forget everything they shared?

Ben should have come sooner. He should have left Dustin months ago, maybe a year ago, and gone straight home. If he had, he could have saved them all the grief. Abigail wouldn't have to wear that dingy black dress and maybe she wouldn't have been so desperate to agree to courting this man. Maybe then he could have helped raise his son, the little boy sitting on the carpet in front of the fireplace.

But the longer he sat in his rage, fuming and holding back the shift for as long as possible, he knew that coming back to Georgia that soon would have been a mistake. As much as he despised Dustin for turning him, for spreading lies that leaked back to his family, and for trying to manipulate him into going to Alabama, Ben had to admit that his mentor had been right. He wasn't ready to come home. If he shifted now, it was likely that the beast would find its way into the farmhouse and kill all of them. Though the innocence of Abigail and the colonel were debatable, the boy was an unarmed civilian in this battle. No matter what Ben or Abigail did, the boy didn't deserve the outcome.

Hot gusts of breath sputtered from his nostrils as he tried to gain control, forcing his body to hold on just a little longer to its human form. Part of him waited for Abigail to come to her senses and take it all back. The other part was suicidal and waited for what did come next.

Abigail's voice would forever ring in his ears and the profession of admiration for the colonel that affirmed it all. Over the sound of his own heavy growl and rapid heartbeat, he heard her say that she had been denying her feelings since they met, because she felt it would be a defilement upon Ben's memory and the love they shared.

The colonel had an answer for everything and consoled her until Abigail was able to be herself, to bear her heart to him as she had done for Ben so long ago. She smiled that beautiful smile that had been reserved for only him. Those blue eyes that had captivated him as a boy, looked to the colonel with abounding love. How could she do this to him?

They embraced, and they kissed.

Ben finally looked away and felt his once fleshy heart turn to stone and shatter. He felt betrayed, abandoned, alone. If he couldn't have Abigail, if his family was beyond his reach, then what else was there for him? What was he to do? What could he do?

He could storm into the house in the morning, reveal that he was alive so this unholy companionship would end. He could claim the son he never knew and they could be a family again. But would that solve anything? He was still a werewolf, a monster. His golden eyes couldn't be ignored and tinted spectacles – if he could find another pair – would only last for so long. Would she cast him off as his own mother had? Could she accept him? Was it worth the risk?

Or he could leave. Leave Abigail to this new love that was greater than the one they once had. Why else would she be so willing to forsake everything for this man? He could go somewhere far away to heal from this new wound, and fester in this pain that no amount of morphine, chloroform, or laudanum could dull. He could let Abigail be happy and give his son a step-father that he could look up to.

He hung on tighter to the tree he was hiding in, forcing himself to stay rooted in place until he could bear it no more. The wolf yowled in pain, both physical and emotional, sharing in everything that Ben experienced as he leapt from the tree and fled from the farm.

The farther he ran, the more he gave his body over to the shift, Ben realized that he wasn't quite as alone as he had once believed. The wolf was with him. It would always be there, sympathetic to his grief and anger in a way that no other man on earth could come close to.

Ben tripped and fell as the final stages of the shift took hold, conquering him body and mind. He gave himself to it, letting the darkness close in over his soul one more time. It was better than seeing her so happy without him, knowing it was better this way in the end.

Though the fact that Warren Taggart was to leave Bainbridge that afternoon with the rest of his cavalry regiment saddened her heart to a degree that she couldn't possibly explain to her mother or Mrs. Fleming, Abigail caught herself humming a sweet and lively tune. A burden had been lifted from her and if she wasn't careful, she knew she'd blow away in the cool morning breeze. It was a fine day, clear and crisp.

Donning her apron and taking up the collection basket, she set out early for the chicken coop as she recalled the tumultuous emotions from the night before. The kiss wasn't expected, or completely wanted, but in the moment, she was too taken by his sincerity.

Warren had a way with words, and though she could usually spot a liar from a mile away, she saw no deception in him. He wasn't a confidence man, though the skeptic side of her was tempted to believe so. Yet, there was nothing to gain from her. Nothing but love and a son that wasn't his. She was virtually destitute, without a home or way of making a station for herself in the world. There was nothing that she could give him that he would need to trick her in order to achieve.

As dangerous as it was initially perceived, this might have been one of the safest and most logical decisions she had ever made in her life – apart from marrying Ben. Then why did she still feel ashamed for the way she gave into him so quickly?

Should she have dragged out her decision? Should she have waited or even refused him? Would that have made her feel any more comfortable with her choice?

She opened the wire mesh door to the chicken coop and stepped inside, cooing to the hens and roosters as she closed it behind her. Tiny beaks pecked at the hem of her shabby calico dress, one of the only ones that remained from her old home in Franklin. The time of mourning was over, and her mother would see it as soon as they sat at the table for breakfast. The scores upon scores of questions would come flying at her for days to come and she resolved to answer as plainly and passively as she could.

Abigail dispensed out the corn kernels and shooed out the hens who were too stubborn to leave their nests. The collection process barely took ten minutes before she turned back to the coop door.

There, tucked in the frame where the latch held the door in place, was a neatly folded letter. The parchment was stiff and new, not worn by the transfer between hands or bent after being stuffed into a mailbag with other letters like it. She paused and touched the corner of it, half expecting the letter to disappear like a mirage. She had just opened this door a moment ago and there was nothing there. Someone must have slipped it in while she had her back turned, but there was no one out this early in the morning and she hadn't heard anyone come close to the coop.

Finding that it wasn't just her imagination, she snatched the letter from the crack and saw it was addressed to her... in Ben's handwriting.

The breath was knocked from her as she blinked and turned the envelope over, trying to make sense of it. She knew her late husband's handwriting by heart. She had taught him to write when they were children. It wasn't as careful and neat as hers, but his "B" was unmistakable. It had been his favorite letter, since it was the first in his name and the second in her own.

Abigail hastened out of the coop and to the side of the house where she was sheltered from the wind that might have grabbed the letter from her loose and trembling hold. With the basket of eggs beside her and seated upon a pile of chopped wood for support, she ripped open the envelope and devoured its contents.

My dearest Abigail,

You know I was never one for words, but in this final hour, I know I must impart my last to you and you alone. As you will find, either before you receive this or well after, I am dying. I beg you not to be sad or mourn my passing, because I've served my country the best that I know how. I don't know what the future holds for the Confederacy, for the south, or for you. But know this, my love, that I will be waiting for you in heaven. Know that I regret nothing about our courtship, our marriage, or anything else about my life that some may have called simple and uneventful.

Loving you was an adventure, and I find myself thinking back to those days when we explored the woods beyond the plantation. I remember all the games we played and the good times we shared together as friends, as sweethearts, and as lovers. I hope you will never forget me or the life we had.

As for me, I know where I'm going. The Lord has prepared a place for me, as the Bible says, and I'll be there soon. And as for you, it is my fondest hope that you will carry on, that you will find happiness after this cruel war is over, whether that be as a widow or as a bride to a new man. Don't think I'll be angry if you remarry someday. I will only be angry if you deny yourself the happiness that I wish for you. Black was never your color, so I hope you don't wear it for long after I'm gone.

Tell my folks that I love them and take good care of my mother, if she should find herself alone. Tell your parents that I'm grateful for their generosity toward my family and toward me. They gave me the greatest treasure when they allowed me to marry you, and for that I will be eternally grateful.

I wish I had more to say, but I am weak. I close this with my love. I am always with you in spirit, and I know we will meet again someday.

The letter was signed with his name, "Benjamin Myers", but Abigail could no longer see them. The black scribbles became a watery blur of color as tears welled in her eyes.

If this was written just before Ben died, then why did it look so pristine? Who had delivered it? Had someone in her family been saving it all this time? Why would they keep something from her so important as a letter from her dead husband?

Reading the words, feeling the sentiment behind them, and imagining her husband lying on his deathbed had rekindled her grief, but only briefly. Because in this letter was the blessing she needed. He wanted her to move on, to remarry, to be happy without him. He was giving her permission to live and be herself with someone else. Ben, in his final moments, thought only of her and the life they had before the war. How merciful he was, to love her so dearly to know that someday she would need this approval. She had never loved him more, never cherished him as fully as she did now, tightly clutching his last words.

"I'll never forget," Abigail whimpered. "I'll never forget."

TERMS TO KNOW

Maryland Campaign/Battle at Antietam – With Robert Lee freshly appointed to the Army of Northern Virginia, and still on a victory high after beating back Union General McClellan from entering Richmond, the Confederate army decided to make the offensive move to invade Maryland. At the time, it was believed by General Lee that Maryland was virtually being held hostage by Lincoln as the rights of habius corpus were suspended and political leaders were thrown in jail to prevent the state from joining the Confederacy. As a slave state, he imagined Maryland would by sympathetic to the southern cause. Part of this campaign involved the acquisition of Harpers Ferry, which was a weapons manufacturing center for the north. Several small battles were fought before the climax of the campaign at Sharpsburg on September 17th, 1862. The battle at Antietam became somewhat of a Union victory, though the losses were heavy on both sides, amounting to the bloodiest single day in American history with over 20,000 casualties. General Lee took his army back over the Potomac on the evening of September 18th, ending the Maryland Campaign.

Bivouacked – A temporary encampment made of no shelters or improvised shelters.

Haversack – A one-compartment bag carried by soldiers, sometimes along with a knapsack. In the haversack, they'd keep extra boxes of cartridges, rations, etc. The confederate haversacks were made of canvas cloth and not weather-proof, while the Union haversacks were often leather or weather-proofed. These were worn on the left side with the strap reaching across to their right shoulder since their cartridge box and percussion cap box were worn on their right side for easy access during battle. If the soldier was left handed, this would be the opposite case.

Kepi – A short military-issue hat. Sometimes decorated with symbols or numbers of their regiments. The rimless design of the kepi was ideal for bringing a rifle up to aim, but provided little protection from the sun and elements. For this reason, many Confederates wore their own rimmed hats and either pinned one side to the cap of the hat or had it tilted to one side so it wouldn't interfere with their aim.

Johnny Reb/Billy Yank – Ambiguous nicknames given to Confederate and Union soldiers.

Hardtack – Also called "hard crackers", "sheet iron crackers", "molar break-ers", "cabin biscuits", "Tooth-dullers", and "worm castles". A soldier's ration item comprised of flour and water. As the name suggests, these were difficult to eat after they became stale and provided little nutritional value for their diet. They'd sometimes be dipped or broken up into other watery foods to soften them. Some stories told of soldiers who would use hardtack as ammunition in cannons or throw them at their enemy. Then, when advancing upon the field, they could pick up their hard crackers and keep running. Sometimes before the hardtack could get to the soldiers, it would mold and become infested with weevils during transport, which was a common occurrence for most army rations.

Civil War Coffee – As the Union blockade tightened around the Confederacy, coffee grounds became a luxury and soldiers had to roast other foods. The goal was to make a warm, flavorful drink rather than make genuine imitation coffee. Other ingredients included peanuts, chicory, acorns, beans, cotton seeds, corn, okra seeds, peas, yams, potatoes, rye, and wood splinters.

Special Order 191 – One key factor in McClellan's victory in the Maryland Campaign was the discovery of a letter intended for D.H Hill from Robert Lee. Written by Robert Chilton, adjutant general (chief military administrative offi-cer) to Robert E. Lee, they detailed the intended movement of the Confederate army in and around Sharpsburg. They were found utside Fredrick, Maryland near a campground that Hill had just vacated, and wrapped around three cigars. Sergeant John Bloss and Corporal Barton W. Mitchell of the 27th Indian Infantry were the finders of the plans and immediately gave them to their commanding officers, who passed them onto McClellan.

Dunker Church – One of the most well-known landmarks at the battle of Anti-etam near Sharpsburg Maryland. The white church has a modest construction and is situated near the West Wood portion of the battlefield near Hagerstown Pike. Its congregation were made up of German pacifists who refused to enlist or participate in the Civil War. In 1708 the denomination was formed with the baptism of eight believers by full immersion. The name Dunker derives from this method of baptism. However they were more commonly known as the German Baptist Brethren. In 1908 the official name became Church of the Brethren. The primary fighting around Dunker Church occurred in the morning of September 17th. On September 18th, it was designated as a "no man's land" were the wound-ed were brought and treated by both sides of the army.

Civil War Rifles – One major innovation to the small weapons used in the Civil War was the rifled musket. The method of rifling involves creating spiraling grooves within the barrel of the musket. This allows the bullet to spin as it's being fired, which can increase its range and accuracy. This, along with the invention of the "mini ball" added to the devastating casualty reports from the war. Civil War rifles were also designed in such a way that they can be easily taken apart and cleaned using a portable kit that many soldiers carried with them.

Tintype – A tintype, also known as a melainotype or ferrotype, is a photograph made by creating a direct positive on a thin sheet of metal coated with a dark lacquer or enamel and used as the support for the photographic emulsion. Tintypes enjoyed their widest use during the 1860s and 1870s, but lesser use of the medium persisted into the early 20th century and it has been revived as a novelty and fine art form in the 21st.

Sunken Road/Bloody Lane - The Sunken Road, as it was known to area residents prior to the Battle of Antietam, was a dirt farm lane which was used primarily by farmers to bypass Sharpsburg and been worn down over the years by rain and wagon traffic. Union and Confederate troops dug in at the Sunken Road on September 17th, 1862. For nearly four hours, from 9:30 a.m. to 1 p.m., bitter fighting raged along this road as General French, supported by Gen. Israel B. Richardson's division, sought to drive the Southerners back. Outnumbered but with a well-defended position, the Confederates in the road stood their ground for most of the morning. Finally, the Federals were able to overwhelm General D.H Hill's men, successfully driving them from this strong position and piercing the center of the Confederacy's line. However, the Federals did not follow up this success with additional attacks, and confusion and sheer exhaustion ended the fighting in this part of the battlefield. In three hours of combat, 5,500 soldiers were killed or wounded and neither side gained a decisive advantage. The Sunken Road was now Bloody Lane.

Cláirseach Harp – The Celtic harp is a triangular harp traditional to Wales, Brittany, Ireland and Scotland. It is known as telyn in Welsh, telenn in Breton, cláirseach in Irish and clàrsach in Scottish Gaelic. In Ireland and Scotland, it was a wire-strung instrument requiring great skill and long practice to play, and was associated with the Gaelic ruling class. It appears on Irish and British coins and coat of arms of the Republic of Ireland, the United Kingdom and Canada.

"Riam Nar Dhruid O Spairn Lann" – (Reeve naw-r ghruid owe spairn lon) – Irish for "They shall never retreat from the charge of lances" and the moto for the Irish Brigade.

"Fág an bealach" – (Fawg on byal-ockh) – Irish for "Clear the way" or "Get out of the way". A commonly heard battle cry of the Irish Brigade.

Casualties – An important thing to remember when hearing the casualty reports after a war is that "casualty" does not necessarily equal "killed". This term encompasses the total number of dead, wounded, missing, and captured during a battle or engagement. For instance, at Antietam, there were approximately 22,720 casualties reported from both sides, however there were 3,650 considered dead or killed in action.

"Acting a maggot" – Slang for "acting like a jerk/asshole"

Blue Ridge Mountains - The Blue Ridge Mountains are a physiographic province of the larger Appalachian Mountains range. This province consists of northern and southern physiographic regions, which divide near the Roanoke River gap. The mountain range is located in the eastern United States, starting at its southernmost portion in Georgia, then ending northward in Pennsylvania. The Blue Ridge Mountains are noted for having a bluish color when seen from a distance. Trees put the "blue" in Blue Ridge, from the isoprene released into the atmosphere, thereby contributing to the characteristic haze on the mountains and their distinctive color.

Shenandoah Valley/River – The Shenandoah Valley is a geographic valley and cultural region of western Virginia and the Eastern Panhandle of West Virginia in the United States. The Shenandoah Valley was known as the breadbasket of the Confederacy during the Civil War and was seen as a backdoor for Confederate raids on Maryland, Washington, and Pennsylvania. Because of its strategic importance it was the scene of three major campaigns. The first was the Valley Campaign of 1862, in which Confederate General Stonewall Jackson defended the valley against three numerically superior Union armies. The final two were the Valley Campaigns of 1864. First, in the summer of 1864, Confederate General Jubal Early cleared the valley of its Union occupiers and then proceeded to raid Maryland, Pennsylvania, and D.C. Then during the autumn, Union General Philip Sheridan was sent to drive Early from the valley and once-and-for-all destroy its use to the Confederates by putting it to the torch using scorched-earth tactics. The valley, especially in the lower northern section, was also the scene of bitter partisan fighting as the region's inhabitants were deeply divided over loyalties, and Confederate partisan John Mosby and his Rangers frequently operated in the area.

French Leave – Requesting furlough in the army during the Civil War could often be a long, tedious, and disappointing endeavor. Instead, soldiers would sometimes leave their regiments for a day or two if they were close to their homes. This was done without consent from commanding officers and sometimes went unpunished.

Rope Petticoat/Hoops – A style of women's dress at the time of the Civil War involved the use of hoop skirts under their dresses. These hops ranged in diameter based on class and wealth. The idea of the hoops was to create the attractive hourglass figure in the waist and to conceal the shape of the woman's legs. Since this style was still desired, but sometimes impractical for working women or ladies who couldn't afford the wire hoops, petticoats sewn with stiffened rope were worn. The ropes helped to give the skirt its bell shape, but still pliable and easy to maneuver in. It could also be a cheaper alternative to the wire hoops.

"Bully" – Slang for "great" or "fantastic". The phrase "bully for me" can be taken as sarcasm in some contexts.

Gettysburg, Pennsylvania – Considered the bloodiest battle of the entire Civil War – and in American history – it took place in a small town in Pennsylvania between July 1st and July 3rd, 1863. Fighting was primarily done in the town and to the northwest and southern areas surrounding the town. General Robert E. Lee was engaged with newly appointed General George Meade. Casualties at Gettysburg totaled 23,049 for the Union (3,155 dead, 14,529 wounded, 5,365 missing). Confederate casualties were 28,063 (3,903 dead, 18,735 injured, and 5,425 missing), more than a third of Lee's army. Some famous engagements during the battle are the charge upon Little Round Top involving the 20th Maine under Colonel Lawrence Chamberlain, and Pickett's Charge where the Confederacy suffered close to 9,000 casualties and where the largest artillery barrage in American history took place.

Contraband Camps – The term "contraband" was applied to runaway slaves to the north who were looking for freedom. These runaways formed camps where they were utilized by the Union army as a source of labor for the war effort. They were not paid at first, but later in the war, wages were issued. Many man from these contraband camps went on to join Union regiments once people of color were allowed to enlist. Contraband camps were also safe places for negro children and adults to be educated and prepared for life as freed people.

Secesh Mail – A term for Confederate mail between soldiers and family, or any mail traveling within the states where there is fighting. "Secesh" being the shortened word for "Secession". It was a common thing for mail to travel slowly, so if a letter was said to be taking too long, citizens would blame it on "Secesh Mail".

Copperhead – A political term used to label Democrats in the northern territories who opposed the Civil War and wanted immediate peace negotiations between the north and south. They were likened to the venomous snake by the Republicans because of their dissenting opinions.

Battle at Blountville, TN – A minor engagement during the Knoxville Campaign that took place September 22nd, 1863. It was considered a Union victory where Union Col. John W. Foster, with his cavalry and artillery, engaged Col. James E. Carter and his troops.

Silver Half-Dollar – The Confederacy primarily printed paper money between the years 1860 and 1865, but in the early days of the war, silver half-dollar coins were minted in New Orleans. In January of 1861, the Federal government produced about 330,000 silver (actually 90 percent silver and 10 percent copper) half dollars at New Orleans. When Louisiana seceded the state took over the mint and continued production, turning out about 124,000 of the coins. They used the original die (the die is what actually creates the image on the blank coin) so their coins still said "United States of America." The Confederate Treasury Department then took over and minted another 963,000 United States half dollars. Coins of this period contained approximately the amount of metal equal to the face value of the coin and these Louisiana- and Confederate-produced coins had the same amount of silver as the U.S.-produced coins and were thus just as valuable. There is no way to determine if an individual coin was minted by the U.S., Louisiana, or the Confederacy as the same workers used the same die and machines and the coins had the same amount of silver. (Reference: https://www.money.org/blog/ConfederateCoinsMeisky)

"A chonách san ort" – (Ay hohn-ahck sehn orht) Irish for "serves you right".

"Cúl tóna" – (Cool toh-nah) – Irish for "ass hole"

"Eejit" – (Ee-jiht) Irish form of "idiot".

Chickamauga, Georgia – The Battle of Chickamauga, fought on September 18 – 20, 1863, between U.S. and Confederate forces in the American Civil War, marked the end of a Union offensive in southeastern Tennessee and northwestern Georgia — the Chickamauga Campaign. It was the first major battle of the war fought in Georgia, the most significant Union defeat in the Western Theater, and involved the second-highest number of casualties after the Battle of Gettysburg.

Chattanooga, Tennessee – The Chattanooga Campaign was a series of maneuvers and battles in October and November 1863, during the American Civil War. Following the defeat of Major General William Rosecrans' Union Army of the Cumberland at the Battle of Chickamauga in September, the Confederate Army of Tennessee under General Braxton Bragg besieged Rosecrans and his men by occupying key high terrain around Chattanooga, Tennessee. The siege ended when Grant replaced Rosecrans, opened a "Cracker Line" to resupply the city, and the high ground was taken in late November. This effectively beat the Confederacy back into Georgia and paved the way for Major General William Tecumseh Sherman's Atlanta campaign in spring of 1864.

Siege of Knoxville/Knoxville Campaign - The Knoxville Campaign was a series of battles and maneuvers in East Tennessee during the fall of 1863 designed to secure control of the city of Knoxville and with it the railroad that linked the Confederacy east and west. Union Army forces under Major General Ambrose Burnside occupied Knoxville, Tennessee, and Confederate States Army forces under Lieutenant General James Longstreet were detached from General Braxton Bragg's Army of Tennessee at Chattanooga to prevent Burnside's reinforcement of the besieged Federal forces there. Ultimately, Longstreet's own siege of Knoxville ended when Union Major General William Tecumseh Sherman led elements of the Army of the Tennessee and other troops to Burnside's relief after Union troops had broken the Confederate siege of Chattanooga.

Song List

The Vacant Chair - written by George F. Root in 1861

Hard Time Come Again No More – written by Stephen Foster in 1854

Just Before The Battle, Mother – written by George F. Root

Maryland, My Maryland - written by James Ryder Randall in 1861

Darling Nelly Grey – written by Benjamin Hanby in 1856

The Southern Wagon – A 1861 variation of lyrics written by Geo. P Knauff in 1851

Bonnie Blue Flag - written by Harry McCarthy in 1861

Lorena – written by Rev. H. D. L. Webster in 1857

Goober Peas – Though sung throughout the Civil War, the first sheet music publication was by A. Pindar in 1866

Weeping Sad And Lonely – written by Charles Carroll Sawyer in 1863

Regiments

7th Georgia Infantry - 7th Infantry Regiment was formed in May, 1861, at Atlanta, Georgia, and in June moved to Harper's Ferry, Virginia. Its members were raised in the counties Coweta, Paulding, De Kalb, Franklin, Fulton, Heard, and Cobb. Assigned to Colonel F. S. Bartow's Brigade, Army of the Shenandoah, it was active in the fight at First Manassas. In April, 1862, the regiment had 611 effectives and served under the command of General G. T. Anderson until the end of the war. It participated in the campaigns of the Army of Northern Virginia from the Seven Days' Battles to Cold Harbor, except when it was detached with Longstreet at Suffolk, in Georgia, and at Knoxville. The 7th was not involved in the Battle of Chickamauga. It was active in the long Petersburg siege south and north of the James River and later the Appomattox Campaign. Total casualties reported for this regiment were 624.

5th Alabama Infantry - The Fifth Alabama Infantry was organized at Montgomery, 5 May 1861, with recruits from the counties of Barbour, Clarke, Dallas, Greene, Lowndes, Monroe, Pickens, Sumter, and Talladega. It moved to Pensacola and a few days after, it proceeded to Virginia and took post near Manassas Junction in the brigade of General Richard Ewell. It was in the skirmish at Farr's Cross Roads and was on the field (but not engaged) at 1st Manassas. It remained in the vicinity of Manassas during the fall and winter, and General Robert E. Rodes became the brigade commander in October -- the 6th and 12th Alabama, and 12th Mississippi being the other regiments in the brigade. Moving with the army to Yorktown in March 1862, it there reenlisted and reorganized. It was under fire at Yorktown and was on the field at Williamsburg. At Seven Pines, the regiment engaged for the first time. The 5th was hotly engaged at Cold Harbor and Malvern Hill. It was not at 2nd Manassas but moved into Maryland and fought at Boonsboro and Sharpsburg. At Chancellorsville, where its flag was captured by members of the 111th Pennsylvania Regiment, it was in the line under General Rodes that swept everything before it. It moved into Maryland and Pennsylvania in the Gettysburg campaign, and its loss was severe in that battle (60% casualties among 317 present). Having wintered at Orange Court House, the 5th, now reduced to a skeleton, participated in the battles of The Wilderness and Spotsylvania without severe loss. It took part in the subsequent operations as the lines began to be drawn around Petersburg, losing slightly at 2nd Cold Harbor. It went with General Jubal Early into the Valley and across the Potomac, taking part in numerous engagements with the enemy and losing severely at Winchester. It soon after took its place in the trenches of Petersburg and wintered there. Only 4 officers and 53 men were at the final surrender at Appomattox, under Captain T. J. Riley. Of 1719 names on the rolls, nearly 300 died in battle; 240 others died in the service, and 507 were discharged or transferred.

1ˢᵗ Georgia Infantry – 1st (Ramsey's) Volunteers Infantry Regiment was formed at Macon Georgia, in April, 1861. The men were raised in the towns and cities of Newnan, Perry, Augusta, Sandersville, Atlanta, Bainbridge, Quitman, Dahlonega, and Columbus. After being stationed at Pensacola it moved to Virginia, served under R. S. Garnett and H. R. Jackson, then during Lee's Cheat Mountain Campaign was attached to General D. S. Donelson's Brigade. In December, with a force of 918 officers and men, it was sent to Winchester and later Lynchburg. The regiment was soon ordered to Macon and mustered out of service. However, many of the soldiers enlisted in other Georgia, Alabama, and Florida regiments as infantry, cavalry, and artillery volunteers.

19ᵗʰ Georgia Infantry - 19th Infantry Regiment was assembled during the summer of 1861. Its companies were raised in Henry, Jackson, Douglas, Coweta, Carroll, Mitchell, Heard, and Bartow counties. Comprising 900 men, the unit was sent to Virginia and placed in the Potomac District. In April, 1862, it totaled 395 effectives and during the war served under the command of Generals W. Hampton, Archer, and Colquitt. The 19th fought in many battles from Seven Pines to Chancellorsville, then moved to Charleston, South Carolina, and later Florida where it took part in the conflict at Olustee. In April, 1864, it returned to Virginia and continued the fight at Proctor's Creek and Cold Harbor and in the

Petersburg lines south and north of the James River. In 1865 the unit participated in the North Carolina Campaign and surrendered with the Army of Tennessee. Total casualties reported by this regiment were 417.

35th Georgia Infantry - 35th Infantry Regiment was organized at Atlanta, Georgia, and mustered into Confederate service at Richmond, Virginia, in October, 1861. The men were recruited in the counties of Troup, Haralson, Bartow, Walton, Chattooga, Harris, and Gwinnett. It was first assigned to General French's Brigade and in April, 1862, had a force of 545 effectives. Later the regiment served under Generals Pettigrew, J.R. Anderson, and E.L. Thomas, Army of Northern Virginia. It fought in numerous battles from Seven Pines to Cold Harbor, then was active in the long Petersburg siege south of the James River and the Appomattox Campaign. Total casualties reported by this regiment were 275.

50th Georgia Infantry – 50th Infantry Regiment was organized at Savannah, Georgia, during the spring of 1862. Its members were recruited in the counties of Ware, Coffee, Lowndes, Thomas, De Kalb, Clinch, Colquitt, Berrien, and Brooks. After serving in the District of Georgia, the 50th moved to Virginia and was assigned to General Drayton's, Semmes', Bryan's, and Simms' Brigade. It participated in the campaigns of the Army of Northern Virginia from Second Manassas to Gettysburg, then was ordered back to Georgia. However, the unit did not arrive in time to share in the Battle of Chickamauga. It was involved in the Knoxville operations and later the conflicts at The Wilderness, Spotsylvania, and Cold Harbor. The regiment fought with Early in the Shenandoah Valley and ended the war at Appomattox. Total casualties reported by this regiment were 487.

2nd Georgia Cavalry - 2nd Cavalry Regiment, assembled at Albany, Georgia, in February, 1862, contained men from Randolph, Dougherty, Clayton, Marion, Fulton, and Decatur counties. It moved to Chattanooga and after skirmishing in Tennessee was placed in Forrest's, Wharton's, J.J. Morrison's, Iverson's, and C.C. Crews' Brigade. The regiment participated in various conflicts such as Perryville, Murfreesboro, Chickamauga, Philadelphia, Campbell's Station, Bean's Station, and Mossy Creek. Later it was involved in the Atlanta Campaign, the defense of Savannah, and the campaign of the Carolinas. On April 26, 1865, the 2nd Cavalry surrendered with only 18 men.

69th New York Infantry - The 69th Infantry Regiment is an infantry regiment of the United States Army. It is from New York City, part of the New York Army National Guard. It is known as the "Fighting Sixty-Ninth", a name said to have been given by Robert E. Lee during the Civil War. An Irish heritage unit, as the citation from poet Joyce Kilmer illustrates, this unit is also nicknamed the "Fighting Irish", immortalized in Joyce Kilmer's poem *When the 69th Comes Home*. The

69th Infantry Regiment traces its Civil War honors through three units, the 1st Regiment of the Irish Brigade (69th Infantry New York State Volunteers (NYSV) (1st Regiment of the Irish Brigade)), the 182nd New York Volunteer Infantry (69th Artillery, serving as infantry, the 1st Regiment of Corcoran's Legion) and the 69th National Guard Infantry (State Militia). The Irish Brigade was noted for its ability to tackle tough missions. As one war correspondent said during the Civil War, "When anything absurd, forlorn, or desperate was to be attempted, the Irish Brigade was called upon."

Paying Honor to These Soldiers

References:
https://www.ranger95.com/civil_war
http://www.culpepperconnections.com/ss/p32436.htm

7ᵗʰ Georgia Infantry

Alman E. F. – 7ᵗʰ Georgia Infantry, Company G - Private - July 30, 1861. Wounded at Garnett's Farm, Virginia June. 27, 1862. Died of disease October 10, 1863.

Beck, John R. – 7ᵗʰ Georgia Infantry, Company G - Private - May 31, 1861. Supposed to have been killed at Sharpsburg, Maryland September 17, 1862.

Brittain, J. Thomas - 7th Georgia Infantry, Company G - Private - July 30, 1861. Killed at 2nd Manassas, Virginia August 30, 1862.

Second Lieutenant Thomas Brown (CSA) – 7ᵗʰ Georgia Infantry, Company G - Private - May 31, 1861. Elected 2nd Lieutenant September 16, 1861. Died of brain fever at Camp Sam Jones near Centreville, Virginia January 18, 1862.

Lieutenant Colonel George Carmical (CSA) – 7ᵗʰ Georgia Infantry - 2nd Lieutenant - May 31, 1861. Elected Captain December 16, 1861; Major July 1, 1862. Wounded in knee at 2nd Manassas, Virginia August 30, 1862. Elected Lieutenant Colonel September 1, 1862. Wounded in shoulder at Knoxville, Tennessee December 4, 1863. Elected Colonel July 27, 1864. Wounded in face at Fussell's Mill, Virginia August 16, 1864. Surrendered Appomattox, Virginia April 9, 1865.

Cotten, James F. (or Cotton) – 7ᵗʰ Georgia Infantry, Company D - Private - May 4, 1861. Appointed Surgeon July 22, 1862; Assistant Surgeon, C. S. A., and ordered to report to Medical Director, Army Northern Virginia July 22, 1862. Relieved from field duty on account of disability and ordered to report to Medical Director at Macon, Georgia August 16, 1864. Served as Assistant Surgeon 10th Regiment, Georgia Infantry in 1864. Roll for October 1864, last on which borne, shows he was transferred to Post duty in Georgia. No later record. Born 1839.

Captain Noah Culpepper (CSA) – 7ᵗʰ Georgia Infantry, Company G - Private - May 31, 1861. Appointed 4th Sergeant September 16, 1861. Elected 2nd

Lieutenant January 27, 1862; 1st Lieutenant May 12, 1862; Captain February 16, 1863. Wounded at Deep Bottom, Virginia August 15, 1864. Surrendered, Appomattox, Virginia April 9, 1865. Born 17 May 1839 in Meriwether County Georgia. He married Martha Henrietta K. Almon at Heard County, Georgia, on 15 Nov 1859 at age 20. Fathered nine children between 1861 and 1878. He died at DeKalb County, Georgia, on 25 Apr 1929 at age 89.

Duke, John A. - 7th Georgia Infantry, Company G - Private - May 31, 1861. Wounded at Garnett's Farm, Virginia June 27, 1862. Died in Winder Hospital at Richmond, Virginia November 20, 1862.

Favor, William A. -7th Georgia Infantry, Company G - Private - May 31, 1861. Wounded and captured at Funkstown, Maryland July 10, 1863. Paroled at Baltimore, Maryland September 25, 1863. Received at City Point, Virginia for exchange September 27, 1863. Roll for February 28, 1865, last on file, shows him absent, wounded. No later record.

Hester, Henry - 7th Georgia Infantry, Company G - Private - July 30, 1861. Killed at Malvern Hill, Virginia July 1, 1862.

Lane, A. M. C. - 7th Georgia Infantry, Company G - Private - May 31, 1861. Wounded at Funkstown, Maryland July 10, 1863. Died from wounds in Seminary Hospital at Hagerstown, Maryland July 21, 1863.

Pitman, William Dempsey - 7th Georgia Infantry, Company G - Private - May 31, 1861. Wounded at Thoroughfare Gap, Virginia August 28, 1862. Captured at Gettysburg, Pennsylvania July 3, 1863. Paroled at Point Lookout, Maryland February 18, 1865. Received at Boulware & Cox's Wharves, James River, Virginia, for exchange February 21, 1865. Furloughed for 30 days February 21, 1865. Furlough extended 30 days, on account of disability, March 31, 1865.

Rooks, William R. - 7th Georgia Infantry, Company G - Private - May 31, 1861. Supposed to have been killed at Sharpsburg, Maryland September 17, 1862.

Spearman, William S. - 7th Georgia Infantry, Company G - Private - May 31, 1861. Captured at Gettysburg, Pennsylvania July 3, 1863. Died at Point Lookout, Maryland December 21, 1863.

Stewart, D. W. - 7th Georgia Infantry, Company G - Private - May 31, 1861. Captured at Gettysburg, Pennsylvania July 3, 1863. Died at Fort Delaware, Delaware September 30, 1863.

Taylor, James Josiah - 7th Georgia Infantry, Company G - Private - July 31, 1861. Accidentally wounded near Luray, Virginia October 31, 1862, and sent to hospital. Absent, wounded, February 28, 1865. No later record.

Wilson, Jack M. - 7th Georgia Infantry, Company G - Private - July 30, 1861. Wounded at Garnett's Farm, Virginia June 28, 1862. Died from wounds in hospital June 29, 1862.

50th Georgia Infantry

Carter, Alexander – 50th Georgia Infantry, Company F - Private - March 4, 1862. Wounded in arm, necessitating amputation below elbow, at Chancellorsville, Virginia, May 3, 1863. Discharged, disability in 1863. (Born in 1839.) Died in Decatur County, Georgia in 1885.

Lieutenant Colonel William Fleming (CSA) – 50th Georgia Infantry, Company F - William O. Fleming was born in Liberty County, Ga., the son of William Bennett Fleming and his wife, Eliza Ann (Maxwell) Fleming. He married Georgia W. Williams in 1860 and became a planter near Bainbridge, Decatur County, Ga. At the start of the Civil War he was a lieutenant in Captain John W. Evans' company, the Bainbridge Independents, 1st Georgia Regiment; and in 1862-1865 he became an officer in the 50th Georgia Regiment, rising from lieutenant to lieutenant colonel. After the war he returned to his family at Bainbridge, was appointed solicitor general of the Albany circuit in 1876, and in early 1881 was elected a judge by the state legislature.

The Outlaw

Legacy Series Book II

Sheritta Bitikofer

MOONSTRUCK WRITING

CONTENTS

Dedication   #

Terms to Know   #

1. Chapter 1   #

2. Chapter 2   #

3. Chapter 3   #

4. Chapter 4   #

5. Chapter 5   #

6. Chapter 6   #

7. Chapter 7   #

8. Chapter 8   #

9. Chapter 9   #

10. Chapter 10   #

11. Chapter 11   #

12. Chapter 12   #

Here's to all those cowboys and cowgirls at heart.

Terms to Know

"Fifth Ace" – Often a gun or knife that a gambler would hide – or flaunt – to ensure none of the other players would risk cheating during a game.

Bowie Knife – Also known as an Arkansas Toothpick. Invented in the early 19th century. A fixed-blade fighting knife with an iconic clip-point blade type and wide flat. Typical length varies between 12-18 inches with a 5-12 inch blade.

"Swinging a wide lasso" – A slang term for cattle rustling.

Running Iron – A branding tool used to modify preexisting brands on cattle or livestock.

Claim Jumping – When a person takes a piece of land or mining rights that was already reserved or "claimed" by another settler.

Herd Cutting – A process where a cattle rustler takes only a few head of cattle or livestock from a larger herd to amass their own.

Grubstaking – A form of investment between a financier and a miner. The financer would pay for the miner's equipment and supplies to go mine for gold or silver, and if the miner should find anything, he gave a percentage of the yield to the financer as payback with interest.

Mart Duggan – Born Martin J. Duggan in County Limerick, Ireland on November 10th, 1848. He immigrated to New York with his parents, but in July of 1864, moved out west to Colorado. He took jobs as a bouncer for saloons and gained a reputation as a gunfighter when he bested his opponents in duels. Elected marshal over Leadville by the mayor, Horace Tabor in the spring of 1878. In the booming silver town, previous lawmen had been intimidated out of office. Mart immediately began taking out corrupt officials and replaced them with men he could trust. There are several noted cases of Mart's unique way of dealing with violence and crime in Leadville. He was in and out of office until 1880. For further reading on his exploits, I refer you to "Deadly Dozen: Forgotten Gunfighters of the Old West, Volume 3" by Robert K. DeArment. It could be argued that Mart Duggan is one of the most underrated western gunfighters in history.

Ute Indians – Primary lands took up most of Colorado and Utah (named after the tribe), but their hunting grounds extended well into Wyoming, New Mexico, Arizona, and Texas. They traded with many other smaller neighboring tribes and intermarried to make borders between these tribes merge and indistinguishable. Before acquiring horses, any conflict with other tribes was mostly defensive, making the Ute not as warlike as the Comanche to the south or Lakota to the north. After horses, most warrior parties went out with the intent to steal other horses, gain prestige, or to exact revenge for a wrong done to them. When settlers like the Mormons came to Utah territory, Utes were pushed off their land and into reservations starting in the 1860s. For the most part, their cohabitation was peaceful until 1879 when a raid was conduction on an Indian agency. Eleven men were killed, including Nathan Meeker. This incident caused the reservation to be reduced from a generous portion of Utah and Colorado to a smaller reservation.

Sinapi – "Sinaævi" – Ute for "wolf".

Bear Dance – The first report of the Bear Dance reaches back to the fifteenth century when Europeans first witnessed it. The origins trace back to a legend about two brothers who encounter a she-bear in the woods while hunting. The bear was scratching on a tree and promised to teach one of the brothers the ways of the bear for one year. When it was time for him to return to the village, he had turned into a bear. The dance is to honor what the brother learned about bears and nature, but also to celebrate the arrival of spring. It's said that when the Ute hear the first thunder of spring, it's time for the Bear Dance celebration. The dance was also a way for the people to release some tension after being cooped up all winter. In the Bear Dance, the musicians use instruments made of bone that create a sort of growling sound similar to a bear. Women pick their dance partners. Festivals for the Bear Dance are still held today on the reservations.

Quantrill Raiders – A band of pro-Confederate guerilla fighters under the command of William Quantrill. Also known as bushwhackers. Quantrill was given a field command by the Confederate government under the Partisans Ranger Act during the war to fight in the region of Kansas and Missouri, but the gang soon became something more like a terrorist group or gang comprised of pro-slavery and Anti-Federal radicals. They're most known for the massacre in Lawrence, Kansas – one of Quantrill's hometowns – where they killed 180 citizens (mostly male) who were supposed to be anti-slavery. After the massacre, the Confederacy frowned upon their actions and no longer supported them. By 1864, the band fell apart and Quantrill was killed in Louisville, Kentucky in 1865 a couple of months after the war ended. Other notable members of the gang include Jesse James and "Bloody" Bill Anderson.

CHAPTER 1

MAY, 1878 - FAIRPLAY, COLORADO

"Now, son," the marshal started, "I know you're lookin' for justice. I would be too. But I doubt if you'd ever find a soul in all of Colorado who knows where Clarence Biller hides out. He just vanishes into thin air after every crime. You see all them wanted posters?" He gestured to the wall that Sarah had been glaring at during his speech. "I got my hands full tryin' to rope in these fellas. I've got a better chance of findin' any of them than I do of findin' Clarence's gang."

Sarah bit at her chapped lips, wishing she had the nerve to say what she truly felt. She would have blasted the man into next Tuesday and accused him of being a lazy lawman. If he was truly bent on finding any of those outlaws, he wouldn't have been lounging back in his chair with the two front legs hovering off the floor. He wouldn't have been sitting around in the jailhouse with his deputy and a half-empty bottle of whiskey on the table.

But something of her mother's teachings stuck like cactus needles in her skin. She wouldn't call Marshal Jenkins all the foul names she wanted to scream out against the other marshals who said they couldn't help her either. She stood, her hands balled into tight fists until the blisters on her palms smarted with the pressure.

"My suggestion to you is to take this up with the sheriff of Park County or – "

"I already did," Sarah spat, minding to keep her voice deep. "He said the same as you."

The marshal folded his arms over his thick chest, making the silver star on his vest flash in the afternoon light. "Then the best you could do is get down on them knees and pray some man will find Clarence one day and bring him in for the mile-long list of debts he owes to families like yours."

That wasn't what she wanted to hear. She couldn't move on from this. Never. She needed to see Clarence Biller hanging from the end of a rope, even if it was the last thing she'd ever witness.

Without another word - because she had nothing nice to say and wouldn't thank him for his time – Sarah stormed out of the red brick jailhouse and down the steps onto the grassy lawn. The soft clink of a bottle neck upon the rim of a glass could be heard from inside. Sarah strode away, convinced there wasn't any other way she could influence the marshal to take back his decision.

A hot gust of wind kicked up a thin cloud of dust as a few cowboys rode past on their way to the main street. They paid her a brief glance, but nothing more. The baggy clothes concealed any curve that her feminine figure possessed, making her like any other speck of dirt in these parts. No one tipped their hat to her or gave her those lurid looks. She preferred it that way.

What she didn't prefer was how her disguise had backfired. As a woman, she received a heap of sympathy and lies. The lawmen said they were doing all they could for her, searching night and day. But they weren't, and she knew it. Sarah was sick of being lied to and coddled. As a man, she thought she could get somewhere with the authorities.

She might as well have been spitting into the wind.

Sarah looked to the green and perfectly formed mountain range to the west. That thin strip of hills and peaks told her that she was nearing the edge of her search. She had banged on the doors of marshals in almost every town from Trinidad to Denver, no matter if they were eating dinner with their families or in the middle of an arrest. She'd make her case known and do everything short of beg at their feet for help. None would give it, and she was running out of towns.

The heavy clod of boots down the stone stairs from behind made her turn. The younger deputy marshal approached with his thumbs slung in his belt loops as if an unoffending posture would pacify her, eyes squinting in the bright sunshine.

"He means well," the deputy said in a hushed tone, so his superior wouldn't hear. "And I know you must be tired of being told the same thing. He may suggest that you lay down like you're licked, but if you wanna have any chance of getting at Clarence, you might need to step a little outside the law."

Sarah's brows rose in the faintest bit of astonishment. It wasn't every day that a lawman would suggest such a thing. "You're saying I go after Clarence myself?"

The deputy scoffed at the idea. "Hell, no. Clarence would chew you up and spit you out like tobacco juice." His eyes roamed over her body, seeing what any other man in Colorado saw – a rangy kid with dirt smeared across her sunburned cheeks and hair tucked under a hat to complete her disguise. But one thing that no one could mistake was her determination to find the outlaw and seek her revenge. It's all she had thought about for two months. All she had left to hope for. "You got any money?"

She shrugged in her big coat. "Some."

"Better hope it'll be enough." The deputy stepped closer and pointed toward one of the saloons settled on the secondary thoroughfare that ran along the shores of a meandering segment of the Platte River. She could only see the rear of it behind a few other buildings along Main Street, its red brick façade towering higher than its roofline. "There's a man at the Summer Saloon who might be able to help you. I don't know his name. I don't think anyone does. But they say he's a tough character. Comes around from time to time to gamble for a few hours and then leaves. My guess is that he's some kind of bounty hunter, but he doesn't talk to too many folks and all I hear is rumors. Might wanna go ask if he'll help you for a price."

Sarah was glad that the wide brim of her hat shadowed out the way her face paled at the thought of confronting a hardened gunfighter. Lawmen and store owners were one thing, but she'd never said a word to any of the uncouth ruffians in the saloons. Again, something of her mother's cautionary tales echoed back to her from childhood. This quest for justice had taken her outside of her comfort zone plenty of times, but she had never done more at a saloon than beg for a glass of water or light wine and spoke as few words as possible to the bartender.

"You got a name?" she questioned again, careful to keep whatever fear or timidity she felt from affecting her voice.

"Nope. Never really ever got a good look at him either. Keeps his head down all the time." He straightened and Sarah heard the way the deputy's back popped as he rolled his shoulders. "I wish you luck, kid. If you're the first one to take Clarence into custody, I'll be sure glad I had the chance to meet you."

The deputy turned and ambled back into the jailhouse to leave Sarah with this ultimatum.

She could keep pressing westward to Granite or north to Breckinridge in search of a marshal or sheriff who would be willing to go after Clarence. Or, she could take a chance and employ a bounty hunter. For all she knew, this mysterious man without a name might know Clarence personally. Her mother always said rough men somehow always knew about one another. They were all cut from the same cloth, forged in the same fires as The Dalton Brothers, Jesse James, Billy the Kid, John Wesley Harden, or The Reno Gang. They were all equally bad men who should be avoided by those who don't want trouble.

But Sarah straddled the edge of trouble. This quest had taught her that she wasn't going to get anywhere with the law, and now it seemed that she needed to step outside of it. Just this once.

Straightening her shoulders, feigning confidence, she crossed the street to the boardwalk that rounded the corner and made her way to the Summer Saloon.

Sarah compressed her lips and took one more big gulp of fresh air before plunging herself into the thick miasma of cigarette smoke, whiskey, astringent perfume, and manly smells that were poorly masked by it all.

Light from the two large windows on either side of the door illuminated the inside. The modest kerosene lanterns that hung from the ceiling would replace the natural light once the sun set. Round tables covered in green felt dominated the room, with a bar counter opposite the front door that stretched from one end of the hall to the other. A mirror reflected back the afternoon sun behind the bar, its edges rimmed in a dark mahogany that matched the countertop. Liquor bottles lined the space along the back, their labels proudly displayed for customers.

Fairplay was a sizable town, but this was not the only saloon worth visiting, and therefore did not have as many occupants – which she was grateful for.

Two groups of men were deep in their card games on either side of the room, muttering the occasional comment to their neighbors that was followed a grisly laugh or grunt. No music played and the only soft, pleasing sound would have come from the smiling, painted lips of the soiled doves who whispered in the player's ears. There were four in all, each one pretty in her own right with long hair, faces as flawless as porcelain and eyes bright with the prospect of gaining a potential client.

The cowboys, miners, and farmers with cards in their hands looked as grimy and filthy as they smelled. Her father, a man who had been unafraid of dirtying his hands, at least had the sense to bathe every so often. These men, however, looked as if they had just come out of the mines or in from the fields.

Sarah was virtually ignored when she entered and kept a steady, but casual pace as she crossed the floor to the barkeep.

The proprietor with his white, rolled-up sleeves greeted her as he might any other customer. "What'll ya have?" he asked as he slowed in his task of cleaning the polished wooden countertop. She presumed him to be the one whose name was engraved on the plaque above the sign on the façade, Leonhard Summer.

"Beer," Sarah replied flatly, suddenly feeling her throat choked with the fear of confronting any of these men. To ask if she could pay them to help her track down a killer might as well have made her like one of the men who petitioned to the ladies of the street. If she didn't dislike the way whiskey scorched her mouth, she might have asked for a shot of the firewater to steady her nerves.

Leonhard poured a glass from a keg underneath the counter and presented it to her. With a few coins, she paid the man and used the convenient placement of the mirror to watch the two coinciding games. With her elbows leaning against the edge and one heel hooked over the brass foot rail, she studied each of the men with no risk of discovery. They were all so engrossed with the state of their hand in the games that they didn't pay her, or the prostitutes, any mind. While they all gave the impression that they could fire a gun with some level of accuracy, none of them struck her as potentially dangerous or vicious. Ill-mannered, yes, but not vicious.

The bartender resumed the task of cleaning and when he came back in her direction, she decided to be brave.

"I was told there was a bounty hunter here," she began in a faint whisper. "Would you happen to know if he's still playing?"

Leonhard glanced directly to the occupied table on the right side of the room and motioned with his rag. "That one in the glasses, I'd think. I know every man in here, except for him. Never gives his name or nothin'. Just comes and plays a few rounds, then leaves."

Sarah leaned enough, so she could get a look at the man through the mirror. Like the others, she had discredited him upon first inspection. Now, she saw him in a different light. Slumping in his chair, one hand tilting down his cards while the other relaxed lazily upon the felt, he looked a hair older than herself.

A hat shadowed much of his features, giving them an enigmatic quality that both frightened and intrigued her. A dark bit of stubble graced his bold jaw, eyes almost completely obscured by the amber-tinted glasses he wore. Though she couldn't see the direction of his gaze, she felt it upon her, burning straight through and rendering her motionless under its power. Every line of his fit, powerful body warned her against attempting any interaction with him. The way he stared so fixedly, and yet calmly, told her that he was well aware of her interest. Something about him made her want to run and burrow into the ground to hide until he was gone, but without saying a single word he commanded her to stay.

How she could have overlooked such a character was incomprehensible now. He stood out in this crowd but evaded the unfocused eye without even trying.

She tightened her hold over the glass of beer in front of her, only two sips taken from its measure. Thirst had left her entirely as a cold sweat beaded along her back and neck. The spell was broken the moment his head angled away from her enough to let her know that he was no longer staring.

Sarah swallowed hard and lowered her gaze, fortifying herself for when the moment came to talk to him. Contrary to how she felt, she refused to be cowed by this subtle intimidation. Justice and honor were at stake.

From the looks of the pot in the middle of the table, there was plenty more on the line. Greenbacks, gold and silver coins, and other trinkets of value were piled high, each man putting a fortune at risk over the five cards they held.

For some time, none of the men spoke. No new bets were placed as fate's guiding hand hovered over them, waiting to deal the blow or bestow the reward. One man took a long drag from his cigarette and blew the smoke into the air as he tapped out the ashes into the tray on the table. He had a lady on each arm who favored his company above the others. Sarah could see the leg of another player bouncing nervously as he contemplated his hand. It was as if he were trying to will the faces to change to a more favorable combination. The remaining two – the one with the glasses and another with a gnarled scar across his left eye – silently assessed one another like two circling predators ready to pounce.

The game on the other side of the room was far more relaxed, the source of boisterous laughter and slapping of knees as men exchanged stories and jokes, betting only on pocket change and poker chips that held little to no value. The atmospheres were divided. It was like when a storm front was halted upon the heights of the mountains. One half remained sunny and bright, while the other was darkened by thunderheads. Lightning would soon strike, and Sarah was sure a fire would manifest from the sparks and destroy this whole place if someone didn't break the tension soon.

"Stop movin' your damn leg," the smoker reprimanded. "You're gonna spill my whiskey."

The jumpy one snapped out of his concentration and all jittering stopped. "Sorry."

"What're you waitin' for? You foldin' or what?" the scarred man grumbled to the man in the glasses, one hand bending his cards almost enough to crease them.

The mercenary thrummed his fingertips upon the table once in a show of impatience before replying, "I've already got my all in. You gonna fold that wimpy hand of yours or keep fingerin' that fifth ace?"

At this, Sarah turned in her seat and could see the glint of a knife blade laying across the agitated man's lap.

A bit of her composure slipped, and she cagily watched each of the men for their reactions. The armed gambler's piggish nostrils flared and if it were possible for him to be any more grotesque, Sarah doubted it. The cigarette dangled from the smoker's mouth, all amusement gone. The two women edged further behind the man they thought would win this round. The one who wasn't scared to show his anxiety finally folded and threw up his hands.

"I don't want no trouble, Morgan," he said to the one hiding the bowie.

The third gambler leaned back until he was balancing on the back legs, wholly unfazed by the unease that began to make its way across the room to purge the cheerful mood on the other side. Lips that were smiling now turned down into a worried frown as they stared at the scene unfolding.

Beside her, Leonhard's hand reached for the shotgun underneath the counter. Either he had seen these situations enough to know the outcome, or he knew Morgan well enough to predict how he would react.

"Take it easy, Morgan," the bartender warned. "Don't make me holler for the marshal like I had to last week."

"You stay outta this, Leonhard!" Morgan thundered, swiveling around to point an angry, calloused finger toward the bar. Much to Sarah's chagrin, she flinched and looked away.

"We're just playin' a friendly game of poker," the mercenary said coolly. "Ain't no need to get all excited."

Morgan spun back and slammed his hand on the table. "Show your hand or fold!"

This jostling of the tabletop caused the whiskey in the smoker's cut crystal glass to slosh over the rim. The only repercussion Morgan would receive was a nasty look. The sole level head in the saloon was the one whose eyes she couldn't see and whose face she couldn't read.

A few seconds passed and the five cards were finally laid upon the table. A neat row of diamond royals stared up at Morgan and the other gamblers.

Jaws went slack, eyes went wide, and calculating minds added up the total value of the pot on the table. Only the brave exclaimed over the high sum and the dumb luck that anyone could pull a strong hand like that on the first try. Sarah might have assumed the man was cheating, but as the others inspected their own cards, they didn't say another word about it. There were only twenty cards between them and none were available to draw or exchange. A hand like this only came around once or twice in a lifetime.

The face of the scarred man wrinkled with a contemptuous sneer. "I think you been cheatin'. Ain't nobody can win ten games in a row," he said to his rival.

A long slow breath was expelled from the young man. "I ain't gotta cheat. You been bluffin' since you walked in the door and you can't hide it any better than a rooster can hide its tail feathers."

Sarah mutedly begged the man not to rile his opponent. The last thing she wanted was to be caught in the middle of a shootout in a saloon. She had been fortunate enough to avoid them thus far.

The smoker took a long drag of his cigarette and threw down his hand, showing only one pair of tens and an ace of hearts. Morgan's bent cards weren't so weak, but his triplet of kings would have beaten the nervous man's two pair.

When the mercenary was done collecting his winnings, he left the table and ambled toward the bar counter to stand right beside Sarah. He counted out the bills and gave a few to Leonhard. "Their drinks are on me."

Now would have been the time to ask him about her predicament, but her tongue was held tight when the harsh scraping of chair legs upon the wooden floor jarred her out of her fascination.

Someone shouted and the only thing she saw was the mercenary catching the blade of the bowie knife in his fist. Morgan was on his feet, chest heaving and eyes wild for payback, but it came to nothing. If the knife had been allowed to follow its projected path, it might have found its way into the man's back. Instead, it was flipped around and the mercenary stabbed the counter, the tip stuck firm in the wood.

Sarah stared, lips parted in amazement. He had caught the knife in midair so swiftly that it defied logic itself. How could he have known it was coming? And why didn't he fight back? Any other man would have taken the invitation and returned the blow instead of rendering the knife useless, now jammed in the bar top.

A few of the older men fled to Morgan to calm him down while the mercenary slipped from the saloon, much without Sarah's notice. It all happened so quickly, so suddenly that she had to remind herself to move and carry out her purpose for coming here. This man, this even-tempered mercenary gambler, had to help her find her parents' killer.

Ben flexed his hand and took his first look at the cut on his palm. Morgan's blade had sliced him deep, and some residual blood stained his roughened skin, but the wound itself was gone. He had been a werewolf for sixteen years, but his healing abilities still astonished him on days when he could almost forget what he was.

The people that he passed by in town, the men he played poker with, none of them knew the truth. None would have even suspected it. Out here, superstitions were reserved for the mines, the Indians, and the unexplored reaches of this vast territory. No one would have thought a beast could walk in their midst as he did.

He attempted to wipe a bit of the blood onto the seat of his dark pants, but little transferred. He'd have to wash before making one last stop at the telegraph office. Turning down an alleyway, Ben made his way to the creek that ran along the western edge of Fairplay. A few washerwomen were gossiping downstream and he made sure to stay well out of their way, slipping practically unnoticed between a pair of tall bushes that could mask his presence.

But he knew that he couldn't be alone for long. She was following him, and the pounding of her hastening footsteps were hard to miss, even over the voices of the women on the other end of the creek.

After he tucked the money safely in his coat pocket, he plunged his hands into the cold water and waited, unsure why. In any other circumstance, he would have escaped through the forest until she lost interest or gave up in her pursuit. Maybe it was the fact that she had called him a bounty hunter to the bartender, or the fact that she was wearing men's clothing and that intrigued him more than it should have. Why would a woman go masquerading as a boy? Unless she had something to hide – or something to lose.

She clumsily slid down the grade that led to the creek's shore, panting as if she had run all the way from Summer Saloon to catch up with him.

"I don't know what you want," Ben began, not even bothering to look over his shoulder, "but you ain't gonna get it from me."

She paused and the breaths that came out quick and rough were withheld for a moment while she recovered. He half expected the girl to turn around and leave. Any other person in their right mind would, but she stayed rooted a couple of yards behind him and pretended to not hear his refusal.

"Mister, I need help," she said, her voice deep to match her disguise. "And after I saw what you did in the saloon, I – "

"Drop the play, girl," he interrupted. "I know you ain't a boy, so do us both a favor and quit actin' like it."

Again, there was a pause of wonder as he wrung his hands in the creek. Plumes of red drifted with the current and he hoped that it would dissipate by the time it reached the washerwomen. The last thing he wanted ringing in his ears were the screams of a few frightened ladies. He'd had enough of that.

"Fine," she said, her feminine tones emerging. "Like I was saying, I need help and I'm willing to pay for it."

Ben snorted as he rose from the embankment. "And what makes you think I even want your money?" he asked, shaking the water droplets from the tips of his fingers. "I just won over a hundred dollars in that saloon. I could double that in the next town over if I wanted."

He turned and faced the girl. The one look he had paid her in the saloon was enough to tell him that underneath the dirt, she was rather plain. Her dark blue eyes were thin, lashes pale like the long hair tucked under her hat. The baggy clothes did a fair job of hiding her sex, leaving little for any man to speculate about. At a glance, she certainly looked like a boy. Her face was round, cheeks hollowed, and lips thin. Her only redeeming quality might have been her nose, which was well shaped and almost so regal that it seemed out of place with the rest of her.

Yet, something in those eyes spoke to him even louder than her words. A spark was nestled there, a boldness that contradicted her hesitance in confronting him. He understood it, sympathized with it. He had seen it before in a prettier face, one that haunted his dreams almost every night. Maybe it was that resemblance that made him want to hear her out.

So, he folded his arms and waited.

"Well, I can't pay you a hundred," she said. "I don't have that much... But I... I'm desperate, mister. The marshals won't help me and since you know I'm... I'm just one person. I can't go after him alone and I thought maybe – "

"Who's 'him'?"

She swallowed hard. "Clarence Biller."

Ben lowered his chin. "You're jokin'."

"I'm not joking," she replied firmly with a grim shake of her head. "He killed my parents two months ago. I've been trying to get a marshal to go after him, but they say it's hopeless. No one knows where he is and no one's willing to help me look. He needs to be brought to justice and no one has the guts to do it."

"Except you," Ben said, the edges of his mouth curling into a mocking smile. He knew full well that this girl was terrified. Whether that fear was of him or of Clarence, he wasn't sure, but it was there all the same like the glaring of a train spotlight coming from a mountain tunnel. She could have fooled the marshals or the people in the saloon, but she would never fool him. Under it all, she was scared, but she didn't dare show it.

"Someone has to," she exclaimed. "But I know I need help to track him or maybe get some idea of where he might be. I thought... I thought maybe you'd know."

If Ben's hat wasn't pulled down so far over his brow, she would have seen his alarm at such a statement. "What makes you think I'd know where he is?"

She gestured to him, as if it should have been obvious. "Well, you seem like someone who would, that's all."

Ben shifted his weight and sighed. "Let me make one thing clear. Just because I look like an outlaw, don't mean I am one. And even if I was, not every outlaw knows one another like that."

Her shoulders slumped half an inch. "So, you don't know where he is?"

"I didn't say that."

Hope sprung again in those sapphire eyes, and Ben immediately hated himself for saying it. Clarence was no ordinary outlaw, and though he had heard plenty of stories around the saloons, he didn't know the man or any of his gang personally. One thing he could say with more confidence than most, however, was that the renegade didn't scare him. Not much could scare a werewolf who had been to the deepest depths of hell and survived more than any mortal man should ever have to suffer.

"I have an idea of where he might be," Ben continued before the girl could ask too much. "But I know someone who could confirm it."

Fear gave way to excitement as the girl took a daring step forward. "So, you'll help me?"

Ben ground his teeth as he debated. He had kept his distance from this kind of involvement for years. He had lived day to day, traveling from place to place without a name or explanation to give to anyone. They avoided him, fearing what secrets lay behind his tinted glasses. And though the law wanted to pin something on him, they never could. He had no warrants, he violated no ordinances, he didn't even carry a gun. He was a rover and after all he had been through, he wanted to stay that way.

But this girl came to him, braving a refusal and defying her own fear to make this proposal. She was alone in the world, just as he was, without family or friends who were willing to come to her aid. The beast wanted nothing to do with her, to tell her to go find Clarence on her own. Then, he could run off to complete his business at the telegraph office. The man in him, the one speck of humanity still left in his soul, couldn't turn away.

"I've got somethin' to take care of in town. Wait for me outside the general store."

CHAPTER 2

The longer Sarah leaned against the column outside the grocery store, the more she began to wonder if the man who promised to help her had lied. What was there to gain from deceiving her? She hadn't given him any money yet, so why should he disappear unless he found some kind of enjoyment in leading on a helpless woman.

She craned her neck to peer down the street in both directions, searching for the man whose name she didn't even know. He had made such a hasty retreat from the creek that introductions were overlooked completely.

A mother and child came toward her down the boardwalk and she lowered her chin until her face was hidden from their view. For the last hour, she had nervously fidgeted with her clothes, pulling them further out from her body and constantly adjusting her hat to settle further upon her brow. If one man could see through her disguise, then it was likely that others could.

Behind her in the store, a man laughed loudly, startling her for only a moment. Following the episode in the saloon, Sarah wanted nothing more than to leave this town. If only she didn't have to wait so long for this man who was her best bet at finding Clarence Biller.

Her dapple-gray mare, Jemimah, snorted and stamped her hoof in the dust at the hitching post. Sarah left her place by the column and went to comfort her horse's subtle sign of distress, assuming it was because of the boisterous voices of the men inside the store.

The horse tugged furiously on her reins, bridle clattering and head snapping from side to side in an effort to free herself. Sarah reached for the harness and tried to shush Jemimah, but the horse wouldn't be quieted for anything. She continued to kick and knicker, her dark eyes rolling.

Sarah couldn't understand it until she happened to glance up and see the lone figure of her mercenary standing several yards off. With his hands slung in his pockets, he stared at her horse and seemed to be waiting for something. It took her only a moment to realize that it wasn't only Jemimah. The other horses along the street were defying their masters' directions and resisting their tethers to the hitching posts. One even managed to slip the knot loose and had bolted down the lane, scared for its life.

After some observation, she made the connection. Their fear had nothing to do with any sudden noise or appearance of a snake in the dirt. It had everything to do with the new arrival at the end of the lane, the tails of his coat flapping in the breeze; her mercenary in the amber glasses.

Sarah gave him an apologetic, almost pleading look as if she were trying to make sense of the commotion. He was only a man, standing quietly without a weapon or any hint that he would harm them. Yet, the animals were frightened by him all the same.

She didn't want to believe that it was truly the man who could inspire such widespread fear, but when she remembered the edginess that pervaded the saloon during the poker game, she could see the similarities. All those at the table were anxious, even the smoker. She recalled the way he obsessively puffed on the cigarette and rotated his whiskey glass.

This stranger had some sort of affect upon the masses that Sarah could somewhat attest to, though her steadfastness to see Clarence in chains served as a barricade against any crippling fear or doubt that might dissuade her. The mercenary would not intimidate her, and perhaps that's why he had agreed to help.

There was the most miniscule change in the way he held himself that if Sarah hadn't been watching him, she might have missed it. Elbows relaxed, shoulders slumped, his chin lifted no more than half an inch, and the rise and fall of his chest came less frequently, his breaths deeper and calmer.

The tension in the air suddenly shifted and as if by some magic that only he could command, all agitation among the horses dissipated. A few, like Jemimah, had worked up a nervous sweat in the hysteria and Sarah petted down her damp neck until she was satisfied that she could untie her reins without the mare running off as the gelding had.

Wondering if this lull could even be maintained, Sarah guided her horse with some difficulty toward the man. The customers who had been talking in the stores had thundered out onto the boardwalk to attend to their own, and she could feel their curious eyes upon her and the mercenary.

The man only glanced to her before they unitedly made their way out of town and to the north, with Sarah elected as the buffer between him and Jemimah. Not a word was exchanged between the two, and she blindly followed his lead around corners and past shops.

Some witnesses muttered to their neighbors about the strangeness of seeing these two newcomers walking side-by-side, but she didn't care about what they thought. She had her guide and whether he was reliable or not, only time could tell. Her mother had always talked about trusting God and how faith could change the course of someone's life. Sarah only hoped that her mother was right.

The tightness in her limbs eased once they were away from Fairplay and out of sight from the townspeople. Sarah said nothing in order to keep the balance of peace between man and beast, but a more pressing need drove her to open her mouth.

"My name's Sarah McDaniel," she said, somewhat grateful that she could tell a stranger her Christian name for the first time in over a month.

The man didn't look to her, nor did he answer, emboldening her as he unintentionally had at the creek. His silence and unique flavor of arrogance drove her to press him harder, to prove that she was capable of the task at hand. Why his opinion should matter more to her, she wasn't totally sure.

"If we're going to be – "

"My name's Ben." The words came flat, clipped, and impatient, as if she had been harassing him for hours.

A little startled by how little it took to provoke him, Sarah stared dumbly for a second and then nodded. "Thank you for agreeing to help me, Ben."

"Don't thank me yet," he replied. "The fella I know was in Alma, last I heard. And it ain't a guarantee that he'll know where Clarence is. I might not be able to help you any more than the marshals."

Sarah found herself smiling. "But you're trying. That's already helpful."

Ben's attention diverted toward the mountains for a moment, and then back to the road that wound its way along the banks of the Platte River.

"I take it you're not from Fairplay?" she asked, more out of a desire to fill the air with more than the sounds of their shuffling feet.

"Nope."

"Where are you from, then?"

He didn't answer right away, and she saw how the corner of his mouth tugged down, as if her question left a bad taste in his mouth. "Not Colorado."

"That's mighty vague," she returned.

"You're mighty nosy."

Sarah was taken aback, but she would not be silenced by his curtness. Ever since she'd set out from home, she had met her fair share of rude men and dealt with them all – as a woman and as a man. "No reason to get snippy," she muttered. "As I was trying to say before, we're going to be working together, so I don't see any reason we can't be civil with each other." When Ben gave no response, she bravely continued with, "Were you sending a telegram to your family?"

His head whipped around to pin her with a fierce stare. "What?"

"I saw you go into the telegraph office in Fairplay. Sending a telegram to your family?"

Ben stopped cold and that same power he had projected in the saloon and the street outside the store poured from him once more. Jemimah nearly wrenched the reins from Sarah's gloved hands.

"I can be civil with you, but I'm gonna tell you right now that what I do ain't any of your business."

Sarah was only half listening as she turned to Jemimah to help settle her irrational fear. There wasn't a man on earth who would hurt her horse, not even Ben. That gray mare was all that was left of her home and the life she knew before Clarence Biller came barreling onto her farm with his gang. It was only because of Jemimah that Sarah was spared the same fate as her parents.

"Fine," she snapped, feeling a hot rage creep up her neck. "Keep your secrets. I don't need them. If you want to just give me the name of this fella you know in Alma, I'll go find him myself."

For the first time since she had seen him in the saloon, Ben seemed to start at her blatant challenge. She meant it as a dare to straighten up or leave her alone. Sarah had thought she had found an ally, someone willing to tolerate her long enough to help. She didn't care if he disappeared after they parted ways or not, but she did care if he would maintain this attitude for their entire connection with one another.

That radiating dominance lessened and poor Jemimah was calmed once more. If this was any sign of how their journey together would be, Sarah thought she'd come to regret it and she half-expected for Ben to give her the name of his associate and move on.

Instead, he heaved a sigh, and said, "I ain't gonna leave you out here all by yourself. Besides, the fella in Alma... He's a different bird, for sure. It'd be best if I talk to him instead of you."

Sarah tossed a scathing look his way, but was instantly humbled by the hint of contriteness in his expression. Even with his eyes masked by the glasses, he still portrayed a wealth of feeling that astounded her almost as much as his admission. And she wasn't so blinded by her pride that she couldn't see the muted petition for them to forgive and forget.

After all, he was a rogue and a mercenary. She couldn't expect him to have the gentlest manners in the world. Now, Ben knew that she could fire back with just as much of a kick as he could give.

"You don't have a horse?" she asked skeptically, changing the subject. As soon as the words left her, she realized how silly of a question that must have been. Surely he understood his affect upon the startled horses in Fairplay.

Ben passed a look toward Jemimah and she saw his nostrils twitch. "Never had a need for one." Sarah pondered on this before he spoke again. "Are you gonna saddle up or is it gonna take us all afternoon to get to Alma?"

Befuddled by his sudden turn to the aggressive again, she replied, "I can walk fine. Just because I'm a girl doesn't mean – "

"It ain't got nothin' to do with you bein' a girl. We'll get there faster if you ride the damn horse."

Accustomed to rough talk, she let his obscenity slide. "You're not going to run with the horse, are you?"

"I intend to."

She didn't hide her disbelief, but he didn't waver. So, more or less to avoid an argument with her guide, she mounted Jemimah. Almost as soon as she did, Ben started off at a jog that slowly increased into a full run. Sarah urged her horse into a canter, but soon found that she couldn't keep up with the man who was kicking up a whirl of dust behind him.

Much to Jemimah's disapproval, Sarah kicked her into a gallop and stayed at pace with the mercenary. It wasn't natural, but Ben kept at that steady gate. He never tripped, lost his footing, or slowed, not even when the path rose over a hill or twisted in sharp turns that Ben completely cut across for the sake of time.

It was impossible. Unthinkable. Sarah gaped at his inexhaustible stamina, wondering how any man on earth could outrun a horse. Who was this man? Where did he come from? Did this inhuman talent have to do with the aura of authority he exuded so naturally? What had she gotten herself into?

Alma

Ben's underhanded scheme to hush Sarah's incessant questions had worked. It was a risky move to show her a fraction of his werewolf speed, but he hadn't done it unthinkingly. She had seen the invisible evidence of his wolfish nature first hand when he'd arrived on the street in Fairplay. Animals, especially herd or prey animals, could sense the predator in him and responded to it without fail. The only way to quiet their spirit was to momentarily blanket his own.

It was unlikely, however that she would ever suspect the truth. Few would. Not in this age where oceans were connected by railroads and the world no longer seemed the scary and mythical place it had once been. The humans around him had more to worry about, especially when their own kind could be greater beasts than the ones tucked away in fairytales.

There was one person, however, who did know about his cursed nature. And if he was the same sort of man that Ben remembered, then it wouldn't be hard to find him in Alma. Unlike Fairplay, there were only a small handful of saloons and it wasn't hard to pick up Henry's scent amongst the population of miners and farmers in the streets. With luck, he'd be sober enough to not make a scene, but just drunk enough to leak the information he needed.

He left Sarah waiting down the street near a dress shop, ordering her to stay there until he returned. It wasn't until he heard the dissenting whispers of the women who passed by the shop that he realized that his choice of establishments might have been problematic. Ben's initial thought was to keep her far from the roaming eyes of men, but he hadn't given any thought to how others of her sex would perceive her loitering in such a place. He didn't intend to be long with Henry, so hopefully no well-meaning matron would call on the marshal to report a suspicious young man outside the shop.

Ben pushed his way through the swinging doors to enter the saloon. His keen eyes sifted through the faces until he spotted a familiar backside and distinctively tooled leather belt and holster. One look to the obliging mirror behind the bar confirmed his identity and Ben slipped his way past the other tipsy patrons.

This late in the evening, the tables and counter were packed with men willing to gamble away their earnings or drink away the thought of a hazardous tomorrow in the mines. Saloons, above all establishments, seemed the most profitable these days.

"Stayin' out of trouble?" he asked once he came to stand beside the scamp he had known for almost a decade.

Henry practically jumped out of his skin and spilled a bit of the whiskey he had been holding. "Damn it, Ben! I swear you've got some Indian blood on those Georgian roots of yours."

Ben allowed himself a smile, somewhat glad that he could relax after metaphorically walking across broken glass for months on end. Henry knew more about him than any other man in the country. "You know I always walk softly."

Henry looked him over with a pair of dark hazel eyes. "Yeah, I remember. How could I ever forget?" As if to chase away the sudden disturbing thought, Henry downed the last of his liquor.

He took the time to inspect his old friend. His ashen brown hair was matted with dirt and sweat, which acted like a holding agent to keep his hair slicked back from his forehead. His clothes were equally filthy and the odor that made Ben's nose wrinkle rivaled that of the miners who stood toward the end of the counter. His boots were muddied, his pant legs torn a bit at the hem, and the bandana around his neck looked as if it had seen much better days. One thing that hadn't change was the way the corners of his mouth seemed to pull into a perpetual smirk, as if he found life and the whole world amusing in some way. Those eyes sparkled with a fervency for life and fun that Ben couldn't always understand.

"You look like shit," Ben mumbled.

Henry scoffed. "You ain't no daisy yourself. What have you been up to?"

The barkeep came to take his order, but Ben turned him down. Once they were alone again, he replied, "Nothin' worth mentionin'."

"In other words," Henry said as he waggled his brows, "the same ol' stuff you've been doin' for the last... how many years? Five? Seven?"

"Eight," Ben corrected with a note of annoyance. "You still swingin' a wide lasso? Or is that why you're here in Alma and not down south near Pueblo?"

Henry took a nervous glance over his shoulder and gave a slightly exaggerated gesture for his talkative friend to shut his mouth. "No need to talk about all that," he whispered, knowing the werewolf would hear him over the din of saloon noise.

Ben met the stare of a stranger in the mirror who sat halfway across the saloon hall, hat tucked low over a severe, careworn face. His clothes were perhaps the cleanest in the entire place, save for the bartender, and he was the only one not participating in the game at his present table. His tumbler of whiskey was only half-full and focus wholly settled upon Henry and his new friend at the bar.

"It wouldn't happen to have anythin' to do with the Pinkerton agent that's been watchin' you, now would it?" Ben wondered aloud, knowing how sly and completely correct he was.

Henry let out a low groan and pushed away his empty glass. "The man's been followin' me. I swear, those cows didn't have a brand when I found them."

"Did they not have a brand, or did they suffer a new one before you sold them in Denver?"

The cowboy slid him a distrustful look. "You ain't in league with that scumbag, are you?"

Ben let out a low chuckle. "Nope, but I know you too well, Henry. You've always been handy with a runnin' iron and if you ain't out claim jumpin', herd cuttin', or swindlin' someone out of their life's earnin's in a game of poker, you're bored out of your mind. Those years we spent workin' on the Kansas Railroad were the most respectable you ever spent."

Henry gave a hearty laugh at his speech and slammed his hand on the table before leaning in close to mutter with a smile, "If you were any normal man, I'd gut you where you stand."

In return, Ben eased his tinted glasses down his nose and locked the golden eyes of the wolf upon his old compatriot. "Good thing I ain't normal."

Henry shuddered and stood up straight again. "Good Lord, Ben. Put those things away. I didn't like lookin' at them when I was seventeen and I don't like them now."

Ben pushed up his glasses again to conceal the one aspect of his preternatural condition that could never be willed away. He had left his mentor too soon and never sought the guidance he needed to learn how to make his old brown eyes return. He hoped that one day the wolf would recede somehow and relinquish its hold without effort or a struggle. Until then, he gave into his fate of never being able to hide completely in plain sight as the one who had bitten and turned him years ago.

"So, how bad is it?" Ben asked, paying another glance to the agent in the mirror.

After a few beats of silence, Henry replied, "Two warrants. Maybe three. I can't remember if they issued one for that one incident in Utah or not. I swear it was a fair fight and it should've been deemed as self-defense. That don't count everythin' else, though. I'm sure there's plenty they could peg on me, but they ain't got no proof... as long as some whores don't go runnin' their mouths... Come to think of it, there may be one warrant from Cedar Point. That man just got on my nerves."

Ben turned his head slowly to regard the outlaw with mild annoyance. Henry only gave a helpless shrug. "Like you said, I get bored. Hell, I'm bored now. I've been waitin' for the guy to either move on or arrest me all ready. He hadn't budged for at least an hour. I was plannin' to get outta Colorado until I knew he was followin' me."

With a sigh, Ben assessed his options while Henry poured another shot of whiskey. He carried no gun on him, and Henry had his own pair of Colt double-actions. The cowboy to his left was too far in his boots to realize if Ben would have stolen his gun, so that gave him some access to a weapon. One bouncer at the door was busy talking with a barmaid while the other was keeping his eye on a tense game of poker not too far from him. No doubt the bartender had a shotgun under the counter somewhere and with so many scents to filter through, Ben couldn't tell where exactly it was. The other factors he couldn't count on were the sheer number of guns still present in the saloon. If they made a run for it, would the drinkers and gamblers side with the Pinkerton or mind their own business?

Then, there was Henry to consider. Ben could take a bullet or two. He'd done it before. But Henry was still human, and one lucky shot in the right place could prove fatal. This escape had to be executed delicately or there would be a bloodbath.

"This place have a backdoor?"

He shook his head. "I all ready asked about that. Unless you wanna run upstairs and escape out a window, the only way out of here is through the front."

Ben ground his molars and thought harder. "I'll tell you what," he began, "if I get you outta here and take care of that Pinkerton, will you take me to where Clarence Biller and his gang hide out?"

He didn't have to even look to know that Henry was giving him a hard, sidelong stare. "Clarence Biller?" he questioned slowly. "Did I hear you right?"

"You heard me right. I'm in a bit of a fix right now and whatever information you can give would be appreciated. I remember you mentionin' a few years back that you had almost helped them with a bank job, so I figured you'd be the best one to ask."

Henry ran his hands through his hair, his fingers weaving amongst the stiffened locks. "You sure we're talkin' about the same guy?"

Ben struggled to keep his calm. "Yes. Clarence Biller, the man who's wanted for the murder of countless families, robbed over a dozen trains, stage coaches, and a couple of banks, and kidnapped the wife of the mayor of Denver for three weeks."

"Same Clarence Biller who stole that one captain's uniform from Fort Laramie?"

"While the captain was sleeping in it," Ben finished. "Yes, we're talkin' about the same one."

When Henry didn't respond quickly enough, Ben looked to see a countenance riddled with indecisiveness. "I know you're not that drunk. You can see the sense in helpin' me. You get out of here in exchange for a little information. What's to think about?"

The cowboy pulled a face. "Plenty. You might save my skin from that Pinkerton fella, but who's gonna save me from Clarence if he finds out I snitched?"

"If all goes well, you won't have to worry about that either. There's a lady outside who's itchin' to get him measured for a noose and I think she could do it if we only knew where he was."

At this, Henry's eyes glazed over with interest. "A lady, huh?"

Ben let out a low warning growl that the cowboy would have felt in the soles of his boots. "Don't even think about it. Clarence killed her family and she's out for revenge. You gonna help or not?"

Henry scratched at the bit of light stubble on his chin and finally nodded to whatever logical end he had come to. "Truth be told... I really don't know where he is. But I know a fella who does. And he's in Leadville."

Ben looked heavenward and rubbed at his rough cheeks. This was turning into a wild goose chase with too many hands in the kettle as it was. Involving another man in the operation would make things more difficult; not necessarily for Sarah, but for Ben. He didn't feel right about passing her along to strangers. Part of him didn't even want to give her over completely to Henry's guardianship.

He began to wonder how far he was willing to go for this girl. When would he deem it suitable to sever his involvement in this vigilante mission? When would he decide that her safety was no longer his responsibility? For now, Ben resolved to see it through. He'd protect Sarah from Clarence Biller and Henry if he had to.

"It's about half a day's travel through Buckskin Gulch to get to Leadville. From there, it may be another long stretch to get to Clarence. That kind of journey, she'd need supplies," Henry mused. "I got a little cash leftover from my last payout. This lady gonna finance the trip?"

"She ain't got much to speak of," Ben said. "But I know a store owner in Leadville that owes me a favor. He could probably get us some supplies on account. He deals in that sort of thing with miners. Grubstakin', I think he called it."

Henry nodded, probably knowing all about such dealings as grubstaking between starry-eyed prospectors and entrepreneurs. "Sounds like a plan... So, how do we get out of here without the lawman seein' us?"

"Oh, he's gonna see us," Ben grumbled, still not quite satisfied with his plan. "Just get ready to skin that pistol and run like a bat outta hell."

A wide grin split the cowboy's face. "I must be dreamin'. You got a wild streak in you after all."

"I'm too used to tryin' to stay alive. I was bound to get creative after a while... Still got that deck of cards?"

Henry, confused by the question, reached into his vest pocket and withdrew the dog-eared stack. The cards were worn, stained, and he knew a few to have some special, discrete markings in the corners of their intricate designs. As long as Henry played with his own deck, he couldn't lose. Ben drew the first ace and handed the rest back to him after slipping it up his sleeve.

"Stay at the bar until I give the signal," Ben instructed.

"What's the signal?"

"You'll know it."

After carefully pocketing the unprotected gun from the drunken cowboy, Ben moved away from the bar at an ambling pace, averting his eyes from the Pinkerton and keeping his natural dribbling dominance to a minimum. If he became the prime focus of the detective, then none of this plan would work. Henry, like a fool, cagily continued to watch his friend's progress as he went from poker table to poker table. Ben would linger for a few moments, and then move on, laid-back and innocuous.

When he came to the game that was being watched so fiercely by one of the saloon bouncers, he stayed planted just long enough to make the other gamblers comfortable with his presence. There were other spectators, some who were drawn by the large pot in the center or by the need to give well-meaning advice to their friend who had a stake in the game. Ben was barely noticed and after one last look to the bouncer, Henry, and the detective, he made his move.

He let the ace fall to the floor, the soft tap of the edge upon the planks undetected among the stamping feet, swishing skirts, and general clatter of glasses and poker chips. When he was assured that no one took notice of the incident, he turned as if he would walk away. Playing the innocent, he looked down to the card and then squatted to scoop it back up.

"This yours, friend?" he asked to the gambler beside him.

Wide eyes looked between the unsuspecting miner, the ace, and their own hands.

What followed sent the entire saloon in an uproar. Hands reached out to reclaim their winnings, angry mouths shouted obscenities and insults upon the accused cheater, cries of distress and pleas for a pardon were issued, but it was too late to stop this raging fire. Guns were pulled, knives unsheathed, whiskey glasses toppled over in the scuffle to investigate the allegations, and the most important – no one was paying attention to Henry anymore. Not even the Pinkerton detective.

The bouncers rushed to detain one burly farmer who was ready to lift the hair of the guilty party, while the Pinkerton believed it was his civic duty to rise from his chair and finally take action. Ben managed to slip through the jostling, smelly bodies that hurried away from the center of the chaos. From his place on the wall, he spotted Henry standing near the bar like a dumbstruck dupe, clearly oblivious to what Ben had done.

He bit back the snarl that swelled in his throat and kept his eyes riveted upon the operative. These sort of saloon fights could be like Chinese firecrackers or dynamite explosions. There was no in between, and it was becoming more and more evident that though the men of Alma were hot-headed, they could be settled down with a heavy hand or threat of a bullet between their eyes. That was not what Ben was counting on. And Henry hadn't moved yet. The window of opportunity was closing fast.

There was a brief second where Ben made eye contact with his friend and he jerked his head toward the door as the sign to run. It was too obvious, and the Pinkerton saw it.

He turned his focus back to Henry and, seeing that the incident was being well taken care of by the bouncers and barkeep, moved to make his arrest. Henry bolted from his place by the counter and put a crowd between himself and the Pinkerton, but Ben knew it wouldn't be enough.

Ben pulled the pistol from his coat pocket and took aim at the detective. One shot through the back of his knee not only sent him crumbling to the floor, but acted as a catalyst to the final explosion of pandemonium that rippled through the saloon. Women screamed and rushed for safety behind the bar. Gunmetal gleamed in the afternoon sun as they all turned to try and find the source of the shot. By then, Ben had used his inhuman speed to some advantage and shoved everyone out of his way, so he could accompany his friend out of the building. If anyone guessed it was him that had fired the shot, they never acted upon it.

Once outside in the clean air, Ben grabbed at Henry's sleeve and whipped him into the street to get clear of the doors. He had already heard the hammers lock on several pistols before the shots rang out. The shattering of broken glass added to the tumult and now, pedestrians were searching for cover.

Except one.

Sarah was no longer hitched outside the dress shop and was riding toward the saloon, oblivious to the furious shouts of men coming from within. She looked from him to Henry, and back to the saloon as her horse weaved in objection to her promptings. Thankfully, Henry thought she was just another snooping citizen and didn't pay her a second look... yet.

He jumped upon his horse and it took a moment for him to orient himself to the west, toward Pennsylvania Mountain. But once he had his bearings, he kicked his dun stallion into a full gallop, and he went flying out of town like a scorched cat. Sarah also didn't make the connection that they would all three be traveling together and shouted to Ben, "Well? Where are we going?"

"Follow him!" He pointed to the fleeing outlaw and she obeyed without further question.

Ben stayed on the boardwalk outside the saloon for only half a minute to make sure that the Pinkerton was well dispensed with, and then he took off down the alleyways in an attempt to catch up with the others. Out of sight from the frantic townspeople, he could let a bit of the wolf's speed into his limbs.

He beat them to the edge of town, less than a mile from the base of the towering mountains that divided them from Leadville. Golden eyes glared brighter behind his tinted glasses, and though the humans would never see them, the mare instinctively shied from Ben as they approached.

Henry's stallion was less afraid since he had known Ben from a colt, but Sarah's mare reared and almost threw her into the road. Ben, as he had been tempted to do so many times before, restrained from reaching out to calm the animal. Growing up on a farm in Georgia, he had once been known for his soothing way with horses and other livestock. As a werewolf, a predator trapped within human skin, he could never be so useful.

Familiar to these innate reactions to Ben, Henry grabbed for Sarah's reins and managed to ease the mare to a more practicable temper. What unfolded afterward troubled Ben more than it should have.

Their gazes met and realization dawned in Henry's eyes before a slow, charming smile spread over his lips. Sarah's sun-kissed cheeks colored under his attention, the same as any other woman's had when they were being unwittingly wooed by the cowboy.

"Howdy, miss," Henry drawled as he lifted his hat onto his head. "You must be the lady Ben mentioned. Name's Henry Blair."

He offered out his roughened hand, but she didn't take it. The irritation in her eyes contradicted her flushed face and Ben tried to make sense of her reaction.

"Sarah," she replied, "Sarah McDaniel."

His grin widened at her staunch refusal at physical touch, seemingly undaunted. If only she knew that Henry would take this as a challenge rather than a deterrent.

"Let's get movin'," Ben interrupted, startling them both. "We may not make it to Leadville by nightfall, but we need to get as far as we can through the mountains."

Sarah, now in control of her horse, moved along toward the path that led to Buckskin Gulch. He could sense the unspoken questions, but there would be plenty of time to explain everything on the way.

Henry came up alongside Ben, the only dismounted one of the party and gave him a meaningful look that told him enough. The young woman might be a target, as he feared, and Ben's former notion that he'd need to stay as a chaperone for the two was reinforced, much to his displeasure. With luck, they would all get to see Clarence hang from the gallows by the end of the week. He wasn't sure they would all make it longer than that.

CHAPTER 3

BUCKSKIN GULCH

Henry considered himself the only sensible one of the group. With Ben's unnatural ability to see through the pitch blackness, he thought it best to push on through the nighttime hours, since they had encountered too many delays. Sarah, strengthened by the obvious need for retribution, agreed with the werewolf. She couldn't have any clue as to what Ben was. But as the stars of twilight appeared against the darkening sky, Henry spoke his mind.

"There ain't no need to endanger the horses by traveling through the night. They'll twist a foot in a heartbeat if they can't see where they're goin'."

Ben stood upon a high boulder on the path ahead of them, his silhouette cutting a lone and determined figure in the gloom. He had rightly taken control of the party, calling the shots and directing them down the shortest route through the mountains to get to Leadville. It'd be his call whether to camp or keep going, because a bullet from Henry's pistol meant nothing to the werewolf.

After some time of waiting, Ben finally nodded and Henry dismounted with relief. He had ridden in the saddle for longer stretches before, but the last few days of running from the Pinkerton agent left him sore and with an aching backside. With a tinge more regret than her guide, Sarah also stepped down from her horse and untied her pack.

As Ben loomed like a sentinel, Henry could only guess that he was listening for something that neither of their human ears could perceive. Crickets and other twilight critters called out in the brush and slopes around them, a high wind whipped through the gulch and disturbed the tall grasses, but Henry knew more lurked in the shadows. None of it, vicious or not, could compare to Ben.

After years of separation, Ben had found him again somehow. Had he known his wanderings all along? Or was it a good guess to find him in Alma? Even after the few infrequent visits over the last eight years, Henry still didn't know the full extent of his enhanced abilities. Even after one year of working together on the railroad, he often felt like he didn't know the man at all. How far he could track, for how long, how he could possibly know the things that he knew, and where exactly his limits lie. Henry knew absolutely none of it and each time they came back into contact with one another, he learned something new.

One constant, however, were the eyes. Those piercing golden eyes that never went away, no matter how hard he concentrated on pushing back the beast that lived within him. Once, Henry tried to listen to his story and understand his condition, but so much remained a mystery to the farm boy from rural Kansas. With only a third grade education and over a decade of rough living, there was still plenty of which he was ignorant.

Henry looked to Sarah, and once more felt a twinge of gratitude for what Ben's reappearance had also produced. He had met plenty of girls in his life; painted ones, plain ones, ones that could make him ache with a bodily need and others who could make his skin crawl. But Sarah... she was something else.

Fiery, and pretty in a modest sort of way. Her dark blue eyes were like the color of the velvet sofa cushions in a bawdy house, calling to him to take his rest in her as long as he wanted. She was the kind of girl he had always wanted, but could never find. All the good girls married early and the widows had their babies to take care of. Anyone else dealt in the carnal trade and weren't willing to give up their livelihood for a piece of land they would have to work and a houseful of brats to run after. Plenty of other eligible girls came with their own ornery father and a loaded shotgun.

But here, Henry found himself presented with a priceless opportunity. He had a score to settle. The one bank job he had given aid to had almost ended in disaster for him because of Clarence. Henry didn't care if he was a famous outlaw. When you do a job, you don't leave men behind to take the fall. Henry got no cut of the spoils and felt no obligation to keep Clarence safe from the law. He cared about finding the bastard for himself, but also because she cared.

Henry saw that fortitude in her eyes with every look, every glance, even the ones that weren't directed toward him. Sarah was wound up tighter than a two-dollar pocket watch and Henry thought himself the only one willing to take apart those gears and help her to relax. Someone so beautiful should never have to be saddled with such a burden. But she was certainly brave for trying.

When he turned back to Ben, he saw that the werewolf had come back several yards toward their intended campground and pinned Henry with an unyielding stare. His brows arched in question to his old friend's harshness and received a subtle prompting for him to come closer.

Leaving Sarah to tend to her horse and sleeping arrangement, Henry obeyed.

"May I help you?" Henry wise-cracked.

That elicited a low growl from Ben that would have left any man shaking in his boots. "Don't start with me. I've been seein' the way you look at her."

Henry, unafraid of aggravating the wolf again, glanced over his shoulder to Sarah. He could barely see her outline near the river, but a pale moon began to peak up from behind the mountains to shed more light upon the golden hair she had loosed from her hat.

"You got a point?"

Ben's brows compressed. "I'm goin' to get food, so I'll be leavin' you two alone for a while."

Hope surged within Henry and his friend noticed it. "Great. Have fun." He thought he could get away with giving Ben a slap on the back and turned away to see if Sarah needed any help watering her horse, but a hand grabbed his collar and yanked him back.

"Do not," Ben began, low and his voice filled with all the malice that a snarling dog like him could muster, "touch a hair on her head or I'll have to take yours off your shoulders."

Henry paused and felt an unpleasantly familiar sensation course through his blood. He had felt it a few times before when Ben became this angry, but it had been so long that he had almost forgotten how it could sober a man so effectively.

"Is she spoken for or somethin'?" he asked, genuinely trying to make heads or tails of Ben's dramatic reaction to his interest in Sarah.

"All I know is that she's been through enough and she don't need some rake comin' in and meddlin' with her head. I've seen what you've done to womenfolk before. You can't just do what you want and throw her away when you're done."

An indignant line etched between his brows. "Ben, I know our paths haven't crossed in a long time, but I'm not the same seventeen-year-old kid who pounded railroad spikes."

"No, you're worse," Ben grumbled, releasing Henry's collar before he turned his back and blended into the coming night.

"What do you want me to tell her?" Henry asked before he could have a chance to fully disappear. "I can't exactly say you're off hunting with your bare hands."

"Lie to her," Ben said. "You should be good at that."

Henry pulled a wry face. If they'd had this conversation a few years ago, he would have been tempted to throttle Ben – werewolf or not. Henry had been insulted on two accounts, as a philanderer and a liar. Thankfully, age and some maturity had gotten the better of Henry and he didn't feel compelled to challenge his friend for the simple fact that he was telling the truth.

Henry straightened out his shirt and vest and sucked in a tight breath to keep himself from firing back some unwarranted accusation about some of Ben's faults. But he held his tongue. It was true that he wasn't the same man, but Ben didn't know about the change that had taken place in Henry over the last month or so. Nights were spent lying awake, wondering how long he could keep it all up.

The cattle rustling, the gambling, the drinking, the girls. It was fun for a while, but his sins had caught up to him and it might have been high time he retired. Whatever options were available to him remained unexplored, but the first step had been made. Henry was looking for a wife, a home, and something permanent.

Eight years had hardened him into the rough character that he never thought he would become. Yet, he stood in boots that he had stolen off a drunk cowboy, holstered two pistols that he had won in a card game, and there was a small bounty on his head for crimes that he had committed. If he had any common sense, he would leave Sarah alone like Ben demanded, not only because she had too much going wrong in her simple little life, but because he was no good for her.

However, Henry wanted her to be the judge of that.

He waited until there was no sign of Ben anywhere near that section of the river and then made his way toward Sarah, who fumbled with the flint striker. In the course of their talk, she had managed to dig a shallow pit and filled it with kindling from nearby. A smile tugged on his lips and Henry squatted beside her.

"Allow me."

Sarah's steely eyes met his, and after a silent battle with her own pride, she relinquished the flint and striker. Their fingers brushed, and Henry hoped he wasn't the only one to feel the bit of tingling that spread across his skin when they touched.

After two tries, he had created enough sparks to ignite the bits of dried grass. The embers burned and spread as Henry stoked them with a gentle breath. Soon, the flames caught and a dancing orange glow illuminated Sarah's softened countenance. Henry stared, memorizing that almost peaceful expression. He wondered what thought had crossed her mind to make her brows slacken and her lips part just enough to give them an impression of fullness.

But one glance to him frightened away the memory and she regressed to the seriousness that had been his only companion for the last four hours as they wove their way through the mountain pass. She rose to her feet and dusted off her knees before she walked some distance away where the fire's light couldn't touch her.

"Don't wander far," he warned.

"I'm not going anywhere," she replied curtly. It was then he realized that she had decided to busy herself with unsaddling the horses by the river.

Henry quickly jumped up and attended to his own horse. Anything to stay close and watch for that hint of the delicate woman that he had glimpsed a second ago. Her movements were confident as she unfastened buckles, as if she had done this a million times. Such deft precision was reserved for seasoned ranch hands or cowboys who had been on the drive for months. It only piqued his curiosity.

When they walked in unison back to the fire, Sarah finally took the time to look around her. "Where's Ben?" she asked. The first bit of willing conversation out of her all day and it had to be about the werewolf.

Instead of being discouraged, Henry seized his chance. "He's off hunting for supper. He should be back soon."

Sarah seemed caught off guard, and he suspected it had to do with the fact that they were now alone together. He had seen the way she kept Ben within a constant visual, how she had ridden ahead to stay close to his side. A pang of unfounded jealousy might have provoked him to think that she fancied him, but a bit of reticence lingered when it came to how they interacted. She would draw close to Ben, but still kept at least a few yards between them.

"So, how'd you meet up with ol' Ben?" he asked her. "He's not exactly a social creature, ya know." He heavily set down his saddle by the fire and worked to unfurl his bedroll.

A fraction of her certainty waivered, but Sarah maintained her staunchness. "I saw him in a saloon. He handled a fight pretty well, so I figured he'd be able to help me find Clarence."

One side of his mouth quirked up. "Did you ever figure he'd end up ropin' me into all this?"

"No." The word came out biting, squelching the stab he made at redirecting the conversation to himself.

"Well, I'll admit that I never thought I'd see him again," Henry continued, attempting to call to her imagination. "I mean, the last time we met, he just showed up out of the blue, stayed for a few hours in town and left. He tends to do that."

As he lowered himself to the ground, a stick in hand to help coax the flames higher, Henry could feel her gaze upon him and gloried in it.

"That's what the deputy marshal in Fairplay said, too," she replied a little softer. "He comes into town, gambles a bit, and leaves. They didn't even know his name."

"So, he was in Fairplay this time around? I reckon he's been just about every-where in these parts. That one likes to roam."

There came the rustling of flattened grass as Sarah took a seat within Henry's peripheral. "He doesn't have a home?"

Henry slid her a cunning look. "Men like him – and men like me – typically don't. It's a little easier that way, sometimes."

Once more, she refused to deviate from Ben. "He doesn't have a family?" The soft laugh that came unbidden from Henry's throat almost made her sheepish. "I'm sorry I'm prying, but... Well, he won't talk about it with me."

"He's barely talked to me, darlin'. I only know all this, because he kind of took a likin' to me years back. I was a kid workin' on the Kansas railroad in sixty-nine. We were extendin' the line from Salina to Denver and aimed to get there about the time the Union Pacific was gonna lay down the last of their ties. Ben showed up one day and the foreman gave him a job. Didn't talk with none of the other workers, didn't eat with anyone... Hell, I don't think I ever saw him eat anythin'. He came to the job, did his work, and left."

Of course, so much more could have been said, but Henry refrained for the sake of her feminine mind. If he had told her all about the one night when he had followed Ben onto the open plains and watched him devour a buffalo, she might have fainted. Then again, she might have been strong enough to handle such a story. Henry, on the other hand, wouldn't survive the beating from Ben if he found out that he had revealed his secret.

"But, where is he from?" she asked, her tone more feverish and demanding than it had been. "Where did he go at night if he didn't stay with the rest of the workers?"

Henry grinned, somewhat consoled by her enthusiasm. He didn't expect the polar change in her attitude to be so great, but he decided to enjoy it while he could. With luck, this shift would be permanent, and he could show her that it was possible to be strong and vulnerable at the same time. It was clear she hadn't learned that yet, and he wanted to be the one to help her heal.

"He told me once – and only once, mind you – that he's from Georgia."

"That's a long way from home," she remarked, curling her legs behind her and leaning upon one hand as she eagerly waited for the rest.

"It sure is. And all he ever mentioned about his family is that he's got a ma still there. She ain't right in the head, so all the money he earned from the railroad and gamblin', he sends it back to Georgia so someone can take care of her."

At this, Sarah fell speechless and turned her stare to the growing fire. Once more, she seemed lost in some thought that broke down the walls she had raised up against him. Henry wanted to dismantle them further until he knew for a fact that they would never be erected again, but something stopped him. It might have been something akin to respect. Women could be so emotional about these things – family, homes, valor, loyalty. All things that he didn't have.

"That must be why he went to the telegraph office in Fairplay. He was wiring money to his mother." Her voice came almost imperceptible over the rising chorus of crickets.

"I reckon so," Henry replied in just as low of a tone, as if he were afraid to break this seemingly fragile spell of fascination. "After we were done with the railroad, he went off west. I don't really know where he went. California, maybe. Or Oregon. I wouldn't be surprised if he spent some time in Canada. We ran into one another every now and again, but he never told me what it was that he did between towns. He likes to keep his secrets."

And that, Henry knew to be an understatement. He was sure that there wasn't a single soul in all the world who knew as much about Ben Myers as he did. The werewolf didn't seem to be the kind to confide in many.

Henry thought to mention that Ben had served in the war between the states, but there was no reason to confuse her. The man looked to be in his early twenties, but most veterans – whether Yankee or Confederate – were well in their forties, if not older. Another quality that he could never get used to. Ben never aged. He never looked a day older or walked with a limp or seemed to be anything other than the strong, dangerous beast that he had proclaimed himself to be long ago. If it wasn't for that, and all the things he had seen in between, Henry might have thought him a lunatic.

In the relative silence, there came a noise that Henry recognized almost instantly. He tossed the prodding stick into the fire and stood to peer into the darkness around the encampment.

"What's wrong?"

He wouldn't answer her. Only when he saw the glint of something metal peeking through a nearby bush did he draw his guns. It took that one quick move to set forward an even swifter chain of events.

He fired at the stretch of dirt in front of the bush, only startling the spy. Less than a second after he did, seven men seemed to materialize from the shadows, charging into the encampment. The horses were apprehended, Sarah was snatched to her feet, and Henry found himself on the business end of three pistols, all pointed at his head.

"Drop the gun!" one of the outlaws ordered.

If he were alone, Henry would have told the man to go to hell and put a bullet in each of their guts. As it was, however, he had more to think of than himself. He was a couple of bullets shy from having enough, and they had guns on Sarah as well. It'd be pure foolishness to oppose them.

He let the pistols roll on his fingers and lowered them to the dirt. One of them scuttled forward and kicked the weapons away for good measure as Henry raised his hands.

"We don't want no trouble," he told them, knowing it would do him little good. He might not have wanted trouble, but these ruffians did.

By the looks of their clothes, Henry knew they weren't so dissimilar to him. Thieves, for sure, and it was likely they had each killed a few men in their time, and judging by the way they had come upon the encampment so suddenly, they knew what they were doing.

He glanced to Sarah, who was too busy shooting daggers with her eyes at the men who detained her. Those who held her firmly by the arms had no idea what kind of spitfire she could be, but they would find out soon enough.

With one gun still trained on Henry, the other two went to rifling through the saddlebags.

"Don't move or I'll put this bullet right between your eyes," the leader of the gang warned, his crooked and discolored teeth flashing behind dried and dusty lips.

His eyes hardened. "Wasn't plannin' to, friend. We ain't got anythin' worth fightin' for."

"Speak for yourself!" Sarah growled.

He looked to see one of the outlaws pulling out trinkets and family heirlooms. A silver locket, a few framed photographs, a hairbrush, and a golden pocket watch with some sort of engraving. The men whooped and hollered at each article they pulled out, including a wrinkled calico dress.

Their eyes met for a brief second and he conveyed the message that they both needed to remain calm and do as the men asked. The only way to get out of scrapes like this was to cooperate. They could get everything back in due time with the right firepower and a clean trail to follow.

"Got anythin' in your pockets?" the gunman asked Henry.

He shook his head. "Just a deck of cards that's missin' an ace." Henry refused to forgive Ben for stealing that prized card back in Alma. "Won't be any good to you."

"What about her?"

Leering gazes turned upon Sarah, and for that, Henry would move.

"She ain't got nothin' either," he replied, bolstering his voice. "Leave her alone."

They didn't listen to him, and Henry wasn't sure why he expected them to.

"Say, I think I know you!" one of the more squirrely of the outlaws mused as he drew closer. After close inspection, he nodded. "Yeah! This is Henry Blair! I heard there's a bounty on his head. Two hundred dollars."

"Three," Henry corrected, though his vanity might prove to be his downfall.

The one who still held him at gunpoint seemed intrigued. "Three hundred? Well, looks like it's our lucky day."

Henry didn't give much mind to what would happen to him. Even if they did turn him in for the reward, he had busted out of jail once before and he could do it again. His concerns rested with Sarah and Ben. Why the werewolf hadn't heard the commotion and come running to the scene was disturbing. Ben once said he could hear buffalo grazing from miles and miles away. He couldn't have gone too far in search of some game. Why hadn't he returned?

Then, there was Sarah. One of the outlaws began patting down her hips and legs, searching her for any concealed weapons or valuables. She kicked and thrashed against him, screaming and insisting that she be freed. All but Henry laughed at her expense. And though she was feisty, her thin arms were no match for the strength of these hardened criminals.

He had been able to hold his composure for a startlingly long time during this frisking before the other outlaw curled his fingers around her shirt collar and threatened to rip it open.

Heedless of the gun still pointed at his head, Henry leapt toward the trio. Before he could take two steps, he received a harsh blow to the back of the head – a feeling he had known all too well. The outlaw had pistol whipped him, striking with the barrel of the gun. At first, the world spun and then dimmed, as if someone were choking the fire until it died away completely. Darkness crowded in and Henry fell unconscious.

Sarah wouldn't take her eyes off Henry's limp body, willing him with every step that he would wake up.

The rough rope they had tied around her wrists bit into her skin and the bones of her ankles rubbed together uncomfortably over one side of Jemimah's saddle. By morning, a nice deep bruise would appear upon her arm where the outlaws manhandled her, jerking her one way and then another as they coordinated the robbing of their encampment.

Though they hadn't violated her, she imagined that it was only a matter of time. The reward on Henry's head compelled them to make their way through the mountain pass as quickly as possible, darkness or not. One outlaw led the way, holding a lantern to light the path ahead while the others followed in line along the river. One man stayed beside her while another monitored Henry's condition as closely as she did. The rest trotted along in single-file.

Without a gun of her own or any means to truly defend herself against the thieves, she felt helpless. At the start of their return to the east, she had studied their faces carefully in the moonlight. A few, she recognized from the wanted posters that had been nailed to the walls of marshal offices all across Colorado.

Others were complete strangers to her, but just because a man didn't have a warrant for his arrest didn't mean that he wasn't dangerous.

Why they kept her shouldn't have been a mystery. Her mother had scared her with vague stories of men who would do anything to fulfill their more lustful needs. Without a defender, they could take Sarah whenever they wanted. But they didn't.

Over the creaking of saddle leather, the steady plodding of hooves, and jingling of harnesses as the horses chewed on the bits in their mouths, Sarah knew they were talking about something they didn't want her to hear. The low tones of their voices were evidence of that. The words "Denver", "profit", and "no one will miss her" were faintly heard and despite the warm summer night, Sarah felt cold. She knew what they were talking about now, and it wasn't their own needs that they had in mind.

"Hush y'all's damn mouths," the leader scolded when one of the men spoke a little too loudly. "Don't want the lady overhearin' nothin'."

At the mention of her, Sarah looked away from Henry and to the shadowed faces of her captors. The glare she maintained for the last hour caused the finer muscles in her brows and jaw to ache, but she refused to let them see her scared, even when her heart pounded with biting force against her ribcage.

"She ain't gonna tell nobody," the blackguard beside her crooned. "Ain't ya?"

He reached out and made to stroke the back of his dirty fingers against her cheek, but Sarah jerked away and struck out boldly against him.

"Don't touch me!" she cried, knowing that she had given them a peek at her hand. Up to now, she had kept up a good poker face, but at the thought of being sold like cattle to the highest bidder, she could no longer continue to seethe. She might as well have been a rattlesnake, waiting for her chance to lash out.

Instead of warding him away from any further provocation, most of them laughed and the man whom she had resisted recoiled his hand and brought it back to slap her. The sharp crack echoed through the ravine. Sarah reeled and brought up her arms to shield herself from another blow that never came. If she wasn't strapped to the saddle, she would have tried to make a run for it, Henry or no Henry.

"Hey!" The leader of the gang broke rank and barreled down the path to end up in front of Sarah and the offender. "You leave a mark on her and you'll have me to deal with."

Progress slowed as men eagerly turned to witness the fight that was sure to break out. Still tethered to the outlaw who had hit her, Sarah could do little to take advantage of this distraction.

They stared one another down like two animals ready to fight, but the inferior soon relented and nodded to the leader in agreement. Disappointment spread through the other five, but another emotion soon displaced it.

A sudden rustling in an expanse of bushes on the other side of the river startled two of the men into drawing their pistols.

"Put them smoke wagons away!" the leader ordered, steering his horse in their line of sight. "Probably ain't nothin' but a deer or somethin'."

"What if it's a mountain lion?" one asked, as he eased back the hammer on his gun.

"There ain't no mountain lions out here," another contested.

"Are to!" one exclaimed, convinced enough to pull out the rifle from his saddle holster. "I spotted one just last week. Remember, Bob?"

Bob, one of the outlaws who had remained fairly silent during the ordeal, gave a hasty nod of affirmation.

"No mountain lion's gonna attack all of us," the leader insisted. "Keep movin'!"

Those who hadn't brandished their weapons kicked their horses into a faster walk to make up for the lost time, but they soon discovered that their animals wouldn't cooperate. None of them would.

In a scene that Sarah had witnessed once before, all nine horses became thoroughly riled by something that none of their masters could see. Jemimah fought the hardest and nearly threw her captor's horse off balance. Only Henry's horse, whom she understood to be called Buck, preserved his calm with his rider still hanging unconscious across his back.

The movement in the bushes came again, this time noticeably closer to the riverbank. The horses continued to stamp their feet and pull at their reins. The outlaws looked to one another in utter confusion and some of their attention was redirected to the immediate problem with their mounts.

Sarah dared to hope and took a deep breath before shouting out to whom she believed frightened the horses. "Ben! Ben, help me!"

"Shut up!" they yelled at her, probably thinking that it would only spook the animals further.

In the moonlight, Sarah could hardly make out what happened next. Something darted across the shallow river, splashing water in three great bounding leaps. By the darkened outline, the men's earlier fears about a mountain lion seemed confirmed. But the sounds that rose above the cries of both men and horse were not the screams she had sometimes heard outside her family's farm late at night. A roar like nothing she ever heard caused her to tremble and drop over Jemimah's neck. She had some thought that pressing herself into her horse might make her less of a target.

Sarah's vision was limited from her position. She saw the frantic legs of the horses stamping and searching for a route of escape. Confusion erupted as the predator leapt into the gang. Guns were discharged, the black powder flashes at the end of the barrels casting brief moments of light into the ambush. Clothes were torn, saddlebags fell to the ground, horses without their riders bolted into the darkness. The lantern that had led the way for almost a mile went dark, the light snuffed out when it was dropped by the lead outlaw.

The shouts became nothing but a mass of garbled, terrified questions, unheeded orders, and the wails that preceded death. The man who had hit her fell to the ground next to Jemimah's front hooves. In the sporadic bits of light, she saw his face frozen in the same expression he had held in his last moments of life. Wide, horrorstruck eyes stared up at her. Blood splatters across his cheeks and nose stood out sharply, unable to be mistaken for anything else. A bit of the moonlight glistened off the laceration in his throat that had been torn open by the creature.

Somehow, Jemimah's tether had been cut and the moment she was free, the horse turned to the west and galloped without any instruction from Sarah. Dazed by the suddenness of the attack, she simply held on and squeezed her eyes shut against the fading noises.

Once she heard nothing but her own quickened breaths and the pounding of Jemimah's rapid gate, Sarah groped blindly for the reins to make her slow down. They eased to a stop, but the nightmare wasn't over.

She thought of Henry, who would be an easy meal for the mountain lion or coyote or whatever it was. She tried to remember if she had caught a good look at the beast, but everything was so blurry and muddled. It would have been hard to see anything. The only memory that stood out in stark relief was the face of the dead outlaw. She had seen dead bodies before, but never one so mangled as he had been.

For the first time, she straightened in the saddle and looked back in the direction they had come. Several turns in the ravine blocked her view of the massacre, which she was thankful for. She gulped down breaths in an effort to quiet herself, so she could listen for any sign if the creature had followed her.

Apart from her heartbeat thudding loudly in her ears and the panting of Jemimah, she heard little. Not even the crickets. It was as if the beast had killed everything in the mountains, leaving only her and her horse. After waiting for a moment, another sound broke through the stillness. At first, she thought it to be another escaped horse. And it was. Henry's stallion, along with its insensible rider, came scampering into view.

She let out a long breath of relief when she saw Henry's hair and feet bobbing in time with the horse's gait. But before she could go to him, Jemimah suddenly tossed her head. Sarah looked and would have fallen from the saddle if she hadn't still been tied to it.

Ben stood there, one hand gripping Jemimah's harness to keep her still.

More relief washed through her and Sarah pressed her joined hands to her chest. "Thank the Lord, it's you!" The cry was stolen by the consuming fear that had wreaked havoc upon her nerves, but it wasn't too much to keep her from telling him the whole story.

"I have no idea what it was," she continued after Ben had wordlessly retrieved Henry and Buck. All through her outpour, he hadn't said a thing. Not an apology for leaving them, not even a look of astonishment when she talked about the beast. "But whatever it was, it had to have killed them all."

Leading the two horses, Ben finally spoke. "I hope it did."

The coldness, the utter lack of feeling in his words suspended anything Sarah might have said next. She had expected his first words to be something along the lines of, "I'm glad it didn't kill you" or "I'm glad you're both safe." The only comment he could make pertained to the fate of the outlaws. And though they might have deserved to die, Sarah would have never wished such a brutal, savage death upon anyone.

They went along in silence for a short distance along the river. Only then did Ben pull out a knife from one of Henry's saddlebags and he made quick work of her bonds. In the midnight glow of the moon, she saw dark stains upon his hands that covered his fingers and palm. When her gaze traveled to his chest, she saw similar blemishes upon his shirt.

Sarah opened her mouth to ask, but he had already turned away to slip Henry's body from Buck's back. Not trusting her legs to keep her standing, she stayed upon Jemimah and watched closely.

The sight of something caught her notice amongst the grass. Bags. Saddlebags stained with blood. And though most saddlebags were fairly generic in style, even from a distance, she could see the unique tooling and knew who it had belonged to.

How could Ben have run all that way to the scene where the outlaws were killed, come back to dispense with the bags, and still meet up with her? Had he seen the beast? Could that explain the blood on his hands? How long had it been since she had escaped and did that span of time reasonably allow for him to accomplish all of that?

It didn't make sense and her mind couldn't cope. One touch of Ben's hand brought her back from the edge of madness and he helped her from her horse.

"Don't ask me," he whispered.

That hushed request was heeded and Sarah gave in to the fatigue that her panic had staved off for the last few hours. Suddenly, she felt weary and didn't want to think anymore. All she wanted to do was sleep and pray that the beast didn't visit her in her dreams.

CHAPTER 4

LEADVILLE, COLORADO

The list of mistakes that Ben had made in the last sixteen years as a werewolf could stretch from here to Denver. Countless encounters had gone wrong, close-calls, and slipups outnumbered the instances where he had saved himself from discovery. But the night before, when he'd killed those outlaws, could be counted amongst the more idiotic of his blunders. It sat near the very top of the list, right beside the moment when he had decided to tell Henry what he was.

The act of rescuing Sarah and Henry might not have been the most damning part of this two-fold mistake. The first component had been that he refused to attempt a willful shift, which could have saved his clothes from becoming tarnished by the evidence of his deed. If he had charged upon the group in his more beastly form, Sarah would have assumed they were attacked by a creature and would never have thought it could be Ben. However, he argued with himself that if he had shifted, he would have been uncontrollable. The wolf would have taken complete dominion over his mind and body. If that happened, no one would be safe. Not even Sarah or Henry. Ben thought he needed rational thought far more than he needed the guise of a monster.

With his clothes bearing the bloodstains and bullet holes, and not more carefully hiding the saddlebags until the following morning – when he could have made the excuse that he had gone off to investigate the massacre – Sarah would certainly put the pieces together to understand what he had done. Though, to her sheltered mind, it wouldn't have made sense. No man could tear out the throats of another with their bare hands, and she knew that he carried no weapons. The gun he had pinched off the drunkard in Alma had been tossed aside shortly after their getaway.

The moment he helped her from her horse and he saw the trigger of comprehension in her eyes, Ben knew there was little to protect him. He thought he could utilize this curse for better purposes, more noble endeavors. Instead, he proved his former mentor, Dustin Keith, to be right. Their kind were better off in hiding, away from humans if at all possible until they could be properly trained.

The decision to save them, to take the lives of the ruffians who whispered about selling Sarah into a heinous circulation of abuse, was well worth the danger of exposure. His human soul knew it, as did his wolf's. Neither of them could watch as they carted her away to a fate worse than death. He had accepted the institute of slavery once before, but he could never condone it now. Not after living this long in solitude with only his past to haunt him. It might have been easier to let them go, to be rid of this obligation to see Clarence put away for good, but he knew he could never forgive himself if he sat by and did nothing for her and Henry.

When dawn broke, Henry still hadn't recovered from his state of unconsciousness and Sarah slept longer than he'd anticipated, which set them behind a few hours in continuing on the path to Leadville. He found a new shirt in one of the saddlebags, cleaned himself off in the creek, and took that time to dispose of the bodies. The sight of their marred corpses couldn't faze him anymore. He had seen worse on the battlefields and the wolf within him galvanized his stomach to handle the gore.

It had been a few years since he had felt it necessary to kill another human being. In the war, before he had been turned, Ben had almost become desensitized by the art of killing. As a werewolf, he thought little of it anymore, which terrified him more than he would ever admit to a living soul. He thought of the men he buried, one by one. Did they have families? Mothers who worried themselves sick at homes far away? Did they have lovers waiting for them in Denver or Leadville? What drove them to commit these crimes and earn a level of notoriety for themselves? Would his soul, one day, end up where theirs had undoubtedly gone?

As his mind wandered to the deep and dark void of empathy, he remembered the words of his regimental commander. *All hands and feet. Don't think about what you're doing and just do it.*

When he arrived back to the camp, Sarah had busied herself with nursing a barely awakened Henry. Few words were exchanged, a fire was made and a portion of the fawn he had hunted the night before was cooked to feed the two humans. Ben distanced himself from the others, especially when Henry started asking questions about the night before. Sarah told what she could and when it came time to talk about the beast that killed the outlaws, she stumbled through the recitation as if she was confused or looking to explain herself more thoroughly, but couldn't come up with the words.

Because of that, Ben wondered how much she remembered and if the fear of the moment blocked out much of what she might have witnessed against him. It might have been a fortunate thing, but Ben wouldn't rely on a faulty memory to save him.

Against his better judgement, Ben decided to keep a little more distance between himself and the others. If Sarah did suspect anything, he didn't want to be under her scrutinizing stare for the rest of the journey to Leadville. And if she wanted to talk to Henry about what she had seen, he didn't want to be in the way. The truth would be better received from the cowboy than from him, and Ben could see that attachment forming already.

All the way through Buckskin Gulch and around the mountains that morning, Ben could hear their small discussions wandering from topic to topic, but little of the disaster from the night before was mentioned between them. Whether that was attributed to his presence, Sarah's addled brain, or Henry's wounded pride, Ben couldn't tell.

They talked about farming, of Sarah's home back in Trinidad before it was taken over by the bank, of the family and childhood she had lost. Henry imparted little of his own past in return, but entertained her with anecdotes about his many travels and escapades throughout Colorado, Utah, and Kansas. Ben knew most of these stories already, but didn't mind hearing them again. He could tell that something new flourished in the way they so easily talked to one another now. They still had a long way to go before becoming anything close to friends, but it was a start. It was as if their shared trauma forged a connection that would soon develop into something more.

All he knew was that by the time they entered the outer limits of Leadville, they all seemed ready and willing to continue in their mission. Ben, however, found himself blindsided by the sheer growth of the town. The last time he had been in Leadville, there were a few shops, a saloon or two, and it was mostly inhabited by miners. The spread before him made him wonder if he was looking at a new Denver.

While Henry rode ahead, completely comfortable in the bustling streets lined with saloons, general stores, hotels, and restaurants, Ben's steps slowed and his senses became overrun by the mass of civilization.

"I don't remember any of this bein' here last year," Ben said, the first words he had uttered for over an hour.

Sarah gazed at the storefronts and pulled down her hat over her face to further conceal her feminine identity from those who passed by. Henry steered his horse back to face them.

"You ain't heard? It's a regular boomtown," he said, beaming with self-importance as if it were his own town. "They found silver in the mines."

Ben grimaced. Henry, no doubt, could be worked up by the exciting prospect of striking it rich. For a werewolf, silver was a bane, the one weakness that made him ever hesitant to touch a coin in these parts or even draw close to a mining establishment. He dealt only in paper money when at all possible.

"How are you gonna find your friend in all this?" he asked. "It'd take days to look."

Unconcerned with the task, Henry waved off Ben's estimation. "Everyone knows Mart Duggan. And if they don't, they wouldn't soon forget the man. We met at a saloon in Georgetown and even then, he had a reputation. If he's still here, someone will know where to find him."

As if to prove his point, Henry solicited the attention of a man who looked to be an entrepreneur or perhaps a bank clerk. Well dressed in a suit and bowler hat, Ben doubted that he would know the whereabouts of any rough character in town.

"Hey fella," Henry began, "do you know where I could find a man by the name of Mart Duggan?"

At the sound of the somewhat infamous name, the man blanched. "You mean Marshal Duggan? I don't know, mister. He might be at his office or in one of the saloons. I try to avoid run-ins with the law, if you know what I mean."

Now it was Henry's turn to go pale. "Marshal?" he repeated, though his smile slipped. "Well, I'll be damned."

Ben stepped in, seeing that his friend might not be capable of closing the conversation and thanked the stranger for his help. Only when the three were relatively alone again did they speak.

"If Mart's a marshal," Ben said, "then he'll know you have a warrant for your arrest."

Henry tore off his hat to comb his fingers through his hair, then thought better of it and quickly jammed it back over his brow.

"You think Marshal Duggan would give you some leniency?" Sarah asked.

He gave a slow shake of his head. "Mart's... Well... He'll do anythin' for justice. And I mean anythin'. He shot a drunk man just for bein' disorderly. I don't think he'd let me off with a slap on the wrist... Then again, he's got a sense of loyalty, so..." Henry's last words drifted, and he gave a half-hearted shrug. It was clear he wasn't fully positive in this venture anymore. If they couldn't go to Mart, they'd have no lead to finding Clarence.

"I got you out of one fix, and I'll keep you from gettin' yourself in another," Ben declared. "You go find yourself a place to sit outside of town and I'll go ask him about Clarence." Then, he looked to Sarah. "You comin' with me?"

Sarah didn't quite squirm under his pointed question, but he could see it in her eyes. He had his answer and didn't wait long before turning away.

"Take care of yourself, Ben."

Henry's words weren't simply a polite goodbye, but a pointed caution that he grasped all too well. Ben hated crowds. Loathed them with a passion beyond what any man had a right to feel. He disliked being jostled about and neither did his wolf. So many odors and noises convoluted together in one place had sent him through a whirlwind of agitation. Putting Ben in a crowd like this in Leadville was like striking a match near an open gunpowder keg. He was one accident away from spiraling out of control in the middle of a busy town.

When his shoulder received the first grazing shove, Ben could feel the growl surge up his throat. The man apologized, but words could do little for a riled beast. He took a stabilizing breath and continued toward the marshal's office on the other end of the street. Carefully navigating through the hustling patches of women, farmers, miners, and peddlers, Ben was only touched three more times before he stepped onto the final sweep of boardwalk. Only then did he see the sign on the marshal's door that read, "Be Back Soon".

Ben finally let a bit of that building growl ease out between his clamped teeth. His anger was invalid, he knew, but with his temper flaring, he could think of nothing else but the inconvenience of the thing.

Instead of turning to make his way back through the crowd to search the saloons as the stranger had also suggested, Ben leaned beside the doorframe and decided to wait. So much time had already been wasted in letting the two humans recuperate from their ordeal, and the longer it took for them to find Clarence, the longer he had to tolerate them clasped about his ankles.

He folded his arms over his chest and let his glowing golden eyes skim over the crowd, looking more or less for the glint of a star badge. Henry hadn't the time to explain what Mart Duggan looked like, but Ben imagined him to be like the other marshals in Colorado. Portly, lazy, and useless. Then again, if what Henry said could be true, Mart Duggan might not have fit the mold of the typical lawman in these parts. To be considered an associate with Henry's circle, the man must have been tough and unafraid of the risks that came with being a man who couldn't be paid off or bullied into submission.

"Can I help you?"

Ben started at the familiar cadence. Irish. The west was made of all sorts. White men, black men, Indians, Chinese, German, Hungarian, and Irish. But it had been years since he heard that lilting accent and it struck him in the heart.

He turned and regarded the man who spoke to him. Of medium height, blonde hair and blue eyes, and a strong build, the man looked able and confident enough to brandish the star of a marshal. The rather patchy beard that covered his square jaw came in thicker around his chin and lips, while his eyes seemed to be permanently squinted against the bright summer sun. He didn't quite fit the bill for a lawman - as Ben saw them - but as a fellow shootist and cowboy with Henry or the men he had killed last night. The two holstered guns on his hips helped to complete the image.

Altogether, he didn't seem conceited, as some marshals could be as well. Mart Duggan opened himself to Ben, amiable while still being on his guard toward a stranger in town.

"Yeah, I had a couple of questions if you have the time."

Mart nodded and gestured toward his office. "Certainly. Come on in."

They stepped out of the hot, dry air and into the slightly cooler, musty office. Ben couldn't help but inwardly remark to himself that this space seemed much too small and modest for a marshal who was put in charge of keeping the peace in a growing town such as this.

A desk sat toward one end of the room, a smattering of papers and other menial office supplies strewn across the surface. The cedar lap-siding of the walls gave the room a unique and oddly comforting smell for his wolf. It reminded him of the forests that he retreated to for solitude. A single chair sat near the desk, and like the rest of the furniture in the room, it looked like it hadn't been used for a while. It was clear he must not have spent much time in his office, and more time out in the streets on patrol.

"You'll have to forgive my absence," Mart said, once more throwing Ben off kilter by the foreign accent. "I've been in this station for only a month and it's been one incident after another. I can hardly get a moment to myself anymore."

Ben closed the door behind him as Mart cleared off a space on his desk big enough for him to lean against without crinkling any papers.

"I reckon you've got your share of busy work here," Ben replied. "Last time I was here, this town was less than half the size it is now."

Mart nodded in agreement. "And it's still growing, which means more and more criminals are coming out of the woodworks. The marshal before me only lasted two weeks before he was shot and the marshal before him only wore the badge for two days before they ran him out of town."

Ben's brows involuntarily shot up at the admittance. "Sounds rough."

Mart folded his arms over his broad chest and shrugged as if it were still nothing. "They threatened my life the first week I was here. But once they saw I wasn't going anywhere, they left me alone for the most part."

"I suppose that reputation helps you quite a bit."

Mart tilted his head. "Reputation?"

"A friend of mine who knows you from Georgetown said that you're pretty well known. You and that gun of yours." He motioned his chin to the brace of Cold Peacemakers on his belt.

The marshal didn't seem ashamed for anything Ben said and only rubbed at his chin. "I suppose it helps. The mayor wouldn't have asked me to take the job if he didn't think I could do some good in it. That was my first order of business. I fired all of the corrupt deputies and replaced them with men who would give this town the attention it needs." He gave a soft laugh at his own expense. "I had to force a few out of office at gunpoint just to make them cooperate... But I digress. Was there something you needed? You were standing outside like you were waiting on me."

Mart's story both impressed and disconcerted Ben for a moment. Henry hadn't been exaggerating when he said that the new marshal was wholly dedicated to his own brand of justice. The figure this Irishman cut wasn't so clean and predictable, but if anyone would be willing to help take down Clarence, it was him.

Steeling himself, Ben began. "There's a girl whose family was killed a couple months ago and I'm workin' to help her find the murderer. I assume you've heard of Clarence Biller."

Mart snorted a laugh. "Who on God's green earth hasn't?"

"That's who killed her parents and she's out for blood. None of the other marshals in Colorado will help her."

Mart nodded. "Because none of them know where he is."

The tone in his voice might have suggested contempt for those lazy lawmen who weren't willing to lift a finger for the girl. At least Ben had that in his favor, but something told him that playing to Mart's ego or pride wouldn't strengthen his case. It was still worth a shot.

"We had heard about you here in Leadville and thought if anyone was willin' to lend a hand to help, it'd be you."

As he had expected, Mart didn't so much as brighten at the compliment. What he got in return was a hard look that seemed to penetrate through Ben's defenses, through the glasses that concealed his supernatural condition, and into the core of his purpose there.

His wolf nettled at the breach and it took some effort for Ben not to react with dominance or an outburst of harsh words that would ruin everything. He had to play along and earn this man's trust somehow, even though that was a skill he had been utterly lacking in for over a decade. One wrong word, one offensive mood would tip the scales out of his favor.

"Is that the whole story or are you going to cut the bullshit and tell me why you want to find Clarence Biller?"

Ben had been charged with being a liar thousands of times, but never had anyone said it in such a way that he actually felt compelled to defend himself.

"That's enough of the story that should matter to you."

A smile danced on Mart's lips and he gave a nod. "Fine. If you don't want to tell me why Henry Blair's here with you and that girl, then I guess we'll have to arrange a trade of information. I'll tell you where Clarence is, if you'll tell me where Henry is."

Shock was an emotion Ben rarely experienced. Not to the degree that he was rendered speechless. That silence confirmed it for Mart, who thought he had taken the high ground in this engagement. Ben would be firing off harmless powder blasts if he tried to hide the truth any longer.

"How can I know for sure that you know where Clarence is?" Ben questioned, stiffening for the verbal sparring that was to come. If Mart was so eager to know where his old friend was and possibly bring him in for arrest, then why hadn't he gone after a more notorious outlaw like Clarence; someone he did know the location of?

"How do you think I knew that Henry was with you? And that the third rider in your party was a girl who is disguised as a man? I'm sure there's a story there, and I'd be interested in hearing it."

"Especially since Henry has a couple of warrants for his arrest."

Mart grinned. "That'd have something to do with it."

Ben's eyes went flinty. "You're makin' it really hard to trust you now."

"I don't need you to trust me," he replied. "I'm asking you to respect me and the authority this badge carries."

With his arms still folded, Mart tapped his finger against the star pinned to his vest. Even from halfway across the room, Ben could see his own distorted reflection in the metal.

This wasn't the first time he'd had to navigate the unpredictable terrain of an Irishman's temper. He had done it before and he came out the victor, but at a terrible cost in hindsight. Now, faced with another ultimatum, Ben had to find an agreeable compromise.

He was about to state his conditions when screams and angry shouts sounded down the street outside the marshal's office. Both men rushed to the boardwalk and Ben caught sight of someone pushing his way hastily through the thickening crowd that hurried in every direction like ants whose mound had been trampled on.

Most of those ants were heading to one location. The Pioneer Saloon.

Mart, the devoted lawman that he was, pushed through the masses who gladly cleared the way for him. Ben followed closely behind, but as soon as the citizens became too much to bear, he retreated to the safety of the boardwalk across from the saloon.

Women kept their distance from the commotion, clinging to their children or fellow ladies beside them, whispering questions that none of them could answer. A good portion of the men in the street gravitated toward the scene rather than away from it.

His keen senses soon picked up traces of blood coming from the saloon, along with the piteous groans of some victim inside. Centering his focus, he blocked out the frightened voices of the women to listen to Mart's questioning.

"What happened?" the Irishman demanded of some eyewitness.

"They was playin' poker and all the sudden, they started arguin' over the pot. Elkins stabbed Charlie and made off like a scorched cat."

"Was it self-defense?"

Ben could almost taste the disdain in his voice when the man replied, "Charlie wasn't doin' nothin' wrong when that darkie stabbed him."

"You're talking about John Elkins?" Mart asked.

Several of the men inside confirmed it, which sent a wave of gossip through the spectators. Spreading from the door of the saloon all the way into the street, men and women began to expound upon the brawl and fill in what they wanted to believe. Soon, it evolved from a simple misunderstanding about a poker game to a downright pre-meditated murder of a beloved citizen by an embittered former slave.

Ben cursed under his breath and charged through the bodies, toward the origin of the spilled blood. This time, he allowed his wolf to help him, heaving people aside and forcing them to get out of his way. The inhuman snarl persuaded many to stand aside without ever being touched.

When he came onto the scene, Mart was still questioning those who had observed the fight in the saloon. The poker table, along with all its contents were overturned onto the floor. Cards, poker chips, and blood marked the place where the two men had scuffled. The weapon, a knife with its blade coated in the deepening crimson blood from its victim, lay not too far off where it must have been dropped moments ago. Three men had lifted the injured gambler to carry him out into the streets. More shouts, gasps, and cries for justice erupted from the crowd, but few mobilized to carry it out.

Mart, somehow aware of Ben's arrival, turned to him and seemed to debate with himself on something. The marshal came forward and before Ben could even open his mouth, the bargain was made.

"I'll make you a deal. I'll forget about Henry ever being here and I'll tell you where Clarence is if you'll find John Elkins for me. Both of you. Track him down, arrest him, and bring him to me alive."

A stiff wind could have blown Ben over so easily after such an offer. "Why can't you?"

He pointed toward the mob outside the saloon. "These people are about to riot and I need my deputies to keep this crowd under control. I can't go after him myself because I need to collect statements. You and Henry find Elkins for me, and I'll return the favor."

Ben realized a little late that Mart was standing far too close for comfort in their private conversation. He took a step back and looked from the crowd to the puddle of blood on the floor and the knife that accompanied it. He could have followed the man easily. One sniff from the handle was all he needed. But did Mart know that? He already knew so much.

He turned back to the marshal who seemed impatient for an answer. As long as Mart could hold up his end of the bargain, give them both amnesty for Henry and the location of Clarence's hideout, then it was worth the questions. It might have been another mistake that would bring him inches from discovery again, but it was a risk he had to take for the good of people he wasn't supposed to care about.

Henry continued to twist and wring the sprig of long wild grass, his gaze locked upon Sarah, whose own eyes were anxiously watching the road that led into town. Their horses grazed some distance off, and unlike Sarah, they were able to put the horrific night behind them to live another day. Her silence, the way her brows sometimes pinched together at a troubling thought, and how she now avoided Ben like he were some cursed and dangerous thing, all of it told Henry that a burden sat heavy on her shoulders.

He wanted to rid her of it, take it onto himself to end her suffering. Conversation and stories had done a good deal of distracting, but it was like putting a bucket over a rattlesnake. It was still there, coiled and ready to deal the final blow and they couldn't ignore it. He had a fair idea of what was the matter. He could infer scores more between what she had been willing to tell him and what was left unspoken.

Ben had something to do with the attack last night. He must have killed those men and rescued them both. What's more, Sarah was beginning to deduce it. Either her mind couldn't comprehend it or she considered herself too mad to think it possible. This time away from Ben could have been used to talk about it, to bring the truth into the light and tell her what his younger self needed to be told when he first learned about werewolves and monsters.

But how to find the words? How could he verbalize something that had taken him years to come to terms with? What could he say to make her realize that she didn't have to carry this alone? The trauma she had endured shouldn't be hoarded so masochistically.

"I would have thought you'd want to go into town with Ben," Henry said. "Maybe go shoppin' or get somethin' to eat…"

"I'm not hungry," she replied with a touch of frustration. "And I don't know what kind of girls you're used to, but I don't go shopping."

Henry smiled, happy to see the fire return to her cornflower blue eyes. "Don't like dresses or bonnets or pretty things like that?"

She turned on him. "I never had a need for pretty things. They'd get dirty anyway."

"Just a plain farmer's daughter, huh?"

Her countenance softened at the inexcusable mention of the family she would see no more. The mouth that had been on the brink of a sneer, loosened its lines to resemble something worthy of an apologetic kiss that he couldn't give.

Contrary to what he expected, her eyes didn't mist over, and a fit of despondency didn't quite take hold. She was within its reach, but that resilience he had detected in her kept it at bay. Sadness, too, was a little afraid to claim her. But it wanted to. It threatened every time she talked about her parents, the farm, her childhood. If he could, he would have shot that depression all to pieces. If only those demons were material, they'd never bother her again. Not as long as he had breath.

"Not anymore," was all she said before resuming her watch over the road.

"If it's any consolation, I understand what you must be feelin' right now."

Sarah's back rose as she breathed in deeply and let it out in a slow sigh that seemed to cleanse her spirit. "Please, don't try to pretend like you know anything about me or what I'm going through. Unless you've had your entire life ripped out from under you, don't talk to me."

Sympathy hardened into offense. "And don't assume that no one else in the world has ever been hurt like you've been hurt. You're not the only one to lose your family or see things that defy logical explanation."

Henry thought her hat would fly off when she whipped around so suddenly. Those delectable lips parted as if she was ready to argue, but the words were choked in her throat, so he continued.

"I know a thing or two about loss. My paw ran out on me, my maw, and my little sister when I was ten. I had to be the man of the house. When my maw passed from consumption, I had to raise my sister alone too. Ben's not the only one who sends money home." Henry almost prided himself in how dumbstruck he had made Sarah, and still he poured out his heart in the hopes that it would be reciprocated. "When Ella found out what I did to help her through boardin' school, how I sold cattle that wasn't mine and cheated at card games, she ran away.

Last I heard from her, she was out in Ohio somewhere workin' as a teacher and married to a blacksmith. That was five years ago, and I'm sure she's got kids of her own that she'd refuse to let me see." Henry looked heavenward to recall the words of the last spiteful letter he had received from his dear sister. "Called me all sorts of names that I'd only ever heard out of other cowboys on the cattle drives. I don't have a home to go to or a family. When I die, there ain't gonna be a soul on this earth who'll know what to put on my gravestone – if I even get one."

As sweet as this small dose of retribution tasted, Henry couldn't take delight in the stunned, humbled look on Sarah's face. The goal of his speech had been to make her realize the world didn't spin on her command, but it became a weapon. Henry, despite the freshly opened wound on his battered and scarred heart, gave her an encouraging smile and said, "If you can help it, don't doubt my honesty. Ben and I are helpin' you, not because you're payin' us or promisin' us somethin' in return for all this trouble. We're doin' it because we both know what it's like to be alone and in need of a friend."

Now, he could see the glimmer of unshed tears in her eyes and Henry thought this might have been his chance to seal the moment. But as he shifted his weight to stand, he heard the rushing of swift feet coming from town. Though Ben wasn't running at his typical pace, he closed on them fast and a trail of dust followed him.

By the look on the werewolf's face, the news wasn't altogether good.

"Did you find him?" Henry asked, rising to his feet before Sarah could fully compose herself.

"I did," Ben replied hurriedly. "But we've got to do somethin' for him first. I'll explain on the way north."

"North?" Henry nearly screeched.

"Get your ass movin' and I'll explain on the way!"

Henry tipped his hat to Sarah, but by the time he had looked in her direction, she was already running for her horse.

"What're you doin'?" Henry hollered.

"I'm going with you." The girl was hauling herself into the saddle and following after Ben before Henry could even get a hold of Buck's bridle.

"Like hell you are! Sit back down and wait for us."

"We don't have time to argue!" Ben roared. "Let her come if she wants. Can't leave her here by herself anyway."

A wave of that strained and terrifying tension rushed over Henry. It was that trick Ben had spoken about before. Dominance. Something the werewolves used to get their way when the situation called for it. If Ben was willing to pull out his wolfish talents to get them moving, this must have been serious.

So Henry didn't say another word and snapped the tip of his reins against Buck's hindquarters, hastening him forward to catch up with the other two who were speeding to the north and away from Leadville.

CHAPTER 5

B en now regretted the decision to allow Henry and Sarah to join him in the manhunt. The idea that Henry's gun would be a powerful tool had been his sole thought in inviting the cowboy to come along. But Sarah's presence was unnecessary and distracting at best. The timidity that marked her behavior since they'd left the mountains had given way to some new type of inquisitiveness, and the girl wouldn't shut up. He thought he had seen the last of this side of her back in Fairplay.

He answered what questions he could, but his attention had been torn in two. By the time he realized it had debilitated his tracking capabilities, it was too late. The trail was cold, and he'd have to reverse his steps to find where he had gone wrong.

Like a bloodhound, he sniffed the air and bent over logs, bushes, and rocks in hopes that the fugitive had touched it in his escape from Leadville. His ears, too, were tuned to any rustling in the brush ahead, searching for the one frantic heartbeat or gasping breath that could lead him in the right direction.

A hot wind brought with it the scent that he needed. Laced with fear, a tinge of blood, and salty tears, beneath it lay the signature of John Elkins. Ben snapped up and held out his hand for the others to be silent. Elkins had to be at least half a mile out, a surprising distance for one man to run in such a short time.

Then, like an old melody of a song he once knew, Ben remembered Georgia. He remembered the days before the war and the few short years he had suffered being in the south while it raged on. On a summer day, not unlike the one he stood in now, he recalled seeing a runaway slave making his way through the cotton fields around their farm. Though his family's employer never kept slaves, there were still plenty in Franklin who did.

Ben, a boy of only eight years old at the time, asked his mother what the man was doing and why he was running. It was that day he understood what slavery was, and how one man had the right to own another based on the color of his skin or his station in life. His mother explained how it was different from the life of a sharecropper, different from the life they lived on the farm under the protection of Mr. Rider.

But more than this, one thought stood out to Ben that night. The thought that he had never seen a man run as fast as that slave did when he made his mad dash for freedom and a life away from the oppression of the white folk. Forced back into the present, Ben linked this thought with the rumors and hearsay that spread through the crowd in Leadville like a poison.

Perhaps a kernel of truth lay in their gossip about John Elkins being a former slave. It had been thirteen years since the south's capitulation, but there were still many hearts who were shackled to that dead and buried era. A time when they thought not all men were created equal under one mighty god. If Elkins was of this battered race, how likely was it that he understood exactly what would happen to him if he were caught?

"You two stay here," he ordered. Neither of them would understand the context and fragility of this situation. Bringing more people into the mix might make Elkins believe that a mob was after him.

Of course, complaints were made.

"Stay here?" Henry repeated. "I thought you needed my help."

Without having to say it in so many words, Ben cut his eyes to the girl and Henry bought his white lie. If he told the truth, Henry wouldn't have understood, and it wasn't something he had the patience to explain.

The cowboy let out a sigh and skinned one of his pistols to toss it to Ben. "Take it, then."

Ben deftly caught the gun with one hand and weighed it in his hands as he also weighed the wisdom in taking it. His lips curled together and he admitted defeat. If negotiations turned sour, a story about a mountain lion attack could only be believed to a certain extent. Though, a bullet wound to the leg wouldn't help his case either. Ben tucked the gun into his belt beneath his coat and hoped the slight bulge on his hip wouldn't be noticed.

Sarah began to make some cross plea, but by then Ben had already made off. Once out of sight from the others, Ben picked up the pace and conquered the distance in less than a minute. When both the creek and the hunched back of John Elkins came into view, Ben slowed to a stop and waited.

The culprit had his hands in the river, washing away the evidence of his crime with furious, noisy strokes. Potent fear stung Ben's nostrils and he wiped at his face as if that would help expel the peppery stench. He hated to see any creature so afraid, whether man, woman, or beast. If he could despise anything about being a werewolf, it was the fact that he would always know the terror of those around him; and sometimes be the cause of it.

He took step after silent step toward Elkins, who was unaware of his presence up until the moment Ben decided to make himself known.

"Hey, friend," he said, feigning a northern accent to further ease the worries of the black man. Most black folks he had encountered on this side of the country became instantly vexed by the cadence of a southerner, but would willingly put their trust in a man who sounded like he hailed from New York or Massachusetts.

Elkins stood and almost stumbled backward into the stream when he turned to face Ben. The wide, stricken look in his eyes said enough. He wasn't a killer, wasn't proud of what he had done, and all he wanted was to be left alone. Ben could empathize.

A dark, coarse beard covered his face, shadowed by a hat that bore some holes in the soft leather hide. His clothes, likewise, were old and in need of repair or replacement. Perhaps the fatal poker game was his attempt at earning some money to improve his attire. With no coat and boots that looked to be on the verge of falling apart as well, he wouldn't survive the winter.

His broad shoulders and built frame were made for labor and carrying heavy loads. He shouldn't have been in want for work, but his ebony skin might have been the only thing in his way from earning a respectable living. Even out in places where the war hadn't been fought, prejudices ran high and men were too stubborn to accept the new reality of a free nation for all.

"That fella drew his gun on me first," Elkins insisted immediately. "He woulda killed me iffen I didn't do somethin'."

Ben stopped and stared, unsure whether to be impressed by Elkins' ability to see through his defusing introduction or pity him for his stupidity. If his trick had been convincing enough, Elkins showed his hand without any coaxing.

With a nod, Ben replied, "I believe you. Why don't you come back with me and tell the story to Marshal Duggan?"

The black man shook his head. "Ain't no white fella gonna believe me."

Ben smiled. "You'd be surprised. I've known the Irish to be fair men. He'll listen to you."

For a moment, Elkins almost looked as if he trusted his word. But the dark eyes still conveyed that primal need to survive, to live another day whether it was on the run or as a freeman. Maybe it was those eyes that once inspired so many abolitionists to rally the Yankees in the war.

Though Ben's attitude had changed over the years, he remembered a time when he had been ambivalent toward the plight of the enslaved. But time had a way of changing minds, and now that he knew what it was like to be held against his will by a force he couldn't contend with, Ben felt a sort of strange kinship with John Elkins and others like him.

"I can promise you that you'll be given a fair trial," he continued. "Running away like this doesn't help, but coming back will. It shows you're not a coward."

Elkins puffed up his chest. "I ain't no coward," he declared. "I just... I just been through too much. I don't wanna die like this. I ain't done nothin' wrong, but all them folks gonna say I did. My brother got lynched in Kansas last fall for talkin' to some white lady on the street. Just asked her for directions, was all. And they lynched him. They ain't gonna lynch me like that. It ain't right. None of it."

That confirmed it for Ben and he slowly let the air out of his lungs. "You're right. And you have to show them all that it isn't right. But you have to trust me first. Trust that when we go back to Leadville, I won't let anything happen to you... Do you trust me?"

If only Elkins knew what kind of man Ben was, not that he was a werewolf, but a former Confederate, a man who had been altered by circumstances and humbled by fate. If only he knew that Ben was the only man in the world Elkins could truly trust to keep his word.

With only the sound of the trickling stream behind him and the distant calls from animals high in the mountains, Elkins made his decision. He nodded and took his first lumbering steps forward to put his faith in Ben and the law.

By the time they arrived back to Leadville, a vengeful horde had amassed in the street near the Pioneer Saloon. Henry had been hesitant to ride into town with Ben, even with Sarah by their side. After he had been told everything about the stabbing, he had a fairly good idea of what they would come back to. He had seen mobs like this form over smaller incidents, and given the nature and perpetrator of the crime, he expected something akin to borderline chaos.

His old friend, Mart Duggan, met them as they reentered town with John Elkins, who was immediately put in handcuffs.

"Thanks, lads," he said to them. "I'm obliged to you both." Giving a pointed look to Henry, his voice dropped. "I'll forget you were ever here, but I can't help you outside this jurisdiction. Am I clear?"

Henry tipped his hat. "Crystal clear."

The black man's panicky gaze shifted from Ben to Mart and to the crowd that was already shouting insults and demands for negro blood. More specifically, he looked pleadingly to the one who had found him, as if wordlessly asking for something that only Ben would know.

"You lot stay here while I take Mr. Elkins to the jail."

Mart had nearly turned away when Ben grabbed his arm and forced him back. "With all due respect, I'm not leavin' him alone. Not in this." He jerked his chin to the multitudes. The marshal's deputies attempted to hold back the tide of hatred with their shotguns, but some men were also armed, and the show of force did little to deter them.

The two defiant men stared at one another while the rest of them could only wait. Finally, Mart nodded, and Henry bolstered his own bravery to hop down from his horse.

"Deal me in," he said as he pulled out his spare pistol with a grin. "Always wanted to be part of a posse."

Both Mart and Ben gave him sardonic looks, but didn't argue because they knew him well enough. Henry had certainly never been part of a posse, but he had been chased by plenty in his time.

Sarah, who refused to be left behind again, also quickly dismounted and led the two horses to the nearest hitching post before joining the men without a word. Henry didn't particularly like the way Mart eyed her suspiciously and stepped between the two as a barrier.

He had no right to be territorial over the girl, and Mart had proven himself to be a respectable man when it came to the finer sex, but something in Henry wouldn't allow Sarah to go unguarded. Not while the mob struggled forward through the blockade of deputies.

The five marched down the dusty street, a small band of heroes against a sea of intolerance. Each believed they were on the side of righteousness, but only one could be right. His maw – God rest her soul – had taught him every man deserved respect until he showed himself to be untrustworthy otherwise. So, when Mart passed Elkins behind him for both Ben and Henry to hold, the man couldn't have been in safer hands.

Luckily, the mob hadn't reached the jailhouse yet and they were able to approach the building safely without walking directly into a fight. However, upon seeing the criminal, their shouts rose to an epic high until Henry could barely hear himself think. They demanded that Elkins be hung, saying that the man he had stabbed, Charles Hines, was on the verge of death. That made the black man a murderer.

Some deputies, upon seeing their boss arrive onto the scene, broke ranks and came to assist them, which weakened the hold on the flood of people who were ready to charge the jailhouse.

Ben, Henry, Elkins, Sarah, and two other men managed to get onto the boardwalk just before the dam broke. Men and women of all ages and occupations stormed forth.

Elkins was handed off to the deputies and brought inside while the rest remained on the boardwalk to back up Mart, seeing as some of his deputies had been lost in the crowd.

A lopsided grin touched Henry's lips when he saw the marshal pull out his pistols and quicken his stride to meet the people he was sworn to protect. Mart lifted himself onto a sturdy crate near the jailhouse, towering above the riot.

The moment he cocked both pistols and glared at the insurgents, their screams and shouts began to lessen. It was as if Mart had fired over their heads without ever having to discharge his gun. They knew that the moment the hammer was eased back on one of his guns, he wasn't liable to waste a bullet.

"I'll shoot any man who comes within ten yards of this jail!" he yelled, his Irish brogue stopping up every rebellious mouth in the street. "A proper trial will be held and if I so much as hear anyone talk about dispensing their own justice, they better say a Hail Mary, because they'll be dead by morning."

Henry and Ben stood behind Mart's platform and he half anticipated to feel that werewolf dominance coursing from his friend beside him. But it didn't come. It wasn't even needed. Watching the faces of the men who had pushed their way forward, nooses and guns in hand, they seemed to debate the soundness of their irrational plan. Women cowered back, colliding with those who were ready to give up the ordeal as well in the face of this official threat.

Soon, the unruly citizens of Leadville dispersed, but not without a great deal of grumbling on their part. It was only after they left that Henry realized his heart had been pounding a little too fast to his liking. Ben, of course, hadn't broken a sweat. What could anyone in the crowd possibly do to him? The man had been shot and stabbed, walking away from each confrontation as if he had never been hurt. If Mart couldn't take on the throngs, then Ben certainly would have been able to.

He let out a slow breath and turned to find Sarah in the doorway to the jail, chin high and blue eyes blazing like hot coals on the backs of the men who dared to think they could get past her. For a moment, he wondered if the farmgirl was even braver than Mart. Without a gun or any weapon of her own, she looked ready to take on anyone who so much as stepped on the boardwalk.

Once he deemed it safe, Mart eased the hammers forward and jumped down from the crate. He gave a nod of thanks to each of them as he made his way past to check on his prisoner. Sarah slid to the side and in a fortunate accident, grazed her hand against Henry's.

Now, his heart was thudding harder for another reason entirely. Her cheeks plumed a pretty shade of pink and he knew that the contact hadn't gone unnoticed.

Before he could stoke her ego with compliments to her courage, he felt something tap against his elbow. Henry turned to see Ben was trying to give back the gun he had been loaned earlier.

"Don't need this anymore," he said.

Henry wagged his head and took the gun. "I still don't get why you don't just carry your own."

Ben tugged on his vest to straighten it. "You know I've never had much use for one. Did my share of shooting during the war and don't care to do any more if I can help it."

"The war?" Sarah questioned, forgetting her manly guise for a moment in the wake of her confusion.

No, Ben still didn't resemble the other veterans who passed through the western territories. He bore no visible scars, told no outlandish stories about his company or regiment, and he certainly didn't look old enough. Had his friend really meant to say that in front of someone who didn't know the truth about him? Or did he suspect, like Henry, that Sarah was too smart not to know by now?

Before anyone could give an excuse to Ben's untimely confession, Mart came out to join them again.

"Much obliged," he said, putting his hands on his hips. "Now, about Clarence Biller. From what I remember, he and his gang set up camp on Burnt Mountain to the west of Roaring Fork Valley. There's a pass through the mountains cut by Maroon Creek. I don't have a map, but you've been there once, Henry."

Yes, he had. The thought of a surging mob of bigots couldn't make his hands sweat, but the idea of trekking through Indian Territory did. "Are the Utes still there?" he asked, hoping his voice wouldn't break as he spoke.

Mart nodded. "Last I heard, they were. This time of the year, I suppose they'll be up in the mountains, so you'll be safe enough in the valley."

"The fastest way to the valley is through Hunter Pass in the Sawatch Mountains. Should only take a couple of days to get there and we'll need supplies."

Henry regarded Ben with raised brows. "You been there too?"

Even behind his glasses, Henry could feel the coolness in the look he was given that told him not to question him in mixed company like this. Ben had been all over and was well traveled for a man who was much older than he looked.

"You can get supplies from Mayor Tabor's old general store," Mart said, pointing down the street to one of the many establishments. "Tell them to put it on my tab and get whatever you need."

Ben stammered for a moment. "Mayor Tabor? You ain't talkin' about the same Horace Tabor I know, are you? I was plannin' on findin' his store anyway."

Mart beamed. It still amazed Henry how this man could switch from being a hardened marshal to the man he used to drink with in Georgetown. Granted, the Irishman could become rancorous after a few whiskeys. "The very same. He grubstaked in a couple of silver mines that paid off and he's a pretty rich man now."

A touch of awe and sadness came to Ben's countenance, but he said no more. Henry, however, wondered how often he came across old friends or acquaintances who had changed so much in his absence. How many had died or married and started families? How many became rich and then piss-poor broke again by the time he reconnected? How many lives had evolved while he stayed the same?

"I hope you find that son of a bitch," Mart said, then tipped his hat to Sarah. "Excuse the language, ma'am. The only reason I wouldn't go after him myself is because I know better that to pull on a mean dog's tail... Are you sure you want to do this?"

Before anyone else could reply, Sarah nodded. "Yes, sir. If we don't do it, I'm sure no one will."

Henry wasn't sure whether to be proud or terrified.

"You know it won't be easy?" By the turn in Mart's own countenance, Henry guessed he struggled with the same confliction.

"What is easy these days?" Ben retorted with a crooked smile.

"Hell, a lot of things." Before his common sense could stop him, Henry began listing them off. "Stealin' horses is mighty easy when the owner ain't watchin'. Above that might be cheatin' at poker. Gettin' through Indian Territory will be rough, but it's still doable. I'd imagine skinnin' a live coyote might be easier than capturin' Clarence Biller."

All three looked to Henry, but only Mart spoke what they were all thinking. "I believe your friend was being rhetorical. Clarence won't give up without a fight, I'm sure. Be careful and don't go running in blind. He's got a way of seeing opposition coming long before it does. Put a bullet in his foot for me."

After shaking hands, the group was dismissed from their temporary duty as Leadville deputies. Ben was the first to move, but not to the general store that Mart had pointed out. Instead, he was following the marshal inside the jail.

"Y'all go get supplies without me," was all he said before disappearing into the coolness of the shadows.

Henry knew better than to ask why and led the way for Sarah, who continued to look back in wonder.

"What's he doing?" she whispered as they made their way down the street.

He only shrugged. "Hell, if I know. Ben does a lot of weird things. I try not to understand him anymore."

That, along with whatever other thoughts must have accompanied his response, silenced her back into half of the state she had been in before they went after Elkins. Pensive and a little nervous, she followed Henry, and he knew that her questions would have to be answered soon. If they weren't, she was liable to burst for sure.

Hunter Pass

No matter how long she sat and contemplated it, no matter how many times she replayed the events and snippets of passing conversation, nothing made sense. Even now, sitting atop a rocky ledge near their encampment and gazing out toward the setting sun, Sarah couldn't find a clear, definitive answer.

The one thing that she did know, the one truth she could comprehend, was that Ben wasn't human. Or, if he was, then there was something entirely wrong with him. All the evidence pointed to something nightmarish, but her heart wouldn't take the plunge to believe it.

No normal man could have done what he had done to the outlaws who kidnapped her. Sarah was far beyond considering it was an animal of any sort. His mysterious appearance and the blood on his clothes obliterated that theory. Added with his inhuman speed and how he could instinctively know exactly where John Elkins had been, all strengthened her near-final conclusion.

But then there was the way he fought for her, how he elected to bring a man to justice instead of letting the mob take him, how he seemed so loyal and devoted to Henry. Monsters didn't have such noble and admirable qualities. They were creatures that murdered and killed. They didn't send money home to their ailing mothers or help damsels in distress like herself. They would sooner eat them or leave them to starve than do something so heroic.

So, what was he? If he wasn't a man or a beast, then what other options were there?

Behind her came Henry's shuffling footsteps and her pulse quickened at his approach. Through it all, Henry had been her own tether to the real world that kept her from floating away on these clouds of indecision and fantasy. It was his constant presence that made her feel like she'd be safe with Ben, even if he was something unnatural. And it was all because of one other theory she harbored. Sarah believed that Henry knew what Ben was and he might have been the only one who could confirm or deny her crazy ideas, if only she had the nerve to speak them.

He sat down beside her on the rock, so near that her skin felt hot all over despite the steadily dropping temperature of the evening. So far, she thought she had done a fair job of hiding whatever feelings she might have had toward Henry, but something must have been encouraging him, because he watched her in secret as much as she watched him.

She shouldn't have cared, shouldn't have wanted his company the way that she did. It started even before he told that sad story about his life and the family he had become estranged to. Every given chance, she made an effort to discourage him from pursuing her. Her mother had always told her to never feed stray dogs, or they'd keep coming back for more food. Well, Sarah had been beating this dog and he still kept coming back.

Instead of letting her gaze drop to admire the way Henry's biceps filled out his sleeves, or the way a bit of his tanned skin peeked out from the unbuttoned front of his shirt, Sarah kept her eyes on the horizon.

Thin wisps of clouds seemed fixed in the sky, reflecting the orange glow of the sunset. A blanket of a fine blue shade backed the mad array of delicate vapors. When one's eye trailed upwards from the shadowy ridges of the mountains, the hues of both cloud and sky deepened, becoming crimson red splashes upon a veil of indigo.

Something about the fresh air and stunning display pacified her spirit, dampening her resolve to be cold and mean to a man who hadn't personally earned her disdain yet. He was a cowboy, an outlaw, possibly a murderer and far too capable with a firearm. Her father wouldn't have trusted him and perhaps that was why Sarah felt this conflict. She didn't want to trust him or like him, but somehow she did. She was unsure whether it was the kind and carefree look in his eyes that promised adventure, or the way he seemed so willing to be her guardian when he knew very well that she had none.

The sedative effects of dusk loosened her tongue better than any liquor could. "My mama used to call these clouds 'Angel Wings'." Her voice came out in soft, pleasing tones as if she were in a dream. "See how they look like feathers? She used to say when God made a sunset or sunrise like this, the day to follow would be filled with blessings."

All tension dissipated immediately. The last brick of her defenses had been ripped from its mortar and they could have their first deep conversation. One that wouldn't begin with Ben or some present crisis. For the time being, all the world was right.

"I knew a fella once that every time he saw this sorta sky, he'd say the devil was smokin' his pipe somewhere 'cause he got a new sinner in hell. Sure looks a lot like pipe smoke to me."

A once pleasant memory from her mother was now tainted by this new interpretation of nature, but Sarah wouldn't let herself be disheartened by it. "I guess it does look like pipe smoke," she replied, tilting her head as if that would change the visage for her.

"It's all a matter of perspective."

At this profound statement, Sarah met Henry's laughing eyes. And though she didn't ask for an explanation, he willingly gave one.

"What your mama saw as a blessing, my friend saw as somethin' a little different. We all have our different way of lookin' at things... And that's not all bad."

What did he mean? Did he intuitively know what had made her so reluctant to give into her desires? Or was he talking about Ben and her obviously incompatible thoughts toward him? Or did this somehow have to do with her need for revenge against Clarence? The walls that had kept Henry out, the walls that were now crumbled in a heap, were the same fortifications she had built to keep the world from caving in on her.

Up until now, she had been able to keep it all at arm's length. Focusing on Clarence's demise helped her to ignore the fact that she was totally and utterly alone. Rejecting Henry's company had convinced her that she didn't want a man in her life. Refusing to let herself believe what her mind already knew about Ben kept her from going completely insane.

Now, what was left to keep her from the edge? Tears pushed at her eyelids, but she wouldn't let them fall. Not now. Not yet.

Sarah passed a wary look over her shoulder to make sure they were alone, and Henry must have understood its meaning.

"He's gone to find us some food."

With a frustrated groan, she covered her face with her hands. "He didn't take a gun with him, did he?"

After a short pause of silence, Henry replied, "No... No, he didn't."

Inspired in the moment, Sarah looked up and her mouth struggled to form the words. "Wha... What is he?" And then, as if the gate on a bursting corral had been opened, she poured it all out. "He runs almost faster than a horse, he goes hunting without a gun, he's always wearing those glasses even when it's dark out, and then last night when he... when he..."

She couldn't bring herself to say it and those tears which had been born for an entirely different emotion, threatened to spill down her cheeks in a fitful rage of bemusement. But she wouldn't let them. Not in front of Henry, Ben, or anyone else.

"When he killed those men," Henry finished for her.

So, he did know.

Sarah nodded and without ever having to ask, Henry finally put her tortured mind at ease.

"Ben's not... He's not like other men. He's... uh... Well, we'll just say he's got this problem that he's been dealin' with for a while and it's gotten him in a lot of fixes in the past. There's a lot about him that I don't reckon I'll ever understand, but – "

"What is he?" she repeated, her words colored with agitation.

They locked onto one another and once Henry seemed to accept that Sarah wasn't going to back down or take back her question, he said, "Ben's a werewolf."

Her jaw slackened, and mouth felt suddenly dry, so dry that she was unable to ask if Henry was joking. By the way he stared so assuredly, she knew he was serious. Ben was a werewolf.

Sarah had only ever heard of werewolves in passing, and since half of the word itself was comprised of "wolf", she imagined it was something ferocious and menacing. Wolves were a bane to ranchers, and that was the extent of her knowledge on the subject.

So, when she asked, "What exactly is a werewolf?" she hoped that Henry wouldn't laugh at her. He spoke the term so confidently, as if he expected her to know right from the start.

"It's a man who can turn into a wolf. Well, it ain't exactly a wolf like you'd see out in the wild. It's a lot bigger and almost walks like a man and – "

"You've seen it?" she gasped, impulsively grabbing for his wrist.

Henry smiled at this and nodded proudly. "I have. And he didn't kill me. That shows enough that Ben's not a monster... Not completely, anyway. He's a sight to look at when he changes, but I can tell you with complete confidence that he won't hurt you."

Incredulity gave way to awe at the thought. "He can turn into a wolf? How is that possible?"

"I don't even think he knows," Henry replied feebly. "He told me once that he's still tryin' to figure the whole thing out. That's why he wears the glasses. His eyes... well, that's the one part of him that don't look human at all. They're gold like a wolf's and he hides it from everyone so they don't get scared. That's also why he don't spend a lot of time in town. He doesn't want people findin' out about him, because if they did, they might kill him."

Sarah dropped her head into her hands once more. "He's a werewolf." Saying it more didn't make the situation any less confounding. It seemed impossible, but she supposed it all made sense now.

After a whistling wind blew through the camp and tossed back the braids she had woven earlier, Sarah looked to the darkening sky. The clouds were moving on, the once dark blue became almost a deep black, the first emerging stars winking at her from the heavens. She liked to think her parents were up there somewhere, watching her and loving her even in death. But now, she just felt small and stupid.

If things like werewolves could exist, then what else walked about in plain sight? What other mythic creatures were real outside of storybooks and fairytales?

"But... he won't hurt me?" she muttered, still trying to wrap her feeble mind around the truth.

"Nope. He's never wanted to hurt anyone. Not when he was fightin' in the war and not now. It ain't his nature to be mean and cruel. It's the wolf that makes him do it sometimes... But he'd never hurt you."

With one burst of courage, Sarah looked to Henry's face, which was painted with twilight, and said, "Tell me more."

Chapter 6

Roaring Fork Valley

The open spaces between the mountain peaks along Hunter Pass gave way to rocky, forested terrain as they entered Roaring Fork Valley. Ben scouted ahead, choosing the best paths for the horses while still following the steadily widening river. Slopes became steeper, some areas became impassable except on foot. They crisscrossed smaller streams and creeks and, more than a few times, Ben and Henry were forced to make their own way through the dense woodlands.

He had been to the valley only a few times, but it had been years since he'd traversed this primitive ground. By himself, the going was easy. In his beastly form, even easier. But this way hadn't been navigated except by trappers and natives, leaving them with no official map to follow. Only Ben's keen nose and ears would get them out of this rough country safely.

Sarah seemed in brighter spirits, in spite of the jarring truth Henry had told her the day before. Ben was miles away tracking a deer when he told her, so he wasn't privileged to watch her reaction himself, but he saw its effects when he returned to camp. For the first time, Sarah met his gaze and her heart didn't shudder in its rhythm. The fear at his nearness had been reduced into something a little stronger than hesitance, but not quite as enervating.

Henry, too, had changed within the span of a few hours and Ben wondered if the events were connected somehow. As Sarah relaxed, so did Henry and the new bond they shared as the only humans on this expedition became slightly sickening to watch.

Ben saw her blushing cheeks, heard the racing pulses when they came near to one another, tasted the sweetness in the few words they shared, and smelled the faintest indication that this infatuation would grow exponentially as the journey continued.

It felt like a lifetime ago since he had witnessed such mawkish affection and something within his spirit writhed pathetically each time he watched them. Like the other day when he tracked down John Elkins from Leadville, something of Georgia resurrected in his soul.

He remembered the raven hair he had once stroked with loving tenderness, and the blue eyes that put the clearest summer sky to shame. He could still hear her voice on the wind when the loneliness became too much to bear. At first, it served as a balm to his tired and weary heart, but when reality reminded him that Abigail wasn't his any longer, Ben thought he would die from the sorrow alone. Sometimes, he wished he had.

So, each time the love between Henry and Sarah bloomed a little more, Ben hurried ahead to escape the reaching talons of misery. He ripped the limbs from the trees, uprooted whole bushes to clear the way, and heaved aside deeply set boulders that barely blocked the path. All of it to burn off the melancholia that he had been trying to avoid for so many years.

When they finally came to the valley and the shores along the river were clear enough to water their horses, the three decided to stop for a short afternoon break. Sarah took this time to clean her face of the grime and filth that marred her womanly features. And while Henry took care of unsaddling the horses, Ben isolated himself upriver.

Hoping the cold waters would dispel the final toxic remnants of the past, Ben took off his hat and glasses and plunged his head into the swift current of the river. The distorted roars of sound, the steady beating behind his ears and the chill that numbed his face was enough to purge. Only then did he lift himself out and breathe again. If he could have, if he thought it would do any good, he would never have come up for air.

Ben shivered for a moment before wiping away the water from his brow and eyes. Regardless of the fact that Henry was so near now, standing a few yards off, he cursed and looked at the world without the impediment of his tinted spectacles. Vibrant colors nearly blinded him, but he forced himself to keep his golden eyes wide open. Only through seeing nature, unfiltered and unmolested by man, could he appreciate the life he had. Otherwise, he would have tried much harder to kill himself after the war. Without home, family, or Abigail, Ben had every reason to search out death. The wolf and his faith in a future that didn't bring so many reminders of his past were the only things keeping him alive anymore.

Henry came beside him and sat at the water's edge with his hat in his hands. Ben could tell he was happy and wouldn't do or say anything to ruin it for him. His time for love and joy had passed, but that didn't mean he could steal it from others. And though Ben wasn't too thrilled by the circumstances, it wasn't his place to say it.

"You two seem to be gettin' along better," Ben said as he rubbed at his tired and slightly bloodshot eyes.

His old friend nodded. "Yep. I reckon she's warmin' up to me right nice."

"Y'all been talkin' a lot too."

The bitterness couldn't be hidden well enough and Henry's smile faded. "Should I not have told her?"

Ben let out a long sigh and wiped his arm across his face to feel the cold remnants of water on his forehead. "Doesn't matter... How'd she take it?"

"Pretty good," Henry replied with a note of satisfaction. "I think it helps that you kept droppin' all them hints."

"Sometimes I didn't mean to." He donned his hat, but refrained from sliding his glasses back into place. If both Henry and Sarah knew the truth, what use was there in hiding it?

"I don't think she'll tell anyone."

"I ain't worried about that... I'm more worried about what we're gonna do when we find Clarence."

That wasn't entirely a lie, but Ben didn't feel the same kind of fluttering in his stomach at the thought of facing down a dangerous outlaw as Henry might have. What could the man do to him that hadn't already been done?

"I'd be thinkin' more about them Indians in the valley," Henry replied, rotating his hat between his hands as he gazed across the river to the wooded shoreline.

Ben shook his head. "You heard Mart. The Ute are gonna be up in the mountains this time of the year. They won't come down into the valley until it starts to get colder. They won't bother us if we don't bother them."

Henry huffed. "Betcha can't say that about the Lakota or Cheyenne."

"The Cheyenne aren't as bad as the Comanche."

At the mention of that one brutal tribe, Henry visibly shuddered. "Damn, I forgot about them."

Finding the conversation mollifying in some way, Ben continued. "The only way we're gonna be able to take Clarence is by surprise. He's bound to have a few extra men workin' for him. I don't know how many. We got two guns, though and – "

"We've got you," Henry interrupted. "I ain't worried about nothin' Clarence and his gang can do."

At this, Ben turned his wolfish eyes upon his friend, ignorant to their affect upon him. It was a stupid thing to say or believe. One werewolf could do the job of twenty men, but that didn't mean he would. "I ain't about to shift just to do the job that a few bullets could do better."

Transfixed by the eyes of the beast, Henry didn't look away as he had so many times before. Sarah wasn't the only one becoming braver by the hour. And something in Ben's hard stare made him realize how dangerous this mission was. If Ben didn't shift, and if all the stories were true, they were walking into live fire with no cover. Staring down the barrel of a cannon was about as stupid as facing down a charging buffalo or hunting a wanted murderer like Clarence Biller. Someone would get hurt.

"If you have it, why don't you use it?" Henry's question came out slow, drawling, as if he were trying to ask the same thing of a child.

Ben kept a hold on his temper and nodded to his friend's gun. "Same reason you don't use that on every man you see. It's a weapon and you don't pull that trigger unless you're aimin' to kill whatever it is you're shootin' at. I ain't gonna shift and risk killin' everythin' within a five mile radius just because one man needs killin'. It ain't worth it."

That point put a stop to any further doubt on Henry's part and he nodded. "Fair enough... You think we've got enough bullets to handle Clarence? I heard the man's been shot plenty of times and kept on walkin'."

Ben pulled a face and looked down the river. Sarah still had her head bent over the water, running her fingers through her long hair. "You gonna let her shoot one of your guns?"

Henry looked with him and mimicked his expression. "Well... Not that I don't think she could fire it, but I don't know how her aim is."

"Then we don't have enough bullets," Ben ascertained. "Best not let her get involved in the fight if it comes to that."

Henry made a rather cynical sound. "I think we're gonna have to tie her to a tree to keep her out of the fight. That girl's got a lot of anger in her."

Folding up the stiff arms of his glasses, Ben tucked them away in his vest pocket. "As sure as a sunrise, she does. Better tell her that killin' Clarence won't help her none in that department."

"Sure helped me a few times. Made me feel better after I pulled that trigger."

"The difference is that you've killed people before. She hasn't... The first is always the hardest." Ben cleared his throat. "Besides, she ain't gonna kill nobody. Right? We're just takin' Clarence to the authorities."

Henry agreed and stood to stretch his back. As soon as the joints ceased their popping, a new and startling sensation made Ben straighten. Alert and trembling, he aimlessly searched for its source.

"What's wrong?" his friend asked.

Ben jumped to his feet and gave a sharp shake of his head, hoping it was nothing but his imagination. The back of his skull prickled like a spindly cactus was being rolled across his skin. Not hard enough to draw blood, but enough to scare the tar out of him.

He didn't answer, but jogged some distance away, hoping to ascertain the origin. He hadn't felt it for almost fifteen years. He thought he had left all of that behind him in Tennessee. He never wanted to feel this way again, not after all he had been through during the war.

Somewhere, hiding from him, was another werewolf.

A sudden splash came from down the river and Ben turned to see Sarah on her feet and staring up at the rocky outcrop to the south. Behind him, Henry drew his gun, but it took a little longer for Ben's rattled nerves to steady before he realized why.

Over a dozen horsemen lined the ridge, their tanned and leathery faces glaring down at the small band of travelers with dark, penetrating eyes. Bright white feathers were tied into their long hair, offsetting its jet-black shade that gleamed in the sunlight. Some were shirtless and bared their broad chests while others were clothed in buckskin shirts with tassels of stringy leather dangling in the wind. Most of them carried long spears, decorated in more feathers and colorful strings. Their horses were not saddled, their mouths and heads not burdened by a bridle that would have jingled with every movement – hence why they managed to sneak up on the river as they did.

No one moved or looked away as white man and red man sized one another up. Half of the band focused on Ben, no doubt because of the odd color of his eyes. They didn't shy away and there was no fear amongst them. Not even in the horses who stood so stubbornly with their riders. The air was thick with an impregnable tension.

Only the sharp click of a gun cocking could break the delicate peace.

"Put the gun away," Ben whispered slowly to Henry, not taking his eyes off the natives.

It took a few seconds longer than he would have preferred, but the gun hammer was safely lowered and then stowed.

"You know how to tell them we're just passin' through?" Henry asked.

Almost in turn, the natives began to mutter to one another, in the same way, in their own tongue that Ben couldn't understand.

"Not a clue," he replied.

"Fantastic," Henry grumbled. "I thought you said they'd be up in the mountains."

"I did. They must've seen us."

"What do they want?"

Ben sighed, "I don't know. They might think we're tresspassin'."

One word he continued to hear muttered amongst the Ute was "sinapi", accompanied by gestures in his direction. A single cautious step backward, instigated by his wolf, set the war party into motion. The natives turned their horses and carefully navigated their way down the ridge to confront the intruders. In a fit of either terror or bravery, Sarah dove in the direction of the horses and Henry went to follower her.

Ben, deeming himself the last line of defense, moved to intercept the natives and give the others time to flee. But someone beat him to it.

A man appeared, emerging from a small cluster of trees near the mountainside. His shoulder-length, dark blonde hair set him apart from the natives, though he was dressed in a similar fashion. Ben tripped to a stop and felt the back of his head explode with the intense needling that had begun moments before. The sensation was coming from him.

Tall and muscular, he didn't have to exude any dominance to tell Ben that he was a superior werewolf. In comparison to the only other werewolf he had ever met, this man looked to be at least another decade older. The tones of his skin told the story of a well-traveled individual and green eyes held a depth of wisdom that he had never seen in any living soul.

Ben stood entrenched where he was, his wolf demanding it of him out of some strange respect to the werewolf who was making his way over to mediate. The man passed one indifferent look to the younger werewolf and then turned to the natives.

The Ute warriors pulled on the manes of their horses, grinding the party to a full and awkward stop. A babbling, incomprehensible discussion took place between the blond man and the head of the group, and after a short time, some agreement was reached.

Now, the werewolf turned his undivided attention upon Ben, who had never been more frightened for no logical reason in his life. This was the first werewolf he had met since leaving the south. Fifteen years were spent thinking he was the only one of his kind in the western territories and, on this day, he had been proven wrong.

He couldn't speak and could only stare and hope that this man wouldn't take him as a hostile. The golden eyes only showed themselves in times of intense stress, and though Ben felt that in abundance, would this fellow werewolf understand that or see him as an aggressor to the whole affair?

The man came forward, casually and calmly as if he were walking up to an old friend instead of a stranger. He smiled and that simple gesture of friendship seemed to be enough to tranquilize Ben's wolf into submission.

"You'll have to forgive them," he said in a foreign accent. "They know of our kind, but sometimes it's hard to trust strangers in these parts."

Ben blinked, and his mind found it hard to digest this new information. The man didn't speak like he was from the south or the north, but from across the ocean. He had heard it a few times before. Gamblers and saloon keepers came in all nationalities, but he never expected this werewolf to be from England.

"It's quite all right!" he called out to Henry and Sarah who were ready to kick their horses into a gallop. "They won't hurt you."

The two humans were just as confused as Ben, but somewhat appeased by the man's cheerfulness, they came trotting back to join the rest.

The werewolf offered out his hand. "My name's Geoffrey Swenson."

Through his daze, Ben did what he rarely did with any other human he met. He reached out and returned the handshake. "Ben Myers."

He nodded and waved the humans closer. "It's a pleasure to meet you, Ben... You might want to hide those eyes, unless these two know you very well."

For the first time, shame crept up Ben's neck at what he would admit next. "I can't."

There would be no doubt that Geoffrey understood him, but still he questioned, "You can't?"

Ben shook his head. "I can't... hide it." With a quaking hand, he took out the glasses he had stowed away in his vest and slid them onto his face to cover the golden irises. Once more, the world became dull and bland under one, unvarying tone of amber. That, however, didn't keep him from noticing the look of bafflement on Geoffrey's face.

Yes, he was damaged, imperfect, and untrained. And soon, he'd have to explain exactly why.

Henry didn't like any of this one bit. Not in the way Geoffrey took after Sarah so courteously, and not in the way the natives eyed him with savage intent. The Englishman assured them that the Utes meant them no harm, but Henry had heard too many stories and witnessed too many Indian ambushes on defenseless settlers. They were better off in the company of a whole pack of werewolves than in the midst of this native caravan that led them further into the valley.

Geoffrey went ahead, keeping Sarah close by his side while Henry and Ben were separated by the mounted warriors. The only one without a horse, Ben could more easily come to her rescue if this deal should become unfavorable. Thus far, however, Henry had nothing but his groundless reservations. Neither Geoffrey nor the natives gave any indication to some malicious plan. Besides the hard looks - which he began to wonder if they were perpetually fixed on the savages' faces -

they had done nothing and said nothing to suggest what Henry believed would happen.

He expected Ben to tear into the natives as he had done to the outlaws the other night. He thought he might have seen Sarah withdraw into herself after witnessing the massacre as she had done before. He was ready to pull out his gun and shoot any savage who dared to come near her. But this turn of events left him skeptic. Who was Geoffrey? Why was he with the Utes? What civilized man would partner himself with these people? He was like them in everything but speech and manners down to his clothes and the way he rode the dark bay mare without a saddle.

Henry wasn't the only one. Through the cloud of intensity amongst the natives, Ben appeared the most anxious. Never had he known the werewolf to sweat, even when he wore a wool coat in the heat of summer. But he could faintly see a light sheen of perspiration on Ben's cheeks and across his upper lip, the droplets catching in his shallow stubble. In the faintest twitches of his head, Henry could tell his gaze bounced from one native to the next. Muscles stiff and hands poised as if he were ready to tackle the nearest offender, Ben was the picture of a caged animal.

And Sarah, despite her first apprehension to their new escort, seemed at her leisure. Over the course of that day and the evening before, Henry thought he had done a fair job of softening the hard heart that beat behind her bound chest. But with Geoffrey, Sarah's cold and icy winter had melted completely into a bright and cheerful spring. Her face alighted with smiles, of which he was not the catalyst. Blue eyes sparkled with interest at Geoffrey's stories instead of his own. And for this, he hated the Brit.

At the sound of her laugh, Henry couldn't watch from afar anymore. He kicked his already restless horse into motion and forced himself between a pair of warriors. They grumbled, but didn't lash out with their spears. He came to the other side of Sarah and shot an antagonizing look to their preserver.

The man wasn't more handsome than him, and was certainly older. Yet, he did have a kind of palliative aura to his person that almost defused Henry's animosity.

"I was telling the young lady a story about my son when he – "

"I heard you," Henry cut him off. "Is your son at this camp you're takin' us to?"

Geoffrey's smile faltered a fraction, but would not fully break. "No, he's not. He's in Alabama at the moment with good friends of ours. We agreed he would spend some time there and I'd come out to visit old friends of my own."

Henry's forehead creased. "You're friends with these... people?" An insult caught on the tip of his tongue and he restrained himself. If Geoffrey knew their language so well, then what was the likelihood they could understand him too?

"They are," Geoffrey replied. "As are many of the native tribes in this country."
Sarah shifted in her saddle. "How many?"

He leaned in as if to tell a secret. "Hundreds. There are so many tribes across the plains and mountains. So many languages, dialects, cultures, and stories. I live for the stories."

The luster in those green, mystifying eyes served as the only thing Henry wouldn't doubt about the stranger. "You talk like you're one of them or somethin'."

He shrugged. "In many ways, I am. I married into this life once, years ago. She was of the Navajo tribe. Do you know them?"

"I've heard of 'em," Henry replied as Sarah shook her head. She hadn't turned once to look his way since he rode up.

"They, like the Ute, have such rich traditions and folklore. I think I could spend a lifetime with these people and only scratch the surface of their ways."

Henry looked back to the grim and angry faces of the warriors. He wondered how anyone could be enticed into wanting to know more about their way of life. That was the farthest thing from his mind and always had been. Ever since he'd heard the first tales coming from the western plains about the Lakota, Henry only knew that Indians were dangerous heathens who would sooner scalp a settler than talk peace.

The complete opposite, Sarah's saddle creaked again as she angled herself to face Geoffrey. "My mama always thought it was a shame what the government was doing to the Indians. Putting them on reservations, starving them, making them give up their way of life. It's so sad. There were a lot of natives who came through Trinidad and my pa always gave them food if they asked for some."

Geoffrey seemed to take heart in her show of compassion and began to go into detail of the depravity to which the United States army often subjected the natives. He listed off the villages which were wiped out by cavalrymen, of raids upon defenseless women and children, of the conditions within the reservations that even made Henry pity them for the briefest of moments. The images of painted warriors slicing open the throats of unarmed pioneers kept such maudlin inclinations at bay.

"Unfortunately," Geoffrey sighed, "there's little we can do about it."

Sarah became more fervent. "My pa sometimes said we can make a difference by talking to the people in Washington. That'd do something, wouldn't it? You could – "

"No," he said. "It won't do any good. I've seen this happen too many times in other places. Once men get the idea in their heads that they can take what they want, they'll do it. They'll take this land by force if they have to, but they'll have it in the end. Greed gives birth to prejudice. Prejudice will give birth to hatred, and all evil comes from one man hating another. The only cure for hatred and ignorance is empathy. But when both sides are beyond listening, nothing will stop them from killing one another. It's a vicious cycle since the dawn of time and, with all due respect, one girl can't change the course of history."

Silence fell over the three of them, the only sounds coming from the steady plodding of horse hooves and rattling of harnesses as they carried on along the river. Henry couldn't help but feel his simple mind had been attacked somehow by Geoffrey's words. Convicted in his own feelings, he saw himself in the speech and realized he had thought wrongly toward the natives. And perhaps, they thought wrongly about him in the same way. But how could it end? To what extent could he let his guard down while around the Utes? These were the men who were rumored to kidnap women and children from their homes and use the intestines of the men they killed in battle for their bowstrings. Even if he were apt to put aside differences and ignore cruel lies, would they be so willing? If what Geoffrey said was true, the Ute had as much right to hate the white men as Henry had to hate the red man.

What's more, Sarah did not go unscathed either. She turned inward and a bit of that summer glow about her tanned face began to dim with some unwelcome thought. Henry had even more reason to hate Geoffrey now. He had set free his phoenix, only to let her burn to ashes again.

Thankfully, this all was put on hold when they heard the cry of a boy up ahead. One boy turned into two, and then three. Soon, there came a small company of young boys barely into their manhood, running toward the warriors with smiling faces and long bouncing braids that hung over their bare chests. Some girls were in the mix, their deerskin dresses slowing their furiously pumping legs as they came to meet them.

There came similar shouts as Henry had heard earlier. The children's shrill voices called out, "Sinapi! Sinapi!", especially when they clamored to Geoffrey's horse and reached out with greedy hands as if he had treats for them.

"What are they saying?" Sarah asked.

A Cheshire smile spread over the Englishman's lips and replied, "It's just something they call me. It means 'wolf'."

Henry peered at their new guide and wondered why the children would call him this, and why the warriors had almost denunciated Ben in the same way. Neither of them looked similar or wolfish in any obvious way. However, he had little time to dwell on it.

No one dismounted, but the somber haze that hung over the party disappeared in the wake of this gust of childlike excitement. Some men grinned to the boys and hoisted them onto the horses to ride along, while others were content to walk near and babble in that otherworldly language.

Sarah smiled to the girls who came to her instantly and pointed to her golden hair as if it were some novelty. Geoffrey translated some of what they said, but it became lost in the din of other voices. The air had shifted so suddenly that Henry hardly knew how to react to this pre-welcome party.

The one nearly forgotten member had vanished. Henry looked behind him and searched through the mass of horses and boys, but couldn't find Ben. Mindful not to accidentally cut off any warrior or trample any scampering child, Henry began to steer away from the gang.

"He'll turn up in a little while," Geoffrey called to him. "No need to go off looking for him."

As if he had been commanded to do so, Henry fell back into their previous formation. After some time spent trying to comprehend snippets of their language – keeping his mind and heart open as Geoffrey had instructed – they came upon a steady rise in the landscape. Once crested, they were met by the sight of a sprawling Ute village.

Teepees were scattered in no orderly formation with campfires sprinkled between the open spaces. Women were in the midst of chores, either cooking or cleaning the hides of recent kills, while others sat in the flaps of their tents and talked to one another in happy, carefree tones. Elderly men did the same, their dark gray hair a mark of their age and wisdom. Young men, who might not have been quite old enough to join the warriors, assisted the women in their duties or passed the time in sport on the opposite side of the river. A corral of grazing horses was segregated from the rest of the village, a collection of stallions and mares, more beautiful than Henry had ever seen.

The children who had been dispatched to greet the warriors disconnected and bounded down the slope that led into their village, shouting to their mothers, sisters, brothers, and grandfathers. Friendly eyes turned to them, but few rose from their spots to receive them with the same enthusiasm.

The warriors, now satisfied that they had done their job in escorting the white folk, rode past them and followed their sons down the hill. Their ride into the village gave the final touch to the scene and Henry wasn't sure how to feel toward it. Any other cowboy he knew would turn tail and run. He wasn't such a coward to feel the same impulse, but neither was his heart warmed by the sight as Sarah's must have been.

She let out a long breath and said, "It's beautiful."

Geoffrey nodded. "It is. If only time could stand still for moments like this."

Henry gave a sarcastic laugh. "You've got a way of ruinin' a moment, friend."

At once, he felt the eyes of the Englishman on him. "I'm glad you consider me a friend."

A stammering rebuttal did little and Sarah's horse bounding down the rise spurred him out of whatever words he wanted to say to Geoffrey. Let him believe that he trusted him. What could it hurt? As long as Sarah and Ben weren't harmed, he wouldn't have to pull his gun on any Indian or Englishman today.

CHAPTER 7

Sarah had never seen anything like it in her life. Being raised on the fringes of society had afforded her little contact with people of different races and cultures. Not directly. Their farm, though it lay in the path of a hunting trail used by the Indians near Trinidad, wasn't frequented often. And when the Indians did visit, her mother kept her cloistered inside. This mission to find her parents' murderer had been her first taste of the outside world.

The teepees were much larger than she imagined from the stories her father had told her. He, like so many, had traveled on a wagon train from the east as a boy and saw the Indians before their land became overrun. He spoke of brightly painted horses and murals on the walls of the conical homes, of beautiful women adorned in beads and warriors who looked as vicious as any blood-drenched ghoul from a child's worst nightmare. She thought the camp would be swarming with wild dogs and grotesque portions of butchered animals left on spits to cook over open fires.

Some of these imaginings were true, but others couldn't be farther from it. The warriors, though intimidating at first, were only scary in look and manners, but not in action. And this behavior was reserved only for the strangers. When in the company of their families and loved ones, a smile so incongruous with their formerly stern faces made them not so frightening anymore.

The women, likewise, were beautiful in their own way with linen strips woven through their braids, golden hoops dangling from their ears, beaded necklaces, and dress embellishments clicking with every subtle movement. Mirthful dark eyes turned to Sarah and regarded her with both curiosity and wonder. The little girls who had fawned over her hair rushed to their mothers and tugged to bring their attention to the same uniqueness. It made her feel a little easier that they were as awestruck by her as she was by them.

"May I help you down?"

Sarah turned to the voice and saw Geoffrey offering up his hands to her. This complete stranger had somehow arrested her fears and kept them under lock and key. She couldn't point to the exact thing about him that made her feel so at home amongst these savages. Maybe it was his eyes, or the way he sweetly smiled to her like a doting uncle.

Whatever it was, there wasn't a single thought to propriety or modesty when she willingly lowered herself into his care and alighted from Jemimah. Henry was by her side almost instantly, while a young woman came to take their horses toward the corral.

Geoffrey said something to the Ute girl, but Sarah's concentration finally deviated.

"Where's Ben?" she asked, scanning through the village and toward the hill where they had come.

"He's probably hiding," Geoffrey replied, and then pointed toward a cluster of tall pines in a shady part of the valley near the base of the mountains. "There. He's fine."

Sarah looked, but couldn't see any form of a man from this distance. For a moment, she doubted him, but then saw the slight movement behind a tree and the sunlight in the west caught the glass of Ben's spectacles.

As much as she might have been uncomfortable in the werewolf's presence, Sarah pitied him. Though the sentiment would be rued on his part, she felt bad for the way he was forced into a life that he didn't want. From what little Henry had intimated to her, Ben was as much a prisoner of his own mind and body as a caged bird or a wild mustang who had been caught for the first time. She didn't want to fear him so much that she couldn't somehow help him. If what Henry said was true, he wouldn't hurt her, even if she tried to free him.

"What's wrong with him? Besides the obvious," Henry questioned, lifting his eyes to the trees where his friend stayed concealed.

Several more children came to crowd around their legs and they, too, looked to the rise where Ben watched the village. Geoffrey pulled a wily smile and squatted until he was level with the children. When he finished a long, engaging speech, they laughed and ran toward the trees in a flurry of buckskin and dark hair.

As he rose to stand again, Sarah thought she heard Geoffrey mutter, "Don't run." But to whom he said it to, she wasn't sure. The boys and girls were too far away to hear him and he couldn't have been giving that order to either Sarah or Henry, who remained stationary.

"What was that?"

Kind green eyes met hers. "I was telling the little ones that Ben's like the coyote. In their traditions, it's because of the coyote that we have people of different races and languages, rather than one population of Utes. The coyote is responsible for all the hatred and prejudices in the world. I told them that Ben stays away from the village just like the coyote because he thinks they'll punish him. So, I told them to make him feel welcome."

In a heartwarming scene that only the unconditional acceptance of a child could demonstrate, the passel of little Utes closed in on Ben's hiding spot. A bit of worry rolled in Sarah's stomach, wondering if Ben would turn them away. But it only took a moment for him to give into their peeling giggles and be led down the slope, a child tugging on each of his arms and more bringing up the rear to guard against his escape.

Sarah felt hot tears barely form at the corners of her eyes at the sight, and she couldn't hold back the victorious grin. Ben looked perfectly mortified, but he didn't resist and he didn't run.

A light hand touched her shoulder and Sarah turned to see that she was about to be carried away in a similar manner. Women from the village pinched at her clothes and examined her hair in wondrous fascination. They crooned and clucked over her like a mother hen would over a baby chick, asking questions she couldn't begin to answer and playfully arguing with their fellow mothers and wives about something pertaining to the white girl.

In the bustle of eagerness, her hand was taken and she was hurried into the village with Henry and Geoffrey following close behind.

"What are they saying?" she laughed.

Thoroughly amused by it all, Geoffrey said, "They haven't seen a white woman like you before. They've been isolated in these mountains for generations."

Henry huffed. "That's pretty tough to believe. How do they hide here?"

Geoffrey went on to explain that some miners venture into the valley, but they never stay long and the Utes are usually left alone in exchange for safe passage through the area. Most of the conversation faded in the flood of excited voices as Sarah was ushered deeper into this new and strange world of buckskin, feathers, and campfires.

Ben stowed away in the darkness near the river, far from the reaching light of the campfires in the village. The moon above cast silver rays that broke across the rippling current like a thousand diamond studded jewels on a sheet of black. He listened to their chatter and laughter, torn between the need to be close to Sarah and Ben, and the niggling of his wolf to run far away.

Yet, Geoffrey's last command, "Don't run", stuck firm in his mind and he stayed. He didn't resist the children when they took him from his first hiding place and he didn't reject the lukewarm attentions of the men in the village. Henry seemed to get along better with them and was even shown how to shoot a bow. It had to be easy for the cowboy to at least try to learn their ways. He had a clean slate with the natives, unlike Ben.

Word of his golden eyes must have gotten around quickly. The guarded whispers, the stolen glances, and even one instance when a young man made a grab for his glasses to rip them from his face. Geoffrey must have known his intent, and harshly reprimanded the child in his language. No matter what they did or tried to convey to him, Ben couldn't feel at home as the other two did.

Even Sarah surrendered to have her hair braided by one of the matrons of the village. Out of all three, she was the star of the evening. And now, of all times, that showed to be true.

They were in the midst of some celebration. That much, Ben could gather. What exactly they did was still a mystery. Two lines were formed, men on one side and women on the other as they faced together in a cleared area amongst the teepees. Meanwhile, a group of men who wielded specially carved instruments sat a short distance away. The long, slightly curved shafts appeared white and smooth, like bone, but ridges were carved on one side and, when briskly run over with another rod, made a rough, growling sound that unnerved Ben more than it should have. The musicians kept to a steady beat and the dancers stepped in time.

There seemed to be a pattern amongst the dancers that the women were permitted to pick their own partners. Sarah was sought after by all the young and single men of the village, taken by her distinct looks. In contrast, Henry sat on the sidelines for half of the dance until a shy, but pretty young squaw came to ask for his favor.

Ben, still unnerved by the primal music and not wishing to become a participant by accident, slipped away from the festivities to sit by the river. Though his werewolf senses would never give him rest from the noise, he could release some of his anxieties more freely in the shadows. He could remove his glasses again and let the eyes glow their menacing and hypnotic gold. He had the freedom to feel his soul and spirit pulsate with the grinding of the bone instruments until he wondered if it would ever end.

Deep in his core, the vibrations swelled and tightened around his sensibilities. The hold over his wolf, the one he had prided himself in, loosened bit by bit and he dreaded for the safety of these people who unwittingly charmed the beast within their midst. But the final release never came, even when Ben relinquished all hold. Nails hardened and extended into claws, once dull teeth sharpened into fangs, and his world swam in a chaotic lightshow of silver and gold. Still, he remained human, remained conscious and in enough control that he knew the beast was unrestrained, but it didn't burst forth in a mad fury as he expected it to.

He wasn't alone for long.

Geoffrey came to Ben, and wolf met with wolf on a subliminal level. A short growl rumbled in his throat, but the older werewolf somehow made it clear that he came under a flag of truce. The growl was cut off and Ben consented to his presence.

Geoffrey lowered himself to the grass beside him and neither spoke for an indeterminant amount of time. Ben could only judge the passing of it in the steady, tireless rhythm of the music that brought on this unprecedented change in him. To have the wolf so close to the edge, but never leaping, was a new sensation altogether and he didn't have reason enough to establish whether it was good or bad. He could only tilt and sway like an addict high on opium and in the middle of a delirium.

The older werewolf's presence grounded him a little, and Ben felt if Geoffrey left, he would lose that piece of stability that he needed to stay in his human form. Perhaps that was why he had come now and not earlier or later when the spell passed.

The growling from the village was cut off abruptly and a series of whoops and hollers rolled through the dancers.

Unfortunately, Ben's fever didn't break with the music. Lucidity came back to him at an achingly slow pace. His vision cleared, but he knew the other manifestations of his curse hadn't receded. The wolf also, didn't withdraw as he wanted it to.

Dizzy and still faintly light headed, he looked to Geoffrey. Eyes that were once green now burned a deep, bright amber hue like his own.

"How... How can you..." Ben could barely find the breath to speak.

"I've grown used to it," Geoffrey replied, somehow knowing exactly what he was trying to ask. "I've been around these people for decades. In some tribes, it's easier to ignore the call. But here, with the Ute's... It's more difficult."

Ben swallowed hard and realized his mouth had gone bone dry. "Why?"

He gave a half-smile. "I think it has something to do with this." He motioned to the disassembling line of dancers. "The Bear Dance. It's a tradition they've practiced every summer since anyone can remember. It comes from a legend about two brothers who wandered into the woods and met a she-bear. The bear was scratching the bark from a tree and offered to show one of the brothers how. Her condition was that he was to spend a year with her and then he could go back to his village to tell them about everything he had learned. When the year was over, he had turned into a bear himself."

"I don't see what that has to do with anythin'," Ben grumbled as he flexed his hands to make his claws shrink back to their duller, less monstrous state.

Geoffrey leaned over his crossed legs. "A man turning into a bear," he said slowly so Ben's muddled brain could catch up. When he replied with nothing in return, the older werewolf shrugged. "Of course, it could be the instruments. Something about sound can certainly bring out the animal in anyone."

Ben shuddered when he remembered the recent impressions of that music. "I hate it. I hate everythin' about it, and us. It ain't right. I didn't ask for this. None of this. I would have rather died sixteen years ago than be this... this thing."

Unsure why he had so hastily unburdened himself to this near stranger, he couldn't find the strength to stop.

"I had a family. I had a wife and a little boy. I could have died defendin' my country. It wouldn't have made no difference if I did die, but at least I wouldn't have to know what happened to them. Saw my ma lose her mind, my pa and brother killed in battle too. And Abigail... I wouldn't have had to see her go to the arms of another man." Ben beat his fist into the ground, making a crater in the dirt that partially enveloped his hand. "I wished for death... too many times to ever count." His voice became thick with all those emotions he had denied through the years. Anger, bitterness, sorrow, and utter detestation for the man who had ruined his life with good intentions.

Geoffrey gave him time to breathe, to gather his wits and become receptive to his reply.

"It doesn't feel like so long ago that I was in the same place that you are. Not by the same means, but I understand the unrest within you, because it was once my own to bear. I have lost almost everything. I've been alive for five hundred years. I've lost my mother, a wife, a brother, and most recently my father who gave me this gift."

Ben scowled at the mere idea that this existence could be a gift, but he continued to listen.

"Seeing your family, your very life, chipped away piece by piece like the eroding waves against a rocky shore... it's a devastating thing. It leaves you wondering what's left of life, now that it's all gone. The world carries on as it always does, but we never can. We'll lose so many before our time comes and that's our eternal burden."

The far-away look in Geoffrey's stare told Ben that he wasn't blowing smoke. He truly knew the grief and pain of this life. He had albeit accepted the consequences of their existence, but Ben was sure that he never could.

"The only solace I have left is my son, but we both came to the agreement that we want different things from life. I'm sure you heard me say that he's in Alabama, but what I didn't say is that he's helping others like us." Geoffrey brightened and the stars that shone overhead danced in his eyes. "There's a town there where our kind are free to live and walk amongst humans without fear of judgement or death. We visited it back when it was first being settled and when it came time to move on, Adam wouldn't. He wanted to stay, but I could never live in a pack." Somehow, Geoffrey had the good humor to laugh at his own self.

Ben, however, couldn't. He remembered this place and when Dustin spoke of it during their training. "Devia?"

"You know it?"

He snorted. "Yeah, I know it. The man who made me into this told me to go there."

"Why didn't you?" Geoffrey asked, his tone rising as if he were ready to scold a disobedient child. In many ways, Ben was.

"You think after all the shit I've been through, that I would just walk on into Devia and be part of all that? I don't care if an alpha can somehow fix these eyes. I don't want to be around any other werewolves and I sure as hell don't wanna be that close to Georgia... There are too many memories there and I can't stand it."

Geoffrey nodded and all aggression left him. "I can understand that too. But you'll go back. One day, you'll miss it enough that you'll go back. If being a wanderer has taught me anything, it's that you can always go back home. No one will ever stop you except yourself."

Ben knew that the older werewolf would see his eyes roll in the darkness, but he did it anyway.

"You may never go to Devia, but I can tell you one thing." Geoffrey settled his weight on his knees and demanded Ben's full consideration. "If you don't accept that the wolf is part of you, you'll never be free of it."

His brows furrowed in confusion. "What're you talkin' about?"

"My son taught me a thing or two and I know this much." Geoffrey pointed at the golden eyes which would never darken again. "If there's ever a problem with your wolf, it's not the wolf's fault. It's yours. There's conflict between you two and it needs to be resolved. If you don't resolve it, that gold is going to stay there. You need to find out what's putting you two out of balance and fix it."

Ben gave a mirthless chuckle at his nonsense. "You're talkin' like I can have a sit-down with this thing and make it behave."

"You can never make the wolf behave," Geoffrey corrected. "But you can come to terms with it. Accept that it's part of you and you're a part of it. It's never going to go away, Ben. You might as well make the most of it. The longer you stay bitter about being half man and half wolf, the longer you'll suffer."

Ben sneered. "I ain't gonna be grateful for this. How can I be grateful for somethin' that ruined me?"

Geoffrey sighed and he could see a bit of his patience slip. "I didn't say you had to be grateful. Just stop being bitter... I urge you to go to Devia one day. I know you three have a long journey ahead to find Clarence Biller, but at least consider going. You're going to live a very long time. Do you really want to have to hide like this and roam around the mountains like an animal for five, six, or seven hundred years?"

Once put in the perspective of eternity, Ben felt a bit of his stubbornness give way. "I might consider it."

This suited the old werewolf and he dipped his chin. "That's all I ask."

Sarah lounged on the dirt floor of the teepee. Geoffrey had graciously relinquished his tent for the group, though he had made the passing comment that Ben was unlikely to stay the night in the village. That left her and Henry to a space of their own, unchaperoned.

Her thoughts were on anything but propriety. Her spirit was heavy with another worry that superseded everything, and had crept up on her so suddenly. Through the last few days, her mind had been occupied by outlaws, cowboys, werewolves, and Indians, each caricature crowding for space in her thoughts. Only when there was nothing but the muffled voices of natives outside the teepee, when her stomach was full, and she was lulled by the alleviating fact that she was safe, did she remember everything all over again.

She heard the gunshots, the screams, how her blood pounded in her ears and chest ached with the ferocity of her frightened heart. She saw their faces, the flash of gunmetal, and their backs as they walked away at a leisurely pace. They didn't run, didn't ride on horses in or out, just casually left the homestead as if they had done no wrong. Above it all, she remembered her inability to move, to act, to confront them with the crime they had committed.

This condemning knowledge that she had done nothing to stop the murderers had pushed her onward. It was the whip that drove her to seek out the next town, to find the next marshal or sheriff who would do what she couldn't. If she'd had enough courage, she could have ended it all right then and there. She didn't have a gun, but she had the nerve now. At least, she thought she had.

In her hand lay a simple golden chain, an etched oval locket pressed in her palm. If she opened it, she'd find the faces of her parents staring back at her. But she refused to look or give some relief to her wounded and guilty heart. Not until she knew Clarence had paid for his crime would she see her family again.

Watching the families in the village had summoned up her own memories. Some sweet, and others forever tainted by the tragedy that would follow her forever. Sarah thought she was done crying when a single tear rolled unbidden down her nose and splashed against the face of the locket. It wetted her skin, bringing her back to the present long enough to hear the shuffle of feet outside her teepee.

The trim silhouette of a man passed around the side of the tent and then paused in front of the entrance, as if he were unsure whether to trespass or not. By the cut of the shadow, she knew it was Henry.

With an air of reserve, he entered, momentarily brightening the interior with the glow of the fire from outside. When he dropped the flap, the space was darkened once more, with only the dim light filtering through the walls of the teepee.

Sarah rubbed the back of her sleeve against her cheeks to hide the evidence of her sadness, but it was too late. He must have seen them glisten.

"You all right?" he asked.

Henry was still out of arm's reach, both of them safe for now. There came the fleeting compulsion to beg for his embrace, to be held until the soreness of the remorse passed. But she didn't deserve comfort. Not when her parents were cold in the grave.

"I'm fine," she replied, betraying herself with an involuntary sniffle as she tucked the locket away in her pants pocket.

He came closer and his voice softened with compassion. "No. You been cryin'. If you don't want to talk about it, I understand, but sometimes it can help."

Sarah watched his form move to the opposite bedroll and sit. Her very bones ached for his nearness, but she didn't know how to ask for it without seeming forward or like she craved more from him. So she stopped up her silly girlish desires and straightened.

"I was just... How long did it take you to get over losing your parents?" She knew it was a delicate subject, one that shouldn't have been embarked upon so coarsely. But she had to know if she was feeling too much, or perhaps too little. She needed something to compare this to. Something with which to measure her own sorrow.

A sigh floated through the darkness and some rustling of fabric as Henry settled himself to mimic her reclined posture. "You don't get over losin' someone you loved. The hole will always be there. Somedays it seems smaller and you can go without thinkin' about them. Other days, it's as wide as a canyon and deep. Way too deep. You gotta walk around it. You can look in and feel bad for a spell, but don't fall in. Make sense?"

It made perfect sense. The only trouble was that Sarah felt she had leaned too far, peered too deeply into the abyss and now she had fallen over the edge and hung by her fingers. Maybe she'd been that way since she first took to burying the graves. Or maybe she had stumbled in more recently and didn't know it. The descent was so gradual, so easy that she didn't even feel it until now, when she missed them the most.

But what could she do to pull herself back over to safe ground again?

"What if you do fall?" she asked, barely above a whisper as lamentations tightened over her throat.

Even if she couldn't see his eyes, she knew that he was looking right at her, their stares locked. Outside, the world grew silent and still, as if it too waited with bated breath for his solution to a broken heart.

"You get someone to help you out. Because you can't do it alone."

So simple, and yet so profound in itself. All this time, Sarah braved the rugged wilderness alone. She had taken it upon herself to find food and shelter. The only help she had ever asked for was in finding Clarence. Never once had she considered that she couldn't live alone, that she couldn't suffer and grieve alone.

Much against her own conscious doing, Sarah rose from her bedroll and went to Henry's side. He didn't reach for her, didn't move, but followed her with his eyes. Now, sitting so close, nearly touching, she could see his face clearly. As if for the first time, she truly looked at him.

She studied the lines in his tanned skin, the scruff along his jaw, and the faint scar on his neck where no stubble grew. With his hat discarded, she could see the fullness of his hair and the way it curled at the ends. His musky smell enveloped her, comforting and warm. With his hands laced behind his head, his torso and arms were exhibited in such a way that made Sarah's fingers tingle with the need to touch.

Taking a breath in an attempt to will away a new aching within her, Sarah tried to gain control of herself.

"Have you ever... ever fallen?" she asked.

Henry slowly shook his head. "No. I never let myself."

A self-defeating smile touched her lips. "Then you're stronger than I am."

When Henry sat up, Sarah refrained from pulling back, though their shoulders were an inch apart. If she could stand to be this close without acting irrationally, then it'd prove how courageous she could truly be.

"I'd say you're plenty strong. I can't think of any woman who could have come this far without a man's help. Two months is a long time to be fightin' by yourself."

Sarah dropped her gaze and squeezed her hands into fists to keep them from shaking. "It doesn't seem that long sometimes."

"Well, it'll be over soon," he said. "Geoffrey said that Maroon Creek isn't far from here. We should be able to find Burnt Mountain and Clarence's hideout by tomorrow afternoon."

Somehow, that didn't send the same skitters up her spine as it would have days ago. Their nearness to her enemy and the approaching climax of their mission didn't seem to affect her like it should. Instead of feeling eager or excited at a chance to see Clarence Biller dead in a heap at her feet, she felt almost nothing.

It had to be the interlude of despair she'd suffered that evening. Nothing else could attest for this echoing hollow. But the more she analyzed it, the more she realized that she wasn't so empty. Not really. Beneath the seething hatred and the dampening despair, through the haze, something else awakened. Warm, thrilling, and insane, it grew and fed off the heat coming from Henry's closeness.

A finger touched the underside of her chin and slowly drew her back to the cowboy.

"That is, if you still wanna go after him."

His words dripped with sympathy and concern. Perhaps he hoped that she would change her mind, but nothing could make her take back her vow.

"I promised my parents I'd find Clarence and make him pay for what he did to them. I can't turn back now."

Henry gave her a faint, but satisfied smile, as if he had been counting on her to say something like that. "Yep. You're braver than any girl I've ever met."

And she proved her bravery again when she saw his mouth descend upon hers. Sarah didn't move, didn't flinch, and gave into it. As untimely and spontaneous as it was, she would have never had him in any other way. And she gave into that nameless quivering in her core, that sensation that told her not to resist.

So, in one fateful moment, she let go of the ledge and instead of falling, she floated.

Floated over the hate and desolation that would have drowned her. Upward, she could feel herself soar as the kiss deepened and his hands drew her in. Together, they flew and there was no more darkness. Nothing else existed except a white-hot heat that plumed from the inside and drove her to madness. Nothing else mattered. Not Clarence, not Ben, not the world outside that teepee, or the uncertain future. This could very well be their last night together. Whether it was right or wrong, she didn't care. For one night, Sarah let herself have this bit of happiness.

CHAPTER 8

"Take this." Geoffrey presented Sarah with the dagger, its thick leather sheath ornamented with the same tassels and delicate beading similar to the dresses of the women in the village. Its handle was made of antler, curved perfectly to fit in one's hand.

At first, the girl didn't want to take the gift and started to shake her head, but the old werewolf silenced her.

"I insist," he said. "If you're not going to carry a gun, I want you to have this to protect yourself."

Sarah slid a glance to Ben and Henry who waited on the northern rise outside of the village. Henry sat comfortably in his saddle atop Buck, while Ben was content to hold the reins of the gelding that Geoffrey had loaned him. The animal was trained by the Utes and conditioned by the werewolf amongst them to be anesthetized to the effects of the wolf. Though Ben was glad to be in possession of a horse who wouldn't run from him, he was as accepting of the gift as Sarah was of hers.

Beside him, Henry gave an approving nod and Sarah gingerly took the dagger.

The night before had been anything but quiet and peaceful. Between the intermittent sessions of music and dancing, and then the disconcerting change taking place within Sarah and Henry's teepee, Ben got little sleep. Geoffrey, thankfully, kept his distance after their talk by the river. That allowed him some time to think on the journey ahead, and the aftermath beyond it.

What would he do when Henry and Sarah left him? What would happen after they brought Clarence to justice? Would Ben go back to Georgia? Or retreat to Alabama for the help he needed? It would be safer to stay in Colorado or even travel further north into Wyoming, maybe even as far as Canada, where he'd heard the wilderness could swallow men whole. Ben wanted to disappear, now more than ever.

But there was still so much to consider. His mother would be the first. Could he flee deeper into the uncivilized forests to escape humanity when she still depended on him? The money had never been refused, but what guarantee was there that she was still alive? Maybe she had passed on years ago and he would have never known it. Would he go to see her one last time before running away from it all, or stay planted to continue in this vicious cycle for another decade or two?

He rubbed at the back of his neck, dampening his hand with the gathering sweat under his collar. How long could he keep this up? He didn't want to wear the tinted glasses for the rest of his life, but did he really want to be looked at as an oddity amongst the other werewolves in Devia? He was sure they could all control their eyes. Dustin could. Geoffrey certainly could, given his age and experience. Was there hope for him in Devia or would it just be another place for people to stare at him and wonder why he wasn't like the others? An outcast amongst the humans and the werewolves. Ben had to find a place soon or he'd go mad.

"You gonna be ready?" Henry suddenly asked.

Ben detested the way the cowboy glowed. He'd never forgive himself for bringing them together.

"Are you?" he returned. "Not gonna let a girl get in the way of what's got to be done, are you?"

Henry blew out a derisive breath. "Of course not. Why would I?"

Ben arched a brow at his friend. "You two seemed to be gettin' pretty friendly last night. I wouldn't want you losing your head if she gets hurt."

"Well," he began as he shifted and leaned on the saddle horn, "the way I figure it, she won't get hurt. She's got us, and we ain't gonna let nothin' happen to her. Right?"

"It goes without sayin'. It don't matter if Clarence's got two guns or a dozen men with him. We'll take care of him and Sarah will have her reckoning... What're you two gonna do when this is all over?"

Henry was quiet for a while and Ben hoped that he remembered the talk they shared in Buckskin Gulch. Though Ben had little say in the personal lives of either party involved, he did feel somewhat responsible. If he thought they were likely to cast one another's honor into the dust, he would have never allowed them to sleep in the same tent alone. Music or no music. But once the deed was done, it could never be undone. For Sarah's sake, Ben hoped she realized the significance of her decision to let Henry have his way.

"You know I take things one day at a time," Henry answered. "We'll see where it goes."

Ben shot him a censuring look. "Don't you dare leave her in some town by herself, or so help me, I'll – "

Henry chuckled, breaking off his threat. "I ain't gonna leave her... I just don't know what we'll do. That's all. Sarah ain't some whore, but she don't sound like she wants to settle down either."

"And you do?" Ben asked with disbelief.

The cowboy tilted his hand back and forth, showing his indecisiveness. "It all depends. One day at a time."

Now, he had heard just about everything. Maybe it wasn't Henry he had to worry about, but Sarah. Would she be the one to run off and leave the cowboy? Ben might have been wrong about the farm girl from the beginning. A person could change a lot in two months and maybe that cord of strength he had seen in her wasn't so buried after all.

In the valley, Sarah mounted her horse and bade one last goodbye to the people of the village before kicking Jemimah into a full gallop. When she came close, she didn't slow down. Her cheeks flushed and eyes bright with eagerness, she charged past both of them. "We're wastin' daylight!" she called out.

Henry steadied Buck, who had been spooked, and laughed before egging his own horse to give chase. The only one not as eager, Ben clumsily slipped his foot in the left stirrup and hoisted himself into the saddle. It had been so long since he'd ridden, but his body found its natural center of balance. The wolf within him wasn't too pleased and would have rather run alone, but Ben secretly savored in this one luxury he had been barred from for sixteen years.

Turning his gaze to the Ute village, he saw Geoffrey standing almost alone, the last one to see them off. Instead of waving or giving some other customary farewell, Ben's werewolf ears heard his voice rumble over the distant stamping of hooves and shuffling moccasins.

"Keep her safe," he said. "Clarence won't be an easy match, even for you."

He had heard similar commands from the humans along their journey, but he hadn't expected it from the older werewolf. Did he doubt his ability to fight? Maybe he should have told him about the thieves he'd killed in the mountain pass on the way to Leadville. Then he'd know that Ben might have been untrained, but he wasn't weak.

Instead of arguing, he nodded and pulled on the reins to turn his horse to the north.

Henry leaned on the saddle horn, twirling the tips of his reins in one hand while glaring melodramatically at the dismounted werewolf. It was all to make Sarah smile, but he couldn't help but feel a bit of impatience with Ben. He had been standing on the ridge for a quarter of an hour, sniffing the air and scoping the side of Burnt Mountain. In a few hours, the sun would be setting, and they'd have to break for camp. All three had been hoping to find Clarence before then, but now it seemed they would have to settle for the big showdown the following day.

The effort it took to quell his irritation couldn't rival the sheer amount of willpower it took to keep himself in his own saddle when Sarah was so close. That morning, watching her sleep with her blonde hair in a tangled halo around her head, Henry knew he was different.

Other women he bedded couldn't capture his full devotion as she had. Within five minutes of finishing the deed in any cathouse, Henry was ready to put his hat back on and leave. Not with Sarah. He stayed and traced the length of her arm all the way to her fingertips. He held her close and buried his face in her neck to memorize her womanly scent. He never wanted to leave that teepee or see the light of day, unless she was by his side.

Had it always been her fire that drew him in? Or was it the need to see her whole and happy once again? The brokenness in her eyes and the repressed anguish in her voice wounded him as if he were the one who put that pain there. He hadn't, but he wanted to take it away. And if that meant killing Clarence himself and carving out the blackguard's heart to present it to Sarah, he would. At this moment, he felt he would do anything for her.

He wasn't the only one who had changed. Sarah, too, seemed to be a more jovial version of the girl from the day before. Her gaze was no longer distant or unfocused, but direct. The very form of her had been something of a fuzzy, ill-defined shape, unsure what she was doing or what she wanted. Now, those lines were clear, definitive, resolute. A young girl had matured overnight into the woman she was always meant to be. It added to her beauty and allure without dulling his desire to enrich her life further in any way that he could.

On the ridge, Ben took off his hat and raked his fingers through his hair in frustrated sweeps. As blind as Henry was to the dangers of taking on the outlaw, he knew one thing. Something wasn't right.

"Anythin'?" he asked, barely raising his voice since he knew the werewolf would hear him well enough.

Ben didn't reply with a nod or a shout. He kicked the dust and a mumbled curse carried to the two humans by the creek.

"Is he all right?" Sarah asked.

"I don't know," Henry replied. "If he hasn't picked up a trail yet, maybe there's nothin' there."

"Or Clarence could be on the other side of the mountain."

Henry sighed and shook his head. "Ben would've been able to tell if he was. That nose can smell for miles."

A strong wind blew through the gulch, tossing Sarah's golden hair over her shoulders. As the breeze would have hit Ben, the werewolf stiffened and turned to the west. He jammed his hat back on his head and burst into a run, becoming almost a blur amongst the pines and tall grasses.

Sarah was the first to move and steered to follow him along the gulch. Whatever scents the wind had conducted to him, it must have been the hint they were looking for. Henry chased after her, snapping his reins at the gelding Ben had left behind to get the horse moving.

They soon lost him as he climbed higher and higher up the mountain, the forest along its slope thickening to conceal any movement. Sarah and Henry wheeled to a stop as they peered into the surrounding trees where Ben had disappeared. Their horses stamped and snorted in protest to the sudden change of pace, their unrest making it even more difficult to get a good look.

"We have to go on foot," Sarah declared, already dismounting.

Henry's stare snapped from her to the mountain and back. "You wanna climb up that without a horse?"

"The terrain is too steep." Wasting no time, she led Jemimah to a grove of twisting oaks. Plenty of grass grew around its roots, providing ample food while they waited for their humans to return. "It'll take longer, but I don't think the horses would make it back down, even if they could get up."

Henry did see the soundness in the plan, but he could already feel his legs ache from the exercise that was in store for him.

The horses were secured, and they began their trek up the incline to find Ben. All the while, Henry called out in hopes that the werewolf would hear him and slow his pace so they could catch up.

When they were about halfway to the summit, Henry caught a flash of black and leathery brown against the lush greenery on a shallow gradient. He called out to Ben again, but he didn't respond.

Sarah, who was now thoroughly winded, almost slipped on a smooth rock as they changed directions to follow after Ben. Henry caught her in time, wrapping one arm about her waist to steady her. God, how he wanted to forget about Ben, Clarence, and the whole damned mission just so he could have this moment with her.

He was alone in this need, because Sarah quickly regained her footing and hurried up the rise, using the sturdy trees to propel herself forward. Henry still couldn't help but smile at her tenacity, and the way her hips swayed with each step. She might have still been wearing men's clothes, but her body still called to him beneath the layers. He discovered what she had been hiding all along and he wanted more of it.

"One might think you've done this before," he remarked.

"Nope. Never."

She didn't even look back, didn't show any need to continue polite conversation. Not as long as Ben was on the trail and they were coming ever closer to Clarence and the end of her quest for retribution.

Henry, however, wouldn't let up. "So, I been thinkin'..."

"Don't hurt yourself."

Now, she glanced over her shoulder, a fresh playfulness in her eyes and a grin tugging at her mouth. He laughed in return, but wouldn't be daunted.

"I been thinkin'... What're you gonna do after this is all over? Is there anythin' left for you that the bank didn't take?"

Though her back was still turned to him, he could see the way her muscles tensed. Even her steps slowed and the hands that have been reaching for trees and limbs for support missed their marks as if she weren't committed to searching for them anymore.

"I... I never gave it much thought. There's really not much left of my home and I don't have any money to buy it back from the bankers, so... I don't know."

Sarah stopped, and Henry almost bumped into her. Her back rose and fell with each labored breath, the air becoming thinner with every yard they climbed. For a long moment, she didn't move. Didn't turn or even speak. It was as if the fear of an unknown future with no purpose, no drive, had left her immobile. If she didn't move forward, she wouldn't have to face what lay after Clarence's demise.

"You could... I mean, I ain't got much other place to go either. Colorado may not be safe anymore, so I might be goin' north. Or maybe to California." Henry strengthened himself for what he was about to say next, knowing it went against every one of his principles. "You could come with me, iffen you'd like."

Sarah's head angled down, but she wouldn't say one way or another. And the more time passed after his suggestion, the more his doubts grew until the hope of a future with her became little more than a speck on the horizon.

"It's just an idea," Henry said sheepishly and scratched at the back of his neck. Now, he regretted ever bringing it up. He shouldn't have ever asked Sarah such a serious question at a time like this. It was too much to think on and now, her once hardened lines became bleary again.

A shout echoed from up the mountain. As if Ben's voice were the bugle's call to battle, Sarah leapt with renewed vigor and scrambled her way upward. Henry followed, being mindful to catch her slipping feet or help her along in any way he could. Anything to erase the awkward, dangerous exchange he had precipitously begun. He should have kept to what he had told Ben. One day at a time.

The forest began to thin and they found themselves upon an even ledge, wide enough for a man to walk along without falling into the ravine. It curved up and around ledges, through a maze of rocks. It was no wonder that Clarence would want to hide up here. Taking a horse along such a path would be treacherous in itself, so few would dare to follow him. And even if they did, there were plenty of alcoves and crevices carved into the mountainside where an outlaw could slip unnoticed.

The path opened up and made one sharp turn to the north where it led onto a flat, spacious shelf about twenty feet deep and at least forty foot wide. The remnants of a campfire sat cold and long extinguished in the center of the outcrop, the only sign that someone else had been there before them. Still, Henry immediately pulled his gun and tugged Sarah to stand behind him.

They crept around the corner and found a cave sinking into the mountain. More signs of life lay near the recess and there came the whisper of footsteps within.

"They ain't here," Ben reported.

Henry let out the breath he had been holding and let Sarah pass him to inspect the campsite. Even though they were alone, he wouldn't holster his gun. Not yet.

Boxes of extra ammunition lay inside the shadows, along with four open bedrolls. The cave stank of men, blood, tobacco juice, and wood smoke. Not unlike a saloon, if a saloon were carved out of a mountain.

The cool dampness of the air within the cave gave some relief to their weary bodies and the two humans unceremoniously dropped to catch their breath. The werewolf, however, didn't appear tired at all, though he had scaled the side of a mountain at a full run. He continued to examine the camp, studying each random article as if it were important in some way. He touched nothing, picked up nothing, as if disturbing anything would destroy the signatures of the outlaws imprinted on the items.

"So, we'll just stay here until he comes back and ambush him."

Henry's suggestion was ignored by Sarah, who was too exhausted to speak.

Ben, despite being engrossed in his detective work, said, "We shouldn't stay here."

"Why not?" Henry asked incredulously. "We can hide in here. They won't be able to see inside the cave when they round up the path."

"I don't think they'll need to see you to know you're there."

Henry narrowed his eyes upon his old friend. "What do you mean?"

Ben slowly treaded into the sunlight, his steps ambling and slowed by the caution written in every rigid line of his body. Something wasn't right at all, and Henry wondered what must have been going on inside the werewolf's head. He normally wasn't so unsure of himself.

Henry watched him stop and gaze out over the vista of mountain ranges that stretched for miles and miles in every direction. The drop into the gulch below could easily kill a man, but Ben stood only a few feet from the edge, closer than Henry would have dared.

"Ben?" Sarah must have seen the difference in him too, though she couldn't possibly know what was normal or not normal for a werewolf. Hell, Henry didn't know either half the time. He could only guess or conjecture from past experiences.

But this was new. Henry didn't have to see Ben's face to know the man wasn't himself. He barely looked to be breathing. Only a constant wind upon the precipice that played in his clothes could tell him apart from a stone statue.

In a startling explosion of action, they were suddenly not alone. Three men leapt from somewhere above the cave, coming to land behind him, guns drawn. Ben didn't even turn when the pistols were pointed at his back.

Sarah jumped to her feet, but Henry had already twisted her around to put himself between her and the aggressors. Their movement drew the attention of two of the outlaws, who spun and now had their guns leveled upon them.

Henry did the same, but one flash of silver stayed his trigger finger from discharging his weapon. They both bore the silver stars of deputies. Upon close inspection, neither of them possessed the filthy resemblance to cutthroats or thieves. Not like the men who attacked them outside Alma. They were clean shaven and well dressed, but unwavering. They didn't even care that they had targeted a woman.

The third man loomed over the others, his shoulders broad and covered in a long coat that barely brushed the dirt as he strode toward Ben. Both hands were gloved in black leather and an equally black hat shadowed over much of his features. Salt and pepper hair masked the back of his neck and touched his collar.

From his vantage point, Henry could barely see what unfolded between the man and his friend. Ben had turned but seemed stricken by the very sight of the man. Distress transformed his expression and Henry didn't recognize his friend anymore.

This face-off only lasted a moment before the older man grabbed for Ben. A scuffle ensued that ended as quickly as it began. Each blow was done swiftly, too fast for even his eyes to follow and for the first time, he saw Ben licked.

His werewolf was on the ground, faced down with his arms behind his back. The man was atop of him and produced a pair of handcuffs.

"He ain't done nothin'!" Henry shouted, taking a step forward that was followed closely by the two gun barrels. Sarah also made a move to go to Ben's aid, but he held her back with one strong arm.

"Drop your weapon!" one of the deputies demanded.

With a grimace, Henry did as he was told. He might not have been outgunned, but shooting a lawman was a worse offense than shooting a drunkard or fellow bandit. He might not have been able to get away with the deed so easily, and for once, he had a future to think of. He let the pistol roll on his finger and he squatted to place it in the dirt for the second time in this journey.

Just as he did, Ben let out a scream. The faint smell of burning flesh met Henry's nose. When he looked up, the handcuffs were on his friend's wrist, the metal searing his skin. Sarah gasped and clung to Henry's arm, but all he could do was stare.

Silver.

Between the two deputies, he could get a good look at the man who knew too much about Ben. His abnormally tanned face told that he must have had Indian or African blood in him. His dark eyes were stern, penetrating, not unlike Geoffrey's in their depths, but they held no tenderness or compassion for anyone on that cliff.

He jammed the pistol under Ben's jaw and his cry of agony was silenced, though he struggled furiously against his captor. His glasses had flown off in the brawl and lay a few feet away, and his eyelids shut tight against the immense pain. How could he be detained so easily? Henry had seen him wrestle a buffalo to the ground and haul railroad ties all by himself. He was strong enough to toss this man over the cliff. Yet, he had lost the match and was completely disabled as the aggressor's knee dug into his spine.

"When?" the older man demanded, his grizzly voice harsh with the unwarranted anger that burnished in his glare.

Blood seeped from beneath the metal of the shackles. Henry could feel Sarah's hold on his shirt sleeve begin to tremble, her breaths coming out short and ragged.

The man pulled back the hammer and pressed the barrel harder. "When?" he asked louder.

Then came the raspy reply of, "Tonight." It had been uttered so slow, so deep, that Henry almost missed it.

However, he didn't miss the curse and while the man lifted Ben to his feet, Henry saw a similar star pinned to his lapel. A sheriff.

"Why are you arrestin' him?" he implored. "He ain't done nothin'. We came up here to catch – "

The black eyes of the sheriff turned on him with such vehemence that Henry's teeth clamped shut instantly. "I know who you were looking for. He hasn't been here for days. You don't need to worry about Clarence Biller."

Henry flinched. Another Englishman? What were the odds? And how did he know so much?

"What's happening tonight?" Sarah asked, somehow finding her courage again to speak the question they both shared.

The sheriff glanced from Henry to Sarah, assessing them for something. "You'll find out."

Ben, stabilized only by the strong grip of the lawman, was doubled over in pain from the silver branding his wrists. The werewolf was no stranger to the damaging metal, but Henry had never seen its affects until now. And Sarah would see the golden eyes for the very first time as Ben looked to them, pleading for help that they couldn't give.

CHAPTER 9

Ben tumbled to the floor of the tunnel. The silver imbedded in the rock stung his hands when he tried to catch himself in the fall.

How could he have been so daft not to know another werewolf was close by? He smelled them coming, felt the prickling in the back of his skull, and heard their low murmurs right before the ambush. His mind had been in a fog, dumb and unresponsive to everything around him. All because he couldn't place one scent in Clarence's encampment.

Beneath the sweat, piss, and blood, it was there, taunting him and his wolf to remember. But the longer he stared out over the ravine, he couldn't place it. Couldn't name it. That combined with the storm raging in his own body, he didn't budge to defend himself or the others against the sheriff and his posse.

A swift kick sent him rolling across the ground, the traces of the hateful metal grazing the skin on his face. Silver was just as he remembered it. Like acid against flesh, it burned without mercy. Not even the eroding effects of the handcuffs around his wrist could dull the lesser burns to his face and hands.

He quickly rose to his knees and tried to catch his breath. The change would come tonight, making his agony complete. Burned on the outside and coming apart on the inside. The date had snuck up on him and it wasn't until noon earlier that day that he realized what would come. He had been afraid of what would happen to Sarah and Henry, especially if they couldn't find Clarence in time. That anxiety, along with the distracting consequences of the coming shift, had made him nearly useless when it came to locating the hideout. If it weren't for the wind and strong smell of ash and burnt logs from the old camp fire, he might have never found it.

And somehow, the werewolf sheriff had known the shift was close.

"Get moving," he ordered. "It'll be dark soon. I don't want to risk – "

"And you think I do?" Ben growled intensely as he pushed himself to his weary feet.

For his remark, the other werewolf in the mine shoved him forward. This time, he kept his balance, though his muscles twitched and threatened to completely buckle him with every other step.

Perhaps a part of him had been hoping this werewolf was actually Geoffrey, come to help them capture Clarence. But this man seemed the total opposite in every way. Everything from his dark complexion to his brusque and callous manner made him realize how other werewolves could be so diverse in attitudes.

The man introduced himself as Bart Croxen to Sarah and Henry, completely gentle to them, even when they discovered that Henry was a wanted man. But to Ben, the werewolf conducted himself like a tyrant, pitiless toward one of his own kind. He wouldn't answer any of Ben's discrete questions while on the road to this abandoned silver mine. The only attention he received came in the form of angry orders to be quiet or to keep moving.

Maybe now, in the privacy of this tangible representation of hell, Bart would be more open to talking.

"What do you want with me?" Ben asked, looking back to Bart as he continued to stumble his way forward.

The sheriff carried a single lantern with him, but neither of them needed the light. They could have easily seen through the immersing blackness.

"I don't want anything from you," he said, his English accent so prevalent that, once more, Ben was caught off guard by it. He wondered if all the older werewolves came from across the Atlantic. First Dustin, an Irishman, then Geoffrey and Bart. Ben wondered if he was the only one of their kind to be of American birth.

"Then what's all this about? I haven't done anythin'. I stay away from humans as much as I can. I haven't..."

He would have said that he had never compromised his nature to anyone, but that would have been a lie.

"I don't care how careful you've been. I won't tolerate lone wolves in this area. Where's your pack?"

Ben tripped over a protruding rock in the floor, but righted himself before Bart could take advantage of his misstep. "Pack? I don't have one. Never have."

"Born or bitten?" Bart's interrogation suddenly brought on feelings of unjustified guiltiness that Ben shouldn't have felt. He had done nothing wrong except live.

"Bitten."

"Where's the one who bit you?"

"He's gone."

Bart growled in frustration. "Where?"

"I don't know," Ben pleaded, knowing that being truthful would only dig a deeper grave for himself. "I think he wanted to go abroad. I last saw him in Tennessee."

"Why didn't you go with him? Did he just leave you?'

Ben remembered that night in November. Remembered the frost on the ground, the faded sounds of the bivouacked Confederates outside Knoxville, the vein of resentment toward the man who had both saved and ruined his life.

"We... We had a misunderstandin'."

Bart uttered an oath under his breath that sounded vaguely French in origin. "How long have you been alone?"

Almost afraid to answer, Ben replied, "Fifteen years."

The gun that Bart had been holding was suddenly thrust between Ben's tight shoulder blades. "Damn it, didn't either of you have any sense?"

This sudden burst of belligerence sent Ben's mind reeling. "Is that my crime? Bein' alone?"

Dustin had never mentioned any kind of moral or legal code amongst werewolves. There were guidelines, to be sure, but never anything that would warrant such hostility against him. If he had done something stupid like shift in the middle of a crowded room of humans or openly flaunt his abilities, then Ben could understand Bart's rage. But if being a lone wolf was his only crime, Ben could at least plead ignorance.

"You've had no alpha for fifteen years to keep you out of trouble. God only knows what you've done."

"I've done nothin'!" Ben asserted. "I swear, I've never – "

Bart seized his arms and twirled him around so they were facing one another. The end of the gun found its way under his jaw again and Ben had a strong feeling there was a silver bullet with his name on it if he didn't stand perfectly still and listen to what the more dominant werewolf had to say.

"Have you eaten human flesh?"

Ben's eyes widened. "Do what?"

"Human flesh," he repeated slowly. "Have you eaten any at all in the last fifteen years? Do not lie to me."

He knew well enough that even if he felt the compulsion to lie, Bart would sniff it out instantly. Thankfully, Ben didn't have to. "Never."

A pulse of enfeebling power radiated from the werewolf, greater than anything Ben had ever succumbed to. He repeated his answer to prove that even under his dominance, he couldn't lie. "I've never eaten human flesh. Ever."

His heart throbbed hard against his ribs and he could feel the wolf wringing his innards, readying his body for the change that was soon to come.

Bart eased down the hammer on the gun. In a dizzying whirl, Ben was turned around again and pushed onward. This time, the sheriff was gentler in his prodding. It was as if Ben's pleas of innocence were finally being listened to, but that didn't stay the judgement that hung over his head. Nothing he said would keep him from what awaited him that night.

"If he ain't got no warrants, then you can't arrest him like this!"

It was the same argument Henry had made to the sheriff and his deputies for the last two hours, but none of them would be moved. Neither did they give an explanation for their actions. Ben was put in the silver handcuffs and all three of them were escorted down the mountain. When they joined the rest of the posse by Maroon Creek, a fellow lawman recognized Henry from his wanted posters, and he too was clapped in irons. Sarah, though she was the only innocent one of the group, refused to leave either of them, even when the sheriff insisted that she be escorted to the nearest town.

"I'd only run away from them and come back," she promised. "I won't leave either of them."

After some time, the sheriff gave up on trying to convince Sarah to do the sensible thing and leave the matter to the men. Not only were they to punish Ben and Henry for whatever crimes they were arrested for, the posse of lawmen were keeping a close watch over Clarence's hideout on Burnt Mountain and all the trails that led to it. They planned to ambush him whenever he returned from his latest exploit. How long they would be waiting was still uncertain.

Sarah's tireless inquiries did yield some information out of the stoic, ruthless sheriff. He told the three that he had been keeping a close surveillance on Clarence, waiting for his chance to take him into custody. So far, they had little luck in either trapping the outlaw or tracking him from the mountain cave, which both frustrated and disappointed her.

She could glean some hope from the knowledge that someone did care enough about the gang to finally do something about their rampage through Colorado, but that didn't satisfy her. They could have been doing more. If they had put half as much effort into finding Clarence as they did into securing two new prisoners, they would have found him already. At least, that's what she was inclined to believe.

Now, sitting around the campfire under the watchful eyes of half a dozen men and Henry still fuming some distance behind her where he was sequestered, Sarah didn't regret her decision to follow. The two guards attending the cowboy repeated their evasive answers, saying they were only following orders or that Bart was the man in charge and knew Ben's crimes better than they did.

Not one soul would answer the most daring question of all. How does Bart know about Ben?

Her eyes continued to glance in the direction of the mining tunnel they had been taken to. The sheriff had practically dragged Ben into its dark recesses and hadn't emerged since they had breaked for camp. What were they doing down there? Was Ben free of the silver bonds? By the time they arrived to the mine, she could almost see the white bones of his wrists where the very flesh peeled off in bloody, mangled shreds around the cuffs. What pain he must have endured. But if what Henry had told her was true, he would heal from it... eventually.

Her heart bled for the werewolf and the embers of hatred toward Bart and these men grew hotter and hotter with each passing minute as twilight fell over the mountain range.

Sarah briskly rubbed at her arms to fight off the chill that came with the night. Though her mind could have been occupied with other things, such as wondering how Bart knew about Ben's weaknesses, it lingered on those moments that preceded their arrest.

She thought of Henry and his offer for her to travel with him. She thought of those shackled hands that had touched her in forbidden places. She thought of those lips which kissed and caressed the curves of her body with undeniable tenderness. What would they do now? What could she do? No longer pure, her flower given to Henry so blindly, what other option did she have?

If she and Henry parted ways, if he were to be hanged for his crimes, then she could never marry. Her husband would learn of her adulteration and she'd be shamed. Such black thoughts brought tears that choked her until she almost couldn't breathe. Henry dead? Forever considered to be contaminated? She didn't want to think of it, but she had to.

"Here, ma'am."

Sarah snapped her eyes toward the deputy and the mug he offered. Steam rolled up from the hot coffee within, promising comfort and vitality to her senses. She took it and encased her palms around the sides to benefit from its warmth. But she had no desire to drink it, not that she thought she could anyway. With how tight and constricted her throat felt, she was sure nothing would make its way down. Not easily.

So she sat with the mug between her hands, watching the entrance to the mine for any sign of Bart or Ben, and listened to Henry's tireless shouts for a straight answer.

As the sun sank lower, disappearing completely behind the hills and mountain peaks, the stars were now loosed from their daytime prison. They winked upon faces of periwinkle and dusky purple, no clouds to obstruct their view of the earth below. Sarah had always liked this time of the day, this brief span when her world was in transition. There was a sense of cleansing about it. All the day's mistakes and blunders could be erased and with the dawn came a new beginning.

But what would be waiting for them at sunrise? The trio was stuck. One way or another, someone would pay for their crimes – whether they were guilty of them or not. It all seemed like a waste of time when they could have been on Burnt Mountain, doing their part to capture Clarence.

Sarah checked Henry's guard detail and found their backs were turned to her. Then, she looked to the other men. Two were switching sentry duty, one was asleep and two more were about to settle into a game of poker. Chewing on her lower lip, she watched for the perfect moment. When it came, when everyone's attention was conveniently diverted away from her, she set her cup in the dirt and rose. Moving as swiftly as she could while making only minimal noise, she went for the mineshaft entrance.

For the first several yards into the tunnel, Sarah found herself in complete darkness. The cool, dank feel of the air made her skin crawl. With one hand on the clammy stone wall, she walked through the murky dimness. At times, she could scarcely tell if she were blinking. The bottoms of her boots scraped against the rocky floor, each step slow and cautious to make sure the ground was solid beneath her.

The way twisted to the right and left, and she could faintly tell that she was traveling deeper into the mountains at a steady decline.

Around one bend in the tunnel, the amber glow of a lantern light allayed her fears that she had gotten herself lost. Now that the path was somewhat disclosed to her, Sarah dropped her hand from the stone and hurried toward the light.

"Ben?" she called, the name echoing through the mine and ringing in her own ears.

There came a stirring up ahead and Sarah could make out something metallic along one of the walls, but it wasn't until she came closer that she realized the purpose of this portion of the mine.

"Go back!" Ben shouted in return. The stone amplified every sound and she could hear a slight hiss, like when red-hot metal was dunked into a vat of water, but not so prominent.

Sarah's hustle slowed to a walk again. The metal she saw on the walls of the tunnel were not merely reflections of moisture on the stone as she had thought. The steady glow of the lantern gleamed against the iron bars of prison cells. At least a dozen had been chiseled out of the mine and Ben was in one of them.

For fear that she'd see skeletons or other grotesque scenes within the cells, she hastened to Ben's prison. What she found both amazed and frightened her.

The walls of his prison were not only made of stone and rock, but of a precious metal that drove sensible men to madness. Silver. Loads of it. Superficial flecks and massive, glossy chunks caught the light of the lantern and made the cell come alive. It was as if she were gazing at the night sky with its brilliant array of constellations.

And in the middle of the floor, stood the captured werewolf, his bare feet planted in a glistening puddle of what she could only assume was blood. His shirt had been discarded on the floor some distance away, along with his boots, vest, bandana, and other effects. Only his trousers remained, and they were unbuttoned, hanging low on his hips.

Dumbstruck by this display, Sarah almost likened him to a god standing amid the heavens. But this god, this powerful, awe-inspiring creature in the dark didn't carry himself like the magnificent being that he was. Fear was written on Ben's perspiring face, brows pinched and eyes wide as if they had never seen another living being before. And in those eyes, she saw the wolf that Henry had spoken of. The one that kept him hostage within his own body. Their brilliance rivaled the stars, the moon, and the silver that burned his feet.

"Why did you take your boots off?" she asked, this startling detail drawing her from her wonder. The inhumanity of forcing him to endure such torment aggrieved her spirit more than she could have vocalized into any cohesive thought.

She took a step and Ben began to visibly shake. "Don't come any closer," he warned firmly, though there rang a clear note of terror in it. "You have to leave."

Sarah shook her head and tried not to let this dread infect her too. "Not until you tell me why Sheriff Croxen arrested you. No one will tell us what you did or how he knows about you."

Ben's throat worked, and a few beats of silence passed before he could answer. "He hasn't arrested me for anythin'. I've done nothin' wrong."

"Then why are you in here?" Sarah pleaded, coming up to the bars so she could test the soundness of the lock. If she could somehow break it...

Ben jumped backward and caught himself on his own injured feet. She could count on one hand the number of times she had seen the werewolf less than graceful. This wasn't like him at all.

"Please, leave me!" His growling voice was raised enough to carry down the tunnel, making the very rock beneath her tremble at the command.

"If it's some sort of misunderstanding, then I'll talk to Bart. Maybe I can – "

"No!" he barked. "Just get out of here."

Sarah's forehead puckered in irritation. "I'm tryin' to help you and all you can do is tell me to leave?"

A flash of pure rage flared in Ben's eyes. "And I'm tryin' to save your life."

"I'll keep her safe, Ben."

Sarah gasped and turned to see Bart standing not too far behind her, his thumbs hooked in his pockets as casually as if he were waiting on a train. It would have been impossible for him to come down the tunnel without making a single sound. There was only one way in or out, so he had to have been hiding in the shadows somewhere since before she arrived.

"Safe?" she questioned, hating how confused she had been for the last few days. For once, she wanted someone to start explaining things to her the way they should be. Why keep her in the dark like this with cryptic responses? "Safe from what?"

An answer did come, plain and definite.

Ben let out a long groan and she watched him nearly fall over as he became wracked by some tremendous agony. The groan was soon displaced by a wail, and then a scream. The lantern revealed all. She watched the way his bones and muscles moved beneath his skin, the wolf laboring to break free of its human cage.

Henry had told her that Ben turned into a wolfish monster once a month, but she had given little thought to the actual transformation.

It was as if Ben's body were being remolded, the man engulfed by the beast. Hands became paw-like with rough pads and long talons raking the stone beneath him. A once flat face lengthened into a muzzle, complete with gnashing jowls and fangs that glinted in the dim light. Ears elongated and folded back against his skull. A tail extended from the bottom of his spine, tangling around legs that jerked and morphed into a canine likeness. The trousers he had neglected to shed lay in tatters on the floor. Now, Sarah knew why he had taken off his boots and shirt before she showed up.

Perhaps the most startling change was how dark fur sprouted from every pour to make his form indistinguishable against the rock. Only the void of sparkling light from the silver gave some hint to his thrashing, tortured movements within the cell.

A firm hand steadied her and it wasn't until it did that she realized how close she had been to fainting. She had never fainted in her life, not even when her parents died. But this scene, that should have only existed within the realm of horror and fantasy, was unlike anything she could have imagined.

When it was all over, the thing that lay heaving and growling in the cell was not Ben. The creature was twice his size and held little resemblance to the man he had once been. The basic skeletal structure was there, and she could almost see the traces of his muscles beneath the dense pelt of midnight black, but that was all. Only his eyes remained the lustrous golden hue that he had been hiding for so long.

Those eyes, full of the feral need to destroy, fell upon Sarah. Some part of her wanted him to know her, to see that she was neither a threat nor a meal. But when he charged the iron bars, she became boneless and nearly crumbled to the floor.

Bart held her up, but didn't move her to safety. The reason lay in the fact that these were no ordinary prison bars. They, like the cell they completed, were laced with silver.

The monster roared in pain and doubled back, only to find himself trapped by the one thing that could weaken his fury. Yet again, he rammed into the bars and reached through, slashing his claws at the air between them. The pain soon became too much and he gave up, slinking deeper into his prison like the wild animal that he was.

"Those bars are fixed so deep in the mountain that he'll never break them," Bart told her, his voice calm and level. "Along with the silver, he's not going anywhere."

Sarah blinked back the frightened tears that had been unconsciously shed during the ordeal. "He kept telling me to go, because he didn't want to hurt me."

"I suppose so," Bart muttered, his eyes fixed upon the pacing werewolf. A trail of blood followed him, the pads of his hands and feet unable to protect him from the silver anymore than his fur could when he brushed against the sides of the cell. "It's not right for him to be traveling alone. He needs a pack, and I intend to put him in one."

Bewildered by this sudden turn of honesty in Bart, she regarded him with puzzlement.

He returned it with a kind smile and began to lead her away from the cell.

Henry didn't care that two shotguns were aimed at his chest. The moment he saw Sarah's pale-white face, he jumped to his feet and ran to her, handcuffs rattling all the way. He briefly saw Bart raise his hand to the guards who began shouting right before he received her. Her arms were about his waist, head buried in his chest.

Only then did she let out the tiny whimpers that were his only clue as to what might have happened inside the mine.

They all heard the screams and the beastly roars. The deputies merely paused to look toward the mine's entrance, but nothing more. No one ran to see what was happening, no one drew their weapon. It was then that Henry realized he wasn't the only one who knew what Ben was. In that same moment, however, he noticed that Sarah was not where she had been before. Only a full cup of coffee saved her place.

But no one would let him go search for her, not in the hills around their camp or into the mine where he presumed she had gone. Relief was an understatement to what he truly felt upon seeing her safe and whole.

"What happened?" he demanded of Bart.

The sheriff's eyes cut to the guards behind Henry and the slightest head movement sent them to the other side of the encampment with the others. The three were now alone near the cluster of tall aspens.

"Judging by the lack of fear in either of you on Burnt Mountain, I would assume that you know what he is?"

Henry held Sarah tighter. "I know more than she does." He jerked his head toward the group of deputies. "And I'd assume all y'all know too?"

Bart, ever the picture of seriousness and occupational devotion, gave a curt nod. "They do. I've handpicked every one of them, along with those who are still on the mountain. They are all well aware of their job and the risks involved."

Henry frowned. "This is what you do? Arrest werewolves?"

There came the slightest, almost imperceptible flinch from Sarah at the word. He slipped his hand behind her neck, letting his fingers tangle in her hair.

"Ben isn't under arrest, unlike you." The sheriff folded his arms over his broad chest. Notwithstanding his obvious age, denoted by the hints of silver in his dark hair, Bart looked as if he could hold his own fairly well. Henry might have thought he could contend with the other deputies, but not him. "Finding lone loups-garous is only part of my job. The other part involves relocating them."

Despite the dropping temperature, Henry suddenly felt a plume of heat spread across his back. His mouth hung open, unable to articulate any of the questions that had been ignited by such a simple statement.

What the hell was a loup-garou? And if Bart's job was to relocate them, did that mean there were more in Colorado? Had he brought many other werewolves here to the mines? How many had he captured in his lifetime? And where exactly would he relocate them to?

Seeing his confusion, Bart understood his need to explain.

"I call them loups-garous, but you'll know them as werewolves. Forgive me for neglecting to translate. And, contrary to what you may believe, there are quite a few in the states. Not many need relocation, as Ben does, but it's my job to find them and ensure that the human population is safe."

"Who's telling you to do it?" Sarah asked, rotating herself as much as she could within Henry's stiff embrace.

Bart softened toward the lady. "No one. I take it upon myself. I've seen the damage a lone werewolf can exact. Without alphas or proper guidance, they can be destructive and murderous. A werewolf who has killed and tasted human flesh is a danger to all society." Even in the dark, Henry could see something of regret flicker behind the sheriff's severe gaze. "Rogue werewolves kill without mercy or partiality. Men, women, children, other werewolves..." His voice trailed off and Henry knew such a look. Some memory, personal and still raw, rose up from the place he must have buried it long ago. It gave him a haunted, troubled look that seemed so contrary to everything the sheriff had shown them.

"Has Ben..." Sarah probably couldn't bring herself to say it, and Henry couldn't believe it.

The werewolf hunter straightened and seemed to push back the emotions he had failed to hide. "He claims that he hasn't, and I'm inclined to believe him. I have a way of finding a falsehood in someone, and I have no cause to doubt him."

Henry hadn't realized he was holding his breath until it came out in one bursting exhale. Sarah, too, seemed to relax and leaned her head against his shoulder.

"If he ain't doin' any harm, why relocate him? He's been fine for years."

"Just because he's been able to stay out of trouble up until this point doesn't mean that he won't find it someday. Without a pack, without an alpha, he won't last long. Even if he can avoid committing the profane, that doesn't mean he won't endanger the rest of... his kind."

Henry's brows grew together. "So, in the long run, you're tryin' to help him?" The thought had entered his mind that this man meant harm to Ben, and would possibly kill him. Knowing what werewolves were capable of, why wouldn't he?

"I've made it my mission to help him and others like him... But if they're beyond help like... Well, if they are beyond help, then they leave me no choice."

Bart wasn't the only one who could sniff out a lie when it was told to him. And Henry could tell that the sheriff wasn't necessarily lying, but he wasn't telling the whole truth either. There was something else under his words that made his stomach knot, but he couldn't quite pick out what it was. He danced around a truth and the more candid he became, the harder it was to avoid.

Sarah snapped her head around to look at Bart in alarm. "If Ben ate... if he did, then you would kill him?"

With solemn remorse, Bart nodded. "I would have. But, he didn't. So, after I've finished this business with Clarence Biller, I'll escort him to Wyoming. I know the alpha of the pack there and he's been helping to take in stray werewolves for several decades now. He'll take care of Ben and may be able to help him with his eyes."

"Decades?" Sarah breathed.

Less snagged on the immortal nature of werewolves, Henry was concerned about another thing. "Ben doesn't wanna be in a pack. He told me so. He won't go willingly."

His grim smile was not reassuring. "You've seen how persuasive silver can be. He'll go, whether he's willing or not. It's for the betterment of society that he goes and I'll take him to Wyoming by whatever means necessary."

The seemingly unrelated thought of the Ute Indians came to Henry's mind. They, too, were forced off their ancestral lands as Geoffrey had explained to them the previous day. They didn't want to leave or be under the control of the government. Their personal liberties were stolen from them, the same as Ben's freedom was being taken from him too.

If he didn't want to be part of a pack, then he shouldn't have to relocate. He should have been free to live how he wanted to live, as long as he wasn't hurting anyone. But there was some wisdom in what Bart said. Just because he hadn't committed any true sin or crime up until today – save for what needed to be done – there was no guarantee that he wouldn't do so in the future. And if an alpha could help his eyes return to normal, how bad could belonging to a pack possibly be?

CHAPTER 10

B en shivered upon the floor of his cell, balancing upon what was left of his clothes after the beast had torn the fabric to near shreds. Naked and cold, he tried not to feel the effects of the silver, not only upon his skin but on his spirit. Surrounded by the only thing that could kill him, there was little he could do. The bars were coated in the stuff and trying to grind his way through the very rock would do him no good. If anything, it would cause the tunnel to collapse and that could end his suffering.

But unlike that autumn night so long ago in Tennessee, he couldn't bring himself to end it all. Not here. Not like this. Not as a captive.

Dawn banished the monster back to its den, leaving Ben with nothing but a numbness that sank deep into his soul. The last thing he remembered was Sarah coming into the mine to find him and Bart ensuring that she would be safe. Then nothing. Total unconsciousness that he dreaded more than the shift of the beast that instigated it.

With the bars still firmly in place, he assumed that Bart had kept his word and made certain that Sarah and the others were safe from the wolf's rage and unmitigated hunger that carried into his wakeful hours as a man. But the damage was done. She had known what he was, but now she had seen him at his worst.

The echoing chambers of the mine prevented him from hearing much of the outside world. He suspected that they would ride back to Burnt Mountain, find Clarence Biller without him, and bring the outlaw to justice. As rattled as Sarah had been the previous evening, he knew that her resolve to have her vengeance wouldn't be forgotten. They would leave him here to rot or to somehow escape. What reason did they have to stay? Why try to convince Bart, a man so set in his ideology, that Ben could survive on his own?

He had been told all about the pack in Wyoming, about the alpha that would be his guardian. From what Bart had related, Joseph Lupus didn't sound like a cruel or heartless man. Nothing like the sheriff who had arrested him, but would he be a werewolf like Geoffrey? A werewolf who meant well and seemed to care for those he barely knew?

For now, Ben couldn't care about the future. Not when his carefully settled position on the strips of cloth was compromised by fatigue. If he swayed in any direction or fell onto his elbows or knees, the corrosive silver immediately woke him up. He would get no rest, and he wondered if that was why Bart had put him here in the first place. Not only did the mine keep him contained and render his senses practically useless, but with little effort at all, it could break him. Body and spirit would be exhausted by noon and Bart didn't have to lift a finger to accomplish it.

A visitor glided down the path, a small flame cutting through the darkness. The lantern on the wall had gone out hours ago. Ben didn't rise when his deaden nose identified the human. He didn't even make a move to hide his nakedness. Turned sideways to the bars, she wasn't likely to see anything, but neither was he inclined to move and risk the fragile balance between pain and relative peace.

Sarah stood in front of the bars, and he knew what she would see. Light brown hair disheveled, his back and shoulders damp with perspiration brought on by a fever that usually wracked his body after a shift, and golden eyes that would reflect back the light from her makeshift torch. What did she think of him now? She had been hesitant from the start, but he smelled no fear on her now. The girl had been through hell in the last few days and she came out even stronger for it. But how would she live her life now, knowing that creatures like him existed in her damaged and corrupt world?

She didn't shy away from his immodesty, but drew closer as if she wanted to see him more clearly. Her fingers curled around the bars and he envied her for that one simple act. There were so many things, as a human, she would never have to worry about. Silver wouldn't hurt her, she could walk through a crowd without wondering if they would turn on her at any moment, and she didn't have to live with a demon breathing inside of her.

"Are you all right?" she whispered into the silence, as if this space were something sacred or special. But this was hell, and Sarah should have known that.

Ben felt his throat go tight and for once, he knew he could answer honestly. Why should he hide now? "No. I'm not."

Sarah bowed her head and he could see the way she cringed. "I feel this is my fault."

Of all the things she could say, that wasn't what he had expected. "Ain't none of this your fault. It's just... it just happens."

"If I hadn't asked you to help me, you'd still be in Fairplay or some other town far away from here." The tightness in her voice told Ben that she was on the verge of tears and that he couldn't abide by.

"Don't go blamin' yourself for stuff. I sure as hell ain't gonna blame you for this."

Sarah lifted her eyes and he could see a single streak of moisture on her cheek. It had been a long time since anyone bothered crying for him.

"Bart says he's going to take you to Wyoming."

Ben nodded. "He told me the same."

Her hand gripped the shaft of the torch a little harder. "You don't want to go, do you?"

A wry smile found its way to his lips. "Don't matter. He's got those handcuffs. I'm goin' whether I want or not." He gave a careful shrug. "Never been to Wyoming. I suppose it's as good a place as any."

"But you shouldn't have to go if you don't want to."

"There's a lot of things we still gotta do, even if we don't wanna do them. Take me for example. I didn't want to be this. But I am, and there ain't nothin' I can do about it. Life's got a funny way of changin' on you. When you think it's over and done, somethin' else happens to stir the pot. You didn't expect your parents to be killed. You didn't expect to meet a werewolf or a man like Henry." At his words, her cheeks turned rosy, but she was too proud to show her true affections toward the cowboy in any other way. "Life dealt me a hand that won't win me a damn thing, and I've got to make the best of it."

Ben surprised himself by parroting back what Geoffrey had told him the other day. Yes, life had a funny way of changing things on a man and showing where he had been wrong.

He let his head droop between his bent knees and sighed. "Did Bart mention when y'all would be movin' out? I'm guessin' he wants to – "

The jangle of metal shortened his question and he perked up once again. In Sarah's hand was a set of keys. One for each of the cells in the mine. Her fingers weren't as nimble to single out each one and try the lock, but she made do.

When he heard the liberating click of the mechanism and the squealing of the door swinging open, Ben's jaw went slack. Words failed him as Sarah stepped aside and motioned for him to come through.

"I don't know how long it'll take for Bart to notice I took the keys. Just go. Henry's cut the straps on their saddles, so they won't follow."

Ben braved the silver that would scorch his feet and he rose to walk toward the open cell door. Sarah shyly averted her eyes, so she wouldn't see his look of complete and total gratitude.

"Thank you," was all he could say before letting his wolf's speed and the need for fresh air power him forward.

Down the twisting tunnels he ran, his bare and charred feet pounding against the rock. Sunlight shone ahead and in seconds, he was outside. The more distance he put between himself and the mine healed the wounds it had created.

He heard the shouts of the deputies, Bart's annoyed voice rising above it all and ordering them to follow. But none of them could. Henry and Sarah had done the kindest thing that any two humans could possibly do for him.

Wyoming might have been his permanent home, with a pack he didn't know and an alpha he couldn't trust. He might have been able to find a cure for his golden eyes, but to lose his freedom of choice, to know that if he went, he'd be giving up a sense of his autonomy, far outweighed anything else. He would get help, but in his own time and when he damn well pleased.

His only regret was that he wouldn't be able to help Sarah as he had planned. Not as long as Bart was with her. He sincerely hoped that she did find peace in capturing or killing Clarence, and he hoped that the sheriff wouldn't go back on the promise he had given last night. If the old werewolf was to take his place and be her aide, then he had to keep her safe. If he didn't, there wouldn't be enough silver in these mountains to keep him from seeking his own revenge, no matter the cost.

Roaring Forks Valley, Two Days Later

Ben was long gone, his scent weaving through the hills and diluted by countless passes through the rivers and streams on his way east. Bart's senses weren't as they used to be. Dulled over the years of excessive use, he assumed. If he had another loup-garou to keep an eye on the loner, he might have had a chance to catch him again.

At least he had a name and a vague idea of his destination. Even if Henry Blair would soon be locked away for his long list of felonies, he had been useful for one thing. Information. His ears might not pick up every sound as they used to, but he could hear the mumbled conversations between the cowboy and the young lady.

The lone loup-garou was certainly a wanderer. It was no doubt that he would continue doing so, or he would go to one of two places. Alabama or Georgia. The states were far out of his jurisdiction as a sheriff in Colorado, but not for a loup-garou. Ben Myers, however, wasn't a prime concern of his.

In the meantime, he still had another job to do. Clarence Biller would not be forgotten simply because a rogue had distracted him. But the two ignorant humans in his group would need to be dealt with, and there was only one place he knew of where he could safely dispose of them. With Ben gone, he needed to rejoin the rest of his men on the mountain when they faced Clarence.

They arrived at the Ute village where Geoffrey Swenson was rumored to be staying. Bart had made a point of avoiding the old werewolf, knowing they differed on too many subjects to count.

He didn't condone Bart's practices, and it was no wonder. Geoffrey had been a lone loup-garou for centuries. His entire life was spent outside the pack structure, without alpha or even a father to guide him. They constantly bickered over the morality of snatching loups-garous away to pass them off to alphas, especially in some cases when it wasn't needed. Geoffrey presented himself and his son as a perfect example of what independence could do for a loup-garou.

Bart would hear none of it. His case was isolated; an exception and not the rule. He had seen rogue loups-garous and rougarous tear apart communities and murder entire families. There was no speck of logic, whether coming from a loup-garou or a mortal man, that could convince him that the life of a loner was acceptable. Not after so many friends had been lost to a careless act of hospitality on his part. Never again would he let such a tragedy befall mankind.

The chief of the village came to greet the small force of men Bart had brought with him. It took that many to detain Sarah. The willful girl, the one to blame for Ben's flight, persisted that she should accompany his deputies to the mountain to catch Clarence. Bart didn't care if the outlaw had murdered her entire family. She hadn't the faintest idea of whom she had been hunting for the last two months. This job was best left to a loup-garou. Better that one of Clarence's own kind take him down than risk the lives of anymore humans.

The sheriff and native greeted one another in the placid way they always had. They had a passable understanding of what one expected from the other. Bart sometimes needed supplies while out in these uncharted regions, and the chief was granted an advocate when it came to matters of the reservation. These kinds of agreements kept Bart in business and on happy terms with everyone in Colorado, along with the rest of the unruly western territories.

"Where's Geoffrey?" Bart asked in the Ute language, glad that he could still remember how the dialect was supposed to sound when rolling off his tongue.

"He has gone to another village. He will return in four days."

Bart suppressed the growl of impatience. "Is there a translator?"

The chief nodded. "My wife knows the white man words. She can translate."

Bart then took the time to explain that he had two prisoners that needed safe guarding until he returned with the outlaw he was searching for. When the chief looked to see Henry and Sarah, his dark eyes brightened, the wrinkles upon his face deepening with a grin.

"I know these two. They will be looked after."

Bart gave a nod of thanks. "See that they don't run off. I don't want them getting in the way. I'm leaving two of my deputies here as well."

The chief, again, agreed and called over his shoulder for someone to come and attend to their new guests. Exactly how the Ute elder knew of them, Bart didn't know and neither did he have the time to ask. For all he knew, Clarence could have come back to his hideout and his men weren't prepared for what would ensue.

Six human men against four loups-garous was no fight at all.

Outside Leadville

The edges of the cards slid over his fingers as Ben shuffled the deck again and again. The gentle slapping and gliding of the stiff, worn paper drowned out all the other noises in the saloon. Just a few games and he'd have enough to make it to Alabama. The stagecoach and train were out of the question, and he could get what food he needed through hunting, but the call of a warm and comfortable bed couldn't be ignored for much longer.

He guessed it would take a few days, maybe a week at the most, to find Devia.

The minor seize of anxiety pierced through the myriad of stifling emotions. Finding Devia meant finding a pack, finding a home, finding a way to get his old eyes back. He trusted what might have awaited him in Devia more than what Bart had in store for him in Wyoming.

This radical, life-altering decision was not reached lightly, and resulted in the culmination of deep thinking for three days. In those three days since he'd left Henry and Sarah in the mountains, Ben understood what he felt. Hollow. Empty. Missing something that he didn't realize he would miss so much.

Being with Henry and Sarah, even for those few days, had restored a piece of himself that he didn't know he had lost sixteen years ago. There was a certain feeling of affinity with the two humans, inexplicable and somewhat unnatural when he thought about it. They should have been nothing to him, but they had become almost everything. He was willing to kill for Sarah, risked his secret for

Henry when the cowboy's misdemeanors finally caught up with him. Even the wolf, who hated the company of other humans and werewolves alike, grieved for their absence.

Ben had found a pack. A small, odd, and eclectic sort of pack, but a pack nonetheless. Not an hour went by that he didn't feel the urge to turn and run back to the mountains. But he knew that would only bring more troubles on himself. He had to trust that Bart, though he was a twisted and arrogant werewolf, would see to their safety. Henry's resourceful mind would find a way out of going to jail and Sarah would finally have her retribution.

Then what was left for Ben? Alone and now discontent with living that way, he decided to give into his baser instincts. He would find his pack and succumb to an alpha's guidance. Devia seemed the best place to start a new life.

But first, he had to find someone who was willing to lose a few rounds of poker to help him get there. If only his eyes weren't warding away potential players.

Ben sat alone, shuffling and reshuffling the cards with a half-full tumbler of whiskey on the table beside him. The evening would bring more gamblers into the saloon, even this far outside of Leadville, but he didn't count on the house being this empty. Including the bartender behind the counter and only two soiled doves to drive business, there was a staggering total of seven people present. And none of them wanted to get anywhere near the man with the eyes lighter than the amber liquor he drank.

Sitting in the shadows, a new stolen hat pulled low over his brows, his eyes were still a hurdle he'd have to face daily until he could find a pair of tinted spectacles to hide behind. Acquiring a pair would be a double-edged sword. Only bigger cities would have a general store stocked with the luxury item, but bigger cities would mean more people. More humans. The very thought made Ben squirm uncomfortably in his rickety chair.

Something even more disturbing took the place of his nervousness. Ben thought he had felt his scalp crawl for the last time when he left Bart in the mountains. So, when it accompanied a new set of loud, thudding footsteps on the boardwalk outside the saloon, he froze and waited to identify him.

Was it Bart or Geoffrey? Though the scent was familiar, he couldn't place a face to it.

The saloon door opened. With the new customer came the earthy smells of grass, mountain air, and the smallest tinge of blood to give Ben the right nudge his memory needed. Dressed in dusty, trail-worn clothes, he had a fairly good idea of exactly how far this man had traveled.

Unafraid of the consequences, Ben looked up and locked eyes with the werewolf. Short black hair was combed back by sweat and dirt, a signature look of a man who spent his life in the wilderness. Eyes like gray storm clouds stared at him beneath dark, thick brows. A cunning smile both softened and denigrated his strong features. The sensation in his skull transferred down his spine at the mere sight of it. His wolf snared and snapped at the stranger, hating everything about him before he even spoke.

And most unfortunately, Ben would have to suffer through a conversation. It was an inevitable thing, since they were the only two werewolves in the saloon.

He wasn't the only one to notice the shift in the air. The gamblers on the far side of the room turned to watch the werewolf stride toward Ben's table. The two girls who had been gossiping up to this point, immediately took refuge in the backroom while the bartender casually edged closer to the hiding shotgun under the counter.

Ben took the deck of cards in his hands and bent the stack. If only he had enough dominance to make this stranger keep his distance.

The man he suspected to be Clarence Biller, whose scent he recognized from the abandoned camp on Burnt Mountain, sat down heavily in the chair across from Ben. How Ben wished he had a gun, so he could have shot that smug look off his face.

"Nice eyes," Clarence drawled out, deep and sarcastic. The sickening comparison to Henry's voice came to mind, but there was a distinct accent difference that he picked up instantly. The outlaw wasn't from Kansas or Colorado. It rang of the south, of the Confederacy, of home.

A muscle tightened in Ben's jaw and he wouldn't honor the quip with a response.

In a move he didn't expect, Clarence pulled out both of his guns and placed them on the table as a show of forfeit. He made a demonstration of opening his coat to show there were no hidden knives or weapons and then eased back in his chair.

"Satisfied? Ya can stop shakin' like a pup now. I ain't gonna do nothin' to ya."

"I ain't afraid of you," Ben grumbled. More or less to prove his point, he set the deck of cards back down on the table and took a swig of the whiskey. His hand was steady, calm, and didn't so much as slosh the liquor. The alcohol did nothing for him, but the biting feel of it flowing down his throat was a decent distraction.

"Sure ya are," Clarence said with a light chuckle. "Everyone's afraid of me. At least, a little. Ya probably know what I'm talkin' about. That little peppery smell whenever ya walk in a room. It ain't someone's cookin', ya know. It's because of us."

Ben sneered. "I know what fear smells like and I know why I smell it. Don't talk down to me like I was born yesterday."

Clarence grinned and jerked his chin. "How old? I'm curious."

"I don't see how it's any of your business, but I'm thirty-eight."

Brows crinkled together. "Only thirty-eight? Shit, ya are a pup."

Ben set the glass tumbler back onto the table, but only so he wouldn't break it in his tightening grip by accident. "You don't look much older than me."

"I'm about a hundred and twenty. Give or take a few years."

"Keep your voice down," Ben hissed, his glance shifting toward the gamblers who passed their own veiled looks to him in return. There were few other noises to drown out their conversation and Clarence, as much as he hated the man already, was acting careless.

"What? Ya afraid one of them's gonna go runnin' to the sheriff and run his mouth about werewolves?" Clarence rolled his eyes and reached for Ben's whiskey. "He'll get thrown in an asylum before we'd ever get arrested."

Ben watched him down the last of the glass and though the alcohol was useless against his nerves, it had been for him alone. "You gonna pay for that?"

Clarence gave him a hard look. "Ya gonna douse that gold?"

He didn't have the patience to explain it all to another werewolf. First Geoffrey, then Bart, and now he'd have to tell Clarence about his one flaw. To the former two, he could suffer the humiliation. But with the latter, he couldn't demean himself in front of the outlaw.

Ben took to shuffling the deck again and dealt them each a hand of five cards. "What're you doin' in Leadville?" he asked, redirecting the subject. "Plannin' on robbin' a bank? Holdin' up a stage? Murderin' a family?"

Blue eyes darted to the bartender and Ben saw that confidence falter.

"Just passin' through," he replied as he took up the cards to examine them. "What about you?"

Ben didn't bother looking. "Same." Some silence passed as he studied Clarence's cool and composed expression. His poker face was too good. "Your gang out somewhere?"

Clarence eyed him for a moment, and then whether out of blind faith or a nearly unjustified feeling of kinship with the werewolf he just met, he said, "They are. Two are in town gettin' supplies and the other's out watchin' the roads. Don't want no lawman gettin' some harebrained ideas."

"You've been able to avoid them for a while now."

He shrugged. "It ain't hard to outrun them when ya ain't gotta worry about horses. And some of these bastards are too damn scared to go runnin' up the mountains or into Indian territory. Makes it easy for fellas like us to disappear."

So, that's how he did it. He and his gang literally ran away from the crime scenes. As werewolves on foot, they could outpace just about anything, including lawmen who were trying to hunt them down. As Clarence said, they could disappear without a trace. It would take another werewolf like Bart to track him down.

"I heard you got someone on your tail. A sheriff by the name of – "

"Bart Croxen," Clarence sighed. "I know. He's been followin' me for months, but I think we've got him where we want him. He won't be botherin' us for long."

Ben's fingers squeezed over the cards that he still hadn't looked at. "What're you gonna do?"

The outlaw smiled again and he didn't have to say a word for Ben to gather that it wasn't anything good. "Let's just say, that old dog's gonna meet his end real soon. From what I heard, his days are numbered anyway. No sense in prolongin' his sufferin'."

Resigned to accepting the ambiguous reply, Ben finally looked to his cards. He held only one pair of jacks, a queen, a nine and an ace. Not a strong hand, but he didn't need anything better to win. He only needed a straight face and a calm heartbeat. This opponent wouldn't be fooled like other humans who couldn't pick up on subtle twitches or smell the sweat on nervous palms.

"Ran into someone else lookin' for you that might be a tougher match for you than Bart."

At this, Clarence lifted his head and seemed to get serious for the first time since he'd walked in. "Who?"

"A lady by the name of Sarah McDaniel." Ben switched two of his cards around to make Clarence think he was arranging them in a particular order. "You did away with her parents a couple of months back. A little farm near Trinidad. Ring any bells?"

The son of a bitch leaned back in his chair and seemed to think hard about it, stoking Ben's righteous anger even further.

"McDaniel... McDaniel... Yeah, I reckon I knew a man by that name. And we were in Trinidad around that time." Clarence snapped his fingers and slammed his hand on the table when the memory finally surfaced. How inconvenient it must have been to have killed so many people that he couldn't tell one from the other. "I remember! That little wench was hidin' in the barn. We left her alone. Didn't see any point in killin' her anyway. It was her pa we were after."

Ben's golden eyes became slits and he laid his cards faced-down upon the table before he could tear them in his rage. "Dare I ask what you were after him for?"

Something in his behavior must have amused Clarence, because the smirk returned to his lips as he collapsed his cards together into one neat stack. "The man saw too much. We robbed a bank in Pueblo about a week before and he saw one of my pack get a little too excited, ya know. Fangs, claws, the works. We didn't much care that he saw the robbery, and we didn't mind about him knowin' what we were. That was until we found out who his family was."

Clarence leaned down and kicked an adjacent chair enough so he could prop his feet up in the seat before continuing. "Turns out the McDaniel family tree's got a few monster hunters in it. What luck, right? One night, the ass had the gall to ambush us with silver bullets. Nearly killed one of my pack. I couldn't abide by that. So, we tracked him down to his homestead. We only planned on killin' him, but his wife got in the way. Apparently, she knew enough to be a nuisance. She was gonna shoot us, but we got her first. Figured we'd leave the girl alone, because that barn reeked of fear. There was no way she was gonna come after us... Guess we should've. I still think Bart's a bigger threat than some girl."

Now, more than ever, Ben had to hold his poker face and stay indecipherable. If Clarence caught on to how he truly felt, sensed any of the fury that almost spiraled out of control within him, then Ben would lose the high ground. And as it was, he had to maintain the field or his enemy would know his true weakness.

"Bart's been takin' our kind and killin' them left and right." Clarence's casual admittance drew Ben out of his anger and into a state of shock. "I heard he started in New Orleans. One of his friends got knocked off by a wolf who wasn't all there." He tapped a fingertip on his temples to make his point. "Ever since, he's been on this rampage to kill any lone wolf he finds. No one's safe anymore and everyone's guilty in his thinkin'. We're gonna put a stop to it." Clarence leaned in. "Ya mighta heard a load of stuff about me and my gang, but somethin' ya better get straight is that we never kill without a reason. Bart don't need a reason, and that ain't right."

And just like that, Ben knew Clarence was full of shit. Even if Bart was stealing away werewolves and killing them in cold blood, the outlaw in front of him was no less guilty. From his time in the war, he understood what murder was. The battle at Antietam was murder. So was Manassas and Malvern Hill. He saw brothers shoot and kill one another over a differing of politics and ethics.

Clarence, like the Yankees and Confederates, believed he was in the right to take another human life, but he was so utterly wrong.

Ben, although he was no angel himself and a hypocrite in this matter, at least understood that he had committed a sin when he slaughtered the bandits to save Sarah. But he couldn't lump himself in with Clarence or Bart. It didn't seem the same. They reveled in what they had done, bragged about it, flaunted it. They continued to wallow in the mud of iniquity and say they were clean of all wickedness.

Something of a plan began to form and Ben took up his cards again. If he could get inside Clarence's gang somehow, then he could at least save Sarah and Henry from being blown away by the outlaws. To hell with Bart and his pseudo-vigilante mission to round up all the lone werewolves in the western territories.

As heartless as it might have been, Ben didn't rightly care if Clarence killed the old werewolf. After the night of complete hell he had spent in the silver mines, robbed of his freedom at the hands of someone who should have helped him, Ben was ready to taste of bit of revenge for himself. Then, he could deal with Clarence and his gang. As he had assessed before, it would take a werewolf to bring one down, and Ben was prepared to do whatever was necessary to finish the job that Sarah's father had started.

But how much did Clarence trust him? He had been fairly candid so far. How much more would Ben have to prove himself to be admitted into his first pack?

"You need an extra hand with the job?"

The question both puzzled and surprised Clarence. "Ya got somethin' against Bart?"

Ben let out a long breath and played the part of a man with a wounded pride. "Let's just say I've got a bone to pick with him and if you're goin' after him, I want a piece of the action."

Maybe that had been the outlaw's hope from the beginning, because that faint smile widened into a pearly-white grin of delight. "Could always use an extra set of claws."

CHAPTER 11

Sarah's movements were slow as she packed the saddlebags with what little worldly things she possessed. The leather creaked less and the buckles didn't jingle when she handled them with ease and care. She couldn't risk waking Henry.

The two deputies Bart had left in the Ute village still sat outside Geoffrey's teepee, but in the early hours before dawn, she could hear them snoring at their posts. Henry, while still bound in the handcuffs he had been judiciously given days ago, was the only one who could stop her now.

She remembered the way to Burnt Mountain and could vaguely recall the path she would need to take to get to Clarence's hideout. She had plenty of provisions and it wasn't as if she had never traveled alone. After going from town to town for two months by herself, she'd never be afraid of solitude again. Not in that way.

Gingerly shouldering her bag, Sarah glanced back to Henry. The steady rise and fall of his broad chest told her that he was still deep asleep. If luck was on her side, she'd be halfway down Maroon Creek by the time anyone knew she was gone.

Sarah had come to a crucial realization. She could no longer wait on the men to do this. She couldn't wait on Bart to bring Clarence back from the mountains, she couldn't wait on Geoffrey to come back from visiting another village, and she wouldn't wait for Ben to return to them. The only man she could count on was in chains and bound for jail as soon as the sheriff returned. If she didn't go to the hideout herself and personally take matters into her own hands, she'd regret it forever. To hell with safety and whatever was the smart thing to do. Her soul needed this vengeance, almost more than she needed Henry.

She lifted the flap over the entrance to the teepee, allowing a column of gray light to brighten her escape.

"Where're you goin'?"

Sarah cringed and turned to see Henry staring at her, his captivating eyes freezing her in place. The two guards also heard him, and they picked up their guns again, giving her further motivation to stay in the teepee.

With a sigh, she dropped the flap, but wouldn't return to the bedroll. "I can't stay here and wait anymore," she whispered apologetically. "This was supposed to be my chance to avenge my family and everyone's trying to ruin it for me. All I wanted was to know where Clarence was. I never asked for so many people to be involved."

Henry sat up, the chains of his cuffs knocking as he did. "You may not have asked, but you still needed the help. Do you really think you can take on Clarence alone?"

"It's not your fight," she spat. "It's not Ben's or Bart's either. It's mine. It was my family that he killed and it should be my finger that pulls the trigger."

One of Henry's brows shot up. "What happened to turning him into the authorities?"

Sarah tucked her chin to her chest, wishing she had the words to explain how she had lost all her faith in the law. When she needed help the most, it wasn't a marshal or sheriff that came to her assistance, but an outlaw cowboy and a werewolf. Now, she was being held back by the law that was supposed to be on her side.

How many criminals had slipped through the fingers of justice and continued to roam free? How many more murderers and thieves walked the streets? If it weren't for people like her who were fully ready to eliminate these threats. If there were no vigilante forces in this world, it'd be a dark and terrifying place, more so than it was now.

"I've been coming out of my skin these last few days, Henry. I can't just sit here and do nothing." Sarah hadn't realized until now that her whole body shook with the rage she had been trying to contain since they were first led away from Burnt Mountain. "I was so close. So close to having him and now Bart's up there, probably planning to arrest him. I doubt he'll even come back to this village if he catches Clarence. I have to go. And seeing as you can't exactly go with me, I'll go alone."

"Like hell you are," he mumbled. Now, he was on his feet... and the handcuffs were left on the bedroll.

Too stunned by this, Sarah barely had the frame of mind to fight Henry as he scooped her into his arms and carried her to the opposite side of the teepee. Now, away from the door and the saddlebags tossed aside, he sat on her outstretched legs, trapping her against the ground.

Sarah babbled and pointed to the unfastened handcuffs, but Henry wasn't ready to explain himself.

"I made a promise to Ben that I'd keep you safe. I heard Bart made the same promise, too. And right now, the safest place for you is right here in this tent. I ain't about to let you walk out of this village and go traipsin' through the mountains. I believe you could kill Clarence with your bare hands if you wanted to, but havin' backup is a smart idea. I want to be that backup for you. I know how you feel. I want to kill Clarence almost as bad as you do, but now ain't the right time to leave." He thumbed toward the door and lowered his voice to a whisper. "Them deputies ain't gonna let us out of here... But I've got a plan."

Sarah shot him an unimpressed look. "Obviously, you have a plan. You've been out of those handcuffs for God only knows how long, without telling me."

Henry smirked. "I didn't think you'd be this eager to leave, so I was bidin' my time."

Sarah tried to push him off her legs, but he might as well have been like a thousand-pound log across her thighs. "Well, I am. When do we leave?"

He leaned forward, nearing dangerously close to her face until she lowered herself backward onto her elbows. In turn, he supported his weight upon his hands that were planted on either side of her. His masculine scent tempted her to forget everything, but thankfully her restlessness didn't concede to him.

"There's a little matter we never settled when we were up on Burnt Mountain."

A tingling spiraled through her chest. She knew what matter he spoke of. "What's going to happen afterward?"

Henry slowly nodded, his eyes roaming over her face as if it were the most fascinating thing on God's green earth. He didn't speak again, and she understood why. Everything that Henry wanted to say about it had been said. The offer to travel together had been put on the table. They could go anywhere they wanted. With no land, no home, no families, they could make their own in time.

But was that what Sarah wanted? She knew nothing of the world outside her farm before the tragedy that took it all away from her. She knew how to farm, milk cows, and take care of a home. But on the dusty trails, on the lush mountains, and across the desert plains, could she find that same fulfillment? Could she be content without four walls and a roof over her head?

Living the life of a nomad, Henry's life, wasn't the future she had imagined for herself. Then again, there was little time to think of those things before. Could Henry make such a living worthwhile for her?

Sarah nibbled on her chapped bottom lip, wishing she had more room to breathe or that her throat wouldn't feel so tight. It shouldn't have been hard. Her choices were clear. Live a life with or without Henry.

"Where would we go?" she asked breathlessly.

Henry, understanding her answer, grinned and bent his head down to kiss her. "Anywhere you want, darlin'. California, New York, Mexico, Canada. Doesn't matter."

Darling. Sarah liked the endearment coming from his lips, though she had thought it almost condescending from everyone else. Her smile didn't last long when a more pressing issue resurfaced. One more important than travel destinations.

"So, what's this escape plan? How do we get the deputies to leave their post?"

Henry's eyes flashed with a mischievous glint, a familiar sight she was growing fond of.

"Let's say I managed to talk to one of the Indian warriors and he's gonna have a talk with their medicine man. By noon, the deputies' breakfast will be givin' them a mighty hard time. When they're away, we'll run. Together."

That last word was spoken so firmly that Sarah was almost persuaded to obey it. Henry made it clear that he wanted her, and though she was ready to run off and leave him in the village, she wanted him too. She would have returned after it was done, but Henry was right. Backup was a smart idea.

Part of Ben had thought that teaming with four other werewolves would at least partially fill the void that his separation from Henry and Sarah had created. But as dawn broke the morning after meeting them, the chill in his bones couldn't be shaken. Being around Clarence and his three associates might as well have been like trying to bond with vultures or baboons. They thought of little outside their own misdeeds, whether past or future, and much of their conversations revolved around death and the inferiority of the human race.

Ben listened, trying to find something in their talks that he could relate to on a deeper level. The only commonality between them all was the fact that they served in the war against northern aggression. However, they served on opposite fronts of the doomed, fledgling Confederacy. Their most cherished memory from those four years was when they rode with Quantrill into Lawrence, Kansas, and slaughtered almost every man in the town.

It was then he realized he could never feel an empathy with these men. They used the war as an excuse to kill Yankees, not to defend their homes and families.

The gang was ready to go, but waited on Clarence to return from his scouting mission to the north. No fire had been made the night before, they carried no bedrolls, and everything they owned, they carried in their pockets or in their coats. On their way to the hideout to confront Bart, they had stopped for the night along the slope of Mount Shimer. By that afternoon, they would face off against the sheriff and Ben could put his plan into play. How he'd dispatch the more experienced killers in the gang, he wasn't completely sure.

"Who'd ya serve under, Ben?" Lewis O'Connor asked during a lull. "Ya said ya fought, right?"

The biggest and strongest of the three brothers stood tall above the rest, his arms as thick as Ben's thigh and nearly bulging out of his cotton shirt. His heavy, dark brows gave him a brutish look, but he questioned the intelligence behind his ever-squinting eyes.

"I was under Anderson in the Army of Northern Virginia," Ben replied as he continued to twist on the bit of wild grass he had pulled in front of his crossed legs.

"Which one?" Lewis asked with a mocking laugh.

Ben couldn't help but crack a smile as the others joined in. Even he had a hard time keeping up with the names of their commanders. At Sharpsburg alone, there had been at least two other Confederate, high-ranking officers under the name "Anderson".

"Was you at Gettysburg?" Silas, the youngest, busied himself in this downtime by sharpening his dagger. The long blade tapered to a point, double-edged and well cared for. Ben had seen many of its kind in these parts and saw plenty of these knives during the war.

The younger of the brothers, with fair hair and lean build, had faced the constant torment and jeering from his two elder brothers. Most of the teasing was harmless, but when Lewis shoved Silas off the side of a mountain, Ben understood the full extent of what a werewolf could endure, and how thoughtless family could be to one another. Childhood memories of his brother, their pranks and games, came back to haunt him. He couldn't help but wonder what their relationship would have been like if the war had never been fought, if their failed country had never called them into the service that ended their futures.

"No, I wasn't," was all Ben would say on that score.

If he told them the truth, he'd have to confess that he was a deserter. After being bitten, his career as a soldier was effectively over after only serving for a little over a year. Something told him that if he mentioned this fact to the others, they would gut him where he sat. Southern sentiments ran strong, even so long after the war was over. Traitors, Yankees, carpetbaggers, and deserters were hated with senseless passion. And though he didn't much care about how he looked in the eyes of the O'Connor brothers, he did care about keeping his head attached to his neck.

Theo, the eldest of the brothers, chimed in with a story about one soldier he knew that did fight at Gettysburg, and was captured by the Yankee army directly after Longstreet's advance on the third day. He painted a scene of utter loss, brave efforts, and utter stupidity on the part of the generals for letting so many divisions march across a mile of open land and straight into the Federal cannons.

Even though Theo had proven himself to be, quite possibly, the smartest of all the werewolves present on the side of Mount Shimer, he also gave evidence to his ruthlessness as well. If one of his brothers questioned Clarence's direction, he was the first to step in with a growling reprimand that preceded a physical lashing. Blue eyes would turn gold in the wake of his flaming temper and dark hair almost rose up on his scalp in every admonishment.

Such forcefulness seemed pointless to Ben's eyes, and he speculated upon the nature of what it meant to be in a pack of werewolves. Would they be this hardhearted? Would the alpha or beta rule like tyrants or could such a dynamic even be called a "family" as Ben had hoped. He wanted to make exceptions and say that these men were not like other werewolves, but his experience had been so limited that he wasn't sure if Devia was the right place for him anymore.

Ben listened, but all this talk of the war brought back memories he wished would stay buried in the past. His brother had been killed on the very battlefield Theo depicted, and his father was killed not long after in some other battle in the north. He didn't want to think of them or the bones that would never be laid to rest in Georgia. Or his mother, who still waited for them to come home.

"You all right?" Silas asked, pausing in the sharpening of his blade.

Suddenly, all eyes turned to Ben and he didn't quite know how to answer. How long had he gone on his mental journey to Georgia and Virginia? How much time had passed while he sat in a waking dream?

"Ya ain't got that soldier's heart thing, do ya?" Lewis followed.

The term wasn't lost on Ben and he shook his head. Though he was as much of a veteran as they were, and probably saw worse of the war than they did, Ben would never admit to succumbing to such a disability. His mind wandered, it was true, but he never relived his battles or flew out in a nasty rage at sudden noises. Those men with a soldier's heart didn't last long after the final surrender. They couldn't cope with a world that wasn't at war, but Ben could.

"Sure looked like you was goin' someplace in your head, though," Silas said.

Theo angled himself to Ben. "Is that why you don't carry a gun? I knew an old soldier who killed his wife, thinking she was a Yankee officer that broke into his house. He was hung, of course, but they said he had a soldier's heart. It's sheer weakness, if you ask me."

Ben let out a sigh, knowing what would come next. The two other brothers then thought it necessary to build upon Theo's passing statement. Once more, they told story after story about the humans they encountered that weren't fit to breathe. In every way, they truly thought werewolves were the superior race. They were faster, stronger, lived longer, impervious to disease, and healed rapidly. The best of human and animal reigned within their bodies, and they would be the masters of the world, with alphas prevailing over all of the country with humans as their slaves.

He had never heard so much bullshit in his life. Suddenly, the gore and tragedy of the past seemed like a preferable place to meander.

"Well, you can take my knife, iffen you want it, Ben." Silas flipped the dagger until he held it by the point and offered the handle to the newest member of their gang.

If he knew what kind of disdain Ben held for the werewolf, the young outlaw wouldn't be handing him a weapon.

"Ya won't need the knife."

Clarence's voice broke through the bushes around the encampment, announcing his return.

"Why's that?" Lewis questioned, sliding the last bullet into his pistol to make it fully loaded.

The outlaw appeared, eyes made golden by some unknown thrill. Ben loathed the sight of them, knowing that whatever the leader of the gang announced wouldn't be good news to him.

"We're going in shifted."

Silas, ever the eager pup, leapt up and gave an elated holler before beginning the task of undressing. Likewise, Theo and Lewis stood to join him, but waited for their alpha to continue.

"People are just startin' to wake up in the village. When we get there, stick to the plan."

A heaviness settled in Ben's stomach at Clarence's words. The nearest village belonged to the Utes. As the other three stripped down to their skin, he remained seated with his poker mask firmly bolted into place.

"Come on," Silas encouraged, a wicked and excited grin plastered on his face.

Clarence came to Ben's side and nudged the tip of his boot against his hip. "Get up and shift. We don't have all day. The men will be goin' off to hunt before noon and we'll miss our chance."

"To do what?" Ben asked, half disgusted and half horrified. "The Ute's ain't done nothin'. They aren't even workin' with Bart. What do they have to do with anythin'?"

"Nothin'," Lewis replied, neatly folding his shirt. "But it'll draw Bart out of the hills."

Theo gathered up his younger brother's clothes and dagger to put with his own under a sheltering bush. "When he hears the screams of the women and children, he'll come running back from the mountains."

"We're goin' in to kill the women and children and turn the men."

Ben became incensed and stood to stand toe-to-toe with the infamous outlaw. "It's senseless. Let's just go to Burnt Mountain and face him there. Why draw him out with a massacre?"

Theo, hearing this, began to bristle toward Ben, but whatever rebuke would have come was stayed by Clarence's hand.

"You're new to this, so let me explain somethin' to ya." Clarence's voice took on a growling and menacing tone that made Ben instantly pay close attention. "This isn't only about killin' Bart. There's a higher purpose here and I ain't gonna pass it up. We gotta make our mark. No more hidin'. Killin' these savages will make the humans fear us. It's about time they started believin' in monsters again. Once Bart's out of the way, there won't be a single werewolf to stop us from movin' onto Leadville, to Denver... Maybe even Washington."

Ben no longer had the will to argue. It all made sense now. All four of them were insane with bloodlust. Clarence and the three brothers weren't only interested in killing Bart. They wanted to create a panic in Colorado, in the whole United States. Four werewolves could easily clear out an Indian village, but once they strengthened their numbers with unwilling converts, they could rally a force together that could wipe an entire city off the map.

The Utes, like all other Indians, had every reason to see the white man purged from their lands. With only bows and few firearms, they were no match for the military forces that could sweep in and quell an uprising. As werewolves, they would finally have the means to fight back and win. Beside Clarence, they could take back their land, and the outlaw would be able to start his empire as the ruling alpha.

It was a future he couldn't live in. If such a movement reached the south, he knew Devia would step up to stop him. Another war would ensue, one that he would not take part in.

He had to stop it before it began.

The gang looked to him, expecting him to drop whatever reservations he had about the plan and shift with them. But he couldn't.

"I... I never learned how to shift at will."

While Lewis thought he was joking and laughed at his expense, Silas seemed horrified, if not a little disappointed. It had been clear from the moment Ben first treated the younger werewolf with some level of respect, that Silas took to him more than anyone else. It had barely been a day, but Ben had been hoisted onto a pedestal.

Theo might have been the only one to show him some pity, and Clarence was simply annoyed and turned away to allow the eldest O'Connor to teach him. Ben, however, didn't want to learn. Not unless he could fully control himself as a beast.

Roaring Fork Valley

Sarah pressed herself against Henry's side, leaning to peek out the cracked tent opening with him. How he would have loved to take her in his arms and stay right there for days, marinating in each other until they were both dizzy and exhausted. But if she wanted to leave now, then he'd rush his plans and whisk her away from this place.

That fire he had seen deep within her, past the fear for her future, beneath the stonewalls she had built to keep herself standing day in and day out, had strengthened into a roaring flame that eradicated everything that threatened to bank it. And he wanted to play with it, tease it, feed it. If risking their lives to kill Clarence would keep his woman alive, he was ready to give it to her.

He watched the two deputies, the seconds ticking away like hours. Their empty breakfast plates sat near the ashen campfire outside their tent. Women filed past, carrying their empty jugs of water propped against their hips and stomachs. Very soon, the two men would be rushing by to relieve themselves of the tampered meal. If the Utes were good for anything, it was coming up with some way to torment the white folk.

The moment finally came. The deputy on the right coughed, pressed a hand to his chest and then mumbled some apology to his partner. He stood up and vanished through the maze of teepees. The lone sentinel, at first bewildered, came to sympathize and he too, rose up to abandon his post.

"Let's go," Sarah whispered and attempted to push him aside.

His hold on the back of her vest kept her in place. "Just a minute, wildcat."

Once he heard the retching of the two deputies, he gave her the nod of approval. They both burst from the teepee and rushed to the horse corral with their saddlebags, but not before Henry collected his effects that were also being closely guarded by the campfire.

Henry vaulted over the rail fence and slapped the rumps of the horses that got in the way of the beeline he tried to make for Buck and Jemimah. They were the only two horses with bridles in the corral, making them easy to find. Sarah waited outside the gate, but when he came close, he realized a little too late that Jemimah wasn't herself.

The mare pulled and resisted his lead. Buck, too, began to toss his head and snort loudly in protest. Henry, knowing that little could spook his horse, stopped dead and waited for them to behave. It didn't happen. Instead, the remainder of the herd within the corral became restless. For a moment, he doubted how safe he could be amongst the stamping hooves and agitated horses.

When he looked for the source, thinking that perhaps a rattlesnake had slithered its way into the pen, his eye caught on something near the southern horizon. Over the crest of a ridge, four black and brown figures prowled through the tall grasses.

Henry froze and distrusted his own eyes. He blinked several times, thinking he could will away the sight, but the beasts were still there with tall ears pricked forward and snarling muzzles pointed toward the village. Seeing his distress, Sarah looked in the same direction. Her body swayed until she propped herself on one of the posts of the corral.

"Is that..." Horror stole her voice, reducing it to a whisper.

Henry nodded. "I think so."

Who the hell were these werewolves? Where did they come from? Why were they even here, of all places? And more importantly, what did they want?

Ben wasn't amongst them. Buck knew the werewolf enough that the horse wouldn't react this way if he were on the same ridge. These four werewolves – and he knew beyond a doubt what they were – eyed the Ute village like a predator would size up a flock of sheep.

His bullets weren't silver, and he had nothing of the metal anywhere on him. He was also sure that no one in the village would be prepared for this sort of invasion. Fleeing on horseback was their only way to escape the monsters, but he recalled how Ben could easily outrun anything with four legs. It might have been useless, but it was better than staying still and waiting.

Henry tugged harder on the reins of the two horses and managed to make them move closer to the gate, but Sarah wasn't there. Her saddlebags lay on the ground and he saw a bit of her golden hair bobbing against her shoulders as she ran toward the river, toward where the women and young girls were drawing water.

Risking exposure, he called after her and left the horses. He drew his gun from the holster, knowing it was little more than a toy against the werewolves anyway. Nothing would stop them and there was no time to warn anyone. Maybe she had forgotten how fast a werewolf could run.

By the time he reached the edge of the village where he'd have to cross to chase after Sarah, he heard it begin. The sound of ripping tent walls, growls and battle cries mingled in a horrific cacophony unlike anything he had ever heard. The screams of the women let him know that the monsters had reached the river already.

He might have been too late, but Henry pushed himself further, dodging past toppling teepees and Ute warriors who rallied toward the one-sided fight with spears and their quivers. A flash of something massive and brown crossed his vision and he momentarily slid to a stop. He fired toward the fleeing beast, but knew he had hit nothing. They were moving too fast, tearing through everything until the village was razed to the ground.

Once he realized he had gone unnoticed, Henry bolted forward again. He broke through the edge of the mayhem into the open space near the river. Sarah was there, along with the other women of the village and their children, broken pottery scattered through the grass and facing a black werewolf. The beast was crouched on all fours, tail swinging side to side and ears laid back against its wolfish head. Henry could almost hear the distinct snarl coming from him.

He leveled his pistol on the beast, but Sarah suddenly shot her hands up as a sign to stop. He hesitated, but only long enough for the beast to turn its head and lock eyes with Henry.

They were brown. Not golden like the rest, but deep and humanlike. Ben had once said that his eyes used to be that brown, so common and plain. And a spark of that old soul looked back at him.

Henry lowered his gun. The women, though terrified and whimpering in their native tongue, were still alive and unharmed. If this was Ben, if he wasn't one of the werewolves on the ridge, then what was he doing here?

The werewolf turned back to the women and began letting out low grunts as he stalked forward. In turn, the humans retreated like sheep in the face of a wild dog. Ben was herding them away from the chaos, and he was taking Sarah with him. He had come to help and not to harm.

She gave a nod to Henry, somehow understanding the whole thing better than he ever could. The chief's wife was among them and somehow in the confusion, Sarah managed to give her something to translate to the others. Not having much choice, they trusted the woman with the golden hair and they all turned to wade across the river and into the forest on the other side. There, they might be safe with Ben guarding over them.

The pandemonium behind him intensified as the Indians were losing this battle. With his pistol still cocked, he returned to the village and resolved to do what little he could. His lead bullets wouldn't kill them, but it could weaken them. They'd have to do until he could reach the deputies' discarded shotguns near the middle of the wreckage.

With the tents now leveled, he could see their movements. The pelts of all four beasts boasted distinctive colorations, making it easier to track which he had shot and which he had not. At every glimpse of fur, he let off a round until both his pistols were empty. Unfortunately, he was sure that none of them had slowed down.

Henry cursed aloud as he leapt over the fallen frames of teepees and mangled bodies of men who looked to still be breathing. Their hands reached for him, imploring him for help that he couldn't give. Not while the hearts of these monsters were still beating.

In the debris, he found the kits of the deputies who were nowhere to be seen. He pulled up the shotgun and fired off the first round into the side of a black and tan werewolf as it darted past him. Acting upon blind faith, he was rewarded. The gun was loaded with silver and the massive beast let out a yowl of pain before it rolled to a stop. The native the werewolf had been aiming for let out a great yell and was joined by others to stab the skull of the creature. Some were injured in the killing, but not mortally.

Henry grabbed for the ammunition belt and loaded the shotgun again, knowing that if one was wounded, the others would soon come to seek their revenge. He had watched packs of dogs enough to know that even in the animal kingdom, there was some sense of loyalty.

Sure enough, two more beasts came running toward him. He got off one shot before a force slammed him square in the chest. The wind was knocked from his lungs, the gun flew from his hands, and he felt a pair of fangs sink deep into his left arm.

Henry screamed and used his free hand to shove the werewolf off, but his jaws were locked over his bicep. Muscles were shredded and he heard the dull snap of bone as it broke.

Somewhere in the racket, he thought he heard his name being called. A feminine voice somewhere out of sight screamed for him, but he couldn't respond, and he couldn't be sure of anything in the tumult of battle that continued to rage on around him.

Through the pain, he continued to thrash and kick at the creature that was over twice his size. Warm blood seeped from the wound and soaked his sleeve and chest. His heart pounded in his ears, almost drowning out every noise. Only his pulse could mark the passage of time as he lay beneath the werewolf, fighting for his life.

Golden eyes glared at him and Henry could feel the heat of its fierce rage cut through to his soul. It was an intelligent hatred, not senseless or even hungry. The beast could have torn his arm off by now, but he hadn't. He simply hung on. But why?

As quickly as it all happened, it was over.

The werewolf was suddenly off of him. Henry stared up into the late morning sky and listened to the growls and yips coming from out of sight. It reminded him of the dog fights he had bet on in Denver. He tried to roll onto his side, but his useless arm hung limp and the loss of blood made his world spin. All he saw were two beasts rolling across a flattened teepee. Streaks of red trailed behind them on the canvas as they clawed and snapped at one another.

The scene became blurred, but Henry refused to give up. The ring of black in his vision would have to wait. Though his arm felt like it was on fire, he reached for the shotgun and managed to brace it against his shoulder. He fired into the tangled mass of werewolves and hoped that whoever he hit, they were with the bad guys.

A yelp rang out, but the shot didn't kill it. It scampered away with the two others, favoring one of its back legs as it went. It'd slow them down, but the job wasn't done.

Henry opened his mouth to call for someone to take up his banner and go after the monster, but no words came out. The darkness continued to close in and the smoldering sensation from his arm began to spread through his core and up into his skull. A shrill, deafening cry rang through his ears.

It felt as if a fire were coursing through his blood, setting his flesh ablaze from the inside out. He squeezed his eyes shut against the intense pain, waiting for the end. But it only became worse. Spasms that he couldn't control shook his limbs. The gun fell from his grip once more and he clenched his teeth together so tightly he was sure he had cracked a tooth.

But that minor inconvenience was nothing compared to the overwhelming anguish that suffused through the rest of his body. The seizures subsided, but death didn't come. He was still conscious, but barely hanging on.

All he could think of was the pain. The pain and Sarah. Did she make it across the river? He dearly hoped it was Ben that led them to safety, otherwise he'd regret not shooting the animal when he had wanted to.

Henry refused to think of what lay on the other side of this darkness. He knew he was going to hell and he'd have a jury of his enemies to put him on trial when he got there. Even if Sarah didn't make it through this, he'd never see her again. A perfect woman like her would get her angel wings soon enough, and he'd feel the scorching flames of hades for the rest of eternity.

A familiar voice stalled death and the hell that awaited him for a moment.

"You're going to be all right."

Something cold touched his forehead to chase away the fever that consumed him. How long had he been laying there? When had Geoffrey returned to the village? The distinct cadence of his accent gave him away, but his presence made no sense.

But as the time passed, and the fiery poison of death that swept through his veins began to lessen, the end still didn't come. Pain dissipated, his heartbeat slowed, and he waited for the moment his breaths stopped coming out in ragged gasps, but it never happened.

CHAPTER 12

Ben first felt his world tilt, though he straddled the edge of consciousness. The sunlight burned through his eyelids, amplifying the pounding ache in his head. Hands were on him, lifting him to his feet. And all at once, the rest of his injuries became keenly aware to him. A bone in his leg was shattered, his neck damp with blood, and a few of his ribs must have been fractured as well. Sharp pain made it almost impossible to breathe for a second, but that didn't keep him from fighting whoever had grabbed him.

His heels dug into the grass as they dragged him somewhere and Ben forced his eyes to adjust to the bright sunlight. The last thing he remembered, miraculously, was tussling with Lewis O'Connor near the river. The cries of the women and children in the thicket encouraged him to bite harder and slash deeper into the werewolf who would have killed them all without hesitation. He remembered seeing Sarah bound across the stream, hip deep in the current as water splashed all around her. If only his wolfish mouth could form the words to call her back to the embankment. She and Henry should have never been there. They should have been on Burnt Mountain, far away from the coming holocaust.

But with the massive werewolf giving him the beating of his life, Ben could barely utter more than the growls and whimpers that terrified the natives he protected. In the midst of the battle, a short, clipped howl rang out over the village. Lewis left Ben, a broken and bleeding mess that somehow found the strength to continue standing.

As his energy quickly faded away with the blood that leaked from the wound in his neck, Ben held his defensive position as long as he could, watching the werewolf lope away with his own injuries. The women were safe, but one more high-pitched scream echoed from the village as he lost consciousness.

So his first thought as he awoke to find that he was back in his human form, naturally gravitated toward Sarah and what had happened to her. His mouth, still tainted by the metallic taste of Lewis's blood, tried to speak the words, but his throat ached and his questions came out in a harsh whisper that he couldn't even understand.

Another werewolf approached, and in his daze, Ben bore his teeth in a growl, not even knowing who it was. He was on his feet, his leg partially healed and ribs smarting less than they had moments ago.

"What happened?" the werewolf demanded.

Bart.

The wolf, as tired as it was, flew into a temper at the sound of the Englishman's voice. Claws came out, fangs extended, and golden eyes gleamed with unrivaled animosity for the sheriff. "Where were you?" he roared, the beastly side of him finally giving him speech.

"We came as soon as I heard the screams and the howl." Bart took the place of one of his deputies that had picked up Ben. "Did you howl?"

He shook his head and made an effort to calm himself. They were on the same side now, even if the man had locked him in a silver mine with no protection. "Clarence... His gang... Where's Sarah?"

Ben's head tilted up to see the women being filed across the river, many of them hurrying to find their men in the village. He could already hear some of the mourning wails when they found the bodies of their husbands, brothers, and fathers. Half of the horses in the corral were gone, the gate smashed through by the crazed stampede that followed their arrival to the village. The dark blue and black coats of the deputies were scattered around the village, picking up what remained of the teepees. Clarence and his gang had torn through the place like a fox in a hen house. But he couldn't see Sarah's head of blonde hair amongst them. Neither could he see Henry's suntanned face.

"We haven't found her," Bart said. "But we have Henry. He's with Geoffrey."

There was some relief in that. If they couldn't find a body, maybe that would mean she was still alive somehow. Knowing that Geoffrey was in the village also discharged some of his anxiety, though death still hung in the air over the valley. How many had they killed? How many were able to fight them off? And why had Lewis been called away before finishing the job?

When Ben's leg finally pieced itself back together, he shoved off the other deputy and tested its stability by taking a few paces toward the water. Still naked as a newborn, he dropped to his knees and cleaned himself off while Bart talked.

"By the time we arrived, Clarence was gone, but I have his scent. We didn't know he would target the village."

Ben cupped the water and rubbed it into his neck to wash away the blood. "He was tryin' to draw you out of the mountains. Figured you'd come runnin' to help them and he'd catch you off guard." He motioned toward the village. "Better check how many of those Utes are dead and which are turned."

He expected to feel the ripple of surprise from the sheriff, but he replied with, "There's four new loups-garous. Many didn't survive the bite."

For once, a bit of sympathy tinted Bart's statement. It was as if he were truly sorry for what happened here in Roaring Fork Valley. He could feel pity for these Utes, but none for Ben when he had been wrongfully detained and practically tortured?

He turned and was ready to give him the verbal lashing he deserved when Bart continued, "There's five if you include Henry."

Ben froze, and the chill of the water was nothing compared to the ice that had been dumped down his back. The questions and plea for an explanation lodged in his throat like a hundred solid musket balls. He thought, for a moment, that he would be sick.

"His arm was badly hurt, but he'll live."

Talons of dread sank into his flesh and Ben almost wished that Henry had died in the attack. Better to have died than to live the life of a werewolf, a life he didn't want or ask for. Whoever did it, whether it was Clarence, Theo, or Silas, would pay for what they had done.

Lacking all sense, Ben stood and didn't bother crossing the river. He didn't need to go to the Ute village and see the destruction. Instead, he charged to the south where he had seen Lewis run. Now, his strength was returning and there was nothing to hold him back.

Nothing but a firm hand against his chest and a pair of searing dark eyes. "You're not going after him," Bart said. "Not alone."

"I've been havin' to do everythin' else on my own," Ben said, his words laced with venom.

A muscle jumped in Bart's jaw and the hand that had braced against Ben's chest moved to the point where his shoulder and neck met. His nails dug deep, the same tender spot where Theo had squeezed to bring about an induced shift. Ben winced at the pain, but it was the dominance that kept him from retaliating.

"I'm not going to let you go after him. Not without me. I can't take my men into the mountains. They'll be too slow on horseback and we've already lost so much time. We need to leave soon, but we need to know exactly what happened and – "

"I can tell you what happened," Ben snapped. "Clarence and his gang were comin' after you and innocent people got caught in the crossfire. Their blood is on your hands and Henry's life is over because of you."

Bart's grip tightened. "No. It's not because of me. Clarence made the choice to attack these people. I couldn't have known what he would do. But you, on the other hand, could have run to warn me."

"I only learned about the plan this mornin'," Ben retorted. "There wasn't enough time, and if it wasn't for me, all the women would have been defenseless. Do you think I fought against a werewolf almost twice my size for nothin'?"

As if the sheriff saw his point, his hold weakened and he nodded. "I see what you did, and I'm grateful, but let me take care of Clarence now. You've done enough."

No, Ben hadn't done a damn thing. He didn't kill Lewis, he didn't stop Clarence, and now Henry was a werewolf and Sarah was missing. Maybe he couldn't have fully stopped this chain of disasters, but he could help to break them.

Geoffrey appeared on the edge of the dismantled village, a folded up bundle in his hands and a look that told them he had something to say. In no way pacified, Ben followed Bart across the river and they met in the grassy field between.

"Henry's stable and resting," Geoffrey said, making a point to give an contrite look to the former human's friend. "He killed one of the gang before he was bitten."

Ben pushed his legs through the trousers he had been given to hide his nakedness, though the water made the cloth cling to his skin.

"Which one?" Bart asked.

"The younger, I believe."

He nearly fell over when his foot caught on the bottom cuff of a pant leg. "Silas?"

Out of all the brothers that could have been killed, he felt oddly sad to hear that the one boy who was on the verge of idolizing him, had been the only one killed in the engagement. He wouldn't have been pardoned by any means, but if any of them had some luck of being reformed, it was Silas.

They ignored his question and the two older werewolves continued their discussion. "Henry had silver bullets?" Bart asked.

"The shotgun I found by him wasn't his. I believe it belonged to one of your men. Both were killed early in the raid."

The sheriff let out a long sigh of regret, but there was far too much death in one morning to mourn for two more lost souls. "Any others?"

"Henry managed to get one more shot off before they ran," Geoffrey said. "It almost hit me, but it crippled the one who bit him. I can't recall if the bullet went all the way through his leg, but that will slow them down."

"Did you see the girl?"

Geoffrey nodded. "Sarah was in the camp when Henry was bitten. They saw her and took her before I could get to her." Now, he finally paid some mind to Ben. "Do you know if Sarah kept the knife?"

The inquiry was almost enough to distract him from the field of red that engulfed his vision. Clarence had Sarah and God only knew what they would do to her. "I don't know. I don't remember her ever tossin' it."

At this, he referred to Bart, who should have disarmed her back on Burnt Mountain.

"We never searched her."

For once, Sarah's gender proved to be beneficial. Despite her insolence, if neither Bart nor any of his deputies thought to search her for weapons, it was likely she still had it hidden on her persons somewhere.

"That knife was made of silver," Geoffrey confessed, shocking both of them. "If she still has it, that'll be her only chance at defending herself against Clarence and his gang."

Ben couldn't count on it. He didn't doubt that she would try, but a knife like that wielded in the hands of someone who didn't truly know how to use it, would do more harm than good.

"Are you sure you want to go after him?" Geoffrey asked, directing his question to the other werewolf. Now that they stood side-by-side, Ben could compare their differences. Bart must have been a few decades older than Geoffrey for him to boast so many more tells regarding his age.

A silent exchange passed between the two men and from what Ben could gather, Geoffrey was convinced that Bart should not be the one to pursue the outlaw. Why, he wasn't sure, but the sheriff didn't share in his reserves and seemed to take umbrage at the very suggestion that he stay behind.

Ben looked to the southern mountains and felt a thousand obscenities on his tongue, waiting to be uttered in hateful oaths against the werewolves. Once more, they had hailed terror and death upon those who didn't deserve it. They hadn't raised their army, and it was clear they hadn't counted on his and Geoffrey's intervention in their scheme.

One thing they were counting on was Bart's righteous anger getting the better of him. They thought they'd get him alone, without back up or support since his deputies couldn't be relied on to follow at his pace. One thing they would never come to expect was the vindictive nature of an orphaned farm girl and a veteran of the south.

"Ya were supposed to look after him!"

The brawny outlaw grabbed the other by the throat and hoisted him almost three feet off the ground. Sarah watched with wide eyes as the two hurled insults upon one another. The smaller of the two, who held a resemblance to the larger, scratched and bared wolfish fangs as his voice was slowly stolen by the hand clamped around his windpipe.

"Who the hell had silver bullets?" he thundered to Clarence, who stood nearby watching this altercation with a look of indifference.

The infamous outlaw didn't seem as distraught over the death of their fourth gang member, but seemed more annoyed about something else.

"I don't know," he sneered, cold blue eyes fixed to the north as if he were waiting for a posse to come after him at any moment. "Bart wasn't there. Two of his deputies were, but why?"

Sarah clenched her jaws together, refusing to speak or aid them in any way. She simply sat against the tree, her hands and feet bound with a bit of thin rope. For the last few minutes, she had been working on loosening the bonds, but all she gained for her troubles were stinging burns around her thin wrists.

The strangle victim kicked furiously at the man he called Lewis. "Put me down! It wasn't my fault he got shot!"

Instead of letting him down gently, Lewis tossed him against a nearby tree as if he were little more than a ragdoll. The trunk of the pine cracked, nearly splitting all the way through as the man collided with it and tumbled to the ground. Sarah wasn't sure if he would be able to push himself up again, but then she reminded herself that all of these men were werewolves, just like Ben.

They had traveled so quickly and so far that she wasn't even sure where they were. None of the terrain in this valley looked familiar. When Clarence dumped her into a patch of tall grass, Sarah had made a few attempts to run, but found herself trapped by one werewolf or another. Soon, they transformed back into their human skins and a bundle of clothes were retrieved from some nearby hiding place.

"Leave him alone, Lewis," Clarence ordered. "Silas was careless and not watchin' his back, like Theo wasn't."

Sarah glanced to the patch of red on Theo's pants, the one who had been thrown against the tree. The bullet wound had unfortunately healed, but the evidence of it had transferred to the fabric. If only Henry's aim had been a little better.

She cringed and tried to push away the image of his arm mauled and blood pooling around him. It wasn't likely that he would survive. Not without serious medical attention, which he wouldn't get in the destroyed village.

How she hated to think of the warriors strewn across the ground, throats and torsos torn apart by the razor claws of the werewolves. Discovering that Ben had been a monster was distressing enough, but to find that Clarence and his gang were actually a pack of werewolves as well beset her mind with confusing ideas about what was real and what wasn't. Had Ben known what they were the whole time? Did he tell them about the Ute village? Was he in league with them? If he was, then why wasn't he with them now and would he come to save her? Who was the werewolf who fought off Henry's attacker?

Too many questions swarmed in and it was too much for her to bear. The only way she could cope was to sit and try to stay in the moment, accept what was, and let the blanks fill in themselves. With luck, the werewolves would reveal all.

Lewis gave a sniff and looked to Theo, who was slowly recovering from his crash against the pine. "Ma told ya to look out for him."

Theo's lips curled back in a frown. "I know she did. I didn't know the shotgun had silver in it."

"Drop it!" Clarence roared. "There's nothin' we can do about Silas now. Y'all need to think about what you're gonna do when Bart gets here."

"Ya think Bart's comin'?" Lewis asked as he rubbed his dirty forearm against his nose.

"I know he will. And if I guess right, Ben will be with him too."

Theo rejoined him, favoring the leg that had been shot. The first words out of his mouth were about Ben and were not, in any way, kind. Sarah heard some words that weren't even uttered in the filthiest of saloons in Colorado.

"There's a lady present," Lewis rebuked, shoving whom she assumed to be his kin. Judging by the like shape of their brows and the way they talked about their mother, she could guess they were brothers.

Theo quickly looked to Clarence and jabbed his finger at her. "Why the hell is she even here?"

"Bart's a softy for the humans," the outlaw replied coolly. "She'll be a good distraction. We'll make a show out of wantin' to trade her and he won't give a second thought to what we're really wantin'."

"And what's that?"

No one had expected her to speak. None had even heard her until now. Three pairs of evil eyes turned upon her and her heart beat against her bruised ribs.

Clarence drew his pistol. "I reckon I know ya."

Sarah tried the ropes one more time, but they still held fast. "You should. You killed my ma and pa two months ago outside Trinidad."

The reminder was lost on Theo and Lewis, or they didn't care. But Clarence nodded in understanding. "You're that girl Ben told me about. The one that's itchin' to see me swing from the gallows."

"Or choke on your own blood. Doesn't matter to me as long as you're dead."

The other two members of the gang chuckled and turned to keep guard over the northern horizon. Amusement sparkled in Clarence's gaze and he pulled back the hammer on his gun.

"I thought ya were pretty stupid for workin' so hard to try and find me and my boys. But now I know you're just one egg short of a basket case. Didn't ya see what we did to those Indians? What we did to that man that shot one of my own?" Clarence paced closer, the gun aimed at her forehead. "I know he was somethin' to ya. I can hear your heartbeat and what it does when we talk about him. And don't think I don't know what you're tryin' to do to them ropes either."

Sarah immediately stopped her covert efforts to escape and swallowed hard as she looked down the black barrel of the gun. If only she could reach the knife, then she wouldn't feel so helpless.

"I remember you and your family," he continued. "I remember how your mama screamed and your pa begged for mercy. They groveled at my feet and I shot 'em both. Just like this." Sarah closed her eyes when the cool metal touched her forehead. "Your pa knew too much about us. Knew all about our kind and how to kill us. But you... ya don't know shit. If ya did, you'd be scared right now... But you're not. I'd smell it all over ya iffen ya was."

She looked up and her lips pressed into a thin, vengeful line. "Why should I be scared of a mangy dog?"

The gun withdrew and came back to hit her hard against her temple. Sarah cried out and fell onto her side. A wave of nausea swept over her as her head throbbed with the pain of the blow.

"Ya should be scared. Ya ain't gonna live to see the sunset. I can guarantee ya that much."

Sarah flinched when she heard the shot, but relaxed when it was immediately followed by a grunt from somewhere behind Clarence. She struggled to push herself up, but the dizziness compelled her to stay down. The outlaws shouted to one another and more shots were fired. Staying low might have been safer, but at least she had the opportunity to try breaking free again.

A bullet ricocheted into the ground near her, spewing dirt in her face. Fighting back the last of the queasiness in her stomach, Sarah wiggled deeper into the tall grass. A hand grabbed for her arm and she nearly screamed until its mate slapped over her mouth.

"Stay quiet," Ben whispered in her ear.

If he was here, then who was firing the gun? Who else had come to her rescue?

Sarah looked toward where she had last seen Clarence. He and the other two were already shedding their clothes again to prepare for the shift, but they didn't go unnoticed.

Lewis turned and saw Ben. Before she could react, Sarah was thrust into the grass that covered her completely, disappearing from sight. Ben had let go of her and not more than a few seconds later, she heard the skirmishing.

Roars and growls destroyed whatever peace was left in the valley. She could see nothing through the thick veil of swaying grass. Only the sounds and the vague impressions of what must have been going on. Her senses followed the tussling combatants as they moved somewhere in front of her.

Sarah tugged harder, whimpering as the rope cut into her skin and rubbed it raw. The curses she thought she'd never utter came hissing from her mouth as she furiously tried to free herself. After what seemed like a year of wrestling against her own body's pain tolerance and listening to the raging battle beyond the grass, her hand finally slipped through.

Her palms were covered in her own blood, but she couldn't take the time to care. She freed her other hand and quickly reached for the dagger in her boot. Geoffrey's gift may not do as much damage as she wished, being a blade of iron, but she had to try. Anything to help Ben. Her days of staying silent, passive, and letting the tragic circumstances of life toss her about like a leaf on the wind were over. From now on, she wouldn't let any man or monster dictate her fate.

Sarah sprang from the grass and found the nearest werewolf. Its tawny coat with marbling golden hues shined magnificent in the noonday sun, and she recognized it as the one who had whisked her away from the village.

It was Clarence.

The beast was turned away from her, standing tall over a silvery werewolf that she didn't recognize. The outlaw's arm was raised to administer a blow. Sarah mustered all of her courage for one jump. She ran and landed squarely on his back. The knife served as her anchor as she plunged it into his chest. Her legs wrapped around him and she braced herself for what would come. A deafening roar mingled with a strange hissing noise. Blood spilled over her hand and claws slashed at her arms and legs, but they could gain no purchase and hadn't enough strength to push her off.

A memory, dusty and hazy, came to her in this, of all moments. Sarah was a child, maybe nine years of age, and her father had brought home an unbroken horse. He worked hard to break it. For days, he took the time to get the mustang used to a saddle. But it only took one long, perilous ride to make it obey him. She remembered watching him from the front porch of their home, how she had held her breath each time the horse bucked and kicked the air. But her father held on tight and never once gave up.

And that's exactly what Sarah did now. She held her breath and rode out the werewolf until he stopped moving.

Sarah could dimly feel herself falling. The werewolf shuddered and jarred as he fell onto his knees, and then forward. A furry arm wrapped around her, but she didn't resist. With a body as black as night and eyes the color of saddle leather, she knew it was Ben taking her away to safety.

Almost immediately, the battle died away and a quiet settled over the valley. She finally looked up and saw only two bodies. One brown and one silver.

Ben's heavy breaths overpowered the whispering of the branches and leaves that rattled in the wind. She could feel a bit of caked blood on the arm that still encircled her. Soon, her thoughts caught up with the scene and she understood.

The knife was silver. That explained the sizzling sound and why one stab to the chest could execute the monster so easily. Clarence was finally dead and she had fulfilled her promise to her parents.

Somehow, murder didn't feel like she thought it would. Sarah thought she'd be inconsolable in some grief over committing the greatest of sins. She thought she might have regretted it all and wanted to rewind time to find another way to solve their problems. Instead, a burst of joy in her heart almost made her smile and laugh. Her legs didn't give out under the weight of her immorality, but were eager to dance around the carcass. She wanted to pull out every bit of fur from his hide and toss it into the air to celebrate the end of his reign. Sarah was happy, truly happy that her hand was the one to end his life. To her, Clarence wasn't a man. He never was. He was a creature from hell and she had sent him back to the dark and fiery hole he had crawled out of.

The gray wolf, whose dark eyes stared into the void of death, remained a mystery. His demise was not so clean, and the testimony of it showed in how his flesh had been sliced through and bones in his chest crushed inward. Blood pooled around him, staining the ground where he had last fallen. No man could survive that kind of beating.

She stared at his corpse, willing it to rise or heal by some phenomenal feat of resilience. Whoever he was, he had come here to fight for her, and she wished to thank him. But the light faded from his eyes. The soul was gone, leaving only the shell of the beast for them to bury.

Peace and sadness washed over her, the dam of emotions breaking now that it was all over. Sarah twisted in Ben's arms and buried her face in his chest, feeling the warmth of his fur and the heavy pounding of his werewolf heart against her cheek. It was all over. All vows fulfilled, all debts paid. And she was still alive. Hot tears came and spilled out in gushes. It was the cry she had been holding in since she had tossed the last bit of dirt over her parents' graves.

Ben didn't move at first, but then his other arm came to envelop her. In the embrace of a monster, Sarah had never felt safer.

"For Pete's sake, quit screamin' at me," Henry groaned. He threw one arm over his eyes as if it would block out the whole world that threatened to make his ears and eyes explode. All he could hear was hammering, the slap of soft leather, shuffling feet, mumbles and weeping. Every bit of it sounded right next to his face.

But he knew they were nowhere close to the village.

"I'm not," Geoffrey replied in a low tone. "Try to breathe and don't move so much."

Laying under the shade of a sheltering grove of trees, the Englishman tended to the wound in his arm.

"Am I gonna need stitches?" he asked, partly knowing what his answer would be.

"No. Only a new shirt."

Henry took a gander to his left, to the tattered strips of bloodied cotton and the cleaned patch of skin where the werewolf had sank his teeth. Not even a faded scar marred his bicep. But one thing would certainly remind him of this day.

Geoffrey wasted no time in telling him the truth as soon as he awoke after passing out. Henry was a werewolf now, like Ben – and much to his chagrin, like Geoffrey and Bart as well. It seemed the west had more beasts in it than he had ever dreamed. And now, there was one more added to its census.

He thought it strange how, just that morning, no less than twelve hours ago, he had been human. He was nothing special, a cattle rustler who was ready to hang up his spurs for a beautiful, passionate woman. Now, everything was different. His senses were heightened, every bit of his surroundings screamed at him in one way or another. Sight, smell, sound, all of it bombarded him with information that he could barely sort through. Was it like this for Ben? Did he, too, feel something new dwell in his chest? Was this the wolf he talked about?

But nothing in this felt as suffocating as he had imagined. Though the world tried to cram its way into his head, there was something almost stimulating in this new existence. Each breath felt new and fresh. He wanted to become acclimated to it all, so he could learn and piece together what it was he smelled. Which trees matched to which scents? What distant bird calls did he hear?

There was only one thing that could ruin it all for him.

Geoffrey had also told Henry about Sarah and how Ben and Bart had gone after Clarence's gang to rescue her. Debilitated and too weak to travel yet, Henry stayed and recuperated with the other Indians who had also been turned during the raid. Still, not one second went by when he didn't think of her and listen for her approach. With his new abilities, he'd be able to sense her coming from a mile off. Though, he wondered if his fondness of her would be enough to help make her stand out.

But it wasn't the sound of her footsteps or breathing that alerted him first. It was her smell. That distinct womanly smell that had imprinted upon his memory since the moment they came close enough to one another.

Against the old werewolf's wishes, Henry sat up and took a deep whiff of the air. She was coming closer, and if he wasn't mistaken, so was Ben. The smell of Georgia soil practically composed his entire essence. One additional scent clung to them both. Blood.

"She's fine," Geoffrey told him with a smile and pat on his shoulder.

Henry caught his breath and relief melted into anxiety. "Yeah, but will I be?"

The smile faded when the older man comprehended his meaning. "If she truly loves you, this won't matter."

"Not matter?" he questioned in disbelief. "Ben's told me everythin' he's been through. It's hell... I don't know if I wanna bring her into this."

There was so much to consider, so much that could tear apart their budding courtship. It wasn't just the wolf, who would forever play the third wheel in everything Henry did with Sarah. He'd never age. How would it look for him to look as he did now when she grew old and wrinkled? Could he watch her fade like that? He wanted to grow old with her, but being a werewolf spoiled those dreams.

Geoffrey nudged Henry with his elbow to stir him from the despondent thoughts. Then, he pointed to three couples amongst the convalescing. "You see that? Those women have seen werewolves and know what they're capable of. They've seen the best and the worst sides of our nature, and they haven't left their husbands. They're here, taking care of them. One of them told me that she wanted to be the first thing he saw when he woke up. That's love and true dedication. My wife, God rest her soul, knew what I was before we ever married, and she still chose me over the other men of her tribe. She accepted our son, loved him and raised him into a fine man, knowing that he had inherited this from me. I'll never find another woman like her, and if Sarah accepts you – all of you – then you'll never find another like her." He leaned in and dropped his voice. "So, don't bugger this up."

Before Henry could panic about the fact that any sons he bore would also carry this curse, Ben and Sarah came to the grove. He met the blue eyes of the woman he had come to love over the last several days. Instead of seeing repulsion, fear, or all the things that Henry had imagined he would see, there was an abundance of warmth, of joy, of the relief that he reciprocated. She was in one piece, unharmed except for some blood on her hands and stains upon her baggy clothes.

He struggled to stand, even with Geoffrey's help. His legs, now strong and forever strangers to fatigue, were still a little wobbly after all he had suffered. But she stunned him once more and ran to meet him first.

She hugged him, and Henry could feel her bring the disseminated, disfigured pieces of his life back together. In her arms, he didn't care about the future anymore and what uncertainty awaited him.

"Ben told me," she said, her words feathered with a tenderness and understanding. For the first time in his life, he felt like weeping. Sarah knew the truth and still, she received him. All of him.

Henry looked up and saw Geoffrey and Ben in conference several yards away, giving them a bit of privacy. But how much privacy could they really have in a grove full of recently turned werewolves?

"Dead?" Geoffrey asked in dismay.

Ben gave him a solemn nod. "Clarence did him in. But Sarah used your knife and... it's done now."

A few seconds of silence were given for Bart, the only one not to return from the pursuit. Though Henry resented the sheriff for countless reasons, he wouldn't have wished death on the man, especially not at the hands of another werewolf.

"What about the others?"

Ben stuck his hands deep in his pockets. "They ran off after they saw Clarence fall. I reckon they won't stick around, but even if they do, they can't do much now. Their little brother's dead and I'm not so sure all the silver came out of that shotgun wound in Theo's leg." Henry saw Ben glance his way, but only for a second. It was enough time to see the hurt and sympathy behind those golden eyes they now shared. "How is he?"

Geoffrey nodded. "He's fine. So are the others. Bart's told me about the alpha in Wyoming. That may be the best place for them."

Henry frowned and held Sarah tighter to his chest, being careful not to crush her. As much as he didn't want to go to Wyoming, he knew he had to. There were still warrants for his arrest in Colorado and now that he was a werewolf, he needed guidance.

Part of him wondered if Ben would finally settle into a pack, now that he had a friend amongst the cursed. But that was too much to hope for.

"And what will you do?" the older werewolf asked Ben. "You might want to go with him. The alpha might – "

"No," Ben gently interrupted. "I... I can't. Not now. I need some time. Time away from all this. No offense, but I still don't want a pack."

A knowing smile brightened Geoffrey's countenance. "No offence taken. I don't either. I'll be taking them to Wyoming, but I won't stay, and I certainly won't force you to join us. You have to make your own path."

They shook hands and thanked one another for things that Henry didn't fully understand. As Ben came to him, Sarah pulled away from her cathartic hug. The sorrow written in her contracted brows spoke enough. She, like Geoffrey, knew that this would be the last time they saw one another. Henry, however, still held out some hope that this wasn't the end. For him, for werewolves, goodbyes couldn't be forever. They lived too long for farewells to have any kind of permanence. This morning proved that life was too unpredictable.

"You're leavin'?" Henry asked, not feeling the need to speak what they already knew into the open. They were now, like brothers in all but kin and, somehow, it felt right. Out of all the people Henry had met in his travels, Ben had always been special. They'd helped each other out in more scrapes than he could count, and he would never forget the day they met on the railroad.

"Yep," he replied, putting on as brave a face as Henry could muster likewise. "Nothin' left for me here."

"Will you go back to Georgia?" The optimistic turn in Sarah's voice told volumes. She knew about his mother, and bits of his past. But he knew his friend better, that Georgia wasn't home anymore.

He shook his head. "No. I'd like to go someplace new."

"Alabama?"

Ben snorted. "Hell, no. That place ain't nothin' new. I was thinkin' somewhere north. Some place I know I won't run into any more werewolves. I've had just about all I can handle for one lifetime."

He might have had a right to feel wounded. He was a werewolf, after all. Did that mean he never wanted to see Henry again, or was this a phase?

Either way, he nodded and offered out his hand. "Safe travels, then. I hope you find whatever it is you're lookin' for."

Ben shook it and looked to him with the golden eyes that no longer made him squirm or fidget nervously. This journey had taught Henry to love those eyes and be thankful for the friend who owned them. "I'd say the same for you, but it looks like you've found it."

Sarah grinned and nodded before tilting her chin up to Henry. "I reckon he did."

The Deviants

Legacy Series Book 12

Sheritta Bitikofer

MOONSTRUCK WRITING

CONTENTS

Dedication   #

Prologue   #

1. Chapter 1   #

2. Chapter 2   #

3. Chapter 3   #

4. Chapter 4   #

5. Chapter 5   #

6. Chapter 6   #

7. Chapter 7   #

8. Chapter 8   #

9. Chapter 9   #

10. Chapter 10   #

11. Chapter 11   #

12. Chapter 12   #

13. Chapter 13   #

14. Chapter 14   #

Epilogue   #

To those who think they don't belong, who feel out of place, who don't think they measure up.
You're more than you believe to be.

PROLOGUE

SOUTH CAROLINA, 1880

Susan sat upon the settee in the front parlor. Her back straight, eyes fixed ahead, she still couldn't bring herself to believe any of this was truly happening. In the span of just a few days, her life had changed so dramatically. Nothing would ever be the same again.

The house buzzed with activity. The constant traffic of caterers, servants, and family echoed down the halls and through the many rooms. The noise of people would have driven her mad if she wasn't so numb to it all. The excited chattering voices, the tramping footfalls, the swishing of full skirts bustling through doorways. It wouldn't stop. Not until the wedding day.

The bride should have been the happiest of them all. She should have been giggling with her friends, gushing with her aunts and elderly relatives who had traveled all the way from Tennessee for the event. She should have taken some control of the arrangements, but everything had been left to her mother and grandmother. Her step-father, or as he was affectionately called "The Colonel", took it upon himself to spend his days in a cloud of cigar smoke with the other men, boasting about what a fine match his daughter had made. Out of everyone, he might have been the most thrilled.

Susan shared in none of it. Her body felt dead, heavy and useless. She couldn't remember the last time she smiled or answered truthfully to any of the million questions from her loved ones. "Ask mama," she would mutter. "Ask granny," she would sometimes grumble. The color of the bridesmaids' dresses didn't interest her. Nor did the faire served at the party after the ceremony. She stood for the wedding dress fitting and allowed the ladies to croon over the long lacy train. To her, it was pointless. None of it held any meaning. The white gown was little more than a burial shroud. Her life was over the moment she realized that she would actually be marrying Jasper Elster.

He wasn't a bad man. Not that she could tell, anyway. But Susan didn't love him. In her lap, lay her hands, cupped and motionless. She didn't want to move, and she was sure that she hadn't for hours. The hollow between her palms might as well have held her shattered, broken heart. The heart that Ilias had carelessly tossed back to her.

That night seemed ages ago, in another lifetime before yards of satin were draped over her poster bed and she couldn't look anywhere without seeing something like invitations or favors that would be given out at the reception. In another life, she wouldn't be here. She'd be somewhere far away with Ilias, wrapped up in his strong arms and the only focus of his bright, crystalline blue eyes. Jasper's eyes were brown like mud with hair to match. She couldn't even pretend that her husband was her true lover. They were so different, so dissimilar that they might have been from other worlds.

Thinking of Ilias now with his dazzling smile and charming ways made her stomach churn again. Nausea was a constant reminder that she couldn't be completely insensible. She couldn't completely shut out everything. Especially not what was coming from within.

Susan swallowed back the pool of saliva in her mouth and closed her eyes as panic rose into her throat once more. This wedding, as much as she hated it, had to happen. Soon. Her dresses were already fitting too tight and she could only blame her vomiting on a bit of bad pork for so long before they would become concerned.

If only she hadn't told Ilias. If only she had kept him for a little longer. Then, she wouldn't even be here. She'd be someplace she had never been before. Somewhere out west, or maybe further south. Or perhaps they would have gone to Europe, where Ilias was from. She would have the life she wanted. It wouldn't have been easy, and she'd have to leave her family behind. But at least she would have been happy.

"Sweetheart?"

The voice as tender and light as the whisper of dove feathers. She'd know it anywhere.

Susan opened her eyes to see her mother standing in the doorway of the parlor, looking from her daughter to the empty corners of the room. She had searched here for solitude and found it for just a moment. Just a moment to be miserable and heartbroken. That's all she wanted anymore. No wedding, no people. Just her and this ache in her chest.

Her mother hurried forward and sat beside her, a look of concern written in the youthful features of her face. As mothers went, Nancy Jenkins was unconventional. She had her first child at a young age, out of wedlock. Susan was the lovechild from a man she had never met. If The Colonel hadn't come into their lives and ignored her scandalous situation, they wouldn't be living as comfortably as they did now. Even with The Colonel's northern roots, Nancy had wriggled her way into the most exclusive circles of South Carolina society. All for Susan and the future she was so willing to throw away for Ilias and the sake of romance. Barely seventeen herself, she seemed to be following in her mother's footsteps.

"What's wrong?" her mother asked, taking hold of Susan's icy hands. "Are you not feeling well again?"

Susan could feel the weight of her secret sitting atop her lungs, pushing the air out of her. Her sorrow could be hidden from most of the wedding party, but it was too exhausting to keep this from her mother, her sole defender in every way. And from the exhaustion and grief, sprung the hot tears that pushed at the corners of her eyes.

"No," she whispered. "I'm not well. I'm not well at all."

Unable to hold it back any longer, Susan flung herself into her mother's lap, burying her sobs in the stiff taffeta of her gown. She let her senses drown in the perfumed scent of the fabric that she wrinkled between her clenched fists. Instead of demanding an explanation for such an outburst, her mother petted her hair and spoke soothingly. It had been so long since Susan behaved like a child, clinging to her mother's skirt as if that would save her from the monsters at the door.

"What's wrong with her?"

Another voice she could never forget. The booming, authoritative demands of The Colonel made her shiver and shrink further against her mother, seeking shelter until it was all over. If she could have just stayed here in the parlor forever, that would be fine with her.

"It's just pre-wedding jitters, dear," her mother replied coolly. "Nothing to worry about."

The heavy thud of his boots strutting away from the parlor was her cue that all was safe again. She didn't hate The Colonel, and she couldn't begrudge the life he had given them. She remembered what it was like at three years old, her bare feet shuffling across the dirt floor of a shack with a roof that leaked and rats for bedmates. She wasn't so ungrateful and spoiled that she couldn't appreciate the mountain of a man that swore to be like the father she never had. But this wedding and everything leading up to it had made him into a person she didn't know. Cold, decisive, insisting. This wedding was his idea, his match, his fault.

"I can't do it, mama," Susan whimpered as she sniffled back the last of her tears. "I can't marry him."

Her mother took her by the shoulders and eased her up. Susan pressed her lips tight as she met the stern, but loving gaze. "Yes, you can. And you have to. For my sake, you have to."

"I don't love him," Susan confessed, mindful to keep her voice low, so no one else might hear them.

Nancy nodded. "I know, sweetheart. I know you don't. I wish you did, but I understand why. It's hard to even think of loving someone else when you're already in love. You have to believe me that it will get easier with time."

The words sounded as if they came from experience, but Susan couldn't believe it. Her mother and The Colonel always seemed so madly in love, so devoted to one another, even during the roughest of times.

"There was someone who came after your father," Nancy said carefully. "He wanted to marry me before you were born, but I didn't." The bittersweet sentiment in her smile would have broken Susan's heart, if it wasn't already broken. "I was waiting for your father. I held out hope for months, for years, that he would somehow come back and find me. But he didn't and I had to move on. I had you to take care of." Her mother reached up and brushed aside a dangling strand of hair that had come loose from her pins. "And soon, you'll have a little one to look after, too. If you don't marry Jasper now, you will regret it. You may not love him, but he will take care of you. And I need him to take care of you both."

Susan's eyes went wide. "You know?" she gasped.

Nancy grinned and they bent their foreheads together. "Darling, a mother knows things. And I know by the way you've been moping, that Ilias is gone." She pulled Susan into a tight embrace. "If I could have spared you the pain of losing the man you love, I would have. Life doesn't always turn out how we think it should, but it's our job to make the best of it."

Shaking arms returned her mother's hug and Susan felt as if she would cry again. Once more, her mother had become her savior in the moment she needed it most. Through poverty, through loss, and through tragedy, they had always had one another. Another tear spilled onto her cheek, but this wasn't shed for Ilias or the uncertain future that awaited her with Jasper. This tear was for her mother and the unsettling truth that once she was a married woman, these talks and hugs would be numbered.

CHAPTER 1

SOUTH CAROLINA, 1898

Logan swung the axe to split one more log. The two thick halves fell to either side of the stump, tumbling and rolling across the ground. That was the last of it. He drew his arm across his damp brow and collected the halves to stack them with the rest. He should have been on his way into town by now. Ollie, the master horseman, would be waiting for him. But these logs needed to be split before the final winter chill settled in. The morning proved unseasonably warm, and it might as well have been the perfect time. It wouldn't be done otherwise.

Over the earthy scent of pine needles and his own acrid sweat, he could smell something else coming from the house. Logan paused and sniffed the sweet aroma of baking apples and cinnamon. He let a smile curve his lips when he heard the groan of the stove door opening, and then closing. His mother was baking again. She hadn't baked anything other than bread in months.

He set down the axe beside the wood pile and rushed toward the open door.

Before he could get further than two strides onto the wide front porch, his mother shouted, "You aren't getting any until supper. No use running in here to get a piece."

Logan let his bony, broad shoulders slump in defeat as he stepped inside their modest, leaky cabin. "I finished chopping the wood, maw. Can't I have just one apple slice?"

The biggest room of the house consisted of the living room and kitchen, with a dining table as something of a partition between the two. The threadbare rug, which had been a wedding present to his parents, lay across the creaking floorboards and dipped in the places where it covered gaps between the planks. The furniture was in need of a reupholstering they couldn't afford, and the only touches of hominess were the short, drab curtains that hung over the smudgy windows.

The kitchen, his mother's domain, wasn't much better in the way of shabbiness. The pump at the wash station leaked when it was used, causing the boards on that side of the room to rot out every six months. The stove pipe that tunneled through the roof harbored a hairline crack somewhere that they had yet to patch up. The pantry was meagerly stocked, the cupboards full of chipped dinnerware, and the one stool in the corner rocked no matter how much Logan tried to fix it.

Every surface, however, was clean and free of rat pellets. The same went for the two bedrooms that encompassed the back half of the house. His mother, though she had little control over much anymore, did ensure that the place was wiped down and scrubbed almost daily. It might have been the only effort made to keep her family healthy.

Standing near the table, was his mother. Her black hair was pulled back with a cord, eyes shining with pride as she set down the freshly baked apple pie. The crispy, golden brown top crust glittered with sugar granules as steam curled from the even cuts that were made before it was put in the oven. Through these carefully made cuts, he could see the mouthwatering apple slices beneath.

Out of all his mother's recipes, this was his favorite and her best. It wasn't every day they could come by fresh apples, and she must have used the last of the seasonings she had set aside after their meager Christmas feast just a week ago. She had told him she wanted to save it for a special occasion. Just what it was, he didn't know. His birthday had come and gone as quickly as the holidays did, so he knew it couldn't be that. And there was no reason to celebrate in their house. Not anymore.

His mother lifted her chin and smiled to him the way she always did when he came into the room. That happy sparkle in her eyes made all the hard work worth it. "Well, maybe just one slice."

He took another step and his toe hit something on the floor. The hollow clink that his shoe tip made against the trash told him enough. He watched the bottle roll across the floor and stop on a slightly uneven board near one of the bedroom doors. When he looked back to his mother, she was no longer smiling. Her eyes had followed the liquor bottle too.

It wasn't his, and it wasn't hers. His father was conveniently absent – again. But that wouldn't keep either of them from blaming him for its presence there. He must have dropped it last night before she had to carry him to bed. He couldn't sleep on the floor all night.

They stood in silence for an agonizing moment before she turned away to scrub her hands with a dish rag. "Don't you need to go to work?" she asked.

Logan looked down to his clothes and then his hands that were speckled in dirt. He should have brushed off before coming inside. "Yes, but I'll leave in a minute."

"You don't want to keep Ollie waiting for long."

"I know." He nodded and took up the dull knife sitting on the table beside the pie. If he was careful enough, he could pick a softened slice between one of the cuts in the crust and not ruin the beautiful effect of the whole. "What's the occasion?"

One glance toward his mother made him go still before he began his probing. That smile on her lips was familiar too. It wasn't for him, or even for his father. It belonged to some other memory from long ago. He'd see that gentle, closed-lipped smile every once and a while when she thought no one was looking. In the quiet hours of the evening when only a candleflame bathed the light of the home in a warm, amber glow, did she smile like that. Her stare would become unfocused, her eyes glistening with some emotion reserved for whatever it was she was thinking about. When she knitted or stared out the dirty window, the lines on her face would relax and she'd look young again. Not the careworn mother and wife she had become.

Logan never brought it to her attention, lest it ruin her blissful peace, the only bit of true, unadulterated happiness life could afford her anymore.

He dropped his eyes out of respect, but his stare fell on the patch of skin on his mother's arm. There, just below her rolled up sleeve, were four, faint, dark stripes that nearly wrapped all the way around. Logan felt a muscle in his jaw jump.

"No reason," she finally replied to his question. "I just..." She turned and their eyes locked. It was then she realized how mad he had become in just a few seconds. That enigmatic smile left her. "What's wrong?"

Logan gestured to her arm, still afraid to verbally call out the sin by its name. He might have been a man now, just a little over sixteen, but there were still so many parts of him that were young and childish. Even though he wanted his father to be there, so he could finally confront him about this, Logan wasn't sure he'd have the courage to say what needed to be said.

His mother looked to her arm and her mouth pulled into a pained, regretful line. "It doesn't hurt nearly as badly as some that he's made before."

Seeing that he had lost track of what he had been doing, she deftly took the knife from his hand and began to pry out a slice of apple for him.

"We... We could leave, maw," he said hastily while he had the courage. "We don't need him. I can support us both. I have been for a while now and – "

She reached out with a thin hand and silenced her son's bold offer. "We can't. Please don't talk about it anymore."

Logan's guts twisted angrily in his core. "We can't keep living like this."

His mother shot him a scowl. "What did I just say?"

Suddenly sheepish, but still seething, Logan lowered his chin until it nearly touched his chest. "Not to talk about it."

"Thank you. Now, take your apple slice and go to town. If Ollie asks why you're late, tell him I had you chopping wood." She offered out the knife with its dangling, light brown bit of fruit coated in cinnamon. "When you come home tonight, I want to talk to you about something very serious, okay?"

Logan took the knife and popped the treat in his mouth, savoring its rich sweetness. It'd be all that could fend off his hunger until lunch. Though he wanted to ask more about this serious matter, she was right about his lateness.

He gave her a quick peck on the cheek and hurried out the door. If he ran fast enough through the woods, he could make it to town in no time. Maybe the sprint would help to expend some of that burning hatred toward his father. Someday, he vowed to himself as he dodged and weaved through the pines and evergreens, they would leave South Carolina. They've leave and never look back, until they were someplace safe. Away from his father, his drinking, and his fists. Someday.

Ollie took the mare's bridle from Clayton Mosby as he continued his rant about her stubbornness.

"She kicks every stallion I present her with," he complained. "If I can't get her to foal, she might as well be useless."

The horse breeder took a quick assessment of the mare's legs, haunches, and general physical condition. "There's nothing wrong with her, Clay," Ollie said. "She may just be finicky. I'll see if she'll stand any of my stallions."

Clayton grumbled, "She better. If she won't let any of them near her, you can have her. All that money for nothing."

Ollie watched the merchant storm off and shook his head. He had plenty of money and spending it on a horse this fine could never be a waste. He turned to the nearly discarded mare and ran his rough hand over the white diamond between her eyes. "You're not worthless," he encouraged with a smile. "You just haven't found your place."

The mare bucked against his arm and snorted. Ollie chuckled and guided her toward the stables just as Clayton climbed into his carriage and steered away from the husbandry. He was nearly to the doors when Ollie heard his unreasonable customer let out a shouting curse, joined by the harsh turning of the carriage wheels.

He looked over his shoulder and saw his apprentice jumping aside to avoid becoming a casualty in Clayton's speedy getaway.

"Watch where you're running!" the driver shouted before snapping his whip on the flanks of his white gelding.

Logan stumbled on the dirt road, but caught his balance and continued his mad rush for the stables. Panting, his forehead dotted with perspiration, and clothes soiled before he ever put a single hand to work, his apprentice was every bit the young teen he took in two years ago. He had grown a little taller, his limbs awkward and lanky but thickening as he labored harder and harder each day.

"You're late," he stated coolly. Ollie could have been mad. This was the fourth time in the last few weeks that Logan had shown up past his designated time.

"I'm sorry," the boy replied through heavy breaths. "I needed to chop wood for my maw. It needed to get done before winter set in. It's coming a little late this year."

Ollie let out a sigh and nodded, understanding the situation of their family better than any other man in town. "It's all right. Try not to let it happen again."

Logan went straight to the water barrel sitting outside the stable doors and splashed his face. "Did I miss anything?"

"Just the morning feeding and our newest arrival." Ollie opened one of the stall doors and led the brown mare inside. "Grab some straw for her."

Neglecting to dry off, Logan did exactly as he was told and gathered up a hefty armful of hay. "Does she belong to Mr. Mosby?"

He nodded and explained the difficulty Clayton had been having with her. "I was actually hoping you could take a look and see if anything's wrong before I handle her. Could be something simple."

Countless times, horse owners had brought in their stock for this sort of temperamental condition, thinking it was something wrong with them or their amateur efforts to breed. In reality, the behavior of a mare or stallion could have been attributed to something as simple as a health issue or they hadn't been presented with the right match. It had been Ollie's job for decades to find these problems.

Leo dumped the hay into the trough just inside the stall doors and approached the mare. Ollie watched as his apprentice inspected every part of her, taking a peek under her tail and at the grooves in her hooves. All the while, he marveled at the boy's resiliency.

The town knew his father, Jasper Elster. And they all knew his mother, Susan. Good people. Both of them. As long as Jasper was sober. Which, lately, wasn't often. In fact, Ollie couldn't remember a time when Jasper didn't have that bleary-eyed look about him. And he couldn't recall once when Susan didn't make a trip into the store with her pathetically small wallet, torn dress, and long sleeves that hid bruises few knew about. Ollie knew, only because their son, a hardworking and dedicated boy, worked for him. These things, as much as they shouldn't have been discussed, came out sometimes when they broke for lunch, or when Logan was late to work.

"How's your mother?" he asked while Logan continued his evaluation.

He nodded, not lifting his pale gray eyes to meet his. Ollie always wondered where he got those eyes from. He assumed it was one of his grandparents, because neither Susan nor Jasper had eyes like that.

"She's all right," Logan replied distractedly. "She made an apple pie this morning and she let me steal a taste. I can't wait to have more this evening. She says she wants to talk about something with me too."

For all the horses in the world, Ollie hoped it was that they would finally leave Jasper and go back to wherever it was she came from. They had been here for almost seventeen years. The first few had been all right, but Ollie saw the change. Jasper started drinking and gambling. Susan started covering up. Logan looked confused as to why everyone in town gave them sad, sympathetic looks. Maybe that was why he took in Logan as an apprentice after he failed to be a competent blacksmithing assistant. He felt sorry for the lad and their troubles.

"Where are your grandparents?" he asked suddenly, while still musing on that thought. "I don't remember if they had ever come to visit."

Logan paused and cut his eyes toward Ollie before pulling up the mare's lips to look at her yellowed, crooked teeth. "My paw's parents died a long time ago. My maw's parents don't want to see us anymore. I only met them once when I was little. My maw says it's because they're just old and can't travel, but I know better. They don't want to see me."

Ollie folded his arms over his thick chest. "Who told you that?"

The boy shook his head and let the mare have her mouth back. "No one. I remember my grandpa's scowl and my maw cried after she had a long talk with my grandma. That was when I was five, I think. They never came back. I know it's because of me, but no one will say it."

By all the evidence, Ollie could understand why he felt that way. He wouldn't lie and try to tell him he was wrong, neither would he agree. All he could do was mourn the bad fortune of a family that needed help badly. If he thought it wouldn't be so scandalous, he would have offered his home to the battered wife and her well-meaning son. Or, perhaps tried to find a safe place for them to escape Jasper's hold.

The man speculated away what little he earned, leaving almost nothing for them to live on. He stayed the night in the bars, while they starved at home. If Susan had enough to make an apple pie, she must have been saving up every penny she could afford to buy the ingredients.

They had lived on the charity of others. He knew Marv Kittenton had gifted them with a chicken for Christmas just last week. And Elton Smith had given them a whole turkey and bag of potatoes for Thanksgiving a month before that. Donations were handed off secretly, especially after Jasper had almost assaulted the banker in town when he offered a loan to Susan to fix up her home.

Almost the entire town hated Jasper, and if Logan had been astute enough to notice his grandparent's disdain after one meeting, then it was likely he noticed the pity from everyone else too.

Because of that, he carefully wiped his face clean of all the hurt and frustration he felt toward their situation when Logan turned around to give his report.

"I don't see anything wrong, but I'd like to watch her for a few days... Unless you see anything, of course."

Ollie took his cue and busied himself with the mare.

"I know what you're thinking," Logan said as his boss lifted the horse's hooves. "But she won't agree to leave. She says we can't."

He wondered how many took Logan's perceptiveness for granted. His natural talent with the horses and colts astounded Ollie every day, but he had never imagined that the boy could understand his fellow humans just as well.

"I don't know what possessed you to believe I was thinking anything like that," Ollie began, "but since you brought it up, why does she think she can't leave?"

Logan shrugged out of the corner of his eye. "She wouldn't say. She doesn't want to talk about it... I'm going to ask again tonight. I'm sure we can figure something out. If we can, you should know I may not show up for work."

Ollie smirked as he ran his fingers along the edges of the mare's hoof. "I wouldn't expect you to."

"So, you'd be all right if we left?"

He straightened and could feel the muscles in his back pull and smart with the effort. He had hoped one day, if Logan wanted, he could have passed along the stables and all the horses to him. It'd be his business, his future. Ollie only had so many years left of this work before it mule-kicked him into an early grave. If he could afford to be selfish, he would have advised Logan against leaving town. But since he admired the boy's spirit, talent, and tenacity, he couldn't think of himself in that way.

Looking Logan square in the eyes, he nodded. "Yes, I'd be fine. You should look after your mother, no matter the cost. If you need a recommendation to another apprenticeship in some other town, all you have to do is ask."

He gave a grateful, but crooked smile. "And leave out all the times I came in late?"

Ollie laughed. "Of course. I want you to succeed in whatever you do." The old man turned away before he could get misty-eyed, running his hands along the mare's stomach and underside. Logan fell silent, deeply engrossed in his observation of Ollie's technique.

It was then, as he had his palm pressed against the mare's underside that he found the problem. "Looks like she's already pregnant."

CHAPTER 2

The sun hadn't quite set yet. Shades of gold and amber seeped through the dense canopy of the forest. Logan could have taken the dirt path that wound its way out of town, but this way was more direct. And since he was already late for supper, he thought it best not to waste any more time simply by taking the easier route.

The day had been long and unexpectedly difficult. Many times, his body was given to a series of spasms that cleared his mind of every thought. Logan would stop and wait for the cramps in his limbs to pass. They would, but it took several long moments of deep breathing before he felt any sign of relief. Ollie had witnessed one episode and asked if he wanted to go home, but Logan knew what would happen if he did. He'd lose half a day's pay, and since he had lost precious hours that morning already, he couldn't afford to cut his paycheck any further.

Perhaps it was a side effect of the muscle aches, but his stomach wouldn't hold any food down. He tried to eat his portion of the lunch he shared with Ollie, but it all came back up half an hour later after a spell of nausea. The only bit of sustenance he could tolerate was water. Still, he hungered and thirsted like he never had before.

Logan sighed as his gut rumbled angrily against him. With luck, he could tell his mother everything and she'd know what to do. She always knew what to do. But talking about his sickness would have to wait until after a slice of apple pie – if he could keep it down – and that talk she had spoken of earlier that morning.

All day, pass the pain and queasiness, Logan wondered what she wanted to tell him. He hoped, against all the evidence, that she had been planning their escape from South Carolina and she was ready to give him the news that they could finally leave. Leave this town, his father, and every evil thing that had ruined their happiness. He pondered if that wistful smile she so often donned had to do with these plans, and if she didn't want to tell him sooner, because not every detail had been arranged yet. Maybe his grandparents were ready to help them and take them back into their home. Maybe she had some long lost relative or friend that was willing to give them a place to stay.

Logan had to hope. He had to hold onto the dream that one day, they'd be free. He would be driven insane otherwise.

Smoke from the stove oven reached him through the forest, assuring him that he was close to home. Close to a warm fire, a hot meal, and a pair of loving arms that would tell him everything would be all right.

Just when he saw the lit cabin window shining through the dimming twilight, he heard it. Shouts. Deep, booming shouts that were slurred and senseless. Beneath it, a voice meek and pleading, almost too soft to be distinguishable.

Logan stopped and listened. He could make out a few words. None of them kind. Fear and fury swirled in his chest, each emotion taking turns as he scrambled to think of what to do. He knew what was happening. It happened too often for him not to know. As much as she hid the bruises, as much as she smiled through it all, he could never truly ignore what that man was doing to her.

When he was younger, he had tried to interfere. He might as well have been a mouse taking on a raging lion. He'd be pushed aside or struck down the moment he tried to defend his mother. By age seven, he learned to look the other way, because there was little he could do. There was nothing left but to wait for the storm to pass, so they could pick up the wreckage; the broken pieces of furniture, the glass, and the wounded hearts that Jasper Elster left in his drunken wake.

Logan squeezed his eyes tight and tried to listen to anything else. The owl flapping its wings up on a high branch, the cold evening wind rustling the leaves, the pounding of his own heart in his ears. Anything but the screaming and the whimpering.

He flinched when he heard the first blow. It sounded so close, as if he were right there in the room. His mother cried out and there came a crash as if she had fallen. Then there came more whimpers, soft and shrill like the warbling of a wood thrush. Logan balled his hands into fists and he could feel every muscle in his body tighten.

This was something he couldn't ignore. Not anymore. The day had started so well, so hopeful with his father gone. The house was peaceful without him. They could breathe. Now, Logan's lungs wouldn't respond. They, like the rest of him, were congested with that immense, heavy indignation.

He had to do something. No more would he be a spectator. He was a man. Sixteen now. Logan looked to his hands and saw them roughened with callouses by the labor he was forced to do, because his father wouldn't. He had been the only one to care for his mother, and for once in his life, he could finally do what needed to be done ages ago.

His eyes opened and courage displaced fear. He let that anger and hatred for his father course through his blood, imbuing him with the confidence he needed.

He took one step, and then another. Soon, he was running. Logan closed the distance between himself and the porch and charged through the door, nearly blowing it off the hinges.

The house was trashed. Once clean and orderly furniture was turned over. He could see the pie tin flipped upside down on the floor, the crust obliterated, and bits of cold, congealed apple slices spilled out from the edges.

In the center was his mother, holding onto a table leg as the monster repeatedly sent his foot slamming into her stomach. Tears streamed down her cheeks, a dark line of blood trailing from her nostril and down her lips. She tried to curl in her legs to shield herself, but her husband, the man who should have been her protector and her lover, would allow her no reprieve.

Logan didn't even hear what he was saying anymore. He didn't need to know. He didn't want to know. All he saw was his back and the whiskey bottle gripped tight in his hand.

Without another thought, Logan reached for the nearest overturned chair and swung it at the man. The legs and stretchers splintered into pieces, leaving only the back and seat. His father stumbled forward and caught himself against the wall. The whiskey bottle fell from his hand and shattered. Shards of glass skittered across the floorboards as the alcohol filled the air with its potent stench.

A deathly silence filled the cabin with only the heavy, labored breaths of his mother who couldn't rise from the floor. His father, once he recovered, turned to look at his son with eyes as black as the night, and just as cold.

Logan remembered a time when his father shaved, when he took pride in his appearance. Now, the man that stared back at him looked like a vagrant, a beggar, a drunk. He didn't even look like the same man, but he knew his father. He had seen the transformation over the years. What stood before him was nothing more than a stranger who paraded around with a name and title he forsook years ago.

They glared to one another and Logan never felt more like a man in his life. He was more than the piece of trash in front of him.

At the absolute worst time, Logan felt his whole body wrack with the painful spasms. His limbs stiffened and his jaw clamped so tight he thought his teeth would crack in half. He groaned, but he wouldn't take his eyes off his father.

"You wanna fight me, kid?" the drunk asked, taking a halting step forward. "You really wanna start this with me?"

"Leave her alone," Logan growled through his gritted teeth. A shiver traveled across his skin and seemed to sink into his flesh, uncontrollable and enough to make him think he'd crumble to the floor. But he had to keep standing. He had to keep fighting.

"Logan, stop." His mother's voice was wispy and feeble, but he could sense the strength in her, as if she were holding on just as tightly as he was.

His father turned and bellowed more insults, but the roaring pulse of his racing heart drowned it out. The pain intensified, and though Logan began to sway with a sudden wave of dizziness, he stayed on his feet. Everything began to tingle and throb, every bone put under an immense tension as if they would snap.

Jasper looked up and his bloodshot eyes went wide. The sneer was all but gone as a new feeling manifested. Logan's jaw relaxed and he heard, more than realized, the breaths he took came out in unsteady growls.

His father bent to the floor to retrieve the neck of the broken whiskey bottle and Logan acted.

He leapt forward, springing like an animal upon his father. Darkness rimmed his vision, closing in over the man's terror-stricken face. There came a deafening roar that eradicated every other sense. Then, all went black. As black as a dreamless sleep.

Susan hid her face in her arms, willing the chaos to stop. The roaring, the screaming, the sound of clothes and flesh shredding. Then there was the pain. Immense, penetrating pain through her core and chest. Jasper had hit her before, but never this hard or this passionately. Maybe he knew what she had planned to do. To tell Logan everything about his past, his real father, and what was now taking over his body.

She had known this was coming for years, but she didn't want to think it was possible. Like The Colonel, she wanted to believe that her mother had finally snapped under the pressure of being everything for everyone. The wife, mother, grandmother, and head of the household believed in monsters. She spoke of them so often when Susan was growing up, but after a while, she had set that obsession on the shelf.

It wasn't until Logan was born that she began to fixate on them again. On werewolves.

Nancy's' friends, the ones who wrote her long, detailed letters, only encouraged the mania. They told her about the creatures she believed still had a hold over her family. No one took her seriously. No one even entertained the idea that Logan would somehow inherit the curse. It was a long shot, even Nancy admitted that to her the last time she visited the Elster home when Logan was five years old. But it was a risk she wanted her daughter to be prepared for.

Susan had seen the changes in Logan. Subtle, minute things that not even she could articulate. Something in her soul told her it was time to tell him everything about his maternal grandfather, about werewolves, and that he had no real kinship with Jasper.

Now, it was too late. He had become what she and Nancy had feared, and there was no more time to explain. Not that it would matter in a short while. The beast would find her cowering in one of the bedrooms. According to her mother, werewolves had excellent hearing and sense of smell. Logan would hear her pounding heart, her gasping, labored breaths. He would find her, and he would kill her, just like he killed Jasper.

Hot tears stung at her eyes and mixed with the smeared blood on her cheeks and lips. Her whole body trembled and shuddered in the nearly useless hiding spot. Tucking herself into a ball behind a trunk, her back to the wall and out of sight from the doorway, there was nowhere else to go. Susan didn't feel strong enough to run into the woods. She was sure that Jasper had broken her ankle during the beating. And her abdomen hurt so badly that the act of standing and hobbling from the kitchen to the bedroom nearly crippled her.

There was silence in the house and Susan bit her lips together to keep any rogue sound from escaping. She couldn't cry. She couldn't wail out in pain as she wanted. It might have been pointless, prolonging the inevitable. But there was still hope. There was always hope.

A guttural growl rumbled through the cabin and she heard the scraping of rough paws on the floorboards. Slow, deliberate, skilled strides. Susan closed her eyes and listened to her son draw closer.

She knew what would happen in the morning. Nancy had told her everything. Logan would change back into his former self, but with exceptions. He'd be stronger, faster. His senses would be on fire. Logan wouldn't be able to eat like he used to. No more apple pies or his favorite roasted potatoes. Only meat would keep him healthy now. This wasn't a phase. This wasn't something he'd grow out of like when he sucked his thumb. It wasn't a sickness like the colds he so often caught at the onset of winter. This was permanent, and he'd live with it forever.

He wouldn't remember what happened tonight, but she wished with every bit of her soul that he would run far away and never come back to this cabin. She hoped that he would get lost in the forest, lose his way and not come back to see her dead body. The body that he would tear apart.

A hush fell over the bedroom and Susan cracked open her eyes, unable to see much in the near complete darkness now that the sun had set. She heard nothing. Not the noisy breaths or the thudding of his paws.

She was almost tempted to peek around the trunk when it was tossed aside. With one powerful sweep of his arm, Logan had knocked it across the room. She cried out and shrank against the wall. But she couldn't bring herself to look away from the thing her son had become.

His clothes had been ripped from his massive body, now covered in a pelt of thick, midnight black fur. He looked every part the half-man, half-wolf creature that her mother had sketched in the journal she had left with Susan. His torso was broad, his arms thickened by strong muscles. A tail grazed the floor behind him as he stood on legs that were better suited for a dog. His head, most of all, had changed. Tall ears stood erect, swiveled toward her in that alert, aggressive fashion she saw on the strays that fought in town. Lips curled over a muzzle that snarled at her. Golden, wolfish eyes glared where blue ones should have been. Blue eyes like Ilias, his real father.

There was nothing of Logan in this beast. No recognition in its stare, no gentleness or mercy. He charged toward her, fangs gnashing and sharp claws ready to steal her away from this world.

Still, Susan couldn't turn away. All she could think about was how she wouldn't get to hold her boy again. She'd never be able to tell him the truth or comfort him through this transformation. She'd never hear his voice again, never feel his arms wrap around her neck in a loving embrace.

She had loved and lost so much. The years she had given to Logan could never be considered wasted. The love affair with Ilias could never be forgotten. He gave her a son and sixteen years of purposeful living. If she didn't have Logan, she would have given up long ago. Her sentence of misery with Jasper had been extended a little longer for the sake of her son, but she could never regret it.

Susan thought of the times she had taught him to walk, the moment he said his first word, the first time he had been able to say, "I love you, maw." And she smiled. She smiled in the face of her son and executioner. She was ready to go, if this was how it would end.

The beast froze, the tip of its wet nose just inches from her face. The gold eyes grew wide, black lips closed over fangs dripping with saliva. He blinked and eased away, staring into Susan's face with what she would have called confusion and fear.

Did he know her? Did he see her? Remember her?

Susan lifted a tremulous hand and reached out for him. The tip of her finger nearly touched that stretch of fur just below his eye when he recoiled and snorted. Logan tossed his head and the shudder transferred through the rest of his body. Her lashes fluttered and then he was gone. She was left in the empty bedroom and the pounding of her son's powerful limbs on the ground began to fade as he ran further and further away from the cabin.

When the shock wore off, when she realized that she wasn't marked for death, the pain returned. Agonizing and magnified, she doubled over onto the floor and gripped around her middle. She thought to call for help, but she knew she would receive none. For the first time since Ilias left her, Susan felt completely and utterly alone.

CHAPTER 3

All he could feel was the cold. A numbing, penetrating cold that made his entire body sore and tender. He could even feel it in his bones as the chill made his flesh shiver. Equally debilitating as the cold was the darkness. The total blackness that terrified him. That fear wrapped around him, enveloping him like it belonged on his soul, leeching everything from him.

He couldn't move, couldn't breathe, or bring himself to think of anything else. Just the cold and the dark.

An eternity passed before two more senses came crashing through, stirring him from his near comatose state. The sound of buzzing flies backed by chirps and the breeze in the trees. And that smell that made Logan's mouth water. It reminded him of the cookouts and barbeques held at their faraway neighbors' homes. The savory scents of the cooked meats would carry on the wind to his cabin.

It took so much effort to open his eyes. At first, he was blinded by the glare of the morning sun streaming through the foliage in front of him. He blinked and his eyes adjusted. Forgetting his fatigue, Logan let out a hoarse cry and scrambled through the bed of dead leaves. Lying there, its black, lifeless eyes staring at him, was a doe. Her neck was shredded, her belly peeled open to reveal what remained beneath ribs that were picked clean.

Logan gaped at the sight, his chest heaving for air. The shock warmed his body, but he now realized why he was so cold. He was naked. He tore his gaze away from the deer and looked for his clothes, but found nothing but the dry and brittle leaves that blanketed the ground.

He didn't recognize this clearing, or these trees. He couldn't remember anything.

Then, like a slap to the face, the memory of last night came to him. He remembered his mother's cries, his father's shouts. Furniture was broken. The pie was destroyed. Glass shattering. The stench of whiskey all over the cabin floor.

Then a roar. Loud and menacing. It was his roar.

Logan lifted his hands and gasped. Every inch of him from the tips of his fingers and halfway up his biceps were the dark maroon shade of dried blood. He looked to his torso, his chest, and legs. All over was the same. Blood everywhere.

He looked to the deer and came to the sickening realization that it was the carcass that put off such a succulent, pleasing aroma. The buzzing he had heard were the flies cleaning up what the predator hadn't devoured.

Why was he here? What happened to make him forget everything that came after he attacked his father? Why was his body now toned and built like a brute? He had been a youth yesterday, stuck between boyhood and full maturity. He had grown overnight? How was it possible?

The darkness was gone now that he was wide awake, but the fear consumed him. He could feel everything come into sharp relief as he hyperventilated and continued to back away from the doe's corpse. His feet slipped on the grass wet with dew, his hands scraped against the rough bark of the tree as he tried to use them to propel himself further and further into the woods.

He wanted to go home. He wanted answers. He wanted this blood off of him. He wanted his mother. He needed to find her.

Logan felt like a newborn colt trying to walk and make his way to a path. Any path. The urgency to find home drove him through the cold, the confusion, the slight ache of hunger, and the crippling fear. Tears that he barely felt slide down his cheeks angered him. He felt weak and helpless. He never wanted to be helpless. That was why he had attacked his father. That's why he made the choice to be his family's defender. Looking at him now, he was anything but that.

Finally, picking his way west, he found a marker. A road sign. It pointed north toward his hometown. Logan took courage at the first sign of hope he'd had all morning and bolted into a run. But even that proved difficult. He continually collided with trees, tripped over logs he didn't see coming, and got caught in bushes that scratched against his legs. He rammed his shoulders enough times he was sure he had broken something, but he could still stand and continue at his frantic sprint as if he hadn't been hurt at all.

The cabin came into view and Logan rushed for it, tripping over the porch steps and nearly crawling his way inside. The scene stunned him just like the carcass of the doe. Dark smatterings of blood speckled across the walls and covered the floor. The only reason it hadn't pooled around the mutilated body of his father was because the gaps in the floorboards allowed the blood to drain away.

He wouldn't behold his father's face, frozen in the last open look of horror.

Every piece of furniture had been broken. The stove was knocked over, the pipe that fed through the ceiling hanging and disconnected. The sink and water pump had also been ripped from its place and, like the blood, the excess water dripped through the floor. The upholstery looked as if it had been ripped and clawed by an animal, the white cotton stuffing scattered across the equally torn strips of the rug and curtains.

Did a bear wander into their home after Logan ran away? By now, he assumed that's what he had done. How else would he have awoken so far away? And if the beast had done this to his father, what of his mother? Had she escaped?

Logan could feel his chin tighten and quiver as he remembered how frail she had been the night before. She could barely push herself up when he had attacked his father. It was likely she didn't get away. It must have killed her too. Why hadn't he stayed?

Then, he thought he heard something through his wheezing, whining breaths that would have preceded a fit of sobs. It was a whisper, so soft he questioned whether he heard it at all. Then, it came again. It spoke his name.

Logan vaulted over the debris and made for his parents' bedroom. He froze in the doorway and saw his mother lying on the floor. Her mouth and the front of her dress was caked with old and fresh blood. Her pale face, neck, and arms were spotted with dark bruises. Likewise, her ankle looked to be bent in some unnatural way. That's why she couldn't escape, but it didn't explain why he had left her like this.

Her glossy eyes lifted, and she smiled when she saw him. Only a mother could smile at her son when he was naked and covered in blood.

He took a few steps forward, but stopped again. Did she know that he had left her? By her first reaction, she didn't seem mad or angry. Could she forgive him? Did she already? Or did she know why he left?

An unsteady hand reached for him and Logan fell to his knees in front of her. He searched for a place to grab hold, but none seemed right. Wherever he touched, he knew he would hurt her. He couldn't do that. Not after all she had endured.

That hand seized his and held on with a strength he didn't know she was capable of.

"You're going to be okay, Logan." Her voice was raspy, but he could hear every word as if she were saying it in his ear.

Logan let his fingers close over hers and minded not to pinch her fragile bones. "I'll get the doctor from town. I just need to – "

His mother shushed him and closed her eyes. "No," she said. "Don't go. Stay here."

Logan nodded frantically and once more tried to look for a way to make her more comfortable. He snatched one of the pillows from the bed and tucked it beneath her head.

"Last night..." she began, "you... Logan, promise me you'll be calm and listen? You never did listen very well when it was important."

This was his chance. "I'm listening," he quickly assured. "What happened? Why did I leave you? Was it a bear? A cougar? What happened?"

Once more, she shushed him, and Logan bit his lips together.

"It wasn't a bear," she replied effortfully. "It was... It was you. You did this."

Logan glanced over his shoulder to the destruction in the other room. He could see his father's boot peeking in the doorway, his pantleg torn and saturated. He shook his head. He couldn't have done this.

"You changed into..." Her explanation was stalled by convulsing coughs that left her weak and breathless. More blood oozed over her lips. Logan could do nothing to ease her pain or whatever it was that was slowly stealing away the light in her eyes.

"You changed into a wolf," she managed to continue. "I wasn't sure if it would happen, but it did. Your grandmother knew, but I didn't want to worry you without reason. I never knew if she was right, but she was. She was right all along." She reached up with her other hand and held onto Logan like she would drift away if she didn't. "In my hope chest, there's a journal. Your grandmother wrote it. I need you to take it and read it. Your grandfather, your true grandfather, is the only one who can help you. Find him. His name is in the journal."

Logan shook his head, refusing to accept any of it. Wolves? Changing? It was ridiculous. He couldn't change. Then again, glancing down to his new body, he had changed in a way. But not into a beast. It was impossible.

"No. You can tell me. Because you're going to live. I won't read anything."

"Yes, you will," she said with a firm, scolding tone. It was the same tone she had used when Logan refused to behave. "I can't remember everything and I can't... I can't hold on."

Logan cocooned her frail, weakening hands between his. "Yes, you can, maw." Fresh tears gathered on his lashes. "You have to hold on. I'm sorry I left you last night. I won't leave you again."

She smiled and her eyes drifted shut. "You can and you will. You have to... I did my job. I raised you right, I think. Once you find your grandfather and learn all you need to learn about being a werewolf, things will get easier. I promise. You just have to have faith, remember? Faith and hope. Everything's going to be fine."

He didn't care about hurting her anymore. He gingerly scooped her into his arms and held her against his chest. His nose buried in the locks of hair that dried his tears. "I'm not a werewolf," he mumbled. "I'm not. You just... just don't remember right. It must have been a bear. I'm sorry I wasn't here."

She might as well have not heard him. "Promise me you'll look for him? Promise me you'll find him? I can't go unless you promise."

Logan held in the sputtering sobs and shook his head again. "No. I won't promise. I'm not going anywhere."

"Try to remember, Logan. Last night, you were here. You changed and killed Jasper. Then you came in here..."

She didn't have to finish. The moment she said it, the flashbacks came. The screaming, the blood, the fangs and claws. The frightened look in her eyes... then the smile. That whimsical, peaceful smile as he came forward with growls. The only thought that he had when he faced her down was pure and unmitigated hunger.

Logan gasped and fisted the expanse of fabric across her back. "I... I did... Oh, God..."

His mother shushed and her head began to list as she grew frailer. He pulled away and looked to her ashen face and eyes that dimmed with each passing second.

"I forgive you," she breathed. "I forgive you for everything... I..."

The sobs he had tried to restrain came bursting out the moment she went limp in his arms. Her body went cold and still. She was gone. His only thought remained repeating in his head, over and over again with dogged spirit.

He killed her. It was his fault. He was here, he had turned into a monster. He didn't understand how or why, but he had. She wasn't lying or hallucinating. Logan was a werewolf, and he had killed her. He did this to her.

The world around him dropped away. Nothing else existed beyond that room. Nothing else mattered other than what was in his arms. He held his mother and cried into her shoulder, wailing and screaming for her spirit to return. He might have looked like a man now, and had committed the crimes only a man could commit, but he felt like a child. Scared and alone. He had never been without her. How was he supposed to survive in the world on his own?

Then, like an answer to that very question, Logan felt something stir within him. Something dark, evil, and terrifying. It was as if something had come awake in him. It was what exuded the fear and hatred. Hatred for the unfairness of life, and at himself. Because he knew, deep down, that his sorrows were his own fault. He brought this upon himself.

Then, there came a sobering thought. He, Logan, the boy raised by the saint of a woman who had died in his arms, didn't cause all of this. He would never have done this. It was the monster within him. It was the wolf that killed her, the wolf that killed his father and that deer.

Logan was blameless, but the beast within him had ruined his life.

Devia, Alabama

Darren slowly ambled around the edges of the classroom, occasionally weaving around the occupied desks and watching his students from the corner of his eye. An open tome of Shakespeare's sonnets rested in one palm while the other was fisted behind his back.

He had chosen Elijah to read aloud, knowing full well that the ten-year-old struggled with the task. If he didn't practice, he would never be better. And Darren knew that Elijah's mother had little time to monitor his lessons at home. They were in Devia for a reason.

He could hear Elijah's racing heart from across the room and smell the sweat on his neck. His hands that held the book were shaking, just as his voice was as he read aloud. The boy knew that he wasn't as far along as the other boys his age in the class. He didn't need loup-garou senses to know when they whispered about his slowness or ineptitude. Darren might have been the only one pushing him to strive for better when he wanted to give up and quit school altogether.

The eighty-ninth sonnet was not the most complex, but it contained those tricky words that Elijah labored over the most. The student did his best to sound out the words, stammering and grinding out the syllables that he knew.

He stopped cold at "acquaintance" and Darren knew that now was the time to step in.

"Ah-quain-tance," he sounded out with Elijah. His British accent was not wholly uncommon for Devia. These boys heard languages and accents from all over the world in their small town. Despite living in France for centuries before coming to America, Darren had never forgotten his roots, his true home that he might never return to.

His young pupil nodded with a bit more confidence and recited the word.

Two boys in the back giggled and Darren's brown eyes snapped to them. Timothy and Josiah were a year ahead of Elijah, not unlike half of his classmates. They, however, had learned long ago that respect was only earned when given.

The younger students were busy practicing their letters, pencils carefully drawing between the lines in their booklets. Those older by five years or more read along, but grew bored quickly of the lesson, since they had already reached the point in their studies that they could recite many of the sonnets by heart. But a few things that Darren would not tolerate in his class were whispered conversations, note passing, or sleeping. They all knew the consequences if any of them should disobey.

Timothy glanced up to his teacher and saw the stern set of his brows. He elbowed his friend and Josiah likewise stopped. This was their first warning.

Darren turned back to the sonnet. He continued his stroll around the classroom, inspecting the work of the children while making sure that all eyes were open and attentive. Two pairs, however, roamed further than they should have.

He had already separated Allie May and Rafe, putting each of them on opposite sides of the school room. Yet, they still managed to speak volumes without saying a word to one another. Rafe was seventeen, freshly changed and a full loup-garou like Darren, except far less experienced by a few hundred years. He and Allie May had grown up in this town, their fathers being good friends. Darren remembered when he would separate them during recess for roughhousing. Now, they couldn't stop blushing and batting eyelashes at one another.

As much as Darren supported budding love, he didn't condone its flowering in his classroom. He stood beside Rafe and simply waited for the young loup-garou to notice. With his superior senses, it didn't take long. His student gave one last look to his sweetheart before slouching further in his chair. Darren gave his shoulder a reassuring pat and moved on.

In his class, there were four other boys who had matured into men overnight. They were given a brief holiday from schoolwork to spend time with their fathers or mentors, learning to control their new loup-garou abilities. Only when they could tune out every subtle noise, every distracting scent, and keep their new wolfish instinct to themselves, were they allowed back into the classroom.

The smaller boys, those who were destined to do the same one day, nearly idolized their older classmates and each time a new loup-garou rejoined them, questions poured in from every tiny mouth. Darren allowed it. They would need to know these things when it was their time. Every change was different, and these boys were far more blessed to live in Devia than they would ever realize.

When the word "acquaintance" came up one more time a few lines further in the sonnet, Elijah paused again. Darren gave him half a moment to try, and when he opened his mouth again to help him as he had before, the giggling resumed.

Elijah froze and his attention was no longer on the page. Several of the students turned in their seats to glare at Timothy and Josiah. For the first time since the lesson began, the schoolhouse fell deathly silent as the constant metronome of Darren's footfalls ceased.

He snapped the book closed and drew himself up to his full height to glare at the boys. "Would you two like to share what is so amusing?"

The blood in their faces drained as they exchanged glances. Only one of them was brave enough to speak.

"It's an easy word," Josiah said.

Elijah, much to Darren's dismay, abruptly sat down and set the book down on his desk. His hands were folded in his lap, eyes downcast in shame. It only proved to enrage Darren further, and his wolf was in one accord with him.

"So was 'compromise', but it took you months to remember the correct way to say it."

He saw the jaws of a few students tense as they resisted the urge to laugh just as Josiah and Timothy had. Darren almost wished that they would, if nothing else than to prove a point.

"My pa says it wrong at home all the time," Josiah defended. "I can't help it."

Darren gestured to Elijah. "And he has no pa to teach him how to say 'acquaintance' at home. He could say that he can't help it either. But he's trying harder than you did."

"But, Mr. Dubose – "

Timothy didn't get the chance to finish. Darren had a closed-fisted rein over his wolf, but the dominance was one aspect that he allowed to seep out every once and a while in the classroom. It got their attention. The other loups-garous in the class shrank and trembled. They were far more susceptible to this subliminal force than most. Everyone felt it in one way or another. Sometimes as a crushing, suffocating weight. Other times as a constricting vice. More subtly as a mere tingle that ran up their spines to make them sit up straighter in their desks.

Luckily, Darren had three and a half hundred years to perfect his dominance. He targeted the two boys and let them feel the brunt power. He was an alpha without a traditional pack, but he would be respected as one.

The faces of the boys pinched uncomfortably and they both knew they had crossed the line.

"Everyone in this class, at one point in their education, has been challenged. Whether it's a word, an arithmetic formula, or memorizing dates in history. We have all struggled, myself included. Learning isn't easy, but it is necessary. And it's easier when you have a friend, a tutor, a family, or a classmate to help you. If you can't support one another as colleagues, then you will never function well in a pack. And each of you boys will be in a loup-garou pack one day. As Abraham Lincoln said, a house divided against itself cannot stand. A pack that quarrels or ridicules one another will be torn apart."

The four loups-garous who were just beginning to learn the full meaning behind this speech, looked to their teacher with respect that was only tainted with a hint of fear. Fear for the unknown, for their future, their families, and the tremendous changes they had undergone.

For several decades, Darren had purposefully slipped these lessons into their studies for their sake. He wanted to have an impact in their lives, to be the one they could go to for help if they needed it. Some of these boys didn't have fathers to turn to, just as he hadn't when he first turned. Not one of them would ever feel as alone and lost as he did.

"You two can stay after dismissal and clean the schoolhouse." Darren's judgement was not as harsh as it could have been. Many parents encouraged him to take more aggressive action against delinquent students. Perhaps the one thing keeping him from taking a paddle to their bums was the fact that he didn't like to wash the chalkboards any more than they did. Making them do it was punishment enough.

"Elijah, please stand again and finish the sonnet."

Whether the boy had taken courage in his teacher's speech or the fact that the bullies were called out for their own academic deficiencies, he did stand again and square his shoulders before continuing where he had left off. This time, he pronounced 'acquaintance' correctly and loudly for all of them to hear.

When he finished the sonnet, Darren opened the floor for discussion of its meaning. They broke down each line, one by one. The advantage of being born within the same generation of Shakespeare's infamy, Darren could translate many of the words and phrases that they couldn't understand.

During this time, a fresh wave of alertness came to Darren's senses. Another loup-garou was approaching the schoolhouse. He didn't know their scent, but he didn't let it alarm him. There were hundreds of loups-garous in Devia. Some were parents of his students, others were without children, but there remained many he hadn't formally met.

He wandered to the window to see if he could spot the visitor. All four of his more aware students turned to gaze out the same window, craning their necks to see what their teacher was looking for. One reproving look killed their curiosity.

Darren ascertained that the scent was coming from the forest that surrounded the schoolhouse. Unlike most of the other buildings in Devia, they were settled somewhat out of the way from the main thoroughfare. There were less distractions out here, and it provided a spacious field for the children's recess.

He watched the tree line, eyes squinting as he waited and waited. Their steps were slow, halting, almost stumbling. He couldn't see the loup-garou yet, but he could smell something else. Blood. It was old. Very old. But still there, clinging to him like a forewarning sign.

One of the older girls – a scholar beyond her peers - continued her elaborate dissertation about the sonnet, unaffected by the swiveling heads in the classroom.

He interrupted her once the silhouette of the loup-garou came into view. Haggard, clothes too big for him, and emanating an aura so strong that Darren's wolf growled inwardly at the sight of him. In the past, he had not trusted his wolf's intuition. Over the centuries, he came to take what he saw was useful and what was not. But if his wolf didn't like the stranger, then neither did Darren. Especially when this stranger was coming toward the schoolhouse, hungry and halfway dead on his feet.

"Haytham, watch the class."

He gave the order to one of the eldest loup-garou in the class, who also served as his assistant when necessary. Darren set down his book on his desk near the front, hurried out the front door, and then down the steps.

The cold wind bit at his face and arms, exposed by his rolled sleeves. By the look of the loup-garou, he wasn't dressed warm enough for this winter weather, which could have been attributing to his state.

Golden eyes stared ahead, unblinking and clouded by some nameless emotion. Darren hesitated to approach, but when he didn't recognize the loup-garou and realized that he was no more then sixteen, he rushed forward.

The youth must have comprehended and came to a clumsy stop. His legs quivered beneath him and Darren wondered if he would collapse. His clothes were torn and stained. How far had he traveled? Whose blood was caked underneath his nails? When was the last time he ate anything?

Their eyes met and Darren did as he would with any frightened man or animal. He made his hands visible and dropped every ounce of dominance he possessed. While the dominance could inspire obedience, it could also be the catalyst for fear. The last thing this stranger needed was an excuse to attack him.

Behind him, he could hear his students run to the window and whisper about the scene. And if he could hear them, the stranger could too. The way his gaze flickered in the direction of the schoolhouse told him enough.

"Are you all right?" Darren asked slowly, drawing the boy's notice.

He parted his parched, cracked lips, but the only sounds that could come out were crackles and shaky breaths. On the border of shock and collapse, Darren took an easing step forward.

"What's your name?"

Still, the boy couldn't reply. It only took another moment of trying to force the words out before he finally crumbled. Golden eyes rolled and the muscles that had been drawn taunt released all at once.

Darren rushed forward and caught him before he could hit the ground, covering several yards in the blink of an eye. The stranger was drenched in sweat, hair disheveled, feet bare, and heart racing despite his unconscious state.

It was then he perceived that the boy was carrying something in his hand. A black leather journal fell to the grass. Once Darren had a good hold on him, he picked up the journal and slipped it into his vest for safe keeping. Perhaps it would have a name or some clue to his identity.

Whoever this loup-garou was would need to be taken into town and tended to.

One look to the schoolhouse window, he spotted Haytham's face through the glass pane. He gave a nod, a silent communication of his plans. He was a capable young man, even if he had no dominance like his alpha father. He could keep the other students busy until he returned.

It was a long walk back into Devia, but Robert or Adam would certainly know what to do with the stranger.

CHAPTER 4

The burning, gnawing hunger in his stomach was gone. His muscles no longer ached. He felt light, almost weightless. And yet, there was a creeping sensation across his scalp. As if someone were rolling a set of dull spurs up and down the length of his back and around his temples.

Is this death? Please let it be death. I need this to be death.

But he wasn't dead. That much he understood. Logan was breathing. In and out. His senses slowly came to him like it had that long ago morning. But there wasn't the smell of the fresh carcass or the buzzing of flies around his head. There were voices whispering, their words intelligible at first. Then there was warmth. Clean clothes rubbed on his skin as his chest rose and fell with each breath.

Logan was very much alive.

Damn it.

A thousand different smells blended together, mingling in his nose like a swarm of mice pushing their way through a tiny hole. It was as if each person in the room were just inches from him, though he knew they weren't. Sounds, so near and so distant, rang in his head. Laughter, talking, whispering, footsteps, shouting, rustling of fabric and the constant clanging of metal and wood. All of it pounded in his ears. For the last three weeks, he had been this way. Driven mad by all of it.

The only thing he could remember, through the madness, was a word. He remembered hearing it far off. Just one word. Loup-garou. He followed it, and the voices. He came to a white house. No, it was a school. And there was a man.

Logan remembered the way he felt in that moment as he faced the first person he had encountered since leaving South Carolina. Deep in his gut, a rage exploded. He didn't understand why. He didn't want to feel it. The stranger didn't deserve it. But that thing in him, the one that craved meat, it hated him.

In the din, he heard that man's voice.

"He must not have eaten for days," he said. He sounded strange and foreign. Logan remembered once when an Englishman came to Ollie's stables for help. He had been passing through, but Logan remembered that unique accent. So different from the southern cadence he had been raised with.

"I'd bet for weeks," said another voice. It wasn't as deep as the first, but gentler and thoughtful. "I've never seen another so malnourished."

"It's a good thing he fell unconscious," said a third. This one was gruff and held more authority than all three of them combined. "He would have been too unstable to be reasoned with." He knew that accent. It reminded him of home. Of South Carolina.

Logan moved his head and a spark of pain shot through his neck and down his chest. He winced and swallowed hard, but the damage was already done.

"He's awake," said the second voice, accompanied by a pair of hasty footsteps.

Logan tensed involuntarily, bracing for a touch that didn't come. It was then he realized he was on a bed. He felt the sheets beneath him and the comfortable padding of the mattress. His head had rolled against a pillow, crisp and smelling of cotton.

More came to his bedside. He could bear the noise and the smells, but if he opened his eyes, he feared it would bring back all the hunger, the fatigue, the anger and the hatred. It would all sweep in like a gust and tip him over the edge.

The trickling of water sounded off to his side and something soft and cold pressed to his forehead. Before he understood what he was doing, his hand shot out and snatched at the wrist. It was thin and he felt the pulse quicken in his grasp.

A feminine whimper shattered his complacency. Before he had the chance to squeeze harder and break her arm as he wanted, Logan released and let his hand close over the air just in front of his face. The fist was a warning and they heeded him.

The man with authority was the first to break the silence in the room. "Leave, Ginny. Your work is done here."

Logan heard her light footsteps and the dusting of her dress hem against the floor. A door closed and he lowered his fist, but he still wouldn't look at the men. He could feel their stares on him, pinning him to the bed in a muted command to remain perfectly still. All he wanted to do was run.

"You're safe here," said the Englishman. "Nobody's going to hurt you."

He wanted to believe it, but everything in him rejected the assurance. He didn't feel safe. He felt lost and unsure why his head continued to tingle like it did. He wanted answers, but he didn't want to speak.

"What's your name?" the softer voice asked.

A weight pressed down on the edge of the mattress near his side and a new, disturbing sound erupted from Leo's chest. A growl. It rumbled low, another warning. But the man didn't listen. He didn't move.

"You are safe here," the deeper, commanding voice reiterated. "We're like you. We just want to help."

Just like me?

The growl died away and he put a greater effort into opening his eyes this time. The light dazed him at first. It poured through a window behind him, shining upon the three men.

"His eyes were gold when I found him," the British man said to the others in a hushed tone. Dark haired with eyes to match, he was indeed the one that came out to meet him from the schoolhouse.

"That's an improvement," replied the gentle one sitting on his bed. He gave Logan a tight-lipped smile, green eyes smiling with him. His long dark hair was pulled back behind him. The prominent cheekbones and darker complexion reminded him of a Cherokee who lived on the outskirts of his home town. But this man was lighter, and he had never seen an Indian with such emerald eyes.

The last, the one who exuded so much confidence, stared at Logan with piercing blue eyes that offset his jet-black hair. There was something unsettling, yet calm about him. If he thought anyone was a threat, it would be this man. Yet, if anyone were capable of protecting Logan, it would also be him.

All were strong, judging by their build and how their clothes were filled out around their shoulders and arms. They seemed capable, steady, and Logan began to believe what the Englishman said. Maybe he was safe.

"What's your name?" the leader asked as he folded his arms.

Logan let his lips separate, but the answer sat on his tongue for a moment before he could force it out. "Logan... Logan Elster."

He nodded, as if the answer pleased him. "I'm Robert Croxen." Then he gestured to the half-blood native and the Englishman. "This is Adam Swenson and Darren Dubose. Do you remember meeting Darren?"

Logan regarded the schoolteacher and nodded in answer.

"How are you feeling?" Adam Swenson questioned, scrutinizing his face for any flaw or sign of distress.

"Fine," he lied.

The three men stared, and he could tell that they saw through his passive answer. However, they didn't press further.

"Where did you come from?" Darren asked, sliding his hands deep into his trouser pockets.

Once more, Logan didn't want to trust them. He didn't want to say too much. What if they already knew who he was? What if they knew about his parents? How far had he fled from home?

"Where am I?" he asked, carefully avoiding any other questions.

Robert was more obliging. "You're in Devia, Alabama."

So, he had made it. Logan let out a long breath. In his grandmother's journal, it had said his grandfather, the werewolf he inherited from, was from Alabama. It also mentioned in a later entry about Devia. This was a safe haven for werewolves, for beasts like him.

Somehow, through the starvation and fatigue, he'd made it.

"I need to see Dustin Keith," he told them.

Darren visibly bristled at the name. The other two looked to the teacher, shock written in their expressions. "Dustin Keith?" he repeated.

Logan nodded. "Is he here? I need to see him."

Now, Darren looked to the others for assistance. Irritation flamed in him at the delay.

"Is he your father?" Robert asked, his tone dropping a note to convey the seriousness of the question.

"My grandfather... on my mother's side."

It was then that the three relaxed, but only marginally. Darren seemed especially peeved. Adam looked back to Logan. "Who is your father?"

Again, Logan didn't want to answer. He looked to the three of them, and then shook his head. "I need to see Dustin. Is he here or not?"

"He's not," Darren curtly replied. "He left when the war started. He's probably in Europe somewhere. We haven't heard from him in years."

Logan let his head drift backward. All that way for nothing. The promise his mother wanted him to keep was for nothing now.

"If you want us to help, we need to know more, Logan." Adam's voice cut through the contained wrath that surged in him.

He had walked for miles upon miles, across state lines and risked death by starvation to find Dustin, and he wasn't even there. Logan wondered if he could book a passage to Europe, if it was even worth it. His mind was already far away from Devia by the time Darren spoke.

"Where are you from?" he asked.

He wanted to lie. To say he was from somewhere else in Alabama, or even Tennessee. Admitting he was from South Carolina might make them inquire about his family. The one he had left behind.

If they found out what happened to them, they might turn him into the authorities. He'd be charged for murder and sentenced to a death of his own. Then again, would that be so bad? He wouldn't have to withstand the noise, the smells, or the constant flaring of some wild entity roaring inside of him. He could be free again and maybe reunite with his mother.

Would werewolves be permitted in heaven? Would it even matter?

"South Carolina," he muttered.

That elicited some shock from the men.

"You walked all the way?" Adam asked. Logan nodded. "When was your last shift?"

It was then that he remembered what Robert had said. They were all like him, and they wanted to help. All werewolves. He looked to each of them, trying to find some clue in their appearance that would give them away. He saw nothing. Besides their brawn, there might have been nothing to suggest they were telling the truth.

"You can trust us, Logan," Darren said. "We've all been in your place and know how scary it can be. You're among friends."

Throughout his childhood, Logan couldn't remember having friends. It was just him and his mother for the longest time, struggling through life with his father breathing down their necks. Now, he had no one. Not even Ollie. These men and this entire town were supposed to be a refuge, according to the journal. Maybe Dustin wasn't here, but Logan could learn from them instead.

Hope was a dangerous thing. He had learned that the hard way. He could never hope for his father to turn sober. He could never hope that his mother would someday see the error in staying. He could never hope for anything more than being a poor boy who wasn't good at much of anything. Could he hope for a future anymore?

"I... I don't know how long... A few weeks, maybe?"

Robert's jaw clenched. Adam's stare grew distant as if he were thinking about something important. Darren seemed to be the only one still grounded in the moment.

"If it's been a few weeks, what happened to you when you shifted, will happen again soon. We want to be ready for it, so we'll need you to..."

Logan didn't hear anything else. He would turn into a monster again? He'd become uncontrollable? He'd kill? The others in the room might have sensed his panic before he even realized it was upon him.

He bolted upright and tore away the blanket that covered half of his body. They were on him faster than it took for him to blink. Adam grabbed his legs while Darren and Robert took his shoulders and forced him back into the bed. Their grips were like iron, their strength far superior to his.

He kicked and clawed at them, resisting. He couldn't stay. He couldn't kill. Not when there were women and children here. He couldn't hurt them. Not again.

"Logan, you have to calm down!" Robert insisted. "We can't let you leave."

Frightened tears streamed down his cheeks, the first he had shed, since he'd left his mother's body in the cabin. He didn't even have the strength to bury her. He saw her lifeless face again and all at once, he could see so many more dead. Mutilated, bleeding corpses across the town. He could see the white schoolhouse in flames, the children screaming and burning. All because of him. He couldn't be responsible.

"We're going to take care of you," Darren promised. "We won't let you hurt anyone. But you have to let us help you."

Logan was too tired to believe, but just terrified enough to fight. That is, until something else struck him out of nowhere.

From all three came a power more devastating than anything he knew. Greater than hunger, than pain, than sorrow, but more calming than his own mother's fond embrace. His limbs lost their strength. His tears dried up. And though his chest continued to heave, Logan let himself be compressed under this power. He let it drown him, entering his soul and silencing that anger that seared inside.

What had they done to him? Was this how they helped? If it was, Logan would stay in this state forever. Anything to quiet that storm of feeling that could never break.

"We're going to take care of you," Darren said again, attracting Logan's gaze.

For the first time, looking deep in the werewolf's eyes, he believed every word.

Darren had often remarked to both Adam and Robert that his house on the outskirts of Devia had been rather empty and quiet, especially since Dustin had left him. He didn't expect them to remember the comment or take it so seriously.

Now, instead of living all alone, he shared his home with the newest member of their community. Logan's room was across the hall from his.

It was clear the moment the boy stepped up onto the porch that he hadn't been so accustomed to a house of this size. Darren kept it immaculately clean and orderly. The furniture was sparse, but with help from some of the mothers of his students, it had become homey and comfortable. Rugs, paintings, meaningless knick-knacks, a full set of chinaware he rarely used, and bedding enough for a family of six. All of it gave the right touch to make this once deserted farmhouse on untillable land into a proper home.

Yesterday evening, Logan had stared in awe at the details and walked so carefully through the rooms that Darren wondered if the boy had ever lived in a house to begin with. Despite the unsettling arrangement that Robert, the founder and prime alpha of Devia, had made for the boy, Darren tried to make the best of it.

He didn't want a pack. Not after Dustin had fled to the north, complaining about adventure and a need to get out of the south. The heat and mosquitoes were intolerable at best, but Darren had been endeared to the noble cause of Devia since the moment he was told about it in France. A society built for loups-garous and their families to live without fear of judgement or exposure. Packs coexisted together in relative peace and young boys were trained up to be stable and balanced.

Darren didn't give it a second thought when he was asked to cross the ocean and become part of the dream. Dustin, however, wanted nothing to do with it.

Before, when Darren only had to take care of his wife and young daughter, he didn't care for the responsibility of a pack. He was an alpha in character and dominance, but not in practice. Dustin had come along and proved him wrong. Now that he didn't have a family or his beta, Darren was content to let his students be his pack, indefinitely.

Logan was not what he had asked for. Robert had assured it would be a temporary arrangement. Once a foster family could be found for the boy, he would be out of Darren's house. He knew better; that wasn't the truth. Robert had managed this town for seventy years and knew its residence too well. He knew Darren's fondness for the youth and how his raw alpha talent was not being used to its full extent. A new pack, a new start, was what Robert had in mind for Darren. Nothing temporary.

Knowing that he had been sufficiently fed the afternoon before when Darren took Logan unconscious to Robert's mansion in the heart of town, he didn't offer supper. The next morning, however, he knew the boy would be hungry.

Eggs, ham, and a slab of thin steak should have been enough. Though, he remembered what it had been like at that age and freshly turned. He, too, had nearly starved himself on the long journey from England to the south of France. Darren knew how weak and desperate he had been for some bit of food, and how he had resisted his own urges to hunt and eat raw meat. Logan would be no different.

It became clear to all of them that the boy had a past and a family he didn't want to talk about. Why was anyone's guess. Perhaps that was another reason Robert wanted to pair them. Darren had a special knack for listening and prying out the truth from someone without ever directly asking. Hopefully, after a good night's rest and a hearty breakfast, Logan would be a willing donor of the information they needed. They needed to understand the boy in order to help him.

He finished the preparations in the kitchen and then made his way to Logan's room. Before he had to even tap on the door, he heard the youth stir in his bed.

"I'm not hungry," he grumbled.

One corner of Darren's lips pulled into a smile. "Yes, you are. Come downstairs. My cooking isn't that bad."

He walked away, confident that the boy's stomach and curiosity would get the better of him.

However, it took longer than he expected. Darren had finished off all three of his own eggs and half of his slice of ham before Logan opened his bedroom door. He turned up his eyes from the volume of Tennyson in his hand to watch the boy enter the dining room. The untouched, now cold, plate of meat at the other end of the table was waiting for him, and Darren gestured to the empty chair with his fork.

"Go on," he said. "I have to be at the school house shortly. Eat so we can leave soon."

Logan's eyes, which were now a bright and stunning shade of gray-blue, wandered from his new mentor to the plate he had prepared. Still, he didn't move from the threshold. The fear wasn't as strong as it had been yesterday when he'd revived in Robert's front room, but it was still there, stinking up his house.

"I know you don't think you should eat it, but you must." Darren turned his attention back to the book. "I even cooked it for you. I don't normally do that, so please respect my efforts."

It was another moment before Logan took one cautious step, then another, and eventually sat down in the chair. Still, he didn't touch the food. Darren glanced and saw the boy staring at his food.

Studying his features, he could see the resemblance to Dustin Keith. Same nose, and hair thickness. They didn't share the same chin or mouth, which he assumed belonged to his mother. But their mannerisms, their stubbornness, their innate fear of what they had become, all of that made them like twins. He remembered when Dustin had done almost the very same thing when he recovered from his long swim from Ireland to France. Of course, that convalescence took more time and Dustin didn't have the advantage of that handy journal Logan had arrived with.

Against his better judgement, Darren kept the journal and read it while Robert and Adam force-fed Logan in his unconscious state. If the boy had read the book from cover to cover, he knew everything he needed to know. He should have known that refusing to eat would only create more problems for himself. So, why did he just sit there and stare?

"I'd say it's not going anywhere, but if you don't eat it, I just might," Darren remarked before using the edge of his fork to slice off a bit of his ham.

Out of the corner of his eye, he saw Logan pick up his own fork and begin eating. Slow at first, and then a little faster. He finished even before Darren could eat the last bit of his steak.

He slid the bookmark to hold his place in the volume. "Adam said you might have been starving yourself before you came here."

Logan didn't respond and only continued to stare at his now barren breakfast plate. Darren waited and finished off his meal before speaking again.

"I won't be able to bring you to the schoolhouse, so Robert's elected to take care of you today. His son is about your age, so I presume you'll be spending time with him."

Still, nothing. Not a word.

Darren understood, probably more than most. The majority of the loups-garous in Devia had been raised by their fathers, whom they had received this condition from. Others were raised in a pack since they were children. They knew nothing about the hardships of growing up without a mentor and only learning of their kind when it was too late. Logan, as unfortunate as his mysterious circumstances were, couldn't have been in a better place. They had tried to explain that to him yesterday, but after they had told him that Dustin was no longer in the country, he seemed uninterested in anything else.

"Go on and get dressed or I'll be late."

Logan took this as his dismissal and quickly fled upstairs. Darren slid his plate away and rubbed at his face. He searched his memory for what had been the key to helping Dustin cope with his condition, to make him open up. But he realized that there was nothing in particular that he had done or said. Dustin came to him and confessed everything of his free will. It took a while, but it all came out in the end. His home in Ireland, his family, his dead wife, and all the self-hatred he had been bottling up since his first shift. If Logan was so much like his grandfather, he would need to be patient. It would all come out in the end.

CHAPTER 5

Robert pinched the bridge of his nose and gave a deep sigh. He had never thought it possible for werewolves to suffer from headaches as he did. Then again, he remembered that his kind were only invulnerable to sickness, not stupidity.

"I've told you time and again not to use that soap, Ginny." He snatched the shirt from the maid servant's hand. "It has too much fragrance. If I wear this, I'll smell rose water for days. It'll be so ingrained in my nose I'll never be able to smell anything else."

The girl, little older than fifteen, lowered her chin. She muttered a shuddering apology. Past the flowery scent of the clean shirt, he could smell her fear. The rumor in Devia was that Robert could never retain a servant for longer than a month before displacing them elsewhere. Ginny had made it two weeks and already he'd had enough of her mistakes.

But one look to his son, Forrest, leaning against the doorframe, stayed his judgement. He, above all others, understood the rumor to be both true and justified. Over the years, Robert's patience had run short with everyone, human and werewolf alike. It took a calming force, like his son, to pull him back from making a rash decision.

He turned back to Ginny and handed the shirt to her. "Here," he said, "go let it hang on a pine tree for a few days. Maybe then the soap smell will fade."

She immediately took the garment with a shaking hand, gathered it together with the other clothes she had improperly washed, and hurried past both of her bosses.

"We agreed you would keep this one," Forrest said, meeting his father's blue eyes with his own. "If you don't, it's likely you'll never find another."

Robert took one last scathing look to the washhouse and followed his son into the morning air. "If anyone could follow simple instructions, I wouldn't have to advertise so often."

Unless they were acquainted with the family, few would ever suspect that Robert and Forrest Croxen were so closely related. They were opposites in looks and temperament on all scores.

In the sunshine, Forrest's red hair shined ever brighter. Not a day went by that Robert didn't look to his son and think of his own mother. The trait had skipped a generation, and though his wife – Forrest's mother – had hair as black as her husband's, Forrest defied all probability and came out of the womb pale and ruddy.

Their attitudes could not have been more dissimilar. While Robert had sculpted himself into the role of alpha over all of Devia, mastering his dominance and cultivating it from the meager skill it had been in his youth, Forrest showed no interest in leadership. He was content to spend his days with friends or finding his place in a world somewhat apart from his father. He tried one skill after another, searching for a hidden talent that had nothing to do with being the son of a prominent alpha.

Robert saw much of himself in Forrest's calm, almost passive attitude. He had once been the same, but not necessarily by choice. Quiet and thoughtful, he had the luxury of stepping back from responsibilities to watch the world with an open mind and open heart. That was how Devia had come into existence.

But Devia was also the reason that Robert couldn't be a spectator anymore. He'd taken the task by the horns and had never let go. Werewolves and packs came and went. Alphas, betas, and omegas passed through. There was a handful who had stayed since the founding, including Darren Dubose and Adam Swenson. There were more who'd moved on, including his own father, James Croxen.

Remembering his father, Robert might have been glad for Forrest's unadventurous disposition. It meant that he might stay and not go galivanting off to join some navy crew or circumnavigate the globe. That was James' life, not Robert's, and thankfully not Forrest's.

"Ginny's mother is ill," his son informed him. "It's likely her mind isn't fully dedicated to her work. You know how worry can have an impact upon productivity."

Robert narrowed his eyes upon his son. "How did you know her mother was ill?"

Forrest smiled. "I listen. Not just to Ginny, but to the town's people. You should try it one day."

"I do listen," he replied with a measure of crossness. "I listen plenty to their needs. When have I turned away someone at the door looking for help?"

Forrest fully faced his father, stalling their progress across the yard to the mansion house. "Yes, you listen to their grievances, but there's more to running a town than solving one conflict after another."

Robert folded his arms. "I don't need my son telling me how to run a town. I've been doing this for longer than you've been alive."

"Only by fifty years."

While his son appeared a young man, barely into his nineteenth year, in actuality, he would be turning thirty the following month. It seemed only yesterday that Forrest was a child, playing with toy soldiers under Robert's office desk. Time raced ahead, while Robert felt stuck in the same cycle of work and politics.

"You see things from the inside," Forrest continued, "while I see things from a different perspective."

Robert cracked a smile, perhaps the first all morning. Maybe there was more of his old self manifesting in his son every day. Then there was hope that once time took its final toll on Robert, Devia would pass into capable hands.

Their conversation was cut short when they both heard footsteps coming up the walkway to their front door. With Ginny away tending to the laundry, there was no one to receive their guest.

Robert let out a long breath, knowing it must have been another citizen coming to make some petition to him about a petty disagreement. He often felt like Moses or Aaron from the Bible, solving all the problems of his people and suffering for it.

"Just come around the back," Robert said, knowing the man would hear him well enough, even from the back of the mansion.

Still, the doorbell was rung.

Robert and Forrest looked to one another and then tested the air.

"I don't know him," Forrest declared skeptically.

"Neither do I," Robert said. "And he's not werewolf."

A human in Devia wasn't all too uncommon. Children and women were more numerous than the werewolves in the town. An adult human male was an oddity.

They hurriedly climbed the back porch and made their way through the house. Forrest stayed out of sight in one of the sitting rooms to eavesdrop while Robert answered the door.

Standing on his porch was a slightly overweight man in an expensive suit that was tailored to his robust, but strikingly short frame. A bowler hat covered the greasy combover that wreaked of cologne water. The edges of his mustache were waxed into neatly even curves that distracted the gawker from the deep crease of flesh trailing from his nostrils to his mouth, indicative of a man who smiled far too much. The tops of his cheeks were flushed as if he had been walking a great distance, but his horse and buggy sat waiting in the street. Dark eyes sparkled with ambition and one hand gripped the handle of a leather briefcase.

Robert already knew this man, or his type at least. Salesman. Pushy, arrogant, presumptuous. He'd had plenty of their kind pass through over the last few decades. They would try to start their own businesses, make trades, sell their wares out of their trunks and wagons. None stayed. He wouldn't permit it.

"Good morning!" the man greeted as he held out a pudgy hand to Robert. "I'm – "

"Not interested," he grumbled, his dark brows slanting.

The salesman laughed, but kept his hand extended. "No, no. I'm not selling anything, Mr. Croxen."

Robert nettled and he could feel the hairs on the back of his neck stand on end. "I don't know you."

"Not yet," he replied before lowering his hand. "But we're going to become very good friends. May I come in?"

He had never let a human man step foot in his home, stranger or not. "Whatever you have to say to me can be said right here."

The man chuckled again and patted his briefcase. "That'll make it a little difficult for me to lay out my proposal for you."

"So, you are selling something."

"No, not at all," the man said, his smile widening. "I'm looking to buy."

Logan maintained a pace or two behind Darren, his gaze wandering from house to house and face to face as they made their way through the heart of Devia. The day before had been overwhelming, to say the least. There wasn't much of an opportunity to observe this new and strange place.

It wasn't so different from his own hometown. The people dressed the same. Fashion and trends were kept with the changing times, though he had been told that some residents were hundreds of years old. Buildings were not modeled after castles or elaborate palaces from bygone eras. The houses appeared new, well-made, and brightly painted.

Women gathered at the corners of shops and talked. Some men did the same and sat in chairs on the boardwalks between the various establishments. There was a blacksmith, a bakery, a butcher, seamstress, bank, taverns, a barber shop, restaurants, and all manner of stores. If it weren't for the needling sensation in the back of his skull, he could have forgotten that he was walking through a town full of werewolves... just like him.

Logan didn't have to face the truth when he ran from South Carolina. He didn't have to think about what he was or how his new life had changed for the worse. Being here, amongst men who were supposed to be like family, he couldn't ignore it anymore. They all looked to him with encouraging eyes, nods of their heads as if he were already accepted. They knew nothing. Or he hoped they knew nothing.

Could they see through him? Did they know that he was a murderer? Or was that such a common thing among werewolves that they instantly assumed he had killed someone before he arrived and that was why he was there?

Then he remembered the journal. His grandmother had written that werewolves were not the stuff of nightmares and legends. They were often good, misunderstood, rejected by society because of fear and hatred.

So far, the people of Devia had shown that to be true. Everyone, from the baker who gave him a friendly wave to Darren who had gone out of his way to fix him the biggest breakfast he had ever had, assured Logan that he was welcome here.

If he could help it, he wouldn't do anything to ruin it.

They came to the mansion they had left the day before. Outside stood a horse and buggy, the first he had seen in the town, and the first he had seen since he left home.

Logan looked to the brown gelding and froze. Even from a distance, he could tell the animal was frightened. Sweat on the horse's neck glistened in the morning sun, ears swiveled in all directions and though blinders blocked much of his view, that didn't keep them from roaming wildly in his head. The gelding was one loud noise away from becoming startled and bolting into a run.

That's what his human mind reasoned. The other side of him, the side that he could never trust, didn't pity the horse as he should have. It saw prey. A meal. Something to chase.

Foreshadowing images flashed through his mind of blood pouring over the chestnut brown fur. He could almost feel its flesh quivering between his claws and feel its heartbeat pounding against his fangs. His stomach, still full of egg and ham, now growled in perverse hunger.

The horse knickered and tossed its head. The driver pulled back the reins, but it continued to thrash.

If it weren't for that, and Darren's grounding hand upon his shoulder, Logan might not have realized what he was doing. The claws from his beastly fantasy had truly grown from his nailbeds. The fangs that were once dull and harmless, made his gums bleed.

When Logan looked to the man who had opened up his home to him, he could see that his eyes had turned a menacing gold.

"Take a deep breath," Darren advised. "Close your eyes and give it a moment. Ignore the horse."

That was easier said than done. Now that he knew the animal was there, it was nearly impossible to ignore the enticing aroma of its flesh. There was something else there too, peppery and exotic like one of the dishes the oriental woman cooked in his hometown. It only added to the primal urges to hunt and kill, which Logan despised.

If he were a man, he would have gone to the horse and eased its fear. He would have petted its thick and powerful neck, whispering calm words to sooth it. Now, they were no longer equals. Logan was a predator, and always would be.

He curled his hands into fists and the claws cut into his palm. Let the pain be his punishment for frightening a defenseless creature. He deserved it.

"Darren!"

A voice broke his concentration and Logan turned to watch another man come around the side of the mansion house. His orangish-red hair bounced as he hustled forward to meet them and leaned over the picket fence.

He smiled to Logan and all at once, he noticed the total withdraw of that peppery aroma. Logan looked to the horse and noticed something had nullified its anxiety. He wondered if the redhead's approach had anything to do with that.

"Forrest, who's talking with your father?" Darren asked, casually propping his wrists on the posts of the fence. Logan kept his distance and slid his hands into his deep trouser pockets to keep the others from noticing the blood. Then again, they could probably smell it just as well as he could.

"I'm not sure. He said his name was Abel Morris." They both looked toward the front door to the mansion. No one was on the porch, but Logan could hear the voices coming from inside. Their words were garbled to him. Their tones were clear, but he hadn't learned to pick out the conversations over the multitudes just yet. There was still so much he needed to learn, none of it that he wanted to.

"What does he want?"

Forrest, the redhead, shrugged. "They're talking about buying land on the edge of town. Something about a railroad, I think." Then, as if the meeting inside held little interest to him, Forrest offered out his hand. "You must be Logan. I wasn't home when you woke up, but my father told me everything."

Logan eyed him warily. Everything? How much did Robert know that he hadn't revealed during their long talk the previous evening? He reached out and took Forrest's hand, but didn't return the shake with as much enthusiasm.

Darren peeled his attention from the mansion and fixed it upon the two boys. "Logan, this is Robert's only son, Forrest. I told you he was close to your age, but I suppose he's almost twice as old as you."

Logan's brows arched in surprise. "Thirty-two?"

Forrest beamed. "You know your arithmetic! That's excellent. But no, I'm actually twenty-nine for the next month."

"You... You don't look almost thirty."

He nodded. "You're right. I don't. I won't look thirty for another century or two."

Logan cringed. Would he still look so young, so immature for that long? The thought of a century of waiting to grow up didn't appeal to him. He had always dreamed of being an adult and earning the respect that came with age. Now, he'd be nothing more than a child to everyone he met.

"I've got to get to the school," Darren said hastily. "Can you show Logan the town and keep him occupied for the day?"

Forrest nodded. "Absolutely. He can come help me at the furniture shop. Do you know anything about carpentry?"

Put on the spot, Logan stammered at first. "I... A little. I was an apprentice for half a year."

A soft, hopeful smile graced Darren's lips and he nodded. "You two have fun, then. I'll come by to fetch you at the end of the day."

With that, he gave Logan a hearty slap on the shoulder and walked away in the direction they had come. That left him alone with the zealous Forrest and his eager eyes.

Shouting came from inside the house and Logan nearly jumped at the thunderous boom of Robert's voice. The words rang loud and clear, drowning out all others.

"How dare you come into my town, into my home, and try to convince me to practically give you all this land! You have no possible idea how important this land is to us! I don't care if you offered five million for that acreage. You won't get one damn tree! Get out!"

A feeble voice tried to contend with the alpha werewolf, but it was useless. Robert only yelled louder, reiterating his final answer. Logan shrank closer to Forrest. If he had the ears and tail of a dog in that moment, they would be tucked low. He could almost feel the reaching dominance all the way on the sidewalk.

"He's not always like that," Forrest said. "He's just having a bad morning."

The front door swung open and a short, stout man came stumbling out. A briefcase followed him, sliding across the porch deck and then tumbling down the steps. The latch sprung open and papers went flying across the lawn. The wind didn't help matters and blew a good number in the boys' direction.

Forrest snatched one up and held it up for them to inspect. It was a map of Alabama with major cities marked by thick dots. Some smaller dots existed, but what drew their attention was the hatch-crossed trail that snaked northward from the Florida state line and straight through a tiny, unlabeled dot.

"So, it is a railroad," Forrest mumbled.

Logan looked up to see Robert standing on the porch, his arms crossed over his barrel chest and glaring down upon the businessman who frantically gathered up his documents.

"You'll regret this, Croxen," he warned, waving a sausage-like finger at the alpha. It didn't take Logan long to figure out that Mr. Morris was completely and utterly human, and clearly didn't know who he was speaking to. "You can't stop progress!"

"Watch me," Robert snarled.

That should have been enough to deter the man, but something in the way Mr. Morris snapped shut his briefcase and marched back to his buggy told him that this fight wasn't over. Not by a long shot. He gave the orders to the driver and they pulled away from the mansion to speed down the main thoroughfare. The horse, like the driver, must have been glad to be on its way out of Devia and away from the werewolves.

Mr. Morris, however, held that scheming glint in his eye. Did Forrest see it? Or did Logan simply imagine it?

Before Logan could make any comment, Forrest folded up the map and slipped it into his vest before vaulting over the picket fence.

"Let's go," he said. "I was supposed to be at work twenty minutes ago."

Logan cracked a smile and hurried down the street with his new friend. For the first time, Logan felt a little comforted. It didn't come from some wise platitude or assurance, but in the simple, utterly human admittance. Forrest might have been a werewolf, but he was late. He wasn't perfect. Perhaps no one would expect Logan to be perfect either. Some pressure was relieved, but not all.

CHAPTER 6

Forrest continued to sand the unfinished dovetail joint. The harsh grinding of the sandpaper against wood was the only sound inside the carpentry shop. Logan might as well have been nothing more than a ghost. He simply sat on a stool near a mountain of assembled dining chairs, eyes cast down and rotating a scrap piece of wood no longer than his forearm between his hands. He hadn't said a word, hadn't asked any questions or even offered to help.

He could remember being sixteen and scared for the future. He remembered what it was like to hear everything, whether he wanted to or not. After a while, he could tune it out, but despite being trained by his father, Darren, and Adam, there was still much he needed to learn. It was a slow, grueling process to become a capable werewolf, or loup-garou as Darren liked to call them.

"It will get easier," Forrest finally said, breaking the quiet that had lasted for almost an hour. "The werewolf thing... And it's not so terrible. You'll always have a pack and someone who understands what you're experiencing. You'll never be alone."

He could hear the tension on the discarded wooden peg in Logan's grip and looked up just as it snapped in two. The piece was at least an inch thick. Logan stared at the two jagged bits.

"What if I want to be alone?" he mumbled.

Forrest's brows pinched together with concern. "No one wants to be alone. Not our kind anyway... Well, I take that back. There are some who are lone wolves. But they don't survive for long. It's much easier with a pack." He returned to his sanding, but part of him remained alert to Logan, nose and ears peeled to any shift in mood. If he turned violent, Forrest didn't want him anywhere near the chairs he had spent weeks making.

"Why would you want to be alone?" Forrest asked before blowing some of the sawdust from the open joint.

Logan proceeded to pluck away at the exposed splinters of the broken wood. "It's better if I am."

"So no one will get hurt?" At last, Logan lifted his head. Forrest smirked and nodded as he adjusted his sheet of sandpaper. "I think every werewolf has had the same thought. But it is possible to live amongst humans or your own kind without ever hurting a single soul." He gave a soft laugh and went back to grinding away at a stubborn sharp angle. "Now, I've heard some scary stories from werewolves who have turned outside of a pack. One man came and told how he had woken up in his neighbor's chicken coop, covered in feathers. Not a chicken or rooster in sight."

"Anyone ever kill someone by accident?"

The two young werewolves regarded one another. Forrest knew that look in his eyes. The one that tried so hard to hide the true terror and shame of some sin. To the untrained observer, it would have gone unnoticed. But even though Forrest was only twenty-nine, enough werewolves had passed through his father's parlor to educate him in that exact look.

"A few have," he replied quietly. "But they always regret it. And it's that regret that keeps them from doing it again. That's why they come here. They need accountability. That's what a pack can provide."

Logan tore his gaze away, his hands stilling over the broken piece of wood.

If he were anything like his father, Forrest would have pressured him for the full story. No question came about simply on a whim. There was always a reason for the words a man chose. Perhaps Logan, like so many others, had believed the warped myths and legends about their kind. He didn't want to become a ravenous killer. No one truly did. Then again, like lone wolves, there were the exceptions. Forrest and Robert knew that all too well.

He slid another glance to Logan and wondered. The tension, his mysterious arrival, the aloof behavior, the way the horse had reacted to him, his questions about murder... Could all of it be coincidence or could they have a true rougarou in their midst? Forrest had never met the werewolves who had turned rogue and bloodthirsty, but his father had. After the accident in New Orleans, Devia vetted its citizens a little more carefully. Could someone as young and seemingly innocent as Logan slide under his father's scope?

With a shake of his head to rid himself of the idea, Forrest resumed his sanding and tested the joints again. Now, they were too loose. He cursed under his breath and glowered at the ruined project.

"I can never get these quite right," he complained.

Running footsteps sounded toward the back of the shop. Logan braced to stand, but Forrest waved him down. Seconds later, Mitch came speeding in, kicking up dust in his wake.

"Forrest!" he exclaimed, taking him by the arms. "You'll never guess what happened."

Hazel eyes dancing with his usual excitement, Forrest wasn't bothered by the sudden intrusion. Judging by the tangled state of Mitch's dark blonde hair and ruffled clothes, he must have run all the way from the other side of town.

"Logan, this is Mitch," Forrest politely introduced, motioning between the two. "He's my cousin on my mother's side. Don't mind him."

Mitch looked over his shoulder and gave a casual wave to the startled, but intrigued Logan. "Nice to meet ya." He gave Forrest a little shake, mouth spread in quite possibly the biggest grin he'd ever given. "Evelyn Hueser was walking down the street with her sister and I heard them talking about me! Well, they were talking about both of us, but mostly about me."

Now, Forrest was interested. "Chrissy? Chrissy was talking with Evelyn about me?"

Mitch's smile turned sour and he shoved his cousin. "No, didn't you hear me? They're talking about me!"

Logan stood from his place and ambled forward, discarding both sticks onto the dirt floor. Forrest set aside the ruined dovetail pieces of the drawer he had been working on, to give Mitch his full attention.

"Fine, why were they talking about you?"

Mitch excitedly began his story of how the two sisters were discussing their plans for the town's annual festival to celebrate its founding. Details about dresses had been thrown around until they came to the subject of escorts.

"Did Chrissy mention she wanted to go with me?" Forrest questioned frenziedly. He had been smitten with the vivacious blonde since their family had come to town two years prior. Mitch, along with several of their other friends had tried to convince him to ask her to go steady with him, but the matter of her father had kept him from asking. Her father, a pack alpha himself, didn't care for Forrest or Mitch. One was too wild, the other not dominant enough. Robert was blamed, of course, since he had raised the two.

Mitch gave him a cunning smile, which said enough.

Forrest would have howled if the shop hadn't been attached to the back of the furniture store.

"And Evelyn?"

His cousin turned and jumped atop the work table, rattling the tools and bits of useless wood chips. The crown of his head was just inches from the ceiling. If he stood to his full height instead of the eager, halfway crouching stance he was in, he'd hit one of the support beams. "Who else would she want to go with?" he asked and then tapped on his chest. "I've been whittling my way at her for months now. She couldn't think of anyone else, even if she wanted to."

Forrest shook his head ruefully. Mitch might have been a couple of years older, but he had never quieted down. One of the most flagrant werewolves in town, he was always in some sort of trouble. It was any wonder Robert let him out of the house at all.

"When are you going to ask her?" he queried. "The festival's in a couple of weeks."

Mitch lowered himself into a squat and braced his hands on his knees as if he were ready to pounce on the unsuspecting girl right then and there. "Soon. Very soon. I just need some of your brains to help me come up with the right way to ask."

He scoffed. "No way. I'm not going to help you snatch up Evelyn when I have to worry about my chances with Chrissy."

With a dramatic flair, Mitch leapt from the table and grabbed one of the spare aprons laying across a workbench. "Chrissy is fawning over you like a blushing bride already." He draped the apron over his head to mimic a poorly fashioned bonnet. "Forrest is so sensitive, so kind and generous," Mitch's voice rose to mock the young girl. "I don't think there's a wolf in town so gentle as he is."

Forrest dove to seize the apron from his cousin, but Mitch dodged and continued replaying the conversation he had overheard. All of it exaggerated, of course. Forrest knew Chrissy too well to think she would ever confide in her sister so explicitly.

They chased one another around the shop like schoolboys. In many ways, they had never grown up. Both Forrest and Mitch, though they were adults in age if not looks, were still pups in the eyes of the werewolf community. The way they behaved, it wasn't all too surprising.

"Got it."

Forrest came to a sliding halt near the rack of carving tools and looked to Logan. In his hands was the section of the drawer he tossed earlier. Only, the dovetails were no longer loose and useless. They appeared flush and perfectly formed.

Ignoring Mitch, he dashed over and took the two panels to inspect his work. Something like wedges had been pushed into the empty space he had sanded down too vigorously. However, the repair was seamless. Unless one was looking for the repair, they would never notice it. The raw edges of the pin ends had also been filed down to create a smooth finish.

"How did you..."

"The carpenter in my hometown showed me a lot of things," he said. "I can show you an easier method. It'll make for a tighter joint and no sanding required."

Forrest looked to Logan in amazement as Mitch came to examine the piece as well. He knew nothing of carpentry and wouldn't even know what he was looking at, but he was good at faking interest.

"Seriously?" Forrest questioned. "No sanding?"

Logan proudly shook his head. "None. It's in the way you carve out the pin and tails. The angles are a little more involved, but it's not so difficult after you've cut them a few times."

Wherever this werewolf had come from, Forrest was ready to forget every skeptical idea prior to this moment. If he could teach a better way to make sturdy dovetails, he was a Godsend in his book.

"Show me."

Adam tried to quiet his wolf, but it had persisted ever since he first touched Logan after he awoke in Robert's front parlor. There was something different about the boy, something that the wolf needed to understand. Adam could sympathize, but he also understood that Logan would not want so much attention. He was new to Devia, and unsure of himself. That much he could tell just by a quick assessment.

The youth, though he would never admit it, was terrified. Of what, Adam could only guess. Was it his new nature? His new surroundings? Or something deeper?

It was this mystery that continually pulled on his wolf to seek Logan out. It needed answers, just as much as they all did. No matter how much he tried not to let his mind drift to Logan, he found himself passively seeking him.

Darren had agreed to take him, but his English friend had enough sense not to bring Logan to the schoolhouse so soon. Too many noises and new scents to sift through. But, it would have been unwise to keep him home alone.

But when he heard the laughter and rapid conversation coming from behind Hubert's furniture store, Adam knew he couldn't ignore the not-so-gentle prodding any longer.

He entered the store and found the master furniture maker standing behind the counter, a newspaper open in front of him. The older man lifted his stare and grinned at the sight of Adam.

"It's not every day I have an important man in my shop," he exclaimed as he folded the paper and moved to greet him.

Adam returned the smile, though part of him wished that he could go somewhere without being recognized or fussed over. Since he had arrived in Devia, he had become known for his superior intuition and connection with his wolf. Once such a reputation had been established, his home was frequented by werewolves seeking advice or healing. His presence and reputation alone had helped the population of the town grow. Mothers who knew nothing of their child's transformation had sought him out. Fathers who were unsure how to properly teach their sons, begged for assistance.

He had to remind himself this was why he had come to Devia, and why he had parted ways with his father. All this intuitive knowledge could not be hoarded. Though it took some time to adjust to a pack structure, after living as a lone wolf with his father for over a century, Adam had developed a fondness for the town and its people.

When he was a child, he had wanted to become a medicine man in his Navajo village. He thought becoming a werewolf had destroyed those plans, but it only delayed them. Now, he was able to do so much good for his own kind that he could never lament the way things had turned out in the beginning. Even on the days when he was unable to find a moment alone, Adam went to sleep with the surety that he had helped someone in need.

He wanted that someone to be Logan.

"Who's working with you today?" Adam asked Hubert after shaking his hand and glancing toward the door that led to the workshop.

Hubert was a man well past his prime, turned in his old age by the bite and possessing no dominance of his own. He had been admitted as an omega with Robert's pack after his recovery period, which was eight years ago. He, above most, needed Adam's guidance and supervision, since he had stopped shifting on a consistent basis. He, more than anyone else in Devia, understood the significance of this deficiency. His involvement in the Devia community might have been all that kept him from an early grave. Age got the best of many werewolves, and Hubert was no exception.

As a result, he was forced to take an apprentice, Robert's son, to build furniture for him while he manned the business side of things. His arthritis, which shouldn't have existed, wouldn't allow him to handle many of his tools anymore.

"Forrest is working for me, but it sounds like Mitch and another boy are distracting him."

Adam nodded. Hubert wouldn't have known Logan by voice or scent, and he was still new to the town, so word wouldn't have gotten around about his arrival just yet.

"I'll take one of them off your hands," he muttered to the old man, as if they were scheming to ruin the boys' fun.

Hubert chuckled and motioned toward the door. "Be my guest. Take them both!"

A hush fell over the workshop as Adam strode toward the door. The three boys looked to him as he entered, faces guilty, as if they had been caught doing something wrong. By the looks of it, Adam doubted it. Forrest and Logan were handling unfinished panels, while Mitch observed, no doubt adding his unwanted opinions.

Adam had a different effect on the youth of Devia. While the adults appreciated his wisdom and insight, the younger werewolves tended to be wary of him. Perhaps they thought he would tell their parents of their antics or any unsightly issues they were unwilling to divulge to others. What they didn't know was that Adam made a habit never to betray the trust of someone who needed him.

His amused eyes darted from one face to the next and none moved, even when he took a few moseying steps forward.

"I trust you're being productive," he said, hoping that his smile was disarming enough.

Mitch, the ever bold one, was the first to break the fixation. "Logan was showing Forrest how to... do something with the wood." His shrug was enough to tell that the boy didn't know anything about furniture or carpentry. He didn't need to. His talents were aimed toward a different field entirely. Brewing. And in Devia, such a skill went unutilized, seeing as werewolves couldn't get drunk.

Adam looked to the wood the other two were handling and nodded approvingly.

"I like it when you teach one another." He took the planks and examined the careful marks scrawled along the ends. "It's the only way we can learn."

The unease in the room ebbed when Adam returned both of the pieces to Forrest, leaving Logan empty-handed. When the youth realized that he was under Adam's special focus, he tensed and shifted backward half a step.

Wariness had evolved into unnecessary anxiety and Adam tried to not let it discourage him. If his reputation and subtle dominance wasn't enough to raise alarm, it was his appearance. No other in town possessed the same unique heritage that he did. His dark features contrasted sharply with his bright green eyes that stood out in any crowd. His mixed parentage allowed for some exceptional characteristics that made him instantly recognizable, but also unapproachable. Others, completely sheltered from the diversity of the world, feared what they didn't understand. If only everyone could have benefited from a trip or two around the globe. Then, they would realize there was far more outside of their little country, and Adam was nothing new in perspective.

"Let's go for a walk," he told Logan, more as an order than a suggestion.

Adam could feel Logan's walls thicken and shoot up to guard him against whatever would come. It would take him quite some time to break down those defenses.

Accepting this new assignment, Logan said his goodbyes to his new friends and followed Adam out of the store and into the street. While they made their way down the only road that led in and out of town, he watched the boy closely to see how he coped with the sensory inundation.

What he witnessed was favorable. He didn't jump at too many unexpected sounds and didn't let himself get caught up in unknown scents. For the most part, he kept to himself and closely trailed after Adam to avoid any contact with the others they passed. He didn't meet their eyes, didn't look up when someone greeted Adam or asked him a quick question before carrying on with their day.

Soon, they came to the edge of town. Houses and buildings gave way to trees and lush greenery. The smells of civilization faded, the sounds became duller. Adam turned off the dirt road and pushed his way through a low hedge of bushes to find the woodland path.

Logan, however, wouldn't leave the road. Adam stopped and looked back to the boy, who eyed the forest like it were an unsavory character that meant him harm instead of good. If he ever intended to be a proper werewolf, he needed to undo that mentality.

Adam trudged back to the edge of the trees and put his hands on his hips. "Why stop?"

No answer came, though he could tell that Logan struggled with understanding his own feelings toward the forest and what he was experiencing.

"Your wolf wants to follow me, but you don't. There's no reason to distrust it."

Logan's face twisted with confusion. "My wolf?"

Adam nodded. "It's that other self you're feeling. It's been there your entire life, ever since you were born. It begins to surface just before your first shift, and fully matures afterward. It's what's giving you all these new abilities. It's what keeps you alive. So, it's best to trust it."

He turned again and strode deeper into the trees, believing that Logan would be enticed by his comparably short speech and follow.

He did, though slowly.

"Out here, you can think a little clearer," Adam continued, speaking in a low and easy voice, knowing that Logan would hear him just fine, though several yards separated them. "If you ever need a moment alone, you can come here. Robert has thousands upon thousands of acres set aside for us."

"You said this has been with me since I was born?" Logan questioned as he forced his way through a dense grouping of shrubs.

"Yes," Adam replied as he lifted his eyes toward the sunlit canopy. "You inherited this from your father. It's in your blood. It makes up your entire being. If you were to be separated from the wolf, you would die. It's that ingrained in everything you are. Decisions, thoughts, moods, all of it has some link to your wolf. Fighting it will only create more dissention between you. It'll lead to unrest in your soul."

Logan let out a hiss and all movement rustled to a halt. Adam found him examining a long cut on his hand, probably made by a sharp, low-lying branch or thorn.

He closed the distance between them and prohibited Logan from attempting to wrap up the wound. Instead, Adam shoved Logan's sleeve up to better reveal the cut.

"This is what the wolf does for you," he explained. "Any cut and any illness, it expels. Time can't touch you as it once did. You won't age. Death is still inevitable, and it's not impossible, but your wolf will do everything it can to keep you alive. Because as long as you're alive, it's alive."

Before their eyes, the edges of Logan's cut began to stitch themselves back together. Within half a minute, all that remained was a droplet or two of blood. Adam wiped it away. Then, it was as if the cut never happened.

Logan marveled at his now, fully healed hand and shook his head. "But... how? It doesn't make any sense."

Adam smiled. "I'm not sure even the oldest werewolf on earth knows the reason behind it all. The wolf shares with us miraculous gifts. Our senses, speed, strength, healing... the shift... All of it manifests because of the wolf. All it asks in return are a few simple things. Enough meat to satisfy its hunger, and time to run as nature intended. It's a small price to pay for the blessings it gives."

Something in what he said became a catalyst for a switch in Logan's attitude. "So... It's the wolf's fault that I turned into a monster that night?"

Assuming that he meant the first night he shifted, Adam nodded. "It is. For one reason or another, it chose that time to shift."

Logan marched back toward the road, but Adam was too quick and moved to block him.

"Tell me what happened," he demanded, holding back his dominance, until he saw it necessary.

The boy wouldn't have reacted that way if something terrible hadn't happened to him and his wolf. Was it a traumatic shift? Was it a surprise to his friends and family? Did he remember his experience as Adam had the first time he shifted? Though it was completely unlikely that Logan's human side was cognitive during the shift, it wasn't impossible to remember bits and pieces. Adam was an unusual case, as his father had made perfectly clear to him.

The sheer anger bottled inside Logan could have set the forest on fire. Adam felt the heat of that rage deep in his own bones, infecting his wolf. If he hadn't been so mindful, it might have spread through the rest of him and the dominance he had been holding back would spill out unmitigated.

"Nothing happened."

Logan was a terrible liar.

Adam narrowed his eyes and seized the boy's wrist before he had a chance to resist. Over the years, he had perfected this skill that no other werewolf seemed to possess. Wolves could communicate in many ways. Growls, howls, yips, all of it vocal and obvious. Other methods were not so clear, but Adam learned long ago that there was one way to communicate that required no sound, no sight, no smell.

The spiritual linking only took seconds. Logan's ire dissipated, clearing from the air around them like smoke carried away on a strong gale. Through their touch, the wolves could speak.

A common emotion Adam witnessed in young werewolves was fear. They were unsure of themselves, their new bodies, and their future. With Logan, there was the fear, but something even greater. A darkness clouded his spirit. Every conceivable negative energy existed within him, amalgamating into one entity that existed where his wolf should have. It was still there, underneath the layers of blackness.

Adam locked stares with Logan as both sets of eyes turned gold.

He had never felt this in any other werewolf, young or old, stable or rougarou. But he did what he had intended to do. His wolf took its time to entreat Logan's wolf to be calm and open. Of course, it took longer than intended, but Logan was patient in the process.

When it was finished, Adam released and let their wolves disconnect. He could have asked a million things. What had Logan done to contaminate his soul with this darkness? Why hadn't he said anything about it sooner?

He remembered what they had discussed when Logan woke up the previous day. Dustin Keith was his grandfather on his mother's side. What about the other side of his family tree? The side that he would have inherited this wolf from.

"You never told us where your father was," he said.

With Logan now composed, he might have been more willing to cooperate. He opened his mouth to answer, but the response took some time in coming. "He's dead."

"Did your mother tell you he was dead?"

It wasn't unheard of for distraught mothers to fabricate stories about the fate of an absent father. Abandonment, though frowned upon, wasn't rare among their kind. Or, often times, the werewolf father was never in the picture. Logan's mother could have lied and said that his father was dead, or a death had been faked for the sake of secrecy.

Logan shook his head. "No. I saw him die."

Adam felt his brows contract. "Are you sure?"

Logan swallowed hard. "I watched him die... I know it was him. He was... murdered."

His heart was racing, his palms sweating, but his gaze never wavered. The obvious tells were there, but Adam was better at catching a falsehood than even Darren or Robert.

The boy wasn't lying. He truly saw the body of his dead father.

"How did he die?" Adam asked, wondering if they needed to worry about hunters following the son of their last target. A band of werewolf hunters was the last thing Devia needed.

"A... A bear killed him. Mauled him inside our cabin."

Now, the lie emerged.

"Tell me the truth, Logan. Was he shot? Who killed him?"

"He wasn't shot," he insisted. "He was mauled, I swear. It was... It was a monster, that's all I know."

In that lay a nugget of truth. Adam sighed. Either way, his father was dead, which explained this unprecedented spiritual cloud.

"He was a drunk," Logan said quickly. Now that the truth had been partially told, the rest seemed to tumble out in a string of confessions that seemed involuntary. "He hit my maw. All the time. Almost every day. He'd get so drunk, he wouldn't have a lick of sense in him. He deserved to die, but maw... She didn't deserve it. She shouldn't have... She shouldn't have been there."

Adam could overlook the hysteric influx of his voice and the way he gradually retreated deeper into the forest, unconsciously looking for the safe haven he needed. But that first statement stuck.

"Your father was a drunk?" he repeated.

"Weren't you listening?" Logan shouted. "It's his fault all of this happened. It's his fault the wolf decided to shift. If he had just... It doesn't matter. They're dead... and I'm here."

Some of that anger returned, but not in the full, ruthless force it had been. Sorrow tainted its power and Logan seemed unsure whether to cry or slam his fist into a tree.

Adam rushed forward and took him by the arms to help ground him in the present. He suspected that he knew what had happened, but he wouldn't betray Logan's trust. He would confess it all in his own time.

"Your father was... he was human?"

Logan seemed to grab hold of his self-possession and nodded. "Very... very human."

Just like the darkness over his soul, this diluted condition was extraordinary. If he didn't inherit from his father, then the werewolf blood had passed down through his mother. It never happened. It was unheard of. Impossible, even. No werewolf could be born from the daughter of a werewolf alone. The spirit didn't carry like that.

Adam had never asked for a challenge, or a mystery. He was content with teaching and guiding the lost. Now, Logan had come to Devia, a miracle and a conundrum. Perhaps this was why his wolf wanted to be near him so earnestly. Logan was special. But why?

CHAPTER 7

"I'm only suggesting that you teach Cal that roughhousing is meant for the home and not for school," Darren told Elliot, one of the alphas and fathers to a troublemaking child in his class.

Elliot, half a foot taller than Darren, did not seem amused by his advice. The burly alpha folded his arms and dark, bushy brows knitted together. "I don't see any reason to."

"When Cal turns, and he comes back to school with his new strength, he'll – "

"The boy is only thirteen," the alpha interrupted. "He still has another few years left."

Darren held in the frustrated sigh. "If Cal doesn't learn proper etiquette now, while he's in school, he'll grow up to think that fighting to solve his disagreements is acceptable."

Elliot showed no sign of understanding. Why should he? The alpha from New York most likely knew nothing about peaceful negotiations. He, and his small pack had come to escape the booming industrial state, only to find that the loups-garous in the south were quite different than the ones in the north. Darren still cringed when he thought of that first decade after the war when the two sides of the country had struggled to find some common ground. They hadn't yet.

Gathering what little patience he had, Darren said, "If Cal engages in a fight with another boy – or girl – in his class, I'll be forced to send him home. I can't police every rowdy boy."

The unreasonable father bristled at the threat. "Send him home? You think I have time to look after him?"

Darren knew all too well that he didn't. He had lost his wife to an outbreak of yellow fever when Cal was just a toddler. Perhaps the lack of a motherly influence in the home had something to do with his outbursts. Elliot kept company with only his betas and other alphas. That much masculinity in one house might drive any boy to seek his father's approval with some show of manliness.

"Please understand, Elliot," Darren beseeched as more alphas crowded into Robert's front parlor. "I do care for Cal, just as much as you do. I want him to grow up to be a fine alpha, like his father. But he needs discipline. I can only do so much. Cal needs a beta to keep him in check."

The metaphorical comparison of Cal's situation to pack dynamics might have made it real for Elliot. The man unfolded his arms and gave a nod. "Fine. I'll have a talk with him."

Darren rubbed at his cheek as the alpha walked away to meet with some of his friends in the other room. A town-wide alpha meeting might not have been the most ideal place to confront a parent about their unruly child, but it was rare that Darren could catch any of the fathers in a private conference. Mothers were easier to meet with, but many were forced to defer to their husbands or brothers for advice on how to properly discipline their budding loup-garou sons.

He pulled out one of the chairs from the dining table and slowly sat himself in it, wishing the muscles around his spine didn't ache so badly. He might have been loup-garou, but his accelerated healing could hardly keep up with his motley bunch of students. And the day wasn't finished with him yet.

He thought of Logan and how he had been content to stay with Forrest and Mitch when he came to fetch him from the furniture shop. Darren tried to take comfort in the fact that the boy was making friends, but perhaps not the right ones.

While Forrest was a fine example of how a loup-garou should behave, his attachment to Mitch spoiled every bit of it. Practically joined at the hip since childhood, their mothers came to town in search of refuge. Mitch's father had been killed in a hunter ambush before he was born, leaving his mother and aunt without any means of supporting themselves. Robert stepped in to be their preserver, only to find himself falling for Caroline, Forrest's future mother.

The rest was history, and the two boys had never been apart since boyhood. Despite Mitch being slightly older than Forrest, they even shifted at the same time. Both of their mothers were lost to an epidemic that swept through the town shortly after they turned. Their deaths were one thing that Robert couldn't control.

The boys couldn't be more opposite, however, and Darren hoped that Logan would not be so susceptible to the worst of the influencers.

"Long day?"

The one voice Darren welcomed more than the rest drew him out of his worry for the new loup-garou in town. He looked up to see Adam standing in the doorway, a smile touching those piercing green eyes that demanded honesty.

With a huff, Darren ran a hand through his hair. "A long day would be an understatement. I had to break up two fights and spend an extra hour with Elijah after class to get him up to speed with the rest of the readers in his grade. If he just had the right encouragement at home..." He didn't need to finish his sentence.

Adam, his sounding board and possibly the best listener in town, knew all about his frustrations with Elijah and the others in his class.

He came to join Darren in the seat next to him. "I suppose now wouldn't be the best time to talk to you about Logan Elster, then, would it?"

Darren froze. "Don't tell me he's in trouble all ready."

The half-Navajo loup-garou sobered and shook his head. "No, no trouble. He's... I believe there's more to him than we originally thought."

"I could have told you that," Darren replied. "He must be hiding a great deal. The boy barely talks to me."

Adam gave a wry smile. "He's told me plenty. Possibly more than I care to know."

He reclined in his chair and let his hands drop into his lap. "Did you have one of your sage walks with him?"

"I tried," Adam admitted before leaning forward to rest his forearms on the tabletop. "We didn't get far before he nearly stormed off on me. The boy has a lot of anger in him... I believe it has something to do with the circumstances of his first shift. I don't have any solid facts, but one thing I know for sure is this..." Adam leaned forward and dropped his voice, though they were the only ones in the dining room, "Logan's father was human."

Darren scoffed. "He couldn't have been human. If his father was human, he would be human. End of story."

Adam shook his head. "No, it's true. Logan told me about how his father was a drunkard. No werewolf can become intoxicated, you know this. Along with that, the man is dead. Truly dead, according to Logan."

Darren held up a finger. "And there's the rub. It's all according to Logan. He could be lying."

"He wasn't lying," Adam assured gruffly. "Logan knows beyond a shadow of a doubt that his father was human. That means he inherited the gift of the wolf from his grandfather. Your Dustin."

There flared a temptation to be taken aback by Dustin being declared "his", but Darren let it slide and thought on what he had just been told. "It's not possible."

"Just because we've never seen it before, doesn't mean that it's impossible."

Darren jerked his thumb toward the parlor across the hall where the other alphas socialized before the meeting. "Gideon's grandson by his eldest daughter isn't a loup-garou. He has a family of his own with two sons and none of them are loup-garou either. I knew dozens of loups-garous in France who had daughters, who then had sons and the condition was not passed down to them. It only follows one generation, and that's all. Logan must have been mistaken or there's another piece to his parentage we don't know about."

Adam shook his head, this time more adamantly. "I know when someone is lying to me, Darren. Logan wasn't lying. I asked him the question a number of ways to make sure I understood him correctly. I don't know how it's possible, but it's true. What's more... there's something wrong with his wolf."

The two lone alphas at the table had become fast friends over the decades. They countered and complimented each other on a variety of different topics. One was this. Adam believed heavily in the spiritual aspects of their condition. Darren did not. He believed in the physical, what could be seen and experienced. To think that his body was nothing more than a void, a cavity, filled with two souls that blended together seamlessly, was too farfetched for him to imagine. He knew too much of science and biology to even consider that being a loup-garou was anything more than it was; a physical and psychological blending of two species in one body. Though he didn't have all the answers, he couldn't fill in the missing pieces with Adam's spiritualism.

"There's a disconnect between Logan and his wolf," the Navajo continued, holding his hands to try and visualize what he had observed. "There's something keeping them apart. It's like... a cocoon around the wolf part of his being. It might be why he has so much anger in him, why he doesn't trust that side of himself."

"I didn't trust the wolf either when I first turned," Darren said, wholly unimpressed. "Apart from you, I don't know who has. Logan's just scared and unsure of himself, and he's using anger as a tool to mask it."

Adam reached out and wrapped his fingers around Darren's shoulder. "I know what I saw," he asserted.

"And I believe that you believe you know what you saw," he replied. "All I'm saying is that we just met the boy. He needs time to adjust and perhaps he'll explain more about his parentage... Perhaps I'll talk to him this evening. He's with Mitch and Forrest right now, hopefully not getting themselves into too much trouble."

Darren wasn't usually so tetchy. On any other day, in any other setting, he might have been more open to what Adam had to say. But something about the subject of Logan set him on edge. He hardly knew the boy, but he worried for him. Just as he had worried for Dustin. Perhaps it was their subtle similarities that made him afraid to care too much or take anything Adam said too seriously. He had pushed Dustin too hard, and it drove him away. Logan was his second chance, but something told him that the boy would leave him just like Dustin had.

Adam sat back and let out a long breath before glancing toward the parlor. "I'd like to help the boy, if you'll allow me."

He gave a shrug and made to stand as Robert readied the assembly for the meeting. "He's not my son. I'm just looking after him, until another family can take him."

Adam stood as well, the legs of the chairs groaning against the hardwood floors. "He may not be your son, but I believe you're something like an uncle. You mentored his grandfather, after all."

"Yes, and see how well that went," Darren quipped. "He ran off during the war and impregnated a woman without marrying her."

It wasn't often that Adam laughed, but when he did, the world seemed to laugh with him. "How do you know they didn't marry?"

Darren slid him a sardonic look. "If he did, Logan wouldn't have come to Devia on the instruction that his grandmother left. He wouldn't be as lost as he is now."

The soft clink of the pebble hitting the windshield might as well have been like a booming crash. Logan winced and watched as Forrest handed Mitch another rock.

"We're going to get in trouble," he muttered to the two.

"All the alphas are at the meeting," Forrest said. "No one's going to do anything."

Mitch tossed the rock in his hand, squarely hitting the bedroom window pane. "Especially not their father. He's at the meeting with his beta too."

"And their mother goes to the weekly knitting circle about this time," Forrest added. "No one will know they're gone."

The twittering giggles of the girls sounded from the darkened side of the window and Logan edged behind Forrest, afraid that he would be incriminated somehow. He hadn't been feeling right, not after his walk with Adam that afternoon. Something told him that he should have gone back to Darren's house, but when Forrest and Mitch invited him to stay, he took the chance. He had never had friends before, and if they seemed to enjoy his company, he wasn't going to forsake the opportunity.

Still, his stomach turned and the hearty roast they ate for supper had threatened to come back up. His joints ached as well, but he wouldn't let on to the others. If he said he felt ill, they might mistake it for an excuse to leave and miss out on whatever fun they intended for the evening.

The sun had begun to sink below the horizon, setting the sky afire with bright hues of orange and violet. Red clouds streaked toward the west, while the dark blue night crept in from the east. The half-moon shone golden with an accompaniment of twinkling stars. Logan might have thought it beautiful, if his new fear of the coming twilight hour hadn't gripped his heart.

Despite the cold air that made their breath fog around their lips, Logan could feel a sweat build on the back of his neck. A product of the nausea, he assumed. He wondered how long he could hold out before his condition became too apparent to the others. The decision to leave without warning or to stay warred inside him when the window opened on the second floor of the house.

A young woman leaned out, her light brown hair in one long braid over her shoulder. She looked to already be dressed down for the evening, her white nightgown nearly glowing in the ethereal light of the sunset.

"You shouldn't be here," she whispered to the boys below. Forrest and Mitch beamed up to her, but Logan looked away from the dark eyes that seemed to fixate upon him instantly.

"You two come down," Mitch insisted.

Another girl squeezed through. Her hair was blonde, eyes the color of a cloudless sky. Logan knew they were the sisters that Mitch and Forrest had obsessed over earlier that day, but which one was reserved for whom, he couldn't tell.

"Why should we?" the blonde questioned with a saucy tone.

"Because we can't come up there," Forrest replied.

The two girls looked to one another, all smiles as they wordlessly communicated their decision as only siblings could do.

The darker one turned back and gave her nod. "Give us a minute."

With that, they withdrew into their bedroom and shut the window. Forrest and Mitch shoved one another and made some ribbing comments about what they would do and say when the girls joined them in the yard.

All the while, Logan felt the stirring in his gut intensify. He knew he would be sick soon, but couldn't predict just when. A gush of heat broke out across his body and he gulped back the stab of pain in his core. His eyes were rivetted upon the dipping sun, begging it to come back, so he could change his decision. He wanted to be somewhere else. In a warm bed with the covers over his head and a cold rag upon his brow. He wanted quiet and rest. A reprieve from the pain and battling impulses that he pushed back one after another.

Logan wished so many things, but right now, all he wanted was home.

"Sentries?" cried an alpha.

"A guard detail?" exclaimed another.

Darren covered his eyes with a hand and slunk down further into his chair. Beside him, Adam stayed erect and seemed attentive to what Robert had to say. Their opinions all mattered, but Adam's held a certain weight that he couldn't ignore. Whether the other alphas of Devia realized it, their opinions would turn at a moment's notice, hinging upon one speech from the wise werewolf. He needed the native on his side.

Robert held up a hand to silence the storm of questions and opposition thrown his way. "I have a reason," he shouted over the mob in his parlor. Two dozen pairs of eyes looked to him with confusion and anger, their expressions lit in the flickering glow of the lamplight around the room. "I know it may not seem necessary, but the times are changing and we need to change with them."

An alpha, one whose pack had been forced from their home in Tennessee before the war, stood to address his host. "We came here because of that change. This is supposed to be a safe place for us, away from the rest of humanity."

"Is Devia no longer safe?" Elliot boomed from the back where he stood with his cannon-like arms folded over his barrel chest.

More voices rose, drowning out any demand for order that Robert could muster. His hand was forced, and he unleashed his dominance. It spread like a burst of wildfire through the parlor and cut through the rest of the house, expanding even into the street. A dominance so thick and commanding that even Elliot was defused by its power.

Only now could Robert fully explain himself.

"Devia is still safe... You might have noticed that a man came into town this morning. I met with him. He calls himself Abel Morris and he made an offer to buy up a stretch of land that would cut dangerously close to town. He's looking to build a railroad going north from the Florida state line and to the capitol. He said that we own the best piece of land for a railroad. Our town and its surrounding woods lie in the path of progress, the path that men like Mr. Morris are trying to plow down. He's the first who's come to make a proposal like this, but I feel there will be many more. They'll come promising prosperity and commerce, when it's really a death sentence for our way of life here."

Darren, not entirely unfazed by the hold of dominance, but not debilitated by it, scratched at his beard and shook his head. "Then keep turning them down," he said. "If you deny them access, what can they do?"

"If they continue to come, and I turn them all down, Devia will fall under scrutiny. We'll draw unnecessary attention, because we refuse to conform."

Now, Adam spoke up, a calm voice among the hysterics. "Then what purpose do the sentinels have? How do you plan to use them?"

Robert nodded, ready to tell them the rest of his design. "We have very specific boundary lines. I want a guard detail to be set up at major points. On every road, every forest path, along the creeks and ravines. It'll be their job, around the clock, to patrol our borders and keep outsiders from coming in at all. Only our kind and their families will be allowed in or out. No exceptions."

A silence fell over the parlor as each alpha looked to one another. Puzzlement and anger were gone. Now, there only existed this sense of worry for their town and packs.

"I know it's a lot to ask, but if each pack can volunteer at least one man, we will have enough. They can work in shifts. Food and wages will be provided."

Points of disagreement erupted. Some remarked that they had none to spare, that they had their own families and jobs. Others questioned the funding for the wages. Would their taxes be raised? Would this be on a donation basis? Most of the town operated on a barter system as it was. Taking laborers and craftsmen away from their trade would create a void in the town's economics that couldn't easily be replenished, especially when money was coming out of his own coffers to pay for the guards.

"It's not a perfect system," Robert assured quickly. "There are parts that need to be worked out, and that's why I've called you here. You all know I run this town democratically. Everyone has a say. I'm not making a proclamation or demanding that this happen overnight. I'm only proposing that we take the first step to ensuring that our families and packs remain safe. I don't want a railroad cutting through our forests any more than you do. I'd like to put this to a vote and ask that we collaborate on the details."

Robert waited for anymore arguments, and then gave a nod. "All in favor of the guard, say aye."

Before a single alpha could give their decisive shout, another cry split through the darkening night outside the home. A howl, long and distressed, caught the attention of the assembly.

Each werewolf had their own howl, unique to their rank and temperament. Robert could tell the difference between Darren's, Adam's, Elliot's, and all the other alphas and betas present. This howl, shrill and solemn, only belonged to one werewolf he knew.

It was his son's. And it was calling for help.

CHAPTER 8

"What's wrong with him?" Chrissy asked, her voice shrill with panic as Mitch led her and Evelyn back toward the main road.

Evelyn fought the hardest to stay and help Logan, but they all knew what was happening. One couldn't live in Devia for more than a month without knowing. Forrest elected to stay, knowing that his father and possibly a few others would be looking for an explanation. The scent of the girls might be masked by the forest, but if they were present when the other alphas arrived, it'd be nearly impossible to explain it in a decent, innocuous way.

There was little to do, but watch and wait for the shift to complete its course. Forrest, though he had shifted and witnessed the shift in others countless times, couldn't help but cringe and wince at every snapping joint and pitiless wail of his new friend.

He had stripped down to his skin and readied himself for the last possible moment when he, too, would need to transform into a wolf to manage Logan's coming rampage. But the time was slow in coming. Logan was holding himself together, suppressing the natural progression of the shift. How he was doing it, Forrest couldn't even guess. New werewolves were often too helpless to even speak. And yet, Logan continued to beg for Forrest to run and save himself from the wolf that was nearly bursting from his skin.

"You can't force this," he tried to tell him. "You have to let it happen or it'll destroy you."

Logan thrashed his head and continued in his agonizing crawl away from the only one who was willing to stay by his side through the ordeal. "I don't want to hurt you."

Forrest rolled his eyes. "There's not much you can do to me. You're only hurting yourself."

"Then so be it." The shifting werewolf found his way to a tree and hugged it as if that would somehow keep him human. His unsheathed claws dug into the bark, latching on and refusing to let go.

Forrest shook his head at the sight, but he could understand the fear that wafted off him. He had a team of seasoned alphas and betas there during his first shift, and his second. He didn't need to worry about hurting anyone or being alone during such a pivotal moment in his life.

Whatever happened to Logan before Devia, it must have been terrible.

"You'll need to take your clothes off," Forrest advised during a lull in the shift when Logan wasn't screaming. "They'll tear otherwise."

Logan curled his legs beneath him in preparation to stand. He wouldn't have the strength. "No. I'm not... I won't shift. I can't... I can't do it again."

"Yes, you can. I know it's painful, but... you'll become accustomed to the pain."

It might have been useless to say. It wasn't a promise that the pain would be short lived or lessen over time. Only a promise that Logan would hardly notice it after his hundredth shift, or his thousandth.

Logan braced himself against the tree, clinging to it with trembling arms, his legs equally unstable. Over and over, he mumbled his declarations that he wouldn't shift. That he couldn't. Not again.

Forrest couldn't understand any of it. "If you shift, the pain will stop. It's just like going to sleep. Tomorrow, you'll be sore, but it'll be over for another month."

At this point, Logan wasn't even listening anymore. It was a good thing, too, because Forrest's father was loping to the edge of the clearing. Darren and Adam were right behind them, shirts discarded and ready to shift.

"What is he doing?" Darren demanded, marching forward while the native stayed back and evaluated the scene.

"He won't shift," Forrest replied. He, unlike the others, was bare naked in the moonlight. Even after thirty years, he had trouble casting aside his embarrassment.

Logan, upon realizing that he had an audience, turned and looked right at Robert Croxen in his fully shifted werewolf form. He let out a shout of horror and fell from the tree. He scrambled through the foliage to escape the alpha who didn't pursue him.

Despite himself, Forrest held in a burst of laughter. He had to remember that not every boy who would grow into a werewolf was raised with one. Forrest had watched his father shift for the first time before he could speak. It was nothing to him. To Logan, it must have been frightening. It was likely this was the first, fully transformed werewolf he had ever seen.

Darren cut his eyes at Forrest and glared. "Will you be shifting? Or are you simply standing there like a useless sack of bones?"

Now it was Adam's turn to suppress a chuckle. He came forward to stand beside Robert, who failed to make himself appear less threatening. Crouching low, his ears folded back against his head. Brown and tan fur that bristled upon his arrival into the clearing had been smoothed back. Still, the hulking half-man, half-beast couldn't easily be passed off as harmless. If there were any way for Robert to communicate to Logan, he would have. But as a man in his human form, Logan would understand nothing.

"Who's going to break him?" Forrest asked as the others began to disrobe the rest of their clothes. All the while, Logan thrashed and resisted the shift some yards away in the darkened woods.

Darren gave a look to Robert, whose golden eyes pinned the teacher with a stare of expectation.

He let out a huff of a laugh and folded up his trousers. "I haven't broken anyone in over a hundred years."

"He is part of your pack," Adam added, joining Robert in his verdict.

"He's temporarily living with me. That's not the same as being part of my pack. I have no pack." A dark look came over Darren's face as he took Adam's pants and stacked them with his own.

Robert prowled ahead to keep an eye on Logan while the others stayed back. This only distressed him more, but it proved to accelerate the shift. The mere presence of another werewolf could provoke the shift in another when the conditions were right.

"Dustin was part of your pack, and Logan is his grandson." Adam gave him a shrug, as if the powers that be had decided the matter and not any of them. "By proxy, I believe he is in your pack."

Forrest grimaced as he saw Logan's form become as black as the night sky, fur seeping from every pour as the shift was in its first stages. "Whoever is going to break him needs to get ready, because he's nearly there."

Breaking, though brutal and horrifying to watch, was necessary for every young werewolf. It established pack rank and formed the bonds that Logan would come to rely on for the rest of his life. Pack bonds could be formed and reformed, but it all began with the breaking. Logan's beast needed to be tamed, and that was why Forrest had howled for his father and the others. They needed an alpha. Though Logan wouldn't understand, he had the most capable alphas in all of Devia looking after him now.

Adam rushed forward, and in all his magnificent, uncanny skill, shifted in mid-leap. One moment, he was a man and the next, he was a beige and black beast, green eyes blazing in the darkness. Forrest was sure that every werewolf in Devia envied his talent and connection with his wolf. So seamless, flawless, perfect.

Darren looked to Forrest and gestured to Logan. "I was serious about my question. Are you going to help? Logan's wolf may not know you, but it'll make the transition easier."

A flash of heat streaked down Forrest's back at the thought of shifting. Once more, he had to set his pride aside. It had been a couple of years since he initiated a willful shift, purely for humility's sake. But, he supposed he could set aside his insecurities for Logan, who needed a friend.

Darren and Forrest shifted, and when the pain died away, two more wolves stood in the clearing. One boasted a deep brown pelt with more accents of beige and silver than the rest of them. The other, a deep and shocking shade of red. Forrest's wolf form had adopted his hair color, and regrettably, he was slimmer than his peers. It might have taken a few more decades before he could kick the impulse to think that he was deficient in some way, but at least none present would ridicule him for his distinctive qualities.

Logan still fought back the shift, but he wasn't slinking away as he had been. Unable to move through the convulsions, his body writhed along the forest floor. All four werewolves waited and watched as the pure black wolf finally rose onto weak, unsteady limbs. Golden, hungry eyes seethed at them and a growl broke the calm.

Robert and Darren moved forward, ears pricked and tails straight to assert their authority. Predictably, Logan became defensive and snapped his fangs at the encroaching alphas.

All at once, the three went still. The building tension broke and Logan lashed out. Forrest and Adam dove out of the way as a fight ensued. Yelps, snarls, and roars followed the tornado of fur and gnashing jowls across the clearing. Claws and teeth drew blood in movements too quick for any human eye to track.

Forrest crouched low, ready to step in and defend his father if the need came. What he could do would be minimal, but part of being in a pack meant that everyone contributed. Adam, on the other hand, herded him away from the fight, using himself as a barrier to push and guide him out of danger. His contribution would come later.

Robert suddenly skittered out of the fray, leaving Darren and Logan alone. They grappled with one another, their human-like paws clinching onto shoulders and hips. Open muzzles tossed in every direction looking for an opening to snap shut over a throat.

For a new werewolf, Logan was proving to be a challenge. Robert had limped to the side and licked a wound on his arm. It would heal in a moment or two, but the ground became stained by his father's blood. Forrest couldn't be angry or vengeful. Logan didn't know what he was doing. No young werewolf did until they could master the cognitive connection.

Like the peeling of a bell, dominance burst from Darren and radiated through the clearing. Forrest shrank and felt the tip of his tail brush against his underbelly as he tried to make himself as small as possible against Adam. The native, on the other hand, wasn't bothered at all by the final phase of the breaking. He continued to stand tall, undaunted by the dominance.

As intended, Logan let out a whimper and tried to escape from Darren. Every talon unfastened from the older werewolf's flesh and if it weren't for the alpha's quick action, Logan might have successfully slipped into the shadows.

Darren was on top of him instantly. Logan squirmed and let out a shrill whine of surrender. But it wasn't enough. His wolf had to understand that Darren was not only an alpha to be feared, but respected. Forrest watched as a pair of glistening fangs closed over Logan's furry mane. His growls drowned out the whine. Logan twitched and made some move to resist him, but a quick, harmless shake made him still again.

Logan was in no pain, but he would know who was in control. Darren asserted his dominance, but also his benevolence. He could kill the youth so easily, but he didn't. As long as Logan submitted, there would be no punishment.

And then, Forrest felt something else join the pulsating dominance. The pack bond was formed. An invisible tethering of their wolves was created between Darren and Logan. It would be there every waking moment, reminding him that he was part of something greater, something better. They would know when one another was in danger and feel the shift coming in the other.

Forrest felt his father's bond, Mitch's, and a few others within Devia. He remembered each of them and treasured the moment they were fused. He could only hope, that come morning, Logan would feel better about all of this. A werewolf that couldn't accept his true nature might as well be dead.

The pounding headache woke Logan up first. When the throbbing in his temples died away, the voices cut through to remind him of everything. All the pain, the fear, the monsters that surrounded him just before the blackness closed in.

He had done what he swore not to do. He turned into the beast again. Cleaned and under a heavy quilt in his bed, Logan wondered how long he had been unconscious. This was an improvement compared to how he'd awoken from his last shift, but that didn't make it any better. He burrowed deeper under the blanket and hugged the feather pillow until he heard a stitch pop.

"It wasn't a bad breaking," said one voice, whom he recognized as Adam's. He and Darren were downstairs, presumably in the dining room. He could smell breakfast already prepared and ready for him. Logan's gut gurgled and made the skin over his stomach quiver.

"No, but..." The pensive quality of Darren's words troubled Logan. What had he done? What happened last night? Did he kill someone? Was that what they meant by the breaking? Logan did feel different than he had the day before, but he couldn't place his finger on what it was or why.

"I can tell you worry for him," Adam said. "I do too. So far, we can be thankful that he doesn't behave differently than any other freshly turned werewolf."

Logan heard the slight thud of a glass being set on a tabletop. "He may not behave differently, but he... he feels different. When I made the pack bond with Dustin, I could feel some of his grief for Cassandra, his wife. I expected some fear and perhaps a bit of anger from Logan, but there's... there's so much more there. I've never sensed so many conflicting feelings in a boy his age. Feelings no child should ever have to deal with."

"It must be what I saw in him yesterday. That disconnect."

"You might be right. I can't see what you see, but I know what I'm feeling. Something happened to him."

Logan crimped his eyes shut against the new wave of emotions that overtook him. There had always been a measure of anxiety stirring in his chest, but it magnified in that moment. Strong and overwhelming, he dug his nails into the cotton pillow case, ripping the fabric. What were they talking about? What did his grandfather have to do with what happened last night? Was there some link between him and Darren that no one would mention?

Questions spiraled in his brain. He couldn't breathe, couldn't form one cohesive thought through the panic. He began to shake, unable to stop.

Pounding footsteps sounded up the stairs and down the hall. His bedroom door flew open and both men were inside before he could order them away. The covers were ripped off and the cold struck his bare back. The shock of it inspired him to take his first breath, but it came out quick and sporadic. He felt dizzy, nauseous, even as he gasped for a good lungful of air to stabilize him. He wanted an end. He wanted it to stop.

Hands rolled him over, but Logan jerked away.

"Calm down," Darren ordered. "You're safe. Nothing happened."

He shook his head wildly at the meaningless words. "Just get away from me."

Adam took a fistful of his hair and forced his head to stay still. "Look at me."

Unsure why he would even honor the request, Logan opened his eyes. Both men were fully dressed, concern etched in their faces as they watched him have this childlike tantrum.

"You shifted last night," Adam said. "Nothing's wrong with that. It's completely natural and you didn't hurt anyone. We were with you the whole time. Everything's okay."

Logan couldn't believe them. Nothing was all right. Not when his mother was dead and he was the monster who killed her. Not when he was surrounded by strangers who kept secrets from him. Not when he felt so out of control.

"I can't do this," Logan grumbled, his throat thick with sobs that he wouldn't allow to surface. "I don't want to."

Darren took his arm, the hold light, but comforting. "You can do this. You're not alone anymore."

"I don't give a damn about being alone," Logan returned scathingly. "I don't give a damn about you or him or any of you. Just kill me. I don't want this. I hate this thing in me. Spirit, monster, whatever it is. I don't want it."

The two werewolves glanced to one another, then to Logan with such immense pity in their eyes that he couldn't even look at them. He didn't want pity. He wanted answers and for this to be over.

"We can't do that, Logan," Darren replied softly. "Death won't help this and there isn't a cure for what we are."

"You have to trust us," Adam joined. "It will get easier."

"I don't want it to be easier," Logan groaned. "I just want it to go away."

Darren's hand tightened over his arm. "It's never going to go away, no matter how much you want it to. This is your life now, whether you like it or not. We can show you how to cope with this, but you have to meet us halfway. You have to trust us."

Logan met Darren's dark gaze. "Did my grandfather trust you?"

An answer sat on the man's tongue for a few extra seconds before he nodded. "He did. Not at first, but he did eventually. In the beginning, I was all he had. We worked together and he turned into a fine loup-garou. That's why I knew it was all right for him to leave Devia, for him to leave my pack. He could take care of himself. One day, when I know that you can take care of yourself, you can leave too, just like he did."

The hasty, reprimanding look from Adam told Logan that Darren must have said something utterly controversial. However, it was hope. It was a kernel of light at the end of this dark tunnel. If he could be a good werewolf, then he could leave and do what he wanted. He could escape their secrets and everything that reminded him of how tainted and condemned he truly was. These men didn't know a thing about what he had been through, what he did. They couldn't understand. Being here only proved that he was an outcast, a rogue. He didn't belong in Devia.

But if he just played along, if he did what they asked and pretended to be what they wanted, then he could leave.

So, Logan nodded and tried to find some peace in the middle of the storm. Because, one day, he knew he could leave. He had to hold onto that.

CHAPTER 9

"They're not even using this land!" Morris exclaimed, gesturing wildly to the acres upon acres of woodlands on the map. "They're all living in the center with this... this buffer around them! Are you sure it's not being used?"

He looked incredulously to his chief foreman, Ransom Wheeler, who stayed indifferent under his boss's tirade. "It's all forest. None of the undergrowth is cleared, and from what we could tell, there's no sign of any expansion."

Morris shook his head in disbelief. "It's ludicrous! What could Croxen want with all this land if he's not even going to use it? He could clear this for farmland, for houses, for businesses. Yet, he keeps it all wild and uncultivated."

He leaned his fat hands on the edge of the table and stared at the crudely drawn survey of the land. No records in the state of Alabama could give him a clear picture of Devia or the surrounding acres owned by Robert Croxen. If it hadn't been for his surveyors reporting that the land he intended to clear belonged to someone else, Morris would have his tracks laid by now.

"And he won't sell any of it," Morris mumbled hatefully under his breath. "Not a single tree."

Ransom reached over and pointed to the boundary line where Robert's property began and ended. "It is possible to cut around their border. It'll mean a slight detour, but – "

Morris slammed his palm on the table, causing the mapping instruments to jump. Ransom snatched up the glass of red wine before it could tip over. "I don't want a detour. I want a straight line to Montgomery. Going around Devia would only cost passengers and cargo more time. Why wouldn't Croxen want the railroad to even stop near his town? Doesn't he know the economic benefits of the thing?"

He straightened and combed back the greasy strands of hair that had fallen over his face in his rant. "Croxen must be hiding something... But what?" Taking the wine from Ransom, he downed the last of it and set the cut crystal glass on the table.

"Your guess is as good as mine, sir," Ransom offered with a shrug. "Any man who could turn down an offer like yours must be either insane or, as you said, hiding something."

Morris smacked his lips, savoring the aftertaste of his drink as he thought over his conversation with the man. He had seemed closed off from the start, as soon as he opened the door. Croxen wanted nothing to do with him, and wouldn't even crack a smile at his tried and proven jokes to lighten the mood. No amount of coercion could make him believe that this railroad would be a good investment for him and his town. To know that the land in question wasn't even inhabited only added to the mystery.

There was practically no history on the town, and what could be found was minimal at best. In fact, there was little that Morris' informants could find on Robert Croxen himself. No record of birth or marriage. Many of his citizens, as well, couldn't be traced. It was as if the town were full of ghosts.

"Every man has a price..." Morris mused. "And a weakness."

The shift in Ransom's expression told Morris that he might have been toeing toward a line that shouldn't be crossed. But, as he had told Croxen at the close of their meeting, progress would wait for no man. Something had to be done.

"If Robert isn't going to use the land, then I will."

Ransom blinked in confusion. "But, sir, he won't sell the land to you."

Morris jabbed his finger at the miles of untouched wilderness on the map. "I'll wager that he's never even stepped foot on the land. If the people of the town aren't farming it, if no hermit lives somewhere in there, then it won't be missed. It's just sitting there, begging to be cleared and utilized. If Croxen won't heed the call, then I will."

A few beats of silence filled the office before Ransom spoke again. "You're suggesting that we steal the land."

"We're not stealing if it isn't being claimed by anyone for any purpose." Morris took up a pencil and marked at a point along the southern property line. "The railroad will enter here..." He dragged the lead tip on a slightly curved path around the center of town and to the northern edge. "And it will exit here. It's not close to town, and as long as you and your men are discreet, we will never be noticed."

Ransom, who should have been used to his boss's underhanded tricks by now, crimped his face with worry. "Hiding a railroad won't be an easy task, sir."

Morris shot daggers with his eyes. "I'm not asking you if it's easy. I'm telling you to do it."

Looking down once more to the line drawn through the forest, the foreman wasn't shy in showing his hesitance. "And if they discover your plan?"

He drew himself up to his full height and clutched his fingertips behind his back, his belly straining against the gold buttons on his vest. "We'll cross that bridge when we come to it. Croxen will see that he's not the top dog here. I am. And if I want this railroad to cut through his land, by God, I'll have it. Once the land is cleared and the tracks are laid, there won't be much he can do about it. And something tells me that he's not the kind of man who can afford to sue me anyway. And even if he does, I have the best lawyers in Alabama. There's nothing that man can do to stop me or my railroad. I will have it, one way or another. Croxen can keep his secrets, but I'll have my railroad."

It had been just over two weeks since Logan's last shift. Unavoidably, the news of the young werewolf's traumatic experience had spread through town. Forrest's howl could be heard all through Devia that night, and Robert wasn't shy in answering their questions. Alphas offered the boy advice when possible, and even after the incident, Forrest and Mitch stuck by him in the days that followed during his recovery. They stayed by his side to keep him company and told stories of other shifts that were equally as embarrassing or traumatic to make Logan feel less like an outcast.

None of this, however, had any effect whatsoever on his disposition. Not even on this day, when Adam took him into the woods for the dozenth time, did Logan show the slightest bit of improvement. Even the worst cases of self-denial could have been remedied with Adam's one-on-one training sessions.

Alphas like Darren and those who were brought up under John Croxen's tutelage in France had their own method of teaching new werewolves how to control their abilities. Jumping through trees, running to targets, all of it served toward a noble purpose, but Adam couldn't see the sense in it.

Though he was a special case, he didn't have to run through obstacle courses a thousand times to master his skills. A better linkage between the spirits was all that was needed. John's method began with melding the physical, while Adam's began with the mind and heart. He found that once werewolves came to terms with their own condition, everything else fell into place.

He knew that Logan would be a difficult pupil. His obstinance, stubbornness, and obvious debilitation all barred him from his breakthrough. Where most young werewolves were ready to enter society after just three of Adam's lessons, Logan was no better.

They sat, just a few yards apart, legs crossed and open to the elements. Birds sang in the canopy, animals scurried through the bushes, the southern sun fought back the chill of the forest shadows. It might have been a peaceful winter afternoon, if only Logan wasn't struggling.

Adam watched Logan, whose eyes were closed and hands knotted in his lap. Part of accepting the wolf was to meet it. In a calm, meditative state, Logan could come face-to-face with that piece of himself that he hated.

"Don't think so much about it, Logan. Just relax and focus on the inside. Feel your inner spirit."

Logan curled his fingers into fists and Adam could sense a new wave of rage rise inside of him. "I don't want to feel inside. I don't want to feel anything."

"You must always feel something," Adam said, keeping his voice low and calm. "You and your wolf will always be there, inside. Unless you learn to accept its presence, you will always be at war with yourself."

"But I don't want this!" Logan shouted, his voice echoing through the tree canopy high above them. "I don't want to have anything to do with it."

Adam's sage green eyes narrowed on his pupil as he made an effort to not let the anger infect him. "Logan, this is your life. Your wolf is your life. To reject it is to reject yourself and the air you are breathing right now. It is by your wolf that your heart beats."

Logan opened his eyes that now blazed a brilliant shade of gold. "Maybe I'd rather my heart stopped beating altogether. Then I wouldn't have to feel this pain."

"It doesn't have to be this hard," Adam said with a shake of his head. "None of it. You see what harmony between you and your wolf can bring. Look at me, at Darren, Robert, Forrest, and all the other werewolves in Devia. They have come to terms with what they are. They have learned to live with the wolf. If you can't do the same, then life will be that much more difficult for you." He didn't want to play this hand, but it seemed to earn Logan's respect when Darren said it. "If you can't accept the wolf, you'll always have to be looked after. You can never be alone. We haven't let you out of our sight for weeks for a reason."

Logan shut his eyes again as if he were trying to will away the gold that had contaminated them. Pity welled in his heart for the youth. He wanted to be a normal human so fervently. Adam remembered a time when even he had wished the same thing. But that was before he realized the true miracle of being a werewolf. If only Logan could come to understand what a blessing it could be.

Then, something occurred to Adam. He sat back and thought for a moment. If he suspected correctly, if Logan had truly harmed his parents while in his beastly form and felt guilt for it, then perhaps he could use that as a way to shatter his recalcitrance. All he understood was that the beast was evil, that it was something to be feared and hated. Everyone had tried to convince him otherwise, but what if Adam simply stopped trying to swim against the current? What if he agreed with Logan, even if he didn't believe it? Would that reach him?

"Lone werewolves can be dangerous," he said, picking his words carefully, so the boy wouldn't catch on to his scheme. "I've met a few. Without alphas or any other werewolf to keep them accountable, they became killers... One killed my uncle, who was trying to protect me."

Logan looked to Adam, a mixture of pain and intrigue in his stare that Adam hadn't seen before. It was as if someone had finally begun to speak his language. That memory of his uncle, however, was still too raw to handle. It had been over a hundred and fifty years since that day, but it was no easier to look back upon than the moment it happened.

So he would turn to a story he could tell, one that had not involved him directly, but still carried the right weight. "There was an incident in New Orleans some years back. Robert's grandfather devoted over a century to rehabilitating these werewolves who had gone rogue. They called them rougarous. Bloodthirsty, unreasonable... psychotic in a sense. They had acquired a taste for human flesh, something we all have the potential of developing if not tempered."

Adam drew in a breath as he remembered the day when Robert received the news about the collapse at Bart Croxen's estate. "There had been a few close calls, when rougarous were not properly looked after or rehabilitated... But one was different than the rest. Nothing worked. All the usual methods to break the addiction failed and the rougarou went on a rampage. Bart, Robert's grandfather, wasn't at the complex, but if he had been, he would have been killed. Not a human or werewolf was left alive. One of Bart's close associates was also murdered. He was a man whose life Bart had saved before he became a werewolf himself. Bart was devastated by the loss. He and his son, Will, were the only ones left."

Logan lowered his eyes to the stretch of grass between them.

"The tragedy tore them apart and Bart was never the same. They went their separate ways, and the rougarou was never caught. Some think that he had no business trying to reform werewolves who had gone rogue. But Bart saw that there was a need to help the rougarous. He might have failed, but that doesn't change the fact that he understood what happened when a werewolf went without a proper pack, without an alpha, without guidance. People were slaughtered, because one werewolf couldn't control himself."

Emotion stayed the rest of his words. Much against his wishes, he remembered the skinwalker who had killed his uncle. He could see Hugo's body lying at the bottom of the ravine, limbs twisted, bones exposed, blood caking the dust of the earth. He remembered his father's mournful howl and how they both tried to look for meaning in his death in the years that followed. He wondered if Bart Croxen tried to look for the meaning in his colleague's death, if he found any at all.

Death and tragedy followed their lives, and perhaps it was naïve to think that Adam or Logan would be excluded from this rule. For beings who could survive for centuries, they were exposed to more sorrow than any human could ever endure. Perhaps that was why Adam strived every day to teach and educate others, so the mistakes of the past, like with Hugo and Bart, would not be repeated.

While Adam tried to gather himself back together after lingering on these dark thoughts for too long, he realized that the energies in the woods had shifted. Logan no longer emitted that hefty aura of bitterness. Displacing it was a feeling of revelation. Looking to the youth, he saw it in his eyes that had returned to the hue of gray storm clouds.

"We all care about you, Logan," Adam said, his words laden with sincerity. "We don't want to see you become like a rougarou, and I know that you don't either. That's why we push you to fight and to learn. We aren't just telling you these things, because we like to hear ourselves talk. We want... we need you to understand... so no one else will get hurt."

That one sentence, as clumsy as it felt to say, made it real to Logan. He nodded, but seemed to withdraw into himself, his mind spinning toward a dangerous place that Adam knew he couldn't pull him from. It was the place he went whenever he thought of his parents, or his life before Devia. Adam and Darren both recognized the dullness in his eyes when it came, the way his expression went slack. There was little that could help him in this state, but Adam had a vivid moment with Logan that would hopefully carry on long after this lesson.

In the stillness, Adam noticed something else. The birds had fled, and there wasn't a squirrel or rabbit anywhere close. Even the wind had died away, leaving a piercing silence that was soon wrecked by the unmistakable sound of man.

The voices came first, and as he reached out with his senses, Adam could hear a saw grinding away at the trunks of trees. He rose to his feet and turned to the south where the noise originated. Logan, too, heard the commotion and pushed himself up.

They listened until the first cracking and splintering of bark and wood rippled through the forest. Both Adam and Logan started when the fallen tree came crashing to the ground. None of this was visible. It was too far away, too out of sight even for a werewolf. Yet, they could feel it in the ground. That light tremor that came with the felling of the first pine.

"I thought Robert didn't sell any of the land?" Logan questioned. "He said he wouldn't."

Adam strained to make out the words of the laborers, but even though they were undoubtedly on Deviant property, it was too far for his ears to pick up. "He didn't... Something's wrong."

Almost immediately after saying this, something else entered the forest. Something wild, powerful, and formidable. It glided through the trees with all the grace and elegance that was expected of a wolf pack. Ten, maybe twenty at the most, rushed toward the crewmen.

All Adam or Logan could do was listen to Robert's sentinels descend upon the intruders. He braced for the acrid stench of human blood, but all that echoed through the wilderness were their frightened shouts and curses. Barks and growls drove them away, but not before a few guns had discharged. Their deafening crack caused Adam to go pale. Beside him, Logan was shaking.

"They're lead bullets," he mumbled as if to quiet the youth's fears. "They have to be."

The metallic odor cut through the earthen aroma that hadn't been disturbed by violence and bloodshed in decades.

They waited for the noise of the ambush to die away before they looked to one another, an unequal level of fear in their eyes. Devia, a place of peace and seclusion for werewolves, had finally been violated by man.

CHAPTER 10

If Robert expected this meeting to be a calm, civil discussion between the alphas of Devia, then he was a fool. Darren sank lower in his chair, his temple leaning against his index finger as his eyes followed the chaotic flow of conversation.

Questions flooded in from every corner of the room. Alphas and betas alike demanded to know why a gun was fired on their territorial boundaries, and why a human labor crew had been allowed to get so close to Devia. The town's leader and founder stood in the center, braving each volley with the steadiness of a military general. Each answer was short, clipped, decisive, and above all, honest.

When Robert didn't have an answer, he plainly stated so. What he did know, he told them and he didn't soften the blow. Only Darren and Adam remained silent, listening and waiting for someone to ask the big question.

After almost half an hour of this deliberation, someone did.

"What are we going to do about this?"

Every pair of eyes, whether in their calm human state or agitated wolfish gold, turned to Robert. Some in this room were older than him. Some had more experience. And yet, he commanded their respect and loyalty like no other alpha Darren had ever met. John, Robert's great-grandfather, must have passed down this quality through his lineage, but not even the roots of this family tree could do as the uppermost branch did in this room.

John's expertise was limited to the orphans and loups-garous he fostered when they had no other. He instilled that trust in them through necessity. Not a single alpha in this meeting owed anything to Robert besides gratitude for letting them live in Devia. Through dominance and hard work, he earned their allegiance. Now, he'd have to do it through careful diplomacy.

"I could say that we'll double our efforts to patrol the borders," Robert began delicately. "I could say that we'll track down the men responsible and find out who they are and what they were intending... But the truth is that I can't say we'll do any of these things. As of right now, we'll do nothing."

Alphas became enraged by his bold, controversial judgement.

"What about my pack?"

"What about my family?"

"What if they come back again with more guns?"

"Are we prepared to fight them if they come back?"

Every man in the room wanted answers and Robert let them all run off him, not replying to a single one as long as they all tried to shout over one another.

Darren glanced to Adam out of the corner of his eye, who in turn had slid a peek his way. They could both tell that things were getting out of hand. Robert, however, was not forcing his dominance. Darren had wondered if it would be inappropriate to try himself. It would have seemed like an act of usurping, to assume that Robert couldn't handle this conflict.

Adam, on the other hand, stood and didn't hold back. His dominance, equal, if not a contender with Robert's, radiated from him to get the attention of every volatile alpha in the parlor.

"Let the man explain himself," he said, raising his voice to match the others.

One by one, their hostilities were defused, and Darren felt he could breathe easier.

Robert gave the faintest of nods to his friend and squared his shoulders. "The men who invaded our borders today aren't likely to come back. They could have been farmers or homesteaders from one of the neighboring towns looking to expand illegally. They could have been men just looking for a few materials for a building project and made the mistake of choosing our trees. I would rather assume that these men won't be back to bother us after the scare our guards gave them."

He then gave a pointed look to the alpha in charge of the guard detail Robert had enlisted. "Neither will I double the guard. They did their job and it'd be foolish to take more men away from Devia because of one incident. If these men hadn't been driven off, then I would have a different opinion on the subject."

Robert turned back to the assembly. "And they, like most humans, were carrying lead bullets. Our guards were not seriously injured. Silver isn't that easy to come by and no man in their right mind would waste it on casting bullets. We may still be in hiding, but many superstitions have died with the old world. I know it's hard not to think that there's a hunter behind every tree looking to exterminate our kind. Some of us grew up in a world like that." Darren couldn't ignore the way Robert's eyes darted in his direction. "But those days are no more. We're safe here as long as we stay low."

The dissention wasn't so great this time. Alphas voiced their concerns, arguing with Robert's assessment of the situation. But their words were wasted. If Robert didn't want to do anything about the potential danger, then nothing would be done.

And like he said, they lived in a different world. As long as their way of life could be preserved in Devia, then Darren would make an effort not to let his mind wander to the subject of hunters. He didn't need to wonder what would happen to his students and their families if Devia were under such a threat.

"I need to get Logan home," he muttered to Adam, who had taken his seat during Robert's speech. "Is there anything I need to know?"

After each lesson, Adam never failed to give Darren an update on the boy's progress – or lack thereof. Logan was progressing in his training as slow as a dying slug.

Adam made a displeased face and folded his arms, the fabric of his coat jacket stretching over his shoulders. "Be prepared for a talk, if one should come. I told him about rougarou today and it seemed to get his attention... I'm not sure if it was the right thing or not, but he responded to that as opposed to encouragement."

Darren huffed. "I don't know whether to rejoice or lament."

"Neither do I," he replied. "There's still much he has to learn, but now he understands the consequences of refusing to do so." Adam leaned in his chair and dropped his voice so low that no other keen ear in the place could hear his words. "Whatever Logan tells you, be receptive. Don't judge. Let him talk. And whatever comes at the end, deal with it then. Just... be prepared."

He narrowed his eyes upon his friend. "Now I am concerned."

Adam shook his head. "What's done is done and none of us can undo it. We have come to accept this, but Logan hasn't learned to let go. That will be his greatest lesson... And you're the best to teach it."

Darren felt his heart sink into his shoes. There were many things that Adam was knowledgeable about. The connection between man and wolf being at the top of the list. His appraisal of people was a close second. If he could make such a profound statement about Darren's ability to teach Logan to let go, when he hadn't fully learned to do it himself, then he had to believe it sprung purely from reason and not a desire to get the boy off his hands. He trusted Darren's judgement, just as most of the alphas in this room trusted Robert.

He could only hope that trust hadn't been misplaced. Darren could teach children the alphabet, historical dates, and how to read, but to teach some of the lofty virtues that stumped even the oldest loups-garous was far out of his expertise.

Still, he had to do it. For Logan, whom he had grown too fond of over the last couple of weeks.

Darren rose from his seat and edged his way out of the parlor. The other alphas were still tangled in the affairs of the meeting and none would miss his absence.

On the porch sat Forrest, Mitch, and Logan. All quiet with their eyes downcast to the planks of the deck. The moon had risen, giving off a pale blue glow over the empty street. Lantern light shined through the windows of some homes in the distance, but no one dared to roam in the streets at this hour. Not when their town might have been in danger. The alphas would come home to give the news and they would pass word along to their packs. Everyone would know the details by morning, if they didn't know already. If they were listening as attentively as the three youths on the porch, every loup-garou in town would know.

"Let's go home, Logan."

The boy passed an apologetic look to his friends, who bade him a soft goodbye before they returned to their fretful eavesdropping.

Together, Darren and Logan made their way to the edge of town, walking side by side in silence. Adam had told him to be receptive, so he would be. If Logan wanted to confide in him, then Darren would let it come out in its own time. Just like with his grandfather, Logan would tell everything when he was ready, when it couldn't be bottled up a moment longer or he'd burst. Guilt had prompted Dustin to confess about his murdered bride, and perhaps whatever Adam had said to Logan about rougarous would do the same.

Over the weeks, Darren had noticed even more similarities between the two. Whether it was a product of Logan coming into his own with the shift, or it had been there all along, he was so much like Dustin. Not exactly in attitude or wit, but in his bearings. The way he ate, walked, and even sulked. All of it reminded Darren too much of the beta he had lost.

"I think Hubert wants to hire me," Logan suddenly said as they neared the house.

Darren looked to him, fighting to repress his surprise. Not at what he said, but at the sure utterance of it. Since Logan had come to live with Darren, he said little to nothing about his time with Forrest and Mitch, nor about any personal matter.

The fact that Logan was now willing to share had stunned him more than he cared to admit.

"That's excellent," he replied, treading lightly into this new conversation. "If he makes you an offer, will you take it?"

They climbed the porch steps as Logan's expression contorted with uncertainty. "I don't know. I'm good at making furniture. Even Forrest says I might know more than he does."

Darren would have never suspected Logan to be a craftsman. "Every loup-garou has a special skill. Some call it a calling. Many never find it, but some do. If making furniture is your calling, you should pursue it."

They entered and Darren set to lighting the sconces along the walls. Logan, however, remained in the hall and leaned casually in the doorway to the dining room. That in itself was a development. It was a rare evening when Logan chose to stay downstairs instead of immediately retreating to his room.

"I... I don't know if I should."

Darren was glad that his back was turned, otherwise the boy might have seen the disappointment in his eyes. He readied himself for another self-defeating rant, but was once again reminded of Adam's admonishment to listen and not judge.

"Why is that?" he asked.

Silence resumed as he went from lamp to lamp, lighting the wicks. The light wasn't necessary, not in a house of loups-garous. They could see well enough in the dark, but Darren made an effort to make sure Logan was in the habit of doing so when he was around humans who wouldn't understand.

Only when Darren blew out his match did he turn to see Logan transformed. No longer open and willing to speak, he looked to be in some sort of mental anguish that he couldn't begin to name. Only seconds later did he feel it in his own soul and recognize it.

Grief. Again. But grief for whom?

It was the same emotion that had consumed Logan for weeks, but he never spoke of it. Why wouldn't he speak?

Then, Darren remembered what Adam had said. Logan responded to that which lived in the dark. He responded to his story about the rougarou. When Adam listed the consequences, rather than the benefits, Logan listened. Perhaps, if Darren could do something similar, it would evoke a response.

So he went to the lone chair in the hall and sat himself down before he did what he had sworn not to do for ages. He remembered. Everything. He brought up the faces of Eleanor and Lucy in his mind's eye. Their smile, their laugh, their scents, and their bodies. He remembered the fire that consumed his home and how the soil felt in his hands as he dug their graves.

He remembered his mother who had saved his life from the mob in England. He let himself relive the memories that had shaped his life up to this point. He had never remarried, never adopted, never built a new pack, because he feared the attachment it would bring. Death was a part of their lives, and Logan had to know that it was okay to grieve and speak it into the open.

When Darren could almost bear no more, he met Logan's shocked and befuddled stare. Through their pack bond, he would finally learn that he wasn't the only one to feel the sapping talons of the mourning demons. Logan could feel his pain just as Darren could feel his in return.

He took a deep breath to fight back the tears that nearly choked him and waited for the youth to speak again.

"How... How did it happen?"

There were few in Devia who knew about his past. Even fewer knew the particulars. But Logan was in his pack, for better or for worse. He deserved to know. "My mother was burned alive by a mob. They were after me and she distracted them, so I could get away. Back then, they thought me a witch... My wife and child were killed by hunters over a century later. I wasn't there to save them, because I was looking after your grandfather during a shift. That was shortly after we met."

No doubt, Logan would feel in himself the stab of pain at this brief, but meaningful confession.

"Did you... blame yourself?"

Darren nodded. "I did. On both accounts. I still mourn them, but I've since... No, I can't say that." He looked away in self-disgust. "It'd be a lie to say that I've moved on and forgiven myself. I haven't. Not fully. I try not to think about them or the others I've left behind." Darren laced his fingers together and leaned on his knees. "I'm sure there isn't a single loup-garou in this town that hasn't felt the sting of death in their lives."

"Adam said that his uncle was killed by a... a rougarou."

He nodded. "He was. And his own grandfather died of an irreversible disease that has killed many elderly loups-garous... I believe they only had a few short months together before death took him too. Robert's father is nowhere to be found. His grandfather was killed several years ago in the western territories. Forrest's mother died, as well as Mitch's." Darren finally lifted his gaze to the youth, almost hating him for bringing up these harsh truths about life and their existence. "As I said, everyone's been touched by death. But we live on to bear it, whatever way we can."

A long, agonizing pause filled the house before Logan let himself slide down the wall to sit with his legs propped up and arms resting out to the sides. He looked as if his limbs simply decided to stop working, too laden with this burden he couldn't speak of until now.

"They... I didn't... I didn't want to do it. The wolf did it, I swear. I didn't know what was going to happen. One minute, I'm fighting my paw, and the next, I'm... I'm in the woods with this deer and... They were... Both of them."

Darren closed his eyes to the boy's words, unable to attach them with the torn, distraught way he spoke, his stare roaming as if in search for meaning. There was none. None at all.

Logan and Dustin were more alike than he ever imagined.

"It's not unheard of," he said as Logan's breaths became gasping and ragged in the midst of his testimony. "It's happened to plenty of loups-garous who don't have someone to help them when they shift."

"Am I a rougarou?" Logan questioned urgently. "Am I going to kill more people? Am I..."

Darren snapped up to glower at him. "You are not a monster. Don't even think it. And you are not a rougarou. They don't feel remorse for the things they've done. You do."

Logan's lips quivered and a tear glistened upon his cheek in the lantern light. "But... I don't... My paw deserved to die. I don't feel bad for killing him, but my maw... She shouldn't have died."

"That still doesn't make you a rougarou," Darren repeated. "What you did... It can't be undone. We can't go into the past and change what happened. I can't bring my mother, my wife, or my daughter back. Not Robert's grandfather, not Adam's uncle... and not Dustin's first wife. We've all lost. But we still have much. We have our packs. I know that may not mean much to you right now, but with time, a pack can mean everything to someone who has nothing."

Logan swallowed hard and Darren could tell he made an effort to keep himself from flying into hysterics as he had done the morning after he shifted. Even if he did, Darren wouldn't stop him. They both needed this release. As grim as it was, they needed to finally let themselves be vulnerable.

"I'm... I'm scared that I'll do it again."

Darren shook his head. "Not on my watch, you won't. We're looking after you, Logan. You won't become a rougarou and you won't kill anyone else. Not while I have anything to say about it as your alpha."

Somehow, that seemed to lessen the torture Logan must have endured night and day since he shifted for the first time. To know that someone was looking out for him, that Darren wouldn't allow his new greatest fear to come true, mended a piece of that broken heart. Just how, he didn't know. All he understood was what was felt through their pack bond. Logan was allowed some relief, so he accepted it without question. If that's what he needed to be motivated, Darren would remind him every morning.

Cyrus had been waiting for almost an hour. He had no appointment with Mr. Abel Morris, but he would see him before the end of the day. Mutely, he watched the businessmen come and go from the waiting room. They passed through the doors that led into the influential man's office, only to be yelled at and belittled by their host.

The receptionist, unbothered by the constant muffled shouts, continued to jab her fingers along the keyboard of the typewriter. He could almost time it when she was ready to push the cylinder carriage to the left for the next line. Invoices, business letters, and other important documents piled up on the receptionist's desk to the point that he almost couldn't see her shoulders from where he sat.

Every anxious partner, foreman, and salesman who sat in the hard, wooden chairs along the walls exhibited the same jitters. Biting nails, jumping knees, fidgeting with the hems of their clothes or briefcase. The tapping of shoes was equally as unhinging as the clicking of the typewriter. Glancing to the clock on the wall, his frown deepened. Cyrus liked to pride himself on his exceptional level of patience. He needed the virtue in his line of work more than any. But how could one railroad tycoon be this busy?

Then, he reminded himself that this opportune moment could wait for a little longer. It had been several years in the making already. Careful planning, studying, and infiltration had prepared him to finally penetrate Devia's defenses. His father had discovered the place, but warned against any attempt to take it. There were too many. It was too risky. Their team would never survive the onslaught, no matter their marksmanship. The budget was never right to afford the bullets they would need to take on a pack that size. The old man was too careful.

His father was gone now, and Cyrus was calling the shots. Devia was in his sights. When he heard that Mr. Morris wanted to take on Robert Croxen, he saw his chance and wouldn't let it go untaken. Soon, his clan would have this coveted prize.

A loud bang came from the man's office. Everyone, even the receptionist, jumped at the sudden noise when the fat hand slammed on the desk top. Cyrus, however, didn't even blink. Steady nerves were also required to do what he did best.

The angry shouts rose to an unprecedented high as the man continued to berate the incompetence of the foreman.

"What do you mean none of them will work?" he demanded.

Cyrus listened closely for the foreman's response. "They say they won't go back. Not after what happened. I told them it was being taken care of, but they won't budge, sir."

"Then hire another crew! I want those trees cleared by the end of the week!"

"I've tried, sir. They all heard what happened. None of them will go."

"Raise their pay. Threaten them. Do whatever you can to get them back on this job."

A silence fell more ominous than the argument.

"Sir... I don't think I can. Hell, I don't even want to go back. You weren't there. You didn't see those things..."

"They're just animals! You have guns!"

"The guns didn't do anything, sir," the foreman pleaded. "They just kept coming even after we shot them. If you can get that forest cleared out, I'm sure the men will work again."

"I'm still waiting to hear back from my contacts," Mr. Morris said, lowering his tone. "You can tell the men that it will be dealt with, but I'm on a schedule. Those tracks had better be laid by the end of this week or none of you will work in this business again. I can assure you of that."

Before he could even finish this last threat, Cyrus rose from his seat and calmly made his way toward the office, his hat in his hand and shoulders back.

"Sir, you can't go in there," the receptionist warned. "He's in a meeting."

Cyrus only waved his hat, more or less to acknowledge that he had heard her, but was ignoring her anyway. The office door wasn't locked and he didn't knock. The moment he slipped inside, both men turned to eye him with complete disbelief.

"What the devil do you want?" Mr. Morris questioned, the buttons on his vest ready to pop off as he puffed out his chest.

"I heard you had an animal problem," Cyrus began, playing the part of a concerned contractor.

The foreman hurriedly looked to his boss as if to say that this was the answer to their problem. Mr. Morris wasn't so convinced.

"Who are you?" he asked.

Cyrus slipped through and closed the door behind him, seeing this as his invitation. "My name is Cyrus Taggart. I specialize in a certain type of animal... extermination."

There was no light way to put it, but neither of the men seemed to care. They both instantly became more intent.

"What type of animal?" Mr. Morris asked. "Dogs?"

"They were wolves, sir," corrected the foreman.

Just as he thought. "How big?" Cyrus asked, almost forgetting himself in the charade.

The foreman seemed at a loss for how to accurately describe them. He stretched out his hand to be level with his waist. "At least this high at the shoulders. I couldn't get a good look at them, though. They had to be at least... two, maybe three hundred pounds."

Mr. Morris snorted at the absurd number, but Cyrus knew it was a low estimate. "Coloration?"

Once more, the foreman was at a loss. "All manner of colors. Black, brown, gray."

"How many?"

"A dozen, give or take a few."

Cyrus nodded. He was sure there were more in the town. "What exactly happened?"

The foreman began to explain how his crew of twenty had begun the task of clearing the trees near one of their sites for a new railroad. After the first tree fell, the wolves ambushed them. "We shot at them, but they wouldn't go away. Everyone ran after we realized the first few shots didn't so much as slow them down."

"Did they hurt anyone?"

Mr. Morris shook his head. "Not one. A bunch of cowards. They probably missed the beasts completely and that's why they didn't slow down."

"The fact that the wolves weren't even spooked by the gunfire is too fantastic," the foreman said to his boss. "And I know I shot one of them. I saw the blood on its fur."

"A wolf that size would barely feel the wound," Cyrus said. "And if they're so invulnerable to bullets, it's likely they don't have any fear of man."

Mr. Morris sat in his leather office chair, his pudgy fingers gripping the arms. "So what would you do about this pest problem? You can't shoot them or scare them away, so what else is there to do? If I'm going to hire your services, you better give me results. And quick."

Cyrus smiled. "I have a team of men who are trained in taking out wolves just like these. I've been doing it since I was a boy, when my father taught me. My whole family has been in this profession since before this country's founding."

The railroad tycoon crooked an eyebrow at him. "You're a wolf hunter?"

"A very good wolf hunter," he corrected.

Only one man in the room began to look hopeful, no doubt because his job was on the line if the wolves weren't taken care of quickly. The other was still cynical.

"And how much does a very good wolf hunter cost these days?"

Cyrus named his price and neither of the men were happy.

"That's highway robbery!" exclaimed Morris. "How can you get away with charging that much for killing a bunch of oversized mutts?"

"These oversized mutts are capable of killing a man in less than five seconds," Cyrus explained, dropping all politeness. "It's a miracle that your crew escaped with their lives. If you sent them in a second time, the beasts might not be so benevolent. And I charge by the wolf. You say there's about a dozen, but I know for a fact there are more around that town. Those forests have been infested for some time now and I've only recently learned about the pack that occupies that territory. It's probably the last wolf pack in the south."

Morris narrowed his eyes. "If they've been there for a while, why doesn't Robert Croxen do anything about it? They're a threat to his town, after all."

Cyrus, once more had to curb his answer. Reveal too much and the man would think he was an escaped lunatic from an asylum. If he told any other man that those were no ordinary wolves that attacked, he'd be thrown out. But he knew the truth. They were werewolves. He knew the signs, knew what to look for. And Devia was a hornet's nest.

"There are some people who think that wolves, bears, cougars, and other predators aren't a problem. I've done my research. No one in the town makes their business in livestock, therefore a wolf isn't a threat. To most, they're a nuisance and can destroy a family's livelihood. If Croxen doesn't have to worry about the consequences of a wolf pack, then he won't do anything about it." Cyrus leaned his hands on the desk. "But, Mr. Morris, you do have to deal with the consequences. If you want that railroad, you need workers. To get your workers, you need those wolves gone. I'm just the man to get rid of them for you. Pay my fee and give me three days."

The portly man huffed in disgust. "Three days? Why so long?"

"Some things take time, Mr. Morris. I have to go to Devia myself and make my plans." Cyrus stood and offered out his hand. "Pay my fee, three days, and you'll have as much wolf-free land as you need for your railroad."

The shrewd businessman examined Cyrus' face, searching for any hint of a trick in this arrangement. There was none, and even if there was, Cyrus had learned from the best how to hide the truth from other humans who wouldn't understand. The world wasn't interested in monsters and fairytales anymore. Science and progress were clearing the way for a new age of hard facts. No one believed what they couldn't see with their own eyes. And even then, like the foreman, they'd deny that any supernatural creatures were involved. Only a man of unsound mind would.

Finally, seeing that he had no other option before him, Mr. Morris shook his hand. The deal was made. Devia would fall in three days. If not sooner.

CHAPTER 11

"Are you sure you'll be all right alone?" Forrest asked, one hand gripping the handle on the back door of the furniture shop.

In Logan's hands was a half-sculpted table leg that would be put through the lathe once he sawed down the basic curves. "Go on. You told me no one shifts alone, and that includes Mitch, right? I'll be fine."

Just thirty minutes ago, Mitch had complained of a coming shift. It was his time of the month for it. He had excused himself from the shop, but Forrest had admitted that he never missed one of his cousin's nights to run wild. It took Logan the better portion of that half hour to convince him to even consider leaving.

It might not have been such trouble if Hubert hadn't left the shop in their hands and Darren wasn't due to pick up Logan for a while. It'd be the first taste of solitude he'd had since arriving to Devia, and he'd be lying if he said that wasn't part of the reason for wanting to push Forrest out the door. Yet, his new friend was hesitant for that same reason.

It had been some time since Logan last shifted, but he was in no danger of another for a couple more weeks. Though noises and smells were still a blur to his senses, it wasn't as overwhelming as it had been. And after his talk with Adam and Darren, he began to feel a piece of himself return.

Confessing to the murder of his parents had done almost nothing. Darren treated him no differently, as if it weren't a sin at all for a werewolf to steal the life of another. He had expected some harsh judgement, perhaps even banishment from Devia. Of course, that was before he had learned that killing a human didn't make one a rougarou. For that, Logan was relieved.

And it was such relief that told him he could survive some time alone. He wouldn't run. He wouldn't shift. He wouldn't kill. He'd stay in the shop until Darren came for him. Until then, he'd work on this table order for Hubert.

Forrest gave him a wary look, but trust and urgency won the decision. He gave his goodnights and left. For the first time in weeks, Logan was in a room, in a building, all by himself. No chaperone, no teachers, no friends. Just him and the furniture. Part of him missed the ringing silence that came with isolation when he was a human. Would he ever hear it again?

He set to work sawing off the excess pieces of the block and then fixed it to the lathe. As Adam had tried to teach him before, he let his ears become attuned to a specific sound.

He focused on it, segregated it from the others to the best of his ability. How could the others differentiate from the cacophony all around them? Footsteps on stairs in houses down the street, the laughter of families eating at their dinner tables, the mumbled conversations in private rooms, and even further beyond, he could almost hear Mitch and the others prepare for their shift.

Forrest wasn't the only one who had joined them. Though he couldn't make out one from the other in the din, he imagined that Robert and some of the other werewolves his age were walking through the twilight on their way to the forest.

Logan shook his head and wondered once more how a place like this could exist. Every other night, a pack would go to the forests to shift. He could sometimes hear their yips and growls from his bedroom. They acted like it was nothing for Devia to exist, as if they weren't something special and haunting at the same time. He had been a werewolf for over a month now, and he still couldn't wrap his mind around the concept. Maybe he never would.

"Hello?"

Logan nearly ruined the table leg as the shaver in his guiding hand jumped off the wood. He had been so focused on Mitch and the others that he hadn't heard the front door open to the store. The scent that carried to him in the shop, fighting its way through the musty smell of wood, was a familiar one, but he had a hard time placing it.

"Forrest? Mitch?"

He straightened and set down his tool. He wasn't so versed on her scent, but he knew the voice. He had heard it many times over the last couple of weeks when Evelyn and Chrissy came to visit. Logan awkwardly continued working while they visited and hardly spoke a word to either of the girls.

Now, Evelyn, the dark-haired one who was smitten with Mitch, had come to see her sweetheart only to find Logan. It had to be too late to pretend he wasn't there. She'd see the candle glowing through the cracks in the poorly set door, and the sound of the lathe was far too loud for another to miss, even a human. It was likely Forrest had forgotten to lock up. With the sign on the door reading that they were closed, and all the lights extinguished, Logan hadn't thought anyone would disturb him either. Especially not a lady.

He looked to his apron spotted with sawdust and made some attempt to brush it off. That only left his roughened hands in a worse state. Though the scent blended in with his surroundings, Logan was sure that he didn't smell all that pleasant either. There was no use trying to better his appearance so with a sigh, he strode toward the door to meet her.

He swung the door open before she had a chance to reach for the handle. Her hand, delicate and white, was outstretched to take it. Her eyes widened upon seeing Logan there, but nothing in them portrayed disappointment.

"Oh... Is Mitch not here?" she asked, glancing past Logan into the dimly lit shop.

"No, he... He's out."

Evelyn, who had been raised with werewolves, understood perfectly and she nodded. "I see... Forrest too, no doubt?"

"Yes, ma'am."

Her giggle made Logan even more nervous. "Don't call me ma'am. We're practically the same age."

Thinking on it, they were. That realization struck him a little harder than he expected. Both Forrest and Mitch were nearly twice his age. His mentors and the other alphas were ten times older than him. Perhaps one thing he had taken for granted was that time affected werewolves differently. The women in this town likely looked exactly how old they truly were. The men, not so much.

Logan, a little ashamed for his forgetfulness, lowered his gaze and let the silence take dominion over the shop. Evelyn, too, was at a loss for words.

Finally, in a moment of awkwardness, they both looked up and took a breath to speak. Seeing the other one in the act, they shut their mouths in unison to wait.

"No, go on."

"What were you - ?"

They spoke at the same time, and Logan could feel his temperature rise. This had to end before he made a complete fool of himself. He had never been alone with a girl, let alone a pretty one like Evelyn. The glances she had slid his way during every visit had not gone unnoticed. The subtle, but powerful shift in her scent when their eyes met had him puzzled. As did the way his chest and stomach tightened at the very utterance of her name. When she walked by, so close they could almost touch, Logan thought he would come undone. It terrified him as much as the beast did. He didn't want to feel something for Evelyn or any other girl.

The blush on her cheeks did little to help him now.

"I was going to ask if you accepted Hubert's job offer." She gestured to his filthy shirt, apron, and trousers. "By the looks of it, I assume you did?"

Logan nodded. "Yes, I did... I wasn't all too sure if I should at first, but I did."

Evelyn gave him a sympathetic smile. "Mitch told me how hard it's been for you since you came to town. I know I'm only a girl and don't quite understand what you boys go through, but... if there's anything I could do to help..."

Did she leave that statement open for a reason? Or had she stopped herself from making a promise she couldn't fulfill? Logan didn't want to assume, nor did he want to hope.

He looked away toward the store display window and how the silhouettes of the chairs proclaimed how dark it had become in the last hour or so. It didn't bother Logan nearly as much as it used to. The dark was equated with the unknown, with the feeling of being lost. He could see through the darkness now. Nothing was hidden or obscured.

But he thought of Evelyn and the fact that these few candles behind him were all she had.

"You shouldn't be out so late," he said.

She wrung her gloved hands in front of her. "I know, but... I came to see Mitch to tell him... Well, you know how the town foundation festival is tomorrow? He was going to take me, but... You know, I'll just talk to him in the morning."

Evelyn turned to go and Logan found himself following after her. "Are you still going?"

"I... I might be," she said, slowing her steps toward the door. "I know Chrissy is going with Forrest, and everyone will be there. I should go, but... Are you going?"

The eager, hopeful look in her eyes made sweat bead down Logan's back, even though it was chilly in the shop. "I don't have much of a choice. Darren's going, and his students are putting on some play. He won't let me stay home. I've already asked."

Her smile once more made his knees almost buckle. "The festival's not so bad. Of course, it might be a bit much for a new werewolf. There's dancing and music. Robert gives a speech. It's great fun if you're interested in that sort of thing."

"Are you?" The question came out so quickly that Logan hardly had the clarity to stop himself.

Evelyn paused at the door. The waxing moonlight cast an ethereal glow upon her face. For once, he had enough control to take a few steps back, putting her well out of arm's reach.

"Not really," she admitted. "I enjoy quiet evenings. Walks by the creek, dinner with my family... private conversations."

Logan swallowed and glanced to the empty street in front of the shop. There was no one supervising them, no one to see that she was alone with him. Was this appropriate? Things in Devia were different. Did that mean social etiquette was different too? Was it common for girls to be in the company of a boy without an adult? Or was that encouraged here?

"Something tells me that a big party isn't something you'd enjoy either."

Logan felt trapped between shoving her out the door and seeing where this discussion would lead them. "Not really. I've never been to one."

She tilted her head in that curious way. "Never? Not one."

"Not one," he parroted. "We... I was never invited."

Evelyn frowned. "That's a shame. Maybe you'll find that you like them. If it helps, I could... Well, I'll see you there for certain. My mother won't let me stay home either, so... I'll just see you there." Her hand was on the doorknob. "Tell Mitch I need to talk to him, whenever you see him next."

Too dumbstruck to speak, he only nodded. She gave him one more dazzling smile and disappeared out the door. He stood, staring blankly into the coming night as if she had just slapped him.

Was she ready to ask Logan to go with her to the festival when she was already committed to Mitch? If she did, propriety stopped her from making that fatal error. But what if she had asked him? What would he have said? He knew the answer and that truth bothered him more than the question that was never asked to begin with.

Logan felt he could scream and collapse all at the same time. What right had he to want a girl that belonged to his friend? What right did she have for making him feel this way? It was all her fault. Every bit of it. If Evelyn hadn't looked at him that way the night he shifted, her hazel eyes gazing down at him with her dark braid dangling over her shoulder, he would have never had these thoughts. He would have never seen something that wasn't there. It couldn't be.

Logan briskly shook his head, clearing his thoughts about Evelyn just in time to smell Darren's approach to the shop. He'd need to lock up and put away his project in the back. His one hope was that his mentor and alpha wouldn't ask why he seemed so distracted. Logan had told him everything about his parents' deaths, but to confess that he might have been sweet on a girl that wasn't his, was out of the question. One thing he did understand about wolves, was that they would fight to defend what was theirs. Logan had no interest in tangling with a more experienced werewolf like Mitch.

Robert watched as his son and nephew wrestled across the clearing. Beside him lay Adam and two other alphas who in turn looked after their younger pack members engaged in play.

The last two weeks had been nothing short of an ordeal. The trespasser incident had set most of the alphas and betas on edge. They came to him at all hours, asking for updates and if he had developed any other plan to aid them in the town's protection. To his own complete dissatisfaction, Robert had to turn them away with the placating answer that he was "doing all he could". It was the truth, but an unsettling one due to one important fact. He felt as if there wasn't much he could do.

The men were gone, their scents faded, and their purposes unknown. Part of him wanted to believe it was the doing of Mr. Abel Morris, the railroad businessman who had come to him some weeks ago looking to buy his land. It had been ages since he'd had to deal with a man so arrogant. Did he really believe that cutting corners would be a viable option in dealing with Robert Croxen?

He might not have been a strong alpha when he founded Devia, but he was now. He wasn't the biggest werewolf in this clearing, but he could command the respect of all present. That, in itself, might have been his only saving grace in the matter. If his town didn't trust him half as much, they would have been gone long ago. If he couldn't develop a better plan quickly, they might leave. It was their choice, and he wouldn't stop them. But if Robert couldn't hold their loyalty, then what good was he as a leader?

He let his wolf-like muzzle rest upon his folded arms, the tips of the grass tickling the hairs on his mane. Beside him, Adam gave a light snort to get his attention, but only Robert's pointed ear swiveled in his direction. As a man, he could hide his anxiety. As a werewolf, little was left in secret among them. Their scents ebbed and flowed with every slight alteration in their mood. It was likely that Adam could sense this change in his energy. If he were in his human form, he would have asked what was wrong. Thankfully, they were all wolves here and did not have such luxuries as articulation.

All that mattered was what was happening right now. Not what happened days ago, nor what would happen tomorrow. Just this moment while his family let their wolves loose. This was what Devia was all about. Connection, togetherness, and family.

Edmund, one of the few alphas that had helped to settle Devia in its infancy, sat up abruptly. His head whipped toward the south, ears erect and deathly still. Adam, seeing this, turned his attention in the same way. One by one, the other alphas, including Robert, took notice of the new noise.

It sounded as if something was approaching, but there were no new scents on the wind. The younger werewolves stopped and crept closer in the general route of the disturbance, more eager than alarmed.

Forrest looked to his father with the question in his eyes. Could they hunt? It might have been a family of deer that had wandered onto their territory. The alphas also looked to Robert, who was essentially in charge of the run. It would be his decision if they hunted tonight or not.

Something about it didn't seem right. Deer would not make so much noise. Their hooves would turn over leaves and twigs, but these made a larger impact on the earth. Leaves weren't just pushed aside, but crushed. Sticks and small foliage were snapped under the weight of the footsteps. The feet that slowly tramped through the forest weren't light in any sense.

It couldn't be rabbits, badgers, or even a hog. They, like deer, put off a distinct scent that was strangely absent. His next thought was a bear, but the time of the year wasn't right. They were all in hibernation. Whatever this was, it was big, clumsy, and blended well with the forest.

Robert rose and gave a jerk of his head toward Adam and two of the other alphas. Before leaving the clearing, he gave a narrow look to the younger werewolves as a sign that they shouldn't pursue. They would go alone. If it was prey, they'd hunt it themselves.

The four werewolves fanned out, each a reasonable distance apart from one another, attentive to the mysterious encroachment. Unlike their potential quarry, the werewolves were light in their steps, almost inaudible in their advance.

Robert and Adam comprised the middle components of the formation, while the other two would flank them. It didn't take long before he realized that his son had disobeyed. Through the pack bond, he knew the boy was following him. There was no time for a reproach. Because as soon as he sensed Forrest, the crunching of leaves and breaking of branches went completely silent.

Ahead, he could just faintly see them. Dark shadows held perfectly still against the silhouettes of the trees. Robert called for an all-stop, and the five werewolves likewise stood as statues. The late winter breeze rippled through their pelts from the north, sending their scent to the prey, but unable to return the favor.

Still, there was no movement. Either the animals didn't smell them, or they weren't bothered. Were these other werewolves coming into Devia?

Then, one shadow changed. An arm was raised. Then came the click of metal.

Before Robert could give the signal, the flash of gunpowder illuminated the mostly concealed face of a man. He was clothed in black to hide his form, the only visible feature being his eyes and brow.

The bullet whizzed past Robert, but found purchase in flesh.

Forrest let out a yelp and doubled over.

The men, at least ten in number, shouted as chaos ensued. Roars and growls broke through the night as all charged ahead. If these were the same men from before, they could be easily scared off again. Though they were fewer in number, they would soon learn that their lead bullets did nothing.

The meaning of their shouts escaped him as the four alphas wove their way through the woods in the assault. They could have taken them easily, but Robert had made it clear to all the werewolves that it didn't matter who the stranger was. No killing.

These men, however, came prepared. More shots were fired, which were carefully avoided. Still, they ran. And once Robert knew they were close enough to the outer boundary of Devia, he ordered the others to halt. They did, skidding upon the fallen leaves.

Rigid and panting, they lingered just long enough to make sure the humans were gone before turning back. Robert, somehow, had fully expected his son to be with them. He wasn't.

Upon a closer listen, he realized that Forrest was still laying where he had been shot. Heart pounding, he charged ahead of the others to find him. The boy had never been shot before, so he hadn't expected him to be unaffected by the pain, but it shouldn't have crippled him from following.

Mitch and the others had gathered around him. Whimpers and comforting nudges made Robert dash forward and shove them out of the way. Forrest was unable to rise. The bullet wound in his hip hadn't healed. Blood oozed over his leg as he lay helpless. He leaned forward to sniff the wound and found a single long wisp of smoke curl upward. Burning flesh.

This wasn't a normal bullet.

CHAPTER 12

"How the hell did they get through?" thundered Robert.

Forrest lay on the settee in the parlor, his claws ripping the velvet fabric as Dwayne McNair, Devia's only physician, probed the gunshot wound with his forceps. His teeth ground into the wooden rod they had given him to bite when the pain became too intense. Though he was naked, a sheet covered most of his body, leaving his hip exposed. Towels and rags soaked up the blood that continued to run from the open cut, which only became more and more agitated with the doctor's efforts.

"They had no scent," Adam insisted. "They most likely slipped past the guards without much notice."

As humiliating as it was, Forrest didn't deny his father the audience as the alphas talked not five feet from him.

"They did have a scent, I'm sure of it," his father debated. "It was just... just too masked somehow. They smelled just like the trees and plants. They tricked us."

Footsteps sped up the porch and Forrest groaned as the forceps dug deeper. He wasn't sure what was worse. The doctor's tactless searching or the searing of the silver bullet through muscle and flesh.

Darren and Logan barged through the front doors and joined them in the parlor. Forrest wouldn't even look at his friend, knowing that being caught in such a position wasn't something to be proud of. He had been shot, because he hadn't listened to his father's orders. He'd be scolded later when the matter at hand was resolved.

"We heard what happened," Darren said, making his way toward Adam and Robert. Logan went immediately to the settee and Forrest could practically feel his apprehension upon inspection of the scene.

"Silver bullets," Forrest mumbled through the stick in his mouth before succumbing to a new wave of agony at the hands of the doctor.

"You've had more experience with hunters," Robert said to Darren. "Do you know of any scent cloaking tactics?"

"Hunters?" Darren cried. "I thought these were the same men from – "

"We don't know for sure," Adam interrupted. Taking turns with Robert, he began to tell all the details of the assault. The masked scents, the black clothes, the silver bullets, the way they put up a stronger fight. All of it pointed toward the conclusion that these men knew what they were doing and knew who they were facing.

"Where's Mitch?" Logan asked as the alphas were talking.

"Still shifted," Forrest answered after unclamping his teeth from the rod. "But he's in town with some others. They thought it'd be safer if – God damn it, Dwayne! Can't you just get it out already!"

The young doctor wasn't amused. "Do you think any part of this is easy?" he grumbled, still engrossed in his task.

"How far could it have gone in?" Logan asked.

"It's not about how far, but a matter of getting a good grasp of the metal pieces."

"Pieces?" Forrest whined. "I only got shot once."

This drew the attention of his father. "Why is the bullet in pieces?"

Inside his leg, Forrest felt the forceps touch the source of the burning and he nearly screamed as it cut deeper. He returned the wood to his mouth and tried to control his tremors as the doctor proceeded to pull out one silver chip.

With a sigh, Dwayne dropped the piece into the china bowl on the floor. "That's one," he said before immediately going back in.

"Why is the bullet in pieces?" his father bellowed.

"I'm not an ammunitions expert, Robert," Dwayne returned with just as much venom. "Ask someone who's ever fired a gun."

Unless any of the werewolves in the room had a secret, Forrest knew that no one could be asked.

Dwayne found the second shard much more quickly than the first and it clinked against the porcelain.

"If they were ordinary woodsmen or game hunters, they wouldn't waste their money on fashioning silver bullets," Robert reasoned to Darren. "Even if they did, why would they be hunting at night with no lantern and be that mindful to cover their tracks?"

"They were loud," Adam added. "But most humans in the forest are."

Darren shook his head. "I've... I've had experience with hunters, but never... I've never faced them personally. I only know what John's told me and what happens after they take on a pack. Never before. I don't know the signs, I don't – "

"Think!" Robert ordered. "What did John tell you? How do they operate? There were at least ten coming toward Devia. Is that normal? Is that too few? Too many?"

"I don't – "

"And why did they run away? They could have easily shot us all dead. Why didn't they?"

Darren continued to stammer, while Robert unloaded his barrage of questions. Everyone in the room, even Dr. McNair, turned to watch the alpha of Devia become completely mad.

"Father!" Forrest shouted, effectively gaining Robert's notice. "Darren doesn't know. None of us do. We've never dealt with this. Leave him alone."

It was rare that he would call out his father in front of others, especially alphas like Darren and Adam. But if he hadn't said something, Forrest knew that it might have come to blows. Robert had been under so much pressure lately. The meetings, the trespassers, the festival the following evening, all of it would break him. As dire as the situation seemed, and as much pain as Forrest was in, he could somehow keep a calm head through it all.

He understood the dangers. He knew how many people lived in Devia, human and werewolf. He knew that this bullet could have very well hit him in the heart or the head and he wouldn't be alive to berate his father at all. Yet, he could think clearly through the pandemonium.

"The guards need to be told about the scent cloaking," Adam said, disrupting the pregnant silence. "We need to tell the alphas that – "

"We're not telling any of them," Robert growled. "There's no need to make them worry. We will resolve this as quietly as we can."

Forrest wasn't entirely sure how he expected to keep this whole affair quiet. If Darren and Logan had heard about the incident only hours after it happened, rumors would be all over town by dawn.

Dr. McNair resumed his search for the last shard and Forrest turned away to suffer through the pain, knowing it was coming to an end soon.

"And the festival?" Logan asked, his voice unexpected in the discussion.

"We won't cancel," Robert said. "We will keep everything in place until we no longer can."

Darren, recovering from his stint of confusion, spoke up. "We need to evacuate."

That simple statement inspired a wide array of reactions. Robert peeled into another invective while Adam worked to defend the idea. Logan was too stunned to close his mouth while Dr. McNair sped up the procedure, probably eager to leave this house and the angry alphas. The dominance stifled the parlor.

"No one is going anywhere!" Robert roared. "We are staying right here and if hunters come, we will fight them until every last one of them is dead. I don't care if there's a hundred of them. Devia will not fall!"

The burning ceased and Forrest could feel his tender wound begin to close up. Dr. McNair dropped the last silver fragment in the bowl. The patient glanced over his shoulder to the bloody mess, and in the dim light he could see the metal glinting against the stained porcelain.

"I told you not to engage!" It was a fortunate thing for Vinnie that Cyrus didn't have his pistol strapped to his belt. Otherwise, the hunter would have been shot through the skull by now.

After the failed scouting mission, Cyrus summoned his team to the stately home of a patron in a city close to Devia. Not only would his colleague be chastised, but the others would need to be updated on the plan that he had almost ruined.

"I had a shot and I took it. That's one less wolf for you to worry about."

Vinnie's argument wasn't convincing. Not to any of the other seasoned hunters in the room. If Cyrus could have done this raid with members from his own clan, he would have. If his father's notes were anywhere near correct, ten hunters would be no match for how many werewolves defended Devia. It had taken him weeks to round up enough men before approaching Morris with his offer. Vinnie was included in the twenty-five he managed to coerce into helping him, and Cyrus regretted it already.

"Now Croxen will know the town's been compromised," Cyrus said, leaning his fists over the table covered in maps and notes. "We might have had more time to carefully scout those borders, but thanks to you, we have to strike sooner."

The resentment of every hunter was now turned onto Vinnie and his clan, who remained unapologetic. Their mulishness surpassed any Irishman Cyrus had ever met. He had thought since they both came from a long line of werewolf hunters, there would be some mutual sense of loyalty between them. Not a bit. They clashed at every given turn, as did the other hunters from across the country who answered his call for brave and daring men willing to take on this challenge.

"How does that change the plan?" one of the hunters from Utah asked, a wad of tobacco bulging in his cheek.

Open on the table lay three journals worth of notes his father had left to him. In them was information he had managed to gather about Devia. Demographics, topography, town layout, names, and most importantly the number of werewolves. Disguised as a carpetbagger just after the war, Cyrus's father infiltrated Devia practically unnoticed. He only spent a day in the town, but he discovered enough to tell him that taking on a pack of this magnitude was suicidal.

Cyrus, along with the other hunters who would loyally follow him in the mission, didn't see it that way. The place might have been crawling with wolves, but they had one weakness.

"It changes little," he told them. His eyes wandered about the room, looking into the faces of those who were ready to charge into hell itself. "We'll strike tomorrow just before sunset. We counted ten guards, not including the wolves who attacked. It's likely Croxen will try to strengthen his defenses. We'll account for fifteen guards, now. Snipers will hold their positions until the appointed time. Everyone fires simultaneously. Be sure not to miss your targets. Once the shots are fired, our presence will be known and the rest of the wolves in town will mobilize to defend their families. That's almost eighty wolves."

A whistle of astonishment sounded from the back of the meeting hall. Mumbles and laughs followed, but Cyrus still had the floor. He only hoped that their eagerness for a good, successful raid didn't hinder their judgement.

"Going in too soon, sharpshooters with an itchy trigger finger, depleting your ammunition too quickly, all of these things will cause the entire mission to fall apart. We can't afford any mistakes. Once you move upon the town – and I can't stress this enough – grenades first, and then you shoot. The grenades will throw off their senses. With their eyesight trying to adjust to the fading light, they'll be blinded by the flash and the explosion will ring in their ears. You'll have ten seconds to take them down before they recover. Don't waste those seconds."

Cyrus turned to the hand-drawn map of Devia tacked to the wall behind him. His fingers traced the paths as he explained the plan for what seemed like the tenth time. "All agents will converge on the town. Two teams will move the blockades across the only road in or out. The women and children will try to evacuate. Cut them off and be sure to switch to your lead bullets. The outer buildings will be set on fire first. Don't spend too much time on this step, as the wolves will begin to get desperate and fight harder when you come closer to the edge of town."

He glanced back to the hunters and was glad to see that they had all come to terms with the fact that they would be killing humans in this raid. The women and children may not have been dangerous, but they were still a liability. He didn't need to tell them that survivors from a raid could spell disaster for any further mission. Once tactics were learned, the beasts would become smarter.

"To promise success would be idiotic. I can't promise that any of you will make it out alive. I can promise that if we stick together, follow the plan..." Cyrus gave a pointed look to Vinnie, "and move quickly, Devia will be nothing more than a black spot in the history that no other human needs to know about. We're all here for our own reasons. Whatever they are, hold onto them. When you're staring down a beast, you'll need that courage. This won't be like any raid you've ever done. Get your affairs in order and we'll convene in the morning."

Cyrus watched as the assembly dispersed. Some came to examine the map, some turned to discuss the plan with their teammates. Others bragged how they would take the head of the first werewolf they killed as a trophy. The clan leader slipped away, leaving his subordinates to answer any questions that remained.

Every detail had been carefully mapped out. Nothing was left to chance. Each man would go in with enough silver bullets to take down five times the number of werewolves they were accounting for. His father's notes were over twenty years old. Their accuracy couldn't be fully depended on, but they were all they had.

As he climbed the stairs to the second floor, Cyrus could still hear his father's voice in his head, telling him not to do this. It'd be too risky. It was a fool's errand. Their numbers were too great, their force unprecedented. But Cyrus felt he was ready. He had enlisted the best. They all came with their own weapons and shared experience. The wolves wouldn't be expecting an army this size. They'd be unstoppable.

This was the moment he had dreamed of for years. Still, the tightness in his chest wouldn't ease. Not even after pouring himself a glass of whiskey in his room. It did nothing to calm his nerves. Cyrus reminded himself that he wasn't afraid of death, not even at the hands of a werewolf. And neither were his men. They were ready. They had to be.

CHAPTER 13

It might have been too much for Darren to expect the children to behave. The girls with new ribbons in their hair, danced and twirled with one another to the music coming from town. The boys, too excited to focus on anything but their games, found amusement in chasing one another around the pews. A select few, the shy, the quiet, and the obedient, were not distracted by the festival.

He should have chosen a better place to rehearse their play. The school was too set apart from the center of the festivities, but the church provided ample space while staying close to the stage that had been constructed for them. Next year, he would suffer the long walk from the schoolhouse.

Darren continued to shout for their attention, snapping his fingers and re-cruiting some of the older children to help him. The author of the play they were to perform had a bit of pull in maintaining some semblance of order amongst the rowdy pack. Mattie Stevenson, a girl of eight with creative aspirations that surpassed Shakespeare, Byron, and Dickens combined, had asked him months ago if she could write something especially for the festival. Of course, he couldn't say no to those wistful, hopeful sapphires for eyes and bright blonde curls.

He knew, better than most, that Mattie was nothing without her make-believe. With a beta for a father who was wholly given to the policing of his pack, Mattie needed to stay occupied for the lonely hours spent at home with only her aging nanny for company. Darren listened to her many stories conjured during those long nights and evenings, understanding that few had his level of patience. Even now, some of the students were not as enthused about the project.

He only wished that the others had respected her efforts as much as he did.

"Logan, why don't you grab those boys and make them sit still?"

Perched upon the bench by the piano, Logan's fingers nimbly braided the strands that had unraveled from a tassel one of the boys had accidentally torn from a tapestry on the wall. The young loup-garou was about as interested in the play as the others were, but for a different reason.

Logan gave one bothered glance to Darren and then stood to herd the boys toward the front. His shouting and barking orders did just as much good as their teacher's.

The play was still a couple of hours away, but if Darren could just have their focus for one more rehearsal to make sure they understood their parts, then he'd be satisfied.

"Your parents will be watching you," he said, unconcerned about who was listening or not listening anymore. "I know you want to make them proud, so we all need to make sure that we know our lines."

This one statement gained the attention of some and they hurried to the front of the sanctuary to join the others who had been patiently waiting for the last quarter of an hour. Others, those who didn't care one way or another about what their parents did or didn't see, were at the mercy of Logan's temper.

Mattie came to Darren's side and tugged on his coat sleeve. In response, he bent low to listen to her tiny voice straining over the shouts of her classmates. "My papa's out on guard duty," she said. "Will he come into town to see the play?"

He made a point not to frown. Robert had been more than clear. No loup-garou was to leave his post, not even for the festival. Few knew about the potential threat of hunters, and they all wanted to keep it that way. That meant no one would know about the extra measures Robert implemented to ensure that Devia would be safe.

"I don't know, but I hope he will."

Logan came forward, a boy dangling from each hand that held fast to their ears. They scowled and grumbled in protest, but Darren couldn't be angry. The games had stopped and all looked up to him for instructions. He'd have to give them quickly before they lost focus again.

He wasn't halfway through the list of key players when both he and Logan heard it. A single, loud, reverberating crack. The younger of the two flinched as if the roof were ready to cave in on them. Some of the children giggled at his startled expression, thinking it was just another game. Darren knew well enough to let only his heartbeat give away his fear.

He looked to Logan and then to the children, his mind working to understand it. The sound came from all the cardinal points. Outside the doors of the church, he could hear some of the other loups-garous question one another. Still, the music played and laughter rang out as if no human ear heard the sound. Over the festivities, it was likely that they wouldn't.

Logan might not have known the sound, but Darren did.

"I think we know our parts well enough," he told the children. "Why don't you all go find your parents. We'll meet at the stage when it's time for the play."

They didn't have to be told twice. A stampede of colorful frocks, bouncing curls, and banging feet sped down the center aisle. A few turned slowly, glancing back to their teacher to make sure he wasn't pulling a laugh, then dashed on with the others.

One remained.

With unshed tears glistening in her eyes, Mattie watched her friends leave. "But... the play..."

He knelt in front of Mattie and took her hands. "The play will be brilliant," he said softly to her. "I'm letting them go have fun for a little while. You should too."

Mattie turned and rubbed the heel of her palm into her eye. "My papa..." She sniffled and there was no need to finish the sentence.

He promptly stood, refusing to allow himself the thought of what exactly her father might have been doing in that moment. She didn't need to think he was in danger. None of them did. "Let's go find Winnie and her parents. You like Winnie, don't you?"

Mattie nodded and seemed to brighten at the mention of the older girl who helped her with her multiplication tables. His goal wasn't only to pair the girl with a friend, but to give her into the capable hands of a family with an alpha who would keep her safe.

As he made his way past the rows upon rows of pews, Darren looked to Logan and saw that the boy fully comprehended the situation. He wouldn't have sent the children away if those gunshots weren't something more serious. With Mattie's attention diverted, he gave a tiny shake of the head, a warning not to do anything that might cause a panic.

"Go to Forrest," he said. "I'll find Robert."

Quicker than Darren expected, Logan rushed out the side door of the church, leaving him and the little girl to make their way into the street. He denied himself one last look to the sanctuary and the wooden cross hanging on the wall behind the pulpit. He didn't want to imagine what this place would look like by morning.

Adam grabbed Ruben Heuser by the arm and, with great effort, swung him back into the alleyway between the two stores. "You are not going to meet them," he growled, being sure to back it with as much dominance as he could muster without causing further alarm in the street beyond.

Half a dozen alphas had confronted him when the shots rang out, leaving their families to question their absence for too long as it was. In any other less perilous situation, Adam might have kept his promise of silence to Robert. But as soon as the breeze carried the first whiffs of blood and carnage into Devia, all promises be damned.

"I'm sure as hell not going to wait around for them," Ruben fumed, his eyes blazing gold in the evening dim. "I'm not about to let these bastards push me out again."

A few others chimed in their agreement to confront the hunters before they could step foot in the town.

"A scout would have come to tell us if there was trouble," Adam said. "No one came. It's likely all the guards are dead, which means they were able to take down twelve of our betas." One alpha present, who had two betas on the outskirts of town, tensed as if he were ready to kill every last one of the hunters himself. "If they could kill that many so efficiently, imagine what they will do to us."

"They caught us off guard," Elliot insisted as he stepped forward. "But we're prepared now. My pack has taken on hunters before. Our speed is our strength, if we just – "

"No!" Adam snapped, furious with not only their ignorance but their arrogance. "It's too dangerous. The best you can do is get your families together and leave before it's too late."

"I'm not leaving," Ruben once more asserted, nostrils flared and harsh lines of determination deepening upon his brow. "This is my home and I won't let them destroy it."

The alpha shoved Adam aside, clearing the way for him to pass with the others who were ready to risk their lives. And for what? A few buildings? The woods? He shook his head at their stupidity. Elliot followed and gave one less than apologetic look over his shoulder to the wise werewolf who tried to convince them to stay.

Only two remained. Two that would hopefully convince more to mobilize and begin the evacuations. Both of them, from what Adam could recall, had sons who had fully matured into their werewolf inheritance.

"Rafe is with his mother," said Seth, the taller and oldest of the two. "We can be gone within half an hour."

Adam nodded. "Do it. Take as many as you can with you."

The other, Jacob, nodded in agreement and rushed out before they could decide on a general direction to take their families.

At the moment, anywhere away from Devia would be the safest. Adam never thought the day would come when he would see this dream die. Robert would never accept its death, neither could Elliot or Ruben. It would be their downfall, and Adam's wolf grieved for the loss. By morning, how many would be totaled among the dead? Twenty? Forty? Over a hundred?

He thought of the children and the women, those who had nothing with which to defend themselves. Who would be left to protect them if all their husbands, fathers, and brothers ran off to battle a force they couldn't contend with? Ruben was right. They had their speed, their strength, their brute force of will, but that was nothing. A hundred years ago, it might have been enough. But now, facing down guns loaded with silver and men who had more courage than most, there was no chance.

The sunset shone a deep crimson, tinting the world below as day gave way to a black and bloody night.

They will be avenged. All of them. Every last one. Robert had never felt the temptation to consume the blood of humans before. But hatred and vengeance blanketed his mind in a dark and overwhelming haze. He wanted them dead. As dead as the guards that were caught so unaware. As dead as the fathers and husbands who gave their lives to defend his town.

As long as he had breath, he would see the hunters dead and glory in the sour, metallic taste of their flesh in his mouth.

His momentum never slowed as he and the other alphas raced to the south. He couldn't smell them. Their scent was masked as the others had been when his son was shot. But he could hear them. Their boots pounded the earth just as his paws did. The waning dusk allowed them just enough light to see by as their eyes adjusted to the darkness. When they came close enough, he would see them clearly.

When he realized their approach was scattered, Robert barked out his orders. They spread themselves out, covering the most ground to charge them. There was no way of knowing their numbers for certain, but Robert could guess. It'd be a close battle, but they would come out the victors. They had to.

Ahead, he could see them. A group of five running at a full sprint. Robert snarled and quickened his pace. But he at last stumbled when a loud crash sounded to his right. From the corner of his eye, a bright flash of light like the explosion of gunpowder dazed him.

He wasn't close enough to sustain its intended damage, but Ruben was. The alpha roared and Robert turned to watch as his friend writhed in pain on the ground. He yowled as if he were being assaulted from all sides, but the hunters were nowhere near him. A glint of something imbedded in a nearby trunk finished the incomplete puzzle.

The hunters had grenades, packed with powder and silver to agonize the werewolves.

Robert took a step in Elliot's direction when a second grenade detonated on the other side of him. Shots rang out. Roars and snarls of anguish erupted across the woods. Flashes brightened up the forest like a series of cannon fire. Yelps followed the crackling of discharged guns. Blood sanctified the ground. And slowly, one by one, the howls and death throes of the alphas ceased, only to be replaced by something more odious. The shouts of victory gushed from the mouths of men who cared nothing for life or peace.

The troop that he had been running toward were gaining ground, closing the gap between them. His fur would serve as camouflage, and if he ran now, there would be no chance they could catch him. Not even if they threw a hundred grenades.

Robert turned and loped back toward Devia, his escape laden by the loss that he never thought he would feel. He needed more men, more alphas to help him. The hunters would still pay for their treachery, but he needed a plan. He needed help, and perhaps a miracle.

CHAPTER 14

L ogan and Forrest charged up the steps to the Heuser's porch and let themselves in without knocking. At the state things were, propriety and politeness didn't exist.

Having fully recovered from his gunshot wound, he didn't hesitate when Logan told him about the rising panic in town. His first thoughts were of Chrissy and Evelyn, and though Logan knew Darren would have rather his time be spent otherwise, he offered to help.

Mitch was on the other side of town, assisting Adam in the evacuations. All celebration for the founding of Devia had fallen to pieces in the wake of its demise. Families hustled from one house to another to assist their neighbors and friends in the packing. Wagons were loaded, horses were rounded up to be harnessed for those who couldn't run on foot, and the general hysteria of crying and lamenting for their fate rose up to such a high that Logan couldn't hear much of anything else.

Even the bustling of skirts and harried talk upstairs could barely be distinguished over the rest of the noise coming from the houses around them. Forrest bounded up the stairs, ignoring the matronly woman who sat as still and stoic as a statue in the parlor. With her hat discarded beside her and chin erect, she wouldn't even pay Logan a glance.

After determining that she didn't want to be bothered, Logan followed his friend.

"Help me with this trunk," Chrissy beseeched to Forrest in one of the bedrooms.

"There's no time! Leave it!"

Logan nearly collided with Evelyn as she came rushing out of a room with a bundle of clothing between her arms. He caught her by the elbows and ignored the uneasy feeling in his stomach when he saw her face, as pale as marble. Startled that he should have been there instead of Mitch, she skipped backward a step or two.

"I have to have my things, Forrest!" Chrissy screeched out of sight from the other two.

"You can't take anything with you. It'll only slow you down. You can get dresses somewhere else."

Logan held up his hands in offer to take the bundle, but Evelyn shook her head. "They're my mother's," she said, her voice so wispy compared to her sister's. "She says she won't leave without our father."

"I don't want to get dresses somewhere else! I want these!"

A bang made the couple in the hall start. "Damn it, woman! If the hunters catch you, there will be no more dresses to wear, because you'll be dead!"

Evelyn turned up her dark eyes to beg Logan for an explanation. "They're on the edge of town."

If it were possible for her to blanch anymore, she would have been as white as the paint on their picket fence. "But... What about the guards? Robert? Where are – "

"I don't know," Logan said. "All I know is that Darren wants us to leave, and that's what everyone else is doing. It's just not safe to stay."

A scuffle was heard in the other room and Forrest came out with Chrissy slung over his shoulder. Her fists beat at his back mercilessly. After being shot with silver, two skinny arms could do little to faze him.

Logan and Evelyn stepped aside to let them through, marveling at the fair-haired girl who put up an admirable fight.

"What about these?" the calmer sister asked, holding up the bundle.

He shook his head in response. "I think you'd better leave everything."

"What about the china?" cried Chrissy as Forrest hauled her down the stairs.

"Damn the china!"

"The linens! We have to take the linens!"

"Damn those too!"

Evelyn, with some measure of regret, tossed her mother's things back into the room, letting the cotton dresses flutter to the floor in a disorderly heap. She then turned and hurried toward the stairs with Logan. He was grateful that he wouldn't have to carry or drag her in any way. She might have been the most sensible of the three.

"Mama, we have to go," Evelyn said from the parlor room door.

The older woman stiffened and wouldn't meet their gazes. "I'm not going anywhere without Ruben."

"Please, ma'am," Logan implored. "He would want you to go with your daughters."

Forrest made it as far as the porch before Chrissy wailed to be let down. Evelyn ran to her mother's side and knelt at her feet. Logan watched as she took the wrinkled, bony hands.

"Mama, we have to go. We'll meet papa when it's all over."

Just when Logan was ready to give up his pride and carry Mrs. Heuser out of the house, Darren came bounding up the walkway calling for him. The teacher, panting with a wild look in his eyes, beheld the scene as if they were all growing a second head.

"What the bloody hell are you lot doing?"

Logan gestured to the staunch woman on the sofa. "She won't leave."

Darren's brows slanted together in a look of pure rage as he turned on Mrs. Heuser. "Cornelia, if you don't stand up and follow us, I'll throw you over my shoulder as Forrest just did with your daughter and I won't put you down until we're a hundred miles away from here."

The old woman finally looked to Darren, eyes wide with shock and disdain. "You wouldn't!"

He only needed to take two giant steps forward before she rose and hurried to avoid being disgraced just as he threatened. The four of them exited the house, leaving the front door wide open.

Families kicked up a cloud of dust in the street that led out of Devia. Some women were astride horses, their young children settled in front of them as they followed the rest. Wagons lazily rattled away to the north, away from where they all assumed the attack would come. Alphas, betas, and other werewolves went from house to house, calling for anyone who might have been left. A few had shifted and were running in the opposite direction of the moseying caravan, toward the source of the loud bangs and gunfire that Logan had been hearing for the last ten or so minutes. The final battle had begun and it was just on the outskirts of the town.

Forrest had let Chrissy down and together they ran ahead to find a family for the Heusers to travel with. Darren's eyes skimmed for Adam in the congestion. Evelyn had taken to caring for her mother, hastening her along to catch up with Forrest and Chrissy.

They exchanged one look and for the first time, Logan truly feared what would become of them. Not just him, Darren, and his friends, but all of them. He saw the crying children who asked for their fathers. He saw the way their faces twisted with fear and dread. Everywhere he turned, they all seemed to understand that this was the end.

Logan barely had any time to come to appreciate this place and what it meant for these people. He hated what he was with every fiber of his being, but that didn't mean he couldn't love Devia. The kindness and compassion he had been shown from the very beginning hadn't fallen on a completely stony heart. People like Forrest, Mitch, Adam, and Evelyn had invested in him. They gave their time, their consideration, and for the first time in what seemed like an eternity, he felt as if he had a family again.

And now, that family was scattering.

Evelyn gave him a faint, strained smile, a half-hearted promise that they would see one another when it was all over. He nodded in acknowledgement, though he wasn't quite sure if anything would come of it. What if he were killed? What if she were? In the midst of the end of the world, could promises like that ever be kept?

"Adam!" Darren shouted.

Logan and Evelyn parted ways and he turned to see the half-Navajo werewolf force his way past a tight cluster of older women trailing behind an overloaded wagon. Adam came to meet them and the sight disheartened him. He was just as afraid as everyone else, if not more. If he was scared, they were truly in peril.

"The roads are blocked," he told Darren. "The hunters moved trees to bar the way."

Darren uttered an oath in a language Logan didn't understand. "None of them will get through." The three of them regarded the loaded wagons and the possessions that would have to be left behind.

"Our only way is through the woods," Adam said.

"Which way?"

At a loss, Adam turned in place, looking to all the compass points as if something in the darkening sky would tell him the right answer. "I'm... I'm not sure. We don't know where they're coming from."

Then, an odor reached them. On the northernly wind came acrid smoke. Soon to join it was the amber glow of fire. Shrieks rippled through the caravan and many slowed to a stop when they realized they were riding right into a trap.

From the south came more explosions and Logan could finally hear them. The shouts of the men that came for their blood. Above the heads of the fleeing townsfolk, he could see the pricked ears of werewolves returning. Some limped, some had blood staining their fur. Others had abandoned the fight altogether and searched for their families.

The dull roar of the mounting flames created something of a second sunset on the horizon, as the fire spread from house to house in such quick succession that it had to be staged somehow. The hunters weren't coming to Devia. They were already there.

Darren grabbed Logan, who had fallen into a mild stupor, and tugged him toward the only reasonable route. They couldn't go north or east toward the stretching inferno. Neither could they go south where the battle was already lost.

The only other way was west. Adam stayed in the street, directing the civilians to follow and leave their belongings. The majority were too far gone to hear him. Panic had gripped them and refused to let go. Even when bullets began to strike at the wagons and fencing around the homes.

Logan spotted Forrest and Mitch without the Heuser family, and called to them. They came running to the tree line, but something made Forrest freeze in place. With Darren distracted by ushering the women and children into the forest, Logan ran to them.

Just a second before he was ready to ask what was wrong, he saw it. Forrest and Mitch had caught sight of Robert. The town's founder wasn't alone. With four other werewolves, they had turned to make a final stand against the invading hunters as they marched through the streets.

Shots were fired. One werewolf went down, and then another as the charge commenced. Man and wolf hurled themselves at one another. The first werewolf that Logan had ever laid eyes on tore into two hunters before a gun was leveled upon him.

The trigger was pulled and Forrest let out an inhuman scream. His father fell and lay motionless. The hunters, oblivious to whom they'd just murdered, continued their assault.

Mitch took Forrest's arm and held him back. Logan, too, detained his friend and dragged him deeper into the trees. There was no time to grieve or slow down. If they stopped, if they looked back, even for a minute, they'd be like Robert and the others who had fallen to the hunters.

Logan kept moving, kept hurrying with his two friends in tow, both shedding tears for the alpha they had lost. The other werewolves, the ones who had managed to escape the carnage, did what they could to hurry along the rest. All around, dispersed in utter disorganization, broken families fled the town. They, like Logan, wouldn't look back. Not for the cries of the children, or the screaming of the women, nor for the roars of the werewolves who fought to their last breath. The rising glow of the burning town was enough to remind them that there was nothing left for them in Devia.

Damn waste. That's what it was. The bloodbath had fallen short of their ex-
pectations. Some of the beasts had escaped. And what was worse, their children
escaped. Sons that would grow up into the monsters their fathers had been.
Daughters who would tell the story of the massacre for ages. There were to be no
survivors, and they had failed. It didn't matter if they collected the paws of over
fifty werewolves and burned the bodies of the families that had been left to the
slaughter. It wasn't enough.

As zealously as Cyrus wanted to pursue, his men and resources wouldn't allow
it. Out of his thirty-five hunters, he lost twenty-three. Damn good hunters, cut
down in a battle that should have been theirs. They were prepared, they had
enough bullets, but some of the wolves fought harder than others. Something
must have tipped them off.

Cyrus shook his head at the image of Vinnie's mutilated corpse thrown upon
the pyre. The bastard deserved it for giving away their scouting mission the day
before the raid. If he hadn't fired those shots, they might have had the element of
surprise on their side.

Those left to deal with the wreckage of Devia had congratulated one another
on their success. The houses and businesses burned to the ground, the citizens
unlikely to return, and Mr. Morris had a clear path for his railroad. But the sight
of the remnants running away into the woods negated every sense of victory. It
filled him with a fury that could yet be doused by reason. He hoped this visit to
Mr. Morris' office would bring some closure to the failed mission. Anything less
than total destruction was a failure.

He hopped down from the buggy seat and reached into the bed of the wagon
to grab the partially charred plank of wood. Some took heads, some paws, others
wanted to strip the carcass of the multicolored pelts and fashion them into rugs.
Cyrus would take this, and only this.

Up the steps and through the halls he marched, shouldering aside men who
were in his way and ignoring the receptionist's urgent orders for him to stop. He
wouldn't.

Cyrus invited himself into Mr. Morris' office. The businessman and a few
associates were huddled around his desk, all pointing at maps and referring to
figures in their little books. The door slammed shut behind him with a definite
bang and all turned to glare at his intrusion.

But the moment Mr. Morris realized who it was, his features softened.

Before anyone could ask what the hell he was doing there, Cyrus tossed the
plank onto the man's desk, spilling a glass of whiskey to the floor and sending
some papers flying. The word "Devia" was clearly painted in block letters upon
the face, and the ominous blackened edges of what was once the sign for the
general store caught their attention.

"It's done," Cyrus announced flatly. "Build your railroad. Hell, build your own town."

Mr. Morris looked from the sign to the man he had hired to kill the wolves. This was more than he had paid him for, but Cyrus wasn't looking for more money. He wanted retribution for the men he'd lost and the total victory that had been taken from him.

"Did... What happened?" asked one of the men, obviously an associate who was invested in the railroad scheme.

Cyrus straightened and prattled off what he had rehearsed. "While we were hunting the wolves, there was some accident in the town. A fire started, and they didn't have the means to stop it. Many were left without a place to live, so they left. The town's empty. Devia's gone."

Jaws went slack, eyes widened. None knew how to respond to such news until Mr. Morris spoke up.

"And the land? What's Croxen going to do with it?"

Cyrus shrugged. "Robert Croxen died in the fire. I'd say that the land is up for grabs."

The moment of silence held for the loss of Devia was short lived when the investors heard his answer. They immediately scrambled for the maps of the area and began to discuss among themselves. The plaque was taken away and set against the wall to make room on the desk. A new route would be made for the railroad, one that could capitalize on all the cleared land in the center of the town. Plans were set in motion, estimates were drawn up, and Cyrus was no longer needed. He had done what he came to do.

He turned and strode toward the door just before Mr. Morris rushed to stop him.

"Wait, Taggert," he said eagerly. "Have a cigar. It's the least I can do."

The short, fat businessman pulled out a gold case from his vest pocket and snapped it open. Cyrus held out his hand to deny the gift.

"I don't smoke, but thank you for the offer."

Slightly disconcerted, Mr. Morris took out only one cigar instead of two and returned the case. "I trust those mongrels didn't give you much trouble."

Cyrus watched the way the top of his match sizzled into a tiny flame, just big enough for the tip of the cigar. The smell and the flash threw him back to the previous day when he had led the raid upon the werewolves. The screaming, the fire, the gnashing teeth and slashing claws. He'd have nightmares for a few weeks, as he did after all the other missions. Then, he'd be steady again. He wouldn't feel this anger about losing good, noble men and letting the monsters escape to kill another day. Everything would return to normal and he'd find a new target. All the while, Mr. Morris would exploit the prime piece of real estate that Cyrus had given to him. He'd make his fortune on the ashes.

"No," he replied. "No, they didn't."

Before any more questions could be asked, Cyrus retreated from the office.

EPILOGUE

"**M**ove over!" Cal complained.

Mattie, who sat beside him, kicked her heels against the legs on the chair that was almost too high for her. "I can't!" she pouted. "Elijah won't move."

Darren, seated at the head of the long dining table, looked up from his plate to the quarreling children. Eight others managed to conduct themselves with no more decorum, all orphans from Devia, all waiting for their new families.

It had been three weeks since the massacre. At first, the citizens of Devia had scattered to the winds. It was nearly impossible to know who had made it out alive and what had become of the others. Letters and telegrams were sent out to all contacts in the surrounding states to keep their eyes open for women and children left destitute. Most had been found, others remained missing.

Today would be the first reunion between many of the neighbors and friends who had lost contact with one another. Darren, Adam, and three other alphas remained to piece together what had happened and where everything had gone wrong. Testimonies were compared and the names of those who were certainly in the battle were recorded. If a definitive account couldn't be given of them, it could be assumed they were dead. The list was long.

Still, many hoped for better news.

Darren, having a rapport with these children, had been elected to look after them. A stately home outside Meridian Mississippi had been donated for their use. Its resident, an elderly widow who was at least aware of loups-garous, if not directly associated with one, had been more than happy to bend over backward for the eleven children who were left without mothers or fathers.

Some had been entrusted to friends during the attack. Others had somehow escaped death by hiding in the woods, only to be found later by someone who knew them. Darren thought of their parents, of the alphas, betas, and brave women who had given their lives to protect what they loved. Devia fell in the end, but he tried not to think of the futility of it all. He would tell every last one of those children that their parents were heroes until he was blue in the face.

There was no need to tarnish their views of their parents who foolishly ran into a situation they couldn't handle.

These last few weeks, taking more and more orphans under his wing while also training Logan, had been an ordeal from hell itself. The mass of letters they received daily about families and other children occupied his evenings and with few supplies or means at all he taught his students in the afternoons. He was mother, father, and teacher to every one of them. Mrs. White, the widow, while a kindly hostess, was little help in anything else but making up beds and cooking. Allie May had been a Godsend, as she had a way with the smaller children.

"Quit touching me!" Elijah hollered, dropping his fork to his plate with a crash.

"Then move over!" Mattie screeched.

The three-year-old Ester sitting next to Allie May began to cry. She pulled the toddler into her lap to sooth her while the others began bickering and name calling. Darren, while annoyed by the proceedings, had little energy to stop them.

Logan, who had been staring out the window of the dining hall for the last quarter of an hour, finally turned to the children, his eyes a burning gold. "Knock it off!" he yelled, causing the crystals of the chandelier to rattle above them.

Elijah, Mattie, and Cal all went incredibly still before meekly turning their attention back to the half-eaten eggs and portion of fried bacon. Darren even sat back and cut his eyes at Logan, wondering if his senses hadn't been deceived. Either he had emitted a faint pulse of alpha dominance, or he truly was exhausted.

The boy's irritability could be understood. Forrest and Mitch would not be coming to Meridian. They had gone north to Chicago where they were to stay with Robert's uncle. Darren had never met the man personally, but he had heard enough stories to wish that he could have adopted the two of them. A bachelor and without any children of his own, Will Croxen was not the ideal father figure to raise two young loups-garous. However, he was next of kin, and perhaps a change of scenery would do them both good. They needed to leave the south and all its memories behind.

Though Darren hadn't seen Robert's death, he heard of it from Logan. He made it sound as if the alpha had truly done something heroic, fending off a group of hunters and killing a few before they had turned on him. In Darren's humble and biased opinion, it was the alphas who decided to evacuate who were the heroes. They saved lives. Robert endangered all of them. He respected the man, but he would not glorify him.

Adam could be counted amongst those who should have been revered. He had been the one to rally alphas together, to direct the first wave of evacuees into the forests, and arrange this gathering. However, Darren wished that he had stayed with Logan. Or that Logan would have gone with him on these errands to reunite the town.

Every spare moment was spent training Logan in whatever small way that he could. They were the only loups-garous in the home, meaning that they were the only ones to suffer from the constant noise of the children. Darren would have preferred if Logan could be placed with another alpha or another pack, but whenever the thought arose, a twisted and uneasy feeling possessed him. That's when he understood that if Logan were anywhere else, Darren still would not have been content.

And if Logan were with Adam, it would be likely they would both go to the west together when all this was put behind them. Adam's father was somewhere out there, and he had written to tell Darren that's where he intended to go. Darren didn't like the idea of Logan in those rough, western towns or around large herds of cattle. It would be too much for him too soon.

Mrs. White shuffled in, a bowl of oatmeal between her bony hands. She crooned over the children and refilled their dishes, but other than that, the dining hall had fallen into a calm hush. Only the scraping of utensils upon plates remained. Even Ester had quieted her little sobs and clamored out of Allie May's lap.

Darren watched Logan, who in turn kept his eyes fixed on the road. "You know they're not coming."

The boy glanced at him, but showed no other sign that he was listening.

"The Heusers have gone to stay with a relative in Kentucky," Darren said. "They're probably on a train headed north right now, if they haven't gotten there already."

A muscle in Logan's jaw tightened, but he said nothing.

"You need to eat." Darren tapped the tip of his fork on the untouched slab of ham.

Logan sneered. "If you keep nagging me, I'll eat nothing."

"You and I both know you'll eat eventually."

The teen rolled his eyes and finally gave in, slicing into his breakfast a little aggressively.

"Who are you watching for?" Darren asked as he took a drink of his water and eyed the way Cal and Mattie elbowed one another, fighting for space.

"No one," Logan said. "I was trying to listen. Isn't that something you wanted me to do?" He stuffed his mouth before giving his alpha a snide look.

Since the attack, Logan's discontent had risen to unparalleled heights. Perhaps it was the perpetual presence of the children or the fact that he had no friend of his own to keep him busy while Darren occupied himself with the orphans. Whatever it was, he hoped it would end soon. It needed to before they left.

"Is your new trunk packed?" Darren asked after a stretch of silence had been given for Logan to finish eating.

He nodded. "Has been for a week now."

"That eager to leave?" Darren chuckled, then excused a few of the girls to go play in the yard. Some of the children had already dismissed themselves and went about their usual business. Lessons had been cancelled for the day in preparation for the arrival of their new families.

Logan slid a glance to the others still left at the table who played with their food and frowned miserably at their plates. Children could be resilient, but that didn't stop them from missing their parents from time to time. Part of Darren's job was to comfort them, but they often took consolation in each other instead.

"I'm... I just want to go, that's all."

He nodded in understanding. Just like Forrest and Mitch, Logan was ready to put this bad memory behind him. If only he knew that there would be more to come in the long future ahead. That was inevitable.

"We'll go to Mobile once all the children have been placed. From there, we'll go to France. I want you to meet John Croxen and train with him for a little while."

Logan sighed. "You've told me this already."

Darren crossed his knife and fork over his empty plate. "I didn't tell you that from there, we'll try to find your grandfather."

Logan regarded his alpha with alarm and the first bit of optimism he had displayed since they met. "We're going to find Dustin?"

"We're going to try." Darren couldn't put enough emphasis on that word. "Your grandfather could be anywhere, but John has many contacts across Europe and Asia. We'll have the means and connections to travel through him, and with some luck, we might find Dustin." Remembering his former beta, Darren let out a long breath. "That's only if he wants to be found."

"And then what?" Logan asked excitedly.

He met a pair of hopeful eyes, ones that hadn't seen the world in all its joys and sorrows. There was so much Logan had to learn and there was still so much Darren felt he could teach him. They had centuries ahead of them and miles upon miles to go together. If Robert had ever done one good thing for him, it was giving Logan into his care. He saw that now. If Darren had no one in the aftermath of this disaster, he would have been without direction or guidance. He wouldn't know the next path to take or what he should do.

Now, he did. He had a reason to act. Logan was that reason, and Dustin would be added to their numbers, even if it took years to find him.

"From there... we'll see."

AFTERWORD

Dear Readers,

I can remember the exact instance when I came up with the idea for Devia. It was long before Logan, Darren, Robert, or Adam had ever entered my mind. And way before the Loup-Garou or Legacy Series began to take shape. There's a small town about an hour north of my hometown, and one day my mom took me there to go shopping through the many antique stores along their main road. At the time, I was bored stiff, but my passion for storytelling had just begun to take root in my subconscious. I walked through the twisting and turning aisles of the antique store when I came across a little wolf figurine on a shelf. I took it down and studied it, and inspiration hit me. Now, the whole plot of The Deviants took a few more years to develop, but the idea of a town full of werewolves was there from the very beginning. I imagined a community founded by werewolves for the purpose of staying hidden from the rest of society. The town we visited was pretty disconnected from a lot of other places and the Victorian architecture only added to the face of Devia.

Now, that story idea came with its own cast of characters that have never been born onto paper, but I grafted Devia into my first book, The Enigma, and instead of making it a town that still existed, I christened it with a disaster that would bring the refugees into the life of Katey McCoy as she learns more about the world of werewolves. As the Epilogue suggests, the story continues for Darren and Logan, who are about to venture overseas for their rather long search for Dustin, training all along the way. On their voyage back to America, they board an infamous ship... I won't tell which one just yet. You'll have to keep reading to find out!

To follow my progress in this series, or to see what other projects I'm working on, you can follow me on social media or go to my blog, www.moonstruckwriting.wordpress.com

Until next time, happy reading!

- Sheritta Bitikofer

ABOUT THE AUTHOR

Sheritta Bitikofer is an author of paranormal and historical fiction. She lives for the deep, engaging stories that enthrall readers from cover to cover. As a wife and mother of eclectic tastes, she can be found roaming Civil War battlefields, haunting her local coffeeshop, or relaxing with a plate of chili cheese fries.

Follow her for upcoming novel releases
www.sherittabitikofer.com
www.moonstruckwriting.wordpress.com

ALSO BY SHERITTA BITIKOFER

The Loup-Garou Series
The Enigma
Becoming the Enigma
Beast Within
Precedents
The Legacies Series (A Novella Series)
Companion to The Loup-Garou Series
The Legend
The Guide
The Frenchman
The Prophecy
The Pirate
The Native
The Irishman
The Scholars
The Convicts
The Soldier
The Outlaw
The Deviants
The Unsinkable
Keeper of Light
Bulletproof
The Nexus
Bewitching Brews Trilogy
Bewitching Fire
Bewitching Darkness
Bewitching Hearts
The Decimus Trilogy
The Beast of Verona

Amber Ashes
Saving the Beast
<u>Redemption Duet</u>
The Rose
The Lion
<u>Standalones</u>
Escape
Clouds
Passions
Silver Screen
By The Book

www.ingramcontent.com/pod-product-compliance
Lightning Source LLC
Chambersburg PA
CBHW032250020726
47495CB00001B/48